TALES
OF THE
EXPRESS

TALES
OF THE
EXPRESS

Ellen Wight

To order additional copies of this book, contact:
Xlibris Corporation
1-888-795-4274
www.Xlibris.com
Orders@Xlibris.com
46058

Dedication

To Silvio Piccinotti, who let me drive his old stagecoach and Hoppy Hopkins, who helped me find the pieces of this historical jigsaw puzzle.

ACKNOWLEDGEMENT

I would like to thank the Bancroft Library, for the archive lithograph of the Hank Monk Schottische sheet music cover art, by J. P. Marshall, which is used on the cover, designed by Martin Scherer.

I would like to thank the Pajaro Museum in Watsonville, for their help in researching Charley Parkhurst.

Special thanks to Martin Scherer, my life partner, for his technical help in writing this book and helping me believe that I could write a book at all.

Thank you to Toni Wight, my mother, who taught me to live my dreams.

I would also like to thank my brother Eric Wight, also Judy and Lloyd Dick, Fred Loebenstien, Vicky Cumbow; Chris Ford, Vern Piccinotti, Art Carpenter; and especially Susan Villa. This novel is based on real people and facts obtained from the newspapers of the day, such as, *the Territorial Enterprise, Carson Morning Appeal, San Francisco Chronicle,* and the *Daily Alta California.*

CHAPTER 1

New Hampshire 1826

Summer's soft breeze grew still, as the slowly forming clouds began to darken the New England sky. Beneath the afternoon clouds lay a farm and there in a run-down corral, was a horse and a girl.

The gray stallion was getting up in years, but the skinny girl brushing his soft dappled coat loved him nonetheless. She stood next to her big friend, dreaming of the days before her father had died.

The horse turned and nuzzled the girl's dirty face and played with her long auburn braid. Charlotte Parker was taller than average and wiry, but strong from hard labor on a farm that looked in need of serious attention. It no longer had the pride it showed when Charlotte's father had run things. The fences were poorly mended, and the paint on the buildings was faded and chipped. The gardens had not been pruned and were overgrown with weeds. Only the vegetable patch was cared for and neat, tended each day by the young girl and her mother.

The barn and chicken yard were also kept neat, worked over by Charlotte, who took refuge there.

The stallion pricked up his ears and whinnied as Charlotte heard the wheels of the buckboard grinding in the driveway.

She untied the horse, then hiked up her stained coveralls, and leapt onto the tall gray stallion's bare back from a fence rail and screamed at her stepbrother.

"You can't leave me, Ephram. You said I could come too! You're not leavin' me again! Come on, Blue!" she hollered, as the buckboard disappeared around the bend. Charlotte turned the stallion around and started him off, jumping a fence in order to catch up to the town-bound stepbrother. Rounding a thickly wooded turn, Charlotte was surprised by her stepfather and mother coming around the blind turn in the spring wagon! To her horror, she saw her stepfather's face turning red with rage and wanted to spur the stallion on and keep going. Fear caused her to halt in her tracks. Her mother's head was bowed as if she was praying for mercy for her wayward thirteen-year-old daughter. At that moment, the stepbrother came along and seeing the trouble Charlotte was in, roared with laughter as he headed into town.

"Be home tonight, Pa," Ephram called to his father.

"You be home before it gets dark!" Isaiah Parker called back, choking back his anger. He had tied his horse's reins to the brake and had gotten down from the wagon.

Isaiah grabbed Charlotte by the coveralls and pulled her off the horse, then ordered her to tie the horse to the back of the wagon. Not a word was said until they arrived back at the barn. Her mother silently went inside the house, leaving her new husband and daughter.

"I told you not to touch that horse!" he said as he began taking off his belt. "Just where the hell did you think you were going anyway?"

"Town, sir," Charlotte quaked as the belt came flying, catching her right in the face and knocking her to the ground! The leather had split the trembling child's lower lip. Explanations at this point were useless; the man took sick delight in the pain of others.

"Take off those coveralls!" he demanded.

Charlotte started to fumble with the buttons when a shadow appeared in the door of the barn.

"Enough!" her mother yelled.

Isaiah turned to the voice; his face was scarlet with rage. "I'm not through with you," he said under his breath, looking down at the girl. She sat kneeling in the barn before him, looking at the dirt floor. Isaiah turned to his wife, then smacked the child in the face with his fist, knocking her down. Charlotte buried her stinging face in her hands and cried.

"Don't ever take that tone with me! Do you hear?" he growled at his wife, slapping her in the eye with the back of his hand as he walked back to the house. It began to rain.

Charlotte's family had once been fairly well off; her real father was once a respected horse breeder. When he and his only son died of cholera two years ago, the farm began to fail. Charlotte's mother eventually remarried, but none too well, unfortunately. Isaiah Parker frittered away most of their money, and life was mostly hard work for Charlotte, who had quit school to help at home.

Her mother was transformed from a lovely and gracious woman to one who showed no emotions.

Charlotte's one bright spot was the gray stallion; he was the last link to the pleasant past. Born a jet-black colt when Charlotte was quite small, he slowly lightened to a dazzling dappled gray. She had always called him Blue, he was her pet, and he followed her around like a dog. Charlotte's mother would never allow him to be sold because it was her first husband's favorite colt. She would not reveal that to her present husband, however, for fear that he would sell him out of spite.

Charlotte woke from her tears to find her tall gray friend standing impatiently behind the spring wagon, waiting for his girl to put him away.

Isaiah was careful never to hit Charlotte in front of the stallion for fear that he may attack and defend her. Parker was a bitter man, who felt that the world owed him, and he would collect on it whenever the opportunity arose. As Charlotte matured, she caught glimpses of lechery in Isaiah's face as he watched her; it made her blood run cold.

Isaiah's son, Ephram, was sixteen years old, the same age as Charlotte's natural brother, John, who had died not long after her father. John had been a wonderful brother who had loved her and taught her things. His passing hit Charlotte hard, changing her life forever. A poor bit of judgment on her mother's behalf and the tables were changed completely around. Whereas Charlotte's father was loving and sweet and kind, Isaiah was coarse and hard and alcoholic. Ephram, Isaiah's son, was a chip off the old block. It tolled hard on Charlotte's mother, to find out that the man she had signed her life over to, and the life of her only remaining daughter and family, was of very dubious character.

Abigail Parker's face turned white as her daughter crept into the kitchen, one eye swollen shut, lips cracked and bleeding as she tried not to cry. Abigail felt the sting of her own newly blackened eye and choked back her own tears.

Just then, Isaiah bellowed for his supper as the pious child beater sat at his dinner table.

"Quiet now, Charlotte," her ma quietly spoke, "just be still now and sit over there."

After Isaiah had finished his supper and was well into his bottle of rye, he decided it was time to lay down the law! "The first law (as if she hadn't heard them before!) was that young women did not ride horses like wild, heathen Indian savages in men's dirty coveralls and astride! If she needed to go anywhere, it would be in proper attire, in a buggy with an escort! Furthermore, that damned stallion was off-limits, or he would be sold. How could she ever hope to be married when she behaved so horribly?" the man ranted.

Charlotte just sat and glared at him with her worried thirteen-year-old eyes, one of which was now quite swollen and blue.

The next day, after all of the chores were done, Charlotte and her ma looked through an old trunk for fabric to make a new dress. The prospect of a new dress intrigued the girl even though she had no place to wear one, except every blue moon that they got to go to church. Isaiah was always expounding that the churchgoers were all hypocrites anyways!

As the two females sat talking about the dress, Abigail explained that the young girl would soon be experiencing the curse of all women. The idea frightened the child until her mother explained that it would soon be a commonplace monthly routine. Her mother gave her a set of cloth napkins and an odd sort of belt and explained what to do.

Sewing a dress by hand seemed to take an eternity, so when the "masterpiece" was finally finished, Charlotte gaily danced around the humble home, imagining a new personality. When she suddenly stopped, she saw Isaiah leering at her from the doorway with a bottle of rye in one hand. A familiar feeling of nausea came over her as she ran past him to the barn.

"Oh God!" she whispered to the gray horse. "Now what have we done!"

"Why are you always running to that damn nag anyway?" Isaiah growled. The young girl turned with a start to find Isaiah staring at her from the next stall. "It's a wonder you don't stink like a horse!"

"He's my friend!" she stammered.

"Horse ain't no friend. Why don't you let me be your friend?" he said as he began creeping toward the girl. "I'll show you what real friendship is!"

"Please don't!" Charlotte said as she opened the stall door and tried to go in with Blue. "Just leave me alone!"

Parker was too quick and strong for the girl, and he slammed the stall door closed before she could scurry through.

"How would you like it if I blew that gray bastard's brains all over the barn!" Isaiah hissed, hovering over the girl, breathing hard his whiskey breath upon her. "Or sold him?"

"You stay away from him. He's mine and Ma's! He's won lots a races! So you just leave him alone!" the girl cried. A very long silence ensued, Charlotte did not know what to make of it, but she felt very uneasy about it.

"You're kinda touchy about that horse, ain't you?" Isaiah said, stroking her face with his filthy hands. "Maybe we ought to sell him before he's lost his value. After all, he ain't as fast as he used ta be!"

"No!" she cried. "You can't, he's mine!"

"Yeah? You got the papers sayin' he's yorn? I'd like to see those!"

"What do you want, besides to torture me?" Charlotte cried.

"Well, if you showed me half of the affection you showed that gray bastard, I might keep him around awhile."

"That's all you want to be friends?" she said warily. Blue was frantically pacing his stall trying to get at the man.

"Well, it's good for a start," Isaiah hissed. "I'll settle for being friendly for now." He put his hand behind her neck and pulled her closer. "Give your daddy a little kiss," he cooed, stroking her beautiful auburn hair. The girl had inadvertently backed herself into a corner.

"Pa?" an obnoxious voice called from outside the barn. "I want to go to town. Can I take the black mare?" Ephram croaked as he sauntered into the barn.

"Why are you always buttin' in, you puny little shit?" Isaiah roared, grabbing Charlotte by a handful of her soft hair at the back of her head. "Take this gray bastard to town!" he said, pointing with his free hand. The girl grabbed at the man's powerful grip on her hair; the struggle was futile. "He needs some exercise!" Isaiah's eyes flickered with devilish torture as he walked her backward away from the stall door.

"But, Pa! He don't like me . . . I . . . um, I a . . ."

"You take that horse to town, or you don't go, you little shit! Be a goddamned man!" Isaiah commanded.

"But, Pa—" The boy trembled, staring at the helpless Charlotte, doubtless taking notes for future reference.

"Take him, or you don't go!" the patron roared, irritated for the interruption.

"Geez!" Ephram moaned as he headed for Blue's halter.

Isaiah's hand was still at the back of Charlotte's neck, holding her still.

"You just mind yourself," he muttered under his breath. "You just let the boy take your little horsy!"

Ephram was scared to death of Blue as he tried to snap the lead rope to the halter without being bitten or trampled. He then wrapped the rope around the horse's nose for extra control the way his father had shown him, then led the high-spirited horse from the stall, and saddled him.

Charlotte's eyes felt like red-hot bullets in her head as the idiot son walked out of the barn with her most beloved.

Ephram may have been an idiot, but he was not a fool. He was well aware that he was over mounted with the gray stallion. As soon as he was at the far pasture, he traded Blue for the older black mare, turning the stud loose with the brood mares. He felt he would get to town in much better shape with a gentler horse. Hopefully his father wouldn't notice; he seemed preoccupied with family matters.

Charlotte was now in her own private hell. She had frozen like a fawn hiding from a predator in hopes that it would just go away. Yet her predator held her fast. The man began to slobber over her face and neck and to explore her body with his free hand. The small victim was petrified. She then woke from the nightmare and began to fight back. She was quite certain that she had landed a serious blow with her knee between his legs. When his grip was loosened, she quickly ran back to the house and the protection of her mother. Later she was watching out her bedroom window and breathed a sigh of relief as she spotted Blue galloping in the distant field.

Last year, the horse had received a lameness and was no longer able to race. He was sound enough for light work, but he could not hold up in a field of racehorses. It seemed now that Charlotte and Blue were both getting the short end of the stick. This new development with Isaiah was something altogether more horrible, especially with the threats to her horse. It was her Achilles' heel, and Isaiah used it. Charlotte was at a loss to know what to do, her intuition told her that he was not going to let up. If she told her mother, what could she do? She was married to him, Isaiah would just call her a liar, beat her up, then just do as he pleased. Besides, Ma had become so distant lately, a shell of the woman she once was, like part of her had just wandered off one day.

As the young girl dozed in her bed, dreaming of traveling in a marvelous new country, she was startled by a sinister-sounding creak in her room. She froze, knowing by the smell who it was, and tried not to shake. Still frozen, she felt Isaiah climb into bed with her. Charlotte felt a profound rigor mortis set in as she smelled the whiskey breath on the back of her neck and felt his hands exploring her young body. Fortunately for her, he was extremely drunk, and she had worn layers of her thickest nightgowns. As soon as she heard him snore, she quickly got up. Looking down at him with disgust, she knew she had to do something about this, but for now, she was going to sleep in Blue's manger as her bed was defiled!

Charlotte woke up early in the morning wondering where she was and then feeling strangely dirty when it came flooding back to her why she was there. She collected the morning eggs in a basket that hung in the barn and went to the kitchen, straw still sticking in her unbrushed red hair.

"You're up early, girl!" her mother remarked. "I didn't even hear you get up! Why are you still in your nightgown, Charlotte? You're gonna get it filthy!" her ma criticized, pulling hay from the unbrushed hair.

The child stuttered, not knowing what to say, "Sorry . . . I . . . ah . . . had a . . . bad dreams and then got up without thinkin', I reckon," she lied. Just as she did, Isaiah stumbled in to the kitchen. "Sleep well?" Charlotte asked sarcastically, staring at the drunkard with contempt. It stopped Isaiah cold for a second, then he bellowed with laughter, and Charlotte knew she would have to do something soon.

Her mother just went on frying bacon, oblivious to everything as though she had blinders on.

"We need to make a trip into town. If you'd like to come, you'd better hurry with your chores!" Isaiah wheezed. Charlotte had mixed feelings about a long ride with Ma and Isaiah, but she rarely got to go, so she ran out the back door and got serious about her work.

All the way to town, the girl fantasized about running away. What to bring, where should she go? She had little money, just twenty-five dollars she had won with Blue, that she had secreted away in a hidden cubbyhole in her room. Every time Isaiah looked at her, she knew she would have to leave soon. Last night was the spurring she needed.

Charlotte rustled her new skirt as she walked behind her folks, peering into the windows, wondering what it would be like to live in a town instead of a farm. She tugged at the restraining stays in her new dress. It felt so restricting and unnatural, she grimaced with displeasure. She could smell the cigars and beer of the tavern and the kitchen's exotic aromas swirling out to the boardwalk. Mrs. Parker was holding pretty firm to Isaiah's arm, using it sort of like a rudder to steer him from evil influences.

"Blue is in good shape, he could take me far away, and I could get some kind of a job, maybe in a stable," the girl mumbled to herself.

"What's that, Charlotte?" Ma asked.

"Can I go look in the stables?" she replied.

"What do you want to go look in some old stable for? Don't you spend enough time in the barn at home?" Ma hollered. "Besides, it isn't proper for young women to go into stables. You'll get yourself covered with filth."

"Well, I just like to see other folks' horses is all," the girl said.

"That's the stupidest thing I ever heard! Just look at them on the street if you have to, but stay on the boardwalk!" Ma snapped back.

The noonday-mail coach arrived just as the three were entering the dry goods store. The elegant vehicle, with its shiny horses and stylish harness, took Charlotte's breath away as she stood in the doorway dumbfounded. It was so impressive to her young mind. The driver smiled at her and tipped his hat so elegantly as they rolled by.

Tales of the Express   15

Charlotte followed along the rest of the trip without saying much more than yes or no, contemplating her next move. All the way home she made a mental list of the things that she would take with her.

When the family finally arrived back home, it was dark but still fairly warm. Isaiah was uselessly drunk and staggered into the house. Charlotte went right to work on the evening chores after first donning an old coat so as not to soil her new dress. She began unhitching and unharnessing the horses and feeding the livestock, happily lost in the fray. She was tired and wanted to be alone with her thoughts. After her own dinner, she chose to relax in Blue's box stall, which she always kept well bedded; it felt safe there. She gave her friend some apples, then opened the stall door to the pasture, and the horse leapt out into the night air to greet his waiting mares.

Charlotte threw the old coat down on the soft sweet straw and curled up on it like a kitten, then closed her eyes. She could feel sleep creeping in on her when a sound told her that maybe it wasn't just sleep that was doing the creeping. The squeaking barn wood above her made the hair on the back of her neck bristle. A dark sense of doom came over her as Ephram emerged from the loft of the barn.

"Well, look who it is! My sweet little sister," the voice laughed from the feed door above. Ephram had remained home and discovered one of Isaiah's bottles of rye. While the family was in town, he had passed out in the back of the hayloft and had slept for several hours. The girl's conversation with the horse had woke him, and he had been watching her from the loft as she lay in the straw until he could no longer resist such a tempting little lamb, all dressed up like Christmas mutton.

"Why are you all dressed up like that, little Charlotte?" Ephram asked.

"We went to town," she replied.

"You look like a little woman!" Ephram laughed.

"Leave me alone, Ephram!" Charlotte snapped.

"Now don't be so unfriendly! I didn't mean you no harm I just meant that I ain't never much seen you as a girl, just a scruffy little thing workin' in the yard . . . I could get used to it, though!" he said eyeing the sweet little package.

The girl could see trouble on the horizon; Ephram was the fruit of Isaiah's loins.

"So what are you doing here in the barn so late, little woman?" Ephram cooed. He was in the loft over the opening of Blue's stall, lying on his belly; he grabbed the cross support and rolled down, dropping onto the straw next to the girl.

Charlotte tried to scamper to her feet, but she was no match for the older boy; she could feel her body stiffening up as it had the night before.

"You feel right womanly too! Relax, Charlotte, I ain't gonna hurt you. I'm just showing you some brotherly love."

"Ephram, please don't, Ephram, please don't!"

"Why, I'm not hurting you! See? I just want to show you my love!" the young man said, grabbing her by the hair as his father had done and kissing her forcefully on the mouth.

She bit his lip, then pulled her face away from his as Ephram ripped at the back of her dress. The drunk boy hit her in the face, giving Charlotte yet another in a long list of black eyes. He was sitting on her stomach and trying to undress her at the same time.

"I'm sorry I ripped your dress. I didn't mean it, it just ripped," Ephram smirked sarcastically. All the girl could do was whimper and thrash as some of the skirt gave way. She landed a knee to the groin, and Ephram gave off with a howl!

Then Charlotte saw rescue's dark outline at the stall door! He was like a freight train, full of steam and fire and fury. He charged in and struck with full force, sending Ephram's skull crashing into the wall of the barn! Ephram barely had time to react to the stallions attack, and then he was dead.

Blue stood over the girl after she passed out, the gore that was once her stepbrother was more than her young mind could endure.

Oh, there was no mistaking it, he was dead! His nose was badly broken and twisted, along with his scrawny neck. His skull was cleanly stove in with an imprint of a horse's shoe in the back of his head.

Charlotte came to, stroking the stallion's face as he blew grassy breath above her. Charlotte felt like she was stuck in molasses, she should be doing something. What? What? First thing was to hide Ephram's body. She grabbed the pitchfork and began to throw straw on him, then stopped. "Maybe he's got some money on him. He ain't gonna need it," Charlotte muttered. The child carefully pulled the straw back off and began to go through his pockets, trying not to look at his twisted face and strangely bulging neck. She had to stop to throw up once.

She found a pocket watch, some coins, tobacco, a pocketknife, and his flint stone—all things that will come in handy in her new career as a vagabond. She quickly piled the straw heavily over the body and tried to make it look unnoticeable, then she put the stallion in the tie stall next to the saddles and gave him a very full measure of grain. She decided to use Ephram's saddle; maybe they would think that he had run away too. As she saddled the horse, she spotted some burlap sacks and filled them full of barley, then tied them onto the back of the saddle with some saddlebags. Charlotte packed as much grain as she felt Blue could carry. Next she had to go back to the house and change from her ripped dress.

Charlotte felt herself trembling as the reality of what was happening began to set in. She blew out the light in the barn and led Blue out, tying him to a tree behind the house until she was ready to leave. She was beginning to realize that her life would never be the same again.

Charlotte needed to get to her room without being seen. She was scared; her dress was all ripped in the back and covered with blood in the front. Isaiah was busy yelling at Ma, but for a change, Ma was yelling back! She too was sporting another swollen eye.

The girl slunk up into her room as quickly and quietly as she could, keeping her head down, it throbbed from Ephram's violent attack. As soon as she was in, she ripped off the remains of her new dress, vowing to herself never to wear another stupid corset and scrambled for her work coveralls. She crept into Ephram's room and gathered up some of his clothes that Ma had just cleaned and retreated back to her room. When she was dressed in Ephram's clothes, she got her money from its hiding place and shoved it into an inside vest pocket. The boy's clothes were baggy, and the pants bunched around the girl's slender frame as she tightened the belt. Charlotte threw what few possessions she felt she needed into a burlap sack and tied it with some old bootlaces, then climbed out the window.

The trembling child could still hear Isaiah laying down the law and became profoundly sad. She said a prayer for her ma.

Blue's call snapped her back to reality, and visions of Ephram's twisted face tore through her mind, and she knew it was time to go!

When she reached the horse, she tied on her makeshift luggage and climbed aboard. Ephram's saddle felt so foreign; she was used to riding bareback. She assumed that after a few hundred miles, it would feel just like home. She looked up and admired the large moon and galloped off!

Now Charlotte greeted the great aloneness. It was strange and frightening but at the same time, thrilling and wonderful! She felt like a bird that had just left the nest or escaped from a cage! She must get her bearings and move quickly, for she had no idea how soon they would find the body and discover her missing.

It was sometime after midnight when Mrs. Parker felt Isaiah get up. She lay perfectly still until she heard him leave the room. Then she put on her robe and went to the doorway. Cracking it open as quietly as she could, she watched Isaiah enter her daughter's bedroom and felt the hatred welling up inside like a burning dagger in her heart. She pulled back into the bedroom as Isaiah suddenly appeared again in the hallway; he was muttering something under his whiskey-soaked breath and didn't notice her. She was standing by the door shaking, but instead of coming back into the bedroom, Abigail was surprised that Isaiah went outside instead.

She quickly went into her daughter's room and saw the new dress in a pile on the floor.

"God have mercy!" Ma looked around. "Charlotte?" Ma whispered, her bed had not been slept in. Ma crept back to her own room and sat on her bed, visions of the trouble that Charlotte must have endured tortured her mind. "Well that's it then!" Ma said to herself with conviction.

It wasn't much longer, when the wayward Isaiah came sneaking back to his bedroom. He kicked off his boots and pants and got under the covers; cupping his hands around his wife's breasts, he fell fast asleep. When she was sure that he was good and settled, Abigail rolled over with the family gun in hand and shot Isaiah in the head. She calmly got up and reloaded the gun, asking God for his forgiveness for her sins and praying for him to watch over her last remaining child. She then took the pistol and pointed it at her own temple and pulled the trigger. It wasn't until several weeks later, when a neighbor brought back some of the horses that had strayed, that anyone discovered what had happened, or even thought to look for Charlotte. No one ever looked for her. She was free and didn't even know it.

CHAPTER 2

Charlotte tried not to look back to her past but be reborn like she had read in the Bible.

"Now I can be anyone I want to be! And I ain't gonna be no stupid girl!" she grumbled to herself.

At thirteen years of age, Charlotte had very strong shoulders and arms from the manual labor involved in working on a farm. She had not yet cultivated any feminine curves; all she really needed to do was cut off her hair, she daydreamed.

"We gotta stop soon." The child sighed to her horse, they were so tired, she had ridden all night, and the sun was just beyond the horizon. Finally, the traveler made out what looked like good grazing for the horse, and the girl got down. She untied a long rope she had brought, then tied it between two trees, then she slipped Blue's bridle off and tied his halter rope to the hemp-hitching rail so it could slide back and forth, the way her pa had shown her when she was very young. Charlotte dropped to the ground next to the tree, closing her eyes; she could sleep just as she was. Some inner something forced her to sit upright again. She sat examining her meager possessions; the most valuable she supposed was Ephram's knife.

"Well, I guess I better do it." Charlotte braided her waist long, honey-red hair as tightly as she could in two thick braids, then tied them off tightly with some of her luggage laces. Taking Ephram's knife she cut off the braids, and tied up the loose ends. She then put the hair in the saddlebags. "I hope I can sell them," she sighed, as she took the knife and trimmed the rest of her hair, trying in vain to imitate a man's cut. Without any looking glass, it came out pretty scruffy. At least she had the presence of mind to take Ephram's hat; it covered up most of the hack job.

As the sun came up, Charlotte found that she had selected a fairly good spot. Untying the horse from the tether, she led him to a stream for a drink. Then returned him to a new graze and settled down for some sleep, taking comfort in the rustling of her beloved friend.

A few hours passed when she was awaken by the Blue's restlessness; he had gotten disenchanted with his stabling conditions, pacing back and forth. Charlotte took it as a signal to go. She packed up her stuff and saddled the horse as he ate a ration of grain, then covered up the horse's pawing marks with some dried brush and leaves and swung up in the saddle. The two paused again at the stream and then were gone.

Charlotte stopped rather abruptly in the middle of a meadow. "I must figure out which way is south." Slowly she rode the horse in a circle. "Ma said that Boston was south. I think that's where I ought to go. Now, the sun rises in the east and sets in the west, so if the sun is on my left side, I must be pointed south. Yes, that sounds right, at least till noontime." The vagabond pulled out her new pocket watch and noted the time. "Nine twenty-three. All right, let's go now." She clucked to her companion. It was a good day for adventure!

After about an hour of meadows and woods, crossing streams, and dense fern groves, on deer trails, Charlotte came upon a road. It wasn't much of a road, just twin paths or ruts with lots of hoof tracks. It was rather exciting wondering where it would lead.

Around midday, Charlotte found another suitable field to graze and stopped for a break. It was a beautiful day for traveling; the summer air was not sticky, but fresh. She tied the horse in the same manner as before. Instead of resting next to the horse though, she sat near the road in case a traveler might go by, and she had the opportunity to ask directions. Her stomach moaned. Looking at the horse, she sighed, "At least you have something to eat!" The girl found some dandelions to chew, they were bitter, but it was better than nothing.

Soon the child's ears perked up; the jingling of harness was ever so faint. There was no mistake, Blue had heard the horses coming too, he whinnied to them. Charlotte's heart was pounding as she spotted the coach horses through the trees, making their way closer. She quickly ran and untied her horse and got on without the saddle and galloped to the road. She felt the stallion's heart pumping like before a race; it was clear that the coach was not slowing down. The stallion was now hopping around like a crazed schoolchild, as the coach, pulled by six horses, roared by. Charlotte galloped up behind it and when she could, she maneuvered next to the driver.

"Excuse me! Where does this road go?" the innocent asked.

"Nashua!" the driver, clearly annoyed, called back as he slowed his eager horses.

"Is Boston near there?" Charlotte asked. The driver laughed out loud at the naive boy.

"No, but you are going in the right direction. Is that all?" the driver curtly answered.

"I guess so, much obliged, sir," Charlotte replied. The driver tipped his hat and cracked his whip in one fluid motion and was gone in a moment, like a dream, leaving only a puff of smoky dust behind. Charlotte headed back to collect her gear, then would be on her way.

"This is the right way. That's what the man said." Charlotte didn't know anything about the towns ahead, but it would be nice to get some food. She had hopes of reaching a town before nightfall. The gray stallion settled in to a nice pace as they passed many creeks and streams. Finally, just before the sun began to set, Charlotte arrived at what looked like an inn or a stage stop and got off her horse.

She had roughly twenty-five dollars and did not have any idea how much that was or how far you could travel on it; she felt the need to save what little she had. Charlotte adjusted her baggy and rough-looking attire. The worn-out hat was too big, but it did help to hide the black eye. She tightened the belt of the trousers and turned up the hems so they wouldn't drag. The girl could feel herself beginning to shake as she got closer to the inn. She tied Blue to the hitch rail and approached the front door. The low and gravely voices of the men inside tumbled out to the night air from the window, and it caused her to shake even more. Waddling up the steps, trying to think up something to say, she stopped just outside the door. There was a boisterous crowd inside, and it wasn't helping her confidence any. She could say that she was lost and had been so for days; yes, that was it. Could she work for food and board for the night? That would have to do. Biting her lip, she could smell the food inside, and it made her stomach roar; hunger pains would be her courage. The vagabond rubbed her blackened eye.

As she opened the door, the men were having a roaring good laugh; then they all turned to see what appeared to be a scrawny little man walk in, causing them to fall silent for a moment. Then, as if on cue, the men all busted out in even louder fits of hilarity as if the odd boy had been the punch line of a joke.

Charlotte could feel her face turning scarlet as she scuffled to the bar.

"What'll it be my, good man? Shot of whiskey?" the bartender asked as another round of laughter spread about the smoky room.

"Scrappy little chap! Get a look at that eye!" A man at the bar pointed out.

"I'm lost," a timid voice spoke, trying to be manly.

"What? Speak up, we don't bite!" the pudgy man roared.

"I . . . I'm a . . . I've been lost. I wonder if I can get food and board for my horse and me! I haven't much money," the vagabond stuttered.

"Well, what line of work are you in?" the bartender asked. Another round of laughter ensued.

"I can clean . . . stuff!" Charlotte meant to say stalls but saw all the dishes all around the bar.

"Would that be with a shovel or with a sponge and hot water?" the bartender chuckled. The kid was relieved that the man was kind even though it was clear that the young boy was the butt of all the laughter.

"What . . . what ever you need!" stuttered Charlotte "I . . . I just need some food and rest for my horse and me . . . Is all."

"Well, I guess I can find something for you. You don't look like you'd eat much, small man such as you are. You go to the barn and tell Jacob you're gonna work for your night's food and lodging and that he should make room for your horse, then you come back inside and do dishes, and tomorra you clean the barn. Does that sound fair?"

"Yes, sir," the boy replied. "Thank you, sir." Charlotte wheeled around nearly doing a pratfall in such a hurry to get out the door.

Looking around, she saw a light coming from the barn and headed toward it with her horse in tow to get settled for the night. This would have to be less embarrassing than the tavern, she thought as she led the stallion into the barn. From out of one of the stalls came an immense tree of a man.

"Well, what have we got here?" the tree spoke. Blue nervously snorted.

"The barman told me to a . . . um . . . he said I could a . . . put my horse up for the night if I did the dishes and cleaned the barn!" Charlotte was shaking again.

"Oh, he did, did he? Well, just where in the hell did the bartender figure on puttin' this horse, in the kitchen cupboard? . . . Well?" the tree boomed. "Jesus, that animal is a stud! Where did a scrawny kid like you get such a fine horse?"

"I raised him!" Charlotte shot back. "I ain't so scrawny neither. I work hard!" the hungry boy shouted rebelliously.

"Well, don't cry about it. All my stalls are full, but I'll tell you what I'll do. You take that old cow over there, outside, and you put him in the corral with them mules out there. Bossy ain't a gonna like it, but that's tough. Then you can put that fine-lookin' horse of yours in here for the night." The big man softened. The small vagabond could see the man's face had a nice smile, and he seemed to like Blue.

"You say you raised this animal, how old is he?" the big man asked.

"Seven."

"Well, hell, you ain't hardly any older than that yourself!" Jacob roared.

"I'm seventeen!" Charlotte lied.

"Well, then you mean that this horse raised you!" Jacob laughed. "You want to sell him?" he asked, taking Blues reins as the young boy got the cow from her comfortable stall.

"No!"

"I was just asking. Don't get mad. Watch out for them mules!" Jacob called out as the odd boy took the cow out to the corral. Bossy had other ideas and planted her feet, determined not to enter the domain of the long-eared devils. After a game of tug-of-war, ending with the cow as the victor, Charlotte tied the cow to an oak tree next to the corral instead. Then headed back to the barn to get Blue settled in.

Charlotte found him already bedded down for the night, munching away happily. "I put your gear over yonder." Jacob pointed.

"I'll just sleep in the stall with my horse," the child yawned.

"Suit yourself, lofts probably more comfortable though. And there's no smoking in the barn."

"Well, I guess I'll go do some dishes then, thank you," the kid said.

"You're welcome, you can call me Jacob," he answered, shaking the boy's hand.

"You can call me Charley," Charlotte said with a sleepy smile.

"Don't worry about your horse. He'll be fine. I'll take good care a him, Charley," Jacob reassured the boy as he made his way back to the noisy tavern.

Bracing himself for another round of jokes at his expense, Charley entered the tavern, and to his relief was put right to work washing dishes. It felt nice to have his arms in hot water for a while, not quite a bath but close.

"Hey, Al, get the kid here a plate a food. I can hear his stomach growling from here!" the bartender barked out to the amusement of his patrons.

Charley wolfed the food down; it was as good as it smelled. Home-baked bread and beef and vegetable stew with a rich broth, and fresh milk, it was just what the young traveler needed. When the kid was back on the job, he was as careful as could be with the glassware, the likes of which he had never seen.

The beverages that the bartender made were equally intriguing. Especially the drink called a flip. Charley watched as the man mixed up a batter of eggs and cream and sugar and rum then added it to a big metal tankard that was filled three-fourths with a thick dark beer. Then he pulled out a funny sort of a poker that was very hot from the fire and put it into the mix with a great flurry; it hissed and foamed and was quite popular with the patrons. When Charley thought no one was watching, he tasted the remains of one and found that it was not to his liking at all. Must be an acquired taste, he thought. It made his head feel funny.

At last Charley was finished doing dishes, and made his way back to the barn with a minimum of questions asked. The child was exhausted, but it felt good to be under a roof even if it was a barn. Charley felt most at home in a barn anyway.

The next morning's activity came before dawn. When Jacob came into the barn to feed the horses, they began to whinny and paw, anxiously defending their not-yet-served portions of grain and hay. Charley brought water to each horse and took orders from Jacob as they came.

"Next we'll harness up these six. They gotta be ready to go in one hour." Each horse's harness hung behind the horse occupying the stall, so at least there was no guessing at who's harness was who's. Charley was used to harnessing up the family's horses, so at least he knew what he was doing, but six of them were a lot more than he was used to.

"Check their feet before you put their collars on, boy," boomed Jacob.

"I think this one has a loose shoe," Charley called back.

"You're right, Charley, good eye. You saved some trouble down the road." Jacob skillfully fixed the problem in a few minutes, moving very quickly for his immense size, clinching the shoe on the hoof with the precise tool and examining his work.

"Well, they look dressed to me!" Jacob said as the morning-mail coach came jingling into the station.

"That outside line isn't buckled, "Charley pointed out.

"Yep, you gotta good eye for detail, boy! That's another problem you nipped in the bud. Where's that good for nothing Trencher?" the big man bellowed.

"He's not here yet," another man who had come to the barn answered.

"That worthless piece of flesh!" Jacob swore. "Charley, go head those horses on the coach. I'll start unhitching them. Move, boy!" Jacob said, shoving the kid in front of the tired, sweaty horses. Jacob began to unthread the reins from the lead team and coil them onto the horse's collars; he then unhooked their tugs, and had Charley take them to the tie stalls the newly harnessed horses had occupied. They repeated the process until the six horses were free of the coach. Jacob then met the boy in the barn and instructed him further.

"Now you take these wheeler horses, and I'll take this swing team, and we'll get them hitched," Jacob ordered. Charley took the two biggest horses to the coach backing them into place, one on either side of the wagon pole, then passed their reins to the driver. Charley then buckled the cross-check lines to the inside of each horse's bit, then fastened their neck yoke chains to the pole between them. By then Jacob had the swing team in front of the wheelers and had attached a set of double trees to the end of the pole as Charley hooked their tug chains to the single trees.

"Make sure those tug links are secure on the single trees. I don't want anyone coming loose. Now take these lines and thread them through these carriers and back to the driver while I go on and get the leaders but watch out for the red horse, he bites. You just bite him back, boy!"

Jacob reappeared shortly with the last of the horses and placed them into position.

"Now you just stand in the front and head the team till they're ready to go, Charley," Jacob said as he was threading the last lines up to the driver, who was collecting them and sorting them to the proper finger locations. Sleepy-headed passengers were now making sure that their belongings were on board and boarding themselves. Charley took it all in with awe, especially the driver on his lofty perch with fancy whip and gloves and hat. This was all quite new for someone who had never been off the farm much.

Charley snapped to attention as the red horse bit him on the arm.

"I told you that red horse bites!" Jacob laughed. "All right, boy, stand aside!" Charley had barely gotten out of the way, and horses were off like the wind! What a feeling of excitement it must be to drive so many spirited horses, he thought; it had taken his breath away and almost run him over at the same time!

"We'll see to those new horses. Then you can go get your breakfast," Jacob said, slapping the young lad on the back. "You done fine, boy."

The lad was exhausted and hungry again by the time he had unharnessed and brushed down the six new horses. This is a losing battle, Charley thought. He needed to press on soon; he wasn't far enough away yet.

After breakfast, he washed the morning dishes and thanked the innkeeper for his hospitality, then went to the barn to collect his things and Blue.

"I hate to lose a good helper such as yourself, Charley. You gotta good hand with the horses. You take good care of that stallion. He looks to be getting a bit sore on that right front foot," Jacob advised. "If you want to stud that horse out, you just look me up," Jacob called after.

"Thanks," the boy said as he turned the gray horse and loped off down the road. At least they both had a full belly and a night's rest, clean fingernails too, Charley thought. "They really thought I was a boy, Blue! That was easy. I ain't never gonna be no dumb girl ever again!" Charley chattered to the horse.

Charley cantered along trying to imagine what it must be like sitting in the driver's box of a great coach. What power to have running through your fingers; it would be so exciting!

Charley rode toward the big city to lose himself in the masses; it was his plan. He would look for work in a stable; that was logical. They seem to always have an endless amount of manure to clean up and such; after all, Jacob had said he was good with horses.

The boy should have been paying more attention to his horse really, for he failed to notice the signs of nervousness until it was almost too late. Blue swerved hard to the right, dropping Charley to the side of the saddle. Blue's head came up abruptly as he danced sideways, the rider hanging on madly to the unfamiliar leather.

"Easy, Blue!" Charley yelled. "What is the matter with you!" The horse was backing up fast as Charley heard a bear cub crying in the tree above.

"Damnation!" Charley yelled. Ironically, the baby bear and the jockey were in the same position, both just barely hanging on. Charley and the cub hit the ground at the same time. "Oh Lord . . . help me," the child moaned; luckily he hadn't lost Blue's reins. Suddenly he heard the mother bear's growl. "Mama was coming, but from which direction? It didn't matter, just get on," he thought.

"Easy, Blue, steady damn it!" Charley pleaded, finally climbing back in the saddle, just as Mama bear came charging. Letting the reins slack, he didn't even have to ask Blue; they were moving fast! Mama followed for a while then went back to her fallen offspring. If the child had taken longer to get on the horse, he may have been their lunch. Charley's heart was pounding; he decided to put some distance between the bear family and himself before he could breath easier.

As Charley rode out of the shadows of the trees to an open meadow, he looked down the road as it crested a hill; his heart was again in his mouth! Coming about five hundred yards away was a traveling tribe of Indian braves.

"Savages!" Charley gulped. He had heard stories, mostly from Ephram, of people being skinned alive and scalped or burned and such, but until now, he had never laid eyes on any Indians, especially not a whole tribe, by the looks of them.

"Shit!" he panicked, having no idea what kind of savages they were or just what to do and what he was up against here, but Lord have mercy, they were an impressive sight! Charley was reminded of the inn with everyone staring! The vagabond was trembling like a rabbit, surrounded by a pack of wolves, not knowing what to do! Blue must have sensed this for he stood right up on his hind legs for a moment as if to make himself appear larger when he came back to the ground the plan was clear. Run!

Charley turned the horse and charged off the road onto a heavily wooded deer trail. The natives, who were now curious, stopped to watch the young boy's retreat. They had been on a hunting party and not particularly interested in the young boy but were rather amused and amazed at his horsemanship and daring. They ran after Charley in mocking and fun, but the boy didn't know this. He smelled their heady animal odor and was truly terrified by their face paint and savage wardrobe. Blue ran his greatest race that day. They must have galloped for four or five miles before they stopped at the edge of a deep creek bank to assess the situation. The Indians had long given up the race and had proceeded on their own merry way, but Charley had veered from his course and was now headed west of Boston.

The last encounter really made the child stop and think about what he had gotten into! As Charley slid off the horse he realized he had wet his pants.

"Damnation! Just like a baby!" On closer examination, it wasn't urine but blood. "Shit! The curse! I forgot about that." Charley felt queasy! It was getting late and time to make camp. Blue was feeling the effects of the day too and was beginning to limp. The pair then waded into the creek for a soak. The cool water would help both of them. As Charley stood in the water contemplating this new predicament, she realized this was part of her sex that wasn't fixed with a simple haircut. Splashing in the water, she noticed that the creek was quite full of residents, some of them attracted by the blood smell she emitted. When she saw the shadow of a four-foot pike, she got the hell out of the water and decided it was time to catch dinner or at least try. Charley found some good grazing for Blue and tethered him out with the rope, then stripped off the wet pants and hung them in a tree to dry. She dug in her bag for the napkins but soon found she had left them behind. She had been smart enough to grab a handful of clean handkerchiefs though, so she made due with a handkerchief diaper then put on the extra long john she had brought. She felt so alone, and she missed her mother; the homesick girl tried not to cry.

Hunger was really taking hold now, but how to catch a fish with no hook or line was the problem. Looking at the knife, the child thought, maybe a spear would work. Looking around, Charley finally found a sapling that looked about right and set about cutting it and sharpening it, trying his best to whittle it so that it had a barb, like her father had carved.

Charley started a small hardwood fire in some rocks to dry his pants. Tromping around in some long johns and a shirt, he looked around for some bait. Charley filled the hem of his shirt with as many varieties of things that he thought would attract fish, then returned to the water, climbing on boulders and rocks, trying all the time to keep low. The first of the bait washed right on down the river; then the kid had an idea and went back to Blue.

"Sorry, boy," Charley mumbled as he cut some of his long tail hairs with the knife. Returning to the water, Charley tied several tail hairs together to make a long line, tying a worm on at the end, then tossed it in the water, tying the dry end to a branch that hung over the water. He would wait on a rock for a fish, then try to spear him. The small fish seemed pretty adept at taking the bait, and the worms were eaten quickly enough. Sitting on the rocks, Charley felt the muscles in her pelvis cramping and the wetness between her legs spreading, even gushing, as she stood to relieve the discomfort in her lower back. "Damn those fish!" she swore as the last worm floated down the stream. Then she tried beetles, without effect. Lastly she tried the handkerchief that was now soaked in blood. She sat motionless, mesmerized by the calming, rippling music of the water, waiting with spear in hand for some dinner to happen by.

"This will never work," the fisherman said in despair, about to throw the makeshift fishing spear in the water when he spotted the long dark shadow again making its way toward the bloody cloth. Charley slowly brought the bait in, trying to get into position without startling the fish. Finally, he got close enough, and Charley heaved the spear as hard as he could and sent it right through him, but he was a big fish and thrashing, and they were both going for a swim!

The pike went into a spasm as soon as he was hit, and Charley jumped into the water to grab the thrashing spear. Grabbing the wood as they hit bottom, he lost his grip coming up for air. It was a good hit though, and the pike was in trouble, but the current was swift, and unless Charley could stay with him, there would be no dinner. Charley caught the end of the stick, but now the fish was fighting and trying to bite. Luckily, they drifted into shallower water, and the spiked pike got wedged on some rocks. The nearly drown child grabbed a ham-sized rock and bashed the ugly fish in the head with it!

Charley rested for a moment with the spear in hand, not anxious to let the hard-won prize get away, then she stood up, and slogged back to her horse and camp. She decided that she would clean her catch in the river to keep the bears away if that was possible. At least she would eat good tonight, unless there were unexpected visitors.

Hanging the fish in a tree, using the spear, Charley commenced to build up the small campfire that had dried the stained pants. There was plenty of wood around, and it wasn't long before the small blaze was ready to cook on. Charley found some large branches and with some rocks, made a kind of a woodland coat rack next to the fire to dry the clothes. Wrapped in Blue's saddle blanket, like a pint-sized squaw in soggy long johns, Charley set about preparing dinner. Nervous about attracting natives, he kept the fire on the small side. Tomorrow Charley would push on for a town; he was not anxious for any more surprises. Snuggling in close to the fire as he cooked, Charley drooled over the huge fish, setting half of it to linger over the hardwood smoke. When stuffed to the brim, and he could eat no more, he looked around for a tree that might be a suitable place to sleep.

Charley chose an old tree that had some very thick branches and retethered the precious horse between it and a maple tree, stringing the portable hitching rope from one to the other, so that he could graze all the grass between the trees. Returning to the fire, Charley collected up the now-dry clothes and put them all on and smothered the fire. Wrapping what would fit of the smoked fish in a grain sack, Charley tossed the rest down near the water, hoping that if a bear came he would be satisfied with that.

The sky was growing dark, and Charley went to the tree, with the fish and a saddle blanket, then pulled Blue up to use as a living stepladder, climbing up as high in the branches as he could. It was a splendid tree, and Charley felt pretty safe up in it.

Keeping the knife in hand in case it was needed, he tried to get some sleep. Aware of the nocturnal creatures about in the woods, it was difficult not to be jittery. Charley wedged himself in some branches but wasn't terribly comfortable. When he did manage to nod off, his dreams were filled with strange-painted faces, with claws and teeth. He couldn't imagine what kinds of dangers the city held, but the accommodations had to be better than this!

CHAPTER 3

Finally, the comforting rays of dawn came without any surprises in the night. Except for some dampness from the dew and dampness at her crotch and stiffness in her joints from sleeping in a tree, Charley felt pretty good. She grabbed her fish breakfast and made her way out of the spreading oak, then untied Blue, and went to the water. She noticed that the extra fish had been dined on, but it looked like it had been raccoons, not bears. Nothing goes to waste in the forest. Charley found fresh grass for Blue and built a small fire to warm her young bones and her fish breakfast. Using Ephram's flint to spark up some dry grass, she felt that her senses seemed to be sharper somehow, for she was aware of every little twig snap and movement in the brush.

Soon the young traveler was under way again, trying to find the road and a big city to hide in.

Charley could feel the stallion's lameness becoming more pronounced; he got off and walked next to his friend. As they went along, Charley met some fellow travelers and found that they were now headed for Worchester, Massachusetts, not Boston. It really didn't matter to Charley, who had no way of knowing if he was missing a thing, never having been to these places. The traveler just wanted to get where he could blend into the background, work, and take care of Blue.

By late afternoon, Charley began to see more and more farms. The recently graded road was full of wagon tracks that snaked around a lovely pond with an island at the center. The child admired the civilization as he walked along, in step with the tall gray horse; it looked inviting and friendly. There were so many different kinds of shops; shoemakers and leather works, butcher shops, tanneries, wagon makers, and wheelwrights all laid out in an orderly fashion. There at a large steepled white church was a sign; at last Charley had arrived at Worchester, Massachusetts. People were going about their business, and the well-kept streets were alive with horse-drawn wagons of all types. Charley and Blue wandered down through town, looking for the livery stable, until the child spotted a big newly painted red barn next to a sign that read Balch House in white letters. The young horseman felt that this might be a good place to inquire.

"I must look a terrible sight!" the child mumbled as he tied Blue next to the water trough in front of the spacious barn. "How pathetic! Well, maybe it will work in my favor." Charley spotted a very stout man in front of the barn, stuffing tobacco in his pipe; he looked friendly enough. Charley took a deep breath, hiked up his trousers and adjusted his hat, then approached him. The child admired the man's shiny brown boots and a broad-brimmed gray hat, which framed his wiry orange beard. He smiled as he looked at the child's dappled horse, playing in the water trough.

"Sir, I am wonderin' if you know of any work that I could do? For . . . um, food and lodging for myself and my horse . . . he's lame."

"Oh, that's too bad, boy. What's wrong with him?" the stout man asked.

"I'm not sure, maybe stone bruised."

"You're kinda young to be out on your own, aren't you?"

"I'm sixteen, sir," Charley lied.

"Where's your folks?"

"I'm an orphan, sir."

"I see. Well, I might be able to use an extra hand around here," Ebenezer Balch said, scratching his ear and looking over his new prospect.

While the two were chatting, a black hearse, with four spirited black horses with intricately braided manes, elegantly harnessed with silver buckles and topped with black plumes on their bridles, stopped in front of the barn. The driver was a serious-looking fellow, dressed entirely in black.

"I've got to leave. I received word at the cemetery that there is a problem at home," the driver related.

"Yes, well, off you go then, Mr. Brenner," Eb said with annoyance barely concealed. The driver's assistant, an awkward-looking, skinny, adolescent, jumped down and began unhitching the horses. This seemed to infuriate the stout man who was now climbing to the driver's seat.

"Damned Jehu, will you look at the mud on those wheels!" Eb mumbled under his breath. "Goddamn it, Felix, don't unhitch those animals yet! First, take those plumes off the bridles before the horses rub on them and ruin them! Jesus, Mary, and Joseph!" The stout man was shaking his head. "Well, don't just stand there, kid. Do you want a job, or don't you?"

"Yes, sir!" Charley dashed over to the magnificent team and began gathering up feathers, with the awkward boy.

"Just set them in the back of the hearse for now. I didn't catch your name?" Eb said, collecting the leather lines off the brake bar.

"Charlo . . . ah . . . a . . . Charley, sir," the boy said, enthralled with the plumage he was holding.

"Put those feather dusters in the back."

Felix smiled at the young scruffy kid, his teeth were uneven and yellow, but his smile was genuine.

"All right now, you and Charley meet me behind the barn," the stout man squawked as he sorted leather in his fat hands; he was like a big mother hen as he clucked to the horses.

Charley trotted along behind Felix as they went through the barn to the back entry to unhitch the horses from the long elegant black wagon.

"We'll park the hearse by hand," Eb instructed as the boys began the unhitching process. They began with the two front horses and worked their way back, as Eb held the reins of the dwindling team.

The huge red barn was full of a wonderful assortment of vehicles, the likes of which Charley had never seen.

"The harness is hung there," Felix instructed as he tied the black horse in his stall. Charley nodded, looking around like a kid in a candy shop.

"These wheels are filthy. Did you take a shortcut through a plowed field?" Eb bellowed. The boys were now backing the vehicle in the barn; Eb steered the vehicle by turning the front wheels with the pole. "The hearse must be cleaned before the mud dries on there!" he said, stopping the vehicle in the middle of the barn. "Well, kid, you seem like a hard worker. If you want a job here, you're hired. My name is Ebenezer Balch. I own this livery and the inn next door. Your name is Charley? Charley what?"

"Parker . . . um, Parkhurst, sir." Charley said, inventing a new moniker.

Ebenezer nearly doubled over with laughter; it was a musical laugh and was contagious.

"Parkhurst, well, then you should feel right at home here. Son, if you work for me, I'll make a man of you!" Ebenezer offered.

"Yes, sir," Charley said, smiling to himself, holding out his hand. The two shook on the deal, and the newly christened Charley Parkhurst breathed a sigh of relief.

"First, unharness the horses. Then, Felix, you show Mr. Parkhurst here how we wash wheels in this livery. Then, see if you two can get it parked without scraping any paint off it! After that you can unbraid the horses," Eb instructed.

"Come on, let's get started. I'm hungry," Felix whined as he pulled on his work smock, then smiled at his new work-mate.

Charley looked outside to make sure Blue was still secure, then the two boys began their chores. Felix was a quiet boy of seventeen, kind of clumsy, but he seemed friendly.

"Mr. Balch likes everything done just so, and he gets real mad when you don't do things his way," Felix explained.

"I could see that," Charley said as the two put the hearse on the wagon jack.

"Now see the wheel can turn freely. It's easier to wash," Felix instructed as he poured water from a bucket over the steel tire into a basin that fit perfectly beneath the wheel. "We wash all the wagons and grease the axles before we put them away, generally, so you see there is a lot of work here, and frankly I'm glad to have someone else here to help out!" he said, smiling a toothy grin.

"Jeez . . ." Charley thought. "What have I gotten myself into." As the young boy spun the wagon wheel, another thought popped to mind. "What's a Jehu?"

"I don't know what the exact meanin' is. I think it means a driver who gets the wheels muddy 'cause that's when I hear it mostly. You should ask Mr. Balch," Felix said, slopping the wet towel on the spokes.

After a while, the hearse was clean and dried, and the two managed to maneuver it to its designated spot without a mishap. Charley was enchanted with the long black vehicle, its craftsmanship and carved, curved lines, he didn't mind polishing it at all, just a little taken aback when he found out that it was for hauling around dead people. Felix thought it was funny that the new man was dumber than him.

"Where can I bed down my horse?" Charley inquired.

"You can put him in that end stall, then help me unbraid these black horses," Felix replied. They were real beauties too, very well matched; in fact, Charley had a hard time telling one from the other. The new employee ran his hands over the beautiful black braiding, cascading down the soft velvet neck; Charley had never see anything so lovely.

"Do you always braid the horses' manes like this?" Charley asked.

"No, we have different styles for different occasions," Felix answered. "Do you see the different types of carriages? After we feed the horses, we'll go to the tavern and get our supper. Then I'll show you where you'll sleep."

"Oh, I'll just sleep in the barn with my horse," Charley replied. Felix just stared at Charley as if he were some sort of an idiot.

"Come on, I'm starving," Felix said, starting off for the tavern, running his dirty fingers through his dark greasy hair and shaking his head in an imitation of Ebenezer. "Jesus, Mary, and Joseph, what an idiot!"

The tavern was warm and filled with wonderful smells that made Charley's stomach growl. There were about ten people sitting around as they came in.

"Don't you track mud in on my clean floors now, boys!" a large woman in an apron called out. Charley stopped short and looked at his boots, then went back outside with Felix and stomped around a bit, then made a fresh entrance.

"This here is Charley Parkhurst, everyone!" Felix called out. Charley could feel his face getting red and hot as the men laughed. He followed Felix over to the large lady who had a kind face, framed with lots of soft red hair, streaked with silver and a smile that told of a generous heart.

"Charley, this is Mrs. Balch," Felix said.

"Pleased to make your acquaintance, young man," Mary Balch said as she stretched out a soft but very strong freckled hand.

"Likewise, ma'am," Charley replied.

"Well, now that that's done, you fellows wash up there, and I'll fix you up a plate!" Mary said, getting back to business.

"It sure does smell good, what ever is cookin'," Charley reported.

"Why, thank you, young man. You have good taste," Mary replied as she began ladling out some food onto two fairly large metal plates. "You come and sit here and eat. Do you want some cider with your dinner, or maybe you want a beer with it instead?"

"A beer please, Mary," Felix replied.

"You can get your own beer, Felix. Charley doesn't know where anything is yet, so I'll wait on him for the time bein' now!" Mary lectured.

"Milk if you have any would be just fine, ma'am. Thank you."

"You have nice manners, Charley. Of course. There now, if you need any thing else, just speak right up," she said, setting down a mug. "After your dinner, I'll show you your room. It isn't much, but you'll be comfortable, I think."

"Charley said he'd just sleep in the barn." Felix laughed.

"Nonsense, he can sleep in the loft with you!" Mary said with finality. Charley nearly choked on a sip of milk.

"You got some coming out your nose there, Charley," Felix said, laughing at his new partner.

The food was hearty and delicious; the slow-cooked stew practically melted in the child's mouth as he inhaled it. Looking at the soft cotton napkin, Charley decided to keep it to help deal with the bleeding problem; she stuffed it inside her shirt until she could get away to the outhouse.

"You want some more, just get it yourself now, Charley. You know where the pot is. We will put some meat on your bones if you stay here with us, ey ah," Mary clucked as she put the clean dishes away that she had been wiping.

"I think he may fit into some of your old clothes, Felix," Ebenezer commented.

"Yes, I think so," Felix retorted as he helped himself to a second mug of ale. "I got some pants that are too small."

"Did you wipe down the harness yet, Felix?" Eb quizzed his nephew.

"No, sir, not yet."

"Make sure you do so after you finish that drink. Then you can call it a day, Felix," Ebenezer lectured, "You know I do not like that harness left sweaty."

"Yes, sir," Felix replied. "Come on, Charley, I'll show you where you'll sleep." Charley and Felix tromped up the stairs to the top floor, to the loft. Mrs. Balch was not far behind them, gathering bed linens and a blanket for her new boarder.

"Yes, I think we have some clothes that will fit you, we'll have you fixed up in no time, and you need a haircut too, but I can fix that," Mary huffed as she reached the top of the stairs.

"Don't forget, I've still got to go back to the barn to wipe down that harness," Felix stated.

"Um, I'll help you, I want to check on my horse and get the rest of my stuff," Charley piped up.

"Oh, you have a horse, do you? That's nice!" Mary cooed, making up the bed.

"Yes, ma'am," Charley replied politely. "His name is Blue."

The loft was sparsely furnished, and the ceilings were low at the edges of the rooms. There was a window in the middle of one wall, where the last light of the day shone through. Charley was anxious to see the view in the morning, for he was sure that it would be a lovely vista of the grounds from this height.

"You can put your things in this trunk," Mary said, opening it and removing some linen that was there. "I wondered where these were!" she laughed. "You go on now, and I'll get you some pie when you come back in. Don't forget the coach will be in tonight at eleven," she reminded Felix.

"Yes, ma'am. Come on, Charley. It's nothin' but a barrel of laughs around here!" Felix sighed as he trotted down the many stairs, Charley following after like a new pup.

"How old did he say he was?" Mary asked Eb when she returned to the great room. Ebenezer was in his most natural place, behind the bar. He was a well-liked fellow, and most of his customers felt at home in his tavern, for this is where many took their meals, and relaxed, after a day's work.

"I believe the lad said sixteen," Eb replied.

"Oh, he can't be sixteen. I'd be surprised if he was even fifteen." Mary calculated.

"He said he was an orphan," Eb added.

"Do you think that he's a runaway? He said he has a horse," Mary asked

"It's a rather nice-looking animal," another voice joined in. It was James Brenner who was driving the hearse and was now sitting at the fireplace, in a wooden rocker, enjoying a warm brandy after tending to his emergency. "He looked like he might have some decent bloodlines, a stallion too, I might add," he said.

"You mean that young boy rides a stallion? You don't say!" Mary mused. "Spunky little thing. Seems to have a swollen eye," she added, taking her pie from the oven.

"The lad mentioned the horse is lame," Eb replied. "I'm sure that is why he stopped here because of the horse."

"I will keep my ears open for any missing livestock that might fit that horse's description, just to be on the side of caution," Brenner added, returning to the bartender for a refresher.

"Still, he seems like such a nice boy!" Mary said with resolve, smiling at her steaming pie.

Charley had stopped at the outhouse on the way to the barn to check on her blood loss. She lit the candle in the small commode and was relieved to find that it had dwindled; she dropped the bloody handkerchief down the outhouse hole and folded the cotton napkin and put it at her crotch, then returned to the chores in the barn.

"This harness is really beautiful!" Charley reflected, wiping it down with a clean soft cloth.

"Well, see if you still say that after you've cleaned it a hundred times!" Felix laughed.

"I still think it's lovely!" Admiring the silver buckles and crests on the bridle, Charley was very much in awe of the fineries in this barn; all she had ever been exposed to was work harnesses and farm wagons. The hearses' elegant woodwork and silver appointments were so rich and beautiful; he loved to run his hands over them and see them shine. Charley looked at the beautiful horses eating their dinner, instead of being told to stay away; they were now in his care to be brushed and fawned over. Charley felt as if he was inheriting treasure, instead of being hired for a job, it was what he had always wanted. Charley was about to be adopted into a society of horsemen, who would make him forget the troubles of the past, and leave behind any feminine life for a life in disguise.

In the great barn, Ebenezer Balch had some lovely carriages. A white sociable, which had passenger room for four, facing each other, complete with an umbrella and striped in blue. Next to it was dark green landau, which had a leather roof that split in the middle and opened, folding to the back and front; it was a popular summer vehicle because of the unpredictable summer rains. It seated six passengers, with room for driver and one groom on a bench seat in the front; they had to endure the rain with the horses. The glory of the barn was a beautiful large coach, with seats on the roof. Felix called it a Park Drag. The body of the coach was painted mustard yellow with maroon striping; the wheels and undercarriage were black. On the sides below the driver's seat hung large black and silver lamps with beveled glass that glistened. The Park Drag held up to twenty-two people, nine people inside, and twelve people on top including the driver. This made the coach rather top heavy and required six horses to pull it fully loaded. Its main popularity was for sporting events and horse races as it served as stadium seating as well as transportation, it was even equipped with a portable bar and picnic necessities in the carefully laid-out back boot, that folded out to make a table. Behind the table when it was upright was a built-in cupboard to keep dishware, food and linen for the most properly set and elegant picnic dining. The interior was elegantly upholstered with soft button-tufted black leather, complete with small silver vases for flowers. This particular vehicle came all the way from England and was Eb's pride and joy.

"How do they get up there?" Charley asked, looking up at the grand vehicle.

"You climb up them steps there, on the side, go and see. The brake is set. How did you get the black eye?" Felix asked sheepishly; he suddenly felt awkward and tried to be funny. "I hope you gave as good as you got!"

Charley was shocked out of his own thoughts by the question, for he had forgotten all about it. Ephram's twisted face flashed through his mind.

"He got his, I reckon, I . . . um, got hit by my stepfather." Charley revisited the events like they had been so long ago as he climbed. "After my real pa died, my ma remarried, and my stepfather and I . . . never got on very well, I guess. He drank a lot and spent all of my ma's money, and then Ma got sick and died," Charley lied, making his way up to the driver's seat. "Things just got kind of ugly, till I felt it was best to leave. So I took my horse, Blue, as he was the only thing I had from my pa, and left . . . after a bad fight."

"I'm sorry," Felix added when it was silent.

"No need to be," Charley said, taking in the view from the lofty perch. It was a grand seat, and Charley pushed the past down deep inside and instead envisioned a team of horses charging down an imaginary road ahead. "Tomorrow maybe I can get a doctor to look at his foot." Charley looked over at Blue, who seemed to be resting comfortably, munching away on his hay.

"He's a nice-looking horse. What kind is he?" Felix asked as Charley climbed back to earth.

"A race horse," Charley said proudly. "He's won races too."

"Ebenezer loves white and gray horses, says they have style. You're lucky he's still a stallion. You can get a stud fee for him."

"What do you mean, breed him for money?" Charley asked naively.

"Sure, people do it all the time. You've been on the farm too long!" Felix laughed.

"Well, I'm beat. I'm gonna see about that pie Mrs. Balch talked about," Charley responded, too weary to think of anything else.

"We'll help with the coach at eleven, but you'll get used to the odd schedules around here soon enough." Felix tossed the covers on the clean harness and extinguished the lamp as the two walked back to the tavern.

There was a nice, friendly fire going in the large stone fireplace, and several people sat around chatting in the main room. The boys made their way through to the kitchen, where there was a pie waiting on the table. Felix, who was right at home, dug in as Mrs. Balch came to greet them.

"Do you want some milk or cider with that?"

"Milk would be fine, ma'am," Charley said, smacking his lips at the treat.

"It's there," she said, pointing to the cups and to the pitcher.

"I'm going to have a brandy with mine," said Felix.

"Just mark it in the ledger, Felix. You know you've got to pay for your own brandy! I won't give you strong liquor, young man. If you drink like a man, you have to pay like a man!" Mrs. Balch was flushed with piety at the thought of young men getting intoxicated at her expense.

"We will eat in the bar, ma'am, if it's all the same?" Felix grabbed his plate of pie and ducked out.

"If it's all right, I'll just eat here and then go to bed. I'm awful tired."

"Well, of course you may, you dear young boy. You must be exhausted," Mary cooed as she ran her hand over Charley's face, looking at his sore eye. "And don't worry about tonight's coach either. I'll tell Felix to let you sleep. You'll get used to the strange rhythms of things around here soon enough. Good night, dear boy, I'm going to turn in too," Mary cooed. She was a wonderful cook and such a kind person, Charley felt strangely safe there. Climbing the stairs to the loft, the new resident paused to look at the needlepoint flowers that hung along the stairway. Charley spotted the clean long johns and cast-offs of Felix that Mary had placed on the young boy's bed. Charley heard Felix talking downstairs and wanted to undress before he came up. Suddenly feeling ill at ease, Charley quickly striped off the soiled disguise and left it in a heap then put on the new undergarments, checking the slightly soiled napkin as she did. She refolded it and placed it between her legs, then got into bed. She felt safe for the time being and knew that she would like to stay, at least until she figured out what to do with her life. For now, it was all a thirteen-year-old girl who was about to live her life as a sixteen-year-old boy could do.

Charley slept deeply with no nightmares, and the morning light came swiftly; he had not even heard the coach come in during the night.

When Felix roused him for the morning chores, Charley had to take a minute to get his bearings. As soon as Felix left the loft, he dressed in the new clothes, then stuffed the crotch-stained old pants in his coat and retired to the outhouse before heading to the barn. The bleeding had stopped, yet Charley retained the napkin just to be on the safe side. Much to her chagrin, it ended up tucked in her boot top by the end of the day. While she was in the privy, she cut the crotch out of the old pants with her knife and dropped it down the outhouse hole, then ripped the pants into pieces to use as cleaning rags.

In the barn, the horses, which were all used to the schedule, awaited their food anxiously. The boys climbed up to the hayloft and began pitching the morning hay down to each stall through a trap door above each manger. There were twenty horses, give or take, at any time, in the barn; therefore, you had to keep up with the chores. Next came the watering chores, then chickens needed to be fed, and the eggs collected. Then the manure had to be cleaned out of the stalls.

Charley thought it all strangely fun, everything was so grand, not like the old dingy barn where she had lived; even the wheelbarrows seemed fancy. She couldn't help but think of how her mother must be fretting at the loss of her daughter. Charley just pushed all of her past into the back recesses of her mind and went on with this new life. "What's done is done," he told himself.

"Now we can get our breakfast," Felix said. "Wait till you've had Mary's griddle cakes. Then you know you're eating!" he added.

The tavern was warm and smelled and looked like heaven to Charley. Ham and bacon and sausage, fresh-baked rolls and breads, with plates of butter and bowls of scrambled eggs, all set out on a big table on large platters with smaller plates and silverware rolled in cotton napkins at one end. Cups and saucers with small spoons, along with pots of coffee and a pitcher of cream and a bowl of sugar were set on a smaller table. The room was full of people helping themselves. Charley figured that they had come on the late-night coach.

"You fellas wash up good now. Charley, you use that basin next to the back door." Mary kept a neat kitchen; it was well laid out, with pots hung within easy reach of a large wood-burning stove and a big table in the center of the room on which to work. There was smaller marble-topped table next to the kitchen door with a wide copper basin and pitcher filled with water setting in it, neatly waiting for use. The table had a tall wooden backboard with a mirror and a few hooks on the top for hats. Next to the basin was a small dish full of soap balls of varying sizes and a clean but well-worn towel, hanging on a rod, mounted on the side of the table. A small drawer on the front of the table held clean towels and extra soap. The young men soon made a mess of the aforementioned, splashing water and soap thither and yon and leaving the pristine towel in a less than perfect heap next to the soap dish.

"It sure smells like heaven," Charley said, blushing at the mess and trying to set the towel out neatly.

"Well, you get yourself in and get it before they eat it all, and you don't get to eat any!" Mary advised.

"Mary, what's a Jehu?"

"Well, my goodness gracious, of all things. That is from the Bible, dear. Jehu drove a chariot, I believe. Most people are referring to a fast, careless driver." She smiled.

"Oh." With that, Charley got right in to the main tavern and helped himself to the spread and found that it was as good as it smelled.

Still early in the morning, the grounds were dewy and fresh as Charley looked around his new home, balancing his plate on his lap as he ate breakfast on the porch. The Balch House was a large three-story place, with large porch outside the kitchen as well as in the front. There was a path from the back porch that Charley would become well acquainted with; it went to the back of the barn through a small yard that lay between the two buildings. The main entry to the barn opened out to the road, and a short way down the road was the front entrance to the house. It was naturally landscaped, with ferns and wild roses that Mary had planted at the entry, dressing up the stacked rock fence and spreading in almost every direction. The Balch House provided food and lodging for any budget, from an elegantly appointed room to the tavern floor in front of the fireplace. For the latter accommodations, Ebenezer charged next to nothing but made his money off the sale of liquid refreshment. At times in the winter, men were laid out all over the floor, in front of the fire. Men would swap news about this area and that and who was raising what kind of grains. It was unheard of for a woman to stay that way; women did not travel around much.

Charley liked it at the Balch House very much and soon became enmeshed in the fabric of the place. He became friends with Felix and Eb and also Mr. Brenner. Mary fell in love with the new youngster, making sure he had clean, neat clothes and keeping his hair trimmed in the fashion of the day; she called Charley her little gentleman, which always made him blush.

It was getting late in the summer, and though Charley had only been with Mary and Eb about a month, it seemed like they had always been a family. Charley was now used to the routines and the schedules of the coaches coming and going, jingling in with such fanfare. It was such fun to get the mail and see who would come in, maybe someone important or famous. The Balch House was a home station, which meant that it was a dining house and also an overnight stop for the stagecoaches, as opposed to a stage in which you merely changed horses. Worchester was a thriving hub of activity that year, 1826.

Eb began letting Charley take the ribbons, as he called them, and trusted him to try driving pairs of different horses under his supervision at various driving jobs or going to church. He recognized talented hands in his new apprentice. Felix showed little promise as a reinsman; he was just too clumsy with his judgment and his hands. The young man was easily distracted and paid not enough attention to the horses. He was a good horse groom though, and Eb saw merit in that.

Mr. Brenner used Charley often to help start his young horses under saddle; they nicknamed the young horseman the Jockey. Charley was finally doing what he had always dreamed of doing, ride and be with horses and be recognized for his talent. And not only that, but paid for it as well. Charley actually had some money to spend, which was a new experience.

"That Charley is a bright boy," the new apprentice had overheard one night, before entering the inn. It made the girl stop and smile.

"They truly believe I am a boy!" She laughed to herself.

Charley loved the atmosphere at the inn, with the big roaring fire in the front tavern and the enticing smells coming from the stove in the kitchen. Mary was cooking something nearly all the time, except when she was sleeping, but even then, she was soaking beans for stews and simmering soups over a banked fire. It was her duty to make sure that no one ever went hungry. Even the Indian neighbors were welcome. The inn was what was called a public house, which became shortened, to pub. It was financed to some extent by taxes collected so that there would always be a place for people to go while in transit or emergency or other need, even if it sometimes meant sleeping in the barn. Meetings were often held there and receptions of almost any kind, in addition to it being a stagecoach station. For a young impressionable mind, it was a cornucopia of humanity.

Charley loved to watch Eb's blacksmith when he would visit, driving his great wagon with the anvils secured to the back. His conveyance was a marvel of travel, complete with a kitchen built on the side and sleeping quarters inside. The canvas roof could be stretched out away from the wagon to make an awning to cook under. The blacksmith, Huge, short for Eugene, was just as colorful, and it was clear he loved horses, judging from his own livestock. He had two great hulking Scottish draft horses he had raised himself, named Maggie and Tilly, each with a colt tied on to their collars most of the time. Charley could not resist playing with the babies and petting them. Huge was a man of gigantic proportions; his dark curly hair framing his face always seemed wet with sweat. His neck and shoulders were immense; even his fingers were like sausages. Yet he was as quiet as a purring kitten most of the time, especially around the horses. After he was finished shoeing horses, he would liven up, especially after a few pints of ale. Charley looked upon him as a teacher and tried to learn as much as he could about shoeing horses when he was there. He was a kind man and was flattered that the young lad was such a good helper.

These days working for Eb and Mary were Charley's happiest days. Ebenezer was very particular about his horses, so he taught Charley all he should know about good horse husbandry. Theirs was a society of horsemen, like their forefathers before them; the art of reinsmanship passed down through generations. Charley would be an adopted son.

He also had frequent opportunities to accompany Mr. Brenner, in the manner of a footman or groom. These were the best times, Charley thought, riding along at a quick paces through town with a glossy team of six black horses, put to the shiny Park Drag, the passengers all dressed up in their finest clothes. Brenner always brought along his splendid brass horn, and he insisted it was proper to announce arrivals with his horn blowing. Charley was taught all of the proper tunes for different occasions. It never failed to amuse him.

Eb had a practice rigging mounted to one wall of the barn that was used to teach drivers to handle teams of horses. It had long leather straps, called lines, that were threaded through an eyebolt on the wall, then attached to weights; the pupil could then practice driving a pair or six or eight or ten horses. There was generally a carriage parked so that you could use the break as you practiced with the lines or as Ebenezer was fond of calling them, "Ribbons." Eb and Mr. Brenner took great delight in teaching their new prodigy lessons and maneuvers, and Charley was discovering a talent and fondness for driving.

Blue was living well and was no longer lame; thanks to rest and Huge the blacksmith, who was always wearing his big leather apron that he strapped around his legs when he nailed iron shoes on the horses. He loved to chew tobacco and would punctuate his sentences by spitting into the fire or on a hot iron; Charley thought it was hilarious, and Huge loved a good audience. He was responsible for teaching Charley to chew tobacco. The impressionable youth imitated him often and loved to see his horses, which were, by the way, the best-shod horses around. Huge said they were Clydesdales, Scottish horses that were rich reddish brown with black manes and tails and black knees. Just beneath the black knees, long silky white hair cascaded down over the great plate-sized hoofs. Their faces had placid large blue eyes, unusual with most horses, with big broad white blazes running down their faces, ending at the lower lip. They were like two peas in a pod; if loose in a field, it would be very hard to tell one from the other. The foals usually nursed whenever they stopped. Huge had a route that he drove, shoeing horses, while his family ran the farm. In the winter, he smithed in his barn at home. His wagon was his home away from home, a forefather to the chuck wagon.

Mr. Brenner raised horses also, fine-boned trotters. He fancied bays, dark brown horses with jet-black manes and tails and black points—that is, nose, ears, knees, and hocks. The bodies were frequently dappled with lighter golden hairs. He liked them well polished, and they were. He also had some very nice vehicles that Charley enjoyed riding on. With all this driving around and fancy harness to keep clean, you can bet they kept Charley busy most of the time.

Charley had little time to ride Blue. He was used as a stud animal though as both Eb and Mr. Brenner thought he might throw good coaching horses and two mares were now carrying his foals—big black sisters, Jet, named for the polished stone used in jewelry, and Night. They were the wheelers or horses closest to the wagon in a team. They were a French breed of draft horse, called Percherons, a spirited breed, bred to carry soldiers, the knights in armor. Full armor for man and horse and including rider could weigh over seven hundred pounds, so the French breeders developed a very large agile horse. Percherons also have high leg action; they pick their knees up high when they trot, making them desirable as coach horses. The majority of the Percherons are born dark brown or black. Many get gray, then turn snow-white within seven years. Eb was hoping that the foals would be the start of a gray team. The mares, Night and Jet, showed no sighs of changing from black, but they already belonged in a hitch. A team had to be developed, Eb felt; it took time to find the right horses to work together. "To make a picture!" as he would say.

In early September, the leaves were giving a hint as to the spectacular show they would be putting on. Charley was sitting on the porch finishing his lunch when Felix came out with a newspaper and sat next to him.

"My God!" Felix cried. "Oh my God!" He kept reading, "Jeez, listen to this, 'A grisly discovery was made at a farm in New Hampshire, the home of Mr. and Mrs. Parker. A neighbor upon returning stray livestock and finding no one about, entered the homestead to find the above mentioned Parkers both dead in the bedroom, apparently a murder, suicide. The wife had apparently shot the husband in the head, then turned the gun on herself. Also found on the property was a young man apparently killed by a horse-kick to the head. All of the deceased were in a badly decayed state. The young man had been partially eaten by animals.'"

Charley could barely see straight and bolted off the porch toward the barn; he didn't make it very far before he was heaving up lunch.

"Are you all right, Charley? I didn't mean to ruin your lunch! I'm sorry," Felix apologized.

"Just leave me be," Charley croaked, not wanting to make eye contact, focusing on the roses trailing along the rock wall.

"Geez, I'm sorry." Felix took his paper and went back inside, shaking his head and mumbling incoherently about the carnage.

Charley tried to get a grip on herself; her mind reeled with pain and guilt. Images of Ephram's dead face flashed through her memory like arrows chased by pictures of her tormented mother. Charley hid beneath the shrubbery and cried.

This was certainly a final ending to the past. Charley vowed to himself never to think of the past again; it was gone. He crawled from the bush and turned toward the inn, this was what was real, these folks were good to him, and he felt like he belonged, these people would be his family now. Charley smiled at the large woman with the basket ambling toward him.

"Are you all right, Charley?" Mary asked, clipping off some roses for a vase. "Felix said that he upset you with some awful news in the paper."

"Yes, ma'am, I'll be fine. I need some water is all." Charley trudged along to the well.

"A fine thing, reading such a horrible story while you are eating!" Mary clucked. Never even considering that Charley had been connected to these people. "Imagine comin' across such a sight though! Makes me light-headed!" Mary pondered.

Charley couldn't stand it and ran out to the barn. The chores were done, so he bridled Blue and hopped on, riding without a saddle. Off they went to town or anywhere; it felt wonderful to be free. There was a lake nearby, and it was a favorite place to gallop Blue. Another lad that used to ride out there had a pretty fast horse, and he and Charley had fun racing around together. Odd name though, Ginnery Twitchell. He was a charismatic young man and rode very well indeed.

Ginnery rode a beautiful bay mare named Ginger, and the two had to be careful with the two horses when the mare was in heat. Ginnery invited Charley to his home, and the two became good friends.

The years went by, and the two boys grew and became young horsemen. Ginnery went on to make a name for himself, riding fast horses for the mail service of the day and broke several speed records. Young Charley, not wanting to be a rival to his friend, put everything he had into being the finest coachman around. As the girl grew to a woman, she concealed her breasts with padded vests and wore high-throated ties and leather gloves. The driving coat and top hat completed the disguise.

It wasn't very many years until Charley drove a regular stagecoach route. Folks always had an extra errand that they wanted performed at different towns for that extra bit of money. Charley didn't mind, and the extra income was always welcome. You never knew who you'd meet on any of these odd treasure hunts.

On one such extracurricular activity, Charley was given charge of a young boy named James Birch, who was to be escorted from his home to the school where he was to live for much of the year.

He was a lovely young boy of about eight years, he had dark brown hair and big green eyes, and told everyone he wanted to be a ship captain when he grew up. Charley explained that driving a coach was a lot like sailing a ship. The boy was still doubtful, but the driver continued. The coach is much like a ship in that it is used for traveling; it has an inside cabin and top deck, where they were. Then, the driver is like the captain, in charge of all the passengers; he has a team of horses that he orders about like a crew. The coach also rocks for and aft like a ship. With that explanation made, the young boy's imagination took over. He rode on the roof like Redbeard himself, ordering the horses about; it was a good thing they couldn't understand. About two-thirds of the way to the school, Felix, who was also aboard and in charge of the cargo and mail, was about fed up with energetic little boys. Thinking of a way to quiet the lad, he put some brandy in his eggnog at the dinner stop. Well, it didn't seem to have any effect on him, so he gives the little fella another shot, and off they go back on the coach. The little fella wanted to ride up top with Charley, and what could he say but come on then, so Charley bundled him up with the lap robe then departed.

They weren't too many miles from the final destination when the driver looked over and saw the boy starting to lean off the coach, so he slowed the team down and asked, "James are you asleep?"

"It's all right, Captain, I can swim," the boy explained. With that, the driver gently slowed the horses to a stop, then had Felix put the sleeping boy inside the vehicle.

Charley drove young James home and back several times throughout the year.

"Ready to come aboard, young man?" Charley asked with mock severity.

"Yes, Captain!" James called back with enthusiasm.

"Well then, stow your gear in the back boot and climb up topside!" Charley said with a grin, taking great delight in the young Birch's joy.

"I imagine you're looking forward to your summer on your farm?" Charley asked the boy.

"Oh yes! I can't wait to drive my dad's team and ride the horses," the young man replied. "I'm sorry I'm gonna miss the big explosion next week. My friend told me that his friend Sam was gonna rig up a raft in the Ware Pond, and on the Fourth of July he was gonna blow it sky-high!" James said in awe.

"Blow up a raft in the water?" Charley inquired.

"Yep, he said it was gonna get blown up, right out of the water!" the young boy swore.

"Well, imagine that!" Charley mused.

It was later noted in the newspaper that young Sam Colt had indeed blown a raft out of the water along with a great deal of mud, much to the chagrin of the spectators, who were covered with the latter.

CHAPTER 4

Worchester, Massachusetts, 1834

Charley Parkhurst sat at the end of a large table in the Balch House eating his dinner. Wearing the smartly tailored suit of a well-paid coachman, he was the most handsome man in the room. His friend, Felix, never progressed further than looking after the livery stables and other assorted odd jobs. He tried to keep a neat appearance, but he usually reeked of horse piss and beer, a smell that kept most respectable people at a distance.

"Hey, Charley! You'll never guess what I just seen," Felix said, plopping himself down at the table and laughing to himself over the hilarious pictures still held in his memory.

"What is it you've seen, Felix?" Charley smiled sheepishly.

"Well, I took that wheel down to French's to get a new tire, and they got this tent set up right across the street. So I go over to see what it is, and it's a show. See? 'The Celebrated Dr. Coult of New York, London and Calcutta!'" Felix said, quite proud of the fact that he had said the name correctly.

"Dr. Coult of Calcutta! That's quite a name. What did he do?" Charley ventured.

"Well, mind you, I didn't see the whole show. I sneaked in about halfway, I expect. This fella was mixing up liquids that changed colors and bubbled and foamed, and then he did some things with fire, made it change colors too. Then he claimed he could make people laugh. That was the best part! He claimed he could make even the most sour person laugh, just by breathing in some of his laughing gas. He had his assistant breath some first to prove that it was safe. That started us all a laughin'. Then he picked out a man that looked real mean and bad tempered and asked him if he would like a good laugh. He even waged a dollar he could make the man laugh, like a little child. Well, sir, the man was real sure of himself and grumbled his way to the front and the doctor claps on a face do-dad.

"A what?"

"Some kinda face cup, the gas comes otta, you see?"

"I suppose, go on."

"Well, within a minute, old crab face was laughing uncontrollably at something the doctor had whispered to him. Soon another volunteer was asked for and again the same results. It was the damnedest laughable thing. After the show, the doctor sold whiffs of his laughing gas to anyone who would pay two bits," Felix concluded.

"So did you try the laughing gas?" Charley replied.

"Of course! I never laughed so hard in my life," Felix responded.

"But what were you laughing at?" Charley inquired.

"Damned if I know!" Felix said, shaking his head and snorting out a belated laugh. "You got to go see this. He's gonna do another show in 'bout an hour."

"Well, I ain't gonna spend no two bits to laugh at nothing!" Charley said wisely.

"Ugh . . . come on, I want to go back and see the whole show. It looks real good," Felix whined.

"Well, I ain't stopping you from seein' it!" Charley reminded him.

"Com'on, it will be so much more fun if we both went. You got to see this. It is so funny," Felix begged.

"All right, what time does the next show start?" Charley asked.

"Eight o'clock," Felix replied.

"That's forty-five minutes, and it takes ten minutes to get to French's. Let me finish my dinner, and then we'll go, all right?" Charley conceded.

"Right! I'll see if I can round up some more of the fellas. I'll see you later," Felix said ecstatically.

Half an hour later, Felix had four other guys rounded up to collect Charley to see the great doctor from Calcutta! The troupe walked down the street to the corner next to the wheelwright and took in the carnival atmosphere around the traveling tent show. The young man hawking his show to the bystanders was scarcely older than Charley, who was now twenty-one. Colt had a magnetic air about him and was dazzling folks with flashing hats and cards and smoking canes to entice them to his chemistry lecture and marvels of science. It cost fifteen cents to see the entire show, held inside a large canvas tent. Charley could not help to notice the beautiful painting on the side of the tent of an airship that was held aloft in the clouds by a beautiful sphere; it was rigged with a sail in front and one behind the balloon. Hung beneath it, an admirably painted ship with what appeared to be a fan rotating in the back of the vessel. Charley couldn't help but to wonder at the thought of such an airship. The name at the bottom said Joseph E. Walker, Inventor.

Soon the handsome Samuel Colt took to the small plank stage inside the tent, getting everyone's attention. It was a very interesting show, mostly consisting of beautiful and violent chemical reactions and black powder pyrotechnics. Saving the moneymaker for last, the nitrous oxide or laughing gas.

Colt had devised a method to transport the necessary ingredients to manufacture his own gas as he traveled, thus selling thrill seekers a whiff at between twenty-five to fifty cents a snort. It made a tidy profit, gathered from the curious citizens in search of a good time. Colt was saving the money to manufacture an invention that he had first carved out of wood, on a ship to Calcutta, when he was just a young lad. It was an invention that would leave its mark in history as one of the great inventions, the great equalizer, revolutionizing the weapons of the day and also bringing the new country into the forefront of mass production. The Colt revolver.

The crowd watched as all sorts of folks made idiots of themselves that night, singing songs and generally being silly. The audience lapped it up.

After the show, the young man was eager to talk with folks about his pyrotechnics, and the man took a keen interest in hunters and their guns.

"You aren't by any chance the same Sam Colt who blew a raft out of the Ware Pond on the Fourth of July several years back?" Charley laughed.

"I confess, I am the one," the young man said with a wry smile.

"Well, I'll be damned!" Charley said, shaking the showman's hand. "Name's Charley Parkhurst, pleased to meet you.

"My reputation precedes me! The pleasure is mine." Sam smiled.

"Can I borrow fifteen cents, Charley?" Felix asked, creeping up from behind.

"Nope! I'm goin' home," Charley said, tipping his hat to the young doctor and smiling at his gassed-up friend. He walked back to the Balch House, not knowing that his new acquaintance would later make such an important mark in history with his yet-to-be-patented six-shooters.

Felix and the rest soon followed Charley back to the tavern.

"Yes, I guess it was pretty funny. Are you satisfied?" Charley surrendered at last to his wayward comrade and his friends, assorted stable boys, and bartenders in training.

"Well, I thought it was funny as hell!" Felix laughed to himself. "Hey, let's go see what Mary has in the kitchen to throw into the fire to make it change colors!"

"You're on dangerous ground now, Felix. Mary will skin you alive if you mess up her kitchen," Charley warned. "I'm gonna go read the news," he added, finding a comfortable place to read in the tavern, far from harm's way. Sure enough, the boys were back in the tavern laughing and throwing salt and sugar into the fireplace and making a good mess. Charley grabbed his paper and fled before Mary caught them and enlisted cleaning detail.

Charley would regularly check the papers for any news of the flying ship. A small article would catch his eye one-day that read that the contraption had failed miserably, and the inventor had mysteriously disappeared. Samuel Colt's name would not disappear from the news, and Charley was ever interested in the progress of this man's invention as well.

Worchester was a thriving town, and the city sprouted new buildings and improvements at every turn.

"Hey, Charley, I heard they was gonna build an armory outside a town. They're gonna make a new kinda pistol that you can shoot five or six times without reloading! Isn't that fine?" Felix said with a grin. "I'm gonna get one, you can bet on that!" He laughed.

"What do you need a gun for, Felix?" Charley prodded, rolling his eyes. "If you shoot someone, even accidentally, you'll go to jail or be hanged. Or injure your own self. Probably shoot off your own foot, or me!" Charley huffed.

"Well, I'm gettin' one just the same!" he grumbled under his breath.

"Who is the gun maker?" Charley asked his insulted and pouting friend, hoping the answer was Colt.

"Allen and Thurber. Thought you didn't like guns, so what do you care?" Felix whined as he poured himself a cup of coffee.

"I'm sure, I don't know."

Six months later, Felix was the proud owner of the newest-model pepperbox. He seemed to stand about a foot taller, walking around town with his shiny new toy in his coat pocket. He became somehow more arrogant, definitely more annoying. Charley must admit it was a fine-looking bit of craftsmanship, a compact pistol; about seven inches long with a three-inch-long barrel that had six chambers. The barrel rotated when you cocked it, thus enabling the shooter to fire six times without reloading. They had no sights; it was simply a point-and-shoot operation, a fact that Felix was just dying to demonstrate. Charley had already heard of accidents in which all six chambers fired at once, called chain fire. A gun like that in Felix's hands, or anyone's hands for that matter, made Charley very uncomfortable.

"Great thunder in the morning! All we need is a town full of idiots running around with loaded pepperbox in their pockets," Charley cursed to the heavens, as he walked back to the livery.

"But don't you want to defend yourself if you're in a bind, Charley?" Felix quizzed his friend later.

"From who? A highway robber? If he stops me, I give him what he wants. I've never heard of coaches getting robbed. Besides, I never carry much money with me. My watch isn't even worth very much. The rest is someone else's problem," Charley reasoned.

"Yes, but what about if you're out of town in a tavern and someone threatens you with a knife? You can pull out the pistol and stop him," Felix reasoned.

"Yes, then he runs outside and gets all of his brothers, and they have guns and knives, and that's the end of that. You will stay alive a lot longer if you just stay out of dangerous places," Charley said piously.

"Ugh, now you sound like Father Hezekia," Felix chided.

"Nevertheless, I am still not getting a gun," Charley retorted.

"What about one of them Derringer pockets pistols? They're small and won't cause much trouble," Felix teased.

"I don't need a gun, Felix," Charley growled.

"Well, I was only thinking of your own safety, that is all, my friend!" Felix said, looking over Charley's shoulder at the newspaper.

"Why, lookey there, our old friend, Dr. Colt, is startin' up a gun factory in New Jersey." Felix pointed out.

"Where?" Charley groaned.

"There!" Felix pointed out.

"Well, I'll be damned." Charley smiled, running his fingers through his short auburn hair.

"Thought you didn't like guns?" Felix said smugly.

"Hmmn!" Charley snorted. "Well, I still don't."

CHAPTER 5

1844

Ten years passed, and Worchester grew and prospered along with the people that lived there.

Charley Parkhurst's excellent reputation as a coachman grew, and the Balch livery was a thriving enterprise.

"But, Mary, we'll make much more money, and we'll have a bigger inn. You'll see, you'll love it. Why don't we at least go and look. You could use a little trip. You've been working so hard," Eb explained to his wife.

"Well, maybe it doesn't hurt to look," she replied with a childlike giggle.

"Then it's all settled. We leave as soon as we can," Eb sighed.

Charley was preparing a coach for a job, when Eb entered the barn.

"Do you have a few moments, Charley? I'd like to talk to you," he said with a fatherly tone.

"Sure I do, Eb. What's on your mind?" Charley replied as he tightened a hub nut.

"Well, Charley, as you know, I've been looking into some property in Providence. Mary and I are going to take a trip to have a real look. I'd like it if you would drive us out and have a little look-see yourself," Eb explained.

"I would love to. When were you planning on going?" Charley asked.

"Well, I'll leave it to you to clear up your schedule. I'd like to be away for at least two weeks. Have a bit of a holiday, eh, Charley?" Eb chuckled. "Your lodgings and everything will be taken care of!"

Charley and Eb were now partners of sorts, like a father and son. Parties would hire the carriages and coaches that Eb had, and Charley did all the driving and looked after the horses with Felix. It was extremely agreeable for Charley, who was his own man now and had even saved some money. The well-dressed dashing coachman was now thirty-one.

Charley cleared his schedule up for the trip, and Eb made arraignments for the care of his establishment and livery. He chose to bring Felix along on the trip to keep an eye on him. He was less apt to get into trouble if he was kept busy looking after Mary. Felix was a little too fond of alcohol; if left to his own resources, he generally ended up in trouble.

At last, the best team of gray horses was hitched to the Balchs' elegant landau, and they were on their way to Providence, Rhode Island, dressed in their finest traveling attire. The carriage had a luxurious leather top that could be raised or lowered depending on the weather. The back of the vehicle had a luggage platform that was equipped with netting of thick leather straps to keep cargo from bouncing off.

Mary brought a cornucopia of culinary delights and insisted on stopping at the most picturesque locations for brief picnics. Eb indulged his beloved wife and took a holiday approach to the ride. The trip was roughly sixty miles to Providence, Rhode Island, from Worchester, Massachusetts. They took a leisurely four days to get there.

It was a fine autumn day as the landau glided into Providence; the sea air was very refreshing and invigorating. Eb sat on the front seat with Charley, pointing and giving directions.

"Turn here, Charley. I think that's it. Yes, the stone house there, with the green shutters. See the sign? The What Cheer House, stop in front there. My, how the city has grown. Felix and I will go inside and make inquires. Stay here with Mary till I can find out where you should take the carriage," Eb said, climbing down.

Charley tipped his hat and smiled. At last a young man came outside with Felix in tow and began removing the luggage.

"Come on, Mary, he's gonna show us our rooms," Felix said, helping Mary from the vehicle.

"Oh, it feels good to walk around," she sighed, fussing with her hat.

After unloading the bags, the young man gave Charley instructions to drive down the next alley to the livery behind the hotel. Behind the stone building was a nicely laid-out courtyard and barn for the housing of carriages, and next to that an immaculate city stable that was entirely paved with bricks and kept neatly swept and sprinkled with water. The horses were housed in two columns of tie stalls that were built of beautiful hardwood. The alley led through the harness room, then out to the brick courtyard. The other end of the horse barn alley opened up to a manure collection area, where wheelbarrows of manure were dumped into manure spreader wagons and delivered to fields for fertilizing. The stable had room for thirty horses; that meant the manure wagons were always moving. The livery always made it a point to have a few empty stalls for traveling hitches; however, it was always a good idea to make arrangements for stalls ahead of time as Eb had done. Charley paused for a moment to examine the harness room and found it much to his approval. The carriage house also seemed very much in order.

Charley found his traveling companions at a table in the tavern drinking wine and chatting. The tavern had an elegance about it that was a far cry from the rustic Balch House.

"So what do you think of the What Cheer House, Charley?" Eb said, standing and pulling up a chair. "Later Sven, the caretaker, will give us the grand tour. Have a glass of wine."

"It's a beautiful livery, neat as you please. Very well planned out," he conceded. The thought of pulling up stakes and moving was agonizing, yet the excitement of something new was definitely alluring.

Later on the tour, the group visited all three main floors of the hotel; the top two were bedrooms. The ground floor was office, tavern, and kitchen with a small room next to it with a bathtub. There was an attic for storage and a full basement that was used as a root cellar and bar storage. Firewood was stacked up along one wall as well.

"Well, I might as well tell you, this place was my uncle's property. After he passed on, it has come to me. I've just got to pay some taxes on her, and she's mine!" Eb said with euphoria. "I remember this place from my childhood. I never dreamt it would someday be mine," he recounted with tears of joy welling up in his soft blue eyes.

Mary, who was busy inspecting the root cellar, was clucking away like a mother hen.

"My word, Eb, do you have any idea what it will take to move all your furnishings here?" Felix asked, feeling the aching muscles in his back already.

"Well, I'm afraid he's right that time. I suppose it won't be easy. Most of this place is already furnished though, so I'll only take the important things and sell the rest with the other house," Eb reasoned. "I was told the property across the way was for sale. I might make inquires about building another barn there."

"Sell my furniture? Not my furniture, we won't! Sell your uncle's furniture. First, I'll look at it again," Mary huffed as she climbed from the basement.

"Are any of the vehicles in the carriage house yours?" Charley asked, changing the subject.

"Yes, the will said four vehicles," Eb related. "We'll go there next." He smiled, winking at Mary.

"This is like a birthday party!" Felix laughed.

"Or Christmas!" Charley tossed in.

"I want to look at the kitchen again!" Mary called out from the corner of the pantry, receiving a cheer from her boys.

"We'll drop you off on our way out to see the carriages, Mama," Eb soothed.

"Oh no! I want to see the carriages too!" she laughed.

"Mama you'll be looking at that kitchen all night. I'll send Felix for you after a while. You'll only look at the carriages for ten minutes." Eb laughed.

"Well, you got a good point, Ebenezer," Mary said thoughtfully.

The men breezed through the busy kitchen, leaving Mary to her new wonderland, and proceeded to the livery. They crossed the courtyard toward the flickering lights of the carriage house. The evening lamps had been kept lit for the late-arriving coach.

"Oh my, there it is, my uncle's old road coach. How I've remembered it from my boyhood. It was . . . and still is my favorite vehicle. The What Cheer coach," Eb mused as he ran his hand over the painting of the racehorse on the door. It must be fifty years old, Eb figured. It had been kept in immaculate condition. The body was twilight blue with black wheels and gold trim and completely outfitted in every way, with portable bar setup with crystal glasses to brass horns and exquisite brass lamps. The other vehicles included in the inheritance paled by this most beautiful road coach, but not by much.

After examining the vehicles, Charley decided to look in on the horses again since they were right there in the next barn. He stopped in the courtyard to light his pipe as he went. As Charley puffed away, he noticed two young men about eighteen years old examining the newly arrived horses. A dark-haired young man was pointing out the good features of a particular horse as a sandy-haired boy nodded his head in agreement.

"Can I help you, sir?" the dark-haired boy asked Charley as he came inside the barn.

"No, I just came to tell my horses good night," he said casually, admiring the boy's beautiful green eyes.

"These your horses?" the boy asked.

"Yep," the coachman said, stroking the neck of his favorite.

"Very nice horses, sir," the sandy-haired boy added.

"Sir, I hope you don't take offense, but haven't I met you before? Are you a coachman?" the dark-haired boy asked.

"Why, I don't rightly know, that is . . . Yes, I am a coachman, the name's Charley Parkhurst."

"I'm James Birch, and this is Frank Stevens. We work here at the stable. We must have been dumping manure when you come in. Pleased to meet you," the dark-haired boy said with enthusiasm as he stared into Charley's face.

Charley studied the boy's features and then quietly replied, "I remember taking a young lad named James to school about ten or eleven years back. Said he was gonna grow up to be a ship's captain." He smiled.

"It is you! Charley, the coachman! It is wonderful to see you again," James said, shaking the coachman's hand. "Are you here on business?" he added.

"Well, sort of, business and holiday, be here about a week. Maybe you'd give us a few pointers where to visit," Charley said in a friendly manner.

"Sure, be glad to," James offered.

"Well, I see my beauties are well looked after. I'll see you in the morning then, boys," Charley said, tipping his top hat just slightly.

"Nice to see you again, Charley, hope you enjoy your stay," James said politely.

"I'm enjoying it already," Charley said with a smile.

"Pleased to have met you, Mr. Parkhurst," Frank said as an afterthought.

"You fellas look me up in the tavern when you're though here, and I'll buy you a beer," Charley offered as he turned.

"We'll see you soon." James laughed, smiling at the dashing figure walking back to the tavern. Parkhurst was wearing his formal driving attire with custom-made boots of calfskin and black pigskin gloves. His beaver top hat was very well crafted, trimmed with black grosgrain ribbon. Parkhurst liked to wear a long gray tweed coat and matching vest, a wine-colored necktie, with black trousers, topped by a black topcoat that had a cape for night driving and cold weather. It was a very impressive turnout as the coachman sauntered back to the tavern.

"Imagine meeting up with Ol' Charley after all this time," he heard young Birch commenting as he walked away.

"Let's finish up. He said he would buy us a beer!" Frank exclaimed.

Charley entered the glowing room of the tavern and sat next to Felix near the fireplace.

"Met some of the stable boys in the livery. One is the boy we delivered to school quite a ways back. Little James Birch. Wanted to be a ship's captain when he grew up," Charley commented.

"Oh yeah, I remember him. I gave him a shot of brandy in his eggnog to shut him up. Kid never stopped talking!" Felix smirked.

"He and his friend, Frank, will be in soon. I told them I'd buy them a beer," Charley added.

"Why don't you ever buy me a beer?" Felix asked indignantly.

"I don't know, maybe I'll buy you one too while I'm on holiday," Charley replied with charity.

"You never buy me a beer!" he added as an afterthought.

"I never seem to have any money," Felix said thoughtfully.

"That's because you spend your money on foolish things, like women and that stupid pepperbox," Charley lectured.

"I feel safe with it," Felix said defensively

"You'll feel safe till you shoot your dang foot off or blow a hole in your hand," Charley insisted.

"I know. Or shoot you. Anyhow, here come your little friends," Felix sighed sarcastically. "Is that the kid there?" Felix said, motioning to the dark-haired boy.

"Yep, that's James. The other is Frank. Over here, fellas. This here is Felix, Frank and James," Charley said informally; they all grunted and touched their hats in respect.

"You were the one that gave me the eggnog. I remember you!" James said, looking closely with great humor.

"Yep, that was me," Felix said, blushing.

"That ride was the most fun I had ever had when I was a kid," James reminisced. He smiled at the young woman approaching the table.

"What'll it be, boys?" Charley said with a flourish. "I want to charge some drinks to my hotel bill." Charley smiled at the young woman. It somehow felt strange to know that this new place would soon be home.

"Fellas, I'd like to introduce you to the new owner of this establishment, Ebenezer Balch. Eb, I'd like you to meet the fellas that keep the livery in order," Charley said, walking to the bar and taking him from the bartender's grasp for a moment. "Some nice young men, I first met one when he's about six years old."

"Well hello, boys. My name is Ebenezer Balch. You can call me Eb, everybody does," he said, holding out his plump hand.

"This here is James Birch and his associate, Frank Stevens," Charley said with dignity.

"If you boys want to stay on with me, I reckon I'll have use of your services. Don't you think, Charley?" Eb reasoned.

"Yes, I expect we will have," he said with authority. He looked over to see the smiles on the young men's faces and smiled back. "To the What Cheer House!" Charley said, raising his glass.

"Maybe these fellas could work out some arrangements to be of service during the moving process?" Felix chimed in as a voice from the silent side of the table.

"That's a great idea, Felix. We shall take that up again before we return to Worchester. Sound all right with you, boys?" Eb said with sincerity.

"That sounds fine, Mr. Balch," James Birch responded.

"Eb, com'er," Mary called out.

"Well then, fellas, duty calls. It was fine to meet you." The rotund man returned to his wife who was still inspecting the business of the tavern.

"He certainly seems like a nice man," Stevens remarked as the owner left their presence.

"He's a very good man," Charley reassured. "Mary's a love once you get to know her and a great cook."

"Yes, but she'll run you ragged, that's no joke," Felix advised as he finished his beer. Charley only smiled. "I ain't at all looking forward to this move," he added.

"Me neither," Charley responded. "Lived there most of my life."

"Tomorrow we can show you around some if you like," James insisted.

"Sounds good, how about one more beer then I'm heading to bed. I'm all in." Charley invited.

"Wow, you buying me another beer. That's two in one night," Felix chided.

"Sure, why not, I'm on a holiday," he said, smiling inwardly. He knew that Eb would be paying the tab anyway. After all, it was his tavern now. Eb had not made such an arrangement with Felix for he knew he'd have drunk the place dry.

Before long, it was back to Worchester to pack. Everything that was not going to Providence was sold. Charley's possessions were few; they all fit in a small trunk. The horses are all he cared about, and they would all be moving with them. Blue had long since passed away; he died one cold winter after an illness, five years after Charley arrived at the Balchs. His descendants were integrated in various teams, and Charley saw bits of Blue in many of them.

The Balch household was another matter. Mary could not part with most of her possessions even though the new place came furnished; she insisted on bringing her own furniture. Their largest grain wagon was crammed full, much to Eb's chagrin. It took eight horses to haul it, and it was several trips before everything was finally transported to their new home and everyone could settle into a new routine. Birch and Stevens became regular members of the family.

Charley took delight in traveling over the unfamiliar roads. He often had Birch accompany him as a groom when hired out for various functions. The young man proved to be a most promising driver as well. The excellent teams and their turnouts became very popular, and the livery prospered.

As the years went by, Frank and James both became smitten with a young woman named Julia Chase, a beautiful raven-haired girl with fine, delicate features. The young men vowed never to let the love of a woman interfere with their friendship. They took solace that the woman was far out of their social reach; thus it would seem that the friendship was in no real danger. The two young men would fantasize about making vast fortunes in various schemes while Charley comforted the lovesick young men, telling them that they were still young, and destiny may still deal them a fair hand.

Each time the men saw Julia, the fire was stirred to greater heights. It was a little sickening to Charley, or perhaps it was jealousy. Except for the attentions she had received incestuously, Charley had never known physical love. She was not willing to risk the loss of her lifestyle and could not bear to be found out; it was sometimes painfully lonely. Tuning thirty-something this year (she had really lost track), Charley was resigned to hang around with Felix who was very unsuccessful with women. Yet women were often attracted to Charley, who was dashing and handsome, which was rather vexing and baffling for ignorant Felix.

One evening, Charley and Felix returned to the What Cheer livery from a society party to find the stablemen Birch and Stevens entertaining themselves with a game of cards in the harness room, using their clothes as gambling chips. Birch was very nearly in the all together. The driver and assistant quickly unhitched the horses and rolled the carriage to its place, taking stock of the card players who were quite embarrassed about their condition. Charley removed his hat and coat and replaced it with a smock from the hook, then began to remove the harness from the horses.

"You boys just continue your game. I don't want to interfere or anything. But a . . . what the hell are you playing?" Charley said with a great grin on his lips.

"It's strip poker. Birch is losing," Stevens chimed in, still wearing all of his clothes, Birch's hat, and coat. Birch was wearing only his long johns.

"Hey, can I play? I got plenty of clothes on." Felix smiled.

"Yes, why don't you let Felix play. Then I can unharness all by myself," Charley said sarcastically.

"I reckon you can play." James Birch smiled.

"Thanks, Charley, that's nice of you," Felix said, plopping down in the chair. "Deal me in, boys."

Charley shook his head and cleaned the horses of their work attire, then gave them each a measure of grain; he brushed them down as they ate their dinner.

"I saw the love of your lives, Julia Chase, tonight," Charley said casually as he took off the harnessing smock.

"What? You saw Julia?" James said, snapping to attention. Felix and Frank took a moment to cheat by looking at James's unprotected hand.

"I fold," Felix remarked after sizing up his competitor.

"Who was she with?" Stevens asked with concern.

"Her aunt, I think, it was a dance though, probably danced all night. I swear she was the most beautiful gal I saw there," Charley added, rubbing it in.

"What was she wearing?" James asked, looking miserable, holding out for his last bit of clothing.

"Are you playing?" Stevens scolded.

"Yeah," James sighed, thinking only of Julia.

"Well, what do you have?" Frank demanded.

"Oh . . . full house. Duce's and fours," Birch said, fanning out his cards.

"Ha! Four sixes!" Stevens laughed. "Take them off!" he said, laughing himself to the floor. Charley and Felix were in convulsions as the poor lovesick youth was deprived of even his long johns. Charley blushed yet could not help admiring the gorgeous young man's body. After a moment, he handed him the smock to relieve his dilemma. Charley smiled with chagrin as the youth, nearly naked, pressed his mentor for details of Julia. He even pleaded that he be chosen as groom for the next party that the lovely Miss Chase was likely to attend this summer. Charley resisted the urge to tell the youth that his ladylove was closely attended to by a tall young man, with startling blue eyes.

The next big horse racing event called for all the carriages and coaches. James and Charley manned the infamous What Cheer coach, with Eb and Mary riding aloft as if royalty. As Charley expected, Julia was present, and Birch and Stevens vied for the young woman's attentions though it was clear to Charley that she obviously favored Birch. Charley took pleasure in the splendor of the day and the beautiful turnouts of the park drags and teams of fine horses. The ladies all wore miles of fabric in their skirts with incredible plumage on their elaborate hats. It was a feast for the eyes; the food wasn't bad either.

Time passed in the east and much news was looked on with interest about the new frontiers in the west. Small companies of people were beginning to stake new claims in the wilds of the faraway land. Then, it was as if someone had shot off a cannon: Gold in California! People were wild with speculation; they were infected with a sickness, gold fever! It was all anyone could talk about. It was an aspect of insanity.

"You have always said that Julia is out of my reach. She comes from a family with money. Well, if I go to California, I know I will become rich. Then Julia can marry me!" James reasoned with Charley one cold evening in the tavern.

"I've no desire to leave my happy hearth to travel into God-only-knows-what situations," Charley reflected. "Go if you must and may God watch over you as you go," Parkhurst prayed aloud.

"Stevens and I are thinking of hiring on as wagon masters for a drive west," Birch related.

"You going too, Frank?" Charley asked.

"It's the future. There will be money to be made, and we'll make it. You sure you don't want to come along?" Frank practically pleaded.

"I'm not in the position to try to impress any young ladies at the present. So I think I'll stay put for the time being. But if you fellers hit it off real square, you send for me. I might be persuaded to go and have a look at that land of milk and honey of which everyone is so fond of talking. When were you planning on leaving?" Charley inquired.

"Two weeks. We'll meet the rest of the company in Boston, then onward to the jumping-off point, St. Joe," James explained. "Could you get word to Julia that we're leaving?" he added.

"You might get to say it in person in Boston. Said her family was going for a big New Year's party," Charley sighed. "You fellers are gonna leave me in an awful lurch," Charley sighed.

"Don't worry, Charley, we'll make our millions, and then we'll send for you to come out and join us!" James cheered.

"Yes, of course you will," he sighed, lifting his glass with mock enthusiasm.

"I think it is exciting!" Felix said in a drunken stupor.

"Well, I was sure you would," Charley said, shaking his head.

CHAPTER 6

1849

The two young pals, James Birch and Frank Stevens, were so excited about their new adventure in the gold fields; they had not really understood the vastness of their endeavor, nor could they even imagine the amount of miles filled with hardship they had signed on for. The pair, who were used to fast horses, slogged along with teams of huge oxen, chained six up, in pairs, hauling the massive canvas-covered wagons at a snail's pace, seeking their fortunes in the unknown.

They had no real idea what far was, until they undertook this journey. For Birch and Stevens, the slow trudging of the wagon train gave them time to dream of the possibilities in the golden hills of California.

James cracked his whip above the backs of the tolerant beasts and dreamed of driving over this rugged and beautiful countryside on the finest Concord coach, with six high-stepping horses. This ox train was no way to travel. The wagon train was fortunate to have Birch and Stevens, their good training and expertise with vehicles saved them from the misfortunes that plagued many travelers. Dry axles were a big problem. Parkhurst had always stressed to the young men the importance of maintaining axle grease and the like. The young teamsters saw many examples of negligence along the way.

"Now look at that! This would be a lovely place for a stage stop," James said to the off ox, which just nodded in step. James stuck his fingers in his mouth and let out a whistle, then called back to the wagon train to make camp.

"Circle them up over there, and we'll call it a day!" James hollered. It was indeed a lovely campsite. God only knew where they were, really. The train just kept ever onward following the tracks ahead, watching for landmarks in the maps, crude as they were.

James admitted to Frank that he rather enjoyed the gypsy lifestyle, never knowing what the next turn in the road would bring.

Frank admitted that he really missed the luxury of a soft bed and was looking forward to settling in one spot once again.

"So, Frank, what are you gonna do with your money when we get to California?" James said over coffee and corn cakes.

"Well, I figure it like this; I'll go to the best city I can, and get me a big hotel or something, fill it with all the beds I can afford, and call it Rest for the Weary," Frank spoke, as he tried to arrange his lumpy bed under the wagon, much to his disgust.

James laughed. "That's a good name!"

"You think I'm fooling, but I'm not!" Frank growled at the bed.

"I believe you!" James said, playing in the fire.

The journey was a tough one, filled with hazardous river crossings and treacherous mountains. It molded the young adults to hard men. When at last they reached California, Frank made good his dream and opened up shop in Sacramento, a shack masquerading as a hotel. James laughed when Frank proudly hung up his shingle, Rest for the Weary. He added "With Storage for Trunks" right below. Much to his chagrin, he was quite successful.

James had other notions. He was in love with this new land, California, and could not wait to be driving a coach again. The hills were full of wild mustangs, beautiful little horses, tough and fast and in every color. Unfortunately there were not many wagons to be had, at least not the kind that pleased the young entrepreneur. After much bargaining, he at last found a sound wagon that was suitable and big enough; it was not pretty to be sure, but it could hold at least ten passengers. Now to secure some horses. The Mexican cowboys or vaqueros, as they were called, were willing to sell him four mares that seemed to be fit enough, but none had ever been hitched to a wagon, so it would take a bit of doing to get them trained. For one thing, James didn't have any harness. The vaquero who sold him the horses introduced Birch to a fine saddle maker named Jesus Salazar, who could make him a beautiful set of four horse harness very quickly and at a very good price. Meanwhile, Birch gentled his mares and broke them to ride so he could teach them to yield to the bit pressure, the only real controlling aspect of a driving horse. When Jesus presented the new harness, James paid him the last of his money. He proudly harnessed his green broke horses and pulled up in a cloud of dust in front of the Rest for the Weary and whistled a familiar tune. Frank came outside on his new balcony to see his friend aboard his new business. The horses were wide-eyed and dangerous looking, but it bothered James not a bit. Steam billowed from the anxious horses' nostrils in the cool morning air, as men came out to see the new enterprise.

"All aboard for the Sutters' Mill, Coloma and Mormon Island, all aboard for the diggings!" James called out, waving his hat.

"Good luck to you, Jim! I don't envy you a bit. I'm going back to bed." Frank, wearing only his long johns, waved with a smile.

The men gathered around asking questions, as the wagon soon filled to capacity, and newly trained mares set off down the road, bucking and seeming to run wild. James kept them all moving straight ahead, and after about five miles, they settled in real nice. Birch was thrilled, he made back his entire expenses on the first trip, and this would be just the beginning. The first trip was slow, considering the horses could only go about fifteen to twenty miles a day. The first thing James did when he got back to Sacramento was to buy more horses and harness and wagons. He spent his money hiring men to build stations and care for his stock of rapidly growing horses. He set aside a portion of his profits for a shipment from the east; the most road-worthy vehicle ever devised, in young James Birch's mind, the Concord coach.

A few months later, he had enough gold to send back an order for five coaches to be shipped around the horn. Money was flowing into the teamster's hands, and he was investing it in his dream, and it was paying off.

He wrote faithfully every Sunday to his beloved Julia, telling her of his adventures and success and dreams for a family. James promised to return to her soon. He set his hope on New Year's day. But this time he would go back in style on a ship! He had finished with slow ox trains forever.

The steamer boats could take you from Sacramento to the San Francisco Bay to catch a ship, then down to the jungles of Panama City to cross the land barrier to the open seas on the other side, then home.

Until then, he would drive his wild horses like a man possessed, up and back, running errands in the diggings, then returning to Sacramento to pick up another load. He even ran an ad in the local fledgling press:

> Birches Express Line to Sutters' Mills at Coloma by way of Mormon Island leaves S. Brannan's store, Sacramento City, every morning at seven o'clock. Returning will leave the St. Louis Exchange, at the Mills, every morning at six thirty o'clock (Sundays exempted). Passengers can leave Sacramento City for Mormon Island (which is one mile from the north fork) in the morning and return the same day, stopping one hour at the island. All business entrusted to the proprietor of this line will be promptly attended to. Seats may be secured and further information obtained by applying at the Stage Office, Front Street, Sacramento City.
>
> James Birch, Proprietor. Sacramento City, Sept. 1, 1849.

There seemed to be an ever-growing flow of humanity coming to the new country; they were all in a hurry to get there quickly.

James employed a lot of the vaqueros as horsemen to take care of his growing herd of horses, but good drivers were not as easy to come by. Men were crazy to look for gold. They could not see that the gold could as easily be mined from the miners; the hardware man, Sam Brannan, taught him that. He reflected back to his mentor, Charley, and wrote his friend of the opportunities here. James must bring back a driving force to help his business grow. California was the future.

"Charley, There's a letter here for you." The postmaster smiled. "All the way from Californy! Eah."

"What? For me?"

"Yep. Arrived last night," the man said, dying to know about the letter but trying not to pry.

"Well, I'll be, I never get mail."

"Well . . . you sure got some today," the mailman laughed.

Charley looked at the worn envelope and carefully opened it.

"It's from James Birch in Sacramento," the coachman blurted out to the amazement of the postman.

"Young James, eah," the old man recollected.

"Says he's fine and making money hand over fist. He needs drivers . . ." Charley stopped reading and gathered himself together. "Say I gotta go. See ya tomorrow, Elbert." Charley suddenly felt the need to read the letter in private.

"Oh sure. I'll see you, Charley. Say Martha did you hear? The Birch boy is getting rich in Californy!" he called to the girl in the sorting room.

California. It seemed so far away. So uncivilized. Charley hated to admit it, but he had grown comfortable. The thought of such a journey made him cringe. He was happy to hear that James was returning and figured Julia was the inspiration for the visit. That headstrong young man said he'd make that girl his own and Charley was sure he would be asking for her hand.

When Birch arrived, he flew straight to his lovely Julia Chase. It was a triumphant return, and the young couple was engaged in style. The entrepreneur paid in newly minted California gold for the couple's mansion home to be built on a piece of land Julia had picked out and purchased with money James had sent ahead. They would name the estate Swansea. It was to be a masterpiece; even the silverware would be specially handcrafted of original design made by Tiffany's of New York for the new palace.

James tried to get Charley and bring him back to California, but the coachman was very busy, and they were only able to visit briefly.

Birch offered a good job in the west for his mentor, but Charley politely declined for the time being. He claimed to be fully booked up for the rest of the year and not yet free to travel, but offered to keep the thought for consideration. Secretly he was afraid of the ocean voyage. Why, he did not know.

"I'll bide my time till you knock some of the rough edges off of the roads out there. I'm getting old. I have to think of my comfort," Charley kidded. But in a way he wasn't kidding at all.

"You just let me know if you get tired of the cities and change your mind. You always got a job with me!" James said as he departed.

Birch made it back to California in twenty-five days through the jungles of Panama. When he returned to San Francisco, he had renewed vigor. The first of the Concord coaches had arrived, and Birch was the talk of Sacramento.

Another company, Hall and Crandall, thought to cash in on the never-ending stream of gold seekers; they too had ordered coaches sent from the east. There was room on the road for all. Crandall and Hall had come to the new country across the vast prairies with wagons too. They had been in the freighting business and knew how to keep things rolling.

Stevens, who was secretly envious of Birch's engagement to Julia, decided to invest some of his earnings in a staging endeavor and opened Stevens Accommodation Line as well. He had evidently gotten enough rest at the Weary and needed to branch out. Another man, Charley Green, opened a Stage Line called Green's Forrest Line.

Each company ran a route in a different direction, and was full all the time. The offices in Sacramento were right in a row, and everyone was real friendly; every morning the coaches and horses jammed the fledgling city. Then like a shot they were off for all the diggings. James put his heart and soul into his business, he was proud of it, and it made him sad that his lovely Julia could not see it. He was eager to be with her, but he loved this new land too.

James branched out as the new gold towns sprouted up over California, so did his bank account. With his gold stashed safely away in the Well's & Fargo vault in Sacramento, he set up another office in Dry Diggins, one of the new settlements at the foot of the mighty Sierra Mountains. The miners there were beginning to call it Hang-town because of its rough nature. A lawman would be up to his elbows in business in California.

The newly built office in Dry Diggings was fancy compared to the rows of tents that most of the residents called home. The office was a simple box affair, built with rough-sawn redwood planks; it boasted a real door and a window. It was still quite primitive for now, but an addition was in construction at the rear. James slept on a cot in the corner of his office when he was there, but he still had to eat. He lit his cigar and left his stronghold for an eatery, leaving the ticket agent in charge.

"See you later, Henry. I'm gonna go eat."

"Seven o'clock gonna be on time?"

"I see no reason why not. Unless my watch gives out," Birch kidded Henry Fitzer.

Birch stood on the new plank sidewalk still looking at his watch; he held it to his ear. Yep, it was fine.

A tall young man was approaching Birch from across the muddy street. He had a decent suit of clothes on, which was a good sign he wasn't a miner. His long sandy blond hair was neatly combed, and he sported a soft mustache that ended in a trimmed blond beard. James noticed he was well armed but was walking with a cane.

"James Birch?"

"Yes. Can I help you?"

"Well now, maybe you can. My name is William Byrnes. I'm sheriff of Mormon Station, over the mountains, out at Genoa. I'm looking for a man named Hasket," Will said, shaking the coachman's hand.

"Well, I see . . . I was just going to get some dinner before I head back to Sacramento. We could talk in there. I meet a lot of people," James said, pointing to the large newly planked saloon next door.

The men walked into a smoke-filled establishment. The place was full of miners that were seeking relief from their daily toils. Somewhere in the back, a grease fire had filled the saloon with a burned stench.

"What did this man Hasket do if I may ask?" James said as they waited for the bartender to take their order.

"Well, I'll tell you, he and I were having a bit of a shooting match back at Mormon Station," Will said, putting some tobacco in his mouth. "On targets you see . . . I shot first. When my gun was empty, that son of a bitch Hasket turned and emptied his gun . . . in me. The skunk high-tailed it out of there, leaving me to bleed to death. He's been spotted around here somewhere. He's a coward and can't shoot worth a shit 'cause I'm still around. I'm gonna take him back and make him stand trial for what he did. Then I'm gonna hang him," Will swore, spitting on the sawdust floor.

"Well, good luck to you then," Birch said, wide-eyed at the tale. "Can I buy you a drink?"

"I don't mind."

"What does he look like?" Birch said studying the lawman.

"Tall, skinny man, about forty. Stringy red hair, greasy mustache, sideburns. Weighs maybe one fifty. Got green eyes. Bartender here says you remember people." Byrnes took this time to scan the room with his own light blue eyes.

"Hmmn. Two beers and two shots of whiskey the best you got," Birch called out.

"Yes sir, Mr. Birch," the bartender said, recognizing a man with money.

"Well now, maybe I did see . . ." James started.

"Never mind . . . he's here . . . Hasket! Turn around!" Will growled loudly for all to hear as he turned from the bar, looking across the room at the skunk playing cards in the smoky corner. The place became silent, except for the nervous tinkling of glasses and the piano player, who was still winding to a halt. The piano player then grabbed his hat off the piano and scampered behind his bulky instrument. Other men, not Hasket, took their cue from the musician and did likewise, scurrying under tables and moving out of the line of trouble.

"Hasket!" Will growled loudly. "I said turn around."

The redheaded man stood and turned slowly from his card game, to look at the nightmare that was taking place.

"Go for your gun now, you coward! My gun's not empty!" Will said slowly but deliberately, as more men dove for cover.

"Oh sweet Jesus!" Hasket said as he wet his pants, recognizing his grim reaper. He stood trembling, humiliated at the ever-increasing stain at his crotch. He laughed nervously for a second, then made the mistake of reaching for his revolver. Byrnes drew his gun effortlessly and without hesitation, shot Hasket through the head. The sandy-haired man walked slowly to the crumpled bleeding man on the floor. He looked down at the coward and spit his tobacco at him, hitting the corpse in the now-missing eye. He then walked back to the bar and had his drink, casually showing the barkeep his badge.

"You might want to inform the undertaker," Will said, finishing his beer. "I don't think it will be necessary to take him back with me now after all," he said, turning back to Birch.

"Well, I don't suppose . . . it will at that. Can I get you another drink?" James said quietly astonished. He had never seen anyone shot dead before.

"I don't mind if you do," Will said, pleased with himself.

"Say, set us up with another round and bring me the steak dinner but make sure it's well cooked. I don't want to see any blood," Birch added as the men dragged Hasket out to the sidewalk. The saloon began to buzz back to life as the piano player came out of hiding.

"Right away! Hey, Sam, get the undertaker will ya!" the barkeep hollered to the kitchen. "Coming right up, Mr. Birch."

"You ever get tired of being sheriff of Mormon Station, you would sure make a hell of an expressman," Birch offered. "You got a job with me anytime. Can you drive a stage?"

"I'm no driver, but I might be interested in riding shotgun. I'll give it some thought."

"You do that William Byrnes!" Birch said as he lifted his refilled glass.

CHAPTER 7

William Byrnes decided to stay in California awhile; he even took Birch up on his job. It was a lot easier and better money than tracking people all over the hills on a horse. He just went along for the ride and looked menacing. Byrnes knew he had what it took to back it up. Shooting a man had never been a problem for Will. He had joined the Texas Rangers and fought in the war with Mexico when he was sixteen. After his capture by the Mexican Army, he was imprisoned in Sonora, Mexico. He made friends with the priests there who taught him to speak Spanish and helped him to escape. After that, he hired on with a party of men to collect the bounty on Apache scalps, a dangerous line of business. Byrnes soon tired of that grisly enterprise and headed to the Sierras to try his hand as a lawman and capitalize on the new found wealth there.

Will's express ride for the day was completed. He had arrived safely to the terminus Rattlesnake Bar. Of course, the coach was just delivering people and mail today. Monday the coach would return to Sacramento full of gold. That's when he would earn his pay as a guard. So far no coaches had ever been successfully robbed. It was Byrnes' job to see that it stayed that way. Tomorrow was Sunday, and he was stuck at Rattlesnake Bar for the night. During the week, the coaches rolled back the same night. The stages made good time at night, with the roads clear of the ever-increasing pack trains and freight wagons that clotted up during the day, so great was the flood of humanity spreading out to the virginal landscape.

Will was inclined to wander around the diggings Sunday and borrowed a horse from the stage line for an afternoon ride. The station keeper wasn't in the horse-lending business generally, but the gold dollar kept his head turned as the horse went out for some fresh air.

The hills were full of song and campfires; it seemed as though men were living under every bush and shrub. Crude tents were the most popular accommodations, but ramshackle log cabins thrived as well. Men were in various stages of inebriation, strewn about, singing songs and cooking, doing laundry, writing and reading letters. Will passed camp after camp. He rode away from the river and toward a meadow where he saw less and less men as he came upon a dry canyon. He looked around at the rocky terrain; it was certainly a good place for snakes. He turned the horse to go back to the livery, then stopped; someone was riding toward him. It was two men with a packhorse. He loosened his grip on his horse's reins and walked slowly in the direction of the travelers. As they grew near, he studied them; there was something familiar about the first man. His wide-brimmed black hat was trimmed with silver conchos on the headband. His horse was a beautiful buckskin stallion with a black flowing mane and tail and a high prancing gait. His distinctive gold coat, with black stockings from his hooves to his knees, was crowned with tiger stripes on the tops of his legs to his chest. It gave him a fierce presence.

"I know that horse," Will said to himself.

"Can it be William Byrnes?" the young Sonoran man asked as he drew near.

"Joaquin Murrieta, I would recognize your horse anywhere." Will smiled. "And who is this, Rosita?"

"Si." A young woman concealed in men's attire peeked out of a wide-brimmed hat.

"Where are you headed?" Will said, turning to the young man.

"My brother is over near Murphy's. He sent word he was doing well there."

"I hear big things about Murphy's. I'm riding shotgun on the Birch line these days, just out for a joyride today. Maybe I might get down to Murphy's this summer."

"I heard about Hasket. Glad you got him, the bastard. Did he really shoot you six times at Mormon Station?"

"Yeah, he pissed his pants as he did. He couldn't shoot worth a damn, or I'd a been dead," Will spit. "Goddamned coward. Nothing I hate more than a coward! He pissed his pants before I killed him too, come to think of it."

"We are going to make camp about a mile from here. You are welcome to share our supper," Murrieta invited his friend.

"That sounds fine. I'll even contribute some quail. I saw a large covey a ways back. You go on, and I'll catch up to you," Will said as he lit off toward his quarry.

When Byrnes found his friend's camp, he had six fat quail tied to his saddle. Murrieta was wrestling with a dark blue sail that was being fashioned into a tent.

"It's not finished yet. It's going to be much bigger," the young Mexican said with pride as he tied off a supporting rope. "I bought this fabric from a Jew who was headed to Murphy's, called it denim, said it will make a good tent," he said, looking at it his new abode.

"Looks just fine." Will smiled. Rosita was emerging from the fabric cave; her raven hair was cascading across her lovely face, and she was startled to find her guest had arrived with lunch.

"How beautiful you look, my dear," Will cooed.

"I must look a fright." Rosita blushed. "But gracias, Will."

"I will get some wood for a fire. I leave my wife in your capable hands for now." Joaquin smiled at his friend. Will set about plucking the birds and gutting them while Rosita got her pan for cooking and set up a fire ring and general cooking area. She had become a gypsy of sorts, traveling the California hills in search of elusive fortunes. After eating, the trio sat reminiscing about Sonora, Mexico.

"That's a good-looking stud colt you got there," Will said, referring to the dappled gray colt that was being used as a pack animal. "Looks like he'll end up white."

"Oh, that's Mozo. I won him in a card game. He's just two years old. I'm gonna make a good saddle horse out of him. He's very fine. Aren't you?" the young man said, scratching the big colt behind the ears. The horse nodded in agreement.

"Speaking of which, I gotta get my horse back to the stable, he's got to work tomorrow, and so do I. If you can call it that. Mostly just sit there with my hands full of shotgun." Will laughed.

"I hope we will see you again soon, Will," Rosita said as Byrnes kissed her hand.

"Anything can happen. I hope so too and good luck with this tent. Looks like you got enough fabric for a whole town there." Will smiled.

"Via con dios, amigo," Murrieta called as Byrnes rode back to Rattlesnake Bar.

When Byrnes arrived, the men in town were deeply in their cups. This town wasn't much more than a sewer.

Byrnes thought about heading out to some of the more sophisticated diggings to trying his luck as a gambler or a card dealer in a saloon. He ended up at Murphy's. It was a grand little town built by the Murphy boys who had come to California early and recognized good property when they saw it. It had plenty of water and the most incredible timber a man ever hoped to lay his eyes on. Trees so big that the folks back east refused to believe in them, until a sample cut was shipped back as proof of the mighty redwood's existence.

A lot of people loved the new land, including the people that were there before all the insanity with the gold. They were being swept aside casually as if they didn't matter. Many of the inhabitants didn't take to well to being swept aside.

Joaquin Murrieta and his brother, Jesus, made money all night long, playing monte and poker at the large blue tent. Many times fights broke out. The Mexicans were a strong force though, when they fought together. So the white population instigated the foreign miners' tax. Which meant that the Mexicans and the Chinese would pay for the privilege of mining the ground they could only lease because they were not allowed to own property, being foreigners and all. Never mind that they had been in the country for years before anyone even cared about California. Animosity between the races was becoming thick.

CHAPTER 8

January 2, 1851

The snow crunched under the wheels as James Birch left the new depot in Columbia, heading back to Sacramento. The passengers were the usual lot, some dejected miners going back to try and salvage the rest of their lives, others who had done well and were headed home. One passenger, who opted for the fresh air of the roof, had a most charming way about him. He had long auburn hair, a nicely trimmed beard of light brown, with exceptional ice blue eyes. He would have been very handsome, except for the most hideously broken nose.

The conversations among the passengers ran the gamut from bold boasts of rich strikes, to the worse, hard-luck story. The men loved to try to out do each other. Finally noticing that the driver had been quiet for the entire time, the man with the broken nose, Dr. Hodges, he introduced, asked James if he had any entertaining stories.

"Having driven through the historic roads of this great country," as the doctor put it. "Surely you must have heard tales of great stage robberies and such from fellow whips and the like."

"Well, I do remember when I was back east, hearing tales of the stagecoach robber, Tom Bell. He was a notorious trickster and master of disguise, who stole horses and was a bold highwayman of the eastern states in the last century. He often dressed as a priest. Tom Bell even convinced an entire town that the real parish priest had committed the crimes," Birch went on.

"What happened to him?" the doctor inquired.

"The priest, oh, he was hung I believe," Birch replied. "Git up now, Sarah," he chastised his lazy horse.

"No, the robber!" Dr. Hodges asked.

"Oh, I believe he was finally hung as well. They all get hung eventually," Birch said philosophically.

"Do they?" the doctor asked.

"Seems to me they do. Even those that don't deserve it," Birch reflected.

"I see." Dr. Hodges smiled.

Dr. Hodges rode on the coach all the way to Sacramento; he was intent on conducting business of some kind and was very disappointed with the outcome. Walking back down the plank sidewalk with a desperate look on his face, he noticed the familiar coachman heading to his favorite watering hole.

"My word, you look like someone just ran over your dog," Birch commented, as the doctor came near. "Say I'm heading into the New Orleans. Can I buy you a drink? I hate to say it, but you look like you could use one, I know I could."

"Yeah, I could at that," Hodges said, looking down at some mail.

"Bad news?"

"Yep. You sure could call it that. Business venture turned sour," Dr. Hodges said, tossing down his whiskey.

It was two days later that Birch learned that the doctor had been implicated in a robbery and arrested. He was tried and found guilty, then sentenced to serve time in the penitentiary near San Francisco on Point San Quentin.

The sheriff seemed rather concerned about his charge. Dr. Hodges was a very soft-spoken man, yet he seemed extremely dangerous. He looked around at his half-stiff deputy and then at his dull-witted son-in-law and was fearful that a clever criminal may get the upper hand. And that wouldn't look good on his already-tarnished record.

Leaving Stockton, the party went by riverboat to the San Francisco bay. Dr. Hodges was mesmerized by the diversity of the waterfowl, geese and duck, herons and egrets by the mile. The sloughs sounded like a vast cocktail party of horns and party favors as the steamboat wound around through the wetlands. The rolling hills in the background were speckled with orange and blue and white patches, like some artist had cleaned his brushes on them.

Dr. Hodges had been to San Francisco several times but never crossed the bay to Marin.

The prison there had been a private enterprise, established by M. G. Vallejo and General Estell, temporarily set up on the barge *Waban*, a 268-ton ship moored at the Point San Quentin. The inmates of the barge were put to work making bricks in a brickyard on the point during the day. The clay was very abundant in the area. The barge was quickly over crowded and brick buildings began to sprout on the point. The newly built prison system was run by an independent contractor whom General Estell was the executive officer. The inmates were also contracted to do hard labor on Angel Island, so named for the large flocks of snowy egrets that roosted in the great trees on the island. As the trees were felled and milled, it became a quarry, with prisoners breaking off rock to be used for building the hotels and houses of a growing San Francisco. The angels had been replaced by something less angelic. It too was overcrowded; the men on Angel Island were housed in barges anchored there and locked down for the night. The most dangerous prisoners were kept locked in cells, on the barge *Waban* still anchored at Point San Quentin.

The sheriff led Dr. Hodges to the charge of the deputy at the prison, who ushered the condemned man to the ledger book to sign in.

The next day, Dr. Hodges found his life would now be hard labor, breaking rocks on Angel Island. The guards herded the new prisoners to the boat. Hodges' companions for the voyage was Bill Gristy, alias Bill White; Red Ned Connor; and Jim Smith, an escape artist covered with a tapestry of tattoos. Also along was Bob Carr, known as

English Bob; and a Montegue Lyon, known as Monte Jack; and a most desperate man by the name of Juan Fernandes, wanted in Mexico for most vile killings, off on a short trip to the island in the San Francisco Bay, Angel Island.

"Don't think about swimmin' off'n the island, mates. There's sharks out there that could swallow you whole, twenty footers, no lies," the young guard said, cautiously surveying the waters, having just recently seen an extremely large fish following the boat several days previous to this.

The crew would work in the quarry during the day and sleep locked up in one of the beached barges at night.

The deputies guided the convicts down the planked walk to the quarry. After seeing that the new trustees were secure with the guards, they walked back to the station house to take the boat back.

Dr. Hodges, Bill Gristy, and the rest of the new men stood on the shore and looked longingly across the bay. Right there in front of them was San Francisco and freedom, it seemed so close, taunting them.

CHAPTER 9

January 1851, San Francisco

The sky was gray and wet as the small steamship *Antelope* chugged into the San Francisco Bay. A small group of people crowded the deck, all wearing thick clothing against the fog. More than a few parasols were turned inside out, causing folks to duck for fear of getting clobbered. The billowing view was exciting enough for the newcomers to brave the weather for a look at the city that gold built. They were now entering the Golden Gate as the bay was called. A young woman stood transfixed on the shores masked in fog and clouds; she felt like she could hear strange singing and odd clicks with heavy breathing and splashing in the waters near the ship. She rubbed her eyes and peered through the fog to see a giant flipper roll out of the water, then just silently slip away. Eleanora turned from the sight toward the people standing around her, She thought about informing them of her odd sighting but changed her mind. Ms. Dumont had traveled from New Orleans to reach this place of opportunity and had grown fond of her traveling companions, but now it was time to begin again.

She was dressed elegantly in a deep blue wool coat that was trimmed in silver fox; it accentuated her lovely dark brown hair and blue eyes.

"I'm sure you will be happy to tuck your little ones in a real bed tonight, Mrs. Gesford?" Eleanora said, smiling at the youngest girl.

"It will be a blessing!" the tired mother replied.

"It won't be long now."

Eleanora Dumont had come to make her fortune, just as everyone in California had, coming with a small bankroll that she had saved, intending to open a house of recreation in the gold fields. She wanted to hire musicians and girls to dance for and with the miners. Eleanora had worked in a restaurant with her mother in the French Quarter, where she had developed a keen business sense. The young entrepreneur had talked several girls into coming to California but knew she needed to look for more dancers and get together a band in San Francisco before heading to the mountains. Eleanora prayed her money would hold out until she could reach the gold-laden miners.

It took some doing, but she found what she was looking for in San Francisco, a card game at a reputable house. Her stunning good looks had men lining up to gamble and lose to the voluptuous woman. Soon she held the bankroll of her dreams and sent out a partner, David Tobin, to find a suitable location closer to the source of gold. The troupe was then packed up and on the road to budding Nevada City.

CHAPTER 10

1851

The town of Downieville, California is set on the northern fork of the Yuba River. The scent of dry pine was like perfume in the crisp summer air as James Birch drove a team of prancing horses into the bustling river, with men busy at work retrieving the gold laced among the gravel in the riverbed.

The men looked up and cheered, as the coach and horses splashed across the river. In June, the river was only two feet deep in the crossing spot, but it was bracing and fast, and the horses danced across. In the midst of a large tent town, Birch sought out General Downie and was invited to dinner to discuss plans for his new town. Downie was putting together a road crew, mostly of Chinese, so they could haul supplies in and gold out. It wasn't long after that, James Birch's stage line was traveling to the far reaches of Downieville. The road was a twisting, turning, marvel of a nauseating, rolling ride, on the inside of the coach. On the roof, it was breathtaking and exciting and sometimes hat and luggage stealing.

The forests were very lush and thick, and one could only imagine what it must be like in the winter or early spring. The woods were alive with bird life; and Birch marveled at the variety of hawks, eagles, and woodpeckers. He was also ever vigilante for big brown bears and wolves. The California wolf was a large black animal with long legs, capable of great leaps and high speeds. They traveled in large organized packs. The miners were making them more and more scarce. The virgin forests still held out surprises though, and it paid to be alert; the bears that lived there were gigantic. Birch read the horses' body language in heavy woods, trying to pick up signs of nervousness, and always being prepared with his trusty and well-maintained Colt revolver; it helped alleviate a feeling of vulnerability.

James Birch liked Downieville; it had nice folks. It wasn't any more or less wild than any of the other gold rush towns. Maybe a little more remote. It was way out there, with very few women. A whore could make a killing there, ask whatever price she wanted.

One woman there, Josefa, was not a whore; maybe it irritated men that she would hold out such a wanted commodity, but she was a married Catholic woman and wanted nothing to do with Anglo men, especially a Scotsman named Cannon. From what Birch could figure, she was married to a small Mexican man named Jose. Often Josefa had given James her mail personally, as she wanted to avoid Cannon, who had a tendency to hang around the express office. He had a very foul mouth, and James found him rather offensive as well and didn't mind taking care of Josefa's mail. The Scot was always trying to solicit the woman to relieve his carnal appetite.

Downieville was planning to have big doings in the way of celebrating California's first Fourth of July as a new state. There were big wagons filled with barrels of whiskey and beer, tins of oysters and big wheels of cheese. A herd of cattle had been driven up especially for the big barbecue. It was a stagecoach driver's nightmare. The roads were clogged up with wagons and supplies and you name it. In some places the roads could only accommodate one wagon at a time, so there were hot disputes over right of ways, with tempers getting out of control. By the time the stagecoach arrived at Downieville on the Fourth of July, they were two hours late, but folks were too intoxicated to care. It was as though James Birch was the last sober man on earth. The passengers were all loaded, everyone in town was drunk, even the stable hands. Birch decided to look after the horses himself, then get some grub and barricade himself in the livery stable until the madness passed, thus protecting the horses from some idiot's attempt at whatever foolishness demon rum had planned.

As he fed the horses, Birch could hear the laughter and foul humor and gunshots of the drunken miners. He tried to think about what his lovely Julia would be doing and took out a locket with her picture. She would be celebrating too, but without the bestial behavior and filth that a place like this could sink to. It made him sick to think of this whole town slobbering and puking in the streets. Down the alley, poor Josefa was thinking the same thing.

The noise did not let up all night. James found that he could hear folks making fools of themselves all over town, even through the redwood barn. Even old Cannon was singing some Chinese love songs and enacting various parts of some obscure story to the great amusement of all within earshot. At last the party seem to disperse about one in the morning, with groups setting off to different parts of the woods.

James was awaken by a crash a few doors down from the livery stable and much swearing and some laughing. It was the Scotsman Cannon who must have staggered into the Mexican woman Josefa's door. The swearing went on for quite some time. James got up for a moment to check outside the barn; Josefa's door was broken, but back in place. The voices outside seemed to be tapering out. He had an early run in the morning, and there was still a few hours of sleep to catch.

As the sun slowly lightened the sky, Birch sat outside the stable, watching the stable boy with the dilapidating headache harness up the horses. James spotted Josefa swearing like a wet hen and trying vainly to fix her front door. It looked like a horse had kicked it in. Josefa swore loudly, and Jose came out to try and make the shattered door work. It was six thirty in the morning, and the coach was due to leave at seven. As the coachman sat on the porch, eating his breakfast and drinking coffee, he noticed Cannon and his friend, Lawson, going into the doctor's office, next door, which infuriated Josefa even more. By the time James was in the driver's box gathering his lines, preparing to leave, he saw Cannon and Josefa arguing outside her shack; then it was time to go.

Birch arrived back in Downieville at six thirty the next day and upon his completion of duty retired to Craycroft's saloon; he stood in amazement when he heard the news. It was the only thing folks were talking about, the hanging, and then Cannon's wake and burial. It took time for James to get the whole story. It appeared that Josefa had stabbed Cannon to death shortly after his coach had left. Cannon and the small Mexican woman had a dispute over the door and certain descriptive words that Cannon had called her. While Cannon was in the woman's house, Josefa stabbed him to death with one blow to the chest with a large bowie knife. Cannon, being a very popular man with the miners, aroused an unsympathetic mob, which turned on the young woman and tried her. Within hours, they had sentenced her to hang, despite a doctor's effort to save her by claiming her pregnant. The doctor was run out of town. The enthusiastic lynch mob, now numbering close to a thousand, had prepared a gallows on the Jersey bridge. Over two thousand men came out of the woods and lined the river to see the gruesome spectacle. The body of Cannon had been laid out for all to view the terrible carnage caused by the small woman. Finally, the hour had drawn to a close, and Josefa bravely walked to her final doom, and after saying her good-byes to her husband stepped up to the gallows and put the noose around her own neck, carefully sweeping her raven tresses aside. She then bravely met her maker, leaving a blemish forever upon Downieville's history, the first city in California to hang a woman.

CHAPTER 11

1852 Spring

It was very early in the morning; the sun had not yet crested the horizon. James Birch sat in the new Stockton office sipping on some coffee, talking to Frank Stevens, who had arrived in town last evening. The two had a quiet moment together before they would depart to various parts of the country.

"I had the most interesting encounter the other day. I was leaving Folsom for Nevada City when a beautiful dark-haired French lady stopped the coach. She had arrived late, but her stunning beauty and that of her companions kept the men captivated, and we soon had them loaded on board. The French woman seemed quite interested in riding on the top, so of course I offered her the seat of honor next to me. She had a lot of baggage, so I made arrangements with the freight man to bring them after us. She introduced herself to me as Eleanora Dumont and said she intended to go to the golden mountains of California and provide the hardworking men of this state with the diversions from their labor that they craved and deserved. I praised the Lord for the unsuspecting men and could not help but admired the woman's confidence and charm. She later informed me that she had grown up in Na'Leans and had several uncles that had taught her well in the use of cards and firearms. We took her to the new hotel at the top of the street in Nevada City; it tickled me to watch the headstrong young women march into the establishment with such confidence. She was quite lovely. I'm curious to see what kind of a establishment she opens." Frank smiled as he finished his coffee.

CHAPTER 12

Spring 1852, Foothills California

There was talk that the Mexicans had lost California, and "they could just get the hell out!" It was an ugly, racist time, but Joaquin Murrieta and William Byrnes remained friends, nevertheless.

"Let them try and collect their tax. I'll give it to them," Joaquin swore at the card table. "I was in California long before those gringo bastards!" He was visiting his brother, Jesus, on a fine day in April. "Brother, I need to borrow a horse to get home. My horse has thrown a shoe."

"You can take my mule home. I need my horse." Jesus laughed. "You can bring him back tomorrow. I'll have a new shoe on El Tigre."

"How humbling to ride on a mule!" Joaquin scoffed.

"It's better than walking," Jesus responded.

"Some people say, once you ride a mule, you never go back to horses. I wonder what they mean by that?" a short vaquero commented.

"Shut up, Alejandro!" Joaquin replied. "Or I'll take your horse!"

"You are better off with the mule!" Alejandro laughed.

Joaquin looked over the long-eared fellow; he was well enough put together and seemed like a nice beast. He saddled him and made his way down the path back to the blue tent and Rosita.

He hadn't ridden long before he came to a large gathering of men, who were drunk and looking for trouble. Joaquin, who was alone, tried to get by quickly, but it was to no avail. The men insisted he confront them.

"Listen, I do not want trouble with you, men. I am simply on my way home," Joaquin explained.

"Mexico is that a way." One man pointed.

"Where did you get that mule from?" one of the men asked.

"None of your business," Joaquin snapped.

"That was the wrong answer, Mexican!" another man yelled, throwing a lasso around Joaquin and pulling him off the mule. They dragged him to a tree and tied him to it with the rawhide.

"I think he stole that mule! That looks just like my mule. It was stole the other night!" a tall, lanky fella named Bill Lang insinuated.

"I did not steal the mule. I borrowed him from my brother," Joaquin tried to explain. The group was getting ugly, and it was clear that no explanation was going to suffice.

"Who is your brother?" Lang questioned the captive.

"Jesus Murrieta. I seen them together at the Monte tables," a disgusted gambling man said, looking at Joaquin's bloody face. The young Mexican knew it was futile to escape and was sure, unless there was a miracle, he would be hung for the sport of these racist drunks.

"I know where he lives. Let's get him too," another man yelled. "We'll have us a neck-tie party!"

"You five go and get the brother, and we'll take care of this bastard!"

"Don't you go hangin' him till we gets back," Lang whined. "We can hang them together."

"We'll just warm him up," laughed another man, who was taking off his belt. "We can at least beat the shit out of him while we're waitin'."

With Joaquins' neck tied tightly to the tree, they stripped him down to his bare skin and tied his hands together behind his back. The men lashed him with their belts while the others got his brother. When they returned, Joaquin's back was dyed red with his own blood.

"I'm sorry, Jesus, I did not mean to get you involved," Joaquin cried.

"I told you to wait till we was back. You damn near killed this one already," Lang was whining.

"I did not steal that mule, and you know it, Lang," Jesus yelled.

"I suppose you got some proof?" Lang interrogated.

"Well, not at the moment. You dragged me out of my house. You bastard!" Jesus swore at the men.

"There, now you see he ain't got no proof, I told you. Now let's string 'em up!" Lang insisted.

"No!" Joaquin yelled.

"Shut up, you!" Lang said, getting in a punch on the bound Joaquin. "I got the rope right here," he said, throwing it up over a tree limb. The mob surrounded Jesus and placed him on top of the mule in question and put the rope around his neck; his arms were tied behind his back, and the animal was soon startled into a run. Jesus struggled for a moment, and then it was over. The mule, sensing the dangerous men, kept on running.

"Say, ain't you gonna go get back your stolen mule, Bill?" one of the men asked as the mule in question galloped off into the woods, braying madly.

"Let's cut this one down. He's 'bout dead anyway," one of the men decided, pointing to Joaquin. There was some dispute over the merit of that idea. Joaquin was regaining consciences; upon seeing his dead brother, he hung his head in grief and pain, then began to feel an uncontrollable rage welling up in his throat.

"You may as well kill me now. For if you don't, I will rise up and kill every last one of you bastards who have done this! So help me God!" the beaten man growled with the last of his strength.

The men just laughed at the wretched man and spit on him, then threatened to stretch his neck as well if he didn't shut up. The mob took all of Joaquin's money and rode off laughing. About this time, another group of men approached, drawn by all the noise and commotion. One of the men was William Byrnes, who immediately came to the aid of his friend and cut him from the tree.

"I'm sorry they did this, Joaquin. Jesus was a good friend," Byrnes said as he tried to make his friend comfortable.

"Not half as sorry as those men that did this are going to be. They should have never left me alive. Will you take me to Rosita?" Joaquin asked as Byrnes cut Jesus from the limb.

"Of course, I will make sure that your brother gets a decent burial too." Will put Joaquin up on his own horse, then spoke with his friends, giving them some gold coin for the burial and explained that he was taking the injured man to his wife, then got on his horse behind Joaquin, and rode to blue tent.

"They should have never left me alive," Joaquin kept saying over and over. "I will kill them all!"

When they got to the tent, Byrnes poured the delirious man a hefty shot of tequila, then had one himself. He put his hands over his eyes and sighed.

"This will not turn out well, I'm afraid." Will stared into his friend's tortured face and saw that the light in Joaquin's eyes had turned black with rage. "God help them for what they have done."

"No one can help them now!" Joaquin said as if from far away. "If I have to, I will summons my cousin, Duarte," Joaquin hissed.

"Tres Dedos?" Byrnes was snapped back into reality.

"Yes, it is just the thing he loves to do the most, kill!" Joaquin finished his tequila. "Please go and look after my brother, Will, and thank you."

"Please be careful, Joaquin," Will replied, leaving the tent and riding back to town, careful to notice if anyone had followed him to his friend's abode.

It was not more than a week before the first men that attended the lynching began turning up dead. There were inquiries made about the supposedly stolen mule, and in a dispute, an eyewitness saw Sam Green, who had been drinking heavily, confronting Bill Lang about the incident.

"You cowardly cur, you had nothing on them Murrieta boys. Jesus paid you for that mule, and you know it! You are a born scoundrel. You never was no good. I ought to kill you, and I guess I will!" And with those words said, Sam took out his revolver and emptied it into Bill Lang. Green was tried in district court before Judge Charles Creaner; the jury found him guilty. He was hanged at Mokelumne on July 31, 1852.

Joaquin had rested from his wounds and sent word to Petaluma for his cousin, Manual Duarte. He sat in the blue tent stewing over his loss. Rosita who was nursing her own wounds, incurred after several miners caught her alone one afternoon and had savagely raped her, tried to keep Joaquin from exploding. A few days later, the devil himself appeared at their doorstep.

"Rosita, it is a privilege," Duarte purred, clutching her soft hand with his own grotesquely mutilated paw and kissing it. His index finger was missing, as well as the thumb and the fingernails on the remaining three fingers were long and dirty like claws. He then slunk past her, entering the large fabric abode.

"I'm glad to see you got my letter," Joaquin said, whispering to the evil presence before him.

"I'm sorry for the loss of Jesus. He was a good man," Duarte sighed. "How many men were involved?"

"Eight men. One is dead. The rest are still in the area. I have men watching them," Joaquin spoke, hatred just under the surface.

"How many men do you have?" Duarte asked.

"Seven I can count on," Murrieta replied.

"Then why do you need me?" Duarte laughed.

"They are not killers. You, I believe, are an expert," Joaquin said, pouring the man a drink.

Duarte smiled an evil grin, then laughed a slow deep laugh that could curdle your blood. Rosita fled like a frightened deer from the talk of bloodshed. She sat close to Jesus' widow, who had taken up residence in the tent. The women then set about to feed the newly arrived guest.

"Tomorrow we shall pay a visit to some of these men, yes?" Duarte smiled, lighting his cigar. "What we want to do is to lure them here, where we can dispose of them one by one. Of course, you must relocate the ladies and your belongings. Just keep a facade that you are mining here and that you've had a rich strike. They will come flooding back like rats. Do you have any gold from this area that you can flash around?" the cousin asked.

"Yes, I have quite a lot if you want to know," Joaquin responded.

"Good." Duarte laughed.

The next morning, the two rode into Angel's Camp and deposited some gold in the bank and then sent some more gold to Duartes' address in Petaluma. They retired to the nearest saloon to boast of good fortune. The men in Joaquin's alliance were introduced to Duarte and were invited to a meeting at the blue tent later that night. It was decided at the meeting that no firearms were to be used due to the close proximity of the other miners in every streambed and gully. The men were all experienced vaqueros and were expert at throwing a rope. They would lure their victims into the meadow of blue tent, then ambush them and drag them until they were dead. Duarte instilled his own technique for roping a man, then dragging him about the neck until he could bash him up against a tree stump or a big rock, thus popping his head off. Then the lariat holder did not have to dismount to retrieve his rope.

Soon the trap was set, and the first rats had arrived. The set up worked beautifully. Duarte had even had a tree felled to facilitate his killing style. The bodies were then hidden in shrubbery, until the next victim came to call. Thus it went on, and most of the guilty men were disposed of.

The location of the denim casino known as blue tent was renamed Los Muertos, the dead, because of the assortment of bodies found there. Notably, all members of the Murrieta lynch mob. No one in his right mind rode there alone, lest they receive a rawhide necktie. The denim tent was relocated somewhere south of Mariposa.

Birch's stage line was running from Mariposa to Hangtown, now being called Placerville. The summer saw the rivers full of men in new canvass cities: Drytown, Chile Gulch, Fiddletown, Columbia, and Sonora. Then you had the more colorful names: Gouge Eye, Humbug, Timbuktu, Poverty Hill, Port Wine, and You Bet. The makeshift cities popped up wherever anyone made a rich strike. Populations ebbed and flowed like the tide.

William Byrnes had taken a job in Placerville, helping to keep some order among the immigrant trains coming in from the east. Tensions were running high due to the news of marauding gangs of Mexicans robbing and killing people as they slept in their camps. No one was safe. The papers were telling of daily accounts of gory murders and robberies. People were found slain by the side of the road with their throats cut.

James Birch saw Byrnes in Placerville, and they discussed the events that happened with the Murrietas near Angels Camp. His face turned pale as a full moon when Byrnes told of the atrocities committed by Joaquin's cousin, who went by the name Tres Dedos, which means three fingers.

Joaquin realized that his life would never be the same. Tres Dedos had become a strong force in motivating Mexican families to join the gangs. He pointed out the inhuman treatment and the persecution of their people; he even talked of taking California back for Mexico, with an army of vaqueros and cutthroats. In truth, he simply wanted to rob and pillage. Yet he had built Murrieta's small gang into a very formidable force. Joaquin Valenzuela and Joaquin Carrillo had also thrown in as well; the gangs had many components and family ties.

The Mexicans were great horsemen and specialized in stealing and herding horses. They had many practices; one was to hobble a stallion with a thick rawhide thong, attached to a three-foot length of a tree, about six inches in circumference in order to keep him from trying to run away. It was cruel, but it worked. The men had a network of ranchos that they would drive the horses to, until they got them to ranchos in Mexico. The gold they stole was hidden in various secured homes and mysterious hiding places. There were several designated rendezvous and signals in which gang members would arrange their meetings. One of the locations was post office rock, an interesting work of geology. The rock had been formed in some volcanic episode and looked like a giant stone sponge, with one face sheered off exposing a shelf, riddled with holes, where messages were often left. The meeting place was generally Las Tres Pietras, the three rocks, large sandstone outcroppings that looked like giant teeth sticking out of the earth. It was a good campsite as it had high walls that hung out at the top, making a nice roof. There was generally good feed for the horses in the meadows nearby and a very convenient spring hidden in the rocks.

The men in the gangs were a closely-knit bunch, many related through marriage and cousins. All were rebelling against the taking over of California by the gold hungry Gringos.

CHAPTER 13

1852 Providence Rhode Island

Charley had been driving the rich to their very first rate doings, as he liked to call them, and had arrived back at the Balch livery in Providence. The What Cheer House was still brimming with good spirits, and the laughter was spilling out into the cool fall night air. As Charley stepped through the front door, elegantly attired with top hat and cape, he was greeted fondly by an old friend. James Birch had come back from California! It was a short but important visit, he assured his friend—part business and part pleasure. Charley was overjoyed to see his young friend so prosperous looking.

Birch was wearing the finest clothes that money could buy; the little boy that could swim had done all right for himself. He excited his audience with tales of the new frontier in California, explaining that he had returned to bring back blooded horses, coaches, and skilled drivers. Oh, and of course, to get married! He presented his friend with a wedding invitation for October 14, 1852.

James asked Charley point-blank if he would come to California and drive for him. Parkhurst's mouth hung open for a moment.

"I will pay you top dollar, I assure you! And your travel expenses and I will give you your pick of teams and harness to drive. I'll even have your initials in gold on your harness if that's what it takes to get you out there. I have contracted Abbott to build me some more coaches, so you will be driving the most roadworthy vehicles available. What do you say, Charley? You won't regret it. The winters there are mild, and it only rains in the foothills in the winter," James bargained.

Parkhurst had begun to get bored with the snooty rich and the harsh icy winters. What was there to think about? Of course, he would come! After this bold acknowledgment, Charley noticed a sad look in Eb's face, and Charley realized what all this would mean. An upheaval in the What Cheer House was becoming inevitable. Charley tried to talk Eb and Mary into relocating to the west as well, but both were afraid that they were too old and set in their ways to start all over.

The next night, Charley waited in the tavern, holding a note he had received from James Birch that said he would be there at seven. He stood at the end of the bar drinking a beer, fussing with his black silk tie, oddly nervous. Many people recognized him as the coachman and said hello.

He pondered the decision he had made and reflected on it as he looked around this cozy, genial, safe atmosphere. At last the door swung open and a familiar, but now mature face showed through once again, Charley knew it had been the right choice.

Her heart soared to see him so dashing and almost heroic. Beside Birch was a stern-looking short young man, who seemed to look longingly at the bar. Dressed in a long black coat with a vest buttoned close to his neck, he was less elegantly attired than his host but seemed dignified in a way that a priest would. His face sported a plush mustache and goatee that made him look quite serious.

"Hank, I'd like you to meet Charley Parkhurst. Charley, this is Hank Monk," James said proudly.

"Why I'm pleased to make your acquaintance," Hank said politely, holding out his hand. "Jim, speaks highly of you."

"Likewise I'm sure," Charley said, sizing up this new companion and shaking hands, marveling to herself of the striking blue eyes that hinted of humor.

"Hank has agreed to come and drive for me too. He's sailing back to California with us," James said with enthusiasm. "He's the man that drove the big eight abreast in the Boston parade last."

"Oh, that was quite a hitch. All black, weren't they?"

"Yep, a German team, came from a brewery. Thar big and drafty, go about fifteen hundred pounds a piece," Hank boasted.

"I didn't see the parade myself, but the newspaper made a big deal of it." Charley smiled. "Have you ever taken an ocean voyage?" he said, changing the subject.

"Have you?" Hank smiled.

"No, I'm afraid not. Rather thrilling to think about. California sounds beautiful, with plenty of money to be made," Charley responded.

"Here's to all the money!" James said, pouring a round of drinks for his friends.

"Well, James, you've certainly done all right for yourself!" Felix said, swaggering into the bar.

"Felix Riggs! You haven't changed a bit!" James laughed.

"Well, you sure did clean up good. Look at you. You look like a prince or something," Felix slobbered.

"California could make a rich man, even of you!" James chuckled.

"Is that an offer?" Felix said with a serious tone.

"I'm sure I could find a place for you in my business. Of course, it's an offer!" James said in a princely way.

"Damn! I'm goin' to Californy too!" Felix whooped, swatting Charley on the shoulder, unable to believe his own good fortune.

"I am planning on returning to California in November," James announced.

"Are we goin' around the horn? I heard that's a wicked ride!" Hank asked.

"No, we'll go through Panama. It's the quickest. They have a small steamer that takes you upriver, then a mule ride through some dense forest to Panama City, where we'll meet another ship. A regular adventure, boys!" James said with enthusiasm. "Well, my fellows, Julia is looking forward to seeing you again. I have a carriage outside. We dine in style tonight! Where's Eb?"

"He's upstairs with a head ache. Mary's with him. I think they're angry at me."

"I'm sorry," James reflected, tossing the bartender a gold coin and whisking his troupe off to the vehicle outside.

Two weeks later, about twenty miles from the What Cheer House at Swansea, Massachusetts, the October wedding was ablaze with the bright colors of the New England foliage. The grand new home, though not fully completed, set a romantic stage. James lavished his bride's dream for a beautiful ceremony, and the guests lingered and enjoyed themselves until dawn. Many stayed in the lavish guestrooms that the new mansion boasted.

CHAPTER 14

On a bitter November morning, the U. S. steamship *Illinois* sat in Boston harbor; she was an impressive sight, a side-wheeler, as she was called, for the two massive paddle wheels on either side of her midsection. She sported two huge black smokestacks that were now only mildly puffing. Soon the *Illinois* would be bellowing thick smoke from coal fires and steam from the engines as the paddles churned the ocean. The ship also had three great masts and could travel on full sail as well, making the ship very fast indeed. New speed records were being broken all the time. She carried only passengers and mail, mostly men, but a few daring women turned over their life and limb for pursuits in the golden hills of California. The *Illinois* was bound for Aspinall by way of Jamaica.

"We're going first class all the way, fellas. Here are your tickets, don't lose them," James said, passing out the packets to Hank and Charley and Felix.

There must have been at least five hundred people huddling against the cold and shuffling aboard in small clusters, in some semblance of a line. The baggage was transferred to the ship, and the men began their tour of the decks, of which this ship had three. The top deck held the smaller hurricane deck and also the officers quarters. The second deck had the first-class cabins and the dining room, with a small steerage area aft and the crews quarters at the bow. The lower deck held the rest of the steerage passengers and the cargo.

James had set up his dear friends in the first-class cabins on the second deck. Each cabin had three narrow beds set closely over each other with a fabric curtain for privacy. Next to the stack of beds was a mirrored cabinet that held a bottle of water with a spigot. Below the cabinet was a small built-in basin with a drain and a plug. Next to the cabin door was a tiny chair that faced the porthole on the opposite wall. Beneath it was a small bench and table. There was hat and coat hooks strategically placed around the cabin and a small closet in a corner; in the opposite corner was a chamber pot that was nestled in a railing that held it in place. The whole affair was quite claustrophobic.

"Well, I guess this is home for the time being." James smiled as Hank piled his luggage in the center of the small room.

"Ain't hardly enough room to swing a cat in here. I can't imagine what them louts in steerage got to put up with!" Monk commented.

"Is this it?" Charley asked, setting his luggage in a pile next to Monks. "It looks like it'll have to be the luggage or us. I don't think there's room for both."

"Well, I'm sure you won't spend that much time cooped up in here. They feed you pretty good on this ship," James reassured, as he stacked bags in the closet. "What bunk you want Charley?"

"Oh, I think I'll take the lower bunk if you fellas don't mind," Charley said, imagining the most privacy there. The top bunk was at eye level and the middle bunk most accessible, the bottom bed seemed the least amount of disturbance, she figured to herself.

"I don't care," Hank said, testing out the chair. I'll take the middle bunk. Jim, you take the top." He settled. "Where can a man get a drink around here?"

"Look they have little shots," Charley said, picking up the glass that was in a wooden holder in the cabinet over the basin.

"Good, bring them here," James said, pulling his flask from his coat. Charley set them on the small table with a railing around the edge by the chair, and James filled them with Jamaican rum.

This was going to be close quarters for a while, Charley thought as he smiled at Hank, smelling his strong body odor and stepping back. Little did Monk know what Charley was smiling at as he took out a cigar and trimmed off the end and lit it.

"Look they got some little boxes of Lucifer's matches with the company name on the box," Hank said, taking out his own cigar and finding the matches in an ashtray.

"I told you this was first class. Cheers!" James said, raising his glass. "Wait till you see the next ship, the *Golden Gate*. It's practically new. Very nice and also very fast. They are trying to set the speed record from Panama to San Francisco. Some say they got a fair chance to do it too," James said with authority as he poured another round.

The dining room was outside of the cabins, and people were gathering and milling around, talking and meeting in anticipation of the food and or of departure; no one seemed to know which would happen first. The fellows had said their good-byes long before and stayed in their stateroom and waited for the dinner bell. Felix had a cabin next to Charley, along with a character named McNulty and a quiet man named Morton.

At four o'clock, the steamer set sail, churning onward over the bounding ocean.

The meals were taken care of with the use of various seatings. It would be impossible to feed the entire ship at once, but the first-class passengers had a cornucopia of foods to choose from, such as ham, turkey, roast beef, and lamb. The tables were beautifully set with starched white linens, and they prided themselves on a first-rate culinary experience, which included fresh butter and bread and fresh vegetables and fruit.

The steerage folks got to eat when the dinner bell rang for them. They lined up and were served stew and soups with crackers as they held out their tin bowls, scuffling along. They then procured a place somewhere among the boxes or on the floor to eat. It was decent compared to some other ships.

Meanwhile, the first-class passengers smoked their cigars and had their brandy in style. The discussions were interesting enough, and many men were quite musical. The captain frequently could be talked into a tune on his accordion, after dinner. The fellows spent many hours sitting and walking around the top deck, watching the land in the distance come and go from view through the temperamental weather. Occasionally, a whale was sighted or a big school of fish, which would cause great excitement in the landlubbers crowding the decks to get a look. Many spent the voyage sick in their beds, the chamber pot or basin the only comforting sight. The hardy amused themselves, watching the plates and silverware sliding around the table as the ship seemed to lope across the ocean, sending things to and fro. Charley, Hank, and James were used to the roll and pitch of a coach and had more problems from indulging in too much brandy the night before. The cabin crew was frequently busy with the business of chamber pots in the first-class cabins during a rough sea.

"So how come you're not down below, puking your guts out with the rest of the blokes?" the weathered Scotsman said to the coachman, who had been walking the deck marveling at the angry sea. Charley was clinging to the ropes on the deck; his gaze was far out on the horizon. The old man's voice startled him, and he turned to see his hard watery eyes searching deeply into his own.

"Oh, I drive a coach and six. I guess I'm used to the rolling motion," Charley said, smiling at the Scotsman.

"A coach and six you say? Going to California with Birch?"

"Yes, going to drive there," Charley said, holding out his strong hand. "Name's Charley Parkhurst.

"McNulty. Pleased to meet chou, Charley Parkhurst," the man said with a thick accent. "This ya first ocean voyage?"

"Yes. I can't wait to get back on land."

"The sea is an unforgivin' mistress to be sure. Can swallow you up anytime she pleases."

"Amen to that," Charley sighed.

"Well, good luck to ya!" the man said, wandering off, fearing his new acquaintance to be of the temperance sort. Charley pulled out a thin cigar and walked down the stairs to the dining room. He spotted Monk at the bar and wandered over in search of a match.

"Pretty rough out there," Charley commented as he reached for the small tinder.

"It's the shits!" Hank said bluntly. "Jamaica suppose to be nice though. At least it will be warmer than this. Gonna get me some rum there," he said, raising his shot glass.

"I'll have a beer please. They say that's the place to get it. Never been really excited by rum, gives me a pain in the head. I like a good Kentucky whiskey. Set me up with a shot of good aged rye whiskey, barkeep," Charley said, setting down a coin and picking up the beer.

"Well, I figure I ought to get some while we're there. Don't know if I'll ever be back these ways again," Hank said, scratching his head.

"Well, you've got a damn good point there! Cheers!" Charley said, sucking back the rye with authority.

"Hey, do you have any dice boxes?" Hank inquired.

"Sure, here," the bartender said, setting the leather cups on the bar.

"You want to play galloping dominos for a shot of rum?" He grinned.

"Why not, I don't have to drink it," Charley said confidently. The pair soon included Felix and James and the bartender, who had a loud, noisy bar full of men banging away on the wood with the cups, laughing and swearing and cheering. It went on until they were again diverted to the dining tables. There the comrades regaled themselves telling tales and jokes, until one or the other would excuse themselves and retire to their receptive bunks and snore. The ship's rocking gave them vivid dreams of driving over the famed California mountains. The salt air gave the seasoned outdoorsmen fierce appetites, and by the time they reached Jamaica, they were robust and ready for adventure. The weather was warm, and breeze was balmy and mild. Most men wore no jackets, just vests and a shirt.

Charley had to be careful about getting dressed and generally changed in the bunk before anyone was awake. She felt almost naked wearing just a shirt and vest, unheard of in New England, even in the summer. This voyage was like peeling away the old to find new life and no boundaries on your dreams, but the world was not ready to accept Charley Parkhurst as she was, she reminded herself. Even though the other men had no problem stripping off their clothes in front of Charley, it would be too shocking for her to do the same. No one even suspected Charley wasn't a man; she relished the show and felt only slightly guilty.

"And wait till you lads get a look at them Jamaica girls. You neva seen nothin' like it in ya whole life! Great big lassies with smooth dark skin the color of strong coffee." The man motioned with his hands on his chest. "Buck naked from the hips up. Nothing on but a bit of cloth around their nether regions and carrying a basket of coal on her head to boot!" McNulty cackled as he regaled Monk, who was inquiring about the rum market.

"Yes, I can hardly wait, but what about the rum?"

"Well, we're only gonna be in port for about six hours. I better go with you so you don't get screwed on the deal," the Scotsman reasoned. "What time is it?"

Charley, who was sitting by the porthole, pulled out his watch.

"It's ten thirty. I heard the captain say we dock at noon."

"Great, then we'll get you the best rum that you can afford!" McNulty cheered. "Make no mistake about it!"

At noon, the Scotsman had a small herd of young men eager to see the strange new sights and smells and experience Jamaica's exotic tastes. The first pleasure was the firm stationary footing; it felt odd somehow, Charley thought.

"Damn it, McNulty, you was right! Look at them women!" Felix said with a slack jaw, fairly drooling.

"That's just the start, wait till you taste the food and the rum!" McNulty said, starting to salivate himself. "Spicy!" he sang as he danced a jig down the pier. Monk was hot on his heels, as were the rest. Felix was craning his neck to see all the boobs, himself being the biggest.

Charley marveled at the lush, tropical landscapes and the incredibly beautiful, clear, blue water. He smiled at the charming native people and took in the exotic smells; he noticed his stomach answering back with high expectations. McNulty and Birch were both familiar with various sights and soon had begun the treasure hunt. The group ate and drank themselves up one side of the town and down the other. They returned to the ship fit only for their beds. The next stop, the Chagres River.

The following morning, most of the fellows stayed quietly in bed, heads throbbing. Charley felt fine. He didn't care for rum and had only drunk beer. He had purchased some rather interesting tobacco, very pungent but quiet restful. Charley spent the day repacking for the trip through the jungle, though it was still two days away.

"What cha doing, Parkie? Packing already? What day is it? Are we there yet?" Hank grumbled in a daze. It occurred to the newly christened Parkie that he had the makings for a pretty good practical joke but hadn't the heart when she looked at the charming but naked man, laying there with a sheet hanging off of him, eyes barely able to open.

Parkie slowly looked back at the case and replied, "No, just puttin' a few things away. Go back to sleep before McNulty comes over."

"McNulty!" Hank moaned as he held his head and lay back down. After more rest and a few of McNultys' eye-opener concoctions, the men began to rally.

"What is the Isthmus like?" Charley asked the Scotsman.

"It's a cesspool mostly," McNulty replied. "A dumpin' groun' for poor lost souls who haven't the good sense ta blow the' brains out."

"As bad as that, really?" Monk encouraged.

"From what I seen and heard about it, it is," Birch added.

"Why so bad?" Charley pressed.

"You've got a lot of poor, sick, and desperate people there, all ready ta pounce on the next available stranger they can find ta suck out any life's bloods that they can get at. Like leaches that they have in the jungle, the thieves and pickpockets will bleed you dry," McNulty said, pulling off the cork to his rum bottle.

"Leeches? They have leeches in the jungles there?" Felix whined.

"Yes, indeed, these slippery slug like varmints crawl on you, and then they digs in and drink your blood till he's all swelled up with it. Then he falls off. Disgusting creatures, like a slimy tick. Makes me sick just thinking about them," the Scotsman said, taking a pull of his bottle. The men around him shuttered to themselves.

"And not only that, the jungle thar has got frogs that are the most beautiful bright colors that you ever did see and are deadly poisonous to the touch. Why, I've heard stories about great water snakes that measure twenty or even thirty feet long and could swallow a man whole. Then there's the fish! There's waters in that country that have flesh-eating fish that can strip a man or cow clean to the bone, in minutes! Do you hear? Minutes! I have heard firsthand accounts of such fish and seen their teeth. Piranhas! They call them," McNulty said out of breath. "Why, the jungles are thick with incredible bloodsucking bats and them that have fabulous wingspans of four feet. Then there's the spotted tigers and crocodiles and God knows what else lurking out there," McNultly shuttered.

"Thirty-foot snakes?" Monk quizzed the Scotsman.

"Yes, a great water snake, anaconda, I think they call it. They eat crocodiles, after first strangling them with their powerful body's, wrapped around their prey." McNulty was strangling his handkerchief to demonstrate.

"Well, how come the flesh-eating fish don't eat them?" Charley inquired.

"I don't know. That question never come up!" the Scotsman proudly proclaimed. "Why don't the flesh-eating fish eat them, what a marvelous question!" He puzzled to himself over and over. Then the peculiar man sat up and looked them all square in the eye and spoke in the most serious tone.

"Ah, but it's not the great creatures you should fear. It's the wee creatures you must look out for. The bloodsucking mosquitoes and the tiny spiders, they are the deadly ones. You may not even feel their bite, but they can spread sickness and pain and even death. Then there's the cholera!" The man grew silent. They all paused, as if someone was walking on their collective graves.

The *Illinois* pulled into the bay at one in the afternoon; it had been thirteen days since they left Boston.

The Chargres River emptied out to the ocean in a great crescent-shaped bay, with a tall rock outcropping on the left that held the remains of the castle of San Lorenzo, still keeping watch for the ghosts of Captain Morgan, who once ravaged her. The center of the bay was considerably lower and flat and peopled with various thatched dwellings. The mouth of the river lay to the right and was landscaped with lush palms and ferns. There was a great deal of activity on the water, smaller boats greeting ships and boatloads of gold seekers heading up river toward the Pacific.

Birch's men were eager to be back on terra firma as the small boats rowed them ashore. The beach was alive with humanity as the villagers sold goods to the new arrivals. James set out to the newly built section of town, where in just a few years, it had mushroomed because of the gold rush to California. The weather was steamy, and the noisy jungle was alive with strange birds and monkeys. Charley felt like an adventurer.

The one product that seemed to sell the most was the hat. The craftsmanship was truly remarkable; everyone bought one. They were tightly braided palm leaves, sewn together to make a sturdy lightweight, broad-brimmed hat that shed water quite nicely. The men then softened the crown to shape it any way they pleased.

The city was a churning mass of humanity and filth. The natives made a living off of the traveling hoards. The comrades hung closely together, wary of pickpockets or bandits. They checked into a hotel for the night, eager to start their adventure upriver. Tomorrow they would take a small steamer to Gorgona. James went out after they had settled in for the night to make sure everything was ready.

"She's out of commission you say?" James said with disappointment. "Maybe you could get me a good boatman to take me and my party to Gorgona. I've got a ship to meet in Panama," James said, pouring the miserable steamship captain a drink.

"Yes, I can arrange for your men to leave on some bungos tomorrow, James. I'm sorry there is nothing else I can do," the captain said, downing his drink.

James finally returned to his traveling companions and related the changes. They all took the news in stride. Hank and Charley were especially looking forward to a better look at the exotic creatures. The next morning, the crew was up bright and early only to be told that the boats, or bungos as they were called, would not be leaving until four o'clock that afternoon.

There were five bungos that would be traveling together; they were about twenty feet long and had a canvass top over about a third of the middle of the boat. All were equipped with oars and poles and lots of rope. The crew was both black and natives, but the man in charge was a rough white man with a strange European accent and red eyes. He smelled of rum and strange tobacco, not unlike the kind Charley had bought in Jamaica.

At last they began their safari into the jungle; McNulty blathered on about the various birds flying about and was adept at pointing out snakes hanging from the branches. Charley thought it was thrilling and could see by the expression on Monk's face every time a snake was spotted that they made him most uncomfortable.

The river was swarming with bungos; it was also swarming with mosquitoes. The native crews preferred to boat at night, which infuriated the travelers, who had little to say in the matter as they had left their own civilization far behind. Felix noticed the green glowing eyes all around them in the water and cowered to himself in a blanket, trying to keep from being eaten alive by mosquitoes. The boat ride would last five days, with good weather and no incidents. As the night's mantle covered the river, it became even more alive and noisy with strange sounds from the treetops and deep in the forest beyond. The flickering torches reflected in the river, casting strange light on the jungle's mysteries.

As the dawn's light roused the sleepy passengers, they arrived at the first stop— Gatun, a native village that had become a boarding house for expectant gold miners. The native people were friendly and welcomed the travelers to palm-thatched huts. They were crude two-story buildings with cane floors that had an occasional hide rug. Chairs were a novelty. The huts had poles with notches cut for footholds to climb to the second floor, where the guests would bed down, until the bungos departed again.

James, who had stayed there before, was greeted by a mob of children followed by an old native woman. He was escorted to a fine hut in the center of the village. The rest of his men trailed behind, trying to act natural. Felix, as usual, openly stared at the native women, who wore only fabric wrapped around their hips.

Upon entering the hut, they could not help but notice an old woman sitting on the floor. Beside her, stretched on a frame, was an incredible pelt of the softest golden fur, with black rosettes and spots mottling its shimmering coat. Charley gasped in amazement as he ran his hand across the big cat's face.

"El Tigre," the ancient woman said as she smiled a toothless grin. "Jaguar."

"Grand!" Charley replied to the old one.

"Look at this!" James said, motioning to the great snakeskin hanging around the room. For it stretched a full twenty feet.

"Great ghost of heaven, you see! You thought I was just telling tales, and here it is, right before ya eyes! Anaconda!" McNulty spouted off. He crept near to examine it better. The thatched building was a regular museum of nature.

"I don't know that I'll get a lick of sleep, just a knowing that thing is down here," Hank commented as the troupe climbed up to their beds for some rest. Later they would be fed some exotic stew of unknown content.

Charley was back up in a few hours, determined to get at least a glimpse of this strange new country. He sat near the edge of the village and marveled at the beautiful birds flying and even hovering overhead. The sky was very busy as monkeys leapt from tree to tree; even the lizards could fly, it seemed. Everything was bigger and grander and more colorful, especially the flowers, even the ants. The children were curious and friendly; Charley soon had his own small herd following him around.

By the time the crew was ready to go, it was beginning to rain again, a common occurrence in this jungle. It bothered the natives not a bit as they wore almost nothing. The canvas roof on the bungo was a joke; everything and everyone got soaked to the skin. Monk and McNulty stayed blissfully drunk as James pointed out the plantations of coffee and tobacco that were being cultivated in this wild place. The river was not a bit straight; one never knew what would be around the next turn. The men eagerly awaited their arrival at Gorgona, where they would leave the boating world, temporally, for a mule ride. James was worried about missing the *Golden Gate*; he had originally planned to ride the steamer, which only took one day. Now anything could happen. He kept his fears to himself however; it would serve no purpose to make everyone worry.

On the fifth afternoon, as the boats neared their destination, James pointed out the smoke up ahead. They could hear the fires roar as they neared Gorgona.

"Cholera!" McNulty whispered in horror, reaching for his bottle.

As they drew near the shore, they heard the warnings to stay out of town because of the plague. Buildings, crude as they were, had been cleansed with flame, along with blankets and bodies. It was a sobering thought, even for Felix who had remained blissfully drunk for most of this adventure.

"What are we gonna do?" Felix said, stumbling off the boat and dragging his luggage.

"I know what I'm gonna do. I'm gonna get the hell out of here! Have a nice trip, mates!" the bungo captain spoke as James handed him the balance of his money.

"Yes, I think we ought to do the same. I'll make arrangements for the mules. Stay here with the bags till I get back. Better stay out of the village and don't drink any water!" James rambled as he took control of the situation. Birch shuttered at the thought of being trapped in the wilderness with hundreds of migratory people who don't know what they were doing and are beginning to die from a nasty sickness that basically makes you shit to death.

"I'll keep to my Jamaican beverage," Hank mumbled. Charley patted his own pocket with a wink.

The men grabbed their bags and walked over to some trees and sat down. Some children were playing around the dock, and a small boy decided to sit near the new travelers. He made himself quite at home next to Charley. The boy's lunch consisted of a small bunch of bananas, and he proceeded to eat one; as he did, a small monkey crawled down from the boy's neck to his hand to help himself to a sweet treat.

"Look at that!" Charley said, nudging Felix.

"Ask the kid if I can have a banana," Felix said sleepily.

"No, look at the little monkey!" Charley said with enthusiasm.

"Yeah, ask him if I can have a banana!" Felix said, not seeing the wee creature.

"Look, the boy's got a baby monkey as a pet. He's a cute little critter," Charley cooed.

"Well then, ask the monkey if I can have a banana!" Felix said stupidly.

"You're an ass, Felix, ask him yourself." Charley laughed as the tiny creature left the boy's hand to investigate the tickled teamster. "Look at his little fingers! He looks like a very small old man with those gray whiskers. Look at that face!"

"He's probably a tiny pickpocket!" Felix said unimpressed.

Soon another child was seated next to the travelers. She appeared slightly older than the boy; she too had a pet, only this one was a baby bird. It had a large hooked beak and big clawed feet; its body was covered with spiky pinfeathers that looked like they might be blue someday. The girl was mothering the parrot and feeding it seeds that she shelled in her teeth; the bird looked adoringly at her as it ate.

"I guess they don't have any dolls to play with," Monk remarked.

James soon returned with the news that he had secured a mule train that could leave in a few hours. The men grabbed their gear and waited near the mule station in a seedy tavern. It was beginning to rain again, and the great fire in the square sizzled and popped.

"It's only twenty-six miles to Panama, boys! I guarantee it will be scenic." James cheered, as they were again under way, the rain petering out to a dull drizzle.

"Hope my cigars hold out till then. It's the only thing keeping these little buggers at bay," Charley mumbled, swatting at a mosquito as he mounted his mule, a most sorry specimen as they all were.

"Not quite as dignified as I'm used to," Hank sighed.

The troupe disappeared into the jungle down a muddy path. Soon there was little trace of civilization, except discarded rum bottles and tins or the occasional dead body that had gone unclaimed. Gruesome carcasses of mules were also abundant; the flesh scavenged and left scattered by creatures of the land or of the water. Alligators could be seen sunning themselves on logs down by the water; some were quite large. Vultures circled lazily overhead mingled with the great condors, which looked like they could fly away with a man; so impressive was their great wingspan.

"Looks like somebody had a bad day," Hank said, watching the great birds landing on some unfortunate someone. "Git up now you nasty varmint," he said, whapping the mule on the ass with the end of his reins. "Prob'ly died of the fever!"

"You don' suppose they have any head hunters in this jungle? Eh, Jim?" McNulty quizzed the young businessman.

"None that I ever heard of," Birch replied.

"Head hunters?" Felix mumbled to himself, scanning the trees for a possible raid.

"Don't worry, Felix, I got you covered with my Colt here," Monk chuckled.

The mule train wound around and over hill and dale, crossing creeks and tributaries with every other turn it seemed. The travelers passed mule trains going the opposite way, sometimes narrowly fitting past and sometimes having to wait. The mule had a monopoly on this road; they came along in an endless stream, back and forth, until they died.

The mule train went on even after darkness fell, and the animals of the night took their turn in the wilderness. The nervous men kept their firearms handy. Finally an ocean breeze was detected and the group knew that their ride would at last come to an end. Even the mules felt their destination coming close, as they renewed their enthusiasm for the road or path, with the expectation of dinner growing near. One could faintly hear the sound of music and laughter far ahead. In the distance, the twinkling lights of Panama looked beautiful, but looks can be deceiving.

"Oh my God, I thought we'd never get here!" Felix moaned a sigh of relief. "I'm starving."

"We all are," Charley agreed.

They left their mules with the pack man, at a huge corral outside of town and stretched their weary legs as they looked for the nearest saloon.

"My balls are going to be black and blue for a week!" Monk said, unceremoniously scratching his crotch.

Birch, who was always thinking ahead, did not want to lose any more time and proceeded directly to the Union Hotel office. He instructed the men to wait in the saloon there until he returned. When the desk clerk confirmed that the ship *Golden Gate* was set to depart tomorrow at 5 p.m. James let out an audible sigh.

"Do you have any rooms available?"

"How many in your party?"

"Fifteen," James hoped.

"I'm sorry, the best I can do for you is four rooms."

"Well, I'll take those at least. Can I get some extra blankets?"

"Well, I'll have to charge extra," the clerk whined.

"Fine. Is there a bathhouse near?"

"Across the street," the man pointed. James turned and looked at the house, then turned back to the clerk.

"I thought the *Golden Gate* was supposed to set sail yesterday?"

"Had to be fumigated . . . Cholera," the clerk said with disdain.

James shuttered uncontrollably for a moment at the thought. He studied the man's face as he signed the register, then paid the man and received some keys.

"You need to have your men sign in," the clerk announced

"Yeah, I'll run them by you in a minute. I gotta find 'em first. Can I get a man to take my bags to the room?" Birch said, looking toward the bar.

"Ernesto. Take these bags to 17."

"Here, Ernie," James said, slipping the lad a coin.

"Well, fellows, we sail tomorrow at five in the afternoon. I've got four rooms here. You can look around and see if there's other accommodations to be had, or you can camp with me. If you stay in my rooms, I highly suggest that you take a bath, for you're all pretty ripe. Man said there's a bathhouse across the street."

"I don't know if I want to spend any time in a bathtub with this sickness going around, might catch my death," Monk reasoned.

"You got a very strong point there and a very strong odor, but you've got a right to it!" McNulty said with a worried look.

"Well, if you're staying in the rooms I saved, you'd better sign in. I for one am gonna follow my nose and get some food. We can all sleep in tomorrow."

"I'm with you all the way, Jim," Charley said, finishing his beer and getting up.

The group was compelled to stay together like a herd and filed in line at the register desk.

The men deposited their belongings in the rooms and went out for some Panamanian relaxation.

Most of the men wore their hats low on their heads the next day as they boarded the beautiful *Golden Gate*. It was nice to be aboard such a civilized vessel after the primitive experiences they had just endured. She was spotless, and even smelled clean, or at least had a scent of something to her. James sniffed and wondered to himself if it was safe. He opted to spend the evening basking under the tropical stars and listening to the men singing.

The *Golden Gate* was very full, over five hundred people; it's top deck was crowded with gold seekers. Next stop, Acapulco, Mexico. The men rested and got fat as they cruised along on the balmy sea. Four days later, they pulled into the harbor at 2:00 PM and were advised that the ship would be departing in ten hours. Those choosing to go ashore will be left behind if not aboard at the departure time. Most chose to dine off the ship. In the middle of the meal, they experienced a rather strong earthquake, and all returned with haste to the vessel.

Soon after the ship was under way, the weather became turbulent, with a great deal of rain. Most rode out the weather in their beds, usually with a bottle bought in Mexico. The next port was finally California at last, San Diego, to be exact, but the weather got worse as they drew near. The ocean swells were estimated to be close to thirty feet as the wind howled like a deranged demon; the captain was concerned about going in, lest the ship be smashed. The decision to go on without stopping was made and the *Golden Gate* pushed on for Monterey, but the weather did not let up as they chugged north, the elegant ship fighting the elements as she went.

"Did I ever tell you about the great sea serpent Captain Seabury caught off the Sandwich Islands?" McNulty started to a crowded stateroom.

"Every one knows there ain't no such a beast!" Felix remarked with fearful expectations.

"No! You're wrong! I can tell you a man captured and killed one. I read it in the *New York Tribune*, and I met the captain in New Bedford several years ago and know him to be an honest man, not prone to makin' up tall tales!" McNultly huffed.

"In other words, not like yourself!" Monk smiled.

"Go on, let him tell the story!" Charley cheered, rolling a cigarette.

"I don't want to listen to any more snake stories!" Hank complained.

"Ah, sure you do. This one's bound to be a ripper!" Birch said laughing.

Monk smiled a wounded grimace as he settled himself for the account.

"Well, it was just this January last that the captain first laid eyes on the briny beast. It was breakfast time when a call was heard, 'white water!' This was a whaling vessel mind you and a good captain too," the Scotsman said, settling in. "The native man was in hysterics as he tried to report what he had seen. Then all eyes looked to where the man was pointing. Behold, they see a great black skin undulating through the water. It was longer than any whale that they had ever seen. It was a true sea serpent! The captain having his wits about him mustered the seaman together and set out in the boats to bring him in. They rowed out with their harpoons ready to kill the beast, which did not swim away from them but instead turned to attack the hunters. The men struck at the beast, hitting its midsection. It swung his great head around and attacked the boat, spilling the men into the sea. The captain threw his harpoon as the boat tipped, hitting the beast in its blood-red eye. They got three harpoons into the serpent as it churned the sea into a bloody froth before descending to the bottom of the sea. The captain, who had nearly drowned, ordered all the men back to the whaler and extra rope bent on. They bent on over a mile of rope in an effort not to lose the irons off the ship. Sixteen hours they waited till the lines slacked, and the great snake came to the surface. The men set into action with lances and harpoons determined to kill the beast and take the trophy. Just when they thought the creature was dead, it raised its bloody head and screamed its death cry in a mighty roar, then rolled around in a writhing mass of coils churning the sea again to a bloody froth." The Scotsman paused for a brief refreshment.

"What happened next?" Birch waited impatiently.

"Well now, the captain saw that the creature was too massive to be hauled aboard the ship, so he held a council and asked every man his opinion. He then decided to have a trustworthy and talented Scotsman make a drawing of the creature that they had stretched out to his full length. Then they cut off his head and skinned him. It took three days, but they filleted him up and saved every bone to reconstruct him later. It was said that he was one hundred and three feet and seven inches in length and forty-nine feet and eleven inches around the girth. He had ninety-four sharp teeth in his jaws as fat as a man's thumb. His blubber was about four inches thick, and it burned like turpentine."

"Well, what has become of this trophy?" Charley asked.

"It is a strange thing about the ship and its crew, since it left word of its catch with the ship *Gipsy*. She's never been heard of again," the Scotsman finished, seeing the real look of horror in Hank Monk's eyes.

"Well, maybe the sea serpent's mate tracked down the dead serpent and sank the ship." Charley laughed at the storyteller.

"You know that's not a half-bad theory. They must of had the skin nailed out on the ship's rail to dry, and the mate could have sniffed her out, then taken his revenge. Sinking the ship and eatin' the crew!" McNultly said, licking his chops.

"What is that awful sound?" a petrified Felix called out. It sounded like a horrific ripping of metal. People all came out of their rooms to find out what had happened.

The hurricane deck showed fatigue under the duress of the wind, and a section of the roof was torn clean off. Amazingly it did not hurt the paddlewheels that work away on either side of the wind sheared deck. That no one was seriously hurt in the mayhem didn't help calm nerves however, the warning of sickness was aboard the ship, and there was quite a stir over four deaths aboard, who were all young; two were brothers, fourteen and twenty. Everyone was fearful and stayed to themselves.

The fellows' stateroom looked like a hurricane had blown through; clothes and boots were everywhere. Gone was the cosmopolitan atmosphere. The smelly men congregated everywhere, sitting on trunks and the floor playing cards, reading, drinking, and getting tossed around like a child's throwing jacks.

"I understand the greatest shark of them all lives in the waters off this coast here," McNulty started in again later. "A white shark, the Great White, they call 'em. He eats whales and'll sink a small ship if he's a mind to."

"He can't sink a ship this big!" Felix butted in, trying to reassure himself; he was already near panic with the ships wild rolling and the recent snake story.

"There's thirty-foot killer whales out there too," the Scotsman resumed. "And blue whales, the greatest whale on earth. They can get to be eighty-foot long. That devil could do some damage!" he chuckled.

"Oh God!" Felix said, getting up hastily and running down the hall to the stairs to the top deck. He didn't make it outside and barfed on a pile of dirty table linen, just outside the dining room. He had second thoughts about the fresh air and returned to his own room to hide in his bed.

"Hope Ol' Felix didn't get swept off the deck," Hank said, lying in his berth and trying to roll a cigarette. "Parkie, can you roll me one? I ain't haven't any luck at all," he said, passing his pouch down to Charley's bunk.

"Naw, probably barfed in the hall. That guy can't hold his liquor," Charley said pouring tobacco into a small paper. "Shit!" Charley was covered with tobacco as the ship tossed his body wildly to the wall; the rebounding roll caused him to roll all the way out of bed to the floor, followed by Hank and James, who had also been spilled from their comfortable beds.

"I didn't have any luck neither!" Charley laughed, handing Hank's pouch back to him. James was rubbing his head as the trio tried in vain to get to their feet; the ship rolled them into Charley's lower birth as they laughed and grabbed on to the curtains.

"You all right, James? That's a good-sized goose egg swellin' up there?" Charley said as the three wedged themselves sideways with their feet in Charley's bunk to keep from spilling out again.

"I reckon, do you mind if I stay down here time beein'? That was a long way down," James said, rubbing his head.

"Sure, give me back that pouch. I'll give it another shot, Hank," Charley said.

"Here." Monk handed his friend the tobacco.

On the afternoon of December 16, they finally arrived in California. The weather in Monterey was very rough, and the captain wanted to leave for San Francisco as soon as possible and was under way in two hours. Nine hours later, they were anchored just outside of their namesake, the Golden Gate. Yet they were forced to drop anchor at North Beach and wait until the storm subsided. Many ships clotting the harbors were dragging anchor, and it was too dangerous to get in safely.

That night while waiting to get into harbor, another person died. This time a woman, bringing the death total to five. Many of the wealthy offered from ten to thirty dollars to any brave sailor who would row them to San Francisco. But the sea was so violent, there were no takers. Finally the next afternoon, a tugboat was sent to pilot the great ship to her berth, and they at last reached their destination.

Charley and the men stood around the deck and admired the beautiful mountain that lay at the mouth of the bay; the very top was dusted with snow. They gathered their belongings and made their way down the pier to the waiting cabs on the streets, if you could call them that. The torrential rains had turned the sandy soil into a quagmire. The dutiful equines had their work cut out for them! The men finally reached a fine-looking establishment and stepped out onto the wooden sidewalk.

"It'll be nice to sleep in a bed that ain't pitchin' a fit!" Hank said, stepping up the stairs to the fledgling city's finest rest for the weary.

"Hey! The What Cheer!" Charley sang out.

"I thought you'd feel at home when you saw that!" James smiled back. Charley was suddenly sentimental and had to choke back a tear.

"Com'on, Charley, I'll roll you for a drink!" Felix said, slapping his pal on the back and breaking his spell.

"Sure. I want to stow my gear and wash my face. I feel so gritty," Charley replied.

"Hey, Albert!" James called out to the front desk clerk.

"Mr. Birch, I'm so glad to see you back again. Did you have a pleasant trip?"

"Oh hell! It was a ripsnorter, Al! Set us up with the best you got! I could sure do with a bath and a shave!"

"Whatever you want, Mr. Birch. How many rooms do you want?"

"Seven ought to do." James smiled. "Just for the night, be heading out to Sacramento tomorrow morning."

"Rightee this way, sirs," the Chinese bellboy said in his newly learned language, picking up the men's luggage. As the boy gathered up as many bags as possible with another lad, the pair began to ascend the stairs to the bedrooms above, their long braided pigtails hanging down their backs.

"Kinda reminds me of them pack mules in the jungle," Hank whispered to Charley as they followed behind.

"I do believe you're right." He smiled in return.

"At least thar are no bloody mosquitoes!" McNulty boomed out.

"Amen to that, brother!" Monk said, fishing out a cigar from his vest.

Charley deftly pulled a Lucifer from his own vest and scratched it with a thumbnail; it ignited, and he lit Hank's cheroot.

"Thank you."

Albert unlocked the rooms, and the men made themselves at home.

"Oh my Lord, a real honest-to-God bed!" Felix said, flinging his filthy body on the mattress.

"Well, that's your bunk. You stunk that bed up already," Charley half kidded.

"Fine with me!" Felix said, rolling around on the furniture.

"This room is complete with its own tub!" Albert boasted, opening the next door.

"You can bunk in here with me if you like, Charley," James invited.

"That would be fine," he said, eyeballing the beautiful bathroom. He definitely longed to soak the salty adventure from his skin and set about figuring the safest time.

"You have lawndee?" the young lad asked the teamster. "Lawndee? Two hour I take lawndee? Dirt closee?"

Charley looked blankly at Albert who was leaving the room.

"He wants to know if you have any clothes to be cleaned, dirty laundry," Albert explained.

"Did he say two hours?" James asked.

"Two hour. They done," the Chinese boy smiled.

"No, I think I'll just get some new clothes and then burn these," Charley sighed, looking in a mirror.

The next morning, James roused the men early for a big breakfast downstairs in the hotel restaurant. Then it was off on another voyage, upriver to Sacramento.

The weather was still a driving rain, as the men boarded the small paddle wheeler. The bay was crowded with abandoned ships, their empty masts like a dead forest in a flood, as the steamer chugged by. Men sat around playing cards and drinking or just watching the scenery go by, as they snaked along, going deeper into the lush green hills. Great flocks of ducks took flight, as the ship disturbed their peaceful surroundings. The waters were alive with great blue herons and white cranes and egrets; beautiful white hawks could be seen hovering near a hillside, then diving into the wet grass, only to fly away with a gopher or a snake.

Later that night, twinkling lights in the horizon told that they were near the bustling new city of Sacramento. It welcomed them with music flowing into the streets and delicious smells coming from eating establishments.

"I'll meet up with you fellas in a bit, over at the New Orleans. I'm gonna check in at the office and let them know I'm back," James explained as the group walked down the planked sidewalk toward the enticing smells.

Later James confirmed his new driver's routes over dinner. Most would be heading out to Placerville tomorrow. Felix would be hired as an express guard riding with Charley, complete with shot gun and badge. Somehow Charley wasn't comforted by that.

It was a beehive of activity in the streets the next morning; horses and wagons squeezed onto the muddy road, filling with supplies and passengers, heading to all points of the gold fields. A passenger not paying close-enough attention could find he had been ushered aboard the wrong coach. The air was filled with men singing out destinations, which seemed ludicrous to the east coasters, hearing them for the first time.

"This coach for Mormon Island, Rattle Snake Bar, Horseshoe Bar, Condemned Bar, and Manhattan." The chants rang up and down the streets as luggage was stowed and supplies roped down, as the wagons and stagecoaches got ready to leave. Charley took it all in and chuckled to himself. Then as if a starting gun was fired, they all departed for points north, south, and east. He held the leather lines in eager anticipation. Too long it had been; it seemed like a year had passed since he drove, and this day was certain to be full of wondrous new scenery. He would follow a coach for today since it was his first day on his new job! For now it was off to the hills and mountains beyond. It felt quite good to be in one's own element at last. That was the last ocean voyage he had ever hoped to take. His adventures would be on land, thank you very much.

James crossed paths with his friends on regular business trips to the stations. He spoke of returning by ship to visit Julia again and their soon-to-be-expected child.

He wanted Charley to learn all of the routes and rotated him around to give the stations the benefit of Charley's vast driving experience. Parkhurst was eager to see this newly forming America. At first, he was awed by its vast, rolling fields of grass, then by the delicate oak groves with babbling brooks, and fern-laden rocks. As he drove further into the foothills, pine and redwoods joined the oaks, a tree like he had never seen before. The shear mass of the trunks inspired awe. Charley wondered at the remarkably tall trees, each grander than the next. He could tell they were approaching the diggings as he began seeing more and more camps. They were mostly crowded around streams that were being run roughshod over, the men having no appreciation for the pristine land they were fouling. Everywhere makeshift hovels were erected; blankets crudely strung over struggling vegetation would serve as a tent. The populations became thicker and thicker, men from all over the world, returning to a primitive existence, eager to reap the treasure from the golden hills of El Dorado.

CHAPTER 15

Placerville, January 1853

"Look, Charley, a white horse, there," Felix said, pointing down the slushy, mud-filled street. "You always was partial to white horses, I always said."

The two were sitting on the hotel porch after supper, having a smoke. Down the street, a thin Indian man was leading a well-groomed white horse with a profound limp.

"Look at how he's lame. I bet he's takin' him to the butcher," Felix blathered on.

"The butcher?" Charley popped to attention. "Think I'll go have me a stroll. You coming?"

"Yeah, I reckon," Felix replied, setting down his empty glass.

Sure enough, the white horse was tied in front of Armor's butcher shop. Charley looked the animal over. He was an incredible beauty that was unable to put any weight on his front left hoof.

"Don't worry, my friend, all is not lost," Charley cooed, stroking the young stallion's neck. Parkhurst turned and entered the butcher shop. It was a busy evening in the meat store, and the young Indian was having no luck in getting the proprietor's attention. Men in line were sneering at the young man, and he began to feel that he had made a poor decision to capitalize on the misfortune of his masters' horse. The animal was obviously suffering and in need of shooting, so why shouldn't he make something on the body? Murrieta needn't know about that. After all, the horse was dead and disposed of.

"Hey, mister, that your white horse outside?" Charley said, tapping the young man on the shoulder.

"Yes."

"You want to sell him?" Charley asked, staring into the Indian's dark face. He had jet-black hair that flowed down past his shoulders and a thin black mustache that fell past his jaw; he was dressed like a Mexican.

"Yes. Five dollars."

"I'll give you three dollars," Charley said, reaching in his pocket.

"He's yours. I hope he tastes good," Chappo said in disgust.

"Hey, Chappo, you peddling horse meat again?" Armor called out when he saw the Indian. "You know, I run a quality shop in here."

"I'm leaving," the Indian sneered back. He smiled smugly to himself, knowing he never would have gotten two dollars from the butcher.

Charley stepped outside to look over his ailing new horse.

"Chappo? What's the horse's name?"

"Mozo, it means the worker," the Indian said, getting on his own horse and riding away.

"How you gonna get Ol' Mozo to the barn, carry him?" Felix cracked.

"We'll just mosey, that's all." Charley smiled, leading the horse slowly through the mud.

"What do you thinks wrong with him?" Felix called from the boardwalk.

"I don't know, maybe an abscess. Come on, boy." Charley fished in his pocket for a cube of sugar. It was gratefully accepted.

Charley found a stall for his new pet project and set about his doctoring. First he got out some hoof tools and removed the shoe from the lame foot; then he trimmed the hoof down. Using the hoof knife to carve down into the suspected affliction, Charley sniffed at the foot, trying to detect infection; it was pretty rank. The horse was fully cooperative and seemed to be most grateful for the attention. He had been well trained; that much was very obvious. At last Charley struck a foreign object deep in the crevice of the frog, a soft v-shaped pad on the sole of the foot. Charley got some needle nose pliers and pulled the offending nail from the hoof, it was followed by a stream of puss and an audible sigh from the horse and doctor both. Charley and Mozo both rested, as the built-up fluids drained from the wound.

"I think a poultice will do the trick now," Charley said, well pleased with himself. "You sure are a pretty fella. Remind me a little of Blue." Charley left the stable to get a bowl of oatmeal and some other ingredients and some sackcloth to tie his hoof concoction on with. He couldn't help but notice the admiration from the Mexican stable hands. They almost seemed to know the horse.

"Hey, James, come see my new horse later, over at the red barn," Charley called out to Birch as he walked by the office. It was getting late, and James was burning the midnight oil in his office.

"New horse? Yes, I'll have a look. I'll pop in a bit later," Birch said, looking over the company's books. He leaned back in his chair and lit a cigar. Later, he walked over to the barn and found Charley sitting in the straw, braiding the sackcloth up the fetlock of the stallion and tying it off.

"Figures he's a white horse," James said as he appeared at the back of the stall.

"Yep, tomorrow he'll feel a lot better. Looks better already!" he said standing up and patting the horse on the neck. Mozo nuzzled Charley's pocket looking for another treat. "Out of candy, boy, sorry."

"Where did you get him?" Monk asked, poking his head in the stall.

"Hi, Hank. Some Indian named Chappo was gonna sell him to the butcher. So I bought him for three dollars. Maybe I shoulda got some papers, but shit, he was gonna sell him for meat!"

"I hope he wasn't stolen." James smiled.

"Looks like a bandito's horse," Hank countered, spitting his chew.

"When will you find the time to ride him? Don't I keep you busy enough?" James chided.

"Well, maybe I'll just stud him out or better yet, make a leader out of him. Need some more white horses on my string," Charley said in a playful way. "Got a funny name, Mozo, the worker. I kinda like it."

"He's a beauty, all right. I always said you got a good eye for horseflesh. He'd make a grand leader," James said, giving Monk a wink.

"Let's get a drink," Monk replied. "I seen enough horses' asses for one day."

"Charley, I need to talk to you about going down to the Mariposa route. Things are slow up here for now till the weather gets better. Don't worry I'll make sure you can bring your new horsy," James said, squeezing his friend's shoulder as they walked down the newly planked sidewalk.

"What happen, somebody quit?" Charley inquired.

"Well kinda, he died," James stated.

CHAPTER 16

Mariposa, February 1853

Before dawn, a coyote rattling the chicken coop next to the horse barn startled the rooster into his crowing. Charley woke from a fitful sleep. Each day new challenges awaited: wild rivers, bears, herds of wild horses, almost nonexistent roads. There was no end. This country seemed unfathomably large.

The Mariposa landscape in the dawn's light reminded Charley that at least this country had not the biting weather of the east, on the same February morning. He paused on the way to the barn, to admire the soft green mountains in the distance. Charley watched the young Mexican man harnessing the horses in the barn, then stepped outside for a smoke, spending a few minutes in Mozos' corral, scratching him behind the ears. The stallion was not quite ready to be put in a hitch, but Charley was anxious to drive him. He spotted Felix shuffling toward the barn; he was sporting a bad hangover.

Charley was starting to wear due to the stress of traveling for so many hours with no relaxing sleep, only naps. The miners in town kept up spirits until all hours of the night. The saloons and bars never closed. Gunfights were a regular occurrence; most every man was armed and was liable to be in any state of drunkenness.

The teamster carefully checked over each horse and harness and then inspected their feet for loose shoes or problems developing. Now it was time to hitch; Felix and Charley did so methodically and without a word. The stablemen were all Mexican and only spoke in Spanish and a little broken English.

The two eastern friends had ceased to speak to each other due to an argument about Felix's drinking. As they both sat in the lofty driver's box, Charley arranged the lines in his hands. Felix turned away and took a pull off of the flask he always kept hidden in his vest pocket.

"Put that away, goddamn it! You got to pay attention. I'm sick of you fallin' asleep on me! I can't do everything around here!" Parkhurst growled.

There were two passengers this trip, eastern men; both leaving the goldfields well heeled.

As soon as the mail was loaded, Charley sang out to the team, and they were flying across the country. He kept the team at a fast working trot as they can keep that pace for a long time. The terrain was mostly down hill to the next station. The cool February air caused the animals to steam as they warmed up, their breath puffing out in front of them in twin clouds.

There was no real road, just a pair of trails in the high desert landscape, where the wagon wheels and the horses' hooves cut into the ground, guiding the lot to their final destination. The road was becoming steep, and it soon dropped down into a canyon, with rocky hills on either side of the stage. This was a worrisome place for some reason. Charley wanted to slow the team for a break, but he didn't like the looks of this area, with big rock formations for savages and bandits to hide behind. He had the damnedest feeling that he was being watched. The odd thing was that the horses should have been pretty tired, but something other than Charley was compelling them forward. The leaders were pulling and wanting to speed up.

"There must be horses ahead," Charley thought. "Just what I need now, wild horses." Parkhurst loosened his grip, cracked the whip, and let the horses run; he wanted out of this place.

Unfortunately, when he let them run, Charley failed to feel the coach rock back, with an added load, as Tres Dedos cut in behind the coach and jumped from his horse to the back boot. He was carefully making his way to the front to dispose of the purveyors of this fine vehicle and its contents.

Charley never knew what hit him as the bandit, in one swift and almost practiced move, slammed the butt of his huge knife into his temple and then cut Felix's throat on the follow through. All Felix had time to do was looked surprised before he was tossed from the rocking stage. Charley, who was out cold, still gripped the lines, a reflex action, like a cat asleep in a tree. Tres Dedos tucked away his bloody dagger and grabbed the leather away from the driver. Driving wildly and thrilled with his new toy, he kicked the driver off the box, then laughed, as he felt the rear wheel bounce over the body. A slow death by wolves or a bear was good enough for him.

Luck was with Charley, for he landed in soft sand next to a rock that took the blow of the wheel as it bounced over him. As the lights in Charley's eyes flickered from blackness, he swore he heard the devil himself shrieking in delight. The stagecoach lurched off into the distance, leaving the two crumbled bodies in the dirt. The rest of Tres Dedos' men galloped down to join the fun, wildly laughing like madmen, jumping over the still bodies, then disappearing beyond the horizon. The two dozing passengers inside the stolen coach had no clue they would be dead men soon.

Charley lay very still, floating in and out of reality. She felt certain that this had to be a dream, but there were warning bells going off in her head, and she could do nothing about them! She really must do something! Finally, Charley started coming to; her body was lying flat in the sand. "Oh God, it wasn't a dream!" she thought, spitting out blood and sand and getting a firm grip on the earth. For the first time since she could remember, Charley Parkhurst started to cry. Her head was so dizzy, she started to vomit. The pain sang out in waves through the fallen driver's body, she tried to raise herself, but couldn't and could barely see. Charley felt the black angels hopping close and flying around her.

"God help me!" Charley cried, realizing that the black angels were vultures and giant condors.

Swinging her arm and trying to get up, Charley turned and spotted a heap on the road about fifty yards away, circled by black birds. The fallen driver crawled over to her friend; he seemed a mile away. The injury to her back was excruciating, and she could not stand without blinding flashes of pain.

"Felix! Oh God!" she cried, as she collapsed and vomited again. Felix was lying in a puddle of his own blood with what was left of a stupid expression on his face, except that he had only half a face due to the vultures, who had begun to tear him apart. Charley knew she must get up and find shelter, but all she could do was lay sobbing. She felt completely lost, as if cast away in the open ocean. Charley lay there in the sand, the vultures having their way with poor, stupid drunken Felix. She wanted so much to leave, but when she stood, it was hard to tell which part of her body shrieked with the most pain, and she sank back to the sand. Attempts to crawl away were pathetic, and she soon just lay there batting off the bold vulture that couldn't wait until she had quit moving for good.

"Oh God, what was going to appear at night?" she wondered. Surly the smell of Felix's blood will draw other scavengers. Charley had retrieved poor Felix's beloved pepperbox from his gruesome body and clung to it for comfort. "A lot of good it did you, friend," Charley sighed, lying on the desert, crying and praying, reduced from her lofty perch to a miserable mess! She sensed the scavengers, mostly coyote, drawing near. Finally as the day grew to darkness, she felt the presence of something larger coming close. Charley decided to play dead although she dearly prayed for rescue. Out of the corner of her eye, she saw what appeared to be an Indian. He was looking over what was left of Felix, then turned and began to approach Charley, who was still clinging to the pepperbox.

"You are alive?" he asked.

"You speak English?"

"Yes."

"Will you help me?"

"Yes."

"Oh God, thank you!" Charley sighed, rolling over onto her back.

"It looks like your God has forsaken you and your friend there!" the young man said.

"He sent you!" Charley smiled as she looked up at the dark young man.

"Hmm, let's get you out of here. I have a camp near here."

"I don't think I can walk," Charley groaned.

"I have a horse. I'll get her." Yellow Bird returned shortly with a scrawny little mare.

Charley heard her back pop and spasm as the young Indian man helped her on the horse. She held tightly to the horse's mane as she was led to the modest camp high in the rocks. It was more of a cave actually and was very protected. The young man helped Charley to lay on his bed, then proceeded to brew up a cup of bitter liquid, and instructed Charley to drink it. It tasted awful, but it made the pain stop and soon Charley was out cold and sleeping. When she awoke, it was nearly noon, and Charley was startled to find that she was wrapped tightly in a blanket, which smelled very odd.

The teamster also realized that her clothes were missing, and she had strange leaves on her body beneath the blanket. Charley tried to keep a rein on her panic, but realized that she felt better, except for her head, and her eye was swollen shut!

"Do you want to eat?"

"I wish I was dead!"

"You very nearly had your wish! The man that took your coach is a very evil man!" the Cherokee stated.

"You saw what he did?" Charley asked.

"Yes, from up here. He has killed many people. You're lucky he didn't cut your throat. It seems to be a hobby with him. How are you feeling?"

"My head hurts," Charley moaned.

"You don't have any broken bones. Wicked tire track, though." The young man almost appeared to blush; it was hard to tell with his dark complexion.

"What did you put on me?" Charley asked.

"It is a comfrey poultice to help keep the tissues of your body from swelling and bruising. You sprained your leg, and your back was messed up badly. I think I got you straight, though," the young man said proudly. "You should try and stay still for a few days to let the muscles heal up."

Charley stared at him; he was handsome and about twenty years old, so she guessed.

"I had to find out if you had broken bones. Your clothes are there." He motioned. "I didn't know they let women drive coaches?"

"No, they don't. No one else knows I'm not a man," Charley said cautiously.

"My name is John Rollin Ridge. My Cherokee name is Yellow Bird."

"My name is Charley Parkhurst, thank you for saving me, Yellow Bird."

"You're welcome Charley Parkhurst. I'll make you something for your head and your eye. You are a very strong woman. You will heal fast."

"I feel like the devil kicked out my guts! Do you know where my coach and horses are?"

"Yes, I think so. Here, drink this." He handed her a smelly dark potion in a tin cup.

"Thank you . . . I think. What about Felix?"

"The other man on the road? I buried him last night."

"Thank you for that." Charley choked back images of Felix and drank the bitter tea. Soon she would fall back into a fitful sleep filled with dark and stormy dreams, with knives and claws and poor drunken Felix. Charley was left in the dust with nothing but a pepperbox pistol and the clothes on her back and little else but her own fortitude, and now it seems, a new friend.

"I must get my horses and coach back!"

"You're awake, I see . . . The man will kill you or worse."

"You said that you knew where they were?"

"Yes, I saw them this morning. They don't appear to be moving yet, but that could change any time," Yellow Bird answered. "You go in there and try and get those horses, and you'll get killed for sure."

"I have to do something. How long have I been lying here?" Charley inquired.

"Only one day and a half," John replied.

"Shit! I gotta get going!" Charley tried to get to her feet and fairly swayed around to and fro until she finally held her balance; then feeling the toweling start to loosen, she had a bout of modesty and returned to her seat.

"You better take things slow, my friend. Rushing around will only make things worse. I was once in a situation in which I felt the need to seek retribution, but I was held back for my own good, for I would have surely been killed. Then I would not be here in order to save your sorry hide." John sat down and filled his pipe. "Your clothes are there." He pointed, making himself comfortable in his cozy cave. I highly recommend that you leave the herb on. It will help your healing process," he said, drawing on his pipe. "Do you smoke?"

"Yes, I do," Charley replied. "That smells unusual," she said, buttoning her shirt on over the toweling. "Tell me what happened to you?" Charley inquired.

"It happened in Arkansas, fourteen years ago in '39, my father was called to the door and was immediately swarmed by about thirty members of the Ross clan of the Cherokee tribe. My grandfather and uncle were killed that night too at another location. My brother and I witnessed the mob from the second-story window. We took our mother and made our escape through the back of the house, hiding in the lower hedgerows till dawn. We then fled to a friend's home, until things could be sorted out. I vowed to revenge the deaths, but politics being what they are, my mother convinced me to leave the area. Later, after I finished school back east and had married, and had a child, again the trouble started. The Ross men stole my prized stallion, and when I went to retrieve the horse at the farm of my neighbor, David Nell, I was met with laughter. I was returned to me a newly gelded horse, still bleeding from his castration. They pushed until there was gunfire. Nell was dead. I was forced to flee, leaving my family to wait and wonder."

"At least you still have your family and your ma," Charley interjected.

"Yes, but when I did take revenge, it didn't bring my father or my grandfather back. It didn't even make me feel better, just sick to my stomach."

"Well, I gotta try to do something!" Charley stood up and tried to hop into her pants and fell like a sack of potatoes.

"Yeah, sure, you'll get yourself killed." Yellow Bird took a long pull on his pipe and shook his head. "They are many."

"Well, I'm not adverse to any suggestions. All you keep sayin is you're gonna get killed!" Charley had started to tear up.

"You should forget about them and move on," the Indian said calmly.

"Well, thanks for the advice!" Charley had risen again. "And I'd appreciate it if you didn't tell anyone about me being a woman. That is, if I survive," Charley growled. She stood like a newborn colt testing his gangly legs for the first time. The sun hit hard when she stepped from the cave. "Thank you, Yellow Bird," Charley called out as she stumbled away, then turned back and reentered the cave, and nearly collapsed. "I forgot to get directions."

"If you're goin' to get yourself killed, you may as well have something to eat first. Then I'll give you directions."

"Fair enough," Charley said gratefully, making herself at home. John handed her some soup made with dried meat and a cup of coffee.

"What can you tell me of these men?" Charley asked.

"Well, first, they are well organized, and they are mostly family. A dangerous family. The man that killed your partner and took the coach is a notorious killer named Emanual Duarte, alias Bernadino Garcia or Tres Dedos, which means three fingers. You may have noticed the missing thumb and first finger."

"I didn't see."

"He fought in the Bear Flag Revolt a few years back and received a most grisly reputation. You see, he was fighting for General Vallejo. Tres Dedos' good friend Ramon Carrillos' sister married Vallejo. Well, Ramon's girlfriend was raped and killed by two of Fremont's men, Cowie and Fowler. When Tres Dedos and Ramon caught the men, they did not kill them. No, that would have been too merciful. They cut out their eyes and their tongues and used the men for knife-throwing targets. Then they stoned them till their bones broke. One man had his jawbone ripped from his face. It was hanging from a tree. It had been pulled off with a lariat that had been threaded through an incision cut in his neck. After all of this, they skinned the men alive and left them to die a slow and cruel death. That is Tres Dedos' own confession. He boasted about it. For you see, he was caught and did confess but mysteriously escaped. Probably by compatriots or family . . ." Rollin Ridge stopped to light his pipe; he stared at the frightened woman. "So now you know what you're up against. You still want those horses?"

Charley sat there, comparing pictures of what he had just been told to the ones that he had been dreaming of; they seemed manufactured by the same hand. "Yes, I do! I want to at least check on their whereabouts so I can report them stolen."

Yellow Bird looked at the man-woman and laughed. "I think you should be happy you're alive and let it go at that."

"Well, I'm not gonna! So just point me to my horses and let me go."

"So you will die for these horses?"

"Hopefully not!"

"I will show you where they are tomorrow. You must rest another day before you go skulking around these hills. They will hear you moaning and groaning and find you for sure. Besides, you will need all your strength. Here, eat. Do you even have a plan?" the Cherokee asked.

"Not really, I am open to suggestions however." Charley smiled.

They sat at the entrance to the cave and traded life stories. John explained about the division in his tribe and how he had been destined to be the chief and now was in exile from his people. He was looking for direction in life, trying to fit into the expanding white man's world. Ridge was happy to meet someone who could read, as he was an aspiring writer. He shared his own worn book of poetry, always kept at hand,

and Charley was especially taken with a poem about Mount Shasta. She was happy to read his poetry.

John told how he was thinking of writing a novel about how circumstances that are out of our control changed a person. Much like his own life, and it would seem, his new friend. He didn't, for political reasons, want to write his own story, but one that would parallel his. He also told of how he would someday like to write out for history's sake the facts of the various tribes of Indians and their cultures. Charley enjoyed the company of the handsome, intelligent man, with the piercing dark eyes and jet-black hair flowing down his back, as he told about his wife, Lizzy, and his daughter, Alice.

"Why are you out here, in this cave?" Charley asked.

"Well, I was headed to Stockton to send for my wife and daughter. When I spotted Tres Dedos, I decided to hide up here awhile to let them move on before I set out. I didn't want to get caught by them. Then, of course, I had to wet-nurse you."

The next day, John kept his promise and guided Charley to a lookout where they could see the herd. There were about a hundred horses grazing and playing in the meadow. He could see his favorite mare beating the tar out of a rangy bay stud and spotted a few guards watching the fight; they seemed to be wagering on the outcome. Charley told John that he could call the team to him with one whistle, but that would alert the guards, and they would be discovered. So close, but yet so far. The coach, well, that was something else, the evil one was sitting in it, eating. The harness was strewn about on the poles; God only knows what shape that was in. Next to the cliff and out of sight to the pair on their stomachs was a large blue tent.

"Now you see how useless this is?" John asked. "Let's just go and report them."

"Well, I hate to just leave them!" Parkhurst growled.

"Well, maybe with the cover of night you might get one or two horses, but I don't think so. You stay here. I will go and check out the other side of the canyon. You're too noisy. I'll come back for you soon."

Charley just stared at Yellow Bird; she was in pain and very frightened. Even her hands were trembling. "Stay quiet! I'll be back," the Cherokee warned.

Charley got comfortable, lying on her stomach in some rocks, watching the horses. Time seemed like molasses. She was so afraid that John would be caught, and images of Felix kept creeping into mind; her new friend had taken a big risk. The sun was warm, and Charley fought to keep from dozing off.

"See anything you like?" a deep voice came from behind. Charley heard the click of a gun being cocked; her body stiffened.

"Oh God!" She swore, twisting her neck in a painful way to gaze up at a incredibly handsome specimen of a man, with long flowing honey brown hair cascading over his shoulders. He was pointing a new Colt revolver, the brass bead sight shinning in the sun. Charley's heart was pounding somewhere in her throat as she managed to choke out a few words. "I . . . I was looking at my horses."

Joaquin threw his head back and laughed uproariously. Charley began to shake uncontrollably.

"I will take your pistol. You have fortitude. Tres Dedos said he ran over you and killed you." Murrieta ran his eyes over the scrawny man, obviously fresh from the east. Joaquin could smell the strange herbs about him. "Just how did you plan on taking back your horses?"

"Well, a I . . . I wasn't quite sure," Charley stuttered as the teamster gazed deep into the stunning young man's dark blue eyes and handed over the gun. Joaquin laughed at Felix's pepperbox and grabbed the front of Charley's shirt, pulling him to his feet.

"You are not a man! Are you?" Joaquin said, gazing hard into Charley's hazel eyes. "Now I am impressed!"

"How did . . . do you know . . . I wasn't . . . I'm not a man?" Charley stumbled for words; she was fascinated by the man's chiseled and disquieting face smiling down at her. He slowly released his grip on his captive, who slumped back down to the ground.

"The way you looked at me, I see that look only in women's eyes." Murrieta laughed; then he noticed the searing pain written on the woman's face. "Can you ride?" he asked with tenderness in his voice.

"Yes." She was mesmerized by his charm, something she had never experienced before.

"Then come, I am fascinated." His horse was near, and Joaquin pulled her up behind him on a remarkable buckskin stallion. His legs were jet-black up past his knees; then his coat turned tawny gold with the most remarkable black stripes running horizontally across the top of his legs and to his powerfully built chest. His mane and tail were long and silky black. Joaquin pulled Charley's arms around his own waist. "Don't fall off," he laughed. "And don't try any thing stupid!" he warned.

"I'm going to try not to be stupid," Charley replied, trying not to panic.

"So tell me about yourself and these horses that are so important to you." the dark man asked as they made their way down the canyon.

"My name is Charley Parkhurst. I am a stage driver with Birch's stage line. My expressman was killed by a man with a really big knife. Then he knocked me out and threw me from the stage and ran over me. I survived because an Indian, Yellow Bird, picked me up off the desert floor and saved my butt." Charley took a deep sigh. She instantly regretted involving her friend.

"But you are a woman! Women are not stage drivers!" Murrieta puzzled.

"Well, I know, but nobody knows I'm a woman!" Charley replied.

"Really?" he laughed. "I recognized your sex right away!" Joaquin laughed.

Charley could feel her face getting very hot, with a tingling sensation that had never been experienced before. Maybe it was riding behind such a handsome and masculine man, with her hands on his waist and his long soft hair in her face.

"Well, believe it or not, no one else has ever figured it out, except my friend who took my clothes off me to check for broken bones," she said blushing, "Two men in one week! First time in thirty years, and it's twice in one week! That's almost funny!"

"Were you carrying mail on this run?"

"Yes, of course!" Charley realized her ace in the hole. "Why, I'm two days late. They must be frantic by now! They must have a posse out looking for us."

Joaquin took note. She was right; they would be looking. Charley could almost hear the wheels turning in this dark handsome man's head as they loped toward the main camp, dominated by a large blue tent. Joaquin told her to be quiet, and everything would be all right. Charley had no recourse but to play along.

As they made their way to the canyon floor, Charley spotted the man with the knife. He was greeting Joaquin with a smile and waving. "Just act relaxed and listen to what I say and go along with it," Joaquin purred.

"Yes. I will," Charley stuttered.

"I will introduce you as my friend Charley, from Texas. Can you talk like a Texan?"

"Why, you bet, partner!" Charley whispered, involuntarily shaking at the sight of the demon of her dreams.

"Joaquin, who is your little friend?" the evil one smirked.

"It is my friend Charley from Texas, who's been searching for his coach and six horses. You haven't seen the six gray coach horses, have you?" Joaquin questioned his uncle.

"Maybe I have, Joaquin, don't tell me you want me to give them back!" The man was extremely drunk on tequila and stumbled laughing.

"What if I do? What good will a coach with a bounty on it do, but get our men shot?"

"You have a good point there! Come have a drink. We talk about horses later!"

"The coach and six must be returned. It is too dangerous and recognizable. That is the end of it!"

"How was I to know that he was a friend of yours. You shouldn't have so many friends." Tres Dedos slobbered. Charley was hiding behind Joaquin on the horse, when the bandito suddenly threw his leg over the saddle horn and jumped off the horse, leaving Charley sitting alone.

"You take stupid chances. You will endanger this family!" Murrieta roared. Charley slowly slid off the horse, trying not to throw his back out of whack or be noticed, when Joaquin turned to the survivor. "Charley, you can rest in my tent!" He pointed to the deep blue cloth domicile. "Rosita will bring you something to eat."

"The sooner I get out of here, the better," Charley sighed.

Charley was so tired that he lay on the bed practically spread-eagle, facedown, as a lovely young woman came in with a plate.

"I have brought you food," the sweet voice spoke. Charley couldn't resist rolling over to catch a glimpse of this angelic voice. She stood in the doorway, and Charley could see dangerous-looking men standing outside the tent, and it made him queasy.

"Can I bring you water, Charley?" the angel asked.

"Please, a gracious." Charley made an attempt at grace.

The angel noted the gesture. Then departed and returned very shortly with a glass and two bottles, one with water and one with something else; it wasn't whiskey, and it wasn't brandy, but it certainly had something going for it!

"Agave!" the young woman stated. "Tequila."

"Good. Gracious." That was all that Charley could think of as he lifted his glass to the young woman and quietly accepted the drink. Only to be startled by the whoops and hollers of Murrieta's men and a familiar voice pleading for mercy.

"That is my friend!" Charley said bolting upright, his back screaming in pain. "That is my friend Yellow Bird!" Charley was startled by the yells and immediately shot up and out of the tent.

"This man is my friend! He is a writer!" Charley screamed at the men dragging Yellow Bird along with a rope.

"Release him!" Joaquin shouted. The two men reluctantly let the prisoner go, and Charley ran to her friend.

"I don't have time to explain . . . This is my friend," Charley called out, dragging Rollin Ridge into the tent. "It's hard to explain, but the leader, Joaquin, likes me, and we are pretending I'm his friend from Texas. See?" Charley informed the Indian.

"Well, whatever you say, they beat the shit out of me. Do you mind if I sit down? Hell, they even served you supper . . . Do you know who your friend is?"

"I didn't exactly catch his name now that you mention it," Charley whispered

"That's Joaquin Murrieta."

"Oh," Charley said oblivious to the real danger.

"I'll tell you later . . . If we have a later," Rollin Ridge replied. "You gonna eat that?"

"I can't eat." Charley sat on the floor and motioned the Indian to the spot she had been on the bed. "He knows I'm a woman too!" Charlie sighed.

The tent was very large and made of durable blue fabric. It was divided into two rooms, a gambling parlor and a bedroom. The fabric was held up with rope and beams of pine that looked freshly cut. The two could hear the others talking on the other side of the fabric wall, and Joaquin was trying to sort out the details of the coach incident. The men were all in favor of returning the stage; they wanted no part of it to begin with. Tres Dedos swore at the men and called them women.

"He is a writer. Maybe he's gonna write a story about you," Alejando advised the three fingered-cutthroat.

"That's good, someone should write my life story! I like that! But I don't think I like him. I think that we should cut both their throats and feed their carcasses to the wolves! That is what I think we should do," he hissed with resolve. Tres Dedos stood up and stumbled out of the tent.

"Where are you going, Duarte?" Joaquin snarled.

"Why don't you go kiss your little friends good-bye before I cut their throats, Joaquin!" Tres Dedos hissed back. The blood was pounding in his temples, and his head ached. He didn't like anyone to tell him what to do, and he certainly didn't want to give up his new toy. He ran his hands over the gold lettering, slamming his fist into the name as if it would change to his own; then he laughed.

Rollin Ridge and Charley sat in silence listening when Joaquin walked back through the partition, startling the two outsiders.

"You must collect your horses and leave. There is no telling what he will do, maybe just go and pass out, but you never know with him. We will help you catch them," Joaquin instructed.

"All I need is a pail of grain and some halters. They will all come to me when I whistle," Charley bragged. Joaquin was impressed, and some of the men found it an interesting bet; they seem to wager on almost anything. Charley was taken to where the coach was parked and checked over the harness and found it in good order. The coach appeared to have been rolled, judging by the deep scrapes on the side and the imbedded dirt in the upholstery. Otherwise, it was in fine shape. "Gotta hand it to Abbott. They sure know how to build them," Charley sighed. He picked up three of the halters and motioned for Yellow Bird to do the same. Then the men walked out to the edge of the meadow where the horses were grazing. Charley put three halters on each shoulder and took the bucket and bid everyone stay put, which greatly increased the wagering, as he hobbled out toward the horses. Charley stood tall and blew out a very high-pitched rolling whistle, which caught all the horses' attention. The leader's head came up and let out a greeting to his lost pal, and immediately began to circle the mares galloping and calling as Charley continued to whistle. The other horses were stirred up too but were unsure about running toward the man. The leader was glad to see Charley and even more glad to see the pail of grain. The mares were right on his heels, and Charley tried to be diplomatic with the grain and not get stepped on. Most remembered their manners though as Charley quickly haltered the six and led them toward the coach. Some of the men grumbled over their wager, and others were impressed by the man's horsemanship and tried in vain to duplicate the whistle. Charley couldn't harness them fast enough for his own liking and couldn't wait to get the hell out of there before that man with the claw hand, Tres Dedos, came back.

Just as Charley was chaining on the last horse, he heard a voice coming from behind, one that he would never forget.

"Don't think that you are safe, or that I will forget this 'cause I don't forget so easy. Someday, we meet again. I will find you, and just when you think you're safe, I will cut out your heart," the killer hissed.

Charley turned carefully around and looked into the bloodshot eyes of the madman, who began to laugh, it seemed to rise from the depths of hell.

"Hey, you writer!" Tres Dedos looked over at John Rollin Ridge. "You write about me if you want to, maybe I don't kill you after all." The man began to laugh wildly again. The animals began to get nervous as though a predator was near. Charley figured his trembling hands were the cause. Tres Dedos stumbled back into the tent as Joaquin was coming out; one could see the animosity brewing between them.

"I see you are almost ready to leave. You are a brave man, Charley." He smiled. "You don't have to worry about your secret. I won't tell. These are fine horses. I'll be sorry to see them go." Joaquin handed the disguised woman the pathetic pepperbox.

Charley gazed into Joaquin Murrieta's handsome face; it was sad, but very sensual. For a moment, the teamster wanted to just melt into his arms, but it only lasted a second as John who was sitting on the driver's seat coughed, and Charley snapped to attention and put out his hand and shook good-bye. He then quickly climbed up to the driver's box and took the ribbons from his new friend, who's sorry-looking horse had been tied to the back of the coach.

"Maybe we will meet again someday," Joaquin said, as Charley put the lines between his skilled fingers and whistled his horses on.

"Maybe," Charley said under her breath as the coach was again on its way.

"What will you tell the stage company when you get in?" Rollin Ridge asked.

"The truth I guess! I really hadn't thought about that. I wasn't sure I would ever get in." Charley looked at his new driving partner.

"Well, if you tell them you were run over by the coach, they might make you see a doctor, and then you'll be found out. I mean by somebody else," Ridge teased.

"Yes, I see what you mean." Charley said, puzzled. "I'll think about it. It seems wrong not to just tell them a crazy madman cut Felix throat and pushed me from the coach, and then . . ."

"Then what? The nice other bandito just gave you back the coach?"

"Well, he did," Charley said.

"I got a bad feeling about this, Charley. Tres Dedos is a very dangerous man. If you squeal on him after he gave back the coach, he will search for you and cut your throat," John warned.

"Not if they catch him and hang him first," Charley gulped, remembering poor Felix and the two passengers.

"He is very hard to catch, he has many confederates, people are afraid of him, they wake up one morning, and they find themselves dead. You think about it, you cannot bring Felix back to life, save your own self."

"Yes, but you said that about the horses, and look where they are now, right in my two hands!" Charley said with pride.

"Well, you do what you think right. I'm glad you got them back anyway." John and Charley both smiled. "I won't tell anyone your secret. Besides, you drive pretty good for a woman." John Rollin Ridge laughed. Charley laughed also.

"What will you do now, John?" Charley asked.

"Well, I'm not real sure."

"Hope you can find some outlet for you're writing talents. It would be fine if you could make a living at it," Charley replied.

"Yes, there is plenty of time to write after digging in the earth for gold all day, but very little energy left to write with." He smiled. "I might try my hand with the newspapers," Ridge added.

The two sat silently as they rode back to civilization, each contemplating what to do.

CHAPTER 17

Charley and Rollin Ridge made it safely back to Stockton with no further mishaps. The teamster's stomach ached as they pulled up to the budding cow towns Stage office.

"My God! If it isn't Charley Parkhurst, my friend, goddamn it, man, sit down!" James Birch was beside himself as the missing teamster walked through the door. For the past few days, he'd been worried sick that something horrible had happened to his ace in the hole and best driver, Charley Parkhurst. But here he was, larger than life. Next to him stood a broody-looking dark complected man of the native persuasion.

"We imagined the worst possible situation that could have kept you from coming in or getting word to anyone. I thought I'd lost you for good," Birch sighed. "Get word to the posse, Edgar!" Birch hollered to the office manager.

"I lost Felix," Charley said solemnly.

"What happened?" James asked, seeing the extreme pain his friend was in.

"I don't know. It happened so fast!" Charley began. Rollin Ridge just sighed and rolled his eyes. "I just don't know for certain how it happened," Charley started as a spasm of pain shot through his back as he settled into the chair. "When I woke in the sand, dazed and confused, he was dead. A man jumped onto the back of the coach and killed Felix. He knocked me cold, then threw me from the coach. My friend here, John Rollin Ridge buried Felix after he found me. He helped me to recover the coach and the horses. There were two passengers aboard at the time the coach was taken, but I never seen them again," Charley related. John hid in the corner of the room listening intently. "We found the coach and the horses a day or so later and drove back. John Rollin Ridge here helped me to navigate to Stockton since I had gone off course."

"My God, Charley, I'm so glad you made it back safely. It's mighty good to see you. I bet you could use a drink!" James said, rising and clasping Charley's hand firmly in his own and pulled him to his feet with pride; he threw his arms around his friend, and Charley sighed audibly. The hug was excruciating because of his bruised ribs.

"Yes, it's good to see you too, James," Charley sighed, hearing his back pop.

"Hey, Fred, make sure they get word to the posse! Oh my, I forgot, I . . . um, please come inside my office. I have someone waiting. He's just delivered some hardware from Hartford, from Samuel Colt," James said, leading his wayward friend through the doorway to his office.

"Samuel Colt, the gunsmith?"

"Yes! I'm sorry to keep you waiting. Here is your money," Birch said pulling an envelope from his inside pocket. "Charley, the Birch Stage Line just purchased one hundred revolvers of the finest quality from none other than Samuel Colt himself. This is Mr. Stoterman. He has delivered them from Connecticut," James stated as he pulled a bottle out and started pouring shots in some fancy glasses.

"It is an honor, sir," Charley said, removing his hat, poking John to remove his.

The man went into his best sales pitch. He had laid out the various models on Birch's desk.

"This is the '51 model, the Navy Colt, so-called for the engraving of the battle in the Gulf of Mexico on the cylinder. This next model is the police pocket pistol. It's sporting a scene of a stagecoach robbery on its cylinder. Notice the ramrod is separate, making the gun smaller, yet still packing a large punch. They are all the same caliber, and the parts are interchangeable due to the precise machining done on this fine product. Let me demonstrate how I can take the cylinder from this Navy and put it in this other Navy," the man said, taking out a small brass hammer and pounding out the side pin. He pulled off the barrel of the gun using the ramrod as a lever and slid the cylinder off. He did the same with another gun. He then demonstrated how perfectly the pieces interchanged.

"These guns are all cap and ball revolvers. Which means that they use percussion caps that rest over these nipples here. After the cylinders are loaded with measured powder from these flasks, then a lead ball is pressed into the chamber, with this ramrod. These models are six shot a piece and come with a cleaning kit and holster." He slipped the other cylinder on the handgun and reassembled the piece and checked it out, rolling the cylinder in his palm; it moved perfectly. The salesman beamed with pride.

"Go on, Charley, you pick a couple of the ones you want, go on now!" James said like it was Christmas.

Charley remembered Tres Dedos and searched the table carefully for a suitable weapon. He settled on a Navy model, the same kind that Joaquin had pointed at him. He slowly turned the cylinder, examining the battle scene. The smooth wood handle felt good in his strong hand. He cocked the hammer back and looked down the octagonal barrel and smiled.

"At long last my own Colt revolver. I could use a new whip too. Mine got wrecked when I lost the coach," Charley sighed. Tears welling up at the thought of Felix.

"I'm sorry, Charley," James said, resting his hand on Charley's shoulder. "You knew Felix a long time, me too, I reckon. The sheriff will be wanting to talk to you. I'm afraid you'll have to make out a report. Are you looking for work?" James asked, turning to John.

"Perhaps," John replied. "I'm a writer by trade, but times have been hard."

"Well, we need someone to fill Felix's job. Are you game?"

"You mean ride on the coach looking after mail and such?" John inquired.

"Yes, we can give you a full job description, but that's basically it."

"Sounds good! I'll drink to that." John toasted.

"Felix would have." Charley smiled.

"I propose that we all get something to eat," James said, taking his cue from the salesman whose stomach was growling. "My treat!" James rang out. As they were leaving the office, they ran into Frank Stevens, and after greeting and introductions, all headed to a very popular restaurant run by an Italian family. The five ate themselves into a stupor.

James insisted that Charley get the rest he needed, for a merger was in the air. Birch had been talking to some of the other stage lines, and the deal was being talked around about a big partnership, one that would be called the California Stage Lines. The maps were already being drawn up.

The next morning was crisp, and there were many coaches being loaded with passengers and luggage. Charley glanced about the street and noticed a handsome man, full of authority, sitting in the driver's box down the street.

"Who is that man, James?" Charley inquired. "Looks like he knows his way around."

"That's Jared Crandall. He is half owner in Hall and Crandall Line. He and his partner were one of the first to start coaching, along with Stevens and I. He's agreeable to a merger, and so is Charley Green."

"Handsome!" Charley mumbled under her breath, admiring the man. He glanced over and casually tipped his hat. The street was beginning to fill up with men looking at the coaches and trying to determine the proper destination. Coachmen sang out their destinations as the coaches filled up fast and were full to the brim when they left.

Charley kept driving the Stockton to Mariposa route, eyes ever vigilant for Tres Dedos.

Mariposa is Spanish for butterfly. In the spring, the name was not given in vain; the meadows were alive with color, like an impressionist painting come to life.

John Rollin Ridge enjoyed the scenery too, but soon decided to look for work closer to his literary calling and bid Charley good-bye, vowing friendship.

As the weeks rolled by, each newspaper held new terror of murders by Mexican bandits.

The next day was Charley's day of rest, and that was what he intended to do. He wasn't one to spend time in a flagrant manner nor drink too much, lest his true sex be found out and blabbed, but Charley did like to play cards, and it seemed to be the favorite pastime in all of the new towns.

He ventured into the saloon down the street from the livery stable to see if there might be a game worth playing. The establishment was about average and had nothing to distinguish itself from the thousands of watering holes spread though out the gold fields. There were four tables inside, all full of men playing cards. After having a drink at the bar, Charley was recognized as the stage driver and invited to play at one of the tables. The soft-spoken man that did the inviting was about twenty-eight, with light brown hair and mustache and very handsome blue-gray eyes. Next to him at the table was a dark complected Mexican man who had a very dangerous look about him.

"Valenzuela!" a bald man next to him whined. "It's your deal, Valenzuela!" He was an older Mexican man who seemed neither to be dangerous, nor very bright.

"Shut up, you stupid old fool!" Valenzuela swore at the older man. "Do you want to play or no?" he asked Charley.

"Don't mind if I do?" he asked, sitting down for a bit of entertainment.

After an evening of poker and beer, Charley made his way back to the hotel and slept like a rock.

The next morning while sitting on the driver's box waiting for his new express agent, Charley was quite surprised when his sandy-haired card companion, with the gray eyes, flashed his express agent badge, as he climbed aboard the sturdy Concord coach to the seat beside him.

That day, Charley inquired of his new companion, William Byrnes, some of the particulars of his life. He had been born in Maine, then moved around to Texas, and then spent some time in Sonora Mexico. He worked his way up the Sierra Mountains looking for gold and in the capacity of a lawman, or so he said; the two got along well, and that was really all that mattered.

They drove the route from Stockton to Mariposa, up then back, six days a week. Occasionally they heard rumors of Tres Dedos. The very thought of the madman made Charley shake, for he ultimately was not suited for combat. He would practice with his newly acquired Colt, always kept close at hand whenever the opportunity arose.

Charley had always concentrated on driving the horses, not in defending the coach. The teamster had no real experience with a gun, certainly no formal training. He was mighty with the lash, however, and often won money hitting coins out of the air with the whip.

While riding together on the coach, Will had talked of his many exploits with a gun, so Charley asked him if he would teach him some lessons. Byrnes thought it would be fun and made a point of finding a canyon to practice at as soon as they got back to Mariposa.

It was warm that night and still fairly light at six in the evening. The men got a bottle of whiskey and a canteen of water and some roasted venison from the restaurant.

"I'll meet you at the corral in a few minutes. I gotta go fetch my horse." Charley smiled.

Charley kept his stallion Mozo in Mariposa, at a small stable at the end of town. It was so lovely to ride in the hills; now that he had fully recuperated and been fit with a new set of shoes, he was always eager to go for a run. Will rode a very nice black Tennessee mare.

"Where did you get that horse?" Will asked, suprised to see Mozo.

"I bought him from some Indian. He was completely lame at the time, and they were gonna butcher him. Can you imagine that?"

"Do you know whose' horse that is?" Will asked earnestly.

"I just told you he's mine. Were you not paying attention?" Charley said as Will climbed aboard his own horse.

"That's Joaquin Murrieta's horse, Charley," Will stated plainly as he seated himself in the saddle.

"Joaquin Murrieta?" Charley said with shock. She looked deeply into Will's serious eyes for any sign of a joke. "How do you know?"

"I just do! Trust me," Will said.

"Well, he's mine now. Let's go," Charley said, not batting an eye. Inside she was reliving the encounter with the brooding man. She was certain he would not harm her; his bandit men were another story however.

The two rode off to a box canyon about a mile out of town. It was kind of spooky to Charley who kept looking over his shoulder. A wise habit in those hills.

Charley was becoming infatuated with Will, and she knew it. He was so appealing that it hurt her to look at him some times. It was strange for Charley, and she started to feel like she was not in control of her emotions.

But it was only a shooting lesson. Two friends practicing their marksmanship. She couldn't help being a woman though; every time Will put his hands on her, it was so enjoyable. Charley fought many battles within herself about telling him the truth, but never could she find the right time or the right words. Besides, she pondered, he might not want to have anything to do with her, or maybe he couldn't keep a secret. It would have be enough to just be friends.

William Byrnes loved to shoot and brought an assortment of bottles to shoot at. First, he laid the bottles on their side to shoot through the opening; then he stood them up to shoot them a second time. He was a very good shot, and Charley was impressed. Byrnes was very charismatic and popular with the women, but always seemed a little bored with them. Charley never set foot in a whorehouse, yet she had sympathy for the "sporting gals," for she knew they were just trying to get along in life as she was.

The light was beginning to fade, and the two were tired and packed it up and headed out of the canyon. After leaving the horses, the two friends headed to the saloon for a last drink before turning in. The bartender was a big friendly man with a good laugh, and everyone called him Big John. He said that a man had inquired after Byrnes and said he would be in the area for a while.

The night was getting on, and Charley went back to his bunk and dreamed what it might be like to be with a handsome man like William Byrnes.

The next day, Byrnes was bored with the Mariposa card scene and asked Charley if he cared for more lively game, and Charley, being fond of his new friend, agreed.

While they were riding out of town, Byrnes informed Charley that an old friend from his youth was in town, and he had set up a casino of sorts near by. Imagine Charley's surprise when it turned out to be none other than the blue tent of Joaquin Murrieta!

Charley started to shake as the two dismounted, and Will was greeted at the tent flap with handshakes and embraces. Joaquin stopped in front of Charley and their eyes met in acknowledgment.

"I believe your friend Charley, and I have already had the pleasure of meeting," Joaquin's gaze went immediately to the big white horse that Charley had arrived on.

"Where did you get that horse?" Murrieta said in amazement. "Mozo?" he said, rubbing his hand over the horse's face. The animal casually rubbed his head on his master's hand. Joaquin turned with a puzzled look at his old acquaintance; his look demanded an explanation.

"I bought him from that fellow over there. He was going to shoot him. Paid him three dollars. He was stove up with a bad abscess and a nail deep in his frog. Right as rain now," Charley said with pride.

"Chappo," Joaquin said under his breath.

"Yeah, that's his name, Chappo, I do believe."

"Do you want to sell him?"

"No, I don't really," Charley said, swallowing hard. "I kinda like him."

"Well, maybe you will lose him in a card game, eh? Your friend has big balls!" Joaquin laughed, turning to Byrnes, breaking the tension and leading them inside the tent. Joaquin began dealing the cards, and as the game commenced, Charley vaguely perceived a wink coming from Murrieta.

Charley recognized the beautiful Rosita, who was playing cards in the corner with another woman.

It was odd, Charley thought, to have these two men who had stirred her at the same table, and that they had already been friends. They brought up old times in Sonora, Mexico, when they were very young men. Charley was highly entertained, and it didn't hurt that he was doing well at cards, either.

"Have you seen Tres Dedos, lately?" Charley asked. There was a silence in the room.

"Well, last I heard he was down in Petaluma. He has a lady friend there. Her name is Hilaria. Said that he was going back to being a barber so that he can run a razor around rich gringo throats." Valenzuala regaled. The room erupted in laughter. Charley didn't find it amusing, he knew that it was likely the madman was around somewhere close.

As the card-playing wound to halt, Joaquin picked up his guitar near the chair and began picking out a haunting tune. Alejandro found his own guitar and accompanied him in a most beautiful song, full of danger and romance, it seemed to Charley.

Finally the night came to an end and Charley and Will rode back to town. Charley had wisely not wagered the horse. Will was astounded that Joaquin had not taken the horse back; it puzzled him. Along the way, he asked Charley how he knew about Tres Dedos and where he had met Joaquin. Charley just said that they had met when he had first come to California and let it go at that. It was fun to have Will interested, but it was becoming painful too. To have women so attracted to Will and know that he would make love to them and never her tore at something deep inside Charley. She was beginning to think that she should stop spending so much time with him, maybe even transfer to another route, but every time they were apart, Charley wondered what he was doing. Whenever he invited him to play cards, Charley could never refuse. They played at the blue tent quite often. Charley was fascinated with Joaquin as well. Whereas William had the blonde coloring and the soft charm, Joaquin was dark and stormy and exotic while not as dark as most Mexicans, his manners and customs were very Spanish. Joaquin prided himself on imitating dialects and often amused the table with impressions of British or Germans; he even did a fair Irish accent. He had flashing deep blue eyes that Charley could just drown in, but she reminded herself that Joaquin knew the truth about her sex. He teased her in his own way, their own private secret.

Murrieta was resigned to the fact that Charley would not give Mozo up and was pleased to see he was kept in the fashion he deserved. He even delighted the teamster with a display of the horse's full abilities as a trained battle warrior that he was. Charley had new respect for Mozo.

One day, James Birch sent word to Charley that a driver was needed on the Downieville route. It was a good break for the driver as she felt her attachments were becoming too strong. A fresh new route was just the thing. James wanted his top driver to be familiar with all the northern roads. Marysville would be home base for half the time, and then he would overnight at the other end of the ride, Downieville, returning back the next day.

Charley liked Marysville; it was fairly civilized and was a jumping off point for most of the upper California mines. John Rollin Ridge, now a budding journalist, found work at the new newspaper the *Marysville Democrat*. Charley would occasionally run into him in the taverns there. One never knew who he would see in this bustling town.

"Charley!" Murrieta said with a smile.

"Joaquin?"

"Sit down and have a drink with me," he charmed.

"What are you having?" Parkhurst inquired.

"Oh, I am having a little tequila," he responded.

"I don't do well with tequila. I'll make mine brandy and some coffee, please," Charley ordered.

"Have you seen Byrnes?" Joaquin asked.

"No, have you?" Charley replied.

"I was supposed to meet him yesterday." Joaquin examined his friend's face. "Poor Charley, you are in love with Will, aren't you? I can see it in your face!" he whispered softly.

"What? . . . What, I . . . suppose I like the man. I can't help myself, Lord knows I've tried. You never told him about me, did you?" Charley asked, looking down at the table, too ashamed to face her friend.

"No. A promise is a promise. Do you still have Mozo?" Joaquin asked, changing the subject.

"Of course. He's fine. Say, I hear they are going to put in a racetrack at Grass Valley. I thought about entering him in some races," Charley added.

"The miners are in great need of new diversions on the Sabbath. There's money to be made without digging in the dirt." Joaquin smiled. "I would bet on him. I saw your friend Rollin Ridge last night."

"Well, perhaps this calls for a poker game tonight then, maybe a meeting of old friends?" Charley inquired.

Just then, a short bald Mexican man trudged to the table slightly out of breath. "Boss, the hotel clerk said that William Byrnes is stayin' here, and they would leave word that we called," Alejandro recited. "Charley! Nice to see you! We miss you at the monte tables. Do you still have the big stallion?"

"Yes. Mozo is fine. Did you say that Will is here, Alejandro?" Charley asked

"*Sí*. He must be upstairs and busy." The old man leered.

"He'll be here, my friend, soon enough." Joaquin smiled as he stood up. His beloved Rosita came to the table and was seated between Charley and himself.

"It is nice to see you, Charley, you look well," Rosita said as Charley kissed her hand. Joaquin laughed out loud.

"Well, look who it is, Charley!" Joaquin teased, spotting Byrnes as he shook the rain from his hat at the doorway. "It's your old pal, Will!"

"Will, it's good to see you," Charley said, standing and shaking hands. Her beating heart pounding in her chest.

"It's good to see you too!" Will replied, grasping his friend's hand firmly. Byrnes was very gaunt and tired looking, but he was still not short on charm.

"I gave up riding shotgun for now. I prefer a stationary seat to one that sways to and fro. These miners are fair and easy picking when it comes to poker," Will commented.

Charley stood up and walked to the bartender to purchase a bottle of brandy as the front door swung open with a whoosh.

Harry Love was a badger of a man; he entered the tavern with a gust of wind. It was storming out and wet; he was fairly soaked through from riding in the weather. Love was a very large man and dark complected. His shoulder-length, wavy, black hair was dripping with rain, as he ran his hands down a wiry goatee to remove the water. Charley saw great resolve in his squinty dark eyes and could not help but notice the large mole on his right cheek.

"Excuse me," the wet man grumbled.

"Go on ahead, you must be freezing," Charley said, stepping out of his way.

"Say aren't you a stage driver?" Love asked.

"Why yes, I am, have we met before?"

"No, I've just seen you drive coach. I like to remember faces. Can I buy you a drink?" Harry was beginning to thaw out.

"Thank you, but my friends and I were just going," Charley said politely. The men were getting restless, and the group would retire to Will's room to play cards. The towns were ripe for fights, and there was a great deal of racial tension around, especially since everyone was cooped up because of bad weather. The miners could get like a pack of drunken, wild dogs snapping at one another.

"I think I will put the blue tent ova' near Murphy's camp, those blokes love to gamble, and it's not far from the racetrack," Joaquin said in his best cockney voice, raising the stakes to all at the table by ten dollars.

"Do you plan on staying in Marysville awhile?" Charley asked Will. Joaquin laughed, and Charley glared at him.

"I may stay awhile, depends on what opportunities arise. I am entertaining some offers in law enforcement. I may head up to the mountains in the spring when it warms up. I can't seem to get warm enough," Will said, pouring another shot.

"Well, shit, maybe it has something to do with that bout of lead poisoning you had," Alejandro said, laughing at his wit.

"Probably so, my friend," Will said, draining his glass.

"Law enforcement, you didn't have your fill at the Mormon Station?" Joaquin asked.

"You have a point there. I have an offer in Hangtown . . . they are thinking of changing the name to Placerville," Will added.

"Well, I gotta go. I have some horses to look at tomorrow. Besides, you guys got all my money anyway. I'll see you later," Charley said, rising and putting on his coat.

The next day was Monday, and Charley rose early and prepared himself to drive the 8:00 AM stage to Downieville. Charley was prompt as usual and got to the coach at seven to make all of the inspections of the coach and horses. Many drivers were lax and trusted that someone else had done this, but Charley always made his own inspections. A breakdown might mean a horse's life or the drivers, and that wasn't good or economical.

The driver was soon perched on his throne, with his willowy scepter balanced in his strong fingers along with the leather ribbons. With a subtle kiss, the horses all stepped forward and walked up to the station for loading. No mustangs for Charley, but her own gray team. A team that could stand perfectly quiet or gallop off at a moment's notice. They could move together in harness like a school of fish gliding around. Charley's hands moving up and down the ribbons like a musician would finger a guitar.

"Well, look who it is! You want to sit up here, or maybe inside would be better?" Charley said laughing.

"No, I think that up top might be nice. It looks like it will be a nice morning," Harry Love responded with good humor.

"Welcome aboard, sir." Charley expertly shifted the ribbons to one hand without tangling them and offered a hand as the burly man climbed up the boot of the coach.

"Are you going to Downieville?"

"No, I get off at French's. I usually ride my horse, but I feel a bit under the weather and decided to treat myself and let someone else do the driving for a change."

Harry Love entertained the men on the roof of the coach with tales of the Texas Rangers of which he was one. He explained that he was busy chasing down murderous gangs of Mexicans that have been leaving bloody scenes in the Monterey area and elsewhere. He was going to convince the governor that he could organize an army of California Rangers, much like the Texas Rangers, with him in charge of course, to rid the country of the desperadoes. Charley felt that the man was rather conceited but probably made a good leader. He sure took a liking to Charley, though. He insisted that he have the opportunity to buy him that drink that he had earlier declined. But Charley insisted that he did not drink till he was finished driving.

It was night when the coach arrived in Downieville, and the weather was starting to whip up.

The winter just rained and rained, bridges were wiped out, ferries swept away, and men never heard from again. Even as if in vile judgment for its part, the Jersey bridge, the sight of Josefa's hanging, was swept away from its mooring and was dashed to pieces. Travel was at a stand still; except for a few high roads, people just had to hunker down and make the best of things. Tempers began flaring as people got stir crazy and cabin fever. In the foothills and Sierras, people who got stuck in their cabins froze to death or starved.

CHAPTER 18

March 1853

"They are becoming a recognizable force, and it's time to do something about it," Harry Love lectured on the porch of the Marysville hotel.

Harry had succeeded in getting the governor's attention, but it would take time to have legislature authorize any Rangers. Harry, who was an impressive figure standing six foot two, could only go on with his current job of catching cutthroats and stay on the lookout for any likely recruits should his California Rangers be ratified by the state.

Charley had just stepped off of the stage and was stretching his sore back as he heard a familiar voice. "Did you bring me any mail, Charley?" Byrnes asked.

"Who'd write to you?" the driver laughed. "Come on, I'm as dry as burned toast. You owe me a beer I'm sure of it."

The two entered the hotel from the side entrance to the post office.

"Let me throw some things in my room, then we can go." Charley ran up the stairs to his room; looking out the window, he noticed Harry Love, who was now sitting on the porch, reading a paper. Charley threw his duffel bag on the floor by the bed and then locked the door behind him and trotted down the stairs to meet Will. Charley could hear Joaquin's laugh in her head. She was still smitten with Byrnes, but so what? He didn't know, so what was the harm of spending time with him?

"Are you hungry? I could eat a bear!" Charley said as they walked through the lobby. "Harry?" Charley asked as they walked by a tall dark man standing by himself looking for a match to light his cigar. The driver pulled a Lucifer from his vest pocket and struck the match on a striker on a table, lighting the man's cheroot.

"Oh yes, Charley, the coachman," Harry responded. "Yes, thank you very kindly."

"This is my friend, William Byrnes," Charley introduced. "We were just leaving."

"Nice to meet you, Mr. Byrnes. Perhaps we shall meet again," Mr. Love replied.

"Indeed, sir," Will responded politely, as the two walked out to the sidewalk. "Where do you get the best grub in this two horse town. All I've been able to muster is shoe leather."

"I'll lead the way." Charley laughed as they made their way to Big John's tavern. "This man always serves the best steak, says he gets it from a man named Ben Holladay, says the man will make a name for his self. You wait and see!"

"Who? Big John or Ben Holladay?" Will asked.

"Oh, I mean Ben Holladay. Big John already is well known. Well, at least around here." Charley laughed as the two entered the bustling saloon.

The bar was full as usual, and the two scanned the room for a moment for a place to sit. At last a beautiful hostess approached the two, and Charley pressed a gold coin into her hand. She smiled ever so sweetly at Charley, then she caught a glimpse of Will, and she smiled even sweeter. In no time, the two were eating at a corner table.

"Will, you know who Tres Dedos is?" Charley asked as he finished his supper.

"What? Tres Dedos? Joaquin's cousin . . . Yes, I'm afraid I do, Charley."

"Aren't you afraid of him?"

Will who was more interested in the young hostess soon to be on his lap, responded in a light flip manner. "No, why should I be afraid of him. I've got nothing to fear from those folks, and neither do you. You should know that. You are practically part of the family, Charley," he said, pushing his plate away.

"No, I don't care what you say. That man is very sick in the head. My friend John told me what he did to the two men in Sonoma, and look at these news stories." Charley pulled several clipped columns of newsprint out of his pocket.

"You saved these?" Will asked. "Why?"

"Because I'm scared!" Charley insisted. The naive hostess had picked the wrong moment to drop back in on Will. She caught the last of the conversation and laughed as she settled into Will's lap.

"What the hell are you laughing at!" Charley snapped, clearly in no laughing mood.

"Charley! What is wrong with you?" Will burst in. "Whatever has happened to your manners, sir? Now you go along now." He soothed to the girl, pushing her up out of his lap. "I'll be along in a few minutes. Charley, now you should apologize to the lady."

"Yes, I'm sorry, gal. I'm just not myself today, forgive me." Charley groveled, not wishing to anger Will, but wanting to push her stupid sweet face in. "Tres Dedos has threatened to kill me," Charley confided after the woman left.

"You?" Will was puzzled.

"It's a long story, but I am seriously afraid of the man, and I'm sure he will bring no end of grief to Joaquin," Charley lamented.

"Yes, Joaquin, I'm afraid he has sealed his own fate now. I can see no turning back . . . Love has his name high on his list of desperate men to hunt. Don't be afraid, I'm sure that if there is one ounce of respect left in Joaquin, he will let nothing happen to his friend, Charley," Will whispered.

"Well, I'm still going to keep one eye open. You ain't been that convincing." Parkhurst laughed. "Now go and get your little filly, you horny bastard!"

Will smiled at his friend as he left the table.

"I couldn't help but hear you speak of Tres Dedos," a familiar voice from the table behind the wooden coat rack started. "Have you met the man, face-to-face?" Harry Love inquired.

"Yes, I'm afraid that I have," Charley said sadly.

"What does he look like?" the dark lawman inquired, settling into Will's vacated seat.

"Well, he is about five foot ten and has salt-and-peppery hair. His face has several scars, and his thumb and first finger of his right hand are missing. He has a mustache. That is all I remember," Charley added quickly, looking to see if anyone was watching. No one was.

"You seem kind of nervous, Charley," Love said.

"No, I'm just cold and tired. I think I'll head in," Charley said with conviction as he got up and walked back to his room.

Parkhurst had a hard time sleeping. Tres Dedo's evil laugh bounced off the inner recesses of her mind giving her fitful dreams.

The days ebbed and flowed; the bridges were rebuilt, and the roads cleared. Time again was passed jingling through the scenic hills of California. Charley pulled up to the final stage stop at the rapidly expanding tent town named Columbia and handed down the mail pouches as the passengers groaned and clambered down from the gritty lady of the road. It was a pleasant-enough trip, spring was definitely in the air, but yet the sky was beginning to look threatening. Thick dark clouds were beginning to pile up once again on the Sierra Mountains.

Charley had a big thirst to quench, then a nice, quiet evening. He had a newspaper tucked in his vest and intended to hide away in the livery after dinner for some peace and quiet. It was still early in the evening as the distant rolls of thunder were beginning to warm up. The coachman made his way to the newly built and christened What Cheer Saloon and was greeted with the usual enthusiasm. He handed the bartender a San Francisco newspaper as he seated himself at the bar.

"You always think of your friends, God love you!" Donna said, coming out from behind the bar to give Charley a smooch and a hug. She especially looked forward to her paper. God help the oaf who looked at it before she did. The teamster sat at the end of the bar and tried to eat his dinner and look at his own paper in peace, trying hard to shut out a particularly annoying drunk who very shortly would be resting on his face outside.

Charley noticed an extremely gruesome story about a family who's home had been set on fire. As each had run out of the burning building, each had been captured and had their throats cut and been left where they had died, outside the burned-out shell of a building, mother, father and children. An icy chill went down Charley's back as he tore the story from the paper and tucked it in his vest pocket, adding it to the growing collection of gruesome news articles. There was no doubt in his mind that it was the work of Tres Dedos.

Charley's mind wandered back to the night that she and Rollin Ridge had first met Joaquin and his gang.

The teamster jumped to attention as the annoying drunk was tossed out the bar door by the bartender's boyfriend, an ugly big, fat miner. Oh God, it was nice to be in such a reasonably safe place! Even so, Charley had an uneasy feeling in the pit of her stomach and looked for more light-hearted news, then decided to take comfort with Mozo back at the stable. Tomorrow was Sunday, Charley's day off. After sleeping in, he was looking forward to a good long gallop on Mozo to keep him in shape for the big race in Grass Valley. Charley got a bottle of brandy from Donna and said good night and took his paper down the street as the rain began to come down. All the while he had a funny feeling that someone was behind him. Tres Dedos was far away, she told herself.

When Charley got to the stable, he inspected the horses and found every thing in order, then sent the stable boy home. He poured a drink and inspected his precious Colt revolver before getting comfortable on the cot with the paper. The thunder was playing in the treetops, and the rain was sizzling on the tin roof. Charley often slept in the stable to avoid all the noise and riff-raff in the crowded hotels.

He was going to enter Mozo in a race next month and had him stabled in Columbia to train for it. The white horse was looking fit and feeling the oats that were being amply supplied.

Charley's blood ran cold when from the side barn door, a purring, gravely voice broke the monotony of the rain.

"Hello, Charley," the voice said. As Charley froze, his hand rested tightly on his gun. "Now is that any way to greet an old friend?"

"Friend?" Charley feared that her heart pounded audibly as she tried to smile. "What brings you here?" she whispered, taking her hand away from the revolver as she stood up and gazed at the man; he did not look like an outlaw. "Would you like a drink, Joaquin? I'm having one," she said, pouring a shot with shaking hands.

"Thank you. You are well liked in these parts. Everyone knows Charley Parkhurst, especially the children."

"Yes, I take good care of the young ones. I like to bring them things, candies and such," she said, handing him a glass with her trembling hand.

"I'll get to the point, Charley. I need a fast horse," he said, setting down the drained glass and looking directly into his friends' face.

"But you have so many horses, Joaquin!"

"Yes, but I cannot get to them. We were captured by the Tejon Indians; Chief Sepparatta had our horses taken from us. Gonzales, Feliz Reyes, and Rosita, all of our belongings, including our clothes, were taken. And then we were whipped. They set us free into the wilderness, bleeding and naked like babes to die in the woods," Joaquin spoke softly. "I got El Tigre back, but he's lame, I need Mozo." He paused to look at his beloved white horse. "I have a proposition for you," the outlaw said, looking sadly at his friend.

Charley's heart was pounding away, and her knees kept feeling all watery like a young calf as Joaquin fixed his gaze upon her. "Please help me, Charley," he purred, putting his hand on her shoulder.

"Just what is it that you propose?" Charley said, trying to maintain composure.

"I need a good horse, Charley," he said as he lifted his hand to Charley's weathered face and looked deeply into her eyes. Charley had all but forgotten what it was like to be female, but Joaquin knew how to talk to a woman.

"I always knew you'd take him back somehow," Charley rebelled, turning away.

"I now find that I have need of him." The handsome man turned and walked to the horse. "You are just mad that he likes me better!" Joaquin teased as he rubbed behind Mozos' ear.

"I never seen that stud take a liking to anyone but me before!" Charlie sighed.

"He has good taste, Charley. You have not listened to my proposition yet. I will give you one hundred dollars."

"He ain't fer sale!"

"Shh" Joaquin said, putting his fingers to Charley's lips. "You take the money and put it up for a reward o' your horse. I promise to bring him back when I can, but in case something happens to me, you'll get the animal back, just the same. I will take good care of him, I promise."

"You expect me to just give you my horse with my blessing!" Charley said with tears welling up. She was starting to see red, and Joaquin knew it! "Where is Tres Dedos?"

"I don't know, Los Angeles, I think. He's out of control." Murrieta frowned.

"Harry Love has been sniffing around here for him and you."

"I know, that is why I need the stallion," Joaquin reasoned.

"He'll get shot! Can't you take a different horse?"

"I said I'll take care of him!" Joaquin growled. Distant sadness and desperation clouded the piercing blue eyes. The thunder rolled over the roof.

"You're gonna take him anyway!" Charley snapped back. "Why don't you just take him and go!" she cried. Joaquin grabbed Charley's shoulders and looked at her weathered face; the tears were streaming down.

"I'm sorry, I need the fastest horse. I promise I'll bring him back. I must make this look convincing."

"What?" Charley asked as the lights went out.

"Thank you, Charley!" Joaquin cooed after he smacked her on the back of the head with his pistol, "Sleep well!" he said, kissing her forehead and laying her on the cot. He then took her gun as an afterthought.

Charley did not sleep well. Her head hurt, and there was something pressing on her chest. She heard the horses snorting and nickering as the rain pounded down on the tin roof in great quantities. Slowly she opened her eyes. It was her worst nightmare.

"You remember me?" the dirty grinning face was saying. "Maybe you remember this." Tres Dedos held up his mutilated knife-wielding hand. He was sitting astride the coach driver's chest, pinning his arms to his sides with his legs and had his unmutilated hand fast about the coachman's throat. "I am looking for Joaquin. Maybe you have seen him?" He sneered.

"Yes," Charley choked out. "He left."

"Oh, he left, did he? Well, maybe he is coming back?" Tres Dedos said, pushing the blade down on Charley's throat.

"No," Charley gasped as she began to shake uncontrollably. The blood pounding in her brain felt like it would explode. "He took my horse."

"You're trembling, Charley. Surely you're not afraid of you're old friend? We are old friends, aren't we? You wouldn't . . . say . . . give out a description of your friend Tres Dedos to the law, would you? No, I'm sure that's not true, eh, Charley?" The evil one laughed quietly.

"Please don't kill me!" she prayed, unable to move.

"No, I came for something else. Something that has been bothering me since we have known each other. You have been bothering my mind . . . Maybe I'm stupid, but I could not figure why Joaquin liked a gringo like you and defended you, even let him keep his favorite horse, until now. Hmm, very strange . . . but I think I finally figured it out. Ever since I had to give up that coach, I have really hated you . . . You a worthless, stupid gringo . . . I always felt that there was something funny about you, but I could not really know for sure till now. Why, he gave you back that coach." He climbed off the groggy prisoner, holding his neck securely with a hand full of hair that brought back chilling memories, dragging him to the stall vacated by Mozo. Charley was too terrified to fight and was becoming light-headed from the swelling knot on her head. Tres Dedos slammed Charley against the side of the stall, hitting her head again, knocking the victim out.

While Charley was unconscious, the madman tied his victim's hands to the bars at the top of the stall partition, with a neckerchief that was sliced into two. After Charley was secured, the killer again closed in on his quarry, grabbing the reviving prisoner by the face and pressed his grotesque knife to his victim's throat.

"Now let me see, where was I in my story? Oh yes, I remember now! One day, it came to me, you ain't no man! You ain't no man, you're a woman, that's why he spared your life and took an interest in you. He wouldn't have given a shit about you if you'd have been a man," Tres Dedos growled in his throat as he grabbed Charley's crotch and laughed hysterically as the rain pounded on the roof. He sliced the buttons off Charley's fine vest, practically foaming at the mouth as he tormented his captive. Sadistically he removed the camouflage one piece at a time.

Charley's head was spinning, her world was wobbling, and she was having her clothes sliced off by a madman, who was now one of three people in the world that knew she was a woman. "So you have come to collect for the coach?" she croaked.

"Well, yes, I suppose I am," Tres Dedos said, inspecting his goods.

"What about Joaquin? What will he think of this?" Charley said, grasping for straws.

"Well, at this point, I don't much care what that bastard thinks! I don't begrudge Joaquin his charm and persuasiveness, but he does tend to cross the line, occasionally! So you see, I take what I want, and Joaquin can go to hell!" Tres Dedos was relishing the fear that he was creating. Charley was trying to remain calm, but failing; she could see it was exciting the madman as he continued to cut off her clothes. Charley stared at him, her body trembling as if facing down an angry dog. At one point, Tres Dedos came across the news clippings in her inside vest pocket, of his own ghastly murders. He was deeply flattered and took it as a sign of admiration.

"You saved these? So you've been keepin' an eye on me, I am pleased. You can always tell my work, I am very thorough. Most would have left the young, but I say, why leave witnesses to suffer and then tell on you?" he snarled as he let the paper fall from his mangled hand to the ground. Kicking her feet apart as he ran his claw hand between her legs, Charley felt the sting of Tres Dedo's knife with the blood stains of uncounted dead on her throat. His heavy breathing on her neck made her flesh crawl. Charley also felt the breath of the horse in the next stall on her tied wrist and felt her kicking the stall partition that Charley was securely tied to, as the monster ripped at the tender flesh between her legs.

The rain beat down outside the barn in a torrent, making a deafening roar on the tin roof of the stable.

"Are you a virgin, Charley?" The demon laughed as he unbuttoned his leather pants and let free his enraged penis. He was pressing the blade to her throat and watching the blood trickle down her neck. "Or have you turned to men clothes for some shameful reason. Come now, it is the time to confess, for you will soon be meeting your maker," the madman was whispering into Charley's ear as he ran his knife blade softly over her exposed breast. Charley reminded herself of the wild horses being broke and tried to respond in the least resistant way to avoid suffering by the hands of the killer; she said the only thing that came to mind, other than the razor sharp knife on her body.

"I was raped when I was a child! That's why I dress like a man," she confessed.

"Well, isn't that a coincidence? You're being raped now!" Tres Dedos laughed as he scooped up her ass with his bloody claw and plunged himself deep inside.

The rain came down with a vengeance on the tin roof, with the power of a freight train. The horses were all nervous and calling, but the horse at the very end of the tie stall row was busy striking her stall with her front hoof as someone entered the barn.

"Gretal, quit that pounding, or I'll come down there and smack you!" the stable boy hollered as he entered the livery. "I thought Charley was in here, but I guess he went out. You want to go get a drink, Curly?" the boy asked his friend as the thunder played a roll over the clattering rain.

"Sure, I'll have just one," he responded politely as the pair turned and left.

Charley felt the breath of Tres Dedos on her neck and shoulders as he continued to gratify himself despite the intrusion. All the while, he kept his bloody knife next to Charley's throat, so tight that she dare not utter even the slightest squeak. The lightning crashed in horrifying blasts as the hopeless woman prepared to meet her maker, fearing the worse. By the looks of things, God was quite angry and hurtling his thunderbolts in preparation to sending one contrary woman to her ultimate doom, torture, and everything. She thought she had a pretty good idea of what hell was going to be like.

Charley felt strange, almost as if she was watching the terrible event from a distance as the horrible beast gratified himself with her body. At last, when the man finally released his spirit inside her, Charley prepared for her death. Her heart pounded in her chest, she thought it would surely explode and prayed to God for a miracle.

The madman was breathing hard and slowly wiping his blade over Charley's strong body as if still deciding how best to finish her off. In the dim flickering lamplight of the stable, the blood trickling down from the small nicks and cuts left a strange glistening pattern on her skin; the madman was transfixed by it. The tied victim hung from the bars as if crucified on a cross, her head hanging down in despair and shame, preying for mercy. Tres Dedos stepped back to admire the work of art he had created while he fastened the buttons of his greasy trousers. He began to laugh at her, with a low gravely rumble, the weather matching it with a low rolling thunder, followed by blue lightning that flashed through the barn window. The air was so charged that the hair on Charley's head began to rise with static electricity, giving her the appearance of a halo. A lightning bolt struck a tree very close by, accompanied by a deafening crash.

Tres Dedos stood mesmerized by the bound and bleeding body; it seemed to take on an unearthly look to it. The crazed man started to tremble and back away as if God almighty was reminding him of a time that would someday come for him.

As the blue white lightning flashed again though the window, lighting the naked, blood-soaked woman, the deranged murderer saw Jesus Christ on the cross instead. Trembling at this holy vision, he rubbed his eyes and shook his head to remove this apparition. It remained before him as the thunder ripped through the sky above. The killer's deeds lay before him in bloody paper clippings on the ground as a reminder of Judgment Day ahead. Then in horror of his own mortality and damnation, Tres Dedos ran from the stable to be free of this Holy Ghost.

Charley was stunned, her body shaking; she had truly witnessed a miracle. The devil had gone and left her alive!

The madman's blade left small cuts around her neck and torso, none were extremely deep, but her body was painted in blood as she hung in naked disbelief. She tried to free her hands, but they were tied fast. Without help, the woman would be discovered, and her life as a coachman would be over.

Charlie Parkhurst could sure use a trusted friend about then, and Gretal was as good as any. A small palomino with a luxuriant white forelock and sharp teeth had stopped pounding on the stall when Tres Dedos had gone, snorting her disapproval of the evil one. She sniffed her treat giver's hand and licked her fingers, smelling the neckerchief, but finding a treat was not there. It smelled good though, so she began to chew on the cloth that bound her friend to the stall bars.

"Good girl, Gretal. You've got an extra pound of grain if you get me loose before someone sees me, my sweet!" After a little encouragement, Charley had one hand free, shivering and bleeding as she struggled to untie the other, before the murderer regained his senses and came back to finish her off. Grabbing a duster that was hanging on a hook, she covered her nakedness. Charley got fresh clothes out of her duffel bag, then went to the best bathhouse in town and soaked in a private tub.

The hot water stung the cuts and turned the water pink but could not remove the filth from her skin or her mind. She sat in the bath and cried.

Charley realized that she was in no position to go out hunting for vengeance. The gangs were too plentiful, and traveling alone was dangerous, so Charley returned to the job of driving coach, ever vigilant for signs of her beloved horse. And ever weary of the news of Tres Dedos.

In Marysville, Charley again met up with her friend William Byrnes.

"I'm very glad to see you Will," Charley said sadly.

"You cut your hair. It looks real slick. You look tired, though," Will responded

"I'm not feelin' very well, but it's sure good to see you." Charley tried not to get upset. How much she really just wanted to let out her feelings and cry on Will's broad shoulders. "I've had a rough go really. Can we talk somewhere?" Charley asked, looking around for prying eyes.

"Come on . . . . What happened, Charley?" Will asked concerned, walking his friend up to his room.

"Tres Dedos, he found me . . . he . . . um . . ." Charley could not look his friend in the eye. After he closed the door, he took the scarf from his neck to reveal the cut marks. "He found me at the stable when I was alone, Will . . . the man . . . assaulted me." Charley could not keep the tears from coursing down his face. "He raped me, Will! I'm so ashamed . . . I can't talk about it . . . . I'm so afraid . . . Joaquin took Mozo and gave me money for the return . . . some sort of insurance plan. Then to make it look like an official robbery, he knocked me out. When I awoke, he was gone, and Tres Dedos was sitting on my chest, waving his machete, and cutting off my clothes."

"He cut off your clothes?" Will hesitated.

"I'm talking about a man that cuts children's throats! He found the newspaper clippings! That's probably what saved my life. He felt proud that I was an admirer!" Charley laughed in quite an insane way, wiping the tears from his sunburst face. "I truly felt like I have met the devil himself!" Charley looked hard at Will, who had turned away and was scratching his head. "I was looking for Joaquin, but I just gave up. Say, you wouldn't be interested in giving your friend another shooting lesson? Will, I'm so scared!" Charley rambled, sitting on the end of the small bed; he put his hand over his face and very quietly cried. Will put his hand on his friend's arm and then rose and poured him a drink.

"It's a miracle you're still alive . . . Try not to worry, Charley." Will smiled, trying to comfort his friend.

"Tres Dedos must be stopped!" Charley said softly.

"I'll talk to Joaquin, just stick to your routine and don't go off by yourself. Stay around lots of people, and I'll take care of Tres Dedos myself. I promise." William patted Charley on the shoulder in a brotherly way.

Charley realized that Will still didn't seem to know that she was a woman! Was she so well concealed that he still didn't know? Evidently not.

"Now here you are, wipe your face. I don't want anyone catching the Charley Parkhurst with a wet face. You just forget all about it," Will said, handing Charley his handkerchief. It was of fine linen. "Here now drink this. It will calm your nerves. Later we'll go down the street and get you one of those new Derringers. They're small, you can hide it your vest pocket!" Will said reassuring.

Will left Charley at the hotel among friends; with a wink, he was gone into the night. He found the Las Tres Pietras, Joaquin's usual meeting place, and rode around the rocky encampment, but there was no sign of life. He left a message for the bandit in a familiar hole and then tied a piece of blue fabric to a root, above the makeshift post office box as a flag.

Joaquin had rode Mozo hard, eager to catch up with his gang. They met in Los Angeles and soon conspired to do away with Harry Love's superior. Harry was deputy sheriff of Los Angeles, and his boss was Sheriff Wilson, who had hung a few of Joaquin's men and was causing trouble for the gangs.

Tres Dedos, who had arrived just after Joaquin, devised a plan to cause a distraction so that Joaquin could get close to Wilson and kill him easily. The plan worked brilliantly. Tres Dedos and Reyes acted as if about to kill each other, and when the crowd was all excited, Joaquin simply rode up and shot the sheriff in the head, informing him just before passing a bullet through his brain that his assassin was indeed Joaquin.

That assassination led to the need to do away with General Bean who was trying to stir up a posse and becoming particularly annoying. The gang got the upper hand, surrounding the general, who was skillfully deployed in grand style by Tres Dedos. Bean's stallion was seized by the bridle in such a way as to create great pain in the horse's mouth, causing him to rear. The general fell back and was caught around the neck by Tres Dedos and stabbed several times in the chest, then shot in the head twice by the same, to really finish the job. Joaquin was repulsed by the delight that the killer took in mutilating his victims, frequently cutting off heads or gouging out eyes. He was a butcher, never feeling the slightest twinge of guilt or pathos for his victims.

The gang soon got word of some wealthy miners, who had struck it rich and were heading back to their homeland, Australia. They would be passing down the sloughs to Stockton, then on to the sea. Joaquin, Tres Dedos, Claudio, and a few other men were hiding out in the rushes and tulles in wait for the treasure-laden skiff. Soon the sails became visible, and the mosquito-bitten bandits slunk into action. They paddled up to the schooner in the cover of night, then attacked the surprised sailors. The miners had their pistols drawn quickly and began firing back, but they were no match for the well armed, seasoned bandits; not one victim was left alive. The take of gold was close to twenty thousand dollars. Joaquin lit a fire on the deck of the small ship, and it glowed in the distance as the bandits made off into the night with their riches.

CHAPTER 19

Will finally received a reply from his message at post office rock.

A return message was left at the hotel for William Byrnes to meet at the blue tent outside of Hornitos.

"Harry Love is busy gathering recruits for his rangers. They mean to hunt you down," Will said bluntly, leaning in his saddle.

"Do you mean to join and hunt me down too, my friend?" Joaquin responded.

"Not you," Will answered.

"But you do mean to join?" Joaquin asked.

"Tres Dedos must be stopped," Will answered. "He nearly killed Charley . . . he is insane . . . Charley showed me all the news clippings of his murders, said it saved his life having them. Tres Dedos was flattered. Charley was shaking and scared. I've never seen a man so frightened."

"Charley is a brave man." Joaquin smiled sadly to himself. "How much is Captain Harry Love paying these days to be a California Ranger?"

"Love has been petitioning the governor for one hundred and fifty dollars a month for a squadron of twenty men. I was told that there would be a thousand dollars split between the men for the capture of the leader of theses crime sprees, dead or alive," Will explained.

"Do they have any names or descriptions?" Joaquin asked.

Charley gave him Tres Dedos description and told him that he stole Mozo, who I see is doing well." The white horse was busy pawing the ground.

"Charley talked to Love about Tres Dedos?" Joaquin was quiet and very introspect; he was tired of all the bloodshed. Tres Dedos would have to be dealt with. After a long pause, he spoke, "I will pay you five thousand dollars to kill him, but I want you to join Harry Love's company to do it."

"But I don't understand. I don't need those assholes!" Will replied, very insulted.

"I know that you don't, but I want you with them so I have a spy to keep them off of me!" Joaquin explained. His face told of a plan formulating in his mind.

"Oh, I see," Will replied.

"I will feed you information. You can keep me posted about their plans. Then when you kill Tres Dedos, you announce that you have the ring leader, and they will quit looking for me!" Joaquin felt fairly confident that his plan would work. He had spies in most towns that he trusted to carry messages, most which hated Tres Dedos. It was worth a try to be rid of the devil, once and for all. Especially since he was now in the habit of putting Joaquin's name on some of his most hideous crimes.

Joaquin was amused that apparently Will still did not know Charley's true sex, especially since she was so smitten with him, but that was her business. "Go on, muchacho, don't look so worried. It will work. Tell Charley not to be afraid. I will meet you at post office rock next Friday. We will exchange information then. Be careful, my friend."

Will rode back to the same hotel that Charley roomed in and knocked on the door. "It's me, Charley. It's Brynes," he called in a loud whisper.

"Come in. Did you find him?" Charley asked, opening the door.

"Yes, we talked. He wants me to join Harry Love."

"What? He wants you to join the Rangers? That don't make any sense," Charley questioned.

"Yes, he wants me on the inside, and he will help me to assassinate Tres Dedos. Says it would be unfamily like for him to do it. They are cousins, and the family doesn't approve of killing their own. So I will do it, then claim him as Joaquin the ringleader. They will quit looking for the real Joaquin. I will kill Tres Dedos, I promise," William Byrne said quietly. "Speaking of horses, Mozo sends his love. Come on, let's get some coffee downstairs," he added.

"You saw him?" Charley almost forgot herself and hugged Will.

"Yeah, he looks fine!"

"Why didn't you bring him back?"

"Murrieta was still using him."

The two had breakfast, and Charley drove away on the early stage.

Harry Love was in town again, he and Will had a chat on the porch as the dust cleared. With them sat a small group of men, new recruits, William Byrnes surmised, all fine specimens, many over six foot tall. Byrnes, who was six foot two himself, found it unusual to see more than one man as tall or taller than he. Harry Love presided over the men; he was a natural leader. The younger men such as Evans and Ashmore and Black looked up to Harry as he told stories of his adventures as a Texas Ranger. They were his new army and were formulating plans to rid the hills of Mexican cutthroats.

Will pondered getting involved; he hated to participate in group hunts, and he much preferred to operate as a panther on his own.

"So, Mr. Byrnes, what brings you to California?" Love asked.

"I have been recuperating from a wound inflicted by a scoundrel, sir," Will retorted.

"I am looking for some men to make up a company of Rangers," Harry petitioned.

"Who are you hunting down? If I may inquire?" Will asked.

"I have partitioned Governor Bigler to hire a company of California Rangers to capture the Mexican bandits in these hills. There are a number of warrants sworn out on the three Joaquins—Murrietta, Valenzuela, and Carrillo. If we break up the gang, we collect, and then we can write our own ticket politically. We'll be heroes," Love boasted.

"I happen to have been an acquaintance of Joaquin Murrietta. I met him when I was captured by the Mexican army and imprisoned at Sonora, Mexico, back several years ago. He worked at the prison there, taught me to speak Mexican."

Will and Harry became friends and comrades, along with a bright young man named Connor, whom Love intended to make lieutenant; he was keen of wit and very perceptive.

Byrnes was soon offered the position of acting lieutenant after regaling Harry with stories of himself and Joaquin, the dreaded bandit. Harry was thrilled to have an ex-partner of his prey on his team.

Byrnes felt like a heel for it even though it was Joaquin's own idea. He confessed to Charley when he saw him next.

"I don't understand, how can you be helping Joaquin this way?" Charley asked.

"We leave messages for each other through his family and friends. We have signals. It's best that you don't know."

"But I think that I should know!" Charley complained.

"All right, this is a sign." William put his thumb and little finger together and spread the remaining fingers. Then put the remaining fingers, the index and fourth fingers, on the cheekbones and the middle finger on the bridge of the nose. "This means Las Tres Peitres, the three rocks. Are you happy now?" Will snapped sarcastically.

"You don't have to get snippy, Will," Charley chided.

"Snippy? What the fuck is that? I'm gonna have a drink, then hit the hay, and if you're not careful, I will introduce you to the rest of the company," Will warned playfully as they walked down the planked sidewalk.

Byrnes had heard about an independent group of miners getting up a hunting party, and he sent out messengers to the ranchos that he knew Joaquin was affiliated. About a week later, one of the messengers came back sporting a new saddle and boots and handed Will a leather pouch full of gold.

"From Joaquin." The boy smiled as he tossed down the pouch and wheeled his horse away. Evidently Joaquin takes care of his confederates, Byrnes thought to himself.

It was going to be more and more difficult to get messages through as Harry Love was getting more recruits to join the California Rangers, and it looked like the state was going to fund the project. It was almost funny though. Byrnes was making much more money from Joaquin for spying, than they were going to pay the entire company of Rangers.

All Charley could do was wait and keep on driving the stagecoach. There were mornings that he just seemed so mad at the world and sick to his stomach that he found himself vomiting behind the barn. His clothes didn't fit well either.

"God, I'm so hungry. I could eat that old mule you keep tethered behind the barn, Jake! Hello there, Harry!" Charley remarked as he came in from the cold night air.

"You starting to look like you did eat him, Charley!" Harry Love remarked back.

"Yeah, I guess I put on a few pounds. How goes the fight against crime?"

"Very good, the governor has given the California Rangers to legislature, and he is confident of their approval. The Rangers shall be official in May if all goes well. Meanwhile, myself and the other lawmen in these parts are doing everything we can to make the roads safe to travel," Harry Love preached like a true politician.

"Well, good luck," Charley replied.

It was raining hard in Marysville on April 1, 1853, as Charley arrived at his friend Rollin Ridge's small home, near the edge of town. John was standing on the front porch of his house lighting his pipe as Charley waddled up.

"Charley!" John called. "Nice to see you, have a smoke." The two sat on the porch together.

"I don't know what it is, but I can't stomach my cigars lately. I been throwing up."

"You've put on some weight too. Maybe you're pregnant, Charley," Ridge laughed at his joke.

"What?" The thought hadn't occurred to her. John was staring at her, with laughter in his face. The cold, hard panic that it caused left his friend scratching his head.

"Who's the father?" John finally asked. Charley was in shock and couldn't say anything as wave after wave of nausea swept over, until she got up and puked on the heirloom rose, the rain mercifully washing the mess off the new buds.

"Tres Dedos . . . What am I gonna do?" Charley choked out. John handed his friend his handkerchief.

"Want some water? Might help settle your stomach," he offered, not knowing what else to say and saddened by the sight of his friend in such a predicament.

"I guess I thought I was too old to get pregnant. I didn't even figure on this!" Charley said, getting her bearings. "I think I'm about forty!"

"My God, you're lucky to be alive!" John offered.

"It was a very ugly thing," Charley said, quietly gritting her teeth. "So I haven't been getting a lot of sleep, lately. I thought I was getting the flu. This is just icing on the cake, now I carry the bastard devil's own offspring."

"But it is also half you, Charley, and that is surely good!" John tried to shine a ray of hope.

"Well, then you raise the bloody bastard!" Charley sobbed. "But don't ever tell it who his father is!"

"I'll have Beth ask around if any of the folks here are looking to adopt a child if you like," John comforted. "But you should take her into your confidence. You're gonna need some help when the time comes."

"John, you're my friend, I trust you," Charley resigned.

"Let's see if Beth's pie is cooled down enough to eat," John responded. It was, and the two's spirits picked up measurably. As Charley departed, John mentioned that he would explain matters to his wife. Charley agreed. Beth was a lovely young woman with a sweet smile and soft eyes that could melt your heart.

The swelling driver read the news every evening for clues as to the whereabouts of Tres Dedos and was shaken almost daily by some gruesome murder. The gangs were preying heavily in the Calaveras county, keeping the law there running in circles.

Finally on May 17, the State of California stepped in. Captain Harry Love assembled his men at the Orleans Hotel in Sacramento and gathered them at the bar.

"Well, boys, it's official! I've just met with the governor. He agreed to pay each Ranger one hundred and fifty dollars a month. But we only got three months to catch these bastards if we want to get the money!" Love said to his men. "These bandits that we're after are the worst sort, real butchers. So if any one of you wants to back out, do it now."

The men just looked at each other and laughed.

"Good! Now the state isn't gonna pay for any of our guns or horses. That is your responsibility. You can draw against what the state is paying if you need to. I want each man armed to the teeth," Love ordered. "Rifles, shotguns, and at least two pistols each. It's gonna be war, boys! Bartender, a drink for my men. Get your gear ready, and we will assemble in the lobby at six tomorrow morning. Try and get some rest tonight. You're gonna need it," Love said, raising his glass and downing his drink. The men were a rough-looking lot, mostly young and spirited, some older and experienced in hunting and tracking. They had a formidable task ahead of them.

Harry liked to work the men in teams or squadrons, and they were kept busy running through the foothills asking questions, hunting down resources for ammunition and food and following the trail of blood left by Tres Dedos. The bandits were bold and fearless and fast; the Rangers were always just a bit too slow to catch up to them.

The pressure of the Rangers pursuit was causing fear and strained relations between the outlaws. Most of the gang had begun making arrangements to drive a large herd of stolen horses to Mexico and retire, but not Tres Dedos, who still had bigger treasures to reap. He had plans to rob several more locations before he retired and got fat, having designs on several places in Los Angeles and Monterey.

Joaquin just humored him and carefully planned out the final steps in finishing off this demented monster. He wrote out a letter, in code, to William Byrne. Murrieta addressed it to his sister in case his brother-in-law, Jesus Feliz, who was to deliver it, should be caught, thus not blowing Byrne's cover. The letter contained information about the next meeting place and the plans of his cousin.

The Rangers had been roaming the countryside for two months, with nothing to show for it. They had only one month left to collect on the contract and were tired and discouraged; their horses were jaded and foot sore. The bandits' horses always seemed fresh and fast.

Jesus Feliz was headed to Monterey with the letter and a real message for Joaquin's sister, then on to Nile's Canyon to inform Rosita of the new plans. She was to take a ship to Mexico and meet Joaquin there, in due time. Feliz stopped in San Juan Bautista to deliver the fake letter to Byrnes. Whether from fear or carelessness, his timing was bad. He was recognized by a Ranger as a member of the outlaw gang.

"My name is Jesus Feliz. I am the brother-in-law of Joaquin Murrieta, the man you are lookin' for!" He proudly confessed. "I take you to where you call his hideout. You never catch him. It's too late to find Joaquin. He and his men leave for Mexico."

"Leave that to me. Lead me to the hideout, and I'll let you go free," Love instructed.

"Senior Captain Love, Joaquin's friends live close to that place. It's not safe for me to be seen with you."

"Don't worry, we'll keep you undercover, just point out the place, and we'll let you go on your way." Harry Love was chomping on the bit as he wrote out a quick note to the governor about Jesus, and the nature of his next step. The men were ordered to make ready their provisions and give full-grain rations to their tired horses. As soon as they had all eaten, they would go off after the bandits, following their new informants' instructions.

Jesus took the longest possible route to the Arroyo Cantua. It was a concealed valley with a very nice water source, a flowing spring that broadened out to a nice brook. The bandits had corrals for branding and breaking horses and beautiful meadows full of good grazing. There was a stone rancho in the middle; next to the house was a large barn and more corrals. The bandits kept their saddled horses close at all times, and all were always heavily armed. Their saddles had a specially made holster, which fit over the saddle horn, it contained two guns, usually Navy Colts, that fit barrels down, one on each side of the saddle horn, next to four fully loaded cylinders for each of the two guns. Many carried Colt Walkers, manufactured in '47. The bandits, wearing two guns on their body and two more at easy access on the saddle horn and eight more loaded cylinders at the ready, gave each bandit seventy-two shots. This made an organized gang, a formidable adversary.

The summer morning was beautiful, it was not yet dry and dusty, and the sweet morning dew was still lying over the hills in a fog. Jesus Feliz took the Rangers to the arroyo in the most tedious way that he could think of. The captain was riding him like a vaquero on a four-year-old stallion, ever vigilant. At last the group of men were close. Harry Love splintered his army into two groups as they drew near. As Jesus and Captain Love crested the hill, the captive let out an audible sigh, "Shit!"

"What?" Harry questioned, looking down into the business below them. "Oh, shit!" he said as he backed his horse down the other side of the hill. It was too late, though, the guard had already spotted them, and had sent down a warning to the officers of the gangs.

At this time, Harry Love released Jesus Feliz, who skinned out for home immediately.

The Rangers knew it was the confrontation that they had waited for. As he looked down, he and Lieutenant Byrne counted approximately seventy men working approximately five hundred horses; they were in the process of branding and trimming the feet, all things in preparation for a long trip south.

Harry knew that he had been found out when he saw the scout go to the chiefs. He had to design a plan. Losing the element of surprise, he might still be able to bluff. If he kept a bold front, they might not know that he couldn't back it up, so he rode in.

He assembled half of his troops; the others had been sent out to flank and were out of communication. They had no way of knowing what was going on. Captain Love's company, consisting of Lieutenant William Brynes, the Terrible Sailor Norton, Lafayette Black, and six other Rangers rode into the stronghold of the most feared gangs of cutthroats that any one has ever conceived of.

The very fact that William Byrnes took the front line as they rode in proved to Harry Love that Byrnes was indeed a brave man. To Joaquin, it proved that Will was in control of the situation. Several of Joaquin's compatriots were obviously nervous and confused at the sight of Will and Joaquin seemingly on different sides. He silenced them in Spanish and went on with the business at hand.

"What is it that you want?" Joaquin snapped at Harry Love.

"We have been sent by the governor of this state to record the names of the mustagers in these ranges. We are the California Rangers," Harry Love said with pride. He motioned to Lafayette Black who jumped off his horse and made ready with a pen and paper to take down names and notes at the every whim of Captain Love.

Joaquin played a cool hand, with his partner Will, to guide him in the Captain's weaknesses.

The two worked the Captain in an unfair manner, and in the end, Will knew that the end was near for Tres Dedos, who was on the hillside, on his way down to the rancho. Love had no advantage; he tried to just roll with the punches. Harry did his best to have the roster of horse wranglers recorded for the state recorder's office; it was an impressive list of fake names and aliases. Several privates were scared into moistening their britches.

After about two hours, the names were recorded, and many suspicious horses were removed from the gang's possession. Harry Love successfully cleared his men out, staying about five or six miles away from the huge gang. Privates were dispatched to spy on the bandits, but most were too scared to get very far from the home base.

The bandits were totally confused and panicked by the bold move of Harry Love, quarrels ensued, and many figured that the army was soon to descend on them. Most not realizing that the force was only twenty strong. Joaquin ordered the horses rounded up, and men were told to begin taking the herd to Rancho Berrunga in Sonora, Mexico. He himself had to go back to Las Tres Pietras first, but would stay with the herd until they got to the mouth of the Tejon Pass.

Tres Dedos argued that he had still more mayhem to commit before he retired. While the men argued, approximately fifty horses bolted and ran off. It was decided to leave without the missing horses, and the bandits left the site of the Love encounter after two hot-tempered days.

Finally, Lieutenant Connor rode in with the news that the Mexicans had disappeared, and the Rangers moved out after the gangs. Arriving back at the site of the brandings, they found their trail and took off after them. Meanwhile, Connor was instructed to take several men and return the seized horses to Quartzburg.

Murrieta left the gang heading to Mexico and rode north, with Joaquin Carrillo, to his hideout at post office rock. Before he left, he ordered Joaquin Valenzuela to take some men and get the fifty horses left behind. Tres Dedos and his gang also abandoned the herd, leaving Ramon Soto in charge of taking the horses to Mexico.

Following the trail of the herd, the Rangers came across evidence of several departing tracks, the main herd was heading south, but a large party split off, going another direction. Another much smaller party was going another direction and still one more small party headed on a different route. Harry Love, perhaps with Will's advice, agreed to go after one of the smaller sets of tracks. They were headed back to the site of the first encounter.

The country was mostly rolling plains, with scrubby oak trees for cover, but the hills were like a golden blanket that had been spread out then bunched up. The valleys had cover of bay trees, with their aromatic leaves and valley oaks with buckeye trees that sprouted next to seasonal creeks.

The Arroyo Cantua Creek was nothing more than a trickle in the summer, but there was a spring that formed a pool at the head of the Arroyo. In the winter the water rushed fast and furiously and had cut deep walls in the soft, sandy soil, about eight or ten feet high in some places. The springs were a common camping site for travelers. Not far from the springs, the creek banks had been worn down from wagon travel; the road was known as El Camino Viejo. This crossing of the Arroyo Cantua had been used by ox carts, for more than fifty years.

As they approached the road in the dawn's first light, Harry Love spotted smoke coming from the creek bed. The company stopped and divided into two groups, one headed by Captain Love and one by Lieutenant Byrnes. The idea was to surround the men before any attack.

It was just before this time that Joaquin Valenzuela also noticed the smoke, for he and his men were busy running through the hills in search of the missing horses. He went in to find Tres Dedos cooking his breakfast. Chappo, who had ridden with Valenzuela, had found El Tigre, who had been among the fifty that bolted and stayed by the water to wash out a wound the striped buckskin horse had received. The stallion had only a rope around his neck that Chappo tied to a stake in the ground. While tending to the injured horse, he listened to Valenzuela and Tres Dedos argue, as Harry Love unexpectedly strode into the camp, with guns drawn.

At the same time, Byrne's squad approached the other end of canyon.

"Drop your guns, boys," Will spoke softly, punctuating it with a click of the hammer. The two Mexicans were hopelessly surrounded.

The bandit guards, Antone Lopes and Jose Ochovo, had their hands tied and were walked quietly toward the campfire to join the other Rangers.

Meanwhile, Captain Love began to interrogate the Mexicans at the fire, noting that one man had only the last three fingers on one hand.

"Stay with these men," Love ordered his Rangers. He rode up to the man washing the buckskin horse, as he did the Rangers positioned themselves in the camp, guns drawn.

"What are you doing here?" Harry Love demanded of the shaking Chappo.

"We are just chasing mustangs."

"No! We are going to Los Angeles," Tres Dedos spoke up. "Sir, If you have any questions, please address them to me. I am the leader here," he growled.

"I will address myself to whoever I please without consulting you!" Captain Love snapped back.

Lieutenant Byrnes, who had dismounted, was approaching the scene with the captured guards. Tres Dedos used the distraction to reach for his gun and fired at Love. He succeeded in shooting off a lock of hair by Harry's face, leaving him otherwise unharmed. The shot distracted Love long enough for Chappo to pull out the stake and coil a loop around El Tigre's nose. He then leapt on the stallion's back and made a run for it. Byrnes, spotting El Tigre, called out to the men.

"We've got him. That's Joaquin's horse!" Will shouted in the confusion, bullets flying. Henderson and White took off after Chappo as Byrnes came to the aid of Captain Love. Tres Dedos tried to run also but was shot nine times, the last shot by William Byrnes.

"This is for Charley, you bastard!" Byrnes whispered to the seriously wounded Tres Dedos as he pulled the trigger. The bullet exploded through the madman's head, shattering his scull in the back.

El Tigre was giving his caretaker the last of his strength, as he charged up the bank of the river. The going was rough, and the cover poor, so the frighten man galloped the brave horse off the side of the ten foot bank, to the dry riverbed below. The horse flipped in the air, and landed badly, with Chappo landing away from the rolling animal. As the horse came to his feet, the Indian jumped on its back, and made off down the dry riverbed. Henderson was in hot pursuit, as the other men ran around to head the bandit off, further down the bed. Henderson tried the same jump from the cliff, and landed in the same manner, his recovery was not as swift as the young Indians, so when back in pursuit, he aimed his rifle at the running horse and hit Chappo in the small of the back. White, rode up, also fired, hitting Chappo in the back again. Another shot shattered the hand holding onto the mane, which caused Chappo to fall from El Tigre. He tried to escape the Rangers, now arriving in an exited state, who continued to fire at the dying man, until he cried out, "Don't shoot anymore. Your work is done."

When the shooting stopped, the dead totaled eight men. None of the Rangers had been killed and there were two prisoners, Antone Lopes and Jose Ochovo.

"We need to have evidence of this battle," Harry Love told Byrnes. The other Rangers were busy scavenging through the dead men's possessions, looking for gold. Will was staring down at the dead face of Tres Dedos.

"Who do I have here?" White asked riding up, with the body of the Indian, who had bravely tried to escape.

"That was Joaquin Murrieta," Will pronounced, pulling Chappos' hair up to look at his face.

"And who is that? White asked, looking at the mutilated hand of the other deceased, laying before him.

"Tres Dedos," Will said solemnly.

"That means three fingers don't it?" White said laughing.

"Yeah," Will said as he pulled out Tres Dedos homemade Machete that the butcher always kept in a sheath on his boot. Will lay the mutilated hand out on a rock and hacked it off in one powerful, deliberate chop, wincing at the sound of crunching bone. "There, will that serve as evidence?" he asked, holding up the bloody mutilated hand. The three fingers of the severed hand curled up involuntarily.

"No, take his head off too," Love said coldly, lighting a cigar. "That man, the one you brought in, Joaquin." He motioned to the body of the young, Indian who had rode so bravely. "Take his head off as well."

The men were all silent, never had they witnessed such gore as a beheading. The repulsion caused most to turn away and vomit.

Byrnes was in a semi-crazed mood as he hacked off the head of the madman, pieces of broken scull and brain falling here and there. Blood flowed out in a great flood that soaked Byrnes legs. The head did not give up easily. The face seemed to twitch with life as he cut. At last when the head was free of the torso, he held it in front of the bound Antone, blood streaming out the neck and screamed at him like a madman.

"Tell what you know and say your prayers!" To which the prisoner replied.

"Cut away, I'll not tell!"

Will tossed the bloody head down on the grass next to Love, then set off to remove the head of Chappo. He threw the man's body from the horse, and chopped off his head with ferocity, again splashing blood on all who had crept close to view the spectacle.

Love smiled as he smoked his cigar, admiring his trophies. Will waded into the water to rinse the blood from himself. He felt sick to his stomach and waded to shore and vomited. He stood staring at Tres Dedos horse then took the saddle holster from it and put it on his own saddle. No one dared question it, as his face still held the expression of a demented, savage warrior.

The heads and hand were wrapped in cloth and willow boughs, to insulate them from the summer heat. Large cans had been brought containing alcohol, but after almost three months on the trail, the alcohol had either dried up or was drunk. Captain Love gave instructions that the trophies were to be brought to Fort Miller to be placed in alcohol. Byrnes and Sylvester had the gruesome assignment.

The day was warming up to a scorcher that would reach well over 100 degrees. Byrnes also had the two prisoners, Jose, and Antone, to be taken to the fort as well. The rest of the Rangers went in search of other desperadoes, and stolen horses.

The trail was hot and dry for the weary Byrnes, on either side of him hanging from his saddle, were the gory remains of a very violent morning. His stomach was both nauseated and hungry, and his head swam with the hotness of the afternoon sun. He pictured the maniac's face in the evil grimace as the final bullet tore through its forehead. It felt almost as if Tres Dedos was reaching out from the grave, as Will saw the head in the bag bouncing on the saddle, in his own mind it was laughing and moving inside its shroud, he couldn't wait to be rid of it.

When they got to the Tulare Slough, the water felt very refreshing, and welcome, but as they rode to the other side, Antone Lopez' horse stumbled in some roots and fell. Antones' feet were tied under the horse's belly, causing him to be crushed by the floundering horse, and drown. The remaining man was taken to the fort, to be delivered to the civil authorities in Martinez. Later he was mysteriously lynched by a group of Mexicans, who perhaps feared he would say too much.

After reaching Fort Miller, and finding only cheap watered down whiskey, Byrnes decided that the head of Tres Dedos was not keeping well, and buried it at the fort. It repulsed him, for it seemed to have an evil presence still left in it. Forever after, he would have nightmares of that head.

For decades to follow, the remaining head of Chappo, and the mutilated hand of Tres Dedos would tour on exhibit, beginning on August 12, 1853, only 18 days after the battle. They would have an extended stay at Jordan's Museum of Curiosities, in San Francisco, until the great city would buckle at the knees in the great earthquake of 1906.

Will left the grotesque trophies with Connor and Henderson and White, and headed back to Stockton. At least that's what he told his subordinates, instead, he headed back to Post Office Rock.

On the way, he exchanged his mount for a fresh one at the livery, as Charley's stagecoach pulled up to the depot steps.

"My God! That you Will?" Charley called.

"Hey, Charley, right on time as usual. I was just gonna have one for the road, and head for the hills, have one with me!" The Ranger called to his friend.

"I'll be right there, let me get the horses unhitched," Charley called back. After that, the two friends walked to the tavern.

"I'm headed back out tonight," Will explained. "Have you heard about the trophies?"

"No. What trophies?" Charley asked.

"Really? I thought that it would be all over town by now, Charley. My faith in you is shaken. Harry insisted from the start that we have some tangible proof of our work. So he ordered that we cut off their heads."

"Whose heads did you cut off?" an incredulous Charley asked.

"I cut off Tres Dedos hand and head—"

"You cut off?" Charley was staring at her friend.

"I did it with pleasure!" Will confided. "Then Harry picked out Chappo as the other head," he whispered.

"Who else was killed?" Charley pressed.

"Murrieta was not there," Will continued barely audibly. "Valenzuela, Gonzales, some of Tres Dedos men. We took two alive but lost one in the river.

"Your contract is just about up, ain't it? You gonna do another tour of duty?" Charley questioned.

"No, I think that I'm through with this running up and down the countryside looking for desperate characters," Will sighed, pouring another shot.

"Good!" Charley toasted his friend.

Later Will set out for the rock fortress. There was no one there, but evidence proved that there had been campers not long before. He searched the unusual formation for the correct cubbyhole and removed the camouflage rock. There was a letter and a pouch full of gold and a note. "Collect Charley's horse at my rancho." The letter also thanked him for his friendship. Will lit the letter with his cigar and watched it burn as he stuffed the gold-filled pouch in his saddlebag. It was about five thousand dollars. "It seems that I was working for the right man, after all." He laughed as he rode north.

"It's Will!" Rosita called to Carrillo; she was sitting on a rocker on her porch. Carrillo was loading a rifle in anticipation of trouble. He walked out on the porch, rifle in hand.

"You've come for the horse?" Carrillo asked.

"Yes, where is Murrieta?" Will asked, then regretted asking, noticing the black trappings of a new widow. Rositas' eyes were shiny with tears.

"Joaquin and I left Las Tres Pietras and headed to Monterey to see his sister before coming here. We ran into some soldiers near the Pajjaro River and exchanged gunfire. We were riding into a gully when Joaquin took a shot from above. The bullet passed through him and his horse. It killed the horse instantly, went right through his heart. I picked up Joaquin, and we made our escape. Outriding the stupid gringo soldiers." Carrillo was looking at the ranger and spitting at a spider." Finally, we arrived here. Joaquin lived only a short time longer. We buried him yesterday, in the house. His death is to be a secret, but I know you were his partner. That was what he wanted. You understand?" Carrillo threatened.

"Yes, you know I was his friend," Will said, looking at the grieving Rosita. He took her hand in his. "I'm so sorry, gal. Really I am." He was looking into her sad eyes as he kissed her delicate hand.

"Here, have a drink!" Carrillo said, handing the gringo a glass. Will held the glass as it was filled. "To Murrieta!" Carrillo toasted.

It was only a day later that Charley received a message from the sheriff of Pajjaro seemed like someone may have found his missing horse. Charley was elated, even jubilant. Especially after all of the nausea and shock of her condition. At last, some good news. Charley cornered a driver that owed him money and talked him into covering his route for a few days. When the driving responsibility was arranged for, Charley was off to collect his beloved stallion, Mozo. He rented a horse and was down the road. It was a three-day ride. At last, the sheriff at the Pajjaro station greeted Charley.

"Yes, I think we have found your horse. I try to keep up on the stolen animals 'round here. I can take you right to him. He's this way." The small man went out back and got his horse as Charley trotted behind.

"Where is he?" Charley called out.

"Oh, he's back here," the odd sheriff called out. "There," he said, pointing. There was a great heap on the ground, near the river, with a large canvas covering it. The edges were held down with big stones. I'm glad that you got here quick 'cause I was having trouble keeping the bears off him. He's gettin mighty rank. I had a couple of boys and their dogs on it last night. They bagged a bull grizzly and a coyote." The man was hastily tossing the rocks off the canvassed carcass, awaiting the correct reaction and the thoughts of a reward while Charley stood in horror. At last, the canvass was free, and the miserable little man flung back the cloth with glee.

"Oh no," Charley moaned as he sunk to his knees. "Oh no. I'm so sorry. My God, I'm so sorry, my friend."

Mozo had been killed by a bullet that passed through the rider and the saddle that exited between his front legs, piercing his heart. The saddle was still on the animal, but it was covered with blood that was not the horses'. Joaquin had been hit very badly from the looks of it.

"The man ridin' him escaped with a friend, who pulled him up behind him on his own horse," the queer little sheriff stated. "The soldiers wanted to talk to them when they bolted, and the soldiers gave chase, then they yelled halt, but the men kept a ridin'. The soldiers started shootin' and the one man falls off a his horse, and the other feller rides up and grabs him, and they get away."

"They got away?" Charley looked up, shocked, tears still flowing down leather cheeks.

"Yeah, so I looked in my files, and I discovered the description of your missing horse, and here you are!" The sheriff smiled. Charley wanted to punch this little weasel right in the nose.

"Why didn't you tell me he was dead!" Charley growled.

"I was afraid you wouldn't come!" the weasel explained. "I still get the reward, don't I?" he said as Charley punched his lights out.

"I want a decent burial for the animal. I'm gonna stay here till it's done," Charley said, throwing the money on the weasels chest. It succeeded to revive him enough to snap into action, like this sort of thing happened all the time.

"There'll be an additional fee of five dollars for hitting an officer of the law."

"Here!" Charley tossed the chiseler a gold coin. "It was worth it!"

Charley stabled her rented mount and walked into the small town. There was a general store and a tavern at one end of town, and Charley felt in need of some sort of refreshment. Upon entering the store, he spotted some beautiful muslin baby garments and paused to look at them. A young woman came to his side and asked if she could help him find anything, as Charley gazed at the baby fineries.

"Yes, I'd like to get these." Charley motioned to a beautiful red satin baby gown and bonnet.

"Would you like me to wrap them?" she asked.

"Please." Charley was in such an emotional state; he could hardly bare it. He took the package and entered the tavern, walking to the bar. "I'll just have a cup of coffee if you don't mind, lots of cream, please," Charley said politely, looking around the room; the driver then sat at a small table in the corner and wept quietly over the loss of her beloved horse and the thought of having a baby. She figured it must be due in December some time. She sat drinking the coffee staring out the window trying to imagine what it would be like to be a mother.

CHAPTER 20

Upon arriving back in Stockton, Charley was shocked to hear that Byrnes had been shot twice while coming to the aid of a stage-line proprietor. He was presently residing in the new hospital. Charley wasn't feeling well and thought a trip to the medicine counter might not be a bad idea.

"I'm hear to see William Byrnes, Mme. Nurse, please."

"Well, I don't think he's even awake. He's had sedation," the nurse informed Charley.

"Charley! Come in, it's all right, Nurse, I'm awake," a familiar voice called out from behind a curtain.

"Well, don't talk too long. He needs his rest," the nurse cautioned.

"I heard that you got word of your horse!" Will whispered, as Charlie dragged a chair near the bed.

"He was dead, Will," Charley whispered back. "His saddle was soaked with a man's blood as well. Oh, I'm sorry, really. I shouldn't be tellin' you all this, you bein all shot up, and all," the coachman sighed, his eyelids fluttered and closed; the lights faded to black.

"Charley, you look worse than I do!" Will called to the nurse as Charley slipped from the chair onto the floor. The nurse called for help, and they hauled the new patient away on a stretcher to a vacant bed down the hall.

"I'm sorry, ma'am, you've lost your baby," a soft, sweet voice was saying, when Charley's eyelids opened.

"What? Are you talking to me?" Charley was in some dream place she had never been before. There were white sheets covering her and a beautiful woman holding her hand saying, "I'm sorry, you lost your baby. You will stay and rest for a while. Do you want me to tell your friend?"

"Friend?" Charley said in her sleep.

"Yes, Ranger Byrnes?" the nurse was cutting through the fog.

"Oh no!" Charley screamed. "No, he doesn't know. I don't want him to know! Anything!" Charley tried to make the woman understand.

"Take it easy, don't get excited, please, don't worry, lie back, just rest," the nurse soothed as Charley drifted back off to sweeter dreams of Mozo running toward her, in green fields of grass.

She awoke again in the dark of night, shocked to be so naked in such strange surroundings, remembering only snips of strange conversations. No, this was real and she had to get some clothes and get the hell out of there. Charley wrapped the sheet around herself and attempted to find her clothes. All she could find was the top half; the pants were missing. Charley remembered the wetness on her legs before the lights went out; the pants probably didn't recover. "I can't leave without pants!" Charley thought. "I'll take Wills'; he ain't going nowhere soon." Charley looked in the dimly lit hall and found the night nurse fast asleep at a small desk and tiptoed to Will's room.

"Are you awake, Will?" Charley was jiggling the man's arm.

"I am now. Charley what are you doing up? They said you had some sort of a fever and wouldn't tell me much?" Will scolded.

"I'm going to be all right, Will. I gotta get out of this place. I got horses to drive. I gotta take your pants," Charley interjected.

"You gotta take my pants?" Will choked back a laugh.

"You don't need them for a while. I musta made a mess in mine. I can't find 'em. I promise I'll bring them back cleaned and pressed," Charley said, struggling to squeeze into them.

"Go on, bring me some reading materials too and some tobacco and maybe some of that Chinese food. I don't expect that the food here is all too great," Will said, complaining.

"You're starting to feel better I can tell. I'll bring you all sorts of amusement, my friend. I'll see you in two days, I hope," Charley said, pulling the pants on and checking the pockets for anything personal of Will's that he should not be separated from.

"Take good care of my pants," Will whispered playfully.

The next morning, the talkative nurse was in, bright and early, to look after the dashing Ranger.

"Your friend is missing," a fat nurse was saying to the convalescing man even though he was only half-conscious. "Do you know where she is? She shouldn't be walking about after losing her baby like that," she lectured.

"What? . . . She? Who are you talking about?" Will was very unclear.

"The woman that collapsed in here yesterday," the nurse babbled on. "She's left. I don't know what she's wearing. The pants that she wore were completely ruined. Disgraceful for a woman to go around like that anyway, simply disgraceful."

To put it mildly, Will was in a state of shock. A strange look of puzzlement took over his face as he tried to believe. "You mean to say that she lost a baby?" he questioned the woman. As he did, the young pretty nurse came in.

"That's enough now. Didn't you hear her say she didn't want him to know?" The vision of loveliness whispered to the blabbermouth.

"Well, I thought that since she was missing, and all . . . that, well . . . Sorry." The babbling woman excused herself and left the room.

"I'm sorry, she's new. Your friend expressed the strongest wishes that you do not know. Maybe you can find it within yourself to put it out of your thoughts?" the nurse asked.

"Put it out of my thoughts? Well, that was a good one," Will thought to himself, then laughed out loud.

Two days later, Parkhurst returned to the hospital with an armload of goods.

"Here's your pants, Will. And yer Chinese dinner and yer papers. Here's some good cigars too." Charley doled out the favors like the grand friend he was.

"Thanks, Charley." Will smiled. "Where are you heading next?"

"Oh, I'm headed back to the Sierras tomorrow," Charley sighed. "I gotta call on that head nurse and settle my account."

"Yeah, you ran out, and they was a little upset by it," Will stated.

"Oh, a . . . what'd they say?" Charley queried.

"Oh, they went on about how you shouldn't be up and running around in the condition that you were in," Will teased.

"Condition? What do you mean by that?" Charley asked nervously

"Well, they just said that they were very worried." Will smiled.

"Do you know what happened to Joaquin?" Charley said, changing the subject.

"He's dead. He died with his family at his home. His last wish was that it was to remain secret," Will said softly. The two nodded to each other silently.

"Well, I gotta find that doctor and settle up," Charley shot out of his chair, choking back tears. The beautiful blonde nurse appeared in the room, blocking the doorway.

"Oh, I see you're doing fine," the nurse said, as she recognized the strange woman who had miscarried.

"Marion, this is my friend Charley Parkhurst. Marion has been looking after my every need. She is an angel of mercy," Byrnes said his face lighting up as the nurse entered the room.

"Yes, I believe we are aquainted. I must have a bill to settle up," Charley said.

"I'm very glad to see you are well, Charley. Will tells me you are a great horseman. I love horses," she said with the utmost respect and admiration. Charley had a hard time looking her in the eye.

"Come with me, we can take care of your bill simply enough," she said sweetly, taking the teamster's arm and walking the ex-patient to the office.

In a short while, Charley was again with Byrnes and wishing him well soon.

"Now you just make sure that when you're ready to get out of here that you let me know, and I'll be happy to take you, on me, you know!" Charley shook Will's hand.

"What do you think of Marion, so lovely and kind," Will said in a devilish way.

"She is something all right," Charley sighed. "Well, I'll see you soon." With that, Charley pulled on his dusty Panama hat and strode out of the hospital. She still cared for him; her heart was pounding. She was also pretty sure that the nurse had honored her wish not to tell Byrnes that she was a woman. Charley did not have the courage to ask if he knew or not. "Damn I wish I could be a woman like that! Just once!" Charley muttered quietly as he trod down the steps of the hospital and back to the routine of driving stage. It was back and forth, over the mountains and back.

Charley looked in on her friend John Rollin Ridge to keep him abreast of the situation. Especially since his wife was looking for parents that would not receive a child.

Charley walked up the steps to the house. Through the window she saw John sitting inside, bent over some papers, deep in thought. A wisp of smoke was rising above his head; his pipe was clenched in his teeth as he wrote.

"Hello?" Charley called knocking on the open door.

"Charley, is that you? Come on in," Rollin Ridge called out.

"Thank ya, John, good to see you," Charley said, entering the home. I brought them newspaper stories of Tres Dedos, I told you I had," she said, setting the papers on the desk.

"Thank you, Charley," he replied, studying his melancholy friend.

"How is your book coming, John?" Charley asked.

"It's coming along quite well. I'm thankful that you saved these newspaper articles. They will be quite helpful," Rollin Ridge replied.

"They may have saved my life. Now I'm glad they can do you some good. I never want to see them again," Charley said with a shutter.

"I had several talks with Captain Love. He seemed thrilled that he would be immortalized in a book of his heroics." Ridge smiled smugly. "I'm sure he'll roar with disapproval when he sees the title."

Ridge then pointed to the cover of his manuscript in progress. *Joaquin Murieta*. An artist named Charles Nahl had drawn a sketch of a Mexican Bandit, fiercely holding a knife, galloping a fiery stallion across a rocky canyon. Charley smiled.

"You ought to go see Will Byrnes. He's laid up in the Stockton hospital. I'm sure he'd tell you plenty, ain't got nothin else to do all day but lay there and talk," Charley pondered.

"I'm sorry to hear he's bedridden. I may just go for a visit. What happened to him?" Ridge inquired.

"You know, I never did find out what happened!" Charley laughed. Her mood then grew somber again. "Have you seen the head?"

"Yes," John confided.

"Joaquin is dead. I found my horse. He's dead too," Charley confessed, tears welling up in her eyes. "I lost the baby as well," she said, sitting down.

"I'm sorry," John said, placing his hand on the woman's shoulder. "How about a drink?"

"Sure. Will told me Joaquin's wife asked that the truth about his death never be revealed, so don't put it in your book," Charley added. "Don't mention to Will that I ever told you. I don't want him to think I blabbed. It's just that you knew him too, is all," she explained.

"Don't worry I'll not mention that I know anything about it," John said as he poured them both a shot.

"I had a miscarriage at the hospital when I went to visit Byrnes, what timing! Two nurses and I think a doctor know I'm a woman. I don't remember seeing the doctor. I was out cold. When I came to, two nurses were fussing over me. They had all my clothes off, and I was put in a gown and tucked in bed. What a surprise! I was horrified. Later that night, I snuck out of bed and grabbed Will's pants and ran."

"Geez, what a sight." Rollin Ridge smiled. "Do you think he knows you're a woman?"

"I don't honestly know, he might," Charley said, scratching her head. "If he does, he didn't let on."

CHAPTER 21

In '53, the foothills of the Sierras came under another siege, the water cannon, or monitor. The miners made reservoirs high in the hills and funneled water into pipes, with the help of gravity. The pipes got progressively smaller, until they had significant water pressure to wash dirt and stone out of the canyons. Then they mined the earth, newly ripped from its former locations, by way of filtering system.

At one stop, Rabbit Ridge on the way to Downieville, Charley Parkhurst went to stretch his long legs and walked to the edge of a newly created reservoir. The damage to the surrounding areas by the water pressure was devastating. The earth had been stripped of all vegetation and life, and only solid rock remained. The object was simply to retrieve the hidden gold. Trees were washed from their banks, and great torrents of mud were heaped about everywhere. It was disgusting to the horseman. He decided to walk over and look at the newly constructed dam. Along the way, Charley asked a local, one Dissipated Dick, about the new system.

"Oh, you don't want to be messing round any of them thar hydraulic reservoirs. Thar terribly dangerous! Why you remember that crazy old China man, Wat Long, used to wash laundry? Well, he was a monkeyin' around by one of them thar reservoirs . . . and he falls in, see? Well, he gets sucked right in ta one a them pipes, see, and he gets sucked down and down, where the pressure is real high. See? And then he gets shot out'a the end a one of them there monitors, in one big, long, burst! Stretched him out about twenty feet!" Dick laughed to himself like some wild beast. "They had ta coil him around four times ta fit him in the coffin!" He coughed, spitting his *tabac* as punctuation. "I was at the funeral, had firecrackers and sparkly things all over town! The China men dug him up two weeks later and mailed him back ta China!" he said, stuffing a fresh plug of tobacco in his mouth. "So you stay away from them reservoirs! See?" His laugh reminded Charley of coyote chatter.

"Yes, thanks, I think I will," Parkhurst said, backing away from the edge and smiling at the miner.

"Good! Now I hope you bring me a letter next time you're though here! I sure hope I get some mail! I should be gettin' a letter any day now!" he cackled to himself as Charley walked back to the livery scratching his head. "'Course I don't write no letters myself you see . . . Count' a cuz I don't know how to spell . . ." the miner's voice drifted off.

CHAPTER 22

February 1854

Charley was driving a route from Mariposa to Downieville; the trip up took two days running around the foothills of the Sierras. It was a beautiful ride, that is, if the weather wasn't freezing or snowing, or the rivers raging and the wind whipping. This particular route brought Charley and the horses across the Tuolomne River, a river they had crossed countless times. Across this turbulent water was a grand bridge made of giant cedar logs and redwood; it was a marvel to behold, a monument to man's desire to tame the wilderness.

This day the wind howled, and the rain fell in heavy sheets, the air crackled in violent expectation. The bridge across the river tossed and turned like two maids airing out a blanket across the foamy and choppy water, which was racing to the upper reaches of its banks. The braces moaned and creaked in a disturbing manner. Charley pulled the team up to the mouth of the bridge. Looking up river, he saw large a tree trunk, maybe seventy feet long, tossing and turning in the violent current, making its way toward the already stressed bridge. If they were to cross, it would be now or never. The nervous team nickered and snorted as Charley sang out a lullaby to horses as he steadied his jangled nerves. His shotgun partner gave an anxious glance to the reinsman, and then Charley persuaded the team into forward motion.

"Come on now, get in there!" Charley commanded. The entire unit, coach, horses, and the bridge began to sway with the extreme blowing of the wind and waves. Everyone was holding their breath, except Charley and the loud mouth woman sitting on the leeward side of the vehicle, who spotted the tree coming toward the bridge.

"Easy, easy, my beauties, let's go now." Charley tried to drown out the high-pitched screams from the interior of the coach; he was busy talking to his chargers and easing them steadily onward with his whip. As they reached the half way point, Charley heard a loud ripping noise and in looking back saw one of the anchoring piers give way, with the mighty tree caught in its moorings. Charley popped the whip in response and hurried the team across, posthaste; when they reached the other shore, the horses stumbled and slid in the muddy footing of the bank but gave their all to get away from the ripping noise coming from behind. Charley looked back again to see the bridge leave its mooring and descend down the raging river. The tree sweeping the entire structure in its wake. The loud woman, now still in shock, had swooned over in her seat.

"Hopping horny toads! That's one for the camp fire!" The armed guard hollered.

"Damned right!" Charley sighed, out of breath. The horses scampering down the rain-washed road snorted in disapproval and relief.

CHAPTER 23

Sierra Mountains 1854

On a glorious April morning in the mountains, the dogwood blossoms were in full bloom, and the air was sweet with springtime flowers in the meadows; iris, blue lupines, bright orange poppies, and lush green grass covered the landscapes.

Charley was driving a nearly empty coach and six fresh horses to Selby Flats, on the way to Downieville and Sierra City; the cargo was mostly mail. When they pulled into Selby Flats, a small tent town, with some hastily built wood houses mingled throughout, Charley noticed a young woman, sitting on a large leather suitcase, in front of the stagecoach station, smoking a cigar. There were not many women in these parts, and this was a fine specimen. Not what you'd call pretty, but "striking" was really the word for her.

As Charley pulled up to the crude log station, he couldn't help staring at the woman as most of the men; including his very young new expressman did.

"I'm sorry, young woman, I didn't mean to stare, but haven't I met you somewhere's before?"

"I used to run a saloon in Marysville. Maybe you've seen me there," the woman puffed.

"Perhaps that's it," Charley replied. "It would be a privilege for myself, that is, if you would care to ride up on the top of the stage with myself and my expressman, Harte."

"It would be my privilege, sir," Miggles said earnestly. She lifted her skirt alluringly as she climbed up to the top of the stage. The young wiry express guard was instantly captivated by her charms as he helped the young woman to her place between the driver and himself.

Harte was a good-looking young man of about twenty years, with refined tastes of a man brought up in a well-to-do eastern lifestyle. He had yet to realize the best way to make use of his talents, but he was keen on adventure and had taken the job of being an expressman as an inexpensive way to have a good look at the California gold fields, sort of earn as you go. He was brandishing a shotgun that the express company had provided and was rather ill at ease with it.

"Everyone calls me Miggles," the woman laughed as she seated herself.

"Miggles giggles," Charley mumbled. Vaguely recalling the waitress.

"That's right!" Miggles laughed.

"You can call me Charley!" Parkhurst smiled as he started the stagecoach with a flourish.

"Are you traveling alone?" Harte asked.

"Well, for part of the way," Miggles replied. "I will be taking Bill back to the house, after the next stop."

"Who's Bill, if I'm not too presumptuous?"

"Bill is my best friend and love, and now, he's not too well," Miggles explained.

It was a lovely day as they progressed out of the canyon. Men in the landscape were all involved with the object of retrieving gold out of the pristine water. It could just as easily pass for the Garden of Eden if you planted a few more fruit trees. As the miners spotted Miggles, they each let out a cheer, and Miggles couldn't help but to wave back.

The coach and the horses were fresh from the east; they were the best that money could buy. However, soon they were approaching a particularly treacherous stretch of road, one which had been carved out of the mountain and was almost vertical on each side, straight up on the left side and nearly straight down on the right.

Charley soon found it necessary to use the whip to maintain the forward motion, cracking it up above the horses' backs. It was becoming very difficult to keep them moving at all. As Charley forced the horses around the blind turn, the resistance became very apparent!

"Holy shit!" Charley swore!

"Grizzly bear!" Harte cursed as he leveled his shotgun over the horses at the beast.

"Goddamn it, that's a shotgun! You're gonna hit my horses, you fool!"

The bear was standing her ground, all nine feet of her, and the horses were starting to panic! They were rearing and beginning to back up and wanting to go anywhere, but where they were at the moment!

"Don't shoot, you couldn't shoot yourself out of a grain sack! I'll kill you if you hit one of these horses, do you hear me!" Charley was beside himself. "But I can't hold these horses and get to my gun!" Charley was using the whip to make loud cracking reports. The coach, now grinding in reverse, was threatening to jackknife as the back wheels ground into the steep hillside. Parkhurst fought to keep the leaders from pitching headlong down the cliff to avoid the huge standing bear.

"I can't keep these horses still much longer! Hold on!" the driver swore. The bear was holding her ground and approaching the panicky horses.

As Charley focused on the bear and cracked the whip for all he was worth, he heard a shot ring out.

"You killed him with your whip! Charley, I never seen anything like it!" Harte cheered as the bear slumped to the ground.

"What? I didn't kill him, you idiot! Somebody else shot him."

"He's up there!" Miggles yelled, pointing to the trees in the hillside above them.

"Well, I don't know who the hell he is, but I sure am glad he was hunting today." Charley managed to quiet the horses, and then he handed the lines to Bret and jumped down off the coach. He made his way to the front of his horses, then saw the great behemoth of a bear collapsed by the side of the road, in some bushes. A clean shot to the head. Charley quieted the horses who were trembling, then turned back to look at the big bear, mesmerized by the sight of the huge felled beast. As time caught up with Charley, so did the rest of the passengers, including Miggles.

"Oh my God! Oh my God!" Miggles moaned over and over. She couldn't bring herself to look right at the bear but had to distance herself from the bloody scene; as she did, she came upon another pitiful sight.

"Oh my God!" Miggles cried. "The poor things, oh I'm so sorry, you sweet little babies," Miggles cried. Three very young bear cubs, the size of puppies, cowering in the shrubs, began to cry in the most miserable way.

"Oh well, that figures, I'm sure," Charley moaned. Looking down the road on a trio of fuzzy bear cubs.

"Did I get her?" Yank called down as he climbed down the hillside.

"Yeah, you sure got her all right," Charley called back, still calming his beauties as the young man came down from his hunting roost.

"Name's James Folger. Everyone calls me Yankee Jim."

"Well, that was some fine shooting, Yankee Jim! Charley Parkhurst, I thank you!" Charley said, holding out his hand in gratitude. "I do believe you've saved us the bother of death or broken necks if that bear had charged." Charley ran his gloved hand through the long hair of the bear. "That's a fine bear hide, you fetch it down out of these hills, and have it tanned, and I'll pay you good money for it," Charley said, pressing some money in the young man's hand. "Now don't you go letting someone else talk you out of it!" At that time, Charley picked up the notes of some mighty fierce crying, and by the sound of it, from the female of the passengers.

Miggles was standing in the middle of the road with the three tiny baby bears, all balling with about the same intensity.

Charley, whose timing couldn't be worse, came to the scene with gun in hand, intending to put the poor little bears out of their misery. "Sweet Mother of Mercy!" he swore as he aimed at the first cub.

"No!" Miggles screamed, in a moment she had grabbed the cub up by the scruff of the neck, and was shielding it from doom with her body.

"I can't let them suffer," Charley explained.

"You can't just kill them!" Miggles pleaded, tears running down her face.

"Well, what do you propose I do with them? Miggles, look . . . See that bear . . . that mamma bear is how big they're gonna get. She gotta be about six or seven hundred pounds. Well? What am I gonna do with them . . . let them starve or get eaten by wolves? Wet-nurse them? I can't take care of them," Charley said, pointing the gun at the baby bears.

"I'll take them," Yank butts in. "I kin' sell them to some Mexicans I know. They like to put on bull and bear shows!"

"You can't let him do that!" Miggles rang in.

"Oh, how did I ever get involved in this mess!" Charley sighed.

Yank had a cub in each hand, by the scruff of the neck; they were going all limp on him. He had made up his mind and had provisions to look after the two. Miggles defensively clung to the remaining cub, and having been held by the scruff of the neck was also limp as a noodle.

"Miggles, you can't carry a bear on a coach like that. It won't work!" Charley protested. "I just don't recommend it!"

"I know!" Miggles burst out, handing the cub to Harte, who had tied the lines to the brake and had come to see the spectacle. Miggles scampered to the top of the coach and grabbed her case and tossed it to the ground. Then made her way back down. She proceeded to empty it on the side of the road, discarding dresses and other fineries. "There!" she said proudly. "I'll put him my suitcase!" "He'll think he's in a cave!"

"Miggles, I can't believe you're doing this. He ain't a puppy. He's a bear!" Charley scolded. Harte smiled at the soft, brown bundle hanging by the scruff of the neck.

"Cute little fellow." He smiled.

"But at least he'll have a chance!" she said with determination, retrieving a big skirt that she used as a knapsack.

"Well, it ain't my business! My business is drivin' a stage! Now, let's move this bear out of the road and let's get going!" Charley said, looking at his pocket watch and herding shaken passengers.

Harte had his arms loaded with Miggles discarded clothes and was throwing them into the coach and having much to good a time of it. The cub could be heard scratching and crying inside its new leather cave.

"It'a been less trouble if it'a been a bandit!" Charley mumbled.

"I'll have this hide for you in Downieville, just ask anyone in town for Yankee Jim's, and you'll find me."

"Take care with that hide. I want to have a coat made from it for the winter," Charley called down to the young man, who was tying collars around the crying cubs.

"I know a squaw that tans hides real nice. You can pick it up at my store," the young man called back.

"Sounds fine!" Charley replied.

"I think I'll ride inside for now!" Miggles stated. "What's the matter with him. Don't he like animals?" she asked Harte, pointing to the driver.

"No, ma'am, he loves them."

"Come on, Harte, get up here, let's go, theses horses are gettin frisky!" Charley barked. They were back under way once more. The horses were full of power and steam as they let out snorts and blows at the smell of bear blood, exciting them into a high-stepping canter up the mountain.

"I think someone ought to check on that gal, time and again, as that bear grows up, to make sure he ain't et her!" Charley advised.

Now Charley always worried about that gal. The first reason was that she had named the bear Joaquin and Charley knew that meant trouble. He had found out that Miggles was looking after a gambler that she loved, who had suddenly taken very sick; most said he was a goner! Couldn't move nor talk or nothin'. But she loved him and took care of him, so there would be the three of them!

CHAPTER 24

1854

Charley was always amused by the colorful names of the new towns sprouting up along the countryside. Names like Brandy City, christened because a cask had broken there, in a canyon and a rich vein of gold was discovered there. Many towns were Flats or Bars, so named for their locations, Selby Flats, Poker Flats, Rich Bar, Condemned Bar, the ever-popular Horseshoe Bar, then there was Humbug. Charley especial liked the spirited sound of Rough and Ready, a town named after Ol' Rough and Ready Zachary Taylor. The company that founded the town had been named Rough and Ready Dry Goods. While looking for the land of milk and honey and gold, they had come across a ship that had been outfitted with wagon wheels and dragged into the hills with a team of mules, by an old sea captain. He then converted the ship\wagon, into a makeshift saloon and liquor store. The captain had informed the Rough and Ready Dry Goods company, over drinks, that the next hill was as rich a pickins as any other, so the spot was christened after the company, and a town soon developed. Such was the way that oddly named towns developed. Anything from Gouge Eye to Rattlesnake Bar.

Charley had a new stop this evening along his busy route, a budding town newly added to the roster by the name of Timbuktu, a musical name always to bring a smile. It was founded by a black man, who had a big gold strike, and managed to keep it. He was a powerful man with kind eyes and a nasty reputation. Before long, others staked claims and a town developed; the black man named his new metropolis after his homeland in Africa.

The blacksmith shop in Timbuktu, Ficklins' was abuzz with activity as the coach pulled in. Charley smiled to see a beautiful cherub holding court on top of the oversized anvil, in the center of the barn. The tiny honey-haired girl was dancing to an adoring crowd of men, who spilled out on the street, starved to look on such a sweet child. Many men with tears welling up, clutched faded daguerreotypes of their own children, they have missed for several years.

At the end of her dance, the strawberry blonde child was showered with gold that her mother boldly gathered up in her cotton apron. It would be more gold than her good-for-nothing husband had ever seen in his life.

Charley had not enough time to find out who the sweet cherub was, before the coach rocked ever onward.

The evening stage rocked up the hill, the horses at a brisk trot, arriving in Nevada City in style. The driver expertly parked in front of the express office and waited to descend from his perch until all passengers had climbed out; then he tied the lines to the brake as the stablemen took over. Charley stretched his strong shoulders and heard his back pop.

"Jeez, I must be gettin' old," he mumbled to himself as he stepped into the office, before heading out to oil his brake leg.

"Well, Charley, I was wonderin' how long it would take you to finally check out Eleanoras' place!" Will called out from the porch.

"Hey, Byrnes, you're looking fine!" Charley answered, walking up the plank steps. "You know I hear Eleanora this and Eleanora that, so I figure this woman is worth seeing in action. How long have you been in town?"

"I got pretty bored in Stockton, so I ventured over the hills in search of some new game. Everyone's been migrating to this neck of the woods, so I thought I might find some fresh money here," Will admitted.

"I'm glad to see you out and around. I'll be driving this route for a while I suppose. Let's have a drink to old friends," Charley proposed. "Take me to meet this new wonder of the card game. I imagine you and she are close chums by now. When did you get here?"

"Yesterday."

"Oh, well then, you must be best friends by now," Charley teased.

The two made their way through the crowded and bustling card room, thick clouds of smoke circling the tables of men from the various cigars and hand-rolled cigarettes.

The band was comprised of a fiddle player, a piano player, a drummer, an accordion player, and a horn player, who played polkas with enthusiasm in the corner of the parlor. The saloon was done up stylishly with yards of red calico dripping from the walls. It had a fairly large dance floor with a riser in the back that the girls danced and sang on; they would then, for a fee, dance with the customers. The other half of the room held the card tables and bar; it was full of men craning to get a good view of the raven-haired woman in the center of the room dealing cards. She wore an elegant evening gown of deep burgundy taffeta with imported black lace trim. The neckline was round and especially low in the front to frame her beautifully formed breasts. Her petite hands, clothed in black lace gloves with matching jet bracelets were expertly dealing and flipping cards with ease and at the same time elegantly holding her own delicately rolled cigarette. Her long shiny hair was coiled and curled up high on her head and spilled down her back in a cascade of black ringlets.

"She has them waiting in line all day to play at the table with her," Will explained.

"I bet she's raking in the gold too," Charley added.

"I imagine so. Say, I hear Ol' Lola Montez is giving a performance in town here. She's really something. Real theatrical, a dancer, does some kind of a spider dance I think," Will went on.

"A what?" Charley asked in disbelief.

"I think it's called a spider dance. They say she gets a spider on her, and she dances around kickin' up her legs and the like," Will was chuckling.

"You have got to be making this up!" Charley said chuckling.

"No, on my honor." Will smiled.

"I've got to see that," Charley said laughing.

"I think she is performing Saturday, at eight. Will you be in town then?" Byrnes asked.

"I'll make sure of it," Charley resolved.

"Then we'll go, and I'll show you."

"I gotta see this."

"She's quite eccentric. She has a couple of baby bears as pets. Had all kinds of famous boyfriends, the King of Bavaria, I think, and a famous writer, Dumas," Will was rattling off.

"Who Eleanora or the Montez gal?" Charley asked.

"Lola Montez!" Will responded, with annoyance.

"You're a regular fountain of knowledge. How do you know all these things?" Charley quizzed his friend.

"Oh, I get around." Will laughed. "Try some of the oysters, Charley. They are fine. From San Francisco."

"They look good. Eleanora sure knows how to run a classy saloon. I see you can order champagne here," Charley said, examining a card on the bar. "I haven't had that in a long time. You want to split a bottle, Will?"

"Sure. By the way, I forgot to tell you. I'm going to get married," Will said nonchalantly. "I'm gonna have a plate of oysters too. You can get them raw with sauce or fried with bread and butter. Let's get one of each."

"What?" Charley croaked, almost choking on his chewing tobacco, as the bartender came to take their order.

"Hey, Charley!" a familiar bartender greeted.

"Hey, Lenny,'" Charley said still coughing. "I'll have a bottle of this." Charley pointed out on the card, refusing an idiotic attempt at pronouncing the French name. "Two glasses."

"All right, a bottle of number 4, coming up." The bartender had given up trying to pronounce them himself and simply numbered the stock. "Fine choice!"

"So? When is the big day? Tell me everything!" Charley said with a lump in her throat.

"She was working in the hospital, and we met when I was recuperating from being shot. Marion."

"When ain't you recuperating from being shot, Will? I guess it makes sense to marry a nurse, I have to admit. She was very pretty."

"Don't you think so? Anyways, I'll bring her to the show," Will said.

"What do you mean Lola Montez has a couple of baby bears?" Charley said changing the subject.

"I heard Yank telling how he sold the grand dame a couple of baby grizzlies. Said he'd shot the mother, and some other gal got the third little runt."

"Oh no, I saw that mother she was huge! Doesn't that woman have a clue?" Charley said in amazement.

"I guess not. Here comes the oysters," Will said, dismissing the matter and turning his attentions to the delicacies at hand.

After the oysters, the two feasted on grilled salmon, the special of the week as the succulent fish was now in abundance.

"Have you read John's book, yet?" Charley asked her friend.

"Yes, very entertaining," he said solemnly.

"Well, he got most of the facts right, didn't he?" Charley laughed.

"He did well. I hope he profits from his labors," Will said wistfully.

"He made you look pretty good!" Charley added. "What's the matter?"

"I would rather just leave the whole episode behind me, that's all," Will responded, rubbing his head. "I haven't thought about it for a while. The head business, so morbid and all."

"I'm sorry, Will. I heard that a couple of the Rangers are taking the trophies to the cites on a tour and charging admission," Charley sighed.

"Poor Chappo, he wanted to be like Joaquin, now he finally got to be Joaquin, in a jar," Will said under his breath.

"Hey, I think that guy is getting out of the game. There's your chance to play at Eleanoras' table," Charley said with enthusiasm. Will stood and sauntered to the table. No one challenged the famous gunman to the unoccupied seat. The petite woman was busy rolling herself a cigarette, as the men ordered drinks and reorganized for the new player.

"My name is William Byrnes. It is a pleasure to play at your table, Madame Dumont," he charmed. The young woman was instantly enchanted with her handsome new prey.

"The pleasure is all mine," she cooed as she shuffled the deck. "Is that your friend Charley? The coachman?" Eleanora motioned. Charley sat at the bar and watched with admiration, tipping his hat in recognition to the lady. He smiled to Byrnes in his glory at the card table. Charley had mostly lost his taste for gambling, but it was a pleasure to watch Will and listen to the musicians playing with enthusiasm, maybe even dance one or two go-rounds.

"Yes, that's a good friend." Will laughed and shook his head. "He's got a hell of a poker face."

"Why didn't you mention you had already met Eleanora?" Will jabbed at Charley, later that night.

"Well, I met her at the express office. I hadn't been to her parlor, and you was a havin' such a good time showing off, I didn't want to spoil your fun," Charley reasoned.

"You probably already had tea with Lola Montez!" Will mumbled under his breath.

"Well, you know about the baby bears? I'm gonna have a coat made out of their mother's hide. Should be a beauty. Just in time for the winter," Charley smirked.

"How do you know it's their mother?" Will asked.

"Oh, I just got a feelin'," he said with a yawn. "I got to get some sleep. I'm driving early tommorra. I'll see you Saturday. I'll meet you at the show," Charley said, standing to go.

"See ya" Will said, tipping his hat.

The new Nevada City Opera House was filled to capacity that Saturday night. The audience was almost entirely miners; the few ladies in attendance, were given great respect by the men, starved for feminine company in the rugged foothills. Everyone was in great anticipation of seeing Lola Montez. The opening acts would have a tough time winning over a crowd that could barely contain their enthusiasm for the wildly over-advertised spider dance. One small honey-haired girl would enchant them all.

Charley met Will and his soon-to-be-wife, Marion, in front of the theater and went right in, having already purchased balcony seats. It was wonderful to really have a night out, and Charley did so enjoy spending the evening with Will, even though he was with his nurse/bride-to-be.

Marion was a sweet, intelligent woman, and the teamster tried hard to like her, yet somehow, Charley always felt the stinging pangs of jealousy. Marion noticed, but smiled only to herself and was impressed by Charley's total confidence in her masculine disguise.

Looking around the theater from the lofty balcony reminded Parkhurst of the east and the fancy doings he had driven to in the past. At last the lights in the house were dimmed and the lights on stage were lit. They were made up of oil lamps setting in a type of can, which was open in the back toward the actors to throw more light at them; the other side of the can shielded the audience from the direct flame. The inside of the lamp holder was highly polished metal, reflecting even more light; they were called foot lights. The sides of the stage had poles with lanterns fixed to it with polished silver reflectors that focused the light on the stage.

All was silent when the grand dame made her entrance. When the men finally caught their breath, you could hear them oohing and awing in reverence of this divine vision before them. Charley just smiled, as he took in the whole spectacle. Lolas' gowns were sumptuous to look at and she changed costumes frequently. She sang songs and acted dramatic scenes, with various other attractions thrown in between costume changes. A tiny little girl, with a mop of red, cascading curls bouncing down her shoulders, sang and danced a jig; she was the cutest little leprechaun Charley had ever seen.

"I think that's the little gal I seen at Ficklin's one night, a dancing on his O'l anvil," Charley commented to Will, after studying the girl. "She sure is cute!"

At long last, the program drew to a climax; the spider dance everyone had longed for; the Countess of Landsfeld would not disappoint her audience. It was an exotic dance, a combination of classic ballet and strange theatrics. Lolas' raven black hair was tied in the back of her neck in a large chignon, which accented her swanlike neck. Her black silk and lace dress was cut very low and off the shoulder and was very tight to the waist. The skirt was quite a piece of work. Charley couldn't help but discuss that with Marion. It was the fullest skirt Charley had ever seen, and it floated about the stage like a dark cloud even though it was little past her knees, quite shocking. The fabric of the skirt seemed to have a life of it's own as the woman danced on her toes. Then sure enough, on cue, out pops a spider from the depths of the skirt's interior, then another, and yet another. They seemed to be attached to the dress with some string. Charley stifled a laugh. Soon the woman was a furiously leaping and twirling ball of spider mayhem, which took Marion to the limits of her squeamishness; the nurse drew the line at spiders. Charley spotted her clinging to Will's arm for safety, lest one of the spiders should break free from the stage and threaten an innocent bystander. At last, Lola Montez conquered the fuzzy brutes and collapsed elegantly on the floor. Most of the miners had risen to offer assistance to the actress; she elegantly waved them away as she popped up off the floor and took several curtain calls.

"Well, that surely was something!" Byrnes remarked as the lights of the house were relit.

"I've never seen anything like that!" Charley agreed, chuckling aloud as he offered assistance to Marion, whose face was still red from the excitement of it all. The three navigated down the stairs to the main floor and through the milling crowd, exiting the building or bellying up to the bar for one final refreshment upon leaving. The streets were a buzz with the spilling theater patronage; many men commenting on the adorable dancing doll.

The trio strolled down the boardwalk in the soft night air, discussing the shows' finer points and highlights, as they made their way to Eleanoras' polka parlor. They had reasoned since they were all shined up, they might as well show off and enjoy the rest of the evening with a nightcap of champagne.

As they entered the elegant establishment, the men excepted acknowledgments from many of the familiar faces.

"A bottle of number six, I think, Lenny." Charley smiled and tried to act cosmopolitan.

"Coming up!" The bartender set himself into action. "Will you be ordering any oysters?"

"Yes, some cocktails and one order fried, with toast, I think," Will answered, looking at his companions. They nodded. Marion was quite unaccustomed to bar life, but this establishment was a wonder, with its refinements and small orchestra in the corner; she felt safe in the protection of William Byrnes. Her gaze settled on the lovely creature at the center of the room, dealing cards. Her dark and mysterious eyes and graceful confidence set her off like a jewel in a fine setting. She was wearing a crimson silk dress, probably French, trimmed with black lace and small silk roses around the neckline. Her skin was alabaster, and her hair was a dark swirl of rich ebony curls, pulled away from her face and sent cascading down her back. She held a thin dark cigarette in the right hand and seductively blew smoke rings as she played cards.

"This woman holds court better than the Countess of Lansfield, Lola Montez," Marion remarked, looking at all the men, who were taking in the card dealing Venus.

"Yes, she does hold court, you might say," Charley said, handing Marion a glass of sparkling wine.

"Here's to faster horses!" Byrnes said, lifting his glass. "I haven't told you, I'm entertaining ideas of working as a guard at the prison near San Francisco, San Quentin. Course I wouldn't take anything less than captain. Be nice to settle in one spot. Besides, Marion's folks live in that area," Will explained to Charley.

Eleanora glanced up casually from the table and caught the admiring looks from her elegantly attired friends. Charley smiled back.

"I think that the young woman takes a shine to you, Charley, my friend," Byrnes chided. Marion blushed shyly and giggled.

"What? You must be kidding," Charley responded, turning a bit red in the face. Then, as if planned, the graceful proprietor stood and excused herself from the table and approached the trio.

"Charley, I've never seen you dressed so stylishly." She held out her hand, and Charley was compelled to kiss it. "William, who is this lovely lady?" Mme. Dumont inquired.

"Eleanora, this is my bride-to-be, Marion," Byrnes said with charm.

"It is a privilege, mademoiselle, to have such a refined lady grace my establishment. Charley, I do believe that Dr. Wilson is exiting the game. Would you like his chair?" she said, curling her arm around his.

"It would be an honor, my dear," Charley said, smiling first at Eleanora, then at Will, who seemed just a bit envious. That was a laugh. Charley smiled to herself as they walked to the card table. The woman was mesmerizing, and Parkhurst could not keep his eyes off of the stunning card dealer. He could swear that the woman could undress you with her eyes, which gave Charley a new set of feelings altogether.

Soon after Charley sat at the table, the establishment was graced by another stunning lady, none other than the actress Lola Montez herself, followed by an entourage of admirers. Eleanora rose to the occasion and welcomed her charming celebrity guest.

The men all stood as the Countess of Landsfield entered the establishment; the band did its best to play a Viennese Waltz for this occasion. Lola had informed Eleanora earlier in the evening that she might make an appearance. The hostess greeted her with a deep curtsy, designed mostly to show off her own cleavage. The crowd was practically drooling from all the feminine charm in the room this night. Marion, though not in the fashion league with either flamboyant lady, did not lack in her own beautiful charms. She held tightly to Will's arm for comfort and courage, lest she be mistaken for an available woman of less virtue and up for grabs. The nurse was at least the most virtuous woman in the room. Her honey blonde hair softly tumbled down her back to her waist, and her face was framed in curls with delicate silk flowers braided into her hair that formed a soft crown. Her soft pink and white dress made her stand out among the card parlor like a soft blossom that didn't belong.

Chairs were added to the table, and the game commenced. Charley relished playing cards with a couple of women, who lived life on their own terms and by their own rules. The two women at the table, both dark haired and mysterious, seemed to have been cut from the same bolt of cloth.

"Where did you find that charming little girl, Lotta Crabtree?" Charley inquired to the countess on his right.

"Oh yes, the sweet little girl is my neighbor. She comes over and visits with me, and we sing songs. I have given her dancing instructions. I have even taught her to ride a horse," Lola Montez proudly announced in her thick European accent. "So sweet and very talented."

"I heard a rumor that you got a couple of baby bears," Charley said, arranging his cards and throwing in the ante.

"Why yes, that's true. They are kind animals." The woman smiled as she too tossed in her ante.

"If I might be so bold to say, those bears may go on to grow up to be about a thousand pounds a piece," Charley spoke boldly. "I saw the mother if you bought them off a Yankee Jim."

"Perhaps you might come and see them for yourself and see that they are perfectly tame now." The actress smiled at the handsome coachman.

"Thank you kindly, I might just do that," Charley remarked, as the play began in earnest.

The next day in Nevada City, Charley took a moment to go down the street to the mercantile and dry goods store. Charley's eyes scanned the room for some ribbon or feathers or silk flowers, a budding entertainer could wear in her strawberry blonde hair. From behind a curtain, peeked a young woman with long brown braids, who politely asked if she could help.

Charley removed his hat and asked about ribbon.

"I'm looking for something pretty for a little girl's hair. Or maybe even a doll, maybe."

"I might have something you'd like in the back of the store there. It's my sewing room." The woman pulled back the curtain to reveal a dress that she was currently working on and a vast assortment of trims. Charley could only utter an astonished "My, my! Whose that dress for?"

"Oh, that's for Mme. Montez. Of course, it's not finished yet!"

Charley was mesmerized by its delicate beauty, but soon returned to the task at hand. "This ribbon and these feathers, and oh, maybe that little bunch of flowers too, will be all, thank you. How long you been working on that dress?"

The young lady blushed and stated that it had taken about two weeks so far and that she really had lots more to do, but was waiting for Mme. Montez to come for a fitting.

"Can you sew anything? I mean, do you think you could sew me a fur coat?" Charley asked hopefully.

"Well, I suppose so. I never have before, but I think I could," she said bluntly.

"I'll bring the pelt by and maybe you could have a look see." Charley smiled. "What do I owe you for these?"

"I think that it is about five cents there," the young lady replied.

"Well, here's a dime, and we'll call it square young lady, I'll see you in about a week with my fur! Thank you again!" Charley said whistling a tune as he walked back to the livery.

When the driver was in Grass Valley next, he dared to stop by the Montez place to pay his respects. He asked the lady about the child, and Lola took the horseman to meet the girl. Charley pulled the present from his vest and presented it to the child after Mme. Montez was called away. The little girl loved horses, and that made the teamster smile as well.

Charley would frequently stop at Eleanoras', in Nevada City or Lola Montez place to drop off some special delivery. Charley couldn't keep his eyes off the little girl that was frequently there, Little Lotta. She was bright and shiny and had a voice that rang like a bell. She was not afraid of anyone, big or small. Charley always brought something for the little girl, asking her mother first if she could have it. It might be some candy or a doll or a feather fan. Charley couldn't resist the child and called her little fairy dancer.

"Look what Lola taught me!" Lotta chimed, breaking in to a wild Irish jig, ending with a twirl and a curtsy.

"That was magnificent!" Charley applauded. "You should perform for the queen of England!"

"Thank you, Charley," the golden-tressed child responded politely, taking a really professional bow. "Mama says I've got promise as a dancer." Lotta popped to her toes and proudly impersonated Mme. Montez famous spider dance. Her mother, Mary, was a quiet woman that took great pride in her daughter and guarded her jealously.

CHAPTER 25

San Quentin Prison, 1855

William Byrnes and his lovely bride, Marion, stood on the ferry, with the fog swirling around them and their possessions. They had spent the night in the finest hotel San Francisco had to offer and were now looking forward to a new life, across the Golden Gate in Marin. Will hired on to work at the San Quentin prison as a guard. It seemed like easy money and a nice location. With his outlaw experience and marksmanship, he was well qualified for the job.

The newlyweds would set up a home in a little town called San Rafael, near the prison. Will would first escort Marion to their new abode; then he would report to his new job.

Inside the prison, Dr. Hodges still held hopes of escape, even though he had been hold up in the dim and cold brick and stone prison for four years. He had made good use of his medical knowledge, to become a trustee in the infirmary, in order to be spared the rock pile. Yet he had not made great progress with a real plan of escape. The infirmary was a place that had lots of wagging tongues. It was well known that the prison system was extremely crowded, but William Byrnes didn't realize how bad things had gotten. He heard guards talking of reprisals and strikes.

Many inmates mysteriously began coming down with the different ailments. Soon, a few of Dr. Hodges' friends from his first ferry ride, such as English Bob and Bill Gristy began turning up in the infirmary too. After palms were greased and alliances made, a real plan began to materialize.

The prison was being overwhelmed by the flow of criminals due to the mass migration of people to the gold fields of California. General Estell was writing the papers to complain of over crowding. He wanted the state to pay more money for guards and everything connected with housing prisoners, but the authorities were not paying attention.

Bill Gristly had set it up with the transporting guards; there would be an orchestrated prison break. The guards would be armed, but with powder and no balls in their revolvers. The prisoners would be taken out on work furlough to cut wood, then the break would be made on cue. The selected prisoners would then flee into the sheltering hills of California.

The gang in the infirmary miraculously recovered and returned to their labors. Soon the plan was set into motion; the men would be sent on a logging assignment in the foothills. The signal to flee was when the first tree hit the ground. The convicts would each run in a separate direction.

The outlaws scattered through the hills of the country, to meet up again in the budding town of San Jose. The media had a field day with the break, and the prison system was soon overhauled.

Dr. Hodges would breath new life into the legend of Tom Bell, as the inmates stole horses in the darkness of night and rode off to the gold fields, in search of rich pickings, which they found on the back roads of no-man's-land. With newfound wealth, the gang grew strong and set up shop in several taverns and stage stops, paying the less scrupulous to tip off the gang to rich reward.

One such place was the Mountaineer House, on the Auburn road and the Western Exchange Hotel, or Hog Ranch as it was more commonly called, for its generous efforts to satisfy all of man's appetites. Another important set up was the California House located about twenty-eight miles from Marysville, on the Camptonville road, on route to Downieville. The gang was even bold enough to inform their victims; they had just been robbed by the Tom Bell Gang.

Dr. Hodges was no killer though. He had even performed surgery on one victim that Gristy had in inadvertently shot. He stitched him up, then sent the man to town on a wagon, after first exacting his fee from the driver. His kind hearted nature even manifested itself during a holdup. One teamster hauling beer to a thirsty and ironically named Drytown, was returned to him enough money to buy himself a drink upon arrival, so as to forget the incident.

CHAPTER 26

Fall, Placerville, 1855

The weather was getting a serious bite to it. Mountains looming to the east were wearing their first dusting of snow. Charley snuggled in the driver's seat, comfortably warm in a newly sewn bearskin coat. The wheels of the stagecoach crunched through the slushy mud, as they approached the booming town. The passengers could hear the whoops of drunk miners, as they spotted the stagecoach making its way to Placerville. Many miners still preferred the previous name, Hangtown. The majestic hanging oak stood like a shrine at the entrance, hemp necktie dangling in the breeze, waiting for its next customer.

Charley was driving into the busy main street when he drew the coach to a halt. Blocking the road was a freight wagon with grain and produce and a very upset young driver, trying to back four horses and wagon down into a narrow alley. The wagon apparently had a rear axle hub up against the corner of the building. People were yelling, and the teamster was swearing and all traffic was stopped.

"Get that heap off a' the road!" the express guard called out into the fray.

"Shut up, Albert, that ain't a gonna help none!" Charley snapped back at his guard. "Poor man could use some constructive advice about now," he added.

"Yeah well, we ain't got all night, I got to go kick the bushes!" Albert whined.

"Geez, hold on to your pecker. I'll see if I can navigate around this road block," Charley said, gathering up the lines. "How's my backside?" he called to the rear rooftop passengers. "Anyone behind me?"

"Nope!"

"All right, my beauties, step back now." Charley backed the coach up about ten feet, then swung the team to the right and down a narrow side street and around the backside of town. The coachman then approached the station from the other side of town. He could see that the poor wagon driver was still struggling, while Charley parked the coach. He shook his head and entered the express office. When he was finished with business, he noticed that the freight wagon had finally been parked and the horses unhitched, and put up down the street.

There was a fair-sized chunk taken out of the corner store, where the wagon wheel had hit.

"Hey, Charley!" The bartender greeted the coachman as he entered the saloon.

"Set me up, Ol' John!" Charley called back. "There's your papers. *The Sacramento Union*, hot off the presses!" he said, setting the bundle on the bar.

"Thanks, Charley. Say did you see that idiot blocking main street awhile ago?" John laughed. "Kinda filtered folks into the saloon," he said with a wink.

"Yeah, I saw him. We went around the back street. Poor guy, everyone was yellin'! He hit the dry goods store," Charley said with a snort.

"He hit the dry good store? How come nobody told me he hit the dry goods store. I'm stuck in here, and nobody tells me nothin," the bartender whined. "So who was this idiot?"

"Don't rightly know, but he's coming in the door now. You can ask him for yourself," Charley said, enjoying his beer.

The man approaching the bar was a strapping young fellow, with a genuine look of disgust playing about on his face. His eyes were of the most startling light, sky blue; they were framed with wavy blonde hair on his head and chin. He mumbled to himself with an unusual accent, as he stepped up next to Charley and ordered.

"I'll have a short beer bartender," the disgusted young man called.

"You the idiot that blocked up the road a while ago?" the bartender asked.

"Dat is myself," the man sighed, setting his worn felt hat on the bar and running his strong hands through his gold hair.

"Here, have one on me," the bartender said with a whisper and a wink, setting a big mug down.

"Tank you very kindly I'm sure. Dat's da best ting to happen all day." The man smiled. "Say I got to get a vheel vixed. Do you know a good vheel right?" he said turning to Charley, who was mesmerized by his ice blue eyes.

"Yep, I think I can help you out there. Charley Parkhurst's my name," he said extending his leather-covered hand.

"My name is John Thompson," he said, grasping the friendly appendage with his big paw.

"That there is Ol' John," Charley said, motioning to the bartender who was busy elsewhere. "I seen the fix you was in a while ago. I was driving the incoming coach."

"I'm sorry, I bottled tings up good, I expect," Thompson said, looking at his beer. "My lead horses fuss vis each uder, and I have a hard time swinging da team," he confessed.

"Maybe you need to adjust your cross-checks to spread out the horses. I can show you if you like," Charley offered.

"Dat vould be very nice of you. Can I buy you a beer?" Thompson offered.

"Sure, later I'll have a look at your lead lines if you want," Charley said to the nice young man.

"John ve'll have two more here," Thompson said lightening his mood. "I'd like vone of dose newspapers too, please," he added.

"Sure thing, there ya go," the barkeep said, slapping down the paper and fetching two more glasses. "That'll be two bits," he said on his return.

"Tank you," Thompson said, fishing out his money.

"I can take you over to see Studebaker. He can fix your wheel." Charley smiled as she secretly admired the man's strong shoulders and chiseled handsome face. He had a sweet naiveté about him and seemed modest and kind of shy. Charley had instantly liked him. The driver's face suddenly slumped as he spotted Albert making his way toward the bar.

"Hey, Charley, I got a message for you from Birch in Marysville. I thought it might be important," Albert said, handing over the dispatch.

"Thank ya, Albert," Charley said, opening the letter. "Oh, by the way, this here's John Thompson, that's Albert," he said, trailing off, as he read the message. "Hmm, says that the line is going to be trimmed down for the winter. I got to go see Edgar in the office," Parkhurst said, finishing off his beer. "You gonna be here awhile, John?"

"Ya, I tink I'll get some supper and read my paper." He smiled at his new friend.

"Well then, I'll see you in a bit," he said smiling, then turning to Albert. "Thanks, Al."

Charley walked back to the express office to find out about the route changes as Hank Monk pulled up to the front with a full coach.

"Hey, Parkie! That you? You look like you been swallowed whole by a bear!" Hank Monk grinned at the fur-covered man. "You just get in? I heard you was coming on this route!" Monk asked.

"No, I been and had two beers already. Came back to talk to Edgar about the route changes. Got a letter from Birch." He held up the letter.

"Guess it was good luck running into you, or I might get trimmed," the whip said sarcastically as he climbed from his perch. Say, looks like someone ran into the dry goods store."

"Yeah, a friend of mine." Charley smiled.

"Was he drunk?" Hank laughed, shaking his friend's hand.

"No, I don't believe so," he said, as they entered the office.

"Charley, I'm glad you came back. I got a letter from Mr. Birch about the new schedules here, take one if you like," Edgar said pensively. "Oh, hello, Hank. Got some more news about the Tom Bell gang, warnings for teamsters and coach drivers."

"Yeah, I got a letter from James myself," Charley admitted. "That's why I'm here. I reckon he headed east, his wife's havin' their first child."

"Geez, did I get any mail?" Hank said optimistically.

"Yeah, you got a letter from your ma," Edgar said offhandedly. "And a Tom Bell circular."

"Good old sweet Mother," he said, holding the letter to his heart and disregarding the wanted poster.

"I don't know where we'll put all the mail that will pile up around here this winter. Use it for insulation against the snow, I reckon," Edgar said to himself.

"Here, Monk," Charley said, handing a schedule to Hank, who was engrossed in his letter from home and trying not to mist up. "Com'on, Hank, I'll buy you a beer," he said, smiling at the sentimental man, who wiped his eye casually and smiled back.

"Musta got some dust in my eyes when I came though town," he lied, as they headed out the door. "Yep, he hit that right square!" Hank remarked as they got to the corner of the dry goods store.

"He sure as hell did!" Charley laughed. "I think he broke the wheel up too. Dang that ain't too funny."

Hank and Charley entered the saloon. It was smoky and full of men drinking and eating and playing cards. A piano player was working away in the corner of the room. Charley spotted Thompson at a small table next to the wall. He was busy reading or hiding behind a newspaper. Charley made his way over to his new friend.

"I'm heading straight for the closest drink. Set me up, Ol' John, and put it on Parkie's tab!" he called out. John looked over at Charley who was nodding.

"You bet, Hank," John sang back.

"Hey, Thompson, ja eat yet?" Charley greeted her friend.

"No, I just had another beer and vas reading in da newspaper," Thompson said, looking up and smiling.

"My friend Hank and I were probably gonna have some dinner too, mind if we pull up a chair?" Charley asked.

"No dat vould be fine." Thompson grinned.

"Hold down these chairs, and I'll get Hank. Looks like chairs is in short supply in here, musta been a fight or something. I'll be right back," Charley told Thompson, who continued pouring over the print.

"I'll have a beer, John," Charley said, stepping over to Hank. "I'm gonna get me some dinner and sit over with Thompson if you want to come over. He's holding down some seats."

"Fine, but first I think I'll oil up my brakin' leg. I got to stand up for a spell to work out the knots," Hank said, slugging down his shot. Charley could certainly understand, in these rugged mountains the brake leg got a real working. His own back ached.

"Yeah, I see your point, but I'm starving! John, I'd like a steak with beans and some rolls with butter. Oh, and a shot of brandy for my brake leg." Charley winked at Hank, as John set down the beer.

"You bet, Charley." Ol' John smiled. "Steak dinner!" he yelled out the back of the bar. A rough-looking kitchen was set up right outside the bar, under an added on roof of the establishment. There a man was busy over a wood fire, set in a rock hearth, grilling cuts of meat and tending pots of stew and beans; the floor was dirt. He had an oven arrangement for baking breads and pies. The establishment made money and provided a needed commodity in this bustling wilderness.

Charley received a plate of food and returned to the table, sending John to go and get his own. Soon Hank ambled over with his supper as well. The ravenous trio was too hungry to talk for a while.

"So where are you from, John?" Hank inquired, finally setting down his fork.

"I vas born in Norway. My family moved to America vhen I vas ten. Vere are you from, Hank?" Thompson asked.

"I was born in Waddington, New York." Hank grinned. "So are you a farmer, or a freight man?" he quizzed.

"Vell, I got a ranch out at Putah Creek, but I don't know if I like it in da valley. I feel much more at home in dese mountains. I don't like mining much," Thompson pondered.

"Don't pay as much as it used to," Charley tossed out.

"Them fellas that went poking around on the eastern side of the Sierras are gonna be stuck out there till spring, cut off from the outside world," Monk stated, noticing a few headlines in the paper.

"Yes, dat's vhat it says. Dose people vill be stranded out dere," Thompson said, looking out the window at the menacing clouds. "Da snow never stopped my people in Norway. Dey travel all over da snow covered mountains, and very swiftly too." He noticed the stunned looks on his new friends' faces. "Yes, you see dey strap on long vooden snowshoes and glide down da slopes effortlessly."

"That is till you plow into a tree, or glide effortlessly off a cliff!" Hank laughed. Charley could not help but laugh too, at the unfathomable feat.

"Dey really do dat. I myself could go pretty fast as young boy. Da snowshoes ve called skis vere very long. I would require about ten foot of ski now," Thompson said; it brought about a new round of laughter.

"So why don't you carve yourself out a set and give her a whirl? Plenty of timber out here," Hank said, still snorting.

"I might just do dat, if nothing else, it vould be fun to try it again," Thompson reflected.

"I hope you don't get yourself broken-up, busted limbs are costly," Charley advised.

"It vas really fun, I remember," John said in reflection.

"I think I'll pass on that entertainment, if you don't mind," Charley said, finishing off his beans.

John Thompson could not get the idea out of his head. When he returned to his ranch, he began his search for wood to make his skis. He chose some oak planks that he had cut before going to Placerville. The wood had good straight grain, but was still green. Thompson was so eager that he started carving away at them anyway. He sat in his cabin each night after his ranch work was done and worked on his project, dreaming of the day he would test them in the snow. He carefully planed the wood and carved a sweeping curve on the front tips. He then worried over the construction of the bindings, since he had only his memory to guide him.

Finally, the pair was finished and Thompson could wait no longer, he headed back to Placerville. Arriving in town with his produce and a much more manageable team, thanks to some expert advice, he hastily did his business at the dry goods store, careful to avoid mention of the corner incident. He was anxious to test his new skis in the new snow. After unloading his wagon, John spotted a familiar face walking down the plank sidewalk.

"Hank Monk, is dat you? Good to see you, come and look vhat I've made!" Thompson said with enthusiasm.

"Don't tell me you've fabricated them snowshoes?" Hank said laughing at the energetic young Norseman.

"Yes, dey are here. I'm going to try dem out now!" he said, like a child on Christmas Day.

"Well, maybe I ought to come along and sort of watch out after you, kinda," Hank said, looking at the great oak planks. Thompson was lovingly cradled in his strong arms. "My word, you did a fine job there. Nice and smooth and long too. Them is ten feet all right," Hank said inspecting the craftsmanship. "Those look right heavy too. Set them up there on the scale and see what they weigh."

"Twenty-five pounds, it says" Thompson said, when the scale settled. "I made a balance pole too," he said, drawing out a polished oak staff. "Let's go!" he said, setting his equipment back in the wagon and climbing up to the seat. "I vas told dere is some perty good snow just outside of town."

"This ought to be amusing." Hank smiled, as he climbed aboard Thompson's wagon.

"Where's Parkie?" John asked.

"He'll be up in about thirty minutes or so. I expect," Monk said, peeping at his timepiece. Then replacing it and drawing out a flask instead. "You want a snort?"

"No, tank you. I'm so excited! Git up now!" Thompson clucked to his horses. He found a spot about a mile outside of town and stopped the horses. The meadow before them was white with new snow and had a mild slope to it. Thompson jumped from the wagon and gathered his equipment and proceeded to give his creation a try. Monk cackled away at the sight of his absurd friend, making his way to the white meadow on the oversized plank shoes. He watched as the man began to slide around, stopping to make adjustments on his bindings and then proceeding again, and Hank had to sit up and take notice. Thompson was ecstatic and called to Monk.

"I'll meet up vit you, down da mountain!" he called, as he pushed off down the hill.

Monk gathered up the lines and turned the wagon around and headed back to town, craning his head to see where Thompson had slid to. He spotted him several times as he had fallen, but the Norseman kept climbing back up and pushing off again, speeding down the mountain at an incredible rate, until he had beaten Monk back to town.

As it was getting quite dark, they headed back to the livery. Charley was just leaving the establishment when the wagon pulled up. Monk was driving, and Thompson was in the back, trying to adjust his ski bindings.

"Well, Hank Monk, have you become a freight man? Where did you get that wagon?" Parkhurst kidded his pal.

"This is Thompson's wagon," Hank explained

"Parkie, is dat you?" a friendly voice sung out from the bed of the wagon. A moment later a familiar blonde head popped up over the side. "It is. I'm so happy. I just tested my skis, and dey vork good!" Thompson said, hopping out of the wagon to greet Charley. "I vill try dem again tomorrow."

"I'll bet you a five-dollar gold piece that he beats you back to town too!" Monk chimed in.

The next morning, the Norwegian woke Parkie at the break of dawn, and the two took his wagon outside of town, where the man practiced his long-lost skill on the freshly laid blanket of snow. Charley sat in the wagon seat and watched the graceful young man. He then turned and called out.

"I'll meet you at da edge of town!"

Charley drove the wagon back down the hill, craning his neck as Monk had done the night before, trying to watch the young man sliding across the snow.

"That was really something there, John," Charley said, scratching his head in amazement. "I had to see it to believe it."

"Pay up, Parkie," Monk said, holding out his hand with a grin.

"I tink I'll go back out again after I eat something," Thompson said, his stomach growling.

"Well, I gotta go. My coach is due to leave in twenty minutes. You stay clear of trees and cliffs and the like now, ya hear?" Charley clucked, as he tossed Monk his coin and sauntered off.

Thompson practiced and played in the snow as often as he could, each week spending time away from his ranch to return to the snowy mountains. He went out in any weather and seldom was injured besides a few scrapes and bruises.

Soon after Christmas, there was a growing buzz going on in the sleepy town about the crazy snowshoe man. Those who saw him were dazzled by the speed the man obtained on the strange-looking footwear. Most thought he would end up mashed into the side of a tree.

"So, John, how far up them mountains can you climb on those snowshoes?" Monk asked.

"Today I made it out about ten miles. It's so beautiful out dere. I tink I could stay out all night long sometimes," the mountain man spoke in reverence.

"You know Chorrpening is still looking for some fool . . . um . . . some one to carry mail to Carson City." Monk smiled. "May as well get paid while you're out there," Hank said, lighting his cigar.

"I tink maybe I'm ready to try it. I've gotten pretty strong. Feel my leg," Thompson kidded.

"Got yourself a regular ham there," Hank said taking notice. "Here have a look at my brakin' leg. T'other leg is kinda puny 'cause it don't get to pushin' on the brake like t'other one. But this leg is pretty good," Monk said proudly.

"Who should I go and talk to about delivering da mail?" Thompson said changing the subject.

"Well, I'd go on in and see Edgar. He knows everything about the mail," Hank said carefully.

"Edgar?" Thompson nodded. "Do you vant to go vith me, Hank?"

"Do I want to go with you, to watch you tell Edgar that you want to carry the mail across the Sierras, in the dead of winter? Why yes, I would like to be there to see his face when you do. Let's go."

The pair strided down, in step, to the express office, just as an angular man with severe features and a suit that looked a bit to tight, was closing up shop for his dinner hour.

"Evening, Monk. What brings you back to the office?" the businesslike Edgar said curtly.

"Hey, Edgar, I brought my friend here, John Thompson, in to talk to you," Monk said politely.

"Pleased to meet you, Thompson, what is it I can do fer you?" Edgar asked.

"I have come about da job of taking da mail to Carson City," Thompson said softly.

"What is this? One of your pranks no doubt, eh, Monk?" Edgar said, with a huff.

"No, I am serious," John pleaded.

"You sent him here just to plague me, didn't you?" Edgar insisted, looking sternly at Monk.

"I swear, Edgar, he's square." Hank couldn't help grinning, in a practical joking sort of way.

"So let me get this straight. You want to carry the mail, over the mountains, in the snow, to Carson City?" Edgar repeated to the young man slowly.

"Yes, I can do it. I know I can!" Thompson replied earnestly.

"Let me ask you this, are you crazy? Is this man crazy? Or just stupid?" he said turning to Monk. "You have brought a lunatic into this office, haven't you?"

"No, he's not crazy, and he is serious," Hank said softly; he was enjoying Edgar's pains with relish.

"So, how are you going to do it? With some sort of reindeer and a sled?" Edgar asked, studying the tall Norseman's face for signs of insanity.

"No, I have skis," Thompson explained.

"Oh, you have skis. Well, that makes all the difference, he has skeeees!" Edgar laughed sarcastically. "What in the hell are skis?"

"I can show you if you vont?" Thompson offered.

"Now he wants to show me! Well, I can't look at your skis tonight. My wife has supper waiting, come by tomorrow morning, and if you still want the job, we'll talk about it then," the exasperated man declared.

"You're as good as signed up, Thompson!" Hank said slapping the man on the back. "Just wait till you see him go, Edgar!" He said giving him a thump too, causing him to nearly stumble down the steps. Of course, Hank had to blab to everyone that Thompson was going to give a snowshoeing exhibition early next morning. He went on about how he would fearlessly carry the mail over the Sierras. He milked it and reaped the reward of many free drinks that night.

Charley arrived in town driving the eight o'clock stage and then retired to Ol' John's saloon to oil his brake leg and found Monk holding court, with Thompson in tow. They seemed to be celebrating something.

"You all seem like a happy bunch," Charley said, stepping up to the bar.

"Ve're celebratin'!" Thompson said, throwing an arm around Charley.

"What is it? Your birthday?" Charley asked, enjoying the drunken bear hug from the handsome man.

"No, I have signed on to carry da mail to Carson City, or at least I'm as good as signed. Right, Hank?" Thompson laughed. He was unaccustomed to drinking strong spirits, and it showed.

"You put him up to this, Hank?" Charley's tone was anything but happy.

"Why sure, he's out snowshoein' anyway. He may as well get paid for it," Hank reasoned.

"He'll be killed or freeze to death!" Charley scolded.

"No, I'll be fine!" John promised. "I'm going to give a demonstration tomorrow morning at seven," he toasted.

"Oh, that's what Edgar was talking about. Said he had to be in early tomorrow to watch some idiot," Charley said scratching his head. Hank burst out laughing.

"I'm going to go and get an early start for tomorrow," Thompson said with a yawn.

"John, you should think about this some more before you go ahead and sign anything," Charley warned.

"I vill, Parkie, zee you tomorrow," John said, pulling on his hat and staggering toward the door.

"Damn, I need a drink. Set me up, Ol' John," Charley said, glaring at Hank.

Thompson was too excited to sleep much, so he rose at three in the morning and collected his equipment and headed out to the mountains. He climbed and climbed, slowly and methodically sideways up the slopes. He paused to watch the warm hues of morning, peeking through the trees on the horizon and eat some smoked trout he had in his pocket. He checked his watch; it was five forty-five. He would climb for another twenty minutes, he figured, then go back down.

Reaching the summit of a beautiful slope, he adjusted his hat and scarf and held the balance pole in both hands, out in front of his body, then pushed off down the mountain. It was a glorious ride. The unblemished snow was powdery and fast, as he slid down the face of the mountain, faster and faster, back toward town. Snowshoe hares bounded for their lives, as the Norseman flew by.

Hank was up early and was anxiously looking about town for Thompson, who was nowhere to be found.

"Damn that Thompson, he's out to make me look foolish, I swear," Monk said, stomping around the street.

"He's probably up the mountain and on his way down," Charley said, sipping on his coffee. "Lest of course he's hurt out there, somewhere," he said, raising his mug to the mountains. Men were starting to gather outside of town, eager to see the snowshoe demonstration.

"Well, where is this marvel of the mail, Monk?" Edgar said with a snide grin.

"Oh, I reckon he'll be around here soon," Hank said, looking at his watch. It was five minutes past seven.

"Look, I see him coming!" a voice from the edge of town was yelling. Everyone began to trot to the edge of town to see for themselves'. There was a moving speck of humanity speeding down the slope in the distance. He disappeared behind a stand of trees and then reappeared, as he came closer and closer. Everyone was very excited by the show and began to cheer, as they witnessed daring jumps and graceful, sweeping turns. As he drew near, Thompson's speed did not diminish, he seemed out of control. Never had the men seen a person move so fast, let alone, on a set of planks. The audience began to murmur of his impending demise. Yet as Thompson arrived, he skillfully turned his body and skidded to a graceful stop, sending powdery snow in the air like a rooster tail. The men all cheered, "Hurrah for Snowshoe Thompson!" The new name forever stuck with him. Edgar was at a loss for words, his jaw was slack, and he just kept shaking his head incredulously.

"I've never seen anything like that in all my life!" Edgar kept saying. "If you want to carry the mail, I'll recommend to Chorpenning that he give you a try. The crowd all threw their hats in the air with approval.

CHAPTER 27

January 1856, Placerville

Edgar Thatcher was a short skinny gentleman, who was busy fussing around his post office. He checked his watch; it was four thirty in the morning. He checked his coffeepot and poured himself a cup, as the door swung open and John Thompson came in with a gust of snow.

"Oh, dat coffee smells very good, Edgar," Thompson smiled.

"So you really gonna risk your life on this adventure, eh, Snowshoe? Come on and get yourself a cup," Thatcher said, lifting the hot pot.

"I got my own cup here," Thompson said, pulling a tin cup from his belt.

"Oh, so you do," Thatcher said, pouring the coffee. "I suppose the fellas all told you about Pierce and Johnson attempt, and how they nearly died out there." Edgar pointed out the window.

"Ya, and Charley told me da story of da Donner Party too, but I know I can do it," Thompson explained.

"You just gonna wear that? Don't you have one of those bearskin coats like the coachmen like to wear?" Edgar said examining Thompson's clothes.

"I got on da best vool clothes for da trip. Dey stays varm, even if dey is vet. Don't vorry, Edgar."

"Well, here it is, weighs about seventy pounds, I couldn't carry it around the block," Edgar said, pointing to the mail sack.

Thompson took off his newly made back-pack and put the sack in it, then hoisted it on his strong back and tied it on securely. He bounced up and down; to make sure it wouldn't shift. Then he turned to the postmaster and shook his hand.

"Tanks for da coffee, Edgar. I'll be back in a few days, maybe five." Thompson tied his cup back on his belt. On the porch, the Norseman hoisted his planks onto his broad shoulders and held his pole in the other hand and trudged out into the dark morning. The full moon lit his way, to the snowy peaks ahead.

"The man's nutty as a fruit cake. He'll never make it," Edgar mumbled to himself, as he peered out the window, watching Thompson attach his boots to the planks, then disappear into the forest.

Outside of town, the countryside was silent, except for the shushing sound of the smooth wood against the icy snow and Thompson's rhythmic breathing. The effort warmed his body and he loosened his coat. Moonbeams shining through the trees gave off ample light, as the outdoorsmans' eyes adjusted. He zigged and zagged up each hill, as he went higher and higher, to the granite peaks ahead. He was still on familiar territory, having practiced his craft there often. The summit would be his challenge; he had ridden and hiked all over this route before it was snowed in, and felt confident he would not get lost. As the sun came up, Thompson seemed like the lone inhabitant in a pristine world, and he relished it, stopping now and then to rest and enjoy the scenery. Nibbling on some jerky, he got his bearings, then was off again, as the snow lightly fell around him. It was ninety miles to Carson City; he planned to make the trip in three days. The return trip should be easier, he expected to do it in two. Thompson looked forward to flying back down these mountains, but for now he went up and up, slowly.

As the evening came around, Thompson looked for an old dead tree, and having found a stump that suited him, he started a fire in its core and set up his camp. He set some green pine boughs near his fire and melted snow in his cup to drink, then ate canned sardines with crackers for dinner, as he lay on his bed, watching the flames crackle and pop.

The fire in the stump still glowed, as Thompson checked the watch his father had given him as a boy. He kicked snow onto the embers, as he picked up his mail sack, which had served overnight as a pillow, and prepared to depart. Today's climb would be the hardest yet; he would try to reach the summit by nightfall.

The wind blew snow in swirls around him, as he methodically skied across the dangerous slopes, gaining altitude as he went along. His progress was slower than he thought it would be, so he kept on after dark, until the wind and exhaustion forced him to stop. He dragged some dead wood to a rocky alcove he spotted and lit a fire in front of it. He slept soundly after dinner in this little cave, but it was a brief snooze. His fire had gone out, and the snow was becoming relentless, so John Thompson pushed on.

Finally, in the early morning, John could see the summit. He danced with exhilaration when he reached the backbone of the mighty Sierras. Reaching in his coat for a cracker and some sardines, Snowshoe Thompson breakfasted on the top of the world, utterly by himself. Below lay the icy blue waters of lake Tahoe. It shone like a deep blue jewel in the snowy landscape.

After he ate, Thompson pushed off for Genoa and finally Carson City, with renewed excitement, for it was mostly downhill to the small town. The eagles in the sky were his only companions in this frozen wilderness, as he flew down the mountainside. The slopes were steep and dangerous and a wrong choice could mean death, for no other men would be in these Netherlands until spring. Thompson navigated down the mountains with care, enjoying himself and the great speed, with gusto.

Later he arrived without fanfare in Genoa, under darkness of night. In fact, no one even knew he was coming! Thompson walked into the one bar that was still open and announced his arrival. His entrance and announcement took the rough-looking lot by suprise. The miners laughed until the snow-covered man took off his mail sack and heaved it onto the bar.

"I've come from Placerville vith da mail, but da post office vas closed," Thompson told a stunned crowd.

"Why that just ain't possible, but here it is!" the bartender said as he looked in the bag. Here's a letter from my sister in San Francisco! Have a drink on me, young man!" the barkeep said, with astonishment at the amazing mountaineer.

"You say this man just brought in the mail?" a man who had just returned from the outhouse asked.

"Yes, I have, who are you?" Thompson replied

"My name is Kinsey. I am the postmaster here. Who are you?"

"My name is John Thompson. I just came from Placerville. Edgar Thatcher said I am to talk to you about getting paid."

"Well, well, well . . . I didn't even know you was comin!" the flabbergasted man replied. "I'm sure we can work something out. You figuring on taking the mail back too?"

"Of course!" Thompson said proudly.

"Three cheers for Thompson!" Kinsey called out to the rest of the bar, as everyone present wanted to meet the brave mountain man.

Back in Placerville, Edgar fussed and fidgeted around the office. He periodically stepped outside to scan the hills for signs of Snowshoe. This time he locked the door and stepped around the corner for a bracer before his dinner.

"What are you doing here. I thought the coach left?" Edgar asked, as Hank Monk approached the bar.

"Dempsey rode in and said a big tree was blocking the road, about a mile outside of town. We're gonna be an hour late. You still worried about Snowshoe? He'll be all right," Hank said, polishing off his beer.

"I just feel sick about this, you never should have put that idear into his head," Edgar said, searching for the bartender. "My wife gives me hell about it every time I come home. Boy, I sure hope he comes back before I gotta go to dinner. If Thompson dies out there, I'll have to build another bedroom on my house to have any peace."

"Don't worry, he'll be back soon. Coon Holler Charley is keepin' watch. He'll ring a bell when he spots him comin'. Hope he comes back before I got to leave," Monk said, waving to the bartender "Put five dollars on seven-thirty tonight, just in case," he said, setting the gold coin on the bar. "See you tommorra night, Edgar," Monk said, turning to leave.

As Monk walked back to the stagecoach, he faintly heard a bell ringing in the distance. He jerked his head around toward the sound and squinted his eyes, then ran back the way he'd come.

"He's a comin'! Snowshoe Thompson is a comin' down the mountain!" Monk yelled into the tavern.

Everyone poured out of the buildings and ran to see the spectacle. Edgar stopped a moment to heave a heavy sigh of relief before trotting after the rest. Monk grabbed the bugle off the coach and played his best arrival song as the young Norseman glided gracefully home, amid boisterous cheers.

"Hurrah for Snowshoe Thompson!"

"I wish you'd a taken a longer lunch break. I had seven-thirty!" Monk whispered to Snowshoe as the crowd lifted Thompson onto their shoulders and carried him to the post office.

CHAPTER 28

California, Early Spring 1856

Charley had given up driving in the Sierra foothills for the winter. The mountain roads got clogged with snow, and the men came out of their mines to spend the harsh months in more hospitable places, such as San Francisco or Monterey. Charley's seniority with the coach line and friendship with James Birch gave him the opportunity to drive wherever he wanted, so he chose to drive from San Jose to San Francisco in the bad weather. It was still cold and rainy, but much less treacherous than the mountains or the eastern winters.

The rain, which had been relentless, let up for the time being, but the roads were extremely muddy. The near wheeler, the horse in the hitch closest to the driver, was in a particularly bad mood, and it was becoming apparent that her left hind shoe was becoming loose. The ground that they were traveling was becoming increasingly rocky, and they still had at least five miles until the next station, in Redwood City. The constantly wet hooves meant that they were very soft and prone to breaking, if they were let to grow too long between shoeing.

"Dang blast it!" Charley cursed. "I got to take that good for nothing shoe offa that cranky horse before she hurts herself with it." It was clanking in the gravely mud and getting small rocks in it and getting looser all the time.

"Lloyd, you get my spares kit out of the front boot and get me my nail cutters please," Charley said to the expressman, as he was stopping the team.

"Great, it's starting to rain again," the driver sighed. Lloyd was off the coach as fast as his long legs could carry him; he had the case out in no time.

"Why don't you chalk up the wheels while you're at it," Charley said, tying up the lines and climbing down. "After you get the wheels chalked, please stand in front of the team so's that they don't move. Folks you can step out of the coach and stretch you legs 'cause we're gonna be here for a few minutes while I remove a loose shoe from one of the horses," Charley addressed his passengers.

There were a few who grumbled at the accursed mud everywhere and the rain that was beginning to fall, but most had a dull throbbing in their lower backs and braved getting filthy to stretch. When all of the passengers were out, Charley unhooked the horses' tug chains from the single tree and then moved the cranky mare away from the stagecoach pole with the inside tug chain. The horse was a nasty biter, new on the line and probably in heat, Charley guessed.

The stage company bought horses from all over, well-bred horses that had developed bad habits that a few years on the stage route would fix or make worse. Biters, kickers, runaways, Charley had seen all kinds, and was always cautious of new horses. The shoe was still on fairly securely on one side of the hoof with three nails; the other side nails were freed up when a piece of hoof had broken off. The horse had been let go too long before shoeing, a sure sign of a kicker. The loose shoe had to come off.

Charley tried to soothe the mare with quiet talk, as he ran his hand down the horses' leg. He lifted it up, then rested it on his own leg, while squatting in a most vulnerable position. Charley tried to cut off the remaining nails and was successful with two out of three, but the mare was not being patient. She violently pulled her leg away, and Charley tried to calm her. As he again tried to pick up the horses' hoof, the mare became increasingly agitated with the shoe flopping around the hoof, causing her to try and rid herself of the offensive shoe by stomping. In her thrashings, she cornered Charley next to the wagon pole and began to kick in earnest. One of the passengers noticed Charley's dilemma and grabbed the horse's bridle, causing her to turn her ass end toward Charley. Before he knew what happened, Parkhurst had been kicked in the face with the loose shoe, knocking him into the single trees and the feet of the bitchy mare's partner. This animal was a mellower-type horse, which allowed the passengers to drag the now unconscious Charley out of the way of more danger.

"Oh my God! Now what are we gonna do?" a city woman groaned. "I hope the other man can drive this team, or we'll be stuck here. Somebody ought to tell him what happened."

Lloyd had been standing far at the front of the six horses, and did not see his comrade fall.

"Is he dead?" Charley heard one voice saying. His head was spinning, and he couldn't see very well. It was evening, but everything looked so weird, his face was all sticky and his head burned and pounded.

"Oh my God, Charley!" Lloyd cried. "That mare got you! You said she'd be trouble, and you sure were right! Can you sit up at all?"

"I think so, not sure as I can drive though. How's the shoe look on that horse?"

"My God, Charley, who cares! We got to get you to a doctor quick!" Lloyd's panic was starting to show in his voice.

"That bad?" Charley asked.

"Pretty bad, Charley, I think you'd better ride inside," Lloyd said, carefully bandaging Charley's face with a handkerchief.

"Hell no, I still got one good eye. I even said I could drive this route with both eyes shut, so now I guess I can prove it," Charley labored, not wishing to relinquish control.

"You wasn't plannin' on driving, were you?" Lloyd said in disbelief.

"Well, there ain't nothing wrong with my hands, is there?" Charley said trying to conceal his panic.

Lloyd shook his head, as he hooked the mare back into position and helped Charley up to the box. The proud driver sat for a moment and tried to stay in control, but found it impossible and handed the leather lines to his partner as he blacked out. Lloyd took the lines from his proud friend's hands and tied them on the brake, then lay the wounded driver down in the front boot. The expressman then drove as fast as possible to the next station. The offending horseshoe was broken off the mare's hoof as soon as they started.

Lloyd pulled into the station and called out frantically for a doctor. The stationmaster took Charley from the coach to the doctor in town, who soon informed him that his coachman would most certainly lose his eye from the incident.

"How much whiskey has this man had?" the doctor asked.

"I don't know. I don't think he's had any," Lloyd replied.

"Well, you can go home. He will have to stay with me for a few days. This is very bad; I will have to operate on him to remove the eye. It's very serious," the doctor firmly stated. Charley had revived in time to hear the report.

"Doctor?" Charley cried. "I'm gonna lose my eye?"

"I'm afraid I cannot save it, sir, I'm sorry. Now if you please, this man needs attention. I must ask the rest of you to leave. Henry, help me get this man into my chair, then light the lamps."

Lloyd sat on the front steps of the office a moment and hung his head.

"Come on, you're gonna have to finish the route. I got a station to run," the stationmaster said getting into his buggy. "That's all we can do for now."

"I know you are in agony, my friend. I will put you to sleep. When you awake, I will give you something to relieve your pain. Lay back in the chair now." The surgeon had a barber's chair, in which he also performed dentistry. He was buckling thick leather straps around his patient's wrists, securing him to the padded arms of the chair. Charley had no choice but to surrender to his care. The doctor and his assistant set about administering the anesthetic ether to the patient, then proceeded to clean the wounds and assess the damage. The eyeball had been pierced with a horseshoe nail, then ripped beyond repair; a jagged facial laceration descended from the corner of the eye to mid-cheek. It was likely that the jaw was fractured and possibly dentistry needed. Charley's face was swelling rapidly. It was imperative to work on the eye before it was swollen shut.

The eyelid was held open with clamps as the surgeon removed the damaged eyeball. He then cleaned the interior of the socket as Charley struggled in a fitful nightmare. The man then set about stitching Charley's face back to some semblance of order. The patient began to revive as the doctor was applying bandages to his head.

"Here drink this, it will help fight the pain." The doctor had poured a measure of laudanum into a shot glass for the patient. "Go on," the doctor said, helping him put the glass to his mouth. "You will have to stay with me for a few days, I'm afraid. I must keep a close watch on you until you are out of danger."

"I'm sorry to be of bother to you, Doc," Charley said through a haze.

"Think nothing of it. I'm sure you will be quite all right, soon. Try and get some rest now. I will check on you again in a while. If the pain gets worse, I will give you some more laudanum."

"Thanks, Doc," Charley sighed, falling to sleep in the dentist chair; it was really very comfortable. Charley soon drifted off, assisted by the trauma and the opium, now swirling around in his system.

The next morning, Charley woke in a bed. At first he did not know where he was. Later the doctor removed the bandages and examined his work. Charley's face looked like a patchwork quilt with all the fancy stitching and colors. The abused eye socket was angry and swollen. He had packed the empty socket with absorbent cotton cloth, and it was excruciating when he removed it. The doctor placed a pad of absorbent bandage over the empty socket and then bandaged the face back up. He gave Charley a good measure of laudanum; then had the patient lay face down on a cot, with his face and chest propped with pillows so the empty socket could drain. Charley experienced surreal opium dreams.

Lloyd and others visited, but everything seemed to be moving in a strange new time and rhythm, things seemed funny or made no sense. He was wide-awake, yet it all seemed like a dream somehow. The doctor kept Charley fairly well oiled with laudanum. He found his patients whined less, and it was easier to look after them if they slept most of the time, which was what they needed to do anyway.

Three days passed in the twinkling of a missing eye, or so it would seem.

"You may return home today, but you must see me at least once a day for a week further so I can change your dressing. You are healing well, but you are far from danger of infection for at least a month or more," the surgeon advised. "I can drop you off in town this afternoon when I make a few rounds."

"Thank you for all you have done for me, sir," Charley said earnestly. "You saved my life I expect."

"You've no need to worry, Charley. Your secret is safe with me. It's your own business. But I must admit you're one of the most courageous women I've ever met," the doctor confided.

Charley took the recovery hard. Since it was a head injury, the doctor was leery of letting Charley drive again. He had bandaged Charley's head up pretty snugly and had not let her look when he had changed the dressing. When the bandages finally came off, it was rather shocking to see such a strange ugly face, with sunken socket, minus one eyeball. Charley had already started to get used to the monocular vision, but this was a depressing sight. Lloyd presented Charley with a new eye patch as sort of a consolation prize.

"This makes you look kinda dashing, kinda dangerous!" he offered.

"Thanks, Lloyd.

"After you heal completely, you might consider a glass eye," the doctor advised.

"Thanks, Doc," Charley said standing to leave the office.

"You know that the stageline could be responsible for the loss of your eye, Charley. You should make sure that they do right by you. Take care with the laudanum, a little goes a long way," the doctor cautioned, shaking his patient's hand.

"Thanks again, I don't hardly need it anymore." Charley smiled.

"That's good news indeed," the doctor said, hurrying on to his next appointment.

When Charley felt up to it, he went to Sacramento in search of his friend and boss James Birch.

"I have to keep driving, James! It's all I've ever known," Charley said with his head down. "It's all I've ever wanted to do."

"Of course you shall, but for now you shall keep to simpler routes, that's all I'm saying. I need you, Charley. As you know I've been planning the Great Overland Stage Line. I'm contracting stations and setting up meetings as we speak. At least I have people working on it. I want my best drivers fit and ready to deliver. On my last trip to Washington, I delivered my bid to carry the mail from the east to San Francisco. If I win the bid, we will begin next spring. It will be the grandest stage company in the history of the world! I have been collecting horses in the numbers, Charley, we shall have an inspection, and you can tell me what you think! I have always valued your opinion about horses. You could stand a rest. We'll let someone else drive. We'll buy horses!" James said, lighting his cigar, then passing the light to Charley. "I like that patch on you, makes you look dangerous, the ladies eat that up."

Charley sat staring at the young man, he had watched him turn to manhood and was now controlling this tremendous business; he could not help but be proud.

"There are several bids in, however. John Butterfield has a strong chance in his. He has chosen the southern route through the deserts and hostile Indian territory. Apache Indians are very touchy fellows. If you get them angry, there's hell to pay! I opted for the southern route as well, for now. The Sierra Mountains are a formidable barrier, but Jarred Crandall has been looking into solving that problem too, seems to think that there's a way through. He's been talking to that Norwegian chap, Thompson. Heard he's a friend of yours, Charley."

"Snowshoe Thompson?"

"Yes, I think that's what he called him."

"Yes, he's a good friend. Monk and I met him awhile back," Charley mused. "After the roads closed down, he took the mail on his back from Placerville to Carson City. Has long planks that he straps on his feet. Keeps him from sinking into the snow. I think he called them skis or something like that. Amazing man, incredibly strong!"

"So I've heard," Birch said. Charley smiled as he looked at his friend and benefactor. Birch was making a great deal of money as he had predicted and was not shy about putting his money back into the company. He thought long and hard about how to make it the best stageline in the world. He truly enjoyed his life, except that he missed his wife, Julia, and his newly born son, Frank, whom he had named for his friend and partner Frank Stevens. Their first child, a daughter, died not long after her birth. Now with a cherished son at her side, Julia was deathly fearful of traveling west and was too used to her pampered lifestyle. To live anywhere but in the east, at her beloved Swansea, was out of the question. She was used to a social life, and the thought of those filthy miners did nothing to sway her into ever consider traveling to California. So James made his pilgrimages back to the east coast as often as he could, via ship, returning to California with more coaching goods from the east, such as kegs of six horse lines, well oiled and coiled into barrels for shipping.

Charley spent several weeks working closely with James and had new respect for the man's enthusiasm and vision of the future. He had worked at consolidating companies that had been rivals and in doing so, had been able to eliminate redundant routes and price wars. The California Stage Company was soon the largest in the country. Jarred Crandall, now a partner, was determined to bring progress through the mountains and attempted to tame the mighty Sierras or at least one stretch of newly dug road.

CHAPTER 29

Marysville 1856

"Dr. Hodges?" Birch asked, as he walked up to the tavern bar.

"Why yes, my good man, have we met before?" the doctor replied, not looking up at the inquirer.

"Yes, it seems that I last left you, you were on your way to . . . San Quentin," he whispered, uneasily.

"Ah yes, the coachman. Birch, isn't it?" Hodges said after studying the face of the teamster.

"That's right. Guess you got time off for good behavior, eh, Doc?" James smiled at the mild-mannered man.

"How true that is, sir. Can I buy you a drink, my friend?" Hodges inquired.

"Don't mind if you do," Birch said with a chuckle. The man seemed harmless enough to be out on his own. James ran into the mild-mannered doctor often, as he was frequently at stops of the California Stage Company.

"Funny how that band of highway men are using the name of Tom Bell, don't you think, Doctor?" Birch asked one evening.

"Not too funny, my friend, I told your story to many in the institution by the bay. Men there are starved for good stories and repeat them to each other often," Dr. Hodges lied. "Now I have an appointment to tend to," the tall doctor said, rising and looking at his watch. "I must bid you good night." As he left the bar, Birch never surmised the mild-mannered man's true nature.

Up until this time, the roads were safe for stagecoaches; everyone else was fair game. The coaches had been off-limits; too fast and well-armed, millions of dollars in gold ran unscathed through the hills of California quite safe, until now.

The Tom Bell gang was hatching another plan. It would be Dr. Hodges' swan song. He would reap a big reward, then retire in the east. Dr. Hodges had learned of a shipment of gold worth over $100,000, coming from Camptonville to Marysville on August 12, 1856. The gold was the property of one miner named Rideout.

The Tom Bell Gang had a spy to make sure that the gold shipment was loaded, then a signal was given, and the holdup men rode off to the site of the robbery. The site was an uphill climb out of a creek bed; it was narrow and rocky.

Mr. Rideout did not like riding in stagecoaches; the rough hills made him nauseous. He elected to accompany his gold to Marysville astride a horse. It was advised that he stay ahead of the coach to avoid dust, another sore point with Mr. Rideout. He took the deer trails on some occasion to avoid the sun, for it was a very hot August day. The coach was full; it held four Chinese men, several businessmen, and a woman, Mrs. Tilghman, the wife of a Marysville barber. The stage was driven by John Gear and guarded by William Dobson.

In August, Dry Creek is as the name implies, dry, but it was shady nonetheless, so Mr. Rideout took the logical trail. The stage was back about a quarter of a mile, so it would be a refreshing little break under the bay trees for him, so he thought.

It was half past four in the afternoon, when three armed men, with bandannas around their faces, stopped Rideout before he could reach the apex of the wooded trail. They ordered him off his horse and searched him for valuables; they found none. However, it was enough of a distraction to take their minds off their duty at hand, which was the approaching treasure laden coach. The rest of the gang, Dr. Hodges, alias: Tom Bell, Bill Gristy, English Bob and Monte Jack were waiting for the treasure on the express road. As the coach arrived in a cloud off dust, the three robbers were still distracted with treasure's owner, who was watching the stagecoach come into a trap and wondering what to do.

The Camptonville stage was stopped by four men, instead of the originally planned for seven. The expressman, Dobson, boldly set his shotgun at the closest bandit and fired. The target tumbled from the saddle, bringing the odds even closer. The driver, John Gear, fired too, as he whipped the horses into a gallop. The three distracted bandits soon caught up to the scene, as the stage was moving off. Lead was flying through the dust, as the coach horses bolted from the gunfire. The expressman, Dobson, was hit in the arm and could barely hold on, as the coach bounded out of the canyon at top speed. The men in the interior of the stage were firing at the bandits, as they made a last ditch effort to stop the vehicle.

Rideout, who had managed to recover his horse and was currently riding for his life, galloped up to the coach and was ordered by the driver to ride ahead and get help, which he was happy to do.

The road became narrow, with steep hillsides on either side of the road. The bandits were forced to abandon their plan.

The galloping coach arrived at Marysville with one woman, shot in the head, the bullet still lodged in the brain; miraculously she was still alive. One passenger, John Campbell, was wounded in the forehead by a glancing shot, which very narrowly missed his eye. Another man was shot through both legs, and the expressman had a badly shattered arm. They still had the treasure though, which gave little comfort to the barber, whose wife would soon be dead. There was never any trace of the four Chinese men, however; they had jumped out of the coach at the beginning of the shooting and were never seen again.

Word of the holdup spread fast, giving daring coachmen something else to dread on the roads. An accurate description was given, and the men identified as the Tom Bell Gang. The dead woman added extra fervor to the already outraged communities.

Captain William King of the Marysville Police was called in to organize an all out search for the gang. And so the chase was on.

Birch picked up the *Marysville Express* and read the paper, while having dinner at the Hog Ranch. He read the following:

> "My dear Captain King, I think you could make more money by not being quite so officious, for I have had opportunities to put several hundred dollars in your pocket. There was the matter of the Walker and the Martin mares, for which there was $400 reward offered. I could have told you where you might find them, but your vigilant search after me keeps me from putting you on to a great many good things. But don't think for a moment that your vigilance causes me any uneasiness or that I seek for an armistice. No, far from it, for I have unfurled my banner to the breeze, and my motto is "Catch me if you can!" Captain, I know you are pretty smart, but I think that if you would only travel with me a short time, I would teach you some tricks that you have never thought of. Probably you have heard a great many things, but you must know I am not guilty of every accusation that is alleged against me. For instance, some malicious scoundrel tried to saddle the murder at Frenchman's Bar on me, but he could not do it, and although I am looked upon as a desperado and know that I could expect no leniency at the hands of the people should they ever catch me, still I am too proud to commit such an atrocious and cowardly murder as that was. Truly yours, Tom Bell."

"Well, what the hell do you suppose he meant by all that!" Birch exclaimed as he set down the paper and lit his cigar.

"I can't imagine why he is writing to the newspapers!" Elisabeth Hood, the owner of the Hog Ranch, replied. "You ready for your pie, James?"

"You bet, ma'am."

"I'll have one of my girls bring it to you." She winked. Elisabeth was a large woman with flaming red hair. Her daughters had inherited the same in abundance. They had pale skin, with sky blue eyes. The oldest, was fourteen years old, with intense stormy eyes. James had had several occasions to notice them, for she was enamored with the fabulous Mr. James Birch. It was rather unsettling.

"Hey, Birch!" a man called to the driver at the bar, eating pie.

"Well, if it isn't Deputy Sheriff Shuler," James returned. "You fellas hot on any trails?" he asked.

"Well, we are closing in on a few leads, I guess you could say. When are you pulling out?" the deputy asked.

"Tomorrow, at seven. You coming along?" the driver inquired.

"Maybe. Have you met my associates? McCormick, McNish, Sands, Palmer, Adams, and Sheriff Clark."

"Pleased to meet you all, looks like you're loaded for bear, all right!" James said, shaking the long line of hands.

"Birch here is one of the finest stage drivers you'll ever meet!" Shuler gushed. "We met on my first trip to the Sierras, and how he drove through the mountains at night, I'll never know."

"Thank you for that vote of confidence, Deputy, most passengers cuss me out for trying to scare them. Gentlemen, it's been a pleasure but I gotta turn in." The men were busy refreshing themselves and hardly noticed his departure.

The next morning, as James drank some coffee, Mrs. Hood abruptly told him that she was going to sell out and leave. "I don't like the atmosphere around here for my girls. Bad men lurking around every bend in the road. I've had enough." The woman was very close to tears.

"I'll be sorry to see you go, Elisabeth. If I may be so bold," James spoke. "Probably best for the girls though."

A month or so later, on October 10, Charley was in the Marysville depot when a young boy, he had helped with his reading, came running in with a newspaper in hand. "Did you see the news yet, Charley?" he said, out of breath.

"No, I just got in, you found something interesting there? Did you?" he asked.

The young boy was very excited. "The *Calaveras Chronicle* says:

"Our county jail now contains five of Tom Bell's freebooters. On Tuesday last, Deputy Sheriff Shuler arrived in the Sacramento stage, having in charge Jack Phillips, a Sydney duck, who was arrested at the Mountaineer House, seven miles from Auburn. Phillips is said to be a harbored of Bells gang and a gatherer of information for their special benefit. Day before yesterday, the Sacramento and Stockton stages brought each two more of the highwaymen. By some means, reliable information has been obtained of the rendezvous of the gang, and two different parties started hence several days since to capture them. Sheriff Clark, with deputies Shuler, Paul, and McCormick, went to Yuba County and under Sheriff Mulford, Deputy Sheriff McNish and Messrs. Sands, Palmer and Adams to Tulare County. So far six of the gang have been arrested, and others soon will be. Near the junction of the Tulare Lake Slough and the San Joaquin River, they came upon the winter quarters of the banditti and arrested two brothers named Farnsworth, the only persons there at the time. They also captured three fine horses, one of which was Tom Bell's favorite horse, Buckskin, and another his fancy mare. These horses were much worn down and had been put there to recreate. Two prisoners named Garder and Sutton arrived on the Sacramento stage. They where arrested at the California House, twenty-eight miles above Marysville, on the Rabbit Creek road by Sheriff Clarke, Deputy Sheriff Paul, and Constable McCormick. This arrest was made at daylight in the morning, the parties being roused from

a sound sleep. From the exertions that are being made by the authorities,
and the success that attends their efforts, we have reason to hope that this
formidable gang will soon be broken up."

"Looks like the hounds have finally treed their quarry. Good job reading, Michael.
Here, go get yourself a piece of pie." Charley flipped a coin to the boy who surrendered
the paper to his idol.

"Thanks, Charley!" The boy skipped out to the tavern.

"I was just gonna tell you the news when the little blabbermouth came runnin' in,"
the clerk grumbled as if a pin had burst his bubble. Charley would keep an eye out for
more news of the gang, and it wasn't long before there was more.

Mr. Price had been out hunting down some stray cows. Suddenly he wheeled his
horse around in a hurry to tell the judge about the lone horseman he had seen in the
willow trees by the river. It had seemed odd is all, especially with all the outlaws running
around. The judge was eager to follow all leads and set out directly, commanding a small
force of men himself. As they approached the area where the man had been seen, he
split his men up. The judge guided his men, as he walked in front of his horse.

Dr. Hodges, who was sitting on his horse under a tree, did not hear them coming;
he was dozing, for he had gone without sleep for days. He looked up only to see two
rifles and a double-barrel shotgun leveled at his chest and head. He was caught and
slowly raised his hands as the men relieved him of his armaments—a Navy Colt, a
Bowie knife, and a rifle.

"I believe," said the judge as he observed the outlaw's broken nose, "that you are
the man we have been looking for."

Dr. Hodges looked deeply into his own demise and answered, "Very probably."

"Tie him up, boys!" the judge growled.

The men gleefully tied Hodges' wrists and then tied him to his horse for transport,
back to the ferry building. The judge then interrogated the prisoner, who it may be
noted had yet to be tried by a court of law.

"Do you admit before this judge and these sworn witnesses that you are one Tom
Bell?" Judge Belt roared.

"I believe that you have already beaten that confession out of me," Hodges said
spitting, out blood and bits of tooth.

"Well, there you have it, boys. You can get that rope ready 'cause this one ain't
gettin' away!" Judge Belt had passed sentence, death by hanging.

Hodges was locked in the feed room of the ferry, the makeshift courthouse and jail.
As the reality of the situation dawned, he looked for any means to stall the inevitable.
Hoping that justice might arrive and at least give him a trial before jury, instead of this
vigilante courtroom. He asked the judge for pen and paper so he could at least write a
good-bye to his loved ones. The judge, who was busy stuffing his face, was unaffected
by the sentimentality, but provided pen and paper nonetheless.

Hodges listened briefly to the men laughing, as they hung the noose in the nearby tree. It would be useless, he thought, to try and touch the hearts of such savage men; they thirsted for his blood. He needed to buy time, so he wrote. As he did, his spirit came to full realization that there would be no rescue. The men were at the door. Hodges froze as tears welled up in his eyes. The light was blinding as they pulled him outside. At four in the afternoon, the light shown in sharply under the trees, reflected in the river.

"Are you ready?" Judge Belt asked, in a fearful tone.

"Yes, my life is worth nothing," Hodges said quietly.

"You can have some whiskey first, if you want it."

"Yes, I would like that," the condemned man replied, looking out at his small group of executioners.

"Do you have anything else to say about your life of crime at this time?" the judge asked Bell.

"I have no further revelations to make at this time," Tom Bell said, hoisting the whiskey to his lips. "But I would be gratified to drink to the health of all of the present company and know that I hold no personal grudges against any of you . . . who will now execute me . . . . But I do ask of you one last favor," he rambled, stalling for time. "Please allow me to read you the letter I have written to my dear mother."

The men muttered under their breath as the judge waved the condemned man onward. The men stood very still and listened with stony reverence.

"Dear Mother," Hodges began, the paper starting to shake as he loosened his necktie. "As I am about to make my exit to another country, I take the opportunity to write you a few lines. Probably you will never hear from me again. If not, I hope we may meet where parting is no more.

In my prodigal career in this country, I have always recollected your fond admonitions, and if I had lived up to them, probably I would not have been in my present condition. But, dear Mother, although my fate has been a cruel one, yet I have no one to blame but myself. Give my respects to all my old and youthful friends. Tell them to beware of bad associations and never to enter any gambling saloons, for that has been my ruin. If my old grandmother is living, remember me to her. With these remarks I bid you farewell forever. Your only boy, Tom." Hodges lowered the letter, searching the room for sympathy and found none.

Tom Bell looked at the faces; he would never reach them. He quickly began tossing out observations of his life of crime, in hopes off putting off the rope.

"Please I have one more letter, please let me read that!" the prisoner pleaded.

"That's enough, get the rope ready," the judge ordered.

"It's ready, put him on his horse there." The men dragged the prisoner to his last moments. They placed the rope around his neck and sent his horse out from under him; Tom Bell, the outlaw, once again did the hemp-necktie dance of death.

Ten minutes later, Sheriff Mulford and his men rode into the ceremonies, just missing the main attraction.

The news spread like wildfire; the Tom Bell Gang was finished! Bill Gristy was given the opportunity to tell his whole story to the newspapers. It was all anyone could talk about.

"So it was Dr. Hodges!" Birch sighed listening in on the narrative. "Well, I'll be a son of a bitch!" Charley set the paper down, then scratched his head and resumed reading.

"That's what Gristy said, 'Our party at this time consisted of Thomas J. Hodges, alias Tom Bell.'"

"I told him, they all get hung in the end," Birch said, raising his glass as a toast.

CHAPTER 30

Placerville, October 1856

It was dusty and dark and still unusually hot that evening when one-eyed Charley Parkhurst and Snowshoe Thompson rode into Ol' Hang Town on the stage. They both looked forward to a well-earned drink.

Thompson had sold his ranch on Putah Creek and moved to the Sierras. He built himself a log house near Genoa and had signed on as an expressman for the California Stage Company. Snowshoe was looking forward to the beginning of the winter snows, but for now, summer's grip held fast. Fall was only in the air at night and in the yellow and orange of the dying oak leaves in the lower valleys.

The coach rocked through the dusty, bustling streets of Placerville. Men were hard at work putting up new buildings, the Sierra town was growing all the time. Charley parked the stagecoach; then the two friends walked down the plank sidewalk to their favorite watering hole to wash the dust from their throats. It was crowded as the two made their way to the bar.

Sitting at the end was a familiar man, who was covered with dust and coming apart at the seams. He was staring cross-eyed into an empty plate.

"Hank Monk, you old jehu!" Charley bellowed, slapping Hank on the back, which prompted the dirty man to vomit his dinner back into the plate! "You look like somthin' a coyote . . . um . . . barfed up!"

"Bartender! This food stinks! Take this shit back and tell the cook to fix me somthin' that I can keep down! That bastard's tryin' to poison me!" Monk roared. "Shit, Parkie, old man, you gonna stand there with your face hangin' out, or you gonna have a drink with your Ol' friend?" Hank cackled, not losing a beat.

"You look like you killed the better part of a bottle already, Hank," Charley said calmly.

"You tellin' me I'm drunk?" Monk started to fume.

"I wouldn't dream of tellin' you nothin, Hank! Three beers, bartender," Charley laughed. "Here's a napkin, you got some of your dinner in your beard there."

"Don't eat here!" Monk said, wiping his untrimmed goatee.

The bartender took the streaming plate off the bar as if handling a skunk and passed it to the man in the kitchen.

"Do something with this, will ya!" the bartender ordered. The cook took the steaming plate and not noticing it had already been eaten once, emptied it back into the stew kettle.

"Oh shit! You moron! . . . Well . . . I'm glad I already ate!" the bartender mumbled under his breath, as he poured himself a shot.

"I can't wait till we get a little rain to settle this damn dust," Charley said shaking the dirt off his hat.

"Still scenic though! Tickles the shit out of me to scare the piss outa some o' those city slickers, anyhow! I had one city asshole the other day, invited himself up ta the box next to me, and proceeds to first comment about how the horses ain't like blooded stock! What he probably wouldn't know if a they'd falled on him! Then he starts in on how slow they was goin' up the grade, till I was ready to make him get out and walk! Shoulda done it too! Soon as we crested the ridge, I popped the lash, and down we goes, lickety spilt. I think I had that Ol' Concord over on two wheels a couple a times," Hank cackled, his face turning red with glee and whiskey. "When we gets to the station, that bastard is white, then green, then white as a ghost again! Next day the bastard hires himself an Ol' mule to go the rest of the way!" Hank was nearly falling off the stool laughing. "Where's my dinner, bartender?" he snorted.

"I'll be right with you!" Al snapped.

"Hank, is dere anyvone you don't consider a bastard or an asshole?" Thompson asked.

Hank pondered it a moment. "Naa . . . Parkie here is a son of a bitch!" Monk laughed like it was the best punch line ever.

"Charley, can I talk to you for a minute?" the bartender asked.

"Sure, Al," Charley said, following Al to the other end of the bar.

"You seem to know Hank real well, you gotta help me out here."

"Well, we go's back a ways, came to California together. What can I do for you?" Charley confided.

"Well, he comes in every night, drinkin' his self sick, an' passing out in the bar. I don't mind that none, but frankly he stinks to high heaven! He's puttin off the higher-class customers and drawin' flies."

"Well, what the hell can I do? He don't like taking baths," Charley laughed. "You know you can't tell him nothin'."

"Can't you take him to the livery, and get him drunk, then when he passes out, you know, throw him in the horse trough and soak him awhile?"

"What, and poison the horses?"

"Come on, Charley, please? He's a right guy. I hate to throw him out of the place. He spends a lot of money, you know. I'll make it worth your while. I'll buy you dinner!" Al pleaded.

"I've seen your kitchen. I don't eat here anymore!" Charley laughed.

"Not here then, where?" Al asked.

"Big Johns', and Snowshoe gets dinner too, I'm gonna need help!"

"He looks like he could eat a whole steer! All right, all right, just get the man a bath and some decent clothes. He's coming apart at the seams. It's disgusting," the bartender protested.

"I ain't promising no bed a rose petals, now." Charley hesitated. "And I'm gonna need some whiskey, good whiskey!"

"Yeah, yeah, I'll give you a good deal on a bottle of rye! Now get busy, he's puttin off customers and drawrin' flies . . . Here, it aged a whole year!" Al said pulling up a dust-covered bottle. "I was savin' it for winter."

"Com'on, Hank, I bet I can drink your sorry ass under the table!" Charley roared.

"In a pig's eye, you son of a bitch!" Hank answered.

The three walked back toward the livery, Charley and Thompson holding up Monk as they went. Along the way, they passed their favorite kitchen and got some ribs to take to the stable.

Charley had underestimated Hank's ability to drink, and he had to send Thompson to get more booze, suggesting brandy this time. Thompson reported to Al the bartender on the bathing progress, and soon bets were being made.

Charley entertained Hank by teaching him a new dice game he had picked up at Eleanoras' poker house.

"Gallopin' dominos!" Hank swore as the dice rolled across the work table and scattered on the dirt floor. Monk conked his head on the table as he bent down to collect his toys, and Charley thought for a moment he would get lucky, and Monk might knock himself out. But Hank was resilient, and the knock only seemed to wake him up.

Thompson came back soon with the bottle that Charley had sent for and was passed out shortly after. Snowshoe's tolerance for alcohol was low, and he was soon snoring away.

Hank and Charley had a fine time, recalling times aboard ship and Jamaica. Charley was beginning to think that Hank was never going to pass out, when quite suddenly, Hank simply leaned over and said, "I'm going under the table now." He was sliding off his chair and curling up under the table as he had previously announced to his friend.

Charley, who had been dumping his booze out as often as he could, throughout the drinkfest, was as drunk as he had ever been. He bumbled along laughing and got the water heating in metal buckets on the stove.

"Lot a help you are," Charley mumbled, stepping over the passed out Norseman. When the water in the trough was good and hot, Charley dragged Hank out from under the table and managed to put him in a large wheelbarrow.

Hank would open his eyes now and then, and babble on about the Whips Ball, in Concord Massachusetts and how "it was such a grand time," or "they were going to go dancing with the Jamaican gals," then pass out again, as Parkie tried in vain to undress him. The boots were off, when Charley decided to drop him in the water-trough clothes and all.

"I'm not going in, if you don't come in too, Parkie!" Hank complained, holding tightly to his friend's shoulders. The tank was good sized, about five feet across and three foot deep. The steam rose in the cool nighttime air. Charley swore loudly as Hank caught him off balance and yanked him into the water with a splash. They had a good laugh as all the horses in the corral came close, looking at the two buffoons in the steaming water. Upon smelling the soap and the current residents, the horses snorted with disapproval and curled up their top lips in disgust. Charley climbed out of the tub and retrieved the brandy. After a few more drinks, Hank was sitting among the soapsuds, snoring away. When they were scrubbed and soaked good, Charley hauled Hank out of the tub and wheelbarrowed him back inside the barn, where he bedded him down in an empty stall, with straw and blankets. He looked pretty clean. Now for the clothes. Parkhurst carefully peeled Monk's wet pants off, but they were coming apart at the seams, so Charley got a needle and some stout thread, and made a few repairs. Parkhurst felt that somehow it wasn't quite enough to hold them together and took out some small harness rivets, putting them on all the pocket corners and major stress seam ends. Charley washed them again in the trough and hung them on a line, near the corner stove, to dry. The horse trough would have to be scrubbed out now, he reasoned, lest he make all the horses sick. It was a long night.

The next morning, Charley felt guilty for Hank's immense hangover; using his own headache for a gauge, Monk's head must be excruciating! Charley woke early to check on the laundry and put on a pot of coffee; he then scuffled across the street to get some fresh bread for breakfast. When he returned to the stable, Hank and Thompson were still snoring away.

Charley felt some type of longing toward this unpredictable teamster as she watched him sleep. Monk was handsome in his way, with his chiseled nose and high cheekbones. Parkhurst was puzzled by his habit of plunging himself deep in a bottle. Hank liked to leave an impression on people; it wasn't always a good one. Many were afraid to ride with him; they thought he was dangerous. Charley knew that he was very skilled and knew the limitations of the Concord coach very well. It was because of this that Hank could do the type of fast driving that he did; he knew his job, and he could really drive. Monk loved it and respected his animals; he had the hands of a master and the face of a poet. At times it seemed like he was mourning some long-lost love.

Charley set Hank's clothes next to his bed and chuckled to herself as he put them on.

"Why, I feel like a new man, Parkie!" Hank groaned. "I feel like I've grown another head, and it's too tight!"

"I made some coffee and got some rolls for breakfast," Charley said.

"I need something in the coffee. Is there any brandy left?" Hank said in a low voice, inspecting the bread, then setting it down with a frown.

"I suppose here," Charley replied, pouring a shot into the coffee.

"Did you give me a bath last night?" Hank asked wearily, sniffing himself.

"Yep," Charley replied stifling back a laugh.

"Why?"

"Because you were filthy, and you stank!" Charley grinned. "That and Al, the bartender, promised me dinner at Big John's if I could get the stink off of you!"

"Do I get dinner too?" Hank inquired.

"I don't think so. You were the skunk. I was the deskunkee. If you catch my drift."

"Well, somewhere that doesn't sound right, I mean you're gettin' somethin'. What do I get?" Hank whined.

"Well, you got a bath!" Charley smiled. "Try to remain tidy for a while, all right, Hank?"

"Why, Parkie? Don't you want to go swimming again?" Hank said as the two pals laughed and drank their spiked coffees together on their day off.

"Oh, my head!" Snowshoe Thompson groaned upon waking. "Tell dem I cannot make it to church dis week," he grunted and rolled over.

The friends sat for a time in silence.

"Have you ever thought about taking a holiday, Parkie?" Hank asked as he inspected the coffee then added more brandy.

"A what?"

"You know, old man, a vacation, a holiday," Hank explained seriously, stirring the drink with his finger.

"Well, no, I don't suppose that I have," Charley thought out carefully. "I have never planned a trip purely for my own recreation, no."

"Well, don't you think that you should?" Hank replied, his eyes just barely open.

Charley could just laugh. The face in front of him was so dead serious that Charley could do nothing else. "I suppose I ought to give that some thought, there, Hank," he chuckled.

"Splendid! . . . Damn that was hot!" Hank said, sucking on his finger.

"Just where would you go, Hank. On your holiday, that is?" Charley asked.

"I think that I should plan a hunting trip. Big-horned sheep or grizzly bear, perhaps," Hank dreamed aloud.

"Really?" I figured you more for the city type, you know, ladies and such," Charley replied.

"No, no, I really would rather retreat from civilization, for a time, instead," Monk said wistfully.

"Yes, I see what you mean, there is definite merit in that idea. But the dangers, grizzly bears are fierce creatures to be greatly feared. That's no joke, you know. I might instead head for the big cities and theaters and enjoy all of the creature comforts that money and any influence might provide," Charley answered his melancholy friend.

"Yes, but when the asshole in the tavern disagrees with you, you can't always shoot him between the eyes. With a bear, you can just shoot him, simple as that," Hank reasoned. "Besides, I want to get me one of them bear-hide coats."

"Hmm, I see your point." Charley nodded.

"I gotta go tease the cat." Hank belched.

"See ya later, Hank," Charley called and headed back to blissful sleep, with strange dreams of hunting trips in the city.

After Hank relieved himself behind the barn, he continued to waddle down the street, not quite sure where he was headed. His slightly damp pants gave him a clammy feeling as he took notice of the new rivets on the pockets and side seams and laughed out loud. Strolling passed a new shop, with clothing in the window, Monk stepped inside.

"I need me some a these trousers," Hank said to the short Jewish man. "But . . . can you put some rivets on, like this?" Monk said, showing off his new hardware.

"Sure, I can fix you up good. I got this nice blue, denim jeans," the man said holding up his newly sewn pants.

"That'd be just fine, put some copper on the pocket corners there, and we're all set," Monk said, smiling through his headache.

The merchant set about looking through a tin of grommets and rivets to find the proper size and quickly had the pants customized. Meanwhile, Hank realized he had left his money elsewhere and started to feel very foolish indeed.

The slender Jewish man soon handed over the agreed upon garment.

"I don't seem to have any money on me, would you take an IOU, for now? I can pay you later today." Monk blushed.

"You're Hank Monk the coachman, everyone knows you, I guess you're good for it," the tailor said adjusting his glasses, as he looked the customer over.

"Whom do I write it out to?"

"You can write, I, Hank Monk owe Levi Strauss two dollars," the tailor replied.

"Well, these ought to last me!" Monk said, scribbling on the paper. He then peeled off his shabby damp pants in front of the world and Levi Strauss and hopped into his new blue jeans.

"They look good on you, don't forget to tell everyone where you got them!" Strauss beamed. "Good idea . . . the rivets, should hold together forever."

"I tell you, a span of mules couldn't pull these pants apart! See ya later, Levi," Hank said wadding the old pants beneath his arm and straightening his hat, as he left the shop.

"A span of mules? That's very good!" Strauss mumbled to himself, as he sat back down at the new Singer sewing machine.

Charley would tease Hank occasionally about his hunting trip idea, but it only seemed to enflame his passion for it. Monk started making lists of things to bring and where to go. He was beginning to get it all mapped out, fishing, hunting, views—it was all going to be there. Charley was being roped into going along on a hunting trip as well. Will had taught Charley well in the use of firearms, but camping with Hank for a week, looking for bears, was another matter.

They were set to go in early November, as soon as the first snows slowed the Sierra stages. It would be getting cold, and the bear pelts would be fresh for the winter. Hank had envisioned the trophy made into the ultimate driving attire for the Sierras, a great coat made from its own denizen of the deep freeze. The grizzly bear was known to reach giant size, with fur four inches thick. It would be high adventure, to say the least. Charley already had such a coat, and Hank envied it.

"Do you know anything about bears?" Charley asked Hank one morning as the snow began to fall.

"I know I intend to shoot one if that's what you mean. You're not going to tell me that damn Miggles story again, are you?" Hank got in.

"My God, you're ornery. I just thought that we could talk to my friend Rollin Ridge, he's an Indian, and he might be of some help. That's all. Or maybe Yankee Jim could come with us," Charley said hopefully.

"You can back out of this trip if you want to, that's just fine with me, but I'm going with you or without you," Hank sneered.

"I didn't say I wanted out, I just said it might be a good idea to talk to my friend. Don't be so grumpy, Hank," Charley sighed.

"What did you say his name was?" Hank asked

"John Rollin Ridge," Charley replied.

"The writer, Rollin Ridge? The man that wrote that *Murrieta* book? Him?" Hank was excited. "I don't suppose it would hurt none to get some advice. Where is your so called Indian advisor?" Hank queried.

"He lives in Marysville. I'll drop him a letter. Maybe he'll meet us."

"Well, you just do that. I'm going over to the store and pick up my new rifle. It's a dandy, just wait till you see it!" Hank giggled like a schoolboy. "A fifty-six caliber, five-shot Colt, I can't wait to try her out!"

"Oh good God!" Charley sighed.

The next week, Charley received a letter from Rollin Ridge, the three met in Placerville.

"If you ask me you are headed for danger, you have no idea what is lying in wait for you out in the bush, be it beast or man. But if you are stubborn and in search of a trophy or good fishing, then try your luck in the Yosemite Valley, or near the coast, and the big trees. When the salmon run in, the bears come in too," Rollin Ridge advised.

"Come with us!" Hank pleaded. "It will be a great adventure."

"I am not in need of adventure at this time," John counseled. "But I may ride out a ways with you to meet some relatives who are visiting."

"Fine," Hank Monk responded, disappointed. He was fascinated with the Murrieta legend and wanted to pick Rollin Ridge's brain for facts about the bandits and such. Hank was impressed with him because he was a writer, but John was very guarded about his ties to Joaquin.

"If you want to know about Tres Dedos, you should ask Charley," John slipped. The three were packing for the big hunting trip.

"Really? Charley met Three-Finger Jack?" Hank looked over at Charley with new reverence. "Parkie, you never divulged these secrets to me, in all this time." Hank scalded.

"Well, you never asked," Charley said with annoyance. "And I didn't feel like bringing up the subject."

"Now is that any way to talk? Parkie, you've kept your adventures from me, do tell," Monk pleaded.

"What's to tell, they're all dead, and so will we be by the end of this huntin' expedition, I expect," Charley sighed.

"Nonsense, you're well armed," Rollin Ridge advised, pointing to Hank's new treasure.

"Thanks for the vote of confidence, John. You got the galloping dominos, Charley?" Hank smiled, strapping his new scabbard to his saddle.

"You bet!"

"Well, let's go then! Yup now!" Monk said swinging into the saddle and starting up his horse.

The three rode together for two days until they got to a beautiful ridge top, near the coast. They had eight horses between them. All, you might say, were armed for bear. Charley knew that Hank always carried a loaded fifty-caliber Derringer in his breast pocket, a practice that Charley had also taken up. The hunting party felt secure in their armaments.

At the top of the ridge, John stopped and motioned to his two companions. "Go down to the water and follow the trail, until you get to the where the river is wide. You'll know it when you see it. The fish will be jumping. Camp near the cliffs and light big fires at night. I am going to meet some cousins. I will look for you tomorrow night." As he turned his horse to leave, he gave Charley a wink and said quietly but clearly to Charley, "Happy hunting." Then he disappeared back over the ridge.

"He said this way, let's go, Parkie!" Hank motioned like an excited child. Hank's string of packhorses obediently following down the trail, Charley and his packhorse bringing up the rear.

The fog was rolling in large billowy, wet sheets that turned to fat droplets in the great trees in the canyon below. It wasn't long before Hank had found his idea of the perfect camping spot in a box canyon, as the foggy gray sky was dimming to charcoal.

Charley was in her own world thinking about John's allusions toward her feminine attraction to Hank; it bothered her. He had blabbed about the Murrieta connection, how long before he blabbed about her sex? She had not come on this trip to seduce Hank, especially now that she was horribly scarred and wearing an eye patch. Charley had come along to make sure Hank didn't get eaten by a bear, but now her lonely heart ached.

The two quietly tethered the horses to some trees and made camp. Hank chose a site next to the canyon wall, so that they would be secure on one side and relatively free from the wind. The landscape was rocky and became steep, ending up at a narrow in the river, about two hundred yards away. There was a well-used game path down next to the water. The two made a fire ring in front of their bedrolls, and Charley set about making some coffee.

"Do you have a hunting plan, Hank?" Charley inquired.

"Well, I think that we ought to rise at the crack of dawn and go to the river and fish. Then when a bear comes along, we shoot him. Then we have fish for breakfast and bear for dinner. How's that?" Hank grinned, sipping on a bottle of brandy.

"Yeah, that sounds all right, unless we get a bear tonight, then I suppose we'll have bear for breakfast and fish for dinner." Charley shuttered, thinking about a nocturnal encounter.

"Well put, my friend. I for one shall be well armed when I retire," Hank said, patting the derringer in his breast pocket.

"Me too," Charley said aloud, thinking of his set of Navy Colts. He had a very healthy respect for bears and was very fearful of another encounter.

"You know, Parkie, I gotta say, I got a lot of respect for you. I mean, you losin' your eye and all. Well sir, a lesser man would have given up drivin, but not you. You're a tough man, and ya got a lotta guts! You can still drive with the best of 'em!" Monk confided after coffee.

"Thanks, Hank, comin' from you that's high praise indeed!" Charley said, as the blood ran to his face in a blush. Charley laughed to herself, as he gathered up some more dry wood and tied the horses close to the fire. He made sure it would not go out in the night.

It was getting very cold in the big trees; winter was in the air. Wrapped in a buffalo skin and topped with a bearskin coat, it was hard for Charley not to think about her femininity, snuggling to keep warm with the dashing Hank Monk. The two, both fully clothed, slept together for warmth like a set of spoons. It was down right cozy. Except for all the snoring by both parties.

Charley noticed the many eyes that glowed back from the edges of the firelight, as he lay with his friend, listening to the many voices of the night. The owls and the coyotes sang hymns to one another, in the not too far distance.

By dawn, Charley had the horses fed and saddled and fresh coffee brewing.

"Get up, Hank! I got coffee on," Charley said, shoving Hank's butt with his boot.

"It smells delicious. I knew I would like camping with you, you're a good cook!" Hank said rubbing his eyes.

"Yeah, I boiled up a couple a eggs, so get your sorry ass up and get 'em before I eat em all my self!" Charley chided.

"God, love you, my friend," Hank, said pulling on his boots and snugging down his hat. "Geez, you must have been up awhile. You got the horses ready too?"

"Yep. I tell you what, Hank, if you want to fish, I'll stay with the horses and you can climb out on the rocks in the river, if you like, that is," Charley said while the two drank their coffee.

"How sporting of you, old man." Hank smiled. Charley could tell that he was still drunk from the night before. Slow thinking in the wilderness could get you killed. Charley knew that. Hank had never been much of a camper, and so its romance hadn't yet worn off.

Charley put out the campfire, and the two made their way to the water's edge, Charley riding and Hank walking with his new fishing gear, two revolvers and a fifty-caliber Derringer in case of a bear sighting. The plan was for Hank to walk and fish up stream, and Charley would stay down stream with all the horses and gear. That way, Charley figured, if Hank slipped off a rock and was swept down stream, there was a chance he could throw a rope to him or something along those lines.

Charley took the pack string to a lovely wide spot in the river. It was shallow, and the horses enjoyed pawing in the knee-deep water. Charley called out to Hank as he waddled away.

"Now remember about the poisoned oak, that shit is nasty, I'm telling you, don't even get any on your clothes!"

"Yah, I heard ya!" Monk said, scampering off to the boulders in the river with his fishing gear. Charley thought what a comic figure he cut, as he splashed along the rivers' edge.

Sitting on the mare and looking into the sparkling waters, Parkhurst soon noticed that it was indeed loaded with fish. So Charley untied his own fishing pole from the saddle and baited it with some dried meat he had in his pocket. The horseman then tied the packhorses to a tree at the water's edge and climbed back on his horse and rode out in the shallow water, fishing pole at the ready. The expert whip artist sent the bait right over to some really large fish, swimming near some rocks, and it wasn't long before there was interest in the bait.

Fishing on horseback presents a host of challenges. Charley soothed the mare with quiet talk and tried to keep her horse facing the fish that Charley was madly trying to reel in. Luckily the horse had been used to rope cattle and soon got into the spirit of the game. As the fish was pulled closer to the horse, Charley jumped into the water and pulled in the salmon; it was a beauty.

"Well, at least one of us can catch fish!" Charley laughed, smacking the silvery prize in the head with the butt of his gun, then stowed it in a saddlebag. "Good girl, Belle," Charley whispered to the horse, as he stroked the soft red hair of her throat. Charley then climbed back in the saddle, retrieved his pack string, and started upstream toward Hank.

Slowly picking their way up the rocky streambed, Charley and the horses noticed something in the dense growth up ahead.

"Hank, that you? Stay out'a that poison oak now you hear me?" Charley scalded. Silence. The rustling stopped momentarily, then the beast, whatever it was, resumed its travels deeper into the thicket.

"Come on, boys and girls," Parkhurst called to the packhorses. "Let's go." Charley followed the winding waters along, until it stretched out to a wide shallow river, which was being filled with water from a ledge higher up, creating a lovely short waterfall. Charley remarked to the horses on the picturesque scene of beauty before them.

"Isn't that lovely?" he said aloud. The occasional fish leapt out of the water in an attempt to reach the higher level. "Gods own beautiful creation!" In the distance ahead, he spotted Hank, who seemed to be tangled in his special-ordered fishing line and was currently engaged in a lot of swearing.

"You all right up thar? Hank?" Charley called up.

"Ya, I'm all right, I jammed my thumb with a hook is all!" Hank's line was a tangled mess at his knees; he was standing in the water facing away from the shore, sucking his thumb, with his fishing pole tucked under his armpit.

As not to disturb the beauty of the moment, Charley decided to take the string of horses back down stream, laughing at the spectacle of Hank at his most primitive. The next few moments of peace and tranquillity would be broken by a great splash and growling. Hank was running and yelling but getting tangled in his line as he did. A bear was charging into the water at Hank, all one thousand pounds of angry male, grizzly bear. He was moving in for the kill, as the two reached the edge of the falls.

Charley swung around with the horses, who all snorted disapproval. He drew Hank's new rifle from its scabbard and gave off with a shot, momentarily stopping the bear in his tracks. It did not hit him, but it did cause him to stop and look at the horseman, who was aiming the new rifle, but then he focused again on Hank, who was fumbling for his Derringer. The tiny gun tumbled from his fingers, into the river, as the bear slapped the man down into the water with his huge paw, then plunged his muzzle in, grabbing Hank's shoulder and shaking him about like a rag doll. Two more shots rang out and the great beast released the drowning man and fell over the lip of the falls, into the basin below. Charley trotted up with the hesitant horses and called out.

"Hank? You all right?" Charley yelled. All he could hear was a lot of gasping and coughing. Charley shot the bear again through the eye, for good measure, then jumped off the mare and tied the horses securely to a tree and scaled the rocks, to the next level of the falls. Hank was trying to crawl from the water when Charley arrived.

"Take it easy, I think you took one on the head, Hank," Charley said, helping him out of the cold water. "That was a close one! You got your bear though!" Charley said with encouragement.

"You shot the bear, Parkie?" Hank coughed. "That's your bear!"

"I don't want a bear! I don't care about the bear!" Charley reasoned. "You can say you shot it, I don't care! It was shot with your new rifle. It shoots good too! Let's skin the son of a bitch and get the hell out of here!"

"I got your word on it? . . . I can say I killed it? Really?" Hank was revived!

"Sure, I don't care," Charley responded, glad to see his pal was only roughed up and relatively unscathed. The two set about hauling the prize to camp.

"I know a gal that can stitch the pelt into a coat for you, like mine. Her name is Ellen. She's in Nevada City," Charley said as they sat in front of the fire, after skinning the bear.

"Oh, you got a gal?" Hank, who was feeling much better, kidded.

"Well, I met her while I was buying some ribbon and such for Little Lotta," Charley related. "She was working on a dress for Eleanora Dumont, you know, the card dealer. It was really something. So I had her make my coat. She is just as sweet as candy too,"

Charley said, putting more wood on the fire. The two were about to cook the fish and portions of the bear when company arrived in the form of John Rollin Ridge and his three cousins.

"I see you were successful," John said smiling. "Don't let us interrupt, tell us more about yer girlfriend."

"I was just saying, the gal sews real well, and she could probably make a decent coat out of the fur, is all," Charley said, smiling up at the Cherokee. "Welcome and throw some more bear on the fire," Charley said happily.

"Did she sew that coat your wearing?" John said admiring its fur.

"Why yes, she did," Charley responded. "She has this new fangled Singer sewing machine. It's the damnedest thing you ever did see!"

"Yes, my wife has been after me for one of those as well," Rollin Ridge sighed, slicing off bear steaks for himself and his family. "You heading back to Marysville?" he asked.

"Yep, we got to check in with the boss when we get back, to see what the winter routes will be. Lots of men coming in for the winter. They'll probably double up the city routes time bein'," Hank said thoughtfully. Realizing his adventure was coming to a close. "Well, at least I'll have my coat!" Monk said, running his hands across the thick fur.

"It's beautiful," Ridge agreed.

"This bear nearly had me I can tell you!" Hank reflected, with a pinch of the devil, twinkling in his eyes.

"Oh, here we go!" Charley smiled, winking slyly to her Cherokee friend.

Hank spotted it and raised an eyebrow. Charley just shrugged his shoulders and grinned, saying nothing, smiling in anticipation of the tale he was about to hear.

"Well, I had just caught this here beautiful fish, see . . ." Hank went on, putting more salmon on the fire. Now it was Charley's turn to raise an eyebrow. Yet he said nothing. "When I hear some rustling in the bushes," Hank continued, 'Charley is that you?' I called out. But it wasn't, see? 'Cause Charley was way down stream eating some boiled eggs I cooked up for lunch. Then! Just like a shot, out of the bushes comes this great hulking beast of a bear! So I get out my Colt and shoot him, but he just keeps coming at me! The next thing I know, he jumps on top of me and starts wrestling with me, right there in the water. Then I gets hold of my knife and just before he bites me in the neck and rips my head off. I stabbed him in the heart and killed him!" Hank said, sweating from real terror, as he relived the bear mauling. Charley was looking at him with a smile.

Later, after they had parted from Rollin Ridge, at his home in Marysville, Charley chastised Monk.

"I said you could say 'you killed the bear.' What was all that bullshit about the fish and the boiled eggs you made me sound pretty feeble!" Charley grumbled.

"Well, I'm sorry, I just got kind of carried away. You know, I never thanked you for saving my life. You're a good friend, Parkie, thank you," Hank said earnestly.

"Well, you'd do the same for me I suppose." Charley blushed.

"You know I would!" Hank responded enthusiastically. "Let's go and get this son of a bitch tanned! I can't wait to have a coat made outa it! Then I'll buy you dinner, how's that?" he added, trotting the horses toward town.

"Well, Mother Mary and Joseph! I never would have believed it!" Charley laughed encouraging the horses on. "It will feel good to sleep in a real bed tonight and have a bath!" he said.

"I already had my bath yesterday!" Hank said proudly.

"I don't really think 'getting dunked by a bear' qualifies as a bath," Charley countered.

"It does in my book," Hank stated firmly. The pair retired the horses to the livery next to the stage office and deposited the prized possession with a skilled tanner. They then retired to the new What Cheer tavern, and Charley was forced again to hear the thrilling retelling of the bear hunt, taking it with a grain of salt and a shot of brandy. The fish lie remained however, but Hank told the lie with such charm it was hard to stay angry.

CHAPTER 31

Sierra Mountains, December 1856

The mighty Sierra Mountains were shrouded in white; winter had come on with a vengeance. For most, the granite landscape was off-limits; one man had realized the ruinous decision that he had made, in venturing out in this harsh wilderness and was freezing to death.

James Sisson trudged through the deep snow, with the last of his strength; his legs now just searing pain. His face was blistered and raw, his lips cracked. With blurry eyes, he thought he had seen the outline of a cabin, in the fading light. The man crawled forward through the blizzard and frozen white landscape, looking for a comfortable place to die. He slumped down at the door of the crude abandoned building, the snow was piled up, and he slowly scraped at it with his raw hands. Grasping the door latch with all his remaining strength and unfeeling bloody hands, Sisson wrestled the door open, then collapsed from exhaustion on the cabin floor. Later, he managed to crawl over to the fireplace, his legs too painful to stand.

With shaking hands, he attempted to ignite the scraps of wood in the fireplace, but wet matches prevented any hope of a fire. Sisson drifted in and out of frozen consciousness. He crawled to the door for snow when he was thirsty, but could only find flour to eat. The pain of his frostbitten feet was excruciating. He begged for sweet relief with death, but was too cowardly to take his own life; he wanted to live, but saw only a slow, lonely demise in the silent Sierra wilderness as a certainty.

On the fourth day, when James Sisson woke in the dark cabin, he crept over to the fireplace and fumbled for the remaining match, which he had carefully protected to dry. His hands shook from starvation and cold, as he delicately maneuvered the bit of treated wood to the striker. He prayed with his whole being as he struck the match, and praised God, as the flame grew forth from the tiny piece of wood. His shaking hand placed the fire on the tinder in the stone hearth and gloried in his warm accomplishment.

The man then focused his existence for the next eight days on maintaining his fire and prayer. His feet were destroyed by the prolonged frozen state, and his hunger grasped him in a delirium of pain. The log cabin was cast with a ghostly frost, as Sisson clutched the last piece of wood for his meager heat source. Laying it on the dying embers, he said his prayers and lay close to the fire and presumed to die.

At midnight, a tired postman smelled the smoke of a wood fire, then spotted a small plume rising from the winter landscape in the moonlight. Thompson had been heading for the abandoned cabin and had intended on resting there, but was suprised to find it already inhabited.

"Hallo in dere?"

Thompson shoved the door open, with powerful jerks, kicking the snow away with his boots.

"Is dere anyvon dere?" Thompson called out, as he entered the room, pushing the door closed against the driving snow. He spotted the glowing ember in the fireplace and the balled up figured next to it.

"Hallo. Are you hurt? I vill help you," the snow-covered outdoorsman called to the huddled mass. Sisson rolled over to see a hulking figure with a snowy beard and red wool hat, fringed with ice setting down a great sack.

"Saint Nick?" Sisson whispered, before succumbing again to the darkness of his delirium.

"No, I am John Thompson, I vill help you."

When Sisson regained consciousness, he found his saint attempting to remove his boots, something he himself had failed at. The pain was excruciating. Thompson was trying to conceal his horror over the man's condition, but Sisson was not fooled. He smelled food and looked at the now raging fire. Thompson had located a stash of wood and an ax, in the woodshed, outside the cabin. He made some soup with crackers and dried meat, which he always carried on these trips.

"My name is John Thompson. I'm going to get you out of here, to a doctor, but I've got to have help. I'll leave you a pot of soup and a supply of wood. Dat's da best I can do. I'll be back soon. You can count on dat," the mailman said, as he wrapped the man's feet in his extra long johns.

"My name is Sisson. I'm much obliged."

As the starving man gobbled the food, he eyed the ax next to the fire.

"You didn't dull that blade, did ya? My feet is turned to mush, I know, I kin smell it. I might have to take them off myself," Sisson said, with tears running down his face.

"Mr. Sisson, please, please don't try to do dis yourself. You vill bleed to death. Please promise me you vill vait for three days, and I promise I vill come back for you. You must promise me not to chop off your feet," Thompson pleaded.

"Well, I guess I can hold on till then," Sisson said, turning his attention back to the soup.

Thompson strapped on his finely crafted wooden conveyances and grabbed his pole and was gone. Down the eastern slopes of the Sierras in the virgin snow, the man flew, toward Genoa, with a fifty-pound sack of mail on his back. Sisson never expected to see him again.

It was Christmas Day when John slid into town; the small community had just started to wake to their holiday. Those who were out greeted SnowshoeThompson with a cheer. Jack Frost had decorated the tiny town with lacy, ice frosting, on all the structures. The church bell was ringing as the town folks migrated toward the Christmas service. Thompson strided into the church and set down his mail sack, then sought out the minister and related the pressing emergency. The minister then looked about in search of Dr. Daggett as the parishioners filed into the pews.

Thompson went to the post office and dropped off the mail, then returned to the church. He was very tired and slumped down on the pew, as he waited for the minister. Reverend Harris then informed Thompson that the doctor was not in town. As the minister called the service to begin, he invited Thompson to the pulpit to relate the emergency. The congregation was moved by the plight of James Sisson, yet few people felt any confidence in traveling to the summit of these great mountains, in such harsh conditions. John Thompson was a hero and a great mountaineer, but most folks could not even imagine trying the trek themselves. To go out into the harsh elements, risking your own death, it was an ominous prospect for such a hallowed holiday. The minister soon found compelling words to convince some men to risk their lives, to trust a local hero and save a dying man. The first young men to volunteer, Jerry McBride and Nigel Brewster were friends of Thompson's and had admired and sought to imitate the Norseman on the snow. The oldest volunteer was the minister, who felt an almost overwhelming desire to find true meaning in his life.

Thompson was then treated to a substantial breakfast, yet the unfortunate James Sisson could not leave his thoughts. He stowed away food for travel, like a squirrel storing nuts for the winter, then set off in search of a conveyance for Mr. Sisson. John needed a long sled in order to transport the afflicted man down the mountain. He spoke with the town carpenter, W. B. Wade, and told him of the need for a sled for the injured man. The carpenter took Thompson to his wood shop, and John picked out some suitable boards for his sled. The carpenter quickly planed them into a crude imitation of Thompson's skis, deciding, as he did, that maybe he should go along too and got his friend Jacob to decide on the same. When the sled and skis were ready, Thompson gathered some wool blankets and lots of rope, then collected his rescue crew.

"I vill have to teach you men how to use your skis," Thompson said clearly to his men. "Dis vill probably not be an easy ting for you," he said with a stony face; using his balance pole to start himself off, he used his legs to push on the snow, looking back to see that the men were following along. "Ve begin like dis," Thompson started off with the make-shift rescue sled, and five men doing their best to imitate the outdoorsman as the group slowly made their way up the steep mountain.

The snow was relentless, and it was getting worse.

After struggling all day and into the night, the rescue crew finally arrived at the cabin. James Sisson was lying in front of the hearth, with the ax in his hands. He set it down and a most appreciative smile grew on his face, as the men entered the cabin and shook off the cold of winter. Thompson set about quickly to renew the stew pot, for he knew that the unseasoned men were quite hungry.

As they ate their Christmas supper, they each took note of the ever-increasing snowfall. Snowshoe Thompson was afraid that the men might panic at the thought of being caught, held prisoner by the prevailing weather. He focused his attentions on the ailing man and tried his best to prepare him for the journey back.

It snowed all night long, but when the cold dawn broke, the storm had let up, and they set out.

Sisson was wrapped in woolen blankets and then tied to the sled. With rope strategically tied, the men each held a line to the sled. They took their places and began the journey back, down the mountains, with their added burden to bear. Sissons' sled sank in the new snow, and it was very difficult going, as the storm again began to rail against the weary men, slowly progressing in the harsh terrain. Thompson led the way, using his pole to guide his men down the mountain. In some places, Sisson had to be lowered alone, using the ropes and trees to hold him.

Thompson had hoped to lead his rescuers safely home in one day, but his hopes were dashed by the slow progress in the harsh weather. They were forced to stop and make camp in a valley, known ever after as the Hope Valley. The men constructed a crude shelter of pine branches and built a big fire in a stump. They slept huddled together for warmth.

The rescue party set out again early the next morning.

When they returned to Genoa, they were a miserable sight, but they had done it! The doctor, who had been retrieved from Carson City, tended to the patient immediately, but he found that unfortunately, Mr. Sisson would have to have his feet amputated because of gangrene. The poor man was growing deathly sick, yet the doctor would not perform such a traumatic surgery without some form of relief for the patient.

Chloroform was the relief of the day; however there was none in Genoa or Carson City. The sure bet was Sacramento or hopefully Placerville. So Thompson headed back over the mighty mountains in search of relief for a man that he had promised to save.

Unfettered by inexperienced men and carrying only a light mail sack, Thompson again traveled the snowscape with speed and skill. He stopped briefly at the cabin he had found Sisson in, to rest and eat. Then he made his way over the mountain pass and back to Placerville with amazing speed.

"What happened to you? We been worried sick!" Edgar chastised the snowman, as he dropped the mail sack on the desk.

"I have to get to Sacramento in the fastest way possible. There isn't any chloroform here," Thompson said in a weary voice.

"Chloroform?" Edgar puzzled.

"What happened?" Monk, who had just come into the office, asked. Thompson told the story as briefly as he could to an office filling with curious men.

"Da new snow is fast, I can get pretty far still vith my skis. I'll get a horse and ride ven I run out of snow," Thompson explained.

The listening men pitched in money for a change of horses, and then Thompson was off to Sacramento to retrieve the needed medicinals, while bets were being placed.

"Godspeed, Snowshoe," Hank said as the Placerville crowd cheered the Norseman, when he returned. Thompson again trudged back up to the steep mountains, determined to save a man. "But for what?" John sometimes reflected. "For a man to live with no feet? How can dat be living?" He pondered as he rested in a familiar cave.

When Snowshoe Thompson again returned to Genoa, the townspeople dropped everything to see the returning hero, flying down the snowy mountains. Among them, with tears running down their faces, was Sissons' wife and children. The Norseman handed the needed medicine to the waiting doctor, as the town folks cheered.

Sisson would survive his amputations, and Thompson got his answer, in the loving faces of the family that would now be kept intact. The loving looks that the father and children returned, brought a tear to his own sky blue eyes as Sissons' wife wiped her tears away and hugged Snowshoe Thompson in gratitude.

CHAPTER 32

Sacramento, April 1857

Hank Monk and his pal Parkie had parted company soon after the bear hunt. Hank stayed in the mountains and Charley to the city for the winter, missing Thompson's heroics. Hank was thrilled with his new bearskin coat; it kept him warm as toast in the worse weather, but he was looking forward to spring.

Charley was also looking forward to the beautiful spring in mountains and headed back to Sacramento on route to the Sierras. While in town, Charley came across John Rollin Ridge, who was working on the new newspaper, the *Sacramento Bee*. The two found themselves at the Orleans bar and spent some time chatting about friends.

"Say, I heard Byrnes is a father," Rollin Ridge commented, as the bartender set down a second round.

"What?" Charley choked on the beer.

"Sorry, I shouldn't have surprised you like that," John said. "Yep, a girl, they named her Nellie."

"Well, I'll be," Charley said, wiping the beer from his face. "I read about Thompson's rescue. That man is really something. I can't wait to get back to Placerville. I'm sick of the city mud. I need to smell that sweet pine air."

"And listen to Monk's tall tales?" Ridge smiled, drinking his beer.

"Yep, I reckon I miss that Ol' cuss," Charley said, rubbing the eye patch.

"Well, Charley, I have to get back to the office, but when the summer heat gets unbearable, maybe I'll head to the mountains with my family and look you up."

"Good to see you again my friend," Charley said shaking his hand.

"And you," Ridge said.

Charley stood at the bar looking at the remaining beer and thinking of friends. When the teamster looked up and saw a familiar figure approaching the bar.

He was a handsome man, but had been well weathered from the elements, like a sea captain might be. Charley noticed the long brown and silver hair cascading down his shoulders from beneath his weatherworn hat. He was carrying a coach whip and the handle shone with gold rings, each signifying another year in California. He carefully hung it on the hat rack and placed his hat over it. Charley could better see his chiseled and leathery face; it was well proportioned and pleasant, with piercing eyes like those of a hawk. Charley was drawn to the leather patch over his own rugged face, as the man approached the bar.

"Say aren't you Jared Crandall?" Charley smiled at the man.

"Yes, I am," the man said, looking over at the teamster. "Oh, you drive for Birch, don't you?"

"Yes, sir. I've seen you in passing many times. Always admired your style. Charley Parkhurst is my name, pleased to meet you," Charley replied.

"I've seen you drive likewise, handle a team real well. Funny we ain't met after all these years," Jared said directly. "Can I buy you a drink?"

"Sure, I'd love to have a drink with you." Charley smiled. "What shall we drink to?"

"We should drink to the mighty Sierras!" Jared sang out, raising his glass.

"Are you really going to get a road through there, like they say?" Charley asked.

"You better believe I will," Crandall said with confidence. "This summer I'll do it. Got them working on the road right now. Have you ever been up there, to the lake? It's so magnificent!"

"I've been up to Sierra City, but I've never been across the Sierras. I came to California by way of Panama. I been driving in the foothills ever since. I haven't had any need to go further," Charley reasoned.

"Well, I'm not going to let those mountains stand in my way. I'm going to put a line right through." Jared said finishing his drink. "Where do you hail from?"

"New Hampshire, originally. I drove in Providence a lot," Charley related.

"Drove in the cities eh?" Crandall inquired

"Did my share, drove to the races with the big park drags. Party on wheels really." Charley laughed. "I like driving in the mountains here. I've made California my home. My life is out here now."

"Well, this summer I plan to get my route through to Carson City." Jared laughed.

"If you want to talk to someone about crossing the Sierra Mountains, you should talk to my friend John Thompson. 'Snowshoe Thompson' we all call him," Charley boasted.

"Yes, I've got him on my road committee. He's a friend of yours?" Jared asked.

"You bet." Charley smiled.

"This country kinda gets under your skin don't it?" Jared said smiling.

Charley had so often seen him in the distance and had admired him. It was wonderful to finally get to talk to him. He was very charming she secretly thought. "It surely does."

"Well, look me up if you ever want to drive with me. I guess I'll see you around," Crandall said finishing his beer and shaking Charley's gloved hand.

"Yes, I'm sure I'll see you around. Nice to meet you," Charley said, looking into his steel gray eyes. Then he was gone.

CHAPTER 33

Placerville, June 10, 1857

It was a hot June evening. Hank had finished his ride about an hour earlier and was relaxing on a chair propped back on two legs, against the outside of the express office. He had his dinner, but was working on a bag of roasted peanuts. A knee-high mutt was sniffing around under Hank's stool for any peanuts inadvertently tossed out with the shells.

"Go on, Pete, you ain't a getting any more a these peanuts, so scoot," Hank said. The dog plopped down next to the stool, never the less. He was a town dog and didn't really belong to anyone, let alone Hank. The summer heat was still in the air, and the dog panted restlessly to keep cool. The businesses in town were shutting down for the night, but the music in the bars was spilling out to the streets.

Inside the express office a young deputy, James Hume, had just concluded some business and stepped outside.

"Sure is a hot one, eh, Hank?" the young lawman said, mopping his brow with a handkerchief, then striking a match on the porch rail to light his cigar.

"There was a fire in Stockton yesterday. Haystack caught fire. Boy, it was a big 'un," Hank reported.

"God, I hate to even think about a fire!" Deputy Hume said, with real concern, looking at his smoldering match. The town was all wood and very dry; the place would be a tinderbox. Many are the mining towns that had been burned to the ground by a careless smoker.

"Maybe somebody ought to make sure all the horse troughs in town are kept full up, just in case," Monk replied.

"Good idea. Say I hear they got a new banjo player at Jake's," Hume said, scratching Pete on the head. "This your dog? You better bring him in tomorra' and get a license for him. Nice boy."

"Yeah? I didn't know they needed a license. No, I think he's Parkie's," Hank said popping a shell and tossing the nut in his mouth. "You want a goober?" he asked, holding the bag out.

"No, thanks, I gotta go. Tell Parkie to bring him in. See you round. Might want to top off this horse trough, it looks low," Hume said, crossing the street.

"Come on, Pete," Monk said, emptying the remaining empty shells out of the paper bag for the mutt. Hank stood up and stretched his back, then scuffled over to the trough and leaned on the water pump handle. The dog, having satisfied his quest for peanuts, joined his friend at the water trough and joyfully bit at the water flowing from the pump.

"Stop that, you're getting me wet, you fool," Monk scolded the dog, who seemed to be grinning. He did not care what the human thought. "Well, that looks full enough. I'm ready for a beer anyhow," Hank said, mopping his brow.

He clomped along the boardwalk; the wet dog, being an opportunist, decided to tag along too.

"Why, you're out and about rather late this evening, Mrs. Gustoffson. You gonna stay out and see Jared Crandall off on the great ride?" Hank said taking off his hat in respect for the banker's wife. She was a rotund woman in her fifties and had no appreciable sense of humor.

"Yes well, Mr. Gustoffson was thinking we might . . . My word! What business is it of yours!" the woman huffed at the dusty teamster.

"Well, I'm mighty sorry I troubled you, Madame," Hank smirked.

"If you'll just step aside and let me pass, I'll be on my way. It's terribly hot," Mrs. Gustoffson ordered. The new railing on the boardwalk and her gigantic new hoop skirt prevented her from passing.

"Well, I'm trying to, Madame, but your fancy dress seems to take up all the room here on the boardwalk," Monk said, pressing his body to the bank front. "By the way, that is a lovely dress if I might say it. Such a perty blue and so sweeping."

"Well yes, you may. It's direct from Paris. All the women are wearing their skirts this full," the fat woman boasted. The dress was supported by the latest wire hoops and was impossibly large. The little dog, which was sneaking along, began to bark and nip at the offending tent.

"Simmer down, Pete, let the lady pass," Hank sang out to the mutt. As the woman pushed past the coachman, the mutt took the opportunity to see the underside of the hoop skirt first hand; in one smooth maneuver, the dog popped beneath the circus tent.

"What is this!" the woman roared. "I've never been accosted in such a manner!" Mrs. Gustoffson shrieked, as the wet-faced dog sniffed around where he had not been invited. The matron danced around swatting at her skirt and making grotesque faces, until she was forced to hold up her skirt in the most humiliating way, kicking the mongrel out to the street.

"Why don't you control your dog! You idiot!" she fumed at Hank.

"Quite frankly, he don't belong to me. You can probably have him if you want to. You better get him licensed though, or the deputy will get after you!" Hank said scooting along. "I'm sorry I can't stay and chat. I gotta see a man about a banjo player." Hank could still hear the banker's wife cussing as he hurried on to Jake's.

"That was a good one Ol' Pete. I might even pony up the two bits for a license, just for that look on old Gustoffsons' face," Monk spoke to the mutt at his heels. "Good dog."

Placerville had been celebrating all evening, speeches were made, and most everyone got about as drunk as they could, except Jared Crandall and his crew.

It was still warm and dusty that night, as the passengers for the historic ride were assembling at their hotel. It was scarcely two in the morning. A breakfast was served in the lobby, and the press had been invited. Driving the historic coach was Jared Crandall himself. He had gone to bed at four that afternoon and rose at midnight, in order to ready things and leave promptly at three in the morning. The moon was bright, and the new road was ready. The revelers filling the streets were more than primed for the historic event. No stage line had ever been able to span this impossible continental divide, but Crandall was determined a transcontinental stage route would become a reality. Jared had set his course; along the route he had teamsters ready with fresh horses. He had shot his mouth off, or so he thought, and as a result, had a full coach for the journey. The passenger list included the following: J. G. McCallum, T. Foster, H. Cheatum, W. M. Cary, C. Stump, also a Mr. Randolph, a newsman. Other passengers, and there were more, did not lend themselves to historical documentation.

The passengers, well oiled from the celebrations, tended to sleep for the first part of the journey. When they awoke, they found themselves at the Sportsman's Hall. It lay about twenty miles from the starting point, Placerville.

Energized by the fresh air and the second breakfast, the passengers cheered to the newly arrived Mormons, encamped by the water, as they drove farther into the unseasoned road. The dawn's first light gave the granite mountains a soft lavender and peach hue, accenting their sharp and unrelenting hardness.

Jared Crandall had a force of men who ran the stage stops and saw the coach over the newly graded road, through the treacherous mountain range. He would make sure that it would be done again and again, and on time, to boot! Much of the route had seemingly impossible turns and incredibly dangerous cliffs, giving the passengers dizzying thrills and breath-taking views. At times, the passengers were asked to step off the coach, to stretch their legs to the top of a grade. Such inconvenience earned the stage line the nickname of Foot and Walker.

As the rolling party progressed up the thickly wooded mountains, big granite rocks became more and more prevalent. The roadbed became gravel and rocks as the grades became steeper and more winding. By afternoon, the first really dangerous stretch of "road" presented itself, nicknamed Peavine Ridge because of the dense growth of wild flowers on the hills resembled peas. It was a steep rockslide prone stretch, with sharp turns and bad footing, but it was tame compared to what came next.

The scenery became more and more dramatic as the coach reached higher altitudes. The passengers were all giddy from the thin mountain air. The granite jutted out of the earth, like gigantic teeth, yet the defiant, giant sugar pine trees seemed to grow right out of the bare rock, in some places. As they passed the treeline near the summit, the driver pointed out the snow, still lingering in the shady crevices. The coach lurched and rocked around the scenic tight turns, as the landscape became filled with grayish white granite boulders with black flecks, which looked like sooty snow. The next pass looked impossible to navigate; it was a steep, uphill grade, next to a river, with a sharp right turn, that had a low waterfall rushing through it. On the other side of the rushing water, a steep slippery, solid slab of granite and a sharp left turn, to God only knows what, around the bend and out of sight.

"I want all you passengers to keep to the left side of the coach till I tell you differ't," Jared Crandall said calmly and distinctly. The passengers assessing the gravity of the man, quickly obeyed. He slowed the horses with his experienced hands and let them catch their wind, before his ascent to the water. When he started them up, it was with firm resolve. The six horses responded with vigor and the maneuver was accomplished without a mishap. The horses then had a hard pull, as they came out of the water, to the slick granite road that wound around, ever higher, through what would be known as "Slippery Ford." The horses on this stage of the journey wore shoes with special cleats for traction.

Eventually, the coach rocked to a halt on a mighty slab of granite, overlooking the most pristine emerald and blue water of Lake Tahoe, thousands of feet below. The sight brought cheers from the passengers that echoed back to them, and the place was named Echo Summit.

More and more men hiked out of the forest to cheer the coach, as they neared their destination, Genoa. The staging routes were changed forever; a through route was under way.

Slippery Ford and Peavine Ridge were names that would now give the best whips pause. However, the roads made some progress during the season, Johnson's Pass being one notable improvement. Though at the time it was greatly debated upon. The wagon road had been carved though the granite mountains, with raw manpower and in many places was just wide enough for one coach to squeak by. Axles and single trees gouged into the cliffs and eventually left ruts in the side of the mountains. Falling rock and wash outs plagued the road; a road crew was always at work on it somewhere. When winter came, it would have to be closed. In all, it was some of the most difficult driving conditions ever devised. Hank Monk couldn't wait to sign up!

CHAPTER 34

"I wish I could have been there to see Jared cross the summit. I'm so proud I could just bust!" James Birch was pacing back and forth in his office in Sacramento. "Julia has me so torn up. I want to spend time here, developing the new routes, and yet I have a son who I've hardly seen. I wish I could convince her to come to California. I've got to go back to Swansea. Look I've got little Frank's birthday present here." It was a silver handled driving whip. Charley Parkhurst thought it a strange gift for such a small boy.

"I bet little Frank's just as cute as Julia is pretty," Charley said examining the piece.

"I'm sure the company is in good hands. I'll be back before too long. I hope I can talk Julia into returning to California with me. I've got my eye on a piece of property that would make an ideal home on this coast. Down near Monterey," James Birch reflected. "We really have something here, and I hate like hell to go, but Julia will be just be livid with me if I don't make it back in time for little Frankie's birthday."

"You leaving tomorrow morning then?" Charley inquired.

"Yeah, I'm taking the steamer to San Francisco."

"Well, I gotta head in, have a good trip. I'll see you when you get back," Charley said, shaking the young man's hand and gripping his shoulder with his free hand.

"Anything you want me to bring you back from the east?"

"Just yourself. Good night." Parkhurst smiled.

Some newspapers had announced that the California Stage Company would soon be the largest stage line in the world. It was ironic that James Birch, a driving force in land travel, should trust his life to an ocean voyage, but yet, the ships were still faster! Especially now that Panama had its railroad. The jungle adventure from one ocean to another took not days but hours and was extremely scenic.

It was August 20 when James Birch bid farewell to his partner Frank Stevens, for a voyage back to the Atlantic coast, to be with his family. He carried a small silver cup given to him on the day of his departure, by John Andrews, an agent of the company. It was inscribed with the words "From John to Frank." Birch stared at the cup in expectant joy of once again seeing his son and beautiful wife, Julia. It was too bad, he thought, that he would not see the first coaches of his new line come in from St. Joseph, Missouri, and arrive in San Francisco—cannons booming, bells ringing—in thirty-eight days! Soon to be done in less than thirty! It was a remarkable accomplishment, a stage line that could take you from coast to coast. But James could only dream of the events as he steamed onward to Panama, picturing his triumphant return home to Swansea. He would purchase the finest cigars in Havana, to smoke with the fat cats that would celebrate the countries newest and most daring enterprise with the dashing young entrepreneur.

The weather was rough when James left the wooden comforts of the Panama Railroad and boarded the luxury steamship *Central America*, in Aspinall, but the weather in Havana was lovely, and most everyone aboard ship had recovered from their seasickness and were now in grand spirits.

Birch sat on the hurricane deck smoking a cigar, listening to the sailors discussing the weather.

"Well, I tink we gonna get us a pretty good blow, maybe tomorra', I don't care for dem big clouds over yonder. They's heavy wid water dey is. No, sir, I tink it may be rough goin'," the old sailor said to the mate.

At first, James thought that the old man was just pessimistic; the first day of travel was sunny with only a brisk breeze. But by the second night, the wind kicked up to hurricane force. The ship pitched and rolled furiously, and the passengers were told to stay off the top deck. Soon after dark, the rain had started coming down in torrents. Water was running into the ship from the hatchways and passengers were cowering together anyplace they could stay dry, as huge waves broke over the bow of the ship, sending cascades of seawater down the stairways, flooding some of the staterooms. In the dark of night, Birch noticed that one of the engines had stopped, causing the ship to rely heavily on the other remaining engine to keep steady on the violent ocean, with swells of thirty feet and tremendous winds. The crew worked throughout the night, bailing water with the one remaining bilge pump that ran off the engine. Water was rushing in from the over stressed shaft as sailors stuffed blankets around the leaks. Before dawn, the remaining coal engine had been flooded and was now stopped as well, shutting down the bilge pump.

As the gray dawn broke, the storm raged ever stronger. Captain Herndon made the decision to enlist every able-bodied man to take up buckets and begin to bail out the ship, which was foundering some where in the Atlantic Ocean, off Cape Hatteras.

The wind was wicked and unrelenting and wet. Throughout the day, the water in the ship rose steadily.

James Birch was bailing water with the rest of the men; he was dead tired, yet the water did not seem to be going down. The crew had been busy trying to fix the storm-damaged pumps, but without the engines, they were not successful.

Birch recognized one of the passengers, a bartender he had met in Rough and Ready several years ago, his name was Dawson. They sat together as they rested from the futile bailing.

"It seems like we's just wearing ourselves out, for the ocean to make faster work of us, is all," Dawson said with finality, running his fingers through his course black hair. "They's not enough boats for us all if and when this ship goes down. I heared tell that one of the lifeboats got plum ripped offa the deck last night. I figure they ain't gonna let no black man in one, anyways," he added with a sigh.

"There's barely enough room for the women and children. Our only hope is another ship," James said, resting his head in his hands. The ship was bouncing around in the violent water, in a circular motion, almost like the water going down a drain.

The sighting of the brig *Marine* gave new hope, and the men set about organizing the small lifeboats, to transfer the women and children. The first boat was smashed to pieces upon lowering, as the ocean and wind toyed with the small vessels. The women cowered with their men folk, praying and arguing about the separation, shuttering at the thought of riding in the small boat in the violent sea; it was daunting, yet remaining on the foundering ship was no comfort either.

The captain ordered the crew to make sure that the men had access to the life preservers. They were grossly inadequate, but better than nothing. A crewmember tried to convinced James that his great duster, which had served him so well while driving coaches, would drag him to the bottom of the sea, but he would not remove it. He declined the cork and tin vest; the mate was passing out, making sure someone less virile received it. Birch then passed out his cigars to all the men who were near him. He retrieved the silver cup he had put in his largest pocket, staring sadly at it, as he secured it to his belt with a strip of fabric that he cut from the hem of his coat.

The women and children were loaded into the small boats with great effort and taken to the brig *Marine*. She had been disabled in her sailing gear and could not control her motions, thus may not be able to stay close by for long, but she was not taking on water and had agreed to take as many passengers as they could.

Many men were angered about the lack of lifeboats aboard the *Central America* and the flimsiness of the ones that they had, as another lifeboat was stove in upon launching. Several men tried to board the last boat, causing a knife fight and giving the first engineer an opportunity to climb into the dinghy himself.

After the lifeboats and the *Marine* had sailed from view, the men began talking among themselves about keeping afloat after the ship sank. There was much speculation about how much longer until she went down, and it would be dark soon. Approximately four hundred men were still on board.

"They say that when a ship goes down, it sucks everything down with her," Dawson said trying to light his cigar as he spoke. "They say if you can get off and get away from her, you won't get sucked down. That's what I'm gonna do. Right before she goes, I'm gonna jump and swim for my life. Yes, that's what I'm gonna do 'cause ain't nobody looking after my hide but me. So that's my plan," Dawson said with determination. He puffed on his cigar with the enthusiasm of a condemned man.

The men had begun to dismantle the top deck for rafts; ropes were cut to lash the wood together. The sea had become savage and tossed the men like rag dolls about the deck, washing poor souls prematurely into the briny depths. A final crashing of the main mast brought the deck ripping out of the ship. As she lurched onto her side, hundreds of men were washed overboard. When Dawson heard the mast crack, he grabbed his wood and dove into the foamy sea; James Birch did likewise. The two hit the water and upon rising to the surface were joined by everyone else that had been on deck. The men swam for their lives, amidst the roar of the ship's departure for the bottom of the sea and the screams of men meeting their doom.

It was dark and rainy as the nightmare wore on, the cries of men brought to mind images of hell, but in place of flames, there was raging water. The ocean played with her new toys, like a spoiled cat, with no regard for any precious life, a cold and heartless predator.

Birch lay on his stomach, on top of a piece of deck that had been freed up when the mast tore loose. Hundreds of men lie scattered about, clinging to anything that floated.

As the night wore on, the cries of men lessened as they drown, many saving their energy for dawn, some dying from exposure or just plain exhaustion. For many, it was the longest, most horrible night of their greatly shortened life.

James's world had been narrowed down to the sea and the small bit of deck that he was clinging to. Throughout the night, the waves lifted him and dropped him and smashed him in the face as he hung on for dear life. Occasionally he came in contact with another survivor; then they would drift off in the storm. Lightning ripped across the sky, sometimes giving a glimpse of the scattered wreckage. James tried to picture his wife and child to keep his spirits from failing. The morning would be better; he kept telling himself. He felt his side; at least he still had the little cup.

The rainy dawn held no hopeful sights; the wreckage of the ship was scattered far and only occasionally would James spot a possible survivor on a bit of debris.

He was sick with thirst, for he had swallowed a lot of saltwater during the night, and his mouth and throat burned savagely. As the waves pounded over his tiny wooden raft, he realized that he was still wearing his great coat and was amused that it had not dragged him to the bottom of the sea, as he had been warned. It somehow gave him comfort, as did the cup, which he used to collect rain. The sea played tricks on him by tossing waves playfully into his collection before he could drink, but James had patience and perseverance and managed to out trick the sea, enough to keep himself alive, at least. He floated along for three days and nights—hungry, cold, and very afraid. Talking to Julia and his infant son in his delirious state, he told of the new frontiers that would be opening up and the great opportunities yet to be had. He described to himself the fabulous dinner that would await him, when he made his triumphant return to Swansea and the grand mansion that he had built for his lovely wife. As James drifted along in calmer water, two men, who were floating about the high seas, also aboard wreckage of the *Central America*, spotted him. They shouted at James until he looked up from his imaginary banquet and began to paddle toward them. The men were on a crude raft, made from pieces of wood tied together with rope. The men were sitting balanced in the middle. As James got closer, he recognized his friend Dawson.

"Birch! I'd knew you's gonna make it!" Dawson creaked, through cracked and bleeding lips.

"Dawson?" James croaked.

"Yeah, it's me!" he said laughing and coughing. He grabbed the floating man and helped him to the center of the raft.

"Name's Grant," the other man offered.

James was soon asleep on the raft, the only real sleep he had in days. When he woke, he was still in a nightmare, only with his eyes open.

"I'm so glad to be home," James mumbled.

"I'm afraid not," Grant replied.

"I have this cup for little Frank. For the rain." James said to Dawson. Birch untied it from his belt and gave it to his friend.

"What?" Dawson said with a puzzled look on his face; he was also in a delirium and disappointed that the cup was empty.

"Keep it safe for him, my sweet," James said slowly. "Take my coat to the laundry, it's in need of cleaning and repair. Please," Birch said, turning to Grant, as he took off his weathered coat. The coachman saw his butler at Swansea.

Grant was in his own world and only opened his eyes briefly as the coat was handed to him. The man used it as a pillow, and James looked satisfied with himself.

"I'm going to the kitchen and get us something to eat," James said with finality.

"No, don't try to swim, stay with us!" Dawson warned, with the little strength he had.

"No, I insist, there is plenty for all, ham and roast beef and potatoes with gravy. I'll be right back with it," James ranted.

"You'll die, you'll never make it," Grant spoke quietly from his fetal position.

"It's all right, Captain, I can swim," James encouraged as he plunged into the ocean. "I can swim, Captain!" the hallucinatory man called out, as he began to swim away from the raft. Grant and Dawson were too weak to do anything about it.

James Birch was never seen again.

Birch's great coat helped as a sail, when Dawson and Grant met up with another survivor, who had happened by on a small vessel, that had broken free from another ship. The three were eventually retrieved from the sea and revived.

At last, when Dawson had rested and recovered from his trauma, he was interviewed by the press. The story was sensational news. Julia paid Dawsons' way, to deliver the surviving cup to its rightful owner.

Julia Birch was seated in the parlor with her young son, when the carriage arrived.

The humble black bartender marveled at the grandeur of the home, as he looked at his own poor but clean attire. The man tenderly held the cup, wrapped in soft cloth, to his chest, like a baby, as he removed his hat.

"The lady is in the parlor, this way. I'll take your hat," the butler offered, as the newsman and the bartender entered the house.

"This is Mr. Dawson and his associate, Mr. Evans. Gentlemen, this is Mrs. Birch and young Frank," the man said stepping to the side of the grieving Julia.

"Please sit down, gentlemen," Julia said softly.

"My deepest sympathies to you, ma'am. Mrs. Birch, I jes want to say, your husband was a smart and strong and brave man! None of us would'a survived without him or dis cup that he had with him . . . For your son . . . We took turns holdin' it and collectin' rain to drink. We would have perished without it. He . . . he . . . slipped away silently at night when we was asleep . . ." Dawson lied, looking down at the bundle and unwrapping it as he spoke, wishing to take one last hard look at his savior. The man was crying, unable to look at the beautiful woman, who was also crying. He at last handed the silver cup over to her, placing it in her trembling hand.

"I'm real sorry, gal. Truly I am," Dawson said, rubbing his handkerchief around his eyes.

"Thank you, Mr. Dawson. I'm pleased you brought this to me yourself, I appreciate that. Please be a guest in my home, I insist," Julia said, transfixed with the last object her husband had touched. "Please excuse me, gentlemen," she said, rising with a great deal of grace. "Please make yourselves at home. Get some refreshments for our guests please, anything they like, Roberts," Julia said quietly, as she retired to her bedroom to compose herself and grieve.

"Did you lose everything in the shipwreck?" Julia asked Dawson, later at the dinner table.

"Yes, ma'am. But I kin' start over again. I'll go back to tendin' bar somewheres. Maybe go back to California, open a bar," the man said, relishing the delicacies spread about the table in front of him. "Or a restaurant, maybe."

The next morning, when Dawson was leaving, Julia came downstairs to say good-bye.

"I hope you open a wonderful restaurant and thank you very much for coming. This visit has meant a lot to me," Julia said putting a piece of paper in the man's hand. It was a check for enough money to start a new life.

Dawson was stunned as he looked at the note. Tears welled up and coursed down his weather-scarred face.

"Thank you, ma'am. Praise God and thank you," Dawson said, kissing the delicately gloved hand.

CHAPTER 35

October 24, 1857

Charley Parkhurst was driving his winter route on California's coast. The weather and the scenery were lovely, compared to the eastern winters or the Sierras. He drove a San Francisco route until the weather again turned mild in the mountains. Hank Monk stuck with the mountains and toughed it out. But Charley preferred to live as well as his station in life allowed, while still saving for a retirement. The teamster was a regular at the What Cheer Hotel in San Francisco, and it became a familiar home of sorts.

"My word, Charley have you seen the paper? It's a terrible shame that's all. All those people lost!" the tavern owner sighed.

"No, I haven't seen it, what happened?" Charley asked, with a bad feeling welling up in the pit of his stomach.

"Here, you may have it. I'm finished reading it," the man said casually.

Charley picked up the thumbed through edition of the *Daily Alta California*, Friday-morning edition, dated October 23, 1857, and the words shot out like stinging arrows:

Total shipwreck of the mail steamship *Central America*! Loss of four hundred! And $1,500,000 in treasure! List of the drowned and missing! Minute details of the awful calamity. Statements of the saved.

It wracked Charley's brain.

"Did you know someone on that ship, Charley?" a man in the corner asked.

"Oh my God, I hope not! Oh, James, I hope not." Charley scanned the article, but it was getting hard to see; his remaining eye was getting waterlogged. "Can I get another beer here please?" Charley tried to focus on the print.

"It lists the names of the lost there, doesn't it?" said the tavern owner, as he set the beer down in front of the upset Charley.

"Yes, it says Names of the Lost. My head hurts, will you look and see if there's a James Birch?" Charley sighed, rubbing beneath the patch on his wrinkled face.

"James Birch was on that ship? My, my! Let me see, they ain't in alphabetical order . . . ah, well there is a J. E. Birch. Could that be him?"

"Good God almighty!" Charley took the paper and his beer and slunk to the corner of the room and was sullen for the rest of the night. He read the article over

225

and over and tried to make sense of it, but there was none to be made. The despair was all there in black ink.

Charley read the story one last time before he set the paper aside, setting his head on his arm and fought back the tears. "God, I hope he's rescued!"

"Are you all right, Charley?" the bartender asked.

"Yes, fine, good night." Charley left the paper on the bar and walked into the night air. It seemed to be swirling around his head, like a weird fog.

CHAPTER 36

Placerville, December 1857

It was an icy morning in Placerville. The streets were a slurry of mud and snow that hugged the buildings. Men congregated in the warm taverns, as long as time and money would allow.

"I tell you, I have never zeen anyting like it," Thompson related. "Dey could have killed me easily."

"What happened, Thompson?" Hank Monk said, inviting himself into the conversation.

"It vas da most frightening ting I have ever zeen! I vas skiing across da Hope Valley, an vas sliding down da last bit of hill and going through da last bit of forest, before I crossed da open meadow, ven I spotted six great gray wolves, digging in da snow. My path vould have to cross deirs. I had no other course, because da mountain vas fairly steep up behind me. Just on the udder side of da wolves before me if I could only reach it, vas a fast downhill slope, vere I might be able to out race dem, should dey make a run at me. Dey vere great, hairy, timber wolves, lean and hungry looking. Dey vere busy digging up a dead deer. My course lay directly across deir path. I knew enough not to try and run, or dey vould easily chase me down. So I kept my course slow and steady, my pole out in front of me, and made my vay closer and closer to da pack, slowly, but steady. As I got about twenty-five yard avay, da leader turned around and faced me. Den, much to my suprise, he zat down. I kept my head down and kept on goin'. Den da next wolf came up and sat down, den da next, an da next, till day all six sat in a row. I pledge you my word! As I slid closer and closer, I felt deir eyes upon me, yet day did not move. At last, I vas making my vay away from da pack, trying to show not an ounce of fear. Ven from behind me rose da most fearful howl I've ever heard! Followed by a chorus vith da rest of da pack. I awaited my attack, but at da same time kept moving forward vith da same steady movement. Ven I finally had da nerve to look back, I saw dat dey had gone back to deir digging! I never did ski so fast in my life! Down da mountain slopes and away from doz wolves!" John Thompson said, out of breath.

"Damn, Snowshoe! I hope you're packin' a lot of iron when you travel," Hank chuckled.

"All I carry is my knife," John said, unsheathing a sword of a knife. "I don't have to worry about misfire or running out of bullets. As long as it's in my hand, I'm armed and dangerous. Guns are heavy and unreliable in bad weather. Dis knife stays sharp all de time," Thompson said, making a point with all that were in earshot.

"But what about bandits? A knife ain't gonna help you against a gun," Hank shot back.

"If dey want to lay in wait for to rob me, dey can, but I carry letters mostly, not gold or money. So vhy vould anyone rob me?" John Thompson asked the driver.

"Well, ya got me that time!" Monk laughed. "Why would they? They'd probly freeze up to death trying." He laughed even harder at the thought. "Say, when you going out again?" Hank inquired.

"Vhy, you vant to come along?"

"Well, see now, I would love to, but unfortunately I am due back in Sacramento tomorrow afternoon," the Jehu reasoned.

"Dat's too bad, yes, because I'm gonna set out tonight about eleven vhen da snow is good and icy," Thompson related to his friend.

"That does sound like high adventure," Monk said in genuine admiration.

CHAPTER 37

Spring 1858

When the spring arrived once more, Charley Parkhurst again sought out the mighty Sierras to lift his spirits from the fog. The coachman decided to look up Jared Crandall to take him up on his offer. He seemed the type to make good on a promise. A new road would be a good distraction from the sadness and loss of James Birch.

Charley found that Placerville had grown since he had left it for the winter. Unlike a lot of boomtowns in California that were beginning to play out, Placerville had become the jumping-off point for the new diggings on the eastern side of the Sierras. Now with the new mountain road and the central cross-country stage route, Placerville was beginning to swell.

Parkhurst took a few minutes to look at the vast, new commodities to be had, in the thriving wilderness village. The forests close to town were gone, all to build the ever-expanding frontier. The place reeked with humanity and vice, each sign advertising another diversion, just name your poison. It took a moment of search, but the teamster spotted a familiar tavern sign and made his way toward it. He had to navigate a series of boards to get across the muddy street, without getting covered with filth.

Jared Crandall was relaxing at the bar, when Charley entered. The one-eyed driver had not seen him, for he was on his blind side. The teamster stood at the bar and waited for the bartender to come around.

"Hey, Parkie, welcome back. You need a beer? Hey, Jared Crandall is at the other end of the plank if you didn't see him," the bartender smiled.

"Yeah, I'm dry as dirt Lenny, set me up, set up Mr. Crandall too, and meet me down there. Thanks, Len," Charley said, handing the bartender a thin cigar.

"Charley Parkhurst. Good to see you again. Thanks for the drink," Jared greeted the teamster.

"You're welcome, sir, good to see you too. Congratulations on the Pioneer," Charley said raising his glass.

"To lost friends," Jared sighed. "Sorry about Ol' Birch, I knew he was a friend of yourn. Say, I was going to set down and get some dinner. Will you join me? I hate to eat alone." Jared smiled.

"I'd be honored, sir." Charley smiled back.

"Jus' do me a favor and quite calling me sir. Jared is fine."

Charley tried not to blush. The two found a table where it wasn't very noisy and ordered dinner.

"You ready to come and work for me?" Crandall said, with a mesmerizing look in his smiling eyes.

"Well, it would be challenging," Charley pondered. "Aren't you concerned about my missing eye?"

"You've been driving. If you're not concerned about your eye, then neither am I," Crandall responded with a laugh. "Your friend Hank Monk talks mighty highly of you, Snowshoe as well."

"Hank's driving for you?" Charley inquired.

"Yep, probably a lot of folk you know, Coon Hollow Charley and Charley Watson. Watson bought out the Strawberry Station house and is rebuildin' it," Jared said, wiping his mustache with his napkin.

"Rebuilding it?" Charley inquired.

"Yeah, it burned down not long after he bought it," Jared replied. "Things are getting quite lively up here these days. I could sure use another good coachman. Besides, I can now pay you twenty dollars more a month than you are making now," the man said with calculation.

"Well, how could I refuse an offer like that," Charley said nonchalantly, trying to cut into the food. He was greatly flattered and excited about seeing the new frontier and his old pals too.

The next morning, Charley woke to what was sure to be an exciting day. He had driven all over California, but the mountains that lay before him today, caused chills to course through his veins. It was still dark, and the owls were still on the hunt. Charley creaked and popped as he put on his boots. The morning air was cold, and he anxiously ambled out of his room to get a cup of coffee. The whale oil lamps in the hall lit the way to the tavern downstairs.

"Mornin', Charley," Jared greeted his new employee.

"Mornin', Jared." Charley smiled, trying not to stare into his piercing eyes.

"This will be an easy day, Charley, you'll see. You just follow right along after my coach, till we get to Strawberry, then we'll give it a rest for the night. The next day you'll see some of the most beautiful sights that God has ever created. Or at least, that I have ever seen!" Jared said, resting his hand on Charley's strong shoulder. He sensed the worry in Charley's eye if that, in fact, was what it was.

"This here is Curly Dan. He's your swamper, oh, I mean your express guard," Jared said, his smile teasing the mop-headed young man lumbering toward the coffeepot.

"Mornin'," Curly snuffled out.

"Charley, pleased to meet you," he said. "How soon we leaving?" Charley asked the boss.

"About twenty minutes," Jared said, looking at his gold watch.

Charley could not help but notice the vast ocean of men that were piling up to use this new road. Most were still trying to sleep, in any available spot imaginable. Every form of humanity, from all over the world, was represented in this new land. All were seeking their fortunes in gold, in them yonder hills.

After finishing his coffee, Charley wandered to the livery; the horses inside the lamp lit barn were being fitted with their new harness. They were beauties. He walked back to the outhouse; there was a line, waiting for a few private moments. Men were beginning to collect themselves for their coach ride to another adventure. It looked to be a full load.

The stars were still shining brightly, as Parkhurst took the lines in his hands and cracked his whip, sending six young horses on a dash for the Sierras. For now, all Charley could see was the dimly lit rumps of his chargers and the puff of dust in the moon light, that was Jared Crandalls' coach. Slowly the shadow of the mountains became a purple haze, as the clear sky lightened to an azure blue. The sun would not shine in the deep cannons for several hours.

Curly had brought his banjo and was plinking along, as the coach rocked and swayed. Most of the passengers that were crammed on the roof and inside were trying in vain to continue their slumber. Charley and the horses appreciated the musical accompany though.

"Why did Jared call you a swamper? What's a swamper?" Charley asked.

"A swamper is the fellar that sits next to the driver, an' when the driver says, I wonder can we get through that swamp, I wonder how deep it is? The swamper jumps down in there, an' then tells the driver that it's too deep." Curly began to sing with enthusiasm. "Oh, do you remember sweet Betsy from Pike?" Many passengers moaned loudly at the nasal voice. "Well, maybe it is a tad bit early for sweet Betsy." Curly blushed.

"Yep, maybe later in the afternoon." Charley smiled, noticing the nasty faces at the sour singing. "I doubt we'll run across any swamps today," Charley chuckled.

As the morning wore on, the road became busier, as men resumed their travels. The horses wore bells on their harness to warn pedestrians that they were coming round the sharp mountain turns. Curly was fond of tooting out a jaunty little tune on a horn, when they got close to a blind turn, to help clear the road.

"We'll be coming round the mountain, when we come! Clear the way!" he would sing, punctuating it with some blasts on the horn. He enjoyed entertaining the passengers; singing songs and playing tunes. He also carried a harmonica in his pocket, that he was quite adept at playing. Curly felt cheated if he couldn't get the passengers to sing "Oh Suzanna" at least once on a trip. By the time the passengers had reached the terminus for the day, they were a regular glee club.

When they reached Strawberry, at about eight that night, the sun had gone down on the other side of the great mountain range. A storm was forming, as the granite peaks scraped through the icy clouds. Great claps of thunder echoed and rumbled in the sky. Flashes of lightning lit up magnificent boulders and trees. It was good to be in for the night. Such as it was.

Strawberry station was not quite complete, and Charley Watson had his hands full, rebuilding, running a station and playing host to the influx of travelers. The storm pelted the migratory people with small hailstones, bringing everyone out of their crude tent accommodations, in search of more water tight arrangements for the night. Charley slept in the coach, away from the hordes of men seeking refuge in the station. Or at least he tried to sleep, between Curly's snore fests in the opposite seat, he dreamt of the lofty heights he would see tomorrow.

Over breakfast, Jared Crandall shared his experiences on the upcoming stretch of road.

"Well, Charley, since this is your first trip over the summit, I elected to let you have the white team. Hank said how you were partial to white horses and such. Our first stop is at Yank's station to change teams before we go over the top. Wait till you see the team waitin' for you in his barn. We got time for a cup of coffee when we stop at Yanks. That man makes the best brown gargle I ever had. I told him he ought to get out of the station business and go into the coffee business full time. He'd make a fortune," Crandall rambled.

"Yep, I met Ol' Jim around '54. He shot a bear for me, had the hide made into a winter weather coat. Probly wear it this very mornin'. Sounds like the thunder is startin up again," Parkhurst said finishing his coffee.

"Yep, the weather out here is mighty unpredictable." Jared smiled deeply into Charley's remaining hazel orb. "Let's git a rollin'."

It was four in the morning and still dark, only this time the stars weren't shining, and the moon was shrouded in a thick veil of clouds. The wind was swirling around with sharp authority; the bear coat was definitely in order. How drastically the weather changed at this altitude, in Placerville; it had been close to ninety degrees. Charley had packed the coat away without a second thought. He pulled the beast from its duffel bag and shook it out. It was an old friend by now.

"We'll probably pass Monk's coach this afternoon," Jared called out from his perch as he collected the leather lines.

"I'm ready when you are," Charley called back, admiring the milk white horses eagerly waiting to run and adjusting his hat to the wind. The coaches were full inside and out as Curly let out a blast with his horn and the vehicles rocked into motion. The road was steep and winding, as up and up they went. Charley heard the familiar groans of passengers inside, becoming motion sick, while the passengers topside were treated to the most picturesque scenery, as the ever-changing magical morning light, painted the mountains with soft, dark colors of purple and green. They sat mesmerized, as the weather pelted them with hail. The storm had left icy drifts that remained throughout the day, nestled in the shadows of great granite boulders. The magnificent giant trees seemed to have grown throughout time, in this land of solid rock, many grandfather trees towering well over two hundred feet tall. Charley was in awe of the formidable granite that lay still farther. Through the clouds, he could see snow on the highest peaks.

Ahead lay Yank's station; it was a nice log-and-rock affair. The barn was large and could accommodate at least thirty horses.

"Hey, Yankee Jim!" Charley called out to the young man standing on the porch.

"Hey, Charley, I see you still got Mama Bear!" the young man said, calling back to the driver.

"She looks after me now. I wouldn't go nowhere's without her!" Charley laughed, as he settled the team in front of the station. "Good to see you, Jim!"

"Good to see you too, Charley. You got time for a cup of coffee, the boss always has one," the young man said, as the folks descended the vehicle, moaning and groaning as they climbed down.

"Hey, you seen Snowshoe around?" Charley asked, climbing from the driver's box.

"Yeah, you ought to see him out Genoa way, this evening. He said he wanted to see Jared and get him up to date on the road repairs. Jared hired him as the road boss," Yank said, as they entered the granite and log station. Jared already had his hands on a steaming cup and was warming his nose over it.

"Enjoying the scenery, Charley?" Jared smiled the smile of perfect contentment. He really loved to drive, and this was the ultimate test of driving skills. In the coming years, the road would become a well-trod highway, but for now it was just a pair of paths carved around the lofty granite mountains. "Ah the best scenery is yet to come my friend."

"Ain't Hank due in soon?" Yank asked the Boss.

"Yep I believe Ol' Monk'll be in shortly. You 'bout ready to head out Charley?" Jared said reaching the bottom of the cup. "I'm just gonna kick the bushes, then I'm set," he added. The line for the outhouse had diminished, and Charley made a visit before they departed.

The thunder had quieted down to a soft rumble, and there was just occasional sprinkles playing about the landscape. When Charley returned to the driver's seat, another beautiful white team was being brought out. They were a lovely sight, as Charley received the lines to the splendid horses. Curly scampered up to his seat, after chaining in the last horse and took out his harmonica.

"You ever seen this here mountain top, Curly?" Charley said with growing excitement.

"Nope, I never been this far to the east of San Francisco, farthest I ever been is Placerville," Curly replied, taking the harmonica out of his mouth for a moment. "I am originally from Boston," he added. "I just love it out heah. I don't ever want to go back."

"What about your family?" Charley inquired.

"Most is gone, those that ain't, I don't miss. I got a brother out here somewheres. People call him Curly Jerry on account he looks like me," Curly chuckled. "Say is that your friend Hank coming down the road there?"

Charley had been concentrating on receiving the lines to the growing horse team and had not noticed the coach that had come around the countryside and into view. It was arriving at a furious rate.

"Yep, that's got to be Hank, nobody drives that fast," Charley said, as he lit a thin cigar. Jared would surely wait until Hank had come in, before leaving.

"Hey, Parkie, I see ya got ya six white horses!" Hank called out, as he appeared in a cloud of dust. "Ya still got ya bear skin coat I see!" Hank said, a grin peeking out of another grizzly coat. "I hurried in, so we didn't have to pass on the grade.

Ellen Wight

"What was the weather like up there?" Jared called out.

"Saw some picturesque lightning, and some pretty good sized hail, so you might what to batten down the windows," Hank said climbing from his perch. "Good to see you Parkie! I gotta piss like a mule!"

"Yeah, all right. Giddup now!" Jared said kissing his team into a canter. "You heard the man people, you might want to tie down the curtains, I leave it up to you folks inside. It's gonna get mighty picturesque" Crandall called down. "Com'on now, get in there!" he sang out to his chargers, as they hauled the great heap of humanity into the timeless wilderness. Curly cupped his harmonica and worked on his "Coming round the mountain" tune.

"Say, that is a catchy little tune, but don't you have any more verses for it?" Charley said offhandedly, getting a bit tired of the redundant doggerel.

"Nope, I ain't thought none up yet," Curly said, pausing to adjust his hat. "You got any idears?"

"Hmn, I might give it some thought . . . If I did not know better I would have thought I had trained these horses myself, they are so nice and easy to the touch. I could get real used to these beauties," Charley said smiling through the mist.

"Hey, I think I got us a new verse! How's 'bout this? He'll be drivin six white horses when we come!" Curly sang out.

"That's not bad!" Charley laughed as Curly roared again his newfound verse, as the rest of the passengers joined in. "He'll be driving six white horses when we come! When we come!"

A passenger called out from the back:

"They will all be there to meet us when we come! When we come!" The verse was accepted and approved with vocalization. The coach was really beginning to liven up, as the terrain became more and more harsh. Then the party came to a grinding halt, as the road grew too steep for the horses to pull fully loaded. The passengers were obliged to stretch their legs up the mountain a piece. The wind was fierce and the air crackled with electricity. Curly's black mop stuck out in fuzzy clumps from under his hat.

The sky flashed blinding arrows, across her angry surface. The thunderous peal that followed made Charley cower on his perch, self-conscious that his whip was the tallest point on the ledge and quite vulnerable to being struck by lightning, he held it as low as possible. At least the hail had stopped, but the wind had grown in intensity.

"This weather is really something. If this is what it's like in the summer, I can't even imagine what the winter must be like!" Curly observed, as a flash of lightning crackled across the sky, followed by an incredible boom! The milk white animals snorted in disapproval. Charley soothed them and clucked to them and followed Jared's coach.

The horses caught their breath, as the passengers again boarded the coach. They then forded streams that splashed their way to rushing falls, below the rocky road. The vehicles wound around switchbacks that had been blasted out of the rugged terrain, and still the thunder rolled and ripped through the atmosphere. The road seemed to dwindle away at times until you could only see down the cliffs, the road base just wide enough for the stage, and that's all. Tops of giant sugar pines were visible at times level with the coach; they were rooted two hundred feet down a canyon. As they rolled ever higher, even the trees gave up the fight, as the coaches traveled beyond the tree line, the strange place, so high in the altitude that trees can not exist.

"Oh my God!" Charley exclaimed as they wound up the final peak. "Holy Mother of Mercy! Will you look at that!" Charley sighed, trying not to look down the deep canyon beneath them. "I can see the lake!" He took note of the tired, shaky horses that cowered, as the sky rumbled, then echoed in the valley below. The view was stupendous. On the left side you could see the tops of the mighty granite peaks that divided California from the great American desert. It gave one the feeling of being on top of the world. In the midst of these harsh peaks lay the pristine blue waters of Lake Tahoe, its shores partially hidden from view behind the mountains.

"This here must be echo summit!" Curly called out for the information of all, his announcement reverberating in the canyon and back. He played a call on his horn, and to everyone's delight, the tune played back miraculously.

"Yep, let's just get down off a here, come on my beauties!" Charley called out. Passengers, who took notice of the steep precipice directly next to the coach wheels, cowered away from the formidable view.

"You will have to sleep with Grandma when we come! When we come!" Curly blurted out in a fit of song writing. The catchy verse echoed back from the canyon, to the amusement of all on board.

"That's a good 'un." Charley nodded with teeth tightly clenched with concentration, as he maneuvered the coach and six horses to the beautiful lake and meadows below. Navigating down the switchbacks, down the eastern slope of the mountains was treacherous indeed. Curly tried his best to keep spirits high with his harmonica, but it even got to him.

"My spit dried up," Curly confessed.

Charley guided the coach slowly to the basin below, then gave the horses a triumphant gallop through the meadows, the jewel-like water of the deep lake sparkling though the trees. Above them, cries of bald eagles arguing over a fish that was caught pierced the air.

"Surely I have died and gone to heaven." Charley smiled, spotting the magnificent birds and breathing in the soft clean air that was perfumed with pine and sweet grasses. As the horses slowed down, the driver scanned the landscape; he noticed men had been busy cutting lumber and were beginning to leave their ugly scars even on this remote paradise.

"Boy, I sure am working up a hunger," Curly boasted. "We will all have chicken and dumplings when we come! Yee Haw!"

Charley laughed at her new found friend and looked forward to seeing another. The next stop was a few miles further. Parkhurst was enchanted with the countryside. The place was glorious in its rugged splendor. The home station came into sight and brought cheers from the passengers and more blasts from Curly's horn. It was a sturdy house with a granite foundation and built out of thick cedar. The large rock chimney wafted fragrant smoke from dinner that was soon to be served; the sight was inviting indeed. The inhabitants all rushed out to greet the coach, among them stood a towering Norseman with a blonde beard, who merrily waved his hat in the air.

"Is dat you, Charley?"

"Yep, I finally made it over the hump! Its good to see you again, John!" Parkhurst said, climbing from the driver's perch.

"It's good to see you too!" Thompson said, giving the teamster a bear hug. "I have a ranch near Hope Valley. I live up here year round now!" The Norseman said as they walked inside the station. "I've made my home up here."

"I can see why. It's a grand place. I can't even imagine the winters though," Charley confessed.

"Yep, it's mighty tough! But I love it. I been teaching folks how to ski, I could even teach you!"

"Oh, Thompson, I want you to meet Curly Dan, he's my swamper. Mighty good with the mouth harp and such too."

"Any friend of Charley is a friend with me!" Snowshoe said pumping Curly's hand.

"That's mighty neighborly I'm sure," Curly said massaging the blood back to his fingers, with a smile, sort of.

"Hey, can you play 'Sweet Betsy from Pike'?" Thompson requested.

"Can I?" The musician grinned.

"Oh, now you've started him a goin'!" Charley sighed.

Charley enjoyed driving on the new Pioneer Stage Line, but the roads often presented treacherous challenges, such as rockslides, or avalanches.

On a hot summer day, as Charley was driving along the granite precipices, the teamster was forced to stop in a most difficult location. The road was a very narrow ledge, cut into the mountain face. It was at least one hundred feet, practically straight down; next to the road and turning around was impossible. Thus the importance of blowing the horn to let other travelers get over or off the road.

Charley sat on the driver's box and surveyed the boulders and rocks piled up on the road.

"There's no getting around that. We'll have to back out and get a road crew out here," Charley sighed.

"How are we gonna turn around?" Curly asked.

"Well, we can't turn around here. We gotta start unhitching the horses one at a time and lead them to the back of the coach so I can chain them to the rear axle. Then we'll haul the coach around the hill backward, till we can turn her around, I reckon. I'll drive the horses from the rear boot and you can steer the pole," Charley ordered, for he was captain of his vessel.

"Gracious heavens, this is a great inconvenience!" Curly whined.

"Yeah, well you got any better idears? Maybe you want to shovel that pile of boulders off the road?" The teamster offered.

"No . . . I s'pose not," Curly replied.

Charley climbed off the box, securing the brake bar with a thick leather strap, then tied the leather lines to the brake bar. He then blocked the wheels with some of the rocks and went to the rear of the coach and produced some emergency chains and several clevis. He then ran the chain from the rear axle, out past the back boot, using the clevis to keep the chain were he wanted it. He set about unhitching the team and squeezed one horse at a time around the coach, to the back and tied their lines to the boot chains. The horses stood obediently. The teamster removed the singletrees from the wagon's pole and attached them to the chain with a clevis, then hooked the swing pole to the end of the chain between the wheel horses. The swing team's single trees were then added to the end of the swing pole in front of the wheel horses. The swing horses one by one were added. The leaders single trees were then added with the rest of the chain. The leaders were then hitched into place. Curly Dan made ready to steer the wagon pole and the whole company set off in reverse. They traveled like that for about a mile, up and down steep grades, with a passenger running the foot-break on the downgrades, before they had enough road space to turn the vehicle around to its proper direction. The express agent was more than jubilant to once again take his lofty seat on the coach, in his proper position. It became common practice to carry emergency chains in such terrain, as rock slides or fallen trees were not uncommon.

Charley decided to try and tough out the coming winter and even suggested trying sleigh runners in place of wheels to extend the coaching season even further. When the storms made the roads impossible, Snowshoe Thompson alone, carried the mail across the Sierras.

CHAPTER 38

Spring 1859

As soon as the winter snows let up and the Sierras eased into spring, road crews would get into the snowy peaks and begin work for the many travelers to come. This was to be the new pathway of the West. Soon there would be other things to worry about on the roads besides rocks.

Charley's route had expanded to include the budding town of Carson City. It was in its infancy as a town and was still being mapped out, but it had high hopes and had been named after the frontiersman Kit Carson, who had lived in the valley in the early '30s.

Parkhurst and his expressman and just about everyone else in town, frequented a hotel and tavern that also served as the stage office; it was called Ormsbys' after the owner, Major Ormsby, who saw the place as a great investment in his retirement, and it was.

"Come on, Maguire. It's time to go," Charley said to the broad barreled man, with the wiry beard, who was sleeping next to the stove.

"I'm coming," the expressman moaned, hoisting himself out of the chair, with a great belch. The two strolled out into dusty Carson City boardwalk. The hotel lamp flickered in the nearly empty street, as Charley walked around the waiting team and coach. He made a final inspection, taking a twist out of the leader's line, then climbed up to the driver's box with authority, holding out his hand for fat Maguire, who took his position next to the driver.

"You got two and a half passengers this morning. They's going all the way to Placerville," the clerk said with a smile, as the small family approached the coach. Charley smiled at the small mother who was clinging tightly to a squirming bundle.

First on board was a young girl of about seven, with long honey-colored braids streaming down her back; she was rubbing the sleep from her eyes. The mother then handed the baby to the girl, as she herself climbed in.

Soon they were flying in the dark morning air, down the newly graded street, toward the impending Sierras.

The dawn was just bringing out the subtle purple and pink colors of the morning light on the granite cliffs.

By afternoon, the passengers were oohing and awing at the sight of Lake Tahoe, newly renamed Lake Bigler, for the governor of California. It was a much welcome scene for the mother, after the monotony of the plains and deserts.

Tahoe, as the indigenous people, what was left of them, called it, was a majestic deep safire blue body of water, in the stoic granite mountains. It was like a jewel, in a crown of lofty white, fed by the snowy mountains from time immemorial.

As the coach rose above the sparkling lake, the cold fresh air pierced the senses; snow on the summit still hung onto its last grip of winter. The coachman steadily urged his team to the lofty heights. He wished that the little girl could experience some of God's great majesty. It would seem that the diminutive passenger had ceased to enjoy her trip as soon as the vehicle had left the flat of the deserts and crossed to the golden state. She hung her head out the window and puked from motion sickness, as her mother held back her hair.

They were heading for Strawberry's, a grand station now, built of the stone from the mountains and stout lumber. Fashioned with a lot of love, great profits twinkled in its' windows, that were hauled all the way from San Francisco. However, running a station requires a lot more than having sound architecture. If that had been true, the place might have been christened Berry's Castle. Instead, because the first owner, Berry, had invested unwisely in horse feed, owing to faulty judgment, he neglected to purchase enough hay or grain for his first winter and had only an abundance of straw, which had to pass off as feed. Thus receiving the new name of Strawberry. It would forever stick, no matter who owned it. Passengers were often disappointed at the lack of fruit.

However a derogatory name it was, it was always a pleasure to arrive there, for it meant you were almost home. Maguire was never one to miss an opportunity for a drink, and Strawberry's always presented that opportunity.

Charley noticed the little girl lying in the grass, heaving from motion sickness and hastened to relieve her with a shot of sarsaparilla. The child gagged on it at first then drank it down. Charley was called back to the station.

"Sugarfoot is in the neighborhood again? Well, I'm ready for him this time. That son of a bitch," Charley remarked to Deputy Sheriff Hume. The topic was a sore one for Charley, as the outlaw had held him up last month and had successfully made off with the express box, forever tarnishing his perfect record.

"I said I'd be ready for him and I will be," Charley snapped sharply at Maguire, who was lighting the coach lamps. Charley climbed the coach and sorted out his leather lines. "He won't stop me again," he muttered under his breath, as he felt for the extra revolver, placed behind his seat cushion.

After Maguire parked his carcass in the shotgun position, they took off with a jolt; they were losing precious light. Charley cursed under his breath, as the baby inside the coach began to cry. The seasoned teamster wanted to finish the ride and return to Placerville without incident.

"Why do they call him Sugarfoot?" a new passenger sitting behind the driver asked.

"He wears sugar sacks on his feet, so's he can't be tracked as easy," Maguire laughed.

The roads were in muddy turmoil with spring runoff, but the hardest driving was still to come, as darkness enveloped the mountains. Trouble came at the end of a long barreled gun.

"He's got me cold!" Charley hissed at Maguire. "Don't do anything stupid."

The road was blocked by three men, with leveled shotguns. A tin lantern placed on a large rock, by the bandits, illuminated the situation.

"Throw down your guns, and we won't have any trouble!" Sugarfoot called out from the road; his face was covered beneath his eyes with a bandanna.

"Now you can see that we are all being real polite," Charley said, raising his hands to the masked trio of robbers, then tossing his revolver to the road. Maguire swore, as he tossed his new shotgun into the mud.

"Tie that brake on, with the lines driver," the bandit ordered. "Then drop the box and get down."

Charley's mind was clicking away as he watched the bandits pull the mother and the children from the coach; it seemed to enflame something deep inside.

"There's your box, mister!" Charley said, throwing it into the gravel, then climbing from his perch.

"Why that's just fine," the bandit said, shooting at the lock on the treasure box. The gun's loud report caused the girl to recoil in fear and hide her face in her mothers' skirt. "Now you, little girl," Sugarfoot said, pulling on a honey-colored braid, as the baby began to cry. "You go and take that lock off that box, now, you hear?" He pulled her from her mother with her hair, then kicked her toward the box with the ball of his boot, his shotgun balanced in his arm.

Charley could feel the hair on the back of his neck raising, as the masked man breathed stale breath above the innocent child, who was afraid to touch the box, as if it would bite.

"Go on now, open it!" he growled with his whiskey breath.

The child was distracting all attention, and Charley, with hands raised, maneuvered himself within grasp of the gun, hidden behind the driver's seat cushion. He could feel the handle was within easy reach.

When the girl pulled the box open with a clunk, Charley made a grab for the revolver; his first shot got Sugarfoot square in the head. The bandit sunk to the ground with a suprised look on his face. His two partners, also surprised, were slow to react, compared to the adrenaline charged driver.

"Whoa team!" Charley called to the nervous horses. "Get behind the coach!" Charley hollered to the mother holding her baby, who collected her daughter and fled like a bird. The other two bandits turned tail to run, one man attempting to empty his shotgun as he retreated. Charley shot him in the chest. Will would have been proud. Maguire was hit by some birdshot, during the panic, as the last man disappeared into the darkness. Maguire was slumped on a rear wheel, groaning and holding his arm, as Charley grabbed the lines to steady the horses.

"Come on, let's get you in the coach," Charley said, trying to comfort Maguire, as he tied his bandanna around the afflicted arm. "You're gonna be just fine. It's just a glancing shot," he soothed the whimpering man. "Well, youngster," Charley said, turning to the child, who was standing beneath the coach lamp.

"Amy, my name is Amy, sir," the small voice said, peering at the wounded man.

"Well, Amy, how would you like to ride up front with me?" Charley asked.

"Mama, may I, please?" Amy pleaded. The young woman gazed at Charley and nodded, much to the delight of the child. The woman handed the girl a wool shawl, which Charley made sure was wrapped tightly around her thrilled body.

"You hold on tight now, Amy, all right? Charley said, starting the team off. The child's face beamed in the moonlight; she was exhilarated with the grand new perspective and watched the fast horses that seemed to fly through the wilderness. Amy marveled at the brave, strong, one-eyed man that could drive in the dark and had saved them. By the time they reached Placerville, she was fast asleep.

"Heard you had some trouble," James Hume spoke, spotting Parkhurst at the hotel the next morning.

"Yep, Ol' Maguire took one in the arm," Charley said matter-of-factly. "I figured you'd be a lookin' me up. You gonna take me in?"

"You took quite a chance. Especially with a woman and children," the lawman stated. "I got to get your statement and such. I already got the passengers' statement and Maguires'."

"I saw an opening. Besides, no telling what scum like that would do with a pretty woman and a little girl . . . One man got away. I seen that Maguire was hit, so my attention shifted and he disappeared in the dark. Shouldn't be too hard to track," Charley reasoned.

"Thank you, Charley, I'm sure Wells Fargo thanks you. You might have a reward coming," Hume said shaking Charley's hand. "Leave your statement at the office. I'm going out with a posse now, to check over the scene. See if we can pick up the last man's trail."

"You know, honestly, when I saw that man standing over that child with a gun . . . I just wanted to shoot him right between the eyes. I guess I did too, didn't I?" Charley said quietly, coming to the full realization. "Good luck, Sheriff. I hope you find him."

That morning Charley was the talk of the town. Maguire, who was nursing a very tender arm and throbbing head, was not too busy to tell and retell the nights' exciting tale. Charley was more introspective, never having shot anyone dead before.

"You ever kill anyone Hank?" Parkie asked his friend.

"No, wanted to plenty of times, but I never did shoot anyone dead before, must weigh heavy on your mind. It was self-defense though, ain't like you got charged with murder or nothin, right?" Monk reasoned. "Why don't you talk to your friend Byrnes. He's had lots of experience in these matters I hear."

"I ain't seen much of Will since he got married." Charley smiled wistfully.

CHAPTER 39

Carson City, Nevada, June 29, 1859

Hank Monk had considered Major Orsmbys' Tavern, in Carson City, his home away from home. Whenever he was in Carson City and was wasn't driving, you could probably find him there with his chair tipped back against the wall, next to the bar room stove, drink in hand.

"Hank, I hear Ol' Horace Greeley is coming though here. Isn't that exciting? I imagine you'll be taking him on through to Placerville, eh?" the bartender, Henry Sharp, asked.

"Oh yeah, I'm just ready to bust," Hank Monk said punctuating it with a fart, sending him into gales of laughter. "Yes, sir, that Ol' politician is gonna go a roaring through here, giving speeches and campaigning for that funny looking, country bumpkin, Lincoln."

A convention of politicians and lawmakers had busied themselves for a fortnight at Carson City, drawing up the constitution for the newest state-to-be, Nevada. Hank had a great fondness for expressing his own wild political theories. It sometimes started lively barroom conversations, angering the bartenders, who had enough trouble keeping the peace.

"Well, I read in Greeley's paper, the *New York Tribune*, that there's maybe a war coming. That the Southern states might succeed from the United States. What do you think of that?" Henry asked the smart alec driver.

"Shit, I don't care what they do! I live out here now. I ain't a fightin' in no war over no slaves. Hell, I don't even own any slaves. To hell with them!" Hank said disgusted, as he polished off the last of his beer.

"Well maybe you could put on a clean shirt for Mr. Greeley just the same," Henry chided the odorous and distressed looking jehu.

"I'm not sure my laundry will be back. I had it sent to the Sandwich Islands to be cleaned," Hank bragged.

"Well, how long ago did you send it, a year?" Henry said, rubbing his nose.

"No only about a month ago, I reckon," Hank said flipping a coin in his empty glass for another beer, much to the disgust of the bartender.

Carson City wasn't much to look at as a city yet, but there was big talk in the high desert mountains just northeast of there. The "new diggins" had just been christened by one of the locals, James Finney as Ol' Virginey; it looked like Virginia City was going to stick. But Carson City was a stage stop, so it was destined to become established,

242

whether Virginia City boomed or went bust. Major Ormsby's corner establishment had room to expand, in the case of a boom. But for now it wasn't much.

Hank had been killing time, waiting for the incoming stage to arrive; it was quite late. His coach couldn't leave until it arrived. So he entertained himself best he could until then. Most of the politicians were going back to Washington and were likewise waiting for the overdue coach and Horace Greeley. When it finally did arrive, about noon, there were great hurrahs for the famous editor and campaign manager.

Hank just sniffed at it all and set about preparing for his job of hauling the great one to his next destination. He had insisted that the axles be greased, on account of his precious cargo, for they had not a moment to lose. When at last the luggage was stowed and the fresh horses hitched, Hank made a quick inspection, while the stable men held the horses. Then he entered the tavern and in a loud and practice voice shouted, "All aboard for Genoa, Friday's, Yank's, Strawberry's, Webster's, Moss, Sportsman's Hall, and Placerville!" After which Hank turned and walked to his coach and climbed aboard, nimbly gathering up the leather lines and sorting them in his long, strong fingers. Horace strode pompously to the vehicle and looked at the rough looking driver.

"I'm scheduled to give a speech tomorrow at Placerville at five. Do you suppose that we will arrive there on time?" Horace asked directly.

"Oh, I reckon I'll get you there on time," Hank smirked. "I could leave, posthaste, if all my passengers would find a seat. Would you like to ride up top here, Mr. Greeley?" Hank asked.

"Why yes, I suppose it will be quite nice this afternoon," Horace said as his aid assisted him up to the roof. "I expect to see some fine scenery yet. The previous days have been a grave inconvenience," the politician continued.

"Hang on, Horace. Git up now. Yup," Hank called to his horses as the stagecoach leapt into motion. "You're gonna see some scenery now, Mr. Greeley," Hank chuckled, as Horace grabbed seat leather.

"Have you had a nice trip so far? Horace? You don't mind if I call you Horace? You can just call me Hank," the teamster prattled on.

"Why no, and yes, I mean . . . I've had an interesting trip, but as I said, the last half so far has been most uncomfortable. We had several mishaps along the way, and I have injured my knee in a wreck," Horace winced, loosening his grip long enough to rub his affliction. Looking over at the rumpled driver, Greeley's confidence in western coachmen was not yet restored. "I have kept a diary of this trip and intend to publish it upon my returning home to New York," the editor warned.

"Do tell! You can go ahead and write about me if you like. Say, Horace, I'm from New York myself, haven't been back since I came to California. Can't say I miss it none," Hank added with a grin. Horace simply smiled and ignored the remark.

The scenery was beautiful, as the coach rocked its way onto a plateau. From there they would soon be able to see the Carson River, and the green grass growing from its shores. Horace was inspired and blathered on about how an industrious America could make this country bloom with harvest and on and on.

"What's this I hear about a civil war?" Hank said interrupting the politician mid speech.

"Well, it seems that it may be a real threat, with the issues of slavery being such a divisive topic in politics, that is," Horace explained. "The next presidential election will be won chiefly upon the candidates views on such matters. By the way, are there any stops that we make on this journey, where one might obtain a bath?" Horace asked, sniffing first himself, then sniffing toward the driver.

"I don't particularly like to bath myself, that is. However, at Friday's, they got a real claw foot tub. And the lady will fill it with hot water for you for fifty cents. You can use a clean towel for twenty-five cents extra. They have real beds, with feather mattresses, clean sheets, and everything, Horace. You're gonna think you made it to the edge of heaven. Then, the next day we're gonna climb to the heavenly valley. Tonight we'll have supper in Genoa. They got some good food in there. I hope you get a chance to meet Ol' Snowshoe. He lives near Genoa. He's a Nor-wee-gen. He delivers the mail in the winter, straps planks on his shoes, so we all call him Snowshoe. Farms some in the spring and summer. You'd like him. Everyone does."

"Planks, I see, how ingenious," Horace mused.

The Sierras were coming closer, as the coach rolled up and down in the sandy soil that was giving way to harder and harder granite. There were traces of snow still visible on the tops of the mountains. The desert landscape changed to pine forests. As they neared Genoa, the Sierra mountains cast vast afternoon shadows over the country.

Genoa was a bustling and beautiful sight as they made their approach. The town folks had turned out for the editor, and he was quite pleased. He was well relieved to be off the coach once again and was whisked off to eat supper. Horace enjoyed the best meal he could remember since he started on this journey. "Go west, young man!" he had been quoted so many times, now he had been compelled to follow his own advice, before the election and before the impending war.

Before long Greeley was escorted from the dinner table back to the coach. Hank stopped the editor at the coach and shoved a tall blonde man at the weary easterner.

"Horace, I want you to meet Snowshoe, eh, um . . . John Thompson."

"It's a pleasure, sir." Snowshoe smiled, holding out his hand.

"Nice to meet you Thompson," Horace said diplomatically.

"The mailman I told you about," Hank reminded as he climbed up the side of the coach and untied the lines from the brakebar.

"Oh yes. Splendid to meet you. Simply remarkable. The pleasure is mine. If you don't mind I think I'd prefer to ride inside this last stretch," Greeley said, climbing inside the coach.

"You don't know what you're missing, Horace. Best views coming up," Hank said, gathering his lines.

"I think I'll be content to look out the window for now, thank you."

"Suit yourself. Git up there, now. Yup. See ya, Snowshoe!" Hank called out, as horses hit the collars.

The ride would be mostly up hill the rest of the evening. Eleven miles to Friday's. The road had been carved into the mountains by Chinese work crews. It was pretty crude. Work was being done on alternate roads, but all were under construction. The ride was a bit perilous, but the views of the Carson valley and the river at twilight were breathtaking. As the shadows grew long, the coach pulled into the yard of a most unexpected site. Maguire blasted his horn as they made the turn, startling Greeley, who had been dosing on his aid's shoulder. Horace poked his head out the window; to see a creamy pink rose rambling on a split rail fence in the long shadow. Then as the vehicle rocked around the driveway, a two-story house came into view.

"Here we are at Friday's, Horace," Monk called down.

Greeley had been eagerly anticipating the bath Hank had told him about. As he climbed from the coach, his eyes grew large with the sight of the beautiful home.

"Now Jennifer here, will look after you now, Horace . . . I think the man was interested in your clawfoot arraignments. Eh, Horace?" Hank said slapping the editor on the back. "Tomorrow, we get an early start," Hank added, wandering into the barn.

Horace indeed inquired about procuring some needed hot water. He then luxuriated in a real bed, the first in many days. The next morning started about three forty-five. The house was filled with the aroma of freshly baked bread. The travelers ate hastily and stuffed their pockets when no one was looking. The food and the high altitude were intoxicating, and the morning air was bracing, as the coach got under way in the dark. They still had a lot of granite to climb before the majestic lake valley.

Next stop Yank's new station. Horace had decided to ride up top in the seat of honor, next to the driver. In fact, all the passengers rode out on the roof. Hank had promised a thrilling view. The passengers had not any idea how thrilling. The lamps on the coach were lit, two large on each side, just under the front seats, then two smaller ones on each side of the driver's foot boards. To the passengers they seemed wholly inadequate, to the driver, they lit enough of the road to keep the wheels from going over the cliff. They were off at break-neck speed up the mountain, or so it seemed to the passengers being whisked around the steep mountain.

The coach crested the mountain on the eastern side and descended to the lake valley just after sunup. The majestic scenery was magically lit, with a pale peach glow coming from the morning sun. The shadows of the forest and rock faces reflected fluidly in the glassy alpine lake.

"I'm suprised we didn't see no bears. I seen a lot a bears in the streams down there, in the wee hours. They like to sleep mostly in the day and rummage around at night," Hank rambled on.

About eight thirty, they rolled into the swing station. They would normally just take time enough to change horses. However, Yankee Jim had a bowl of his own special scrambled eggs, on hand for the famous editor, and they made time to have a plate, with some coffee, before they set out passed the emerald blue lake.

"Upon my word that is the best cup of coffee I've tasted since I left New York, maybe the best I've ever had," Greeley gushed. "What is your name, sir?" he added with genuine interest.

"James Folger, sir, but everyone calls me Yankee Jim," the station owner said smiling. "Have another cup."

"No, thank you, I really must step outside," Horace said, realizing the urgency of his situation. Upon his return he approached his coachman. "Do you still maintain that I will be on time for my speech in Placerville?" Horace questioned his driver, who had just filled his plate up with seconds from the egg bowl.

"Don't worry, Horace. I'll get you there on time," Hank said mindfully, slowly shoveling the eggs into his mouth, as the fresh horses began to come from the barn.

"I think I shall ride inside this time. I can look over my speech," Greeley informed the driver, who was finally at his perch and picking scrambled egg from his beard, as he held the lines to his horses in one hand.

"Suit yerself, Horace," Monk called out as he watched Horace climb aboard. Knowing full well that Greeley hadn't settled in his seat yet, Hank popped his whip, setting his horses off with a jump and tossing Horace onto his head. "Yup now, boys!"

From Yank's new station at the lake, the road took a vertical turn once again. It was the steepest and most dangerous-looking road anyone could ever imagine, with precipices from between five to fifteen hundred feet. The road was wide enough for only one vehicle at a time mostly, stagecoaches had the right of way.

Hank was king of the road, and he had every confidence in his horses and his skill; he drove faster than most. By this time, he and the horses knew the route very well; they had been at it all throughout the spring.

The first hour out would be a very slow, up hill pull and Hank would often pause to let the horses catch their breath, pointing out views when he did. This began to worry the star passenger needlessly. Greeley looked out the window to a chilling sight of the lake. He couldn't see the road they were on unless he craned his head out of the window and looked beneath the coach; the cliff next to the wheels was perilously steep. He shuttered and looked away, wanting to be clear of these dizzying heights.

"Driver, are you sure I will be on time for my speech?" Horace said, poking his head out the window again and trying not to look down.

"I just thought you'd like to get a good look at the view, sir." Hank smiled. "Keep your seat now, Horace." It was time to show that Greeley a thing or two. Monk muttered under his breath. Hank was a daredevil and loved to drive fast. He more importantly knew how to drive very well. He also knew just how well a Concord coach could handle and what kind of punishment it could take. The leather thorough braces, absorbed all of the shock from the rough roads without transferring it to the horses, who were harnessed loosely, unlike an English coach on springs, which would never hold up on the California terrain. Knowing the vehicles capabilities, Hank put his driving to the ultimate test of speed as he crested the Sierras and sent his chargers flying over the rough ground, descending the summit toward Slippery Ford.

Horace and the other passengers flew around inside the coach like dice shaken in a cup. Hank cut every corner he could determined to set a new speed record that day. After a while, Hank looked behind him and saw Horaces' head sticking out the window.

"Mind yer head, Horace!" Hank called back, as the coach swung around a hairpin turn.

"Please, driver," Horace pleaded. "Can't you take it a bit easier. I'm not particular for an hour or two!" he cried.

"Keep your seat! I told you I'd get you there by five o'clock, and by God I'll do it too if the axles hold!" Hank shot back, hitting a chuckhole full on, sending the republican flying back to his seat. A short time later, Horace again had his head out the window.

"I'm not in as much of a hurry as I was awhile ago! Could you please slow down a bit?" Greeley begged.

"Just keep your seat, Horace, I'll get you there on time. Now don't you worry." Hank laughed to himself as the coach descended into Slippery Ford. It had been improved, but it was still a difficult and dangerous water crossing. The water flow in the creek bed seemed to vary hourly, and the slick wet granite caused the horses to slip, even with the cleats in their metal shoes.

When they made the plunge into the rushing creek, the right lead horse tripped and stumbled. Hank stomped on the break and reeled up the leather lines that were quickly growing tight then slack, praying that the leader would pop back up.

"Jehosafat! And snarling coyotes, we nearly lost ya May Belle, God love ya, get your sweet ass out of there!" Monk swore, letting off with the brake, as the mare scrambled to her feet and jumped up and out of the creek bed. "Oh son of a bitch, May Belle you knocked your tug chain loose! Maquire, you got to get down and hitch her back in," Monk ordered, reeling the frolicking wet horses in and once again standing on the brake.

"Why are we stopping?" Horace called out of the window to Maguire, as the man was crawling past.

"Oh, one of the horses got loose," Maguire said casually as he stretched his back and plodded up to the lead horse.

"We'll be back up to speed in no time, Horace," Monk called down to the nauseated New Yorker. "Look over May Bell's knees real good while you're up there Mac," Hank shouted to the expressman.

There would be four more stops before they reached Placerville. Next was Strawberry's. After relieving himself of his breakfast, Horace needed a bit of coaxing to get him back in the coach.

"Come on, Horace, you don't want to be late!" Hank chided. They soon took off in a cloud of dust. The next two stations were just small relay stations, but the road had more traffic. Hank whipped around the slower wagons, leaving just a hairs width between vehicles it seemed. Greeley, or what was left of him, was battered and green with motion sickness, yet they made remarkable time. When the coach pulled into Sportsman's Hall, sometime around three in the afternoon, a small reception was on hand for the inspiring editor. Greeley took the opportunity to abandon the dizzying stagecoach and maniac driver and desperately looked about for another mode of transportation. His reception committee was happy to oblige.

"I shall no longer be in need of your services, sir, as I have procured other traveling arrangements. They have assured me they can have me in Placerville more rapidly than you," Horace addressed his dusty coachman, who was busy finishing his beer.

"Hmm, get there before me, will they? I think not!" Hank said aloud. His horses were ready, and he set off, giving the reception committee's carriage a head start. "Let's see if that new road is finished yet. Yup now, boys!" Hank called to the horses, swinging them onto the new route. It was a good route, and it was indeed faster, for Hank arrived well ahead of his ex-passenger, Horace Greeley.

Placerville was in high spirits over the arrival of the famous newspaper editor. When the stagecoach was spotted, the new fire bell was ringing and musicians were warming up, the whole town was assembled to get a look at Horace Greeley, and hear his speech. When Hank's coach arrived, the town gave off a cheer and the band started playing "Yankee Doodle" only to be greatly disappointed that Horace Greeley was not on the coach.

The driver sat for a moment fumbling for something to tell the expectant town folks, gathered around his coach, as he tied the lines to the brake and lifted the mailbags out of the front boot.

"Well, Ol' Horace wanted me to tell you all that he'd be along shortly, said he needed to take a bath before he made his grand appearance in this here town. Said I made such a fast time. It afforded him that luxury." Monk smiled to his onlookers. "I do believe I set a new speed record at that," Monk said, looking at his plain brass watch.

Awhile later, the new fire bell rang again; Greeley's party was spotted making their way to town. A fine surrey with the reception committee and Greeley pulled up to the hotel, where Horace would stay. The band played a rowdy version of "Turkey in the Straw" as he stepped down from the carriage, surrounded by the madly cheering crowd. Some of them calling out, "Where ya been, Horace? Did you have a good soak?"

Greeley loudly announced, after he hobbled up the stairs to the porch of the hotel, rubbing the soreness from backside, "When the stagecoach arrives, I would like to have words with the driver."

It generated a great roar of laughter from the crowd, which stunned the editor.

Hank, who was standing just behind Greeley, piped up, "I'm right behind ya here, Horace, I been waiting for at least an hour, I think I set a new record!" The crowd, who had been primed by Monk, went wild again with laughter. Horace, turning red, announced that he would like to treat the remarkable driver to a new suit of clothes. Getting both a dig in and being magnanimous at the same time. Hank picked out the most expensive suit that he could find.

The next day, a commemorative daguerreotype was taken on the streets of Placerville, of the famous editor Horace Greeley, sitting next to Hank Monk, on a coach, with four white horses. Hank wore his new suit.

The tale of Hank and Horace made Monk a local hero and would echo through the Sierras for years.

CHAPTER 40

1859

When winter's grip settled on the harsh Sierras, Charley Parkhurst once again traded in the rough life of the mountains for the beautiful Pacific coast. The aging teamster still liked driving the route from Redwood City to San Francisco and marveled at the growth of the cities there. The budding San Francisco was starting to blossom, many stone mansions were springing up on the highest points.

Charley rented a nice room for the winter in San Francisco; it was near the express livery and had a decent pub next door. The coachman liked the luxury of privacy and comfort that a city could provide if you had money, which he did. Driving coaches was an important job and thus a good paying job. Parkhurst had no one to spend the money on, so he saved it and treated himself well, dressing in the best clothes and going to the barber regularly. What Charley looked forward to most was an opportunity to go to the theater and perhaps visit a few friends in San Francisco.

The dapper driver had made good time getting to San Francisco, arriving around six thirty that evening. It was getting dark and the fog had come in like a thick blanket.

The fledgling city was a cornucopia of exotics. People from all over the world were arriving on this shore and weaving into the fabric of the city, the smells and sounds, of many nations. Chinese, Irish, Russian, Australia, from every corner of the world, coming to see the "Elephant" as the easterners referred to the gold country, to make their fortune. At this time, many were beginning to drift back to San Francisco from the gold fields to see a grand city taking form. It was quite a difference from when they had arrived. San Francisco had burned to the ground several times, and the buildings were being constructed of stronger stuff. Brick was replacing wood, and so on.

While making his way through town, Charley noticed the strange sights on the streets of China town, strange smells, good smells, and he felt his stomach responding. Always cutting a dashing figure on the coach, with his broad-brimmed hat and cape and his eye patch, Parkhurst popped the whip and made sharp corners, with the team responding to the cues from his skilled, gloved hands. The driver was sure the horses were paying attention, as he got ready to apply the break, in order to stop precisely at the unloading deck. The men were waiting to take the cargo off of the coach; the arrival was always a greatly anticipated event.

As Charley pulled up to the station, he noticed a peculiar sight coming down the street toward the coach, all the horses seem to look at him simultaneously. It was a strange little man in a formal black uniform, and he was riding a most peculiar tricycle. It had one gigantic wheel in the front, and two little small wheels in the back. Leading the way were two dogs. The first was a very large, hairy, black dog, some type of Newfoundland mix. Next to him was a small wiry-haired little mutt that had a fancy collar on, something of a festive bow tie. The big black dog was wearing more of a wreath than a collar; it was adorned with fabric roses and bows and was very ornate in general. The two bedecked dogs were trotting ahead of the giant tricycle, ridden by the odd man in the uniform; complete with an ostrich plumbed hat, gold shoulder braid, with brass epaulettes and a sword. As they made their way down the street, like a giant child ready to do battle, or perhaps a circus refugee, the man on the tricycle stopped to look at the stagecoach, all his attention was focused on it, as Parkhurst had parked it with professional skill.

Charley kept his eye on the peculiar man, for he had dismounted his ludicrous conveyance and was watching the men at work, as Charley dismounted the more luxurious vehicle.

"Bummer, Lazarus, take a seat," the uniformed man spoke to the dogs. The two dogs plopped down on the walkway as though they belonged there and became completely and utterly at home.

"My good man, I would like to introduce myself, if I may. I am Norton the first, Emperor of the United States." The lunatic saluted.

Charley looked at the man in disbelief. "Charley Parkhurst, sir, it is an honor," he said, removing his hat and playing along.

Emperor Norton I was very thrilled with his audience, as he studied the teamster's rugged face and eye patch. He was especially enamored with the fancy leather coach whip, balanced in the driver's hand.

"You, sir, are a magician with a whip. It would be my pleasure to bestow upon you, the knighthood of the lash!" the Emperor announced, waiving his ceremonial saber loftily, then touching the blade lightly on the concerned driver's shoulder.

"I am honored Your Majesty, Sir!" Charley replied, not wishing to upset the saber-wielding lunatic. He noticed the men unloading the coach were all smiling.

"And now," Emperor Norton I said, putting away the shiny saber and pulling out his watch, "it is time for me to go, for I have a theater engagement." He tipped his hat and called to his dogs, as he climbed back on the tricycle, then pedaled up the street, golden braid blowing with the breeze.

"Onward, fellows! Off to the theater!" the Emperor called out.

Charley stood looking down the street in utter disbelief, fighting back the urge to laugh out loud. He stood for a moment on the sidewalk, as the men unpacked, watching the strange figure of a man peddling along, making his way to the theater, which coincidentally was where Charley was headed tonight. Parkhurst shook his head and walked into the express office. After signing over his mailbags, he then made his way to his room.

Charley walked to a small shop on the way and bought some flowers made of silk, from a small oriental woman with a sad smile. Walking up the stairs of the rooming house, Charley smiled at the soft lilies, thinking of the little girl who had danced on the anvil. Ol' Uncle Charley, that's what little Lotta Crabtree called him. The coachman had always brought Lotta little presents in Grass Valley, candy or some sort of penny fancy that would delight a little girl, living in a world of dirty, smelly men. It would hold her attention until the next time Charley would arrive, with his magnificent coach and horses. As the child grew in popularity and fame, Lotta never forgot the coachman. The family chose to ride on Parkhurst route whenever they traveled on tour, if they could. Lotta rode next to Charley, holding on to his arm or with her hand in his pocket for warmth or sometimes holding on to the end of the lines, making believe that it was really she who was driving.

Lotta's mother kept a sharp eye on her headstrong daughter and a sharp eye on their money. Her husband, who was a poor businessman and frequently gone, was fond of frittering it away. Mrs. Crabtree was no fool, she knew her little Lotta was money in the bank.

Charley Parkhurst had always been a good and decent friend, and the Crabtrees traveled on Charley's coach often. Lotta idolized Charley and the coachman idolized his fairy dancer, which was what he still called the sparkling eleven-year-old girl.

Charley put on his boiled shirt and his fancy vest and slicked back his hair, then off to Maguire's Opera House! He had a balcony ticket.

It was still early, so Charley went to the back door of the theater. Lotta had given him a card that would always get him in backstage. It was opening night, and Lotta had a new review, something a little more mature than she had been doing. Charley lived vicariously through the little girl, indulging her with the fancy things she herself had been denied as a little girl. Not that the coachman complained about the way her life had turned out, but Lotta had gotten to be so beautiful, and that was something that Charley had never been able to experience.

The backstage area was busy with set people and actors milling about, as the out of place coachman found Lotta's dressing room.

"Well hello, Mrs. Crabtree, I've come to pay my respects to your little fairy dancer, Lotta." Charley blushed.

"Uncle Charley, it's been so long! What happened to your eye?" the beautiful young girl called out, as she skipped past her mother and hugged her friend.

"Oh, a horse got me!" Charley replied humbly, as he handed the child the flowers.

"Thank you, they're very pretty." Lotta smiled. Charley stood looking at the growing girl; she was now a young adolescent and growing prettier every day. "I like your new eye patch. It makes you look dangerous and mysterious," the young dramatic gushed, as she ran her hand over the leather patch.

Soon it was time to take seats and begin the show. Charley was surprised to find that his seat was next the funny man in the ostrich feathered hat and epaulets and the rather large and hairy black dog, with the roses wreath about his neck, who was sitting next to the wiry mutt with the bow tie. Charley looked over at the usher, who was bobbing his head up and down, "Yes."

Charley, who was an animal lover, found the arrangement rather delightful. Bummer was a beautiful dog and looked like he was going to enjoy the show, but the little dog, Lazarus, was a bit snarly. The self-appointed emperor was quite a character; as the spotlight was pointed at him, he took a bow as the band played a majestic fanfare. Emperor Norton boldly commanded the show begin and saluted the band with his sword, much to the delight of the crowd.

Soon the house lights were put out and the stage lit up as the program began.

As it was becoming quiet in the room, Charley heard a familiar voice he couldn't quite place. It rang out just before the band began to play.

"Well, the goddamn dogs got a better seat than I got!" To which the audience erupted at once in uproarious laughter. It started the audience off in a good mood, and the show was a thriving success, with Lotta belting out songs and doing dances.

At intermission, Charley wandered out to the lobby to get a beer when he remembered where he had heard the voice. It was none other than his ex-express guard, Harte.

"Harte? I thought I knew that voice in the crowd. How the hell are ya?" Charley chuckled as he walked up to the well-dressed young man.

"Oh, I'm just fine, Charley. Say, was that you I saw sittin' next to the dogs?"

"Yes, those are Emperor Norton's dogs," Charley replied, stifling a laugh, as the Emperor and the two dogs bobbled down the balcony steps.

"Well, maybe the Emperor's dogs would rather go out for a walk and sit out the next act, so we could have their seats, do you think he would oblige?" Harte inquired.

"You'd have to negotiate that with the Emperor for yourself." Charley shook his head.

"Hmm," the young man hummed, then turned to his lovely lady accompanying him. "I am sorry, Elizabeth, this is Charley Parkhurst. Charley, this is Ms. Elizabeth Osgood. Elizabeth, darlin', why don't you and Charley have some wine, and I will be right back," he said kissing her lightly on the lovely alabaster cheek and placing a coin in her gloved hand. Elizabeth had no more turned about, and Harte had scampered out of the theater. The newly aquainted pair just laughed it off. Soon Harte had come back with a package and had sought out the Emperor quickly. Then the four—Harte, Norton, Bummer, and Lazarus—headed out the front door. Charley ordered a set of champagne cocktails for the lovely Elizabeth and his own dashing self, as the bell for the second act was rung.

Harte and the Emperor waltzed through the side doors like long lost buddies, minus the dogs and greeted the waiting pair.

"Ah, the Knight of the Lash, Charley Parkhurst!" The Emperor saluted, taking out his sword again.

"Emperor, where are your companions?" Charley greeted Norton.

"Why they are dining al fresco and taking a tour of the theatrical district," he laughed, puffing merrily on his new cigar. "Come, Harte, let's partake of the second act!" he commanded as he sheathed his saber and tossed an arm around his new favorite subject and waddled up the stairs.

"Shall we?" Charley held his arm out for Elizabeth and walked her proudly up the stairs, to their seats in the balcony.

The foursome was quite jolly and friendly, as the musical comedy resumed. The entertainment was made up of various sketches and songs with juggling and dancing sprinkled through out. Charley was just as entertained with the Emperor, who was having the time of his life, especially when Lotta appeared in blackface playing a small banjo. He had to be convinced it was really Lotta.

"That looks like a small Ethiopian boy I knew in my childhood days in Africa," Norton the first related.

"No, it's really Lotta there." Harte pointed out in the program.

"Well, so it is!"

The tiny redhead later appeared in a comical sketch about an Irishman dealing with a leprechaun, in which she roused the crowd with her perfectly polished jig, complete with a long stemmed pipe.

"I should very much like to meet that diminutive actor, perhaps bestow a title upon her," the Emperor proclaimed.

"Charley knows the little girl personally," Elisabeth remarked, passing on what she had learned about her new friend at intermission.

"Well, I don't suppose Lotta would hardly want to miss an introduction to the Emperor of the United States, though I got an idear that her mama might be a little alarmed," Charley whispered the last so as not to upset his highness.

After the show, the foursome made their way though the crowd, to the stage door, where Charley once again reached for his card. The doorman recognized the Emperor and received him with all fitting respect for his majesty, opening the door wide for his party.

"Charley, what did you think?" Lotta said cheerfully greeting her friend.

"You bowled them over again, Fairy Dancer!" Charley said, kissing the young girl's hand. "I would like to introduce some ardent admirers. For starters, this is the one and only Emperor Norton the first, Emperor of the United States," Charley said sweeping to the side and bowing to this majesty. The actress took her cue and performed a dramatic curtsy, fitting of his stature.

"Very pleased to meet you, Your Highness. I have been looking forward to your proclamations in the newspaper," the sweet girl said, in admiration.

"Ah, thank you, thank you, young lady, after tonight I am forever at your beck and call," the Emperor said, bowing to the actress. Her mother was studying the situation cautiously. She too had heard of the lunatic who declared himself royalty, but he was well accepted in theatrical circles as sort of a mascot and deemed good luck. Mary Ann convinced herself that he might be good publicity as well.

After the introductions and accolades were finished, the party decided that a late supper might be in order. The group descended on a popular late night restaurant in the neighborhood. Even the dogs had caught up and tagged along, filling out the spectacle.

"Tell me, Harte, what line of business are you in?" Emperor Norton asked the young man with a look of concern.

"I am currently employed in the newspaper business. I intend to make my name as a great author someday," the young man boasted.

"Do you intend to use a fictitious nom de plume?" the Emperor said raising an eyebrow.

"I shall sign my work Bret Harte!" he smiled proudly.

"A melodious appellation! I approve!" Norton saluted. "This is indeed a great night! A toast to Lotta Crabtree!" Emperor Norton sang out to the cheering room full of diners. A table was cleared for the celebrities and patrons took turns sending over drinks. Mary Ann making sure that Lotta had only cream soda.

"I believe in equality for all women Mrs. Crabtree," the Emperor expounded, after the food had arrived. "Women should be allowed to be paid equally," he explained to the enchanted businesswoman. "They should be allowed to be in control of their own destinies."

Elizabeth laughed and smiled at Bret.

"Well I for one agree wholeheartedly," Charley said, with an inside grin.

"What ever became of that young gal with the bear?" Bret inquired to his old friend.

"I never could figure what she was thinkin when Miggles took in that bear. It was a brother to your friend Lola Montez bears. I never did think she was using her brain much, but Miggles loved her bear Joaquin, and it protected her and old Bill, the invalid in the wheelchair. Heck, no man in his right mind went over to visit uninvited. She made it well known about the bear and the men accommodated her respectfully, as her company was valuable. She was always tickled if you brought the bear a treat," Charley said smiling at the Emperor. "There were times during the year when the fish were running up the stream, that I would see the unlikely duo of woman and bear catching fish in the water. The bear would wade into the water and catch a fish and rip off the skin and eat it and toss the cleaned fish to his human partner on the shore, who would put it in a sack. When she had all the fish she could handle, she would go back to her outdoor kitchen, a rather crude affair, and prepare fish dinners to sell to the miners in camps. She always made a fair profit on them too. In many ways the bear and the woman had an ideal relationship; they protected and fed each other. It must of been mighty strange for Ol' crippled Bill if he was, in fact, aware of the goin's on. I was always fearful for Miggles though and felt that she was very vulnerable. I asked about her often," Charley related to a captivated audience.

"One evening, I found Miggles beside the road, near her cabin. She was a sobbing, hysterical mess! 'Miggles? What happened?' I called down. 'Joaquin! Bill! Both dead!' she cried. 'I killed Joaquin! I killed him! Oh God, Charley, it was so awful! I didn't want to do it, I loved them, I loved them both,' she wept. 'I came into the house, and he was eating Bill!'

"I climbed off the coach and had squatted down with Miggles, comforting her. 'You stay put, now I'll have a look,' says I. I ran down the path to the house, the door was wide open. Inside it was a shambles, with shelves knocked down. Then I approached the two bodies in the middle of the room. The bear had knocked over the Ol' crippled Bill's chair, and was lying on top of him, apparently dead. All over everything was red shinny goo. It was gory, but sort of sweet smelling. I took a chair and shoved the bear with it. At least if he wasn't dead I'd have something between us. He was dead all right and rolled off the squashed Bill, who was also dead. I grabbed a dishtowel and wiped his face, but he didn't appear to have any injuries. He was covered with jam! Broken glass and the top of the jar labeled strawberry told of a more innocent bear. The weight of the bear probably killed the old man."

"My word!" the Emperor gasped. "What happened to the gal?"

"Well, I closed up the house securely and walked back to the coach. Then I told her, 'There's nothing we can do right now. We'll send some men out to take care of them and bury them decent.' Then I put her on the coach and brought Miggles into Sierra City. It was a home station, the end of the line. I personally made sure that she was made comfortable at the hotel, and bought her some dinner and some more brandy. The next day was Sunday, so there was a funeral. When the news spread about the famous tame bear and cripple, the miners, always searching for a new and better excuse for a party, decided to have a wake! Miggles appreciated the outpouring and was offered many marriage proposals. I mentioned to her that with her skill at handling animals, she could always join the circus!"

"Quite incredible," Mrs. Crabtree sighed.

"I am thinking of writing a new proclamation," the Emperor said, turning to a daydreaming Bret Harte.

"About women?"

"No, not this time. This has to do with travel and commerce. I am going to propose that a bridge be built across the bay, maybe two of them, one to Oakland and another to Marin. What do you think?" His Majesty imagined with perfect calm.

"Well, I don't think your subjects are quite ready for that one, Your Highness," Bret said, trying not to laugh.

"No? Well, perhaps they might need some time to organize the labor and find the right architect, but I will be looking into it further, I assure you," the lunatic said, finishing off his pudding.

"Say, Charley, did you ever get that mama bear made into a coat?" Bret said, changing the subject.

"Yep, get a lot of use out of her too. Be heading back to the Sierras in the spring," Charley related. "You gonna come back to mountains this summer, Lotta?"

"Well, Mama thinks that maybe it's time to go to New York," she spoke with her mouth full of whipped cream.

"Lotta, don't speak with your mouth full. We might make a tour of the East, Boston and New York, we're still considering offers," Mary Ann offered. "My dear, I'm afraid it is very much past your bedtime. You have an afternoon matinee tomorrow," she reminded.

"Yep, I gotta drive to Redwood City myself. I sure had a wonderful time tonight. Thank you, Mary Ann, for letting me treat you to supper," Charley said, looking for the waiter. He paid for the entire table with a newly minted double eagle and told the busy gentleman to keep the change, for which he was ecstatic.

Charley enjoyed the winter months in the city; he saw the Emperor often and looked forward to reading his proclamations in the newspapers. Parkhurst enjoyed many of Lotta's performances that season, but Parkie missed his other friends—Hank, Snowshoe, Jarred, and most of all Will.

CHAPTER 41

Carson Valley, April 28, 1860

Two young Paiute women splashed in the river, unaware of the Williams brothers, Jay and Oscar, spying on them from the grassy banks. The brothers had a trading post and swing stage stop, a few miles away. The young Indian women had been gathering pine nuts and sage; they had separated from the other women and had decided to cool off in the river. It was a big mistake.

The two men drew their revolvers and announced their presence to the young women, who froze, like baby deer. The older brother carefully walked to the waters' edge and motioned with his gun for the women to walk onto the bank.

Oscar's dog, a large black and tan hound, bounded into the water barking and chasing the women onto the bank.

"Well, well, look what we got here! I think we ought to invite these gals up to the house for a little drink, now don't you little brother?"

"Down, Lucifer," the younger man yelled at the mutt. "I think that's a right good idear, Jay."

The women were herded together and forced at gunpoint to the trading post, the dog trailing behind them, snapping at their heels occasionally, as if they were sheep.

The proprietor and owner of the station, Jay Williams, ran it with his brothers Oscar and David.

"Look at what we caught, Davy!" Oscar said with delight, as he shoved the frightened girls at the suprised young man.

"You can't keep the . . . these Injun ga . . . gals here, the stage, and the . . . the . . . them pony boys . . . soooo . . . meone will find out!" David stuttered.

"Shit, no one is gonna find out, and nobody cares about these stupid squaws, anyway!" Oscar drooled, as he ran his hands over the smallest girl.

"The . . . ey must have family lo . . . lookin' for them!" David protested.

"We'll let them go when we're done with them. They won't be missed for a while. I say they was caught, too bad for them." Jay Williams then grabbed one of the women, cowering on the floor, by her silky black hair and dragged her into his sleeping quarters.

Later they were taken to the cellar and bound and gagged. One by one, the women were repeatedly raped, then retied and hidden in the cellar.

After a week had passed, a young Paiute brave, who was searching for his sister, rode to the trading post, leading a young horse to trade for a rifle. The young brave was angry when the Williams brothers would not sell him the ammunition for his newly traded rifle and a dispute ensued. The dog, Lucifer, got involved, biting the brave on the leg. His yells were recognized by one of the imprisoned women, who had removed her gag in time to call out to her young brother, who bid a hasty retreat to get reinforcements, finding himself greatly out gunned. He grabbed his new rifle and departed on his remaining horse to get help from his family.

The young brave rode to the Pyramid Lake encampment, which had been filling with tribes from all over, for the purpose of holding a council. Among the tribes were Shoshone, Bannock, and Paiutes from all over the Sierras.

The brave entered the camp of his uncle Mo-guan-no-ga, who was Chief of the Humbolt Meadows. He was for some reason known to the white men as Captain Soo. Mo-guan-no-ga was a fierce man, much feared, with good reason; he was a cunning ambush fighter, with generally deadly results.

Upon hearing the news of the missing women's capture, the Chief was quickly in action, calling upon eight of his fiercest brothers to reclaim their own and seek justice. Harming women in their culture was considered the most heinous crime, and justice would be severe.

Mo-guan-no-ga and his warriors sat quietly in the rocks on a ridgetop, watching the Pony Express rider galloping out of the station. The warriors then silently rode into the station, catching the remaining men off guard. The Chief confronted Oscar, who was standing next to the barn with Sullivan, and Fleming, two New Yorkers who had stumbled upon an appealing situation, until now.

Surrounding the station men, Mo-guan-no-ga demanded the captive women. The situation turned critical as another man inside the station, named Dutch Phil, tried to make a run for it. He was quickly cut down by the natives and pinned to the ground with arrows. The other white men watched his body, writhing in agony like a skewered rat, dying. They were frozen with fear, as each of them endured a similar fate. David was pulled out of the station, crying like a wounded pup, followed by the young women and brother, who had first heard his sister's cry for help.

The young woman's husband had a piece of burning wood that he used to light the station roof. He led her to the writhing men of the station, who all lay in quivering, bloody, pleading, heaps, in the sandy earth, in the manner of Dutch Phil, even the dog had not been spared. The young brother, following behind his sister, had some bottles of whiskey taken from the burning station. As he came to each offender, he splashed the alcohol over the arrows sticking out of the dying men. The husband handed the torch to his wife and she lit each man on fire, to burn to his death. When she got to the sobbing David, she handed the torch to her husband and walked silently to his horse. The husband unsympathetically lit the young man's shirt, as he howled in pain.

The horses at the station were given to the women as retribution for the harm done to them.

The proprietor of the station, Jay Williams, had been away that evening. The next morning, Williams returned to find a smoldering ruin, where his station had been and the shocking remains of his brothers. After burying what he presumed to be Oscar and David and leaving the rest for some one else to bury, Williams rode out for Virginia City to enflame the military, for the revenge of his brothers.

CHAPTER 42

Carson City

Hank entered Ormsby's Tavern after driving his route and found it brimming with riled up vigilantes with Major Ormsby himself holding court. Hank was only interested in one thing, and that was kept at the bar in the back of the room. Hank spied Parkhurst's familiar face in the back, so he barged through the mob to reach his friend.

"Parkie, welcome back from San Francisco. Are you having any success with the bartender?" Hank inquired of his friend.

"Here, Hank, have a snort on me." Charley shook his comrade's hand as he motioned to the bottle on the bar.

"Ah, sweet elixir. Thanks, Parkie, don't mind if I do." With a practiced wave of his hand, Hank whisked the bottle to his mouth and slugged down a shot. Then with a smile, he wiped off the top of the bottle and carefully set it back on the bar. "Good to see you again. What's all of the commotion about, my friend?" Hank said with a freshened attitude toward his surroundings.

"A few hours ago, Pony Bob Haslam reported that the Paiute Indians have wiped out the Williams trading post, killing two of the Williams boys. Ol' Major Ormsby wants to get up an army to go and settle up with the heathen Indians, or something to that effect. I came in only shortly before you . . . John, may I have another glass? Thanks," Charley added, as Monk took another pull off the bottle.

"Hey, ain't that Ol' Snowshoe up there?" Hank poked at Charley, wiping his mouth with his dirty sleeve.

"Oh Geez . . . What the hell is he doing? He's just gonna get himself killed! . . . We never had problems with them Paiutes before now! I always thought those Williams boys were assholes, probably had it coming to them, and I don't mind sayin it! Probably sold them Indians some poisoned food, wouldn't put it past them. They probably started trouble!" Charley rambled on to Hank, causing some men to turn and stare. "What the hell are you looking at! Did you know them? Well, did you?" Charley said with an intimidating glare from his remaining eye.

"Well, Charley, my friend, I see you are holding down one of the more important seats in the house." Will Byrnes smiled in his charming way, as he walked through the crowd to the bar. At the same time his glare was enough to ward off trouble from the neighbor, who was unsympathetic to Charley's biased opinion. Parkhurst could feel the blood rushing to his face, as the handsome lawman approached.

"Hey, Captain, pull up a glass, Parkie's buying," Hank cut in.

"Help yourself, Will, nice to see you, it's been a long time . . . Bartender, another glass if you please." Charley blushed.

"We've got some sort of Indian uprising brewing here, right up your alley if I'm not mistaken." Hank grinned.

Charley wanted to punch Monk. "Shut up, Hank!" He blurted out.

"My ain't we in a moody sort of way!" Hank snickered. "Tell Byrnes how you shot Ol' Sugarfoot!"

"Charley you shot a bandit? Did you kill him?"

"Yep got two, one right through the head, the other in the chest. They was holdin' up the stage outside of Strawberry." Charley blushed. The men standing near heard the story and had new respect for the one-eyed man.

"Good for you! Sorry about your eye." Will smiled.

"Yeah, horse got me. I'm used to it now, I reckon," Charley said, pouring out another round. The aging teamster noticed that Byrnes has some fresh battle scars himself. He had just returned from fighting the Pitt River tribe in some sort of dispute and had taken an arrow in that battle. He was like a cat with nine lives. How many did he have left? He wondered.

As the night wore on, an army of unseasoned miners signed up; a battle of some sort would be inevitable. Snowshoe Thompson was one of the first in line to pledge his life. After that, he realized what he had committed to and decided to retire awhile to the back of the room.

"Well, I see you've gone and signed up there, Snowshoe," Hank commented, as the Norseman ordered a beer.

"I have no experience fighting Indians. It's true, but I am a fit and able man, and I know da mountains. It vould be cowardly for me not to go. Besides, da coaches are taking da mail now, so dere's no excuse. I'm glad to see you are back, Charley. You have experience with dese matters, Captain Byrnes, vill you join vid da rest of us?" Snowshoe inquired.

"I have not decided, at this time. I am still recovering from an injury acquired from my last association with the natives of the West," Will replied. "Charley I do believe it is my turn to buy. John, if you would be so kind." He lay down a shiny gold coin for Big John, the bartender.

"I bet you twenty bucks, your captain friend signs up tonight!" Hank whispered gleefully to his pal Parkie.

"Go straight to hell! . . . I know he will!" Charley said sadly.

"You're no kind of a sportsman Parkie," Hank advised. "By the way, I noticed you have acquired some sort of mongrel or possibly a rat." Hank was referring to the squirming puppy face, peering from the depths of Charley's coat. "It may be wise to license him with the new authority in Placerville. The Sheriff there is just murder on dogs. Why just yesterday I saw the man shoot two dogs, that he had apprehended." Hank sniffed as Charley lifted the squirming puppy from his inside pocket. He had been a gift from a thankful family, whom Parkhurst had lent some money. A tiny little white dog, with brown spots, he could fit in Charley's cupped hands.

"What did you name the little runt?" Hank inquired.

"I haven't named him yet. I'm leaning toward peanut. What do you think?" Charley replied as the puppy licked his nose.

"Looks like a little bastard to me!" Hank laughed, as Charley groaned.

"Hey, Cody, what time did you get in?" Big John rang out, as the blonde Pony Express rider approached the bar.

"Nine fifty-seven," the wiry youth said, wiping the dust from his face with a handkerchief. All persons stopped to turn and stare at the youth, that had entered the tavern. The crowd grew silent, and each examined their various slips of paper; they had retrieved from some pocket. Most groaned in disappointment.

"Nine fifty-seven, let's see, Snowshoe Thompson had the closest, nine fifty-eight. He wins again. He owes you a drink, boy. He's right over there. You can tell him the good news," the bartender said pointing.

Major Ormsby banged his gavel and called the rough meeting back to order.

"He won twice, already, I ain't never even won once," Hank whined. John kept a lottery on the pony boys. You bought a time on the day's arrival, and the closest guess won the pot. It was a dollar a guess. Those guessing on the same time had to split the pot.

"Did you all hear about Pony Bob's Haslams record? He set a new record for miles ridden." Charley pointed out. "Three hundred and eighty miles, I heard."

"No, I had money on him though!" Hank chimed in.

"Cody, did you see many Paiutes out on your ride?" Byrnes asked the young expressman.

"Yes, I saw some, near Piramid Lake, a large encampment. They waved, and I kept riding, nothing out of the ordinary. Are they really going to start a war with these people?" The blonde young man searched Will's face for the answers.

"I don't know. It looks like they will. They burned down William's station and several men are dead," Byrnes said quietly.

As the night wore on, Charley turned to Hank and sighed. "Well, there he goes."

The recovering William Byrnes stepped closer to the hub of deliberation and found himself caught up in the ravings of idiots, about to incur the wrath of untold natives. All of which had been quite willing to accept the white man's advancements and trade and so far, willing to put up with his encroachments. These civic leaders had no idea of the consequences of their actions. At least that's what went through the mind of the seasoned warrior, as he stepped to the front of the organizers and volunteered his services. Many of the crowd recognized Will, and one man yelled, "Why, he's the man who shot Joaquin Murietti!" to the great arousal of the crowd. Will was an instant success. Charley could only shake his head and say a prayer.

"Well, good luck to them, I'm goin' to bed." Hank saluted. "Good night, Parkie, don't stay out too late," Monk chuckled, as he tottered out into the streets of Carson City.

Charley sat for a while longer, talking to John Thompson, and waited for Will.

"I felt that they needed some guidance," Will remarked, to a visibly disgusted Charley.

"Yeah, well I knew you'd join the minute I saw you here tonight, what do you think of that!" Charley blurted out.

"You know me so well, my friend." The gunman smiled. "I felt that someone with experience should look after our only winter mailman. Don't you think?" He smiled at Charley, who was casting a worried look in Thompson's direction.

"You are the very voice of reason, Will." Charley smiled back.

The next evening, Charley arrived safely back in California without any Indian encounters and turned over the coach and its properties to the stage office and stretched his weary back. He pulled the sleeping pup from his coat pocket, which whined, as he was set on the cold wet grass, near the office and then promptly watered the shrubs near by. The puppy stood about six inches high and tottered about like a small drunk with four legs. Charley laughed to himself, as he gathered the creature up and walked down the planked sidewalk to the sheriff's office, to register the canine with the law.

"Say, I need to get a license for my dog," Charley inquired, holding the puppy in the palm of his gloved hand. It was chewing on the tip of his gloved thumb.

"Hey, Charley. That's the smallest dog I've ever seen! You sure that ain't a squirrel?" the man behind the desk laughed. "I'll get Deputy Hume. Hey, Jim, you got a customer!"

As the man entered the room, Charley was taken by the man's startling blue eyes and calmness; it made him smile.

"How are you doing, Charley?" Hume remarked with a grin.

"Fine! Pleasure to see you again, Jim," Parkhurst said shaking the man's hand.

"I heard something about a dog license?"

"Yep, I wanted to register my pup here," Charley said setting him on the desk, to the laughter of all in the room.

"Why, that's a fierce little fellow! He's not much bigger than a gopher," James added. "I just need to write down a few particulars, and then there's a small fee. You will need to get a dog collar, so he can wear this tag. That's about it. Now what's the dog's name?"

Charley picked the pup up and looked him square in the face.

"Hank."

"And what kind of dog?" Hume quizzed.

"Why, he's a brown-and-white . . . little bastard," Charley answered. The men in the room began laughing out loud with abandon.

"Yes, I guess that will suffice, brown-and-white little bastard. All right, that will be two bits, and here's your tag. Tags about as big as he is! Cute little fellow, make sure he stays out of trouble now, Charley," the young man said, shaking Charley's hand.

"I don't suppose you folks have heard about the Paiute trouble brewing in Carson?" Charley related.

CHAPTER 43

On the tenth of May, the volunteer army commanded by Major Ormsby set out on horseback to Williams' station. It was very cold and beginning to rain. Still feeling the effects of their liquid fortifications at the previous station, many men got sick at the grisly site waiting for them. Three victims still lay in charred remembrance of cruel retribution, unrecognizable. Thompson spotted two crude graves marking Oscar and David Williams, who would soon be joined by their cooked friends, as the men quickly set about burying the remaining dead men. The soldiers poked around the ruins for any remaining clues to the culprits. When the dead men were tucked inside the earth, the army struck out, following the Truckee River toward Pyramid Lake. That afternoon more volunteers joined them.

There were now four detachments of men, totaling 105, under the command of Major Ormsby, Thomas Condon Jr., Archie McDonald, and Richard Watkins, a veteran of the battle in Nicaragua, where he had lost a leg. Watkins strapped his stump of a leg onto his saddle, which was mounted on a powerful stallion and was a fierce warrior despite his loss. The other men were an unruly lot of miners, young and old, who had little experience with soldiering.

William Byrnes, expecting the worst, was armed to the teeth and had the good sense to provide himself with a reliable, fast horse, something that he had learned from previous dealings with savage men. He had equipped himself with Tres Dedos' saddle holster, which he had kept as a souvenir. It carried two Navy Colts, eight extra loaded cylinders and two cans of caps. Byrnes wore two more Navy Colts around his waist and had a rifle in a saddle scabbard. The majority of the men sneered at the Indians and seemed confident that "they would have an Indian for breakfast and a new pony to ride!" Most of the troops carried only one revolver and felt confident enough.

Later that afternoon, upon reaching the big bend of the Truckee River, the company spotted five white men on the opposite side of the fast moving river. The troops stopped and rigged up ropes to tow the miners across the cold water. The shivering men told of an Indian attack and loss of three men. A decision was made to make camp. As night fell, so did the temperature. Liberal amounts of whiskey were used to ward off the cold.

The next morning was very cold and the men sluggish; the ground was covered with a thin layer of snow, accompanied by a persistent and biting wind. The regiment followed a trail with almost suspicious signs of their prey. As they pressed on, the company passed through a narrows in the trail, where the river far below them was quite swift. The banks of the river were quite steep and muddy from the tremendous spring runoff. The trail rose high above the river, then led down to an open meadow on each side of the river. In the meadow, the land closest to the shore was rolling and uneven, due to the river changing course every year. A dense grove of cottonwood trees lined the ever-changing riverbed.

Before they descended to the meadow, William Byrnes remarked to Major Ormsby how dangerous this place might be in the event of an ambush and that maybe a guard should be posted. His suggestion was duly noted. The major selected C. T. Lake and six other men to hold the upper entrance to the big meadow below. From this vantage point, the meadow looked like a giant bowl, with the Truckee River cutting through it. Next to the trail was a rock formation that resembled a huge molar tooth; it would serve nicely as a sniper position. The rest of the company then descended to the meadow below.

Once they got to the bottom, Major Ormsby called a halt. As the horses and men rested, Will checked his armaments and suggested that Snowshoe do the same.

"Dere are a lot of birds here, do you hear dem?" Snowshoe remarked.

"Birds?" Will shot back. "That's not good! Major, on the bluff there." Will motioned to the ridge on their right.

"Elliot, Look through your rifle scope and tell me what you see. Is that a white flag?" Major Ormsby commanded. On the ridge ahead appeared about one hundred Indians, all mounted on horses.

"That's not a flag. It looks like a hatchet, sir," Elliot responded, accidentally firing his rifle. The Indians were out of range and they knew it. Adrenaline charged the regiment, as they swung back into their saddles and the order to charge was given.

"I don't know about this, stay back and guard the rear, Thompson." Will motioned to John as the eager men galloped up to the bluff, where the Paiutes had been. Byrnes was trying to get a view of the terrain as the troops blindly charged into the unknown. When they reached the top, the Indians were gone; they had disappeared into the landscape, only to fan out and circle around from behind. Soon the air was filled with clouds of black powder smoke and the smell of burned sulfur. Arrows singing through the frosty atmosphere from all directions sent the inexperienced miners into a panic. The warriors shot at the soldiers and their horses, sending them crashing to the ground. The army had great difficulty in shooting back and controlling their horses; many soldiers lost their revolvers in the process and now were just looking for escape. The Indians had surrounded the army; the soldiers who had hung back tried to gain security in the cottonwood grove but were alarmed to find that too was full of braves.

The makeshift army was now in full chaos; it was every man for himself. Major Ormsby tried to rally another charge, but it was to no avail, the enemy was too great. The bullets and arrows flew like a deadly swarm of bees.

Major Ormsby ordered Captain Watkins to secure the narrow entrance that had brought them to this massacre for their retreat. As Watkins rode off, Ormsby was shot in the arm and was dumped to the ground. His stout mule had been shot in the flank as well but did not go down however; his wound was unnoticed in the fray.

"Go, go, you are our only hope!" Ormsby yelled to Watkins, as he bravely crawled to his feet. Major Ormsby made it back into the saddle only to be shot in the other arm and rendered helpless. A soldier seeing his plight grabbed the reins of the mule to help the Major escape, but soon spotted the mule's wound that gushed blood with each step.

"Save yourself, I'm a dead man already," the dying man gasped, as a bullet splintered his jaw. The young man, seeing the wisdom of those words, dropped the reins of the bleeding mule and sped off to escape.

Byrnes and Snowshoe had dug in at the cottonwoods and were waiting for a chance to make a run for it. Will knew that without a horse, you'd never make it out alive. Through his experiences, Will found that the braves would not waste ammunition on an already dead horse, so he had taught his horse to lay down and stay that way, until he could be used to escape. Thompson's horse had been killed and was being used as cover, in the gravel of the old riverbed. Will would not leave Thompson without a horse, but he was too big to ride behind him on his own horse, they'd be too slow. Will desperately searched for another mount for his friend, as another soldier on a fine big bay horse galloped toward them, through the trees. The soldier's chest was suddenly impaled by an arrow, which sent him flying from the saddle, facedown into the dirt to die. The unmanned horse, searching for refuge, galloped over toward the horses laying in the gravel. Thompson was speechless; he had never before witnessed such carnage.

"Get him! Get on, let's go!" Will called to John, as he cued his horse to rise out of the grave. Byrnes swung into the saddle, as the horse came to his feet, then passed Snowshoe a loaded revolver as they made their run for safety.

They passed the Major, who looked like a bleeding porcupine, with all the arrows he received; he had died minutes earlier. There was not time to look, as Byrnes and Snowshoe ran a gauntlet of warriors, who had taken positions on the slopes of their escape route. The two could see Captain Watkins bravely shooting at the top of the grade, at the outpost that six soldiers were supposed to guard. The cowards deserted their post as soon as the fighting began and had managed to avoid being trapped. The army was now in full retreat; men were making any attempt to reach the narrow pass. Anyone unlucky enough to be afoot was being mowed down unmercifully; the order of the day was, "Take no prisoners!"

As Will and Snowshoe reached Captain Watkins, Byrnes felt the sting of a bullet ripping into his leg.

"Let's go, Thompson, now!" Will roared in agony. Thompson, unaware of his comrade's wound, was determined to help Watkins hold the pass, until the rest of the men could get through. "This place is a lost cause. You're too important a person to die in this hellhole! Now let's go!"

"He's right, go on. I'll be right behind you! Go, Thompson!" Watkins commanded. With those parting words, the men spurred their horses on. The battle had now become a horse race; the stakes were life or death, with the Grim Reaper swarming in quickly from behind and on all sides.

Unfortunately for the army, the Indians were particularly fond of horse races and took delight in picking off the soldiers one at a time. The fastest braves would race to a soldier, who was generally out of ammo, and slow the riders horse by hitting it in the face or cutting the reins and leave the slowed victim for braves farther back. The braves would work their way through the retreat that way, killing as many soldiers as possible. Once unhorsed, it was a certain and quite possibly a slow death, the only hope was to hang on and go as fast as possible. One dare not even look back, as each victim brought a bloodcurdling howls and cheers from their hellish pursuers.

It was a long race, for the only sanctuary was Bucklands station, almost twenty miles from the massacre. The deadly horse race galloped past the charred remains of Williams' station.

The exhausted survivors finally arrived at Buckland's station after nightfall. Byrnes slid from his blood soaked saddle into a heap on the ground. His face was a ghastly white in the moonlight.

"He needs a doctor or he'll die," Thompson said, as he peeled Will's bloody clothing away from the seeping wound in his hip. "It's remarkable dat he vas able to stay on his horse! I don't tink he can be moved anymore, vithout it killing him, he's just about used up as it is," Snowshoe said, tying the wound with a handkerchief. Looking around the room, he realized that the station was filling with probably the only remaining survivors; most were pretty beat up. So far there were only about twenty. The Indians had not yet attacked the station. Snowshoe realized that he had faired pretty well, just a few scrapes. The men were nervous and scared. What if the Indians attack the station? Most wanted to flee to Virginia City, but the horses were exhausted, and so were they. All they could do was wait and be ready to fight and maybe die.

"Are dere any fresh horses here?" Snowshoe asked. "I vant to go and get a doctor. I'll alert Virginia City and bring back reinforcements." Thompson turned around to be suprised and pleased to see the heroic Captain Watkins hobbling through the door; he too needed a doctor's care.

Thompson walked out to the horses and removed Byrnes' saddle holster, patting the neck of the brave and intelligent horse.

"Do you know anyting about dese horses dere?" Thompson pointed to the six station horses.

"Yeah, that one kicks," the man responded, rubbing his leg.

"Vich one is da fastest?" Thompson inquired.

"Oh, I don't know. If I's to bet on one, I guess I'd pick the kicker," the stockman pondered.

"I'm going to borrow him to get a doctor and bring back help," Thompson said matter-of-factly.

"Be my guest, he ain't my horse . . . I don't suppose you want me to saddle him fer ya?" the man offered.

"Dat would be very helpful, tank you. I have to reload dese guns," Thompson said, throwing the saddle holster over his broad shoulders.

"Say, that's a mighty handy holster ya got," the man said taking Johns saddle and putting it on the kicking horse.

"You bet your life it's handy!" Thompson said as he stepped back inside the station.

"As soon as I reload, I'm going to Virginia City to get help, Captain Watkins, sir," Snowshoe reported. The captain was stretched out on a table next to Will; the news met with his approval. Thompson set about cleaning and reloading the armaments.

"In my saddlebags, I have laudanum, get them, John," Will croaked.

"You taught ahead, I zee," Snowshoe replied, pleased to see Will regain consciousness. "Don't vorry I'll take good care of your guns, Vill," Thompson said before walking outside and placing the holster over his saddle horn. He patted the kicker on the neck and then retrieved Will's saddle bag, before returning to the station.

"Get me that green bottle . . . . Are you going alone, John?" Will whispered.

"Yes, I'm able and da station cannot afford to lose anymore men in case of an attack. I'm sure I can get through better if I go by myself," Snowshoe explained.

"Take my rifle too," Will added.

"I'll be back soon!" the Norseman promised, as he turned and left the station.

"He's a first-rate man," Watkins said, looking over at the apparently dying Will.

"This stuff will fix you right up," Will said, nodding to the laudanum the station master was pouring into a shot glass for Will. "Give the captain there a snort too," he said as the painkiller slipped down his throat. "Hell, better give them over there a snort too."

Snowshoe arrived at Virginia City a little after dawn. The kicker, a mustang, had given his all. As he entered the city, he heard the fire station bell tolling, to rouse the town. C. T. Lake, the soldier who was supposed to guard the escape route and hadn't, was busy retelling the story of how he had daringly escaped certain death. Thompson was busy searching for a doctor with enough guts to return to hostile territory with other men, to rescue the wounded at the station. The rest of the town began erupting in near panic at the thought of an uprising of untold magnitude. Dispatches were sent to California for soldiers; there was to be retribution made.

As Thompson strode up to the crowd, they turned and insisted on more details about the events of the massacre. He sought out the face of his friend, a man he knew had the steady hands to drive a wagon out to rescue the injured. He did not see Charley's face in the throng as he concluded his recitation of the events and as others took the podium. Thompson walked down the boardwalk in search of his teamster, followed closely by a thin, dark haired man, with circles under his eyes and a pad of paper and a pencil in his hands. The man, William Wright, known to the residents of Virginia City by his pen name Dan DeQuille, was hastily writing down the story and asking questions of the strapping Norwegian man, as he made his way to the livery stable.

Charley was just stepping out of the newest station and was stunned to see Snowshoe standing in front of him. The fire bell was clanging away.

"John, what are you doing here?" Charley spoke with suprise. "Where's the fire?" he said with a suprised look.

"Da Paiutes attacked vith great numbers and fiercely. Most of da men are dead, I fear. Ve need to retrieve da vounded men from Bucklands station," John said, exhaustion covering his face.

"Byrnes, was he?" Charley began. He could not help but notice Will's bloody holster on the scruffy-looking mustang.

"He's seriously vounded. He'll die for sure vithout a doctor," John said quietly.

"I'll get together a team of horses and a coach. How many men are injured?" Charley inquired.

"I don't know maybe eighteen or tventy, maybe more. Not many men made it out alive, maybe more vill have turned up zince I've been avay. Do you have any coffee Charley?"

"Yes, you lay on that cot and rest, I'll get you some coffee, and get the horses and a doctor. I'll be back soon," Charley said, bolting from the livery. The cot nearly gave way as the large Norseman collapsed onto it.

Charley stormed into the stage office to announce that a coach was needed to rescue the wounded, and in short order, arrangements were made and the coach suitably armed.

As the horses were harnessed and hitching began, Thompson pulled the saddle from the kicker, who was eating contentedly, and selected another mount for duty. Charley then suggested the animal be tied behind the coach, so Snowshoe climbed up to the lofty perch next to Charley, who now had the lines balanced in his talented fingers. As the rescue party drove out of town, Thompson spotted DeQuille through the window of the *Territorial Enterprise* newspaper office, madly setting type.

The rescue party arrived without incident and the doctor set about administering aid to the wounded. Charley was shocked at the pale figure of Byrnes stretched out on the table. The attitude of the survivors had rallied with the arrival of the coach and the doctor. With the thought of returning to safety, they wanted to leave soon. Charley was worried that the move could put an end to his dear friend. The doctor made such grave faces at the hole that seeped life's blood from Will's body; the teamster was compelled to leave the room.

Charley sat thoughtfully smoking his cigar on the porch, watching the horizon for signs of hostile natives. Little Hank sat in the teamster's lap trying to console his sad master.

"He'll make it, Charley. He's tougher dan he looks," Thompson advised. "He vas so cool and calm out dere ven everyone vas shitting deir pants . . . He knew just vat to do . . . He'll make it back you'll see. Old varriors are hard to kill," the mountain man said, resting his hand on the teamster's shoulder and playing with the small pup with the other.

At last the doctor announced that he would have to operate in Virginia City and bound up the patients for transport. Will was given one whole seat inside the coach and the balance of the wounded filled the rest of the coach and the back boot and roof. The less afflicted rode horses out of harm's way as Bucklands was evacuated.

Upon returning to Virginia City, Charley found the place to have been turned into a fortress. Every sound building had been boarded up in preparation for the next wave of assault. Will was carried inside and preparations made for the removal of his newly acquired lead. Charley waited on the porch nearby.

Dan DeQuille spotted the teamster and asked to get particulars of the events. Charley related the happenings to the best of his recollections. The town was in a panic, and all mining claims would be suspended, until the crisis ended. Even the stagecoaches and Pony Express would be suspended, until reinforcements had arrived.

Several days later, upon returning to Carson City, Charley found Monk in his familiar seat at the Ormsby House tavern, suffering from the effects of a wake, held in honor of his patron of the tavern, Major Ormsby, who had died in the heat of battle. The entire town took the Major's death hard.

Thankfully Parkhurst knew that Hank Monk, even stinking drunk, could drive a six, better than most any sober driver that he had ever met. Charley would drive a full coach back to Placerville, together with Hank's coach; the Pioneer Stage Company believed in safety in numbers.

Will, carefully bound up, would be aboard also, seeking better medical attention closer to the California capitol. Alongside him sat Marion and their three-year-old daughter, Nellie, who was the apple of Will's eye. The balance of the passengers were people seeking safer living conditions or businessmen suddenly discovering that they had urgent business to attend in the golden state. Along the way the coach passed regiments of California soldiers from all over the state, coming to the rescue of the Nevada miners and citizens. At Friday's Byrnes' spirits picked up.

"I see you still got your dog. What did you name him?" Will asked, pulling on the scruff of the puppy's neck, who was nestled tightly in Nellie's coat.

"I named him Hank," Charley replied with a grin. "Cute little mutt, isn't he?" Charley chucked. "Kinda staggers around when he walks like Monk too, you know, kinda bowlegged and such. I registered him in Hangtown, with Sheriff Hume, as a brown-and-white little bastard."

"I'm sure Hank approves of that," Will smiled, receiving a frown from Mrs. Byrnes.

"Excuse my manners, Ma'am, I'm sorry." Charley blushed.

Nellie giggled, as the puppy squirmed in her arms.

"Yep, everyone just loves that little mutt," Charley sighed.

CHAPTER 44

Placerville, New Year's Day 1861

"Did you ever think about joinin' up with that Overland outfit?" Charley asked Monk over a beer.

"What the hell would I want to go and do that for?" Hank snorted beer and coughed.

"Well, I ain't seen the whole country yet. And what with the war going on and on, they need drivers out there. I want to see as much country as I can before I retire," Charley replied, calmly lighting his cigar.

"Retire?" the teamster choked anew. "Hell, you're just reaching your prime!" Monk laughed.

"I don't know, driving with one eye at night, it gets a bit rough, and I hate to say it, but my joints ain't what they used to be," Charley reasoned. "I'd like to see the rest of the country while I'm still fit enough to appreciate the scenery. Kinda like to see them buffalo herds I hear tell of too," he rambled. "Well, I heard a rumor that Ben Holladay is thinking of buying out Overland and investing a great deal of money."

"You go if you like, but I'll stay here, thank you . . . It seems that my glass is empty," Monk said standing with great ceremony, then called to the bartender. "Hell, Parkie, I'd rather sign up for the War, than drive on the Clean Out of Cash and Pour Pay Company, at least I might get a medal for bravery."

"That's a good one, Hank, I heard someone else callin' it that the other day. Well, I wasn't thinking of leaving Pioneer anytime soon, just keeping an eye open for new opportunities." Charley smiled.

Russell, Majors, and Waddell's most exciting and remarkable enterprise, the Pony Express, would be soon put out of business by the telegraph, thrusting the partners into the limelight. The partners other venture, utilizing the same stations as the Pony Express, was the Central Overland, California and Pikes Peak Express Company, or the C.O.C. & P.P. It was not as celebrated; in fact, it was known as the Clean Out of Cash and Poor Pay Company by some disgruntled employees. It took a great deal of manpower to run 155 stations from California to Atchison, Kansas, and it took a lot of money.

It seems that partner, Russell, had been a bit too desperate in his choice of financial aid for his cash strapped company. The aforementioned stage line and the Pony Express had been funded by the partners' freight line, which supplied military outposts. The money that was owed to the freighting company by the U.S. Army was becoming a great problem.

Russell went back East to raise more funds, but the news of their financial hardships had been buzzing around, and no one would lend him money. All due to the Civil War of course, which seemed to have no end. A visit was paid to other of Russell's partners, Luther R. Smoot of Smoot, Russell, & Co and Luke Lea. They discussed at length their friend's plight, though; neither was in any position himself to lend assistance. Lea did know of a man named Godard Bailey of the War Dept. and Indian Affairs, who might be in a position to help. A meeting was set up.

Russell was in need of one hundred fifty thousand dollars, to keep the C.O.C & P.P. and the Pony Express running. Bailey delivered the amount, in Missouri and Tennessee State bonds, to Russell's room at Potentini's rooming house. Russell signed a note on Russell, Majors, and Waddell's holdings for the same amount, then rushed back to his partners, and told of his success in raising financial aid. But they soon found out there were still problems to be met. Their associate, Jerome Simpson, had done the best he could in cashing in the bonds, but found that they were not worth what Bailey had claimed. Simpson was only able to fetch ninety-seven thousand, a sum inadequate to resolve the crisis. Russell again returned to Washington to the War Dept., but found nothing but excuses as to why they could not pay the money that they owed to the freighting firm, at this time.

Again Russell was forced to send Bailey a note requesting another meeting. At that time Russell told of the embarrassment his company had received at the news that the bonds were inferior in value. The shock on Bailey's face was apparent, when Russell asked of the possibility of borrowing more.

Bailey confessed that the bonds in question belonged to the Indian Trust Fund of the Dept. of the Interior, of which he was merely a custodian. The bonds represented unpaid annuities to various Indian tribes and were not even the property of the U.S. government. In short, Bailey was an embezzler. He had thought that he would be making a great profit, yet now it seemed apparent that he would be caught if the bonds could not be retrieved. Yet the only way to get them back was to invest more bonds.

The next day, Bailey delivered another $387,000. of bonds belonging to tribes of Missouri, South Carolina, and Florida, he returned the note for $150,000. and received another, for the amount of $537,000. The only condition was that the bonds be returned before Bailey's term of office expired.

But still it was not enough money. The horrible news of the Civil War was throwing the banks into a frenzy; people and bankers were calling in loans. Even though Russell was able to raise more funds, again he had to return to Bailey, making the total amount in bonds owed $870,000. He gave Bailey a receipt for the full amount.

Now about this time, Bailey being a worrisome sort, started to think about his term of office coming due and what was he going to do about those missing bonds. He wrote a letter to the Secretary of the Interior, Jacob Thompson, confessing all, then gave this letter to a relative and former employee of the Dept. of the Interior to be delivered to Secretary Thompson five days before the expiration of his term of office. Soon all hell would break loose for the foundering Express Company.

"Hey, Parkie, it says here in the newspaper they arrested the president of the Pony Express, Russell. Says he was a fraud. Where do you suppose them Pony boys been a riding to anyways?" Monk sniggered over the paper.

"What? Let me see that. I reckon it was a good thing I didn't sign on with him after all," Charley said lighting his cigar.

"It says here that Russell was being held on $500,000 bail. Well, if he had trouble raising the money to save his company, he was sure as hell going to have trouble raising his bail."

Ben Holladay, keeping note of the proceedings, swooped in with his large bank account to reap the spoils. The partnership of Russell, Majors, and Waddell was soon after dissolved. The company's name was changed to a manageable Holladay Overland Mail & Express. The gallant Pony Express was replaced by the telegraph wire, also an investment made by Holladay. The railroad was soon to follow, another investment of Holladay's, but there would still be the last glory days of the stagecoach yet to come. Ben Holladay would be the new King of stagecoach.

He enlisted coach makers Abbott and Downing to create his own private Concord coach, from which to oversee his travel empire. It was quite opulent, with the finest leather interiors and fineries. It was oversized, with a bed, and bar and all the comforts one could think of for travel, a rocking hotel room on wheels.

Holladay set about searching the West for the best coach drivers that money could buy and set up interviewing sessions. One such session was set up at Ormsby's Tavern in Carson City, where men sat around, each waiting for his turn to start a new career driving stage, after all it was a respected and well-paying position. Many of the men having given up on the idea of striking pay-dirt, wished only to elevate their station in life, even if it was only eight feet to the driver's box.

"If you were driving along a steep precipice, how close to the edge of the cliff would you drive?" Ben Holladay asked the confused applicant. Ben was sitting behind Major Ormsby's oak desk in an expensive-looking suit, immaculately groomed, smoking a dark expensive cigar, while he glared at the grubby-looking applicant.

"Well, I suppose I would be fairly close to the edge, I guess," the man stumbled, looking at his dirty hat.

"Yes, I see, take your coat. I have a stockman position available for you, next!" Ben commanded, as the confused miner stumbled out of the room. Another man was ushered in.

"You, if you were driving next to the edge of a cliff, just how close to the edge do you think you could drive?" Ben dared the next prospect.

Charley Parkhurst sat next to the wall, fairly entertained by the spectacle of the guessing game in the corner of the tavern, cutting a plug of chewing tobacco.

"Well, sir, I think that I would be able to get so close to that edge that two wheels would be a hangin' in the air. That's how close I could get," the braggart boasted.

"You, get out! You are a liar and an idiot!" the lion roared. Charley stifled a laugh; it was not quick enough, the men around him had turned to see who had laughed and the monarch himself had seen it also.

"You! Smiley! Step up here, you're next!" Ben Holladay ordered. "Where the hell did you get all these morons, Thomas?" Holladay asked his secretary.

"We put an advertisement in the paper, sir," Thomas replied quietly.

"Marvelous!" Holladay mumbled, under his breath.

Charley stuffed the small plug of tobacco in his cheek and chewed with a smirk, as he rose and sauntered to the front of the desk, taking his time. It seemed to cause Holladay a lot of annoyance. That kind of pleased Charley.

"Come on, smiley, I haven't got all day!" Ben jeered.

Charley looked Ben Holladay straight in the eye, with his one weather-hardened hazel eye, then leaned in and replied softly, "I don't think you'd want me in your outfit, Mr. Holladay, I'd drive as far away from the edge of that cliff as I could!" Parkhurst purred then spit into the spittoon.

With that remark, Ben Holladay boomed with deep laughter from within!

"What's your name, sir?" the larger-than-life executive commanded, at the end of his outburst.

"Charley Parkhurst, sir."

"Parkhurst, I've heard of you! You drive for the Pioneer?" Holladay asked.

"Yes, sir, that's me," Charley humbly replied.

"You're hired! One-eyed Charley Parkhurst! Thomas, assign him to the next available route. Welcome aboard, sir!" Mr. Holladay extended his large hand with a stern face. "Welcome aboard! . . . Next!" he bellowed.

As Charley exited the room with the studious Thomas, wearing an odd grin at being recognized as the coachman he was, he passed a kinsman, Hank Monk, on his way in.

"Just stay far away from the edge of cliffs and you can't miss, Hank." Charley winked to his fellow comrade of the lash. Charley went back to the main room, after discussing routes with Holladay's secretary, to see how Hank had done with his interview.

"How'd it go with the big man?" Charley quizzed Hank.

"Well, Parkie you can have your new adventures without me, for I'm stayin' in the Sierras. Overland has a contract with Pioneer, I'll just stick with drivin' my old route. You could drive your route too if you asked. Ain't nobody can drive that ride like you and I? Eh Parkie?" Hank toasted his friend.

"No, I 'spose not." Charley smiled sadly, for he had already signed on for a new route.

Ben Holladay bought himself more than an overland stage line; he bought himself a whole lot of trouble with it. The stage line had been fraught with larcenies, petty and otherwise. Horse thievery was rampant, as was cattle rustling. The passengers suffered the most. Lists of travel hints and rules were published to aid the ignorant public of the obstacles and hazards of overland travel:

1. The best seat inside a stagecoach is the one next to the driver . . . you will get less than half the bumps and jars than on any other seat. When any old "sly Eph," who traveled thousands of miles on coaches, offers through sympathy to exchange his back or middle seat with you, don't do it.

2. Never ride in cold weather with tight boot or shoes, nor close fitting gloves. Bathe your feet before starting in cold water, and wear loose overshoes and gloves two or three sizes too large.

3. When the driver asks you to get off and walk, do it without grumbling. He will not request it unless absolutely necessary. If a team runs away, sit still and take your chances; if you jump, nine times out of ten you will be hurt.

4. In very cold weather, abstain from liquor while on the road; a man will freeze twice as quickly while under the influence.

5. Don't growl at the food stations; stage companies usually provide the best they can get. Don't keep the stage waiting; many a virtuous man has lost his character by so doing.

6. Don't smoke a strong pipe inside especially early in the morning. Spit on the leeward side of the coach. If you have anything to take in a bottle, pass it around; a man who drinks by himself in such a cases, is lost to all human feeling. Provide stimulants before starting; ranch whiskey is not always nectar.

7. Don't swear, nor lop over on your neighbor when sleeping. Don't ask how far it is to your next station until you get there.

8. Never attempt to fire a gun or pistol while on the road, it may frighten the team; and the careless cocking of the weapon makes nervous people nervous. Don't discuss politics or religion, nor point out places on the road where horrible murders have been committed.

9. Don't linger too long at the pewter wash basin at the station. Don't grease your hair before starting or dust will stick there in sufficient quantities to make a respectable 'tater' patch. Tie a silk handkerchief around your neck to keep out dust and prevent sunburns. A little glycerin is good in case of chapped hands.

10. Don't imagine for a moment you are going on a picnic; expect annoyance, discomfort and some hardships. If you are disappointed, thank heaven.

CHAPTER 45

There were problems on Ben Holladay's new stage line that needed a strong hand to clean up, so he hired a veteran of the Pike's Peak Express, Jack Slade, as a line superintendent. Slade had been recuperating from multiple gunshot wounds inflicted upon him by Jules Reni, the founder of Julesburg. Reni and Slade had differences of opinions and Reni caught Slade by suprise and emptied his pistol into him. Then for good measure he shot him with one barrel of his shotgun, leaving him for dead.

Some say that Slade wore an iron vest over his long johns, unfortunately for Reni, Jack Slade survived the ambush. After his recovery, he once again became line superintendent, with one clear goal in mind, get Jules Reni.

Jack Slade was a bad drinker. He was quite pleasant when sober, even charming, but when he drank whiskey, he got mean. He loved to shoot up saloons by riding inside on his horse, then creating mayhem. On one of those bad benders, Jack Slade finally caught up with Jules Reni.

It was night when Jack and his men rode up on the small ranch. Slade had a following of young troublemakers that worshipped him, who sought vengeance for the one who had left their hero for the vultures. They approached the house and could hear men inside laughing, unaware of the danger lurking outside. Slade ordered his men to surround the house, as he remained in the saddle. Four men approached the front door as the other two hid to the side. One man banged on the door and called out, that he needed help with an injured horse.

"Is anyone about? I have a horse that needs a new shoe," the young man called innocently.

One of the men inside, not Jules, came to the door and was immediately held at gunpoint, and told to step outside.

"Make a noise or a false step and I'll blow the back of your head clean off," Slades' man whispered harshly, pointing his Army Colt at the quivering man's forehead. He was then told to call Reni to come and look at the horse. A few moments later, Reni staggered out of the station, complaining. A second man shoved his six-shooter into Reni's shoulder blades and told him to keep walking and not to say a word. Jules jaw dropped, as he saw the ghost of Jack Slade, sitting on a gray stallion in the moonlight before him. He had a lariat in his hand and was making lazy circles with it, next to his pawing steed.

"I don't believe it!" Reni kept repeating.

"Believe it and say your prayers, Reni," Slade said, as he threw the rope around Jule's neck and began dragging the choking man toward the corral. One of Slades' men opened the gate for his leader. When he had reached the center of the corral, Slade stopped and got off his horse and grabbed the rope around his prey's neck, dragging him to his feet. Jules was gasping and crying.

"You haven't even begun to feel pain yet, Jules," Jack hissed at the pathetic man. Slade tied the noose around the snubbing post, in the center of the corral, then wrapped it around Reni's neck a few times and tied it tightly, causing Jules to choke. "Tie his feet to the post," Slade ordered one of his men. "I think I'll leave his arms free. That will give me a moving target, I like that. Now I'm getting a might thirsty, you got any whiskey in that shit hole of a house over there?" Slade said taking out his pistol.

"Yes, all you want!" Jules pleaded for his life.

"Good! That suits me." Slade leveled his revolver at Jule's knee and pulled the trigger. "There, you think about that for a while, won't you?" he sneered, then crawled back onto his horse and rode back to the ranch house. It had been cleared of Jules Reni's cohorts, who had either been shot dead, or had run scared into the night like frightened rabbits. Slade and the men enjoyed the hospitality of the roped, hog-tied, and now bleeding and howling Reni, outside. One man stood guard outside with a shotgun, to make sure that no one tried to rescue their victim. After a few belts of whiskey, the fortified Slade revisited Reni, and lodged another slug in his arm, breaking it hideously. He then again retired inside, for more refreshments, as the man in the corral begged for mercy. All the while, the men inside insisted that Jules had shown no mercy to Capt. Jack Slade. So again target practice was bestowed on Mr. Reni. All through the night this went on, until the dawn finally broke and Slade had tired of the pathetic target. He came outside with Reni's own shotgun and shoved the business end in Jules mouth and pulled the trigger. Slade stared at the now lifeless form, dyed red with blood. A hard calculating gaze, like a serpent about to swallow his prey. He took out his knife and sliced off Reni's ears, like a matador after killing a bull and shoved the souvenirs in his vest pocket. Later, Jack had them tanned and made into a watch fob. Perfect for scaring the shit out of bartenders.

Slade was never prosecuted for this crime; witnesses said it was self defense and let it go at that. Generally speaking, he was a good superintendent; he got a lot done. Folks were too scared of him not to jump whenever he hollered, especially when they got a look at his watch fob.

Driving stagecoach on the plains was worlds apart from the foothills of California; the prairies were vast, monstrously vast. The winds sometimes howled with such velocity, it seemed as if it could blow the coach over. It played havoc with the coach lamps too. Keeping them lit was an exercise in futility, when the wind so desired darkness. The stage stops themselves were isolated, like little islands, the prairies seemed like the open ocean, for all of its treacheries. Each station thirsted for news from anywhere. Charley was always greeted with respect and admiration, like a soldier returning after doing battle, which it sometimes was, whether it was thundering herds of bison, or hunting parties of Indians. They seemed handsome to Charley, but unpredictable, and very fearsome.

The sand and the dust and wind would dry out a body, until a person couldn't even spit. Some of the stations had very little water and what there was, wasn't hardly fit to drink, due to the alkali in some areas, even though the water had been brought in by wagons, the alkali dust was everywhere and got into everything. It made Charley's empty eye socket itch and burn.

Even the roads themselves sometimes provided a great deal of added excitement. One such place was the dreaded Devil's Dip.

About two hundred yards from the Devil's Dip, Charley slowed the coach to a stop and asked that the men help the two ladies climb from the roof of the vehicle to ride inside the coach. Parkhurst then asked the rest of the men if they had any heart conditions, advising them that they would be better off inside as well. There was some grumbling, but folks finally got their seating arrangements in order. Charley then turned to his new Express Agent and asked if he had ever been down this stretch of road.

"No," the inexperienced man answered.

"Well then, could you kindly keep your head turned away from me, and holler to the side of the coach and not in my ear? Oh and you might want to get a good grip on the rails, while your at it," Charley recommended, setting his little dog Hank safely in the bowels of the front boot of the coach. With that announcement made and his dog tucked away, Charley bucked his belt around his waist to the back of the seat rail, much to the puzzlement of the shotgun rider.

The Devil's Dip was a stretch of road that ran along the top of a ridge, then made a sharp right turn and descended, at a fifty degree angle, down to a wide, shallow river bed about five hundred yards below. The banks were too crumbly to try a diagonal path; the coach would slide sideways or roll. Before the coach descended, the lead horses would drop down over the edge and were completely out of sight of the driver, who must let the horses move quickly or else the coach would simply slide on top of them, even with the brake on full. As they continued the hard right turn, down to the water, the coach practically leapt over the edge, picking up speed as each pair of horses gallop into the descent. The driver and topside passengers were thrilled to the hair raising, top speed plummet. The horses racing to the shallow river bed below, were in need of the momentum, to help them up the equally steep, poor excuse for a road, awaiting them on the opposite bank of the river. The Devils Dip became an initiation of the true brotherhood of the lash. However, after some accidents, and bad weather, and a lot of complaints, the road was rerouted. Alas, gone, and probably for the better, was the first roller coaster ride.

One day, when Charley was outside of Big Sandy, on the Platte River in Nebraska Territory, he spotted a very large band of Indian warriors, in full-face paint and feathers, riding parallel to them on a ridge close by. They seemed to simply appear from the landscape. The driver knew that the coach was in a very tight spot and could not hope to outrun such a large party. The coachman had to resort to diplomacy. Charley made strong threats to all aboard, to follow his instructions exactly. Any panicking from the passengers or the express agent could result in instant death from the warriors. The driver kept moving forward at an even pace, keeping panic to a minimum. It was very difficult for the passengers aboard, who thought they should be running as fast as they could for their lives. Charley understood that he could not possibly out run the natives, descending upon them, given the terrain and the upper hand the Indians held. The coaching party was certainly underequipt to out-shoot them, so the only thing left was to bluff. So he did.

The driver navigated the coach out of the dry riverbed up to the road on the open plains. He kept the team at a moderate trot, trying to save their strength for a death run if necessary. The natives all surrounded the vehicle easily, there were so many. At least a hundred, Charley surmised, as he felt the end drawing near. He cautioned the passengers not to fire a shot, or even touch their firearms; it would surely lead to their total destruction. The warriors soon stopped the coach by surrounding the lead horses; the Chief was close at hand. Charley presumed the older man was the Chief, he was elaborately adorned with eagle plumes and silver, even what appeared to be gold. He expressed great interest in the coach and horses and made motions to the inside of the vehicle. Charley made a supreme effort to show respect and integrity to the Chief, ordering the passengers off the coach, reminding them to stay calm or else. After examining the interior, the Chief then examined every horse and harness and ordered them unhitched. Charley tried to be as helpful as he could, trying to explain things in gestures. The Chief then examined the entire coach; he was impressed at the architecture of the vehicle and the painting on the door. He ordered the horses rehitched immediately and was determined to experience the entire medium by taking a ride inside, with some of the other warriors. He soon tired of that and climbed out the window for a ride on the roof, seating himself next to the nervous coachman, the small mutt was now riding shotgun.

"Quiet now Hank, show some respect for the Chief," Charley reminded the mutt. The Chief pointed to a hill and spoke, Charley presumed that's where he wanted to go. The Chief smiled, as he watched the driver handling the six leather lines, skillfully controlling the six spirited horses. They could see the encampment of the tribe, as the coach crested the hill. It seemed that the Chief wanted to make an unscheduled stop at his village. Charley obediently drove toward the teepees. The Chief had decided to try standing up on the roof of the coach, as the ground was now flattening out. Charley looked for the least rough ground to drive, as the village greeted the arriving party. Ecstatic at the advancement of horse drawn power, the man stood behind the driver with the wind in his hair and his arms outstretched, as an eagle soaring through the air. Charley sensing the power of the moment and the even and straightness of the road ahead, handed the Chief the lines to the horses as a sort of peace offering. The sunburst man took the leather in his hands and felt the driver's power.

After a short time, he drew the horses to a standstill and handed the leather back to its rightful owner. Before the Chief climbed down, he gave the driver his own pair of quilled and beaded gauntlet gloves as a gift. Then he mounted his own beautiful painted horse, which had been brought along and called his braves to let the coach be on its way. The teamster waived a cheerful farewell and drove quickly back to retrieve his original passengers. Parkhurst heard the natives laughing and thought it was a very good sign, but he never looked back. He was lucky that time and wore the gloves with pride.

"Sorry I ran behind schedule, Captain Slade, sir," Charley said apologizing to the dangerous superintendent. "Had an encounter with some Indians. They have an encampment near Sand Hill, got out of it without any fighting though, Chief was just curious."

"You should have shot that son of a bitch!" Slade smirked at the teamster.

"Sir, we were out numbered, I did what I thought safest for the passengers," Charley replied, poised for any reaction.

"Well I ain't paying you to think," Slade growled back.

"You ain't payin' me to kill, neither!" Charley replied.

Slade threw his head back and laughed at the relieved driver, as he turned to pour himself a cup of bad coffee.

A few days later, at the home station in Medicine Bow, Wyoming, Charley was relaxing in the boarding house, when a young driver started bragging about how the Overland stage would revolutionize the country, and bring growth to the great new land, and on and still on, until Charley couldn't stand it any longer. He had just finished a very arduous ride. Another tribe of natives, not as curious or amicable, had chased the coach, until Charley had nearly lost control and rolled. Even after arriving at the swing-station, the natives continued to fire upon the intruders of their country, they even tried to burn the sod buildings, but they remained secure. The Indians soon became disenchanted with their prey and left after nightfall. Charley could see violent times ahead.

"There ain't no glory in purgatory!" Charley called out to the loud-mouthed whip, slamming his empty glass on the wooden bar. A burst of laughter came over the room, some agreeing with Charley's pearl of wisdom. The loudmouth turned scarlet at the sight of the weathered, one eyed man and became blessedly silent.

Clearly the plains were not for Charley, he longed to return to California, especially the coast and the brisk ocean air, but he had a good work ethic and felt obligated to be where he was needed.

Parkhurst had once wanted to see the buffalo and see them he did. The buffalo on the prairie were uncountable and particularly nervous one day. Charley could see the heads coming up and then giving long bellows and snorts, with their tails swinging up over their backs. The bulls swinging around and displayed their horns, as the coach snaked it's way through the vast meandering bison herds.

The driver made note of the darkening clouds in the distance; even the birds seemed to be taking their leave of the ominous weather coming. On the horizon, the electricity was manifest in large bolts of lightning, flashing down through troubled clouds. The passengers huddled together inside the coach, with the leather curtains battened down securely. The expressman, was likewise, settled in his wraps, still clutching his firearms, only partly cognizant of what was going on. His main concern was to stay warm and dry and hang on.

Charley took it as a bad omen, the herds seemed to be making a hastily retreat from the distant weather formation. The sky was very dark, yet it was still early evening. Rain was now coming down diagonally, and it was growing strangely warm. The wind was picking up at a furious pace, as Parkhurst could see the lights at the station. It did a lot to quiet his nerves.

"Cyril, we're coming to the station," Charley nudged the expressman.

"Yeah, I see it," he said with a grunt, as he adjusted his hat to the rain. Thankfully it was a home station. When they arrived, the stationmaster and his teenage son, Joseph, quickly looked after the horses. The rain was coming down fiercely, so Charley stepped in to help unhitch the team.

"Cyril, get your lazy ass over here and let's get these horses in the barn." Cy was busy looking for the stationmaster's young daughter.

"I'll be right there! I got to kick the bushes," he lied.

"That slacker!" Charley muttered under his breath.

"I heard that," Joseph laughed.

"Well, I don't care if you did." Charley glared with mock aggression at the young man, then laughed. The two laughed together and Charley bellowed for Cy to get his ass to the barn, which he did reluctantly. The wind was really beginning to howl and Charley related the news of the black clouds coming, to the young man and his father and advised them to "batten down the hatches for a big blow!" The boy, Joe, took the advice to heart and scrambled around the primitive barnyard, securing the chickens, as Charley helped feed and water the tired, but nervous team. Cy had ducked out as soon as they unharnessed, in search of his elusive girl friend.

"Make sure you don't leave any lamps lit, or they could be blown over and burn the barn down," Charley instructed, as he left the barn and went into the sod station house. The stationmaster's wife had a plate of food immediately in front of Charley, as if she had been waiting at the door with it, in order to place it in front of him when he first sat down. She then poured a strong cup of coffee and a shot of whiskey and placed them next to the plate.

"You spoil me Mama!" Charley gushed.

"You deserve it, Mr. Parkhurst," she always replied, setting a dish of scraps on the floor for the little dog.

"We got a big storm out there, a big wind, it's real scary. I'm tellin you true," Charley said, as he gulped down the supper. "I'm going to bed down with the horses, in case it gets bad there, I don't want to lose any of them. I think you should hunker down in the cellar, with the supplies and such, it's the safest place."

"It's that bad?" Mama asked.

"I think so," Charley cautioned. Mama trotted off to find her husband.

"Take your breakables and stow them down below too," Charley called after. The door nearly blew off its hinges as the teenaged boy burst though the doorway.

"You were right about the storm, Charley," Joe blurted out, as he plopped on the chair next to the driver.

"You better help your ma get ready for this storm, the stronghold is the cellar. Get some blankets and water down there and anything that she might want that's breakable. This storm might just decide to rip the roof off this place," Charley added as a warning. The roof on the crude sod building was already beginning to rattle; dirt was falling from the crude ceiling. Cy came into the dining room from the back with the young girl, Rachel, inquiring what all of the fuss was.

"In case you two haven't been paying attention, Cy, there is a big storm descending upon us!" Charley cried, exasperated. "Rachel you and Cy help your ma with the water barrels, get them down to the cellar! Make sure all the passengers stay there, until the storm blows over. I'm gonna stay with the horses," Charley said, washing down the last bit of supper and following it with the shot of whiskey. Charley got up and blew out of the door, followed by an admiring young Joe. Little Hank was smart enough to stay close to Mama, in case she had any more scraps.

"Charley, what's that noise?" The two paused in front of the barn. The very ground that they stood on was beginning to shake. An audible low moaning sound was getting ever so slightly louder.

"Shit!" Charley called out. "Buffalo! Stay here with the horses." Charley grabbed the loaded Henry rifle off the coach and trotted off to the bluff near the barn, then strained to listen for the herd. A tornado was chasing the herd toward the express station. Charley ran back down to the barn. "We are in for it good now, if the storm don't rip the roof of the station, the buffalo, may well do us in anyway! They are headed right at us. Go back to the station and get your Pa and his Henry rifle and tell that fat-head Cy to bring one out too. We got to steer the herd away from us or we might be trampled to death. Go!" Charley ran into the barn and grabbed a saddle and put it on the big wheeler mare, and cinched her up. She was a nice three-year-old and had plenty of stamina. By the time the three came back from the house Charley was on the horse and heading out to the bluff. The herd was getting closer, and it made the horse nervous. The lightning helped Charley to see what had to be done. He began firing at the herd, to change their course. It didn't seem to do much, for they were in a sort of blind panic and simply jumped over their fallen comrades.

"You two fire at them from this bluff, behind the rocks, and I'll ride down and see if I can change their course from down there! If the twister starts heading over this way, run back to the house and get in the cellar." Charley wheeled the mare around and rode toward the bison, firing his Colt pistol. The swirling mass of galloping beasts were beginning to turn, just as a bolt of lightning, illuminated an even more imposing threat, nearly struck the horse, causing him to fall.

"Holy Mother of Mercy, that was close," Charley said as he picked himself up from the dirt. The horse staggered to her feet, as Charley grabbed his gun and swung back into the saddle and took off back to the barn. As he did, he stopped to grab Joseph by the arm and swung him up onto the horse. They hollered for Cy to run for the house. The roar of the storm became deafening.

The barn had been built into the side of a bluff so that it was protected on one full side by hillside, it also helped keep the building cool in the summer and deflect the strong prairie winds. Charley hoped that it would come in handy now. He gathered the horses close to the hillside section of the barn and made sure that they were securely tied. He also kept his knife close at hand, in case he would have to cut them all loose to save them. Charley kept the mare saddled, in case he had to round them up after the storm.

Parkhurst's hand settled on a small flask of brandy, kept in a breast pocket, and shared a sip with the boy. Cy had not returned to the barn. "I expect Cyril went back to the house," Charley reasoned to the young man. "Since that's where Rachel is," Joe added.

The two hunkered down as the wind picked up considerably and the barn whistled and shook, a loud bang was heard, as was a great scraping noise. Then there was another deafening bang and crash as the horses collectively shuttered and danced. The noise reached an impossible pitch, when Charley looked up to see the corner of the barn give way and crash, and the light in his eye went out for the rest of the night.

"Charley are you all right?" A voice in near panic kept repeating, until the lights finally faded back in.

"Yes, I think I'll be all right," Charley whispered, rubbing his weather worn face, the eye-patch oddly askew. "Damn I got dirt in my socket."

"You gotta help me, the station house is gone, we gotta get help, we gotta dig them out of the cellar."

Charley moaned as he stood. "What about the horses?"

"They're tied up over by the creek, I'm glad you left Belle saddled, I was able to keep them together and gather them up when the barn caved in."

The two stared at the splintered remains of the station. Most of it was simply gone, but the cellar had remained, debris had kept the door from opening. Joseph valiantly threw the obstructions to the side, as Charley helped open the door. All inside were fine, Mama, the passengers and the stationmaster, even little Hank, but there was no Cyril. He hadn't made it back. All around them were surreal leftovers from the storm. The station and barn were scattered as if someone had tossed a glass of toothpicks into the air. The strange path of the twister and the furious herd of bison carved a giant swath of ground through the prairie, with the dead buffalo scattered about as if massacred in a great battle, some still breathing their last breaths.

Charley looked around the grounds and spotted the coach, it had been blown over and dragged by the immense winds some hundred yards, it lay on it's side next to the riverbank, where it was nestled in some small greasewood trees, intact. Charley got on Belle and rode about looking for signs of Cy, but none were ever found. The team was harnessed and the coach righted and loaded. The things that could not be brought were stowed in the cellar and it was covered with debris for safe keeping until the station could be rebuilt.

"It's all right, Mama, you'll be fine." Charley tried to soothe the shaken woman, who appeared to be in a great state of shock over her surroundings. "Maybe you should go to California, I think I'm going back. I don't like the plains, too violent."

Yet it was not quite that easy to leave. With the Civil War still raging on, replacement drivers were not to be had. Charley felt a sense of duty to his country to continue to drive on these most treacherous roads. All the while, longing to be back in California.

Slowly Charley worked his way back to Salt Lake City. It was different now, without James Birch, Charley couldn't drive any route he pleased, as when his friend was running the roads. Times had changed, the war was using up good men at an alarming rate and no end seemed in sight. Charley had to take the routes that needed drivers; he was just another driver.

The Comstock Lode was getting a lot of attention these days, between stories of massive battles in Bull Run and Shilo. It seemed that everyone not involved in the Civil War was heading out to Virginia City to dig for silver or invest in shares of a mine. Soon Charley would be back amongst friends.

CHAPTER 46

Virginia City, Fat Bills Saloon 1862

Parkhurst had just finished an extremely long ride, having driven from Castle Rock, Nevada, approximately one hundred and fifty miles away. A relief driver was too sick to drive, that meant Charley had driven though thirteen stations, each approximately thirteen miles apart, equaling 18 hours in the drivers seat. It was three o'clock in the morning when the coach rolled into Virginia City. It had snowed along the way and the coachman looked for a place to warm his insides after work and had settled on Fat Bill's Saloon. It seemed more inviting than The Bucket of Blood, next door.

Little Hank poked his nose out of the bearskin coat, into the night air and Charley pulled the small dog from his roomy inside pocket and set him down to do his business. The little dog followed his master along the planked walkway.

Inside Fat Bill's, Parkie found an assortment of locals still up and carousing at this wee hour. He ordered a double shot of brandy, and some hot coffee, as a familiar face flushed with whiskey ambled over. He had been a passenger on The Overland about a year back and had found himself a niche in the local press in Virginia City.

"Hey, Sam how are ya?" Charley piped in. He noticed the man seemed to be wearing a lot of clothing, possibly due to the cold weather.

"Oh, I'm fine, just put the press to bed a while ago, thought I'd have a few drinks for I hit the hay. Any news in about the War?" Sam pressed.

"Haven't had time to look in the papers I brought in. Must be something in there," Charley replied sleepily. "I heared tell that Samuel Colt died."

"That is news indeed! Say you want to play some cards? I think that table is breakin' up," Sam pointed out. "I think DeQuille will be coming along soon, he'll play. He'll be interested in that Colt story too!"

"Sure, I don't mind sitting next to that fire awhile. My knees are damn near frozen off," Charley sighed. The men settled down at the small table as Sam produced a deck of cards.

"That Ol' Pony Bob over there sleepin'?" Charley said, fumbling about in his vest pocket.

"Yep."

"Guess he's out of a job for now, I don't know if this telegraph thing can last," Charley remarked.

"I don't know, the government invests a lot of faith in it . . . You can examine these if you like," Sam said, shuffling the deck and passing it over to his friend. Charley cut the deck without looking and passed it back. He held his cold hands around the coffee cup and wiggled his gloved fingers to help them thaw.

"I'm not worried much, I don't play for more than I can afford to lose," Charley said confidently, as he pulled out a cigar. "What do you want to play?" he said, looking for a Lucifer with which to light his cigar.

"Do you like black-jack?" Sam asked.

"Ah, Eleanoras' game. Yeah, that's a good 'un." Charley said smiling. "Let's make this a friendly little game and play for short bits."

"Fine, I need to get some change, all I've got is a five dollar piece. You want me to get you some?" Sam said, whistling to the small raven-haired woman, who was busy cleaning off tables.

"Hello, fellas, what can I do for you?" the young woman said, in a practiced but sleepy voice. She deftly sparked up a Lucifer match that she always had on hand and struck a flame for the teamster.

"Oh, why thank you very much," Charley said, blushing.

"What's your name, sweetness?" Sam cooed to the young gal.

"Amy. Can I get anything for you?" The young woman could not have been more than sixteen.

"Would you get us some change, Amy, please, short bits if you could, thanks," Charley said handing the girl some silver dollars. Sam then handed her his five-dollar piece and she returned to the bar. As she left the table, another wayward figure in a bearskin coat entered the room and made his way to the bartender.

"Fats! I'll have a beer, I got to drive in a couple of hours. Throw an egg in it!" Monk said, as an after thought. He turned his attentions to the residents of the room, as the bartender cracked the egg into Hank's beer.

"You want the shell in there too?" the bartender asked, with disgust.

"No, just the soft stuff. Better give me a whiskey chaser too," Hank said, laying some coin on the bar. "Keep the rest," Hank said, tottering toward a familiar face.

"Well, well, as I live and breathe! Parkie? Good to see you old man! I thought the Indians got you for sure! Can anyone get in this game?" Hank said, swallowing down his egg beer, then slapping Charley on the back.

"Good to see you too, my friend," Charley replied, rising from his chair, as the two men gripped hands with a smile, looking like fraternal bruins. Amy was returning with the broken money.

"There you are, gentlemen," she said smiling at the familiar Monk. "Anything else?"

"Yes, I'll have another beer with an egg in it, the bartender knows. There, thanks," Hank said handing her some money and making himself at home at the table. "What are we playing?" Hank asked.

"Twenty-one," Charley replied, turning to the girl and tipping her a dime. "Are you driving this morning?" Parkhurst said, turning back to Monk.

"Yeah, in a few hours. I couldn't sleep. I either got to drive at night or in the day, I can't get used to switching around," Hank said rubbing the sleep from his eyes.

"With this weather coming up I don't know if we'll be going out much longer," Charley said looking at the cards. "Oh, I'm sorry, Sam Clemens this here is Hank Monk."

Sam was busy flipping cards on the table.

"Pleased to make your acquaintance," Clemens stopped what he was doing and stared straight at the bearded, blue-eyed man. "Not the Hank Monk who drove Horace Greeley across the Sierras?"

"Yes, sir, the very one." Hank smiled innocently.

"Do you want any more cards?" Sam asked Charley.

"No, I stay," he replied. "Two bits," Parkie said tossing in the silver.

"There's two and one more," Sam said confidently"

"Let's see 'em," Parkhurst replied.

"The dealer has twenty," Sam said turning over his hold cards.

"Twenty-one," Charley said, revealing his hand.

"Shit ! . . . Why, it would be an honor to have you in this game," Clemens said to Monk without batting an eye. "You know I've heard the story of you and Greeley about a thousand times now, and here you are in the flesh . . . I hope you have some 'other' stories."

"Why as a matter of fact, I pulled a good one the other day," Hank began, as he collected his beer and money from the girl, tipping her a half bit. "Thanks, girl. This odd kinda feller, just as green as grass about the world, was sitting up next ta me in the box. He was nervous I guess 'cause of the steep cliffs and the like. Well, he keeps yammerin on and on, asking me about this and that and the other things on board of the coach. And none of the answers that I give seemed to shut the man up. He runs on and on." Hank prattled as he looked at his cards.

"I know the feeling," Clemens responded as he looked at his own cards.

"Well, finally the man notices an ax, that I always keep in my boot, in case you got to chop a horse out of harness or clear a tree or chop off some ones leg that's badly broken. An so he asks me why I got that ax in my boot, an I sez, 'Well, whenever there's a wreck, someone always get injured, then sues the company big, for damages done to them.' So now, whenever we have a wreck and anyone gets hurt bad, I just pops them in the back of their head with the ax, and puts them out of their misery, savin' the company from pesky settlements. Well, sir, that sure shut him up, till we got to the station, anyhow. Then he runs squealing into that office like a stuck pig, crying about the company's policies. The fellers in the office had one hell of a time shutting him up!" Hank unceremoniously stuck his head beneath the table, hitting his head as he reemerges. "Say, is that little Hank under the table there? Come on here, little Hank," Monk sang, as he lifted the little mutt onto his lap. "He's getting fat!"

"Are we gonna play cards here?" Charley sighed.

"I had a horse once . . ." Sam mumbled as he picked up his cards again. "Bought him at an auction. It was my first horse auction, at the Carson City Plaza."

"I'll put in a dime," Monk called.

"I didn't know any thing about horses, still don't know much," Clemens continued. "Don't know why I wanted a horse even. Just seemed like the thing to do and all. Everyone was riding them about town," Clemens said. "I'll take one card. Well, I spotted a real likely looking candidate, so I commenced to bid on her. A professional horseman told me that this was no ordinary horse, but that this particular beast was a genuine Mexican plug. Also thrown into the bargain, I was told that she could out buck any other American horse! I'm in. Well, gentlemen, I can tell you that I seriously believed that these qualities were just what I needed in an equine companion, and so I made certain that I would be the fair owner of such a prize." Clemens laughed as he threw a dime into the pile.

"So you bought him?" Hank said snickering into his cards.

"Indeed, gentlemen, I did," Sam commenced

"Two bits," Charley tossed out.

"I'll see that and add one more," Hank said with careful calculation.

"Three bits to me," Sam said unflinching. "Yes, well, that evening I undertook to ride my genuine Mexican plug, complete with a Spanish saddle, with full *tapidaros*. I took the mount to the plaza, in Carson, and with growing interest, I first planted myself on the back of the beast. I had one man holding the horse's head, while I boarded and another holding her tail. When they released the critter, the crowd jumped back. The horse, which I named Buster, after a woman I once met, launched herself immediately, and I soon found myself quite airborne. During most of Buster's tantrum, she was especially fond of vertical motion, till some resourceful bystander swatted her on the behind, causing her to leap forward, only to be captured several miles from the first mounting point. I myself, landed very close to the beginning of my riding experience," Clemens said, as he laid the two kings and the ace onto the felt.

"Shit!" Hank swore as Sam reeled in the silver dimes on the felt table.

"That's, just what I said, when I got off the ground," Clemens said gathering the cards and passing them to Charley. "The next day, I commenced lending Buster to people, to kind of get her broke in. The first to take her was a young man of Mexican heritage, who seemed well equipped enough to be able to cling to the saddle. I believe speed records were shattered that day by the youth and the nag for there was not a fence nor obstacle that seemed to stand in the way of the two. The father of the boy soon whisked him away, and other people were lent the horse. All returned on foot claiming that they were in need of exercise."

"What happened to the horse?" Hank asked.

Sam took a long deep smoke on his cigar. "Last I saw Buster she was chasing a coyote across the desert," Sam said.

"I hear Jim Hume got elected sheriff of Hangtown again," Hank commented as he finished his egg beer.

"Good! He's a fine sheriff, "Charley responded. "He's gonna need snowshoes to catch some of the roughs around there. Speaking of which, ain't that Thompson coming in, over there? Charley motioned with his head to the huge man stomping the snow off his boots in the doorway.

"Hey, Snowshoe, over here, look who's back!" Hank shot out.

"Hey, Parkie, good to zee you!" Thompson said, giving the one eyed teamster a friendly swat on the back. "You got room for one more?" Snowshoe asked, shaking the snow off his shoulders, like a great dog.

"Shove over, Parkie," Hank ordered. Parkhurst felt refreshing chills as the virile mountainman sat familiarly close to his friend. "Good to see you, John." he smiled. "This here is, Sam. Amy, can I get another brandy, I'm sure Thompson here needs something? Thanks."

"A cup of coffee and zome biscuits if you got dem," Thompson ordered.

"Hank, it's your deal," Charley said, passing the deck. "You still seein' that redheaded gal over at Strawberry's?"

"No. That's over," Hank said shuffling the cards. "She laid into me but good. Funny thing about that," he said dealing the cards. "I had this young greenhorn riding with me the other day, told me it was his first trip to the golden state. Well, when I pulls in to the station, out comes Red, madder'n a wet hen over some important thing I had neglected, namely her, and she yammer's on for the longest time at the top of her voice."

"Sounds familiar," Clemens remarked, straightening his cards and tossing in one bit.

"Well, as soon as the wild cat finishes her lecture, all eyes was a lookin'. You could'a heard a pin drop. So I looks over to the greenhorn and I says, 'I thought you said you wasn't never along this road before. You're a pretty specimen, young as you be, to desert your wife, an' have her come and abuse you before all these people in that there outrageous manner.' I ain't a seed neither of them since."

"Is dat little Hank? Come here, boy," Thompson sang out, as the others muffled their laughter as not to encourage the man's tall tales.

"That is a cute little canine," Clemens chimed in. "I like dogs as a general rule, can't say I'd say the same of cats, however," he said, throwing his cards in and examining the small mutt. "Wonder what's keeping DeQuille?" he added nervously, looking at his watch. "I must confess that I played a bit of a trick on him tonight, I am waiting to hear the repercussions."

"Vat did you do?" Thompson said tossing two bits onto the growing pile of silver.

"Well, it's this way, DeQuille and I share a room at Mrs. Watson's boarding house. She had a particularly annoying tomcat, who had the most insufferable habit of pissing on my bed. I had finally had enough and devised a most treacherous prank. I filled an old boot with water then fastened it to the little varmints tail with a lace. Then, after having tied its other end to the bed post with a long cord, I heaved the offending creature out the window," Clemens sighed, catching his breath. "Killed him deader than a door nail."

"You didn't really?" Hank laughed.

"Oh yes, I did. Then I left a full confession of the deed. I signed DeQuilles' name to it and left it on my own pillow," Sam said chuckling to himself.

"You lousy son of a bitch!" DeQuille said, crashing through the saloon door with a suitcase, quite hastily packed. Pieces of clothing were sticking out through the edges. "What the hell were you thinking? You low down good for nothing. That old bat was waiting up for me and chased me around the house, swatting after me with a broom. Do I have a black eye?" he said, pointing at his eye and looking at Thompson.

"Ya, I tink dat eye is going to show zome color," Snowshoe said solemnly.

"Of all the stupid tricks, this one takes the prize. I suppose you know we were thrown out of the house! How could you do such a thing?" DeQuille ranted.

"Cat pissed in your new hat, Dan," Clemens spoke calmly. Hank Monk was laughing so hard he almost fell backward in his chair.

"What?" DeQuille roared. "That mangy little bastard! I could just wring his scrawny neck!"

"You're welcome," Clemens said. "Here," he said, pulling the offending garment from a bag.

"Lovely hat!" Hank said busting a gut.

"Goddamn it! My new hat!" DeQuille said, lifting it toward his well-groomed mustache and making a sour face.

"Oh no, I got to piss." Hank laughed. "Can I borrow your hat?" Hank said standing, unable to control his laughter and headed toward the back door.

"Well, the least you could do is deal me in!" Dan said tossing the hat on the floor and sitting in the vacated seat. Little Hank leapt off of Thompson's lap and immediately seized the opportunity to intimidate the castaway hat; he stood before it sniffing and barking, then finished off with a fine, hind leg salute.

CHAPTER 47

May 1863

The Civil War was still raging away in the South, yet the mail from the West to the East must continue to flow. Valuable gold and silver shipments from the West added fuel to the war machines.

There was another war erupting in this country, but it was due North. It was with the Indians and the ever-expanding white settlements. While most of the soldiers were currently tied up shooting at each other, reinforcements were sent for from California to keep the restless and violent natives in check.

Harry Love's Lieutenant Patrick Connor, of the California Rangers, had kept on with his career in the military and had been promoted to Colonel Connor, commanding 233 men of the Second Cavalry, California Volunteers. In a great battle with the Bannock and the Snake people, along the Bear River in Wyoming, his victory in battle caused him to be promoted to the rank of Brigadier General. He and the California Volunteers had been summoned to protect the Overland Mail, from the various warring tribes that took their toll daily on Holladay's outfit.

"Patrick Connor, sir?" Charley Parkhurst inquired sheepishly, setting down the mailbags in the Ruby Valley Express office.

"Why if it isn't Charley Parkhurst!" the General said, turning to his weathered acquaintance. "I didn't recognize you with the eye patch."

"Last I saw of you, you had on a lot less brass and braid. Pardon me for my lack of military education." Charley laughed.

"Brigadier General Connor at your service, sir. We are headed up to Salt Lake City," Connor said shaking Charley's hand.

"Well, well, that's quite a title! Yes, sir. Glad to see you done so well . . . for ya'self. This country has some mighty fierce opposition, I'm here to tell you, barely, that is," Charley said shaking his head. "Say I'm going next door to wash the sand from my wind pipe if you care to join me?" Charley offered. "Be nice to talk about the old days in the diggin's."

"I think I'm finished up here," General Connor said, nodding at the station manager. "I'd like to discuss the route with you. You're probably familiar with the troublesome areas," Connor said, as they walked out the door. He was eager to pry open his friendly oyster and receive his pearls of wisdom about these questionable outposts.

"They're all pretty wide open and subject to attack, the stations, I mean. And in between, the coaches are just like sitting ducks. A driver takes his life in his hands each time he takes hold of the lines. I don't know why I'm still out here!" Charley said, shaking his head.

"You seen Byrnes lately? He's knocking on death's door I hear," Connor said, as they entered the drinking establishment. "I can see by your face that you have not."

"What happened?" Charley said quietly. "Bartender," Charley motioned the man at the end of the plank.

"First, he was shot by a woman in Gold Hill, a mining dispute of some kind. Then he was shot again by a man named Keller. I did not get the particulars on that event," Connor concluded.

"That man has been shot more times than anyone I've ever met!" Charley blurted out. Connor smiled. "You want a beer?" he added.

"Fine . . . He always seems to pull through some how though. It seems to me." Connor could see how the news was affecting his old acquaintance.

"Pitcher of beer and two glasses please, sir."

"Right away," the bartender replied, setting into motion.

"Do you know where he is now?" Charley said with a tight throat.

"Still got a place between Gold Hill and Devils Gate outside of Carson City, I believe," Connor said lifting his newly poured beer. "To old friends."

"To old friends. Leave it to Byrnes to take up residence next to the Devil's Toll Gate, he's probably getting a cut." Charley lifted his glass and drank to the health of his friend.

Charley did what he could to get his route back to Carson City, so he could look in on Will. What he found on the first visit was a bedridden shell of a man.

Will tried in vain to sit up and be cheerful, but it was only a thin veneer and it did little to hide the pain beneath. He could barely use his legs. Charley had a tough time choking back the tears welling up inside. Outside the bedroom, Marion sat in attendance with their little daughter, Nellie, sewing on a quilt.

"Nellie dear, maybe you could fetch your Pa some fresh water, while I talk to your Ma for a spell?" Parkhurst softly spoke, while he petted the girl's soft blonde head.

"Take the Bible in and read your Pa a story," Marion said, handing a well-worn black book to the child. After she left the room, Charley asked Marion what could be done, if anything.

"My father wrote me of a surgeon in New York who could perform the removal of the lead balls lodged near Will's spine. The travel involved to get to New York might be enough to kill him though, given his delicate condition," Marion reasoned. "But if he does not have the surgery, he will die anyway," she cried.

Charley sighed. "It's a tough trip, I know, I've driven most of it. But I seen Will pull through some mighty rough goings. Why don't you write your father about this doctor, and I'll see what I can do about gettin' him there. Now you just keep your spirits up, girl." Charley tried to comfort the lady.

"You are the most courageous woman I have ever met," Marion said, wiping her wet eyes. "How can you have lived like this, for so long?" she asked, looking at the coach driver's shaggy gray hair and scarred face and eye patch.

"It's all I have ever known. I don't know how to be anything else." Charley smiled; then her face grew dark. "Have you ever told Will?" Parkhurst said, staring into Marion's soft pale face.

"I never told him. He doesn't know," Marion lied. Fearful that the woman might not agree to save her husband, Marion was somehow convinced that the rugged woman had strong emotions for her husband.

"Don't worry, gal, he'll pull through. I'll make sure he gets to his surgery," Charley soothed as he departed.

"Good-bye, Charley! Thank you for the candy," young Nellie sang out from the porch.

That night, as Charley rode a leased horse back to Carson City, he spotted a vaguely familiar figure on the horizon.

"Sheriff James Hume, is that you?" Charley called out. "Charley Parkhurst, 'Parkie',," he added

"Oh yes, didn't recognize you, without your stagecoach," Hume laughed.

"What are you doing in these parts?" Charley asked dismounting.

"Oh, I just rode in to tie up some loose ends so to speak."

"I was just going to go in and get some dinner, you eat yet?" Charley asked.

"No, I'm hungry as a bear! You know a good place to eat?" Jim replied.

"Yeah, come on," Charley said tying off his horse at the livery. "I sure do miss California. I'd like to go back. Miss the trees mostly, I think," Charley said striding down the new boardwalk. "Made a few improvements around here I see," he remarked, as the two clopped down the new wooden sidewalk. Carson City had bloomed with newfound wealth, as the miners flocked to the new silver mines. The building was constant it seemed, as the streets branched out and filled with hopeful capitalism.

"Yep, don't get to this side of the mountains much," Jim said keeping up.

"I been driving on the plains for Holladay. It's much different from these mountains. Gets mighty hairy at times, what with the Injuns and such. Got some horrifying weather out there as well!" Charley remarked as he boldly strode into the still familiar Ormsby's Tavern. "The steak is as good as it gets here, not the most tender, but plenty of it to fill you up. Tatter's is good too. Snowshoe Thompson grows a lot of tatters I hear," Charley advised, seating himself at the end of the bar.

"Charley! Good to see you!" Big John cried out. "You gonna have dinner?"

"You bet, John, fix me up with a beer and a steak and potato, will ya? This here is my friend Sheriff James Hume, he wants dinner too," Charley spoke out, making himself at home.

"James Hume? It's an honor, Sheriff of Placerville, right? I've heard of you. It's a pleasure to meet you, sir. Would you like to see the menu?" John said hospitably.

"No, I'll just have the same as Charley here, that'll be fine," Hume said humbly.

"Thompson get out a tater crop this year?" Charley called out.

"Yeah, we're cooking some of his spud tonight," Big John replied with pride.

"That's fine! How's Hank Monk doing? Is he staying out of mischief?" Charley asked Hume, as he delighted in the cold libation John was setting down in front of him. "Ah thank you, John. Cheers," he said, quenching a deep and burning thirst. "Set me up another one, just like it, please," Charley said in a practiced tone. "Man, I was dry as burned toast. Just wait till you see that steak."

James, who still had a meeting to attend to, drank with much more reserve. "Same Ol' Hank I reckon'," he said scratching his head.

"Say, John, you got any of them pickled eggs handy. You ever tried these, Jim?" Charley asked.

"Yeah, sure," John replied, setting down a large glass jar on the bar.

"Can I get two of them pickled savories," Charley answered.

"You bet, Charley." John fished his fat hand into the great pickle jar and plopped two eggs onto a plate. "There you go."

"Thanks, John," Charley said, cranking the pepper mill over the treasures then digging in. "Have one, they're good."

James took hold of an egg with delight and sprinkled his with salt and bit into the well-sought-after nourishment.

"Sheriff! I didn't expect you'd be here so soon," a man just coming in to the establishment called out.

"Oh yes, I came in a bit earlier than expected and thought I would get something to eat first," Hume said modestly, swallowing a great mouthful of egg.

"My wife was hoping to have a supper for you, when you arrived tonight," the man reasoned.

"Is she a good cook?" Charley chimed in unceremoniously, chewing on an egg.

"Oh, this is my friend Charley Parkhurst, Otis Stemhorn," James said apologetically. He was trying to look dignified and realized he was still holding his pickled egg. Big John had since arrived with two steaming plates.

"Say, that does look mighty good, my wife is a pretty fair cook, . . . but that's a nice cut of beef, mind if I taste that?" Otis asked.

"Go right ahead, we can polish this off, then go to your house and have your wife's supper. I'm hungry enough to eat two dinners tonight," Sheriff Hume remarked. "Shove up a chair."

"Hey, speak of the devil and there he is!" Charley remarked shoveling potatoes in his mouth.

"Is that Ol' Parkie a sittin' there with a plate a grub? How the hell you doin', Parkie? Hank said sauntering up to the bar. He patted his friend on the back. "Hey there, Sheriff," he added, watching the two men devouring the food off the same plate. "Can't you afford your own plate, being Sheriff and all?" Hank said, laughing with callous jest. The gentleman seated next to Hume became flushed with embarrassment as he set down his fork.

"This here is, Hank Monk, don't pay his manners no mind, he talks that'a ways to every one," Charley reassured his new acquaintance, as he tightly grasped Hank's bear paw and gave it a shake.

"I hope you didn't eat none of them pickled hen pearls, make you fart like a Washoe zephyr," Hank chimed in. "Hey, John, I'll have a steak and potatoes, make mine bloody. A beer and some whiskey too, thanks."

"You want any pickled eggs?" John asked.

"Yeah, give me three of them pickled hen pearls too. I'm feelin' musical tonight," Hank cackled. "You here on official business Sheriff?"

"Yes, I'm doing a little investigation work in town for a few days," Hume said relishing the tasty spuds.

"What kind of pie do you have tonight?" Charley interrupted.

"I think Sally made pumpkin," John said as he poured Hank a shot of whiskey.

"Well I'll have a big hunk of that too, John," Charley ordered.

"Yeah, John, I want pie with a bowl of cream too. Thanks," Hank spoke up. "I am so hungry. I can't eat that shit at the stations. They got that stringy Mormon cattle Holladay buys. Ormsby's buys some beef from Thompson. I think he feeds his stock potatoes all winter. Least them cows eat good. Taste good too," Hank said with a laugh, as John set the dinner plate before the salivating Monk.

"Sally baked up some rolls special for you, Hank," John said in a whisper.

"Why, Sally, you are a dream come true!" the Jehu said, tipping his hat to the fat woman in the kitchen, who was peeking around the kitchen window. "My worst nightmare! But can she bake! You got to love her for that," he said under his breath. "My compliments darlin'," Hank said waving his fork. The fat woman giggled, placing her hand over her mouth and disappearing back to the realm of cookery. "My friend, it pays to compliment the chef, no matter how grotesque," Hank chuckled.

"Why, Hank, that is so ungentlemanly. Pass over some of those biscuits, you devil," Charley remarked.

"So what brings you back to this neck of the woods, Parkie?" Hank went on.

"Oh, I come to check up on a friend, Will Byrnes. He's in a bad way," Charley said sopping up gravy with a piece of a roll. "That Ol' Sally sure can bake some rolls," he added.

"Yeah, I heard about Ol' Byrnes. Too bad. Got one in the back they said," Monk offered, securing a few rolls for a later date.

"His wife, Marion, said a doctor in New York might save him. Thought I might arrange something for him," Charley related as he reeled in his pie.

"Hey, Charley, it was nice to see you. Are you going to be in town long?" Sheriff Hume said settling up his dinner bill.

"No, I'm headed out to Salt Lake City tomorrow. But I'd like to make some arrangements for Byrnes so I will be back soon," Charley stated, shaking Humes' hand.

"Whatever happened to your little dog, Hank?" the Sheriff asked.

"He was adopted by some kids at Cold Creek station, their little brother died. So I left him with them," Charley said a bit misty eyed. "Kids got kinda attached to him. Maybe I'll get another mutt sometime. Nice to have met you, Otis. See you again, Sheriff," Charley said blowing his nose on a handkerchief.

"See ya, Charley . . . Hank, I'll see you in California I reckon," James Hume said leaving with a fully stuffed gut, and a more than slightly tipsy associate.

"Sweet Jesus! Do you think my wife will be able to tell that I've been drinking? She simply does not allow any drinking!"

Hank and Charley had a good laugh at the hen pecked man as Hume smoothed his ruffled feathers on their departure.

"Hank have you ever thought about settling down. Maybe buying a ranch somewhere and making a home?" Charley drifted off.

"Well, no, not till you mentioned it. Driving is all I know. I feel at home in the mountains or on my coach. I'm looked up to. Why would I want to give that up? I like my route. Sure I bitch and moan, but you know me, Parkie, I'll never change," Hank said diving into his pie.

"Well, I've been thinking about it. I've just about had enough, I'm tired and getting worn out. I don't much care for the plains driving. There's not enough trees and too many Injuns. I'm thinking it might be nice to stay in one place for a while. I thought I might go back to the coast sometime. In California you still have lots of trees and the ocean and plenty of good farmland, a person might make a go of it there. Sweet Jesus, Hank, did you just fart?"

"Sorry, I warned you about them hen pearls!" Hand apologized. "So you're lookin' for the big ride, aren't ya?" Hank said, cutting right to the bone.

"Yes, I s'pose I am," Charley said with a sigh. "I got some money set aside for a ranch, but a big payload would certainly be helpful," Charley said, pushing the empty plates away.

"Maybe, if'n you don't get killed along the way. Is it worth risking your life out there?" Hank reminded

"I don't know. Maybe," Charley said stoically. "If I can save a friend's life, I don't know, Hank, why do you ask such questions!" Charley snapped. "Why don't you finish your pie!"

"Parkie, you're still as crabby as ever. I missed your sorry old face! . . . John, can I get another glass here? Parkie, I'm gonna buy you a drink!" Hank resolved.

"Well, it's about time!" Charley laughed.

"I maybe got some information that you'd be interested in as well," Monk said lowering his voice and looking around the tavern, to see if anyone dangerous might be listening. "I heared that there's gonna be a big shipment of silver out of here soon. They're gonna pay big for a driver with guts. Byrnes, is he well enough to ride as guard?"

"That man, crippled up as he is, could probably still out shoot any five men I know," Charley said pondering the worst case scenario. "Maybe," Charley said reluctantly.

Salt Lake City, Two Weeks Later

"Ben Holladay, sir?" Charley Parkhurst greeted the new King of the stagecoach, in his office at the Mormon City.

"Come in, sit down. I got your telegram, I've looked forward to meeting you again," Holladay replied in a cheerful manner. "Have a cigar, your reputation as a horseman precedes you," he added.

"Sir, I'm here to see you today on behalf of a good friend of mine. Also of your friend General Connor, sir. I am an experienced driver, as well you must know and I have a desire to transport a great lawmen to New York, to have surgery performed upon him. Without the operation he may well die. The man of whom I am speaking, William Byrnes, is a most worthy man to carry on any dangerous trip. He was a Sheriff, and a California Ranger and fought in the Paiute war in sixty," Charley rambled on.

"Do not have another thought about your friend's transport. General Connor has told me about Byrnes, and I can work out arrangements for you to accompany Byrnes and a shipment of gold and silver, all the way to New York if you like," Holladay said, shaking Charley's hand.

"Thank you, sir. I could never have hoped for so much," Charley said relieved. Later he stood in the center of Salt Lake City and lit the fat cigar that Ben Holladay had given him. Pulling the little Lucifer from the corduroy vest that Holladay had issued his all of his drivers; he struck the wooden match on the hitch rail and puffed on the expensive cigar. Adjusting the wide brimmed hat, also a Holladay issue, he walked back to the stage livery. Charley looked over the horses. Tomorrow he would head back to Virginia City and make arrangements for Will. As soon as the shipment was ready, they would head back East. In St. Joe, Missouri, they would cross the river, then take the train to New York. Charley would be in charge of both Byrnes and an important shipment of gold and silver.

Two weeks later, all was in readiness, as dawn's light cast long shadows on Carson City. Marion Byrnes had driven the family buckboard to the Express office and was trying hard to be brave and not cry. Will's daughter, Nellie, was holding tightly to her father's hand, eyes wet with emotion.

"Now you take good care of your Mama, you hear? I'll bring you back something from New York," Will spoke tenderly to the girl. "Don't you fret, Marion, I'll be back, right as rain, before you know it," he said, kissing his wife good-bye.

"It's time, Will," Charley said, hating to break up such a touching scene. Marion and some of the Express men helped Byrnes climb up the steps on the side of the coach. He sat in the seat behind Charley, until they were out of town.

"We got her fixed up so's you can stretch out down the center of the roof. The cases on the outside edges will protect you from the wind and rolling off.

"Why that looks right inviting. I don't mind if I try this arrangement out for myself," Will said, examining the roof bed. "Looks real comfortable."

"Be kinda like sleeping in a big cradle. I got an oil skinned canvas we'll lash down over the top of you if the weather gets bad," Charley explained. "See that tin case there? Got five hundred round of cap and balls, two Navies and six preloaded cylinders. In event of any trouble, that is."

"You expecting trouble, Charley?" Will asked, getting onto his bed and placing his hat over his face.

"I'm expecting anything, truthfully." Charley answered, as they headed out to the dreaded Carson sink. For the next few days, the scenery would be an awful, dust filled, hide drying, stretch. The air was so dry it caused your lips to crack and your nose to bleed. Charley carried some sponges, which he wetted down and placed in front of his nose and mouth and then tied his neckerchief around his face to hold it in place. They were headed Northeast to Salt Lake City. There were forty-six stations before the Mormon city, at an average of twelve miles apart, with names as picturesque as Fish Springs and Point Lookout. There were also some more questionable sounding places such as Dry Creek or Cape Horn or the ever popular No Name.

At Sulfur Springs, the gold-laden coach acquired a new passenger, a doctor, who was headed home to New York and the family practice. He became interested in traveling East with Byrnes, in order to see the wounded guard to his surgical appointment. The doctor was fascinated with the gunman; he had never met a man who had cheated death so many times.

When the coach arrived at Salt Lake City, there was a message from Ben Holladay for Charley. Parkhurst opened the fancy oak door to Ben's office and approached the cigar-puffing executive.

"Oh, Parkie, you made good time, you just get in?" Ben said looking up from his paperwork and glancing at his gold watch. He stood and extended his hand to the coachman.

"Yep, we had good horses and good weather so we made real fast time. I received a note you wished to speak with me?" Charley said, as he shook Ben's hand.

"Yes. How is Byrnes holding up?" Holladay asked, as he tapped the ash from his cigar.

"He's holding up very well. Better'n I thought, to tell you the truth." Charley smiled. "We picked up a good doctor and he's been dressing Will's wounds."

"I wanted to know if you and Byrnes were up to a little side trip for another gold chest. It's north at Fort Hall, little over two hundred miles, shouldn't take a week round trip. They had a big gold strike in Montana, I'll be putting in a new route up there before long, but for now I can't spare any of my regular coaches." Holladay paused to puff on his cigar. "Tell Byrnes his old pal General Connor is up there and will escort you back here. Well's Fargo will hold the first chest here, in their safe, until you get back, then you can take the two chests to New York together. If Byrnes is not up to it, he can rest here until you return," Holladay explained. Charley saw in his face that he was not asking, but issuing orders.

"I'll ask Will, sir, more than likely he'll agree to go. He's always been keen on adventure," Charley said as he rubbed his eye patch.

"Fine you can tell me his answer this evening then. I certainly do not want to keep you from your dinner any longer," Ben commented, as his attention began to return to his papers.

Charley was right. Will was not interested in seeing his driver going off after gold, into Indian country without him. Their new friend, Doc Scherer, found business in Salt Lake City to keep him occupied, in the form of a bad wagon wreck, complicated with black powder, until his friends returned.

Ben Holladay crammed the coach venturing North with as many passengers as he could. All were seasoned, rugged men, most who had fled the Civil War in search of gold.

Charley was happy to have Byrnes along; he was feeling quite well now. The doctor had redressed his wounds skillfully and gave him a good bottle of painkiller, laudanum, a mixture of opium and alcohol.

CHAPTER 48

Fort Hall

The six-up of dapple gray horses were walking slowly to the top of the grade; the Snake River below them shushed along hypnotically. The crescent moon glowed through the trees, as the stars came out in force throughout the cloudless sky.

Will had taken his painkillers about fifteen minutes earlier and was becoming much more comfortable on the rocking roof bed. Other passengers had opted for the roof as well and one had brought along his guitar.

"Do you mind if I play for a while?" the man asked the driver.

"No, you should have brought that out before. That would be nice. We will be there soon. I can see lights ahead," Charley said, pointing. Those that heard the driver cheered. As the man on the roof began to strum out a melody, much to Charley's suprise, Will began to sing. It somehow made the driver feel all mushy inside, so he urged the horses into a faster cadence as they crested the butte and headed down the slow grade to Fort Hall. Its effect revved the musician into a more spirited song, and soon Charley was singing along as well. He blew out a fairly melodic greeting on the bugle as they approached the adobe and log fort. Even the surrounding wolf population got into the act. As the music fell away and the coach rolled through the main gate, they were greeted by men eager for any news from anywhere, especially about the raging Civil War. Charley had only to tie off the horses lines and step off the coach; the soldiers took care of the rest.

"Kinda brisk out tonight, Will. You want me to get your other coat?" Charley said, helping his traveling companion off of the coach.

"Quit hovering over me like an Ol' mother hen Charley!" Will insisted, as he stepped from the coach wheel. "You can hand me my cane if you like," he added. It was really more of a well-padded crutch.

"Here ya go, Captain. Let me know if I can be of any further services," Charley said sarcastically.

"I'll rest on the bench until you conclude your business, securing your cargo and the like," Byrnes said with the facial punctuation of a man in pain.

"Well, let me at least help you up the steps," Charley nagged.

"Fine," Will sighed.

"You can rest inside, it's getting cold, it won't take long, and we'll get you set up in a real bed tonight. Tomorrow's Sunday, we can sleep in," Charley explained, as they entered the office.

"I'm Charley Parkhurst, expressman for Ben Holladay and Wells Fargo, here to sign for my cargo," Charley said with authority,

"Yes, sir, Mr. Parkhurst, we've been expectin' you," the clerk said with enthusiasm.

"You happen to have any coffee around?" Charley asked bluntly. "It's gettin' mighty cold out tonight."

"Of course. Lester get these gents a tin of coffee," the superintendent ordered. "My name is Leonard Croft, Mr. Holladay sent a pony boy with word you were coming," he added.

"You got a place around here run by an Eleanora Dumont?" Charley asked, as he set the mailbag on the counter.

"Yeah, I think so. Old whore does laundry and runs a card game, has kinda a mustache, soldiers call her Madame Mustache," the superintendent said.

"Your powers of description overwhelm me, sir." Will laughed, from his stool in the corner. A few of the soldiers in the office laughed as well.

"Runs a regular house, rents rooms, does laundry and has girls and a pie-ana player," a man sorting letters added.

"Splendid. I can hardly wait to sleep in a real bed," Will said drowsily.

"Come on, Captain, let's get you tucked in," Charley said. "How far is it?"

"'Bout four doors down, this side of the fort. Got a real nice place across the other side if you'd rather, brother in-law runs it," the man drawled.

"Thanks, I'll keep that in mind," Byrnes chuckled.

"Hey, tell the Captain that someone heard Injuns outside the fort. They was a whoopin' it up!" a small wiry young man said breathlessly.

"Don't worry, lad," Charley said, patting the boy on the shoulder. "It was only him, singin'," he said pointing to Byrnes. The boy looked greatly puzzled.

The fort had started to liven up. The familiar strains of *Turkey in the Straw* staggered out of a badly tuned piano and danced into the night air, along with it, laughter and the sound of drinking and carousing. When the two entered an establishment, they spotted a crowd of people around the far table, where a dark-haired woman was holding court with a deck of cards.

"Jack, get this man a drink on the house," Eleanora commanded. Jack, the bartender, set down a glass of milk in front of the loser. "Any man fool enough to lose all of his money to a woman should stick to drinking milk," she pronounced, to gales of laughter from the crowd. The man drank the milk, which got more laughs. He then stood and meekly left the house.

"Well, Eleanora, I see you haven't changed a bit," Will called out, as they approached the table.

"Look what fortune has brought through my door, what a pleasant suprise. Charley, It's a pleasure to see you again. Can this possibly be William Byrnes?" she said, holding out her hand. Charley could see the years had worn heavy on her once lovely face. She did indeed sport a thin black mustache, which Charley pretended not to notice as he kissed Eleanoras' hand.

"Yes, it's truly me, what's left of me, anyways," Will said taking a turn on the lady's hand. "We've come to spend the night, if you've room for us and celebrate Ol' Parkie here's, birthday," he added.

Charley sent Will a shocked and hostile glance, as Will let out a good-natured laugh. "Charley's so shy, he probably never would have told ya. Ain't that right Parkie?" Will laughed, visibly pleased with himself.

"No, Ma'am, that's a fact, I probably wouldn't have said a thing. Thanks a lot, Will!" Charley chastised.

"Really? Is today your birthday, Charley?" Eleanora said with real concern.

"Well of course it is, ain't it, Charley?" Will said still laughing.

"Yes, I suppose it is at that," Charley said, giving in to Will's prank with a shrug.

"We'll make sure this is a real special night for you then. Martha, I want you to look after Mr. Parkhurst's every need now, you understand?" Eleanora said winking at the young eager girl, who couldn't have been more than thirteen.

"By the way, happy birthday Charley!" Will said, with tears of laughter welling up in his eyes.

Young Martha Jane Cannary meanwhile, had gone and had a few words with the piano player and soon the sounds of "For He's a Jolly Good Fellow" came crashing out from across the room. It sent Will into another fit of laughter.

"You got a wicked sense of humor . . . you know that?" Charley grumbled to his comrade.

"You a stagecoach driver, Charley?" Martha asked her new john. "That's a beautiful whip."

"Oh yes. I am. I forgot I was still carrying this. I guess I'm just used to having it in my hand, is all. Maybe you could help us settle in. I know my friend here needs a place to lay down awhile, before he gets into any more mischief."

"Why sure, I'll get you fellas all set up, then you can relax," Martha replied.

"If you don't mind, Charley, I would like a private room, you snore something awful," Will said smiling again.

"Fine with me," Charley said rolling his eyes.

"May I carry your whip for you, Charley?" Martha said eyeing the piece.

"I guess, just be careful with it though," Charley said tentatively.

"Look at all the gold rings on the handle!" Martha cooed.

"I think she's sweet on you, birthday boy," Will teased.

"Thanks a lot Will," Charley said with disgust. "And besides, she looks like she's about thirteen."

"I'm sorry, Parkie, I thought you'd be happy," Will said, with an impish grin, his eyes clouded with opiates. He held onto Charley's shoulder, as they slowly climbed up the stairs to the rooms.

"You can have this room, and, Charley, you can have this one. There's even a bathtub in there." Martha pointed out. "You want a bath, Charley?"

"Yes, you need a bath Charley," Will called out from the next room, imitating the girls drawl. He lowered himself on the hand-hewn bed. "You smell a bit horsy!" he added, laughing in glee.

"Well, I do s'pose I could do with one. You got lots of bath soaps, that makes bubbles?" Charley inquired.

"Why, lands yes! Lots," the girl giggled. "I'll get some hot water up here."

"Lovely," Charley sighed, as he sauntered back to Will's room. "You gonna be all right, Will? Is there anything I can get you?"

"No, thank you very kindly, I think I'll just lay here nice and still for awhile. Maybe I'll get something to eat later," Will said, drowsily.

"I'll order you up some supper. You can eat in your room if you like," Charley said, looking down at his friend.

"That sounds fine, Charley, you do that," he said, drifting off to sleep.

Soon Martha was back, making preparations for Charley's bath. Charley wandered back to the bar, and bought a small flask of brandy and a five-cent cigar.

"Are you finding everything to your liking, Charley?" Eleanora asked, as she rolled her cigarette.

"Why yes, I am. How nice it is to see you again," Charley said, striking a Lucifer for the lady.

"Byrnes looks pretty bad." Eleanora Dumont said softly.

"Yes, Ma'am, he's been shot up pretty bad this time, I'm afraid. We're headed from here to the end of the line in Atchison, then up to New York. He's going to have surgery there," Charley explained.

"You are a good friend, Charley." Eleanora smiled, blowing out smoke in a practiced fashion.

"Oh, he's already taken some medicine for the pain. He ain't suppose to drink whiskey, just tell him the doctor said so," Charley confided. "He can have some beer, but just a little."

"Has he eaten anything today?" the Madame inquired.

"Not much. Anything we can get him to eat is good. He's got to keep up his strength or they might not be able to operate," Charley said sadly. "I shouldn't have let him come up here!"

"I'll look after him myself. Now don't you worry, go on and enjoy yourself. Happy birthday, Charley," she said, kissing him softly on the lips.

"Thank you, Eleanora," Charley said, with a blush.

"I got your bathtub all filled up, Charley," Martha Jane said, barging in.

"Well, I guess I'm gonna take a bath now," Charley said, bidding Eleanora fair well.

"You want me to scrub your back?" Martha said, tagging after the teamster.

"No that won't be necessary," Charley said politely. The girl followed along anyway, determined to look after her charge. She was ever so disappointed when Charley closed the door and shut the girl out of the room, to luxuriate in the hot tub privately. Charley striped off the many layers of clothes concealing her womanly figure and draped them over the end of the bed, then set her loaded revolver on the small stand next to the tub, in case of unwanted intruders. The hot water felt delicious on her bare skin. It would be nice to just sleep in there, she thought, until the water got cold, that is. It felt good to wash the grime out of her hair, which had gotten quite long. It was now just over her shoulders, the longest it had been since she was a child. It was becoming fashionable for men out on the frontier to wear their hair that way; besides, it was useful to keep your ears from freezing in the winter. Charley had become very secure in her masculine disguise. Most of the time she forgot that she was not a man. Now, in her nakedness she felt quite vulnerable. This was the reason for the revolver.

Charley was scrunched up and had her head submerged in the water, rinsing the soap from her hair, and didn't hear Martha Jane knocking softly. When she surfaced, she was shocked to see the girl standing in front of the tub with an armload of towels.

"I forgot to bring you some towels," Martha said smiling.

Charley was in a near panic as she scrunched in the water swishing the bubbles from her hair toward her chest.

"What the hell? Girl, you scared me to death!" Charley sputtered.

"You want me to scrub your back?" Martha asked sweetly.

"Well, I guess you're in here, you might as well have a go, but then you leave, all right?" Charley said, softening. The girl seemed not to notice anything unusual. Charley surrendered his back to the girl and enjoyed the massage immensely.

"You have such big shoulders, Charley, you must be very strong." Martha Jane gushed.

"I reckon I am pretty strong at that," Charley chuckled.

"I'll run and get another bucket of hot water to rinse your hair good if you want," Martha offered.

"Sure, you go and do that," Charley said enthusiastically. When the girl left, Charley quickly got out of the tub and wrapped herself in towels, then proceeded to get dressed before the girl returned. "Man, that was too close," Charley sighed, stuffing a pair of socks in the crotch of her pants, just in case the girl made a pass. While wringing his hair into the tub, the girl reappeared with the pail of water.

"Oh, you got out," she said rather disappointed.

"Yeah, I was a getting cold. Here, pour that over my head like this," Charley said, draping the towel over his shoulders and hanging his head over the tub. "Wow, that wasn't too warm," he added.

The girl handed Charley a fresh towel.

"Thanks, gal," Charley smiled, as he wrapped his dripping hair in the dry cloth. He looked at the young, rough looking girl, her long, dirty, brown hair hanging down around her face. Martha's dress was worn and stained from living in the rough world of men. "How old are you?" the teamster asked bluntly.

"I'm sixteen," Martha lied.

"I'm sorry but ain't you awfully young to be working in a place like this," Charley said feeling a lecture coming on.

"Well, I can't do anything about my age," she said innocently. It made Charley laugh out loud.

"I'm just trying to tell you that you could do a lot of things with your life. That you're young and you should not waste it in a place like this.

"But if I didn' t work here I wouldn't have met you. You're a friend of the Madame. Is she a bad person?" Martha asked naively.

Charley had to admit that the girl had a point. It made him feel like a hypocrite.

"I just want to say that a woman is capable of living a free life, in a free world out here. I've known incredible women that have made their fortunes in business. Don't feel locked into this futile job. You'll catch some foul disease, or worse, get beat up and murdered. Though, I think I'd rather get beat up or murdered as opposed to a slow death from some disease," Charley said, pouring himself a stiff drink. He noticed the girl staring at his missing eye. "I lost that a few years back."

"Does it hurt much?" Martha said, trying to change the subject. "How did it happen? In a fight?" the girl rambled.

"No, it don't hurt. I got it kicked out by a rank horse. That was bad," Charley said, then realized the subject had been refocused. Janey reminded her so much of herself, at the last of her girlhood. She longed to reveal the truth, but feared betrayal. Charley was sure she couldn't keep a secret.

"Would you show me how to crack that whip?" Martha asked, changing the subject again.

Charley picked up the lash proudly and rolled the handle around in his palm gracefully, at the same time sending the lash into rolls, until it was fully extended. He then flipped it around the room looking for a target; he spotted a fly buzzing about the wall. Charley flicked the whip so deftly that the fly was instantly incapacitated. Martha was quite impressed.

"Maybe tomorrow, after breakfast, I'll show you a few things," Charley promised. "Tonight I'm mighty tired, Martha," Charley said, taking the girl's face in his hands and then kissing her on the forehead. "Good night, sweet pea," Charley said, gently pushing the girl out the door. He stretched out on the bed and took in the strange new atmosphere. The noise from the bar and card room and the noises coming from the "cribs," the popular name for the tiny rooms the whores used to perform their labors, came right through the thin fabric walls. He heard someone enter Will's room and the sound of cutlery and plates being set down; it was comforting. Charley thought about little Martha Jane and the path her life might lead. Charley felt weary, this ride wasn't even half over.

The next morning about eight o'clock, Charley was startled by a small figure laying on the bed beside him. Charley turned and faced the sleepy young girl lying there.

"Wake up, Charley, you said you'd teach me to crack your whip." The girl was still intoxicated from the night's carrying on. After Charley retired, Martha had found a few soldiers in the bar, out for a good time.

"Martha, what are you doing here?" Charley said in a fog.

"I got bumped from my room, so I just slept here, I came in the window. Please don't tell Eleanora, she thought that I was going to sleep here and gave up my room to Linda for the night," Martha explained.

"God, I'm sorry, girl. I had no idea." Charley felt instantly guilty and confused at once. "You get some sleep, I'll buy you a nice lunch, Charley said rolling out of bed and kissing the child on the side of the head. Charley instinctively looked in on Will, next door. He was snoring away peacefully. The dishes showed that he had eaten a little. Charley walked downstairs to the bar, in search of a cup of coffee and found what looked like a battlefield. Passed out soldiers and fur traders littered the chairs and floor like casualties of war. The bartender was passed out cold, at the end of the rough pine bar. Charley made himself at home amongst the sleeping men, poking around the bar and searching in the crude kitchen for some coffee. He spotted the last remaining relatively clean pan and a solitary egg, left in a wire basket, hanging from a crude pine beam. The stove in the center of the room still had a glow in its belly, so Charley placed the pan on the stove and cracked the egg into the pan. He also spotted a crust of bread and set that on the stove. He took some joy in cooking his own breakfast somehow and sat at the end of the bar enjoying the fruits of his labor listening to the chorus of snoring personnel and enjoying the relative peace.

After Charley finished, he walked out to the front porch and sat on a bench. He reached for a cigar and struck a match on the underside of the bench.

"Did you have a nice birthday?" A familiar voice said softly from the doorway.

"Yes, I s'pose so," Charley said, exhaling a puff of smoke, then turning to look at Will, who was coming over to share the bench. "You sleep all right?"

"Fine. I feel pretty good." Will responded. "Kinda peaceful out here this morning," he said, lighting his own cigar.

"Yeah, everyone'll be sleeping it off from last night, for a while yet." Charley laughed. The two sat quietly. They both noticed an officer coming out of the fort headquarters; he was walking toward them.

"That you, Byrnes?" the voice asked with authority.

"Yep, it's me all right. Is it General Connor now?" Byrnes replied.

"Yes, it is. Nice to see you again, you're looking pretty well, all things considered. Looks like it will be a good day," he stated.

"Every day that I get up and I ain't dead is a good day, sir. It's nice to see you too," Will said struggling to rise to his feet and extending his hand to his old comrade.

"Charley," Connor said. "I've been sent to escort you back to Salt Lake City and through to Fort Bridger."

"That's fine," Charley said with approval.

"We'll leave at dawn tomorrow," Connor said confidently.

"Say, General, do you know where to get a good breakfast in this fort?" Will interrupted.

"Yes, I'm headed that way myself. I'd be honored if you'd join me," Connor said.

The threesome walked to the fort's mess hall. It lived up to its title—mess. The cook was busy frying up bacon and making large quantities of coffee. He was sweating profusely and sported a throbbing black eye, a trophy from the previous nights' revelries. When he spotted the General, he did his best to look alive, as the three sat at the officer's table.

"Good morning, sir, will you be wanting any coffee sir?" The cook said respectfully.

"Yes we all want coffee I think, get them whatever they want. I'll have eggs and bacon with flapjacks," General Connor ordered.

"Yes, sir, right away!" The cook saluted.

"That sounds fine," Charley agreed.

"I'll have that as well." Byrnes nodded. "You get good service when you eat with the General here." Will smiled.

Connor smiled back. "Well, it does have its advantages," he said smugly.

When they had finished, they strolled back outside.

"I feel so full I could just curl up and go back to bed," Charley said with a yawn and a stomach that felt like it would burst.

"I'll bet you do, I spotted little Martha Jane still curled up in your bed when I got up," Will snickered.

"Shit, I forgot!" Charley hissed, as the two men laughed. At that moment Martha appeared at the front of the saloon.

"There you are, Charley," Martha called. The other men began laughing anew. "You said you'd teach me how to handle your whip after breakfast, remember?" she said, running up to the coachman and latching on to his arm.

"Yeah, I guess I did. General Connor this is Miss Martha Jane Cannary. Come on girl," Charley said, turning again toward the mess. "See you fellows later, I reckon," Charley said, like a hen pecked husband. The two comrades walked back to the saloon laughing, and became friends again.

"Feel up to a few rounds of poker, General?" Will said, pulling a pack of cards from his pocket.

"I might be persuaded," the General replied, pulling his own new pack of cards from his vest pocket.

"I see you've kept up your playing skills," Byrnes commented.

"I picked up this pack of cards when I found out I would be traveling with you," the General said, taking the pristine cards from the pack. Byrnes just smiled, not sure if that had been meant as an insult or a compliment.

"Back again so soon?" the cook smiled at Charley.

"Yes. Set this girl up with some eggs and ham," Charley smiled back. "I'll just have some more coffee."

"Right away, sir." the cook responded.

"Ain't you gonna eat, Charley?" Martha asked.

"Girl, I could already just bust," Charley said belching. He just wanted to go back to sleep.

"After I eat I want to show you my horse, Pete," Martha said. "You can show me how to use your whip back at the stable," she said with enthusiasm.

"So you got a horse, that's real nice," Charley said, looking at his new friend. "I'd like to see him."

"You will," Martha Jane said, plying her face with scrambled eggs.

After two stacks of pancakes and a hefty slab of ham, the two finally left the mess.

"Come on," she said, tugging his arm. They walked to the large adobe barn that housed all the barracks horses, where it was a full-time job just cleaning up manure. There was a mountain of it piled on a huge wagon with a dump bed, that they used to transport it out of the fort. The soldiers used wheelbarrows and a ramp to pile it on, it was the lowest job going.

"Here's Pete!" she said, with adoration reflecting off the black and white mustang. He was compact, but quite powerfully built, with an attitude to match.

"Why, he's a real handsome little devil!" Charley said with genuine authority.

"He's real fun to ride. Bucks a little though. You gotta watch him or he'll try to throw you, that's why I was able to buy him cheap. He threw the last owner pretty good, they was happy to get rid of him," Martha Jane said, with pride.

"Well, you just be real careful of him. What kind of a bit do you use on him?" Charley said with interest.

"Over here is my saddle and bridle," Martha said. "Many of the native women who live up here ride in real fancy beaded saddles. They ride astride like men, so I decided to ride that a ways too. Nobody is shocked out in these parts. Hell, they's just happy to see any woman," Martha said frankly.

"Hmm, that's funny to me somehow." Charley smiled.

"You're leavin' tomorrow, aren't you?" Martha said sadly.

"Yes, I'm going to New York. Then I'm headed back to California. I'm hoping to buy a ranch and stay in one place for a change. It seems my whole life has been taken up going from place to place and never staying for more than a few days anywhere. I'm not complaining though. It has been a great life, full of adventures and exciting times. I've lived my life on my own terms . . . But I'm getting tired, and the thought of a regular bed, in one quiet house, is starting to sound real good. I doubt I'll be back in this neck of the woods again . . . That's a real fine bridle you got," Charley said with admiration, changing the subject. "How long have you been riding?" Charley asked.

"About two years, I guess. I've had Pete for about two months. You want me to saddle him up and show you?" she said buckling the halter around his head.

"Sure, bring him out here so as I can have a look at him, then you can show me what he can do," Charley said, encouraging his newest apprentice.

The girl proudly trotted him out of the stall and then tied him to the ring on the stall wall. She immediately set about fussing over him, brushing his back off, then inspecting his feet.

"He's real good about his feet," Martha said proudly, as she placed the saddle on the silky black and white horse. "An old Indian man helped me start off. He knows lots about talking to horses and the like. He made the bridle for me, kind of a present I reckon," she said, slipping the bit into the horse's mouth. "I'll take him out here," Martha said, leading her steed out of the barn to the pens behind the manure wagon.

"That's good," Charley said, admiring the young woman at work with her prized possession. She was a very talented rider, and the small horse responded nimbly to her commands.

"He's fun to ride. Do you want to ride him Charley?" Martha Jane said laughing, as she glided to a halt after setting the small horse through his lessons.

"Sure, Janey, I'll give him a go!" Charley laughed back. The girl swung off the pinto's back and handed Charley the reins. The man swung gracefully into the saddle and started the animal off. Pete cantered around proudly as Charley took him for a lap around the fort. He waved to the General and Will, who were sitting on the porch playing cards, as he galloped up to Eleanoras' house.

"Hello, boys," Charley said tipping his hat.

"Shit, Parkie's got a horse!" Will laughed.

"Yes, and I've got a pair of queens!" the General said, laying down his cards.

"Shit!" Will called out again.

Charley jumped off the horse and tied it to the rail, then trotted past the card players and went to his room to retrieve his whip, so as to fulfill the promise to the girl. He soon reappeared whip in hand.

"Ol' Charley's got himself a girlfriend!" Will teased, as he shuffled the deck. Charley shot back a leering glance for good measure, then tried to reassure the pinto horse that the whip would do him no harm. The pony snorted at the devise, but obediently allowed the horsemen to mount.

"See you fellas later," Charley said, galloping back to Martha Jane.

"You got yourself a fine horse here, take good care of him, and he'll be a good friend. I brought my whip," Charley said to the smiling girl, as he slid off the small horse and handed her the reins. The girl took her horse from the expert and set about unsaddling and treating him to a measure of grain. The horse dove into his feedbag with gusto. The two then strolled back where the whip would not bother any of the livestock. Charley set the whip into poetic motion and showed the young woman the finer points of the craft. He then handed the scepter over to the novice and conducted class. Martha questioned the man about the art of driving four and six horses, and Charley delighted in the interest she showed. In short the two had a splendid time together.

"Do you know how to shoot a gun, Martha?" Charley asked at the end of the whip lesson.

"Well, not that I could hit anything, mind you, but I have fired a gun," she replied coyly. "I bet you're a good shot though," Martha said with a bright smile.

"Well, I've had a few good teachers in my day. I even met Samuel Colt himself once. Then I got this here Navy Colt I always carry. Got me out of a few close calls I'm here to tell you," Charley bragged.

"My word. Can I hold it?" Martha begged.

311 Tales of the Express 311

"Yeah, just be careful. It's loaded. I always keep it loaded. What's the point of having it on you if it's not ready to go?" Charley reasoned. "You want a shooting lesson, girl?" he asked.

"Sure! May I?" Martha gushed.

"Well, I suppose. But not here. I'll have to ask the General where we can shoot. I don't want to cause a problem, Come on, girl," Charley ordered, retrieving the firearm.

"This is so exciting!" the young woman cheered to herself, following the stage driver.

"Hey, fellas!" Charley said to his friends. "Who's winning?" It was quite obvious the General had been quite successful, but Charley wanted to rub it in nonetheless. "I was wanting to show young Martha here the finer points of handling a gun, but I wanted to get the General's permission first," Charley explained.

"Shooting practice. That might not be a bad idea. What do you think Byrnes? We can wager on other skills for a diversion," the General said, bored with gambling on cards. "We can shoot outside the fort, I'll have targets set up. Fifty feet with Navy Colts, what do you say, Byrnes?"

"You're on, General. A dollar a shot! What do you say?" Will responded.

"Fine!" the General said with glee, as the two shook hands.

"Martha, you're going to get a fine lesson today! I'm sure of it!" Charley said, relishing the color in Will's cheeks.

"I'll be in need of my medications. Charley, shall we retire to my room momentarily, sir?" Will said, giving strong facial gestures to his keeper.

"Yes, I believe it is time for your medicine," Charley responded, helping his friend from his chair and back up the stairs.

"You get two spoonfuls, that's all. Now you got to win your money back from the General, remember?" Charley smiled. Will smiled back and sucked the laudanum off the spoon,

"I've got some targets ready Charley," Martha said to her hero, as she caught up with them coming down the stairs.

"Martha, you're a gem. Gentlemen, shall we?" Charley said standing and motioning to the door and the young woman with the target sacks. "Martha may I please?" Charley said taking the load from the girl.

"I got the flour and the bowl in one of these sacks if we need to make more targets. So don't break it," the young woman scolded.

"Yes, ma'am. Charley said, taking care not to knock the rings off the sack. The troops soon set off, outside the fort for a little practice shooting and a little wagering on the side. William Byrnes, aside from his afflictions and intoxicated state, went on to win back every penny he had lost at cards and then some, much to the General's chagrin. As for Charley and Martha Jane, they had themselves a grand time shooting and enjoying each other's company.

After the shooting, the company had worked themselves into a new hunger and retired back at the mess. Charley had realized that he had a new friend attached to his arm

"Well, Janey, it's been nice shooting and riding with you and all but now I think I better go and grease my wheels and make sure the coach is ready to roll," Charley said, trying to rid himself of this young, amorous girl.

"I'd be happy to help you," she shot back.

"No, now I don't reckon I need any help," Charley reasoned. "I'll say good-bye before I leave in the morning," he explained.

"Oh . . . I s'pose so," Janey sighed.

"What does a young gal like you know about greasing wheels anyway?" Charley asked.

"Well, I've always wanted to learn!" Janey laughed.

"You have, have you?" Charley said with a smile.

"Yes!" Martha Jane said, pleading with her face.

"Well, . . . I guess it don't hurt none if you just watch. Maybe you can be of some help after all," Charley reconsidered. Will and the General chuckled together at the pair, each for different reasons however.

Later that evening in the parlor, Charley settled up his bill in newly minted California gold coin. He gave Eleanora an extra gold piece for taking such good care of Will; she looked as though she could use it. Times were getting hard for the independent woman; she seemed to be harboring a deepening sadness.

"I reckon we'll be leavin real early tommorra, I gotta get my beauty sleep," Charley said, tipping his hat to the Madame. Martha Jane was right there like a faithful dog. "Good night now, Martha Jane, oh, this here's for you," he said, pressing a gold coin into the girl's hand. Thank you for everything. Good night," Charley said with finality. The girl looked in her hand and was shocked to see a golden eagle worth twenty dollars.

"Thank you, Charley!" she said, throwing a grateful hug around the teamsters neck.

"Thank you, Janey," Charley said, pulling the girl off his chest. "I gotta get a good night's sleep now, I'll see you in the morning maybe."

"Oh, I'll be up to see you off!" Martha promised.

Charley retired to his room after looking in on Will, who was exhausted and looked half-dead.

"I shouldn't have let you go out shootin," Charley mumbled over the sleeping man.

"I had to win back my surgery money," Will said quietly, with his eyes shut.

"You old fool!" Charley sighed. He was ten years younger than himself, but looked ten years older. It reminded him of the urgency of their mission.

"Don't worry, Charley, I'll look in on him later, you get some rest," Eleanora spoke.

"Thank you, Ella, it's been nice to see you again," he said, kissing her on the cheek.

Charley wasted no time in getting to sleep, for the next day's driving would be difficult. The next morning, Martha Jane was right underfoot like a faithful dog.

"Well, good-bye, Charley," Janey said, shaking her mentors hand. "Don't suppose I'll ever forget you."

"Take good care now Janey and take care of Ol' Pete too. He's a good one," Charley said, climbing up to the driver's box. "You ready, Will?"

"Yeah, go ahead now," Will replied, getting comfortable.

"Bye, Janey." Charley smiled kissing at the horses. "Let's go now, gid' up." The horses responded in kind and set off in a smart fashion. The General and his troops trotted valiantly in the fore.

"You haven't lost your touch with a gun, Will," Charley said, loosening his grip on the leather and letting it slide through his fingers. The horses were nicely stretched out and moving together in a rhythmic, loose trot. "I hope we don't have to impose on you to display your talents again. I don't know what to expect from the natives ahead. I hope they just let us pass without notice, but you never can tell," Charley rambled.

"Did you have a good time with the girl?" Will asked like a schoolboy.

"Oh, Janey? Yes, she's a great kisser!" Charley shot back with a wink and the last laugh. Will threw his head back and laughed with carefree abandon.

CHAPTER 49

Back at Salt Lake City, they picked up a load of mail, and Doc and several others headed East. The soldiers were to escort the coach to Fort Bridger, in Wyoming territory; it would most likely take three days. It was eleven station east of Salt Lake City and still over one thousand miles from Atchison, where they would take the train to New York.

Will was holding up rather well, Charley thought. There were times when he forgot he was even injured at all, which was amazing, due to the degree of danger his wounds presented.

"I told you not to let him have any alcohol, yet this fell out of his pocket," Dr. Scherer admonished, holding up a small bottle of whiskey.

"Well, I don't know where the hell he got that!" Charley rebuffed. "Besides, I'm not the man's wet nurse!" the driver fired back.

"Well, if you don't look after him, your friend could die," the doctor lectured.

Charley reflected at the idea of seeing the East and all of its progress, since he had taken on his new life in the West. It would be the last time he ever saw it, retiring on the Pacific coast as he planned.

The driver had confidence in the U.S. Army's protection and took time to enjoy the ride like never before. Taking pleasure in the beauty of the rolling plains and the interesting natural architecture of places like Hanging Rock and Echo Canon or Needle Rock even Quaking Aspen Springs. The driver wished he was an artist and could paint these sites on canvas, to preserve them for his retirement memories.

Fort Bridger was a welcome sight as they made their arrival. Charley took out the worn bugle and played their arrival tune, aided by the Army band, who had come out to meet them. It was a pleasure to have some accompaniment. The gates were thrown open, as the dusty party entered the fort.

"Hope you had a pleasant trip, General, sir?" the Major saluted.

"Yes, no problems, Major," he saluted back. "My men could probably use a good meal and some liquid refreshment," he added.

"At once, sir!" the Major snapped back, then departed, issuing orders for the General's convenience.

The troops would be bedded down for the night, then leave early in the morning. It was early evening and dinner was exceptional. There was antelope and bison, also elk and quail, the plains menu was at least bountiful, at the most, succulent and varied. They all stuffed themselves, even Will.

"We'll be heading back for Salt Lake in the morning. I hope you have a safe trip to New York. Dr. Scherer, it was a pleasure to make your acquaintance. Hope every thing goes right for you Byrnes. You're still a crack shot and good sport," General Connor said leaving the table. "I got to get a night's rest. I'm all in. Good night, Parkie." The General smiled.

"Oh, I'm sure that everything's just gonna work out fine, General." Will smiled at his friend as he lit his cigar.

There would be at least eighty-six more stops until Will, Charley, and Doc boarded the train for New York. Charley wanted to average five stations a day; they were roughly fifteen miles apart. That was generally seventy-five miles a day, considering of course, the weather and the condition of the horses. It would mean ten hours a day in the driver's box. It was nothing new to the seasoned teamster and worth it, he kept reminding himself. Byrnes could catch up on needed rest on the train.

The stage road followed the path of a most beautiful river called the Platte. Charley could not help but notice the beautiful indigenous people who gathered there. The women were lovely, but the men on the bluff and hillocks looked fierce and dangerous. The coach kept a very brisk pace and all were on alert at the crossings, especially Will, but no incident ever occurred on their journey East. They made the trip in record time.

The trio soon boarded the famous mail train, the Hannibal and St. Joseph R. R. The railroad received its glory by having the forethought to put a mail car on the line to help expedite the Pony Express. The innovation caused other railroads to adopt the same idea, thus expediting the U. S. Mail service.

Charley was happy to be traveling in the company of Dr. Scherer. At last the pressure was off, the silver and gold were safely locked away in the mail car, and Charley could enjoy the rest of the trip; for once he didn't have to drive, so he relaxed. Unfortunately, the dining car had yet to be invented, so the trio had to do without. They did at least have sleeping accommodations. Which consisted of a bed, that had a bed hung above you or below you, depending upon if you had an upper berth or a lower. It had a curtain for privacy and if you were lucky, a place to store your luggage. The end of the train car was a lavatory, consisting of two sinks with running water that was pumped from tanks and an in-train outhouse. It was a marvel of travel. Charley just shook his head as he looked in the mirror and saw how rough and worn he looked.

"What will they think of next!" he sighed.

"A dining car would be my request, I'm so hungry," Doc grumbled, as he splashed in the sink.

The country was still in the midst of its greatest tragedy, the fight of American against American, the Civil War. All around them now were the effects of that conflict, men returning home a shadow of their former selves. Throughout the train, sat soldiers with various limbs missing and horrible wounds, all with the same miserable look on their faces. Charley took stock of himself and reasoned he had some damaged parts, but thanked God, he was doing fairly well.

"At this stop, instead of trying in vain to get something to eat, let's put our time to good use and wire the next stop ahead; to have some food ready to take with us," Doc suggested.

"That's a right good idea," Charley pondered. "You go and do that, and I'll try and get us some coffee!" Charley said, ready to leap off the vestibule as the train slowed, upon arrival to the station. "Order me and Byrnes a steak and potato dinner each," Charley said, waiting for the right moment to spring into action.

"Right!" Doc said, ready to leap from the train himself.

The train let off a great puff of steam and blew her whistle, as she chugged into the station. The passengers, many half-starved, took off in search of the station's closest food outlet. It appeared on the end of the station landing, in the form of a long bar that offered coffee and breads, and very little else. It was a market whose time would soon come. But until then, the traveler must think ahead and be prepared to suffer, or not.

"Well, I got us some coffee and some bread. Were you able to wire ahead for some dinner? Charley said, out of breath as he climbed aboard the slowly moving train.

"Yes, I ordered three dinners. I'm not going to guarantee anything, however," Dr. Scherer confided. "I ordered some chicken 'cause I thought it would be easier to eat without any silverware."

"That's good thinkin'. I hadn't thought of that. Ain't got any plates neither!" Charley reasoned. "Got this here newspaper though."

"How much time do they allow between stops?" Will asked.

"No more than about ten minutes," Doc estimated.

The trio retired to their bunks to read the paper and drink their coffee as the train left the station.

An hour later, when the train pulled into the next stop, the two traveling companions took off like a shot as the train began to slow. They quickly ran to the establishment the stationmaster had contacted, to collect the food. The hungry men were relieved to find three plates of food waiting. Charley quickly paid the man for the food, as the Doc unceremoniously started dumping the chicken on the newsprint wrapping it and tossing it into a pillowcase.

"Got any wine in a bottle?" Charley inquired.

"Yeah," the waiter responded.

"Get me three bottles, any kind," Charley said hastily putting more coin on the bar.

"We got to get back!" Doc scolded. "We'll miss the train.

"No we won't. Will'll hold it," Charley said grabbing the bottles. "Let's go!" The pair sprinted back to the restless train.

"Jeez, this smells good!" Doc remarked as they ran along.

"Thank God you're back, I thought I was going to have to lay on the tracks!" Will said, when he spotted the two with the booty. "Sure smell's good!" he added, as the three climbed aboard the locomotive.

"Let's eat in the berths, where it's more private," Doc advised. The trio picnicked on their beds, picking at the succulent birds and drinking wine, as the train rocked along towards its next destination.

"That sure was a good idear," Charley reflected with a hearty burp.

"My compliments to the chef," Will added.

"If we had some plates and some cutlery we could order some steaks. Let's see what we can get at the next stop," Doc advised.

"If the train people knew what was good for them, they'd serve dinners on the train. Make lots of money too," Charley said.

The trio finally reached New York City.

At the luggage car, Charley signed over the treasure boxes to some armed bank guards, who had been waiting at the station and was now free of the obligations to Ben Holladay and Wells Fargo, at least until it was time to return home to California.

New York was such a very busy place, crammed full of people who all seemed in a great hurry to be somewhere else.

"My father's cab should be along, I'd be happy to take you to my house or wherever you'd like?" Dr. Scherer offered.

"Well, that is right kind of you, Doc. What do you say, Will?" Charley mused.

"I think we should go and check in with my surgeon and get this operation over with," Will said quietly. Get a hold of Marion's pa."

"You can drop us off at this address," Charley said producing a card from his pocket.

"Yes of course," Dr. Scherer fished for his own card and scribbled on it with a pencil. "If you have any problems look me up. If I am not at home, I will most likely be at this hospital," he said, flipping the card over.

The three men soon climbed into an elegant hard-topped carriage, finely upholstered with rich, soft leather, complete with glass windows with silk curtains.

"Nice cab, Doc!" Charley remarked to his friend as they rolled through the bustling city. They arrived at an impressive looking brick building and the carriage driver called out to them.

"Don't forget, if you need me and I'm not at home, you will probably find me at this address." Doc said, as Byrnes and Parkhurst climbed from his family vehicle. The two trudged up the steps, with Charley carrying the luggage; he then set them down in the corner, once inside foyer. Charley adjusted his hat, as he approached the reception nurse's desk, while Byrnes rested on an uncomfortable chair.

"Dr. Levinson has gone to Georgia," the nurse informed Charley.

"But we've come all this way. We had an appointment!" Charley said in amazement.

"Well, I'm sorry, he left yesterday, he won't be back for at least a month, I expect. War and all, the boys are taking a good lickin'," the woman sighed.

"Well . . . I brought this man all the way from Nevada, to have special surgery to remove bullets next to his spine! What do you think I'm gonna tell him?" Charley said, keeping down a rage building in his stomach.

"Look, check him into the hospital on Center St. How does that sound?" she offered, scribbling out a note.

"Look . . . We will check into a good hotel, and I will then consult with another doctor . . . How does that sound?" Charley said tipping his hat to the woman.

"Get word to me where you are staying, and I will send a doctor," the woman said, with sympathy in her face.

"Yes. I will be in contact soon," Charley said in desperation, grabbing the note and breathing heavily, as he turned to face Byrnes. He stared down at the ailing friend and hated to drag him in search of a hotel. Charley stepped outside the building and hailed a cab.

"I need a hotel room as close to this address as possible," Charley directed. The driver nodded and as soon as the two were loaded, they set off at a brisk pace.

"Don't worry, Will, we'll get you right as rain before you know it" Charley remarked.

"I'm not worried, my friend," Will smiled, his eyes in an opiate fog.

The driver stopped before a comfortable looking hotel, next to the hospital. It was large and had a tavern and small store on the first floor. The food smelled very inviting, as Charley registered at the front desk. He set them up in the most comfortable room they could afford. The desk clerk then ordered a young man in a fancy uniform to help Charley and Will to their accommodations on the second floor. It was a large room with two beds and a small sitting room with a nice table and comfortable chairs. The sitting room had a doorway to a balcony, which covered the front porch of the building.

The next morning, after seeing that Will was quite comfortable, Charley set off to locate Dr. Scherer and Marion's father, starting at the hospital next door.

"He won't be back for a month you say?" Dr. Scherer asked, as he looked over a severely burned man in his care. "Well, that won't do. Will it, Charley?" Doc asked.

"Not especially," Charley sighed.

"All right then, let me consult with my father, and I will meet you tonight at your hotel, about eight, how does that sound?" Doc consoled.

"That would be fine!" Charley smiled fondly, with great relief.

The search for Byrne's father-in-law was not as fruitful. He had gone to Boston for family reasons.

Charley stopped off at the tavern and bought some roasted chicken and wine, then returned to the room. The two friends dined on the bird; then Charley ran back down stairs before the doctor arrived, for a pot of coffee.

"I would like to introduce my father, Dr. Scherer, he's in charge of surgery at the hospital."

"It is an honor, sir," Charley responded. "This is William Byrnes."

"Pleased to make your acquaintance," Will said leaning up to shake hands.

"Please don't get up," the elder man said, grasping the ailing man's hand.

"We would like to examine you more closely, Will," Martin said. "My father is quite an expert in this field of surgery," he remarked.

"I will give you some laudanum to ease your pain. I will have to prod around a bit to locate the exact location of the lead," the older man insisted.

"I am in your hands, Doc," Will submitted.

"What can I do?" Charley asked.

"I want you to go downstairs and get a kettle of boiling water and some clean napkins or towels. At least five or six," the senior Dr. Scherer instructed.

"Right," Charley answered, setting off down the stairs.

"This is going to put you into dream land right away, so I'll wait until Charley returns with the water before we begin, all right, Will?" Doc comforted, as he mixed up some powder in a small vile of liquid.

"What is it?" the patient asked.

"It's an opiate, not unlike what you're used to taking, just a little stronger. It will put you right to sleep, you won't feel a thing," the elder doctor advised. "I will then be able to explore your wounds with out pain," he added.

"Good, while you're in there, take them out!" Will ordered.

As Charley trotted down the stairs for boiled water, he passed a young woman in a starched gray-and-white, cotton dress, coming up the stairs. She wore a starched white cloth around her head, reminding him of the nuns he had seen. It made her look angelic as it floated along behind her.

"I'm looking for Dr. Scherer. I was told he was up here. Number 6?" the young woman inquired.

"Yes, I got a pair of doctors up there, you can have your pick. And you are?" Charley asked.

"I'm Beth, Martin's sister. I'm a nurse. My father sent for me," she answered.

"Welcome aboard. Up the stairs, first on the right, number six's on the door, see?" Charley pointed. "Got a regular family reunion going here," Charley mumbled as he lit down the stairs. "Better get another pot of coffee while I'm down here. Maybe I'll get a bottle of brandy to boot. What do doctors drink, gin or brandy? God only knows what they'll send me for next. Geez . . . Poor Will!"

When Charley returned, the makeshift operating room was in full production.

"Well, I got everything that you asked for, towels, kettle of water, even got some brandy. Oh . . . Hello, Beth, I see you found the room . . . Is they're anything else?" Charley asked, tired to the bone.

"No, Charley. Why don't you just lay down and rest for now," Martin said. The two Dr. Scherers looked the man over thoroughly and had decided that it was best to operate here and now. They saw no point in relocating to a crowded hospital; the hotel room was clean and well lit. The patient was pleasantly under the influence of the opiates and everything was ready, two surgical minds, and a patient ever so willing to give up his offending shrapnel.

The bullets were lodged in a dangerous place next to the spine on his lower back, about three inches apart. A wrong move would mean serious nerve damage and loss of function in Will's legs.

"My God, son, you were right, I don't believe I've ever seen a more shot up living specimen of a man. And believe me, I've seen my share." The two men counted twenty-nine separate gunshot wounds and arrow scars.

"Well, I certainty don't see any reason not to continue, I can reach the lead balls," Martin conferred with his elder. "What about cauterizing the wounds?" The son asked his mentor.

"Let's see how much it bleeds when we remove the lead. If she gushes, we'll cauterize. I'll have the instruments heating."

"Let's get on with it then. Beth, are you ready?" Martin rallied his troupes.

Beth woke Charley awhile later to retrieve more towels. It alarmed him and he tore into the chores like a scared rabbit. Upon returning, he arrived at the operation in time to see Will's side laid open like a Sunday dinner. The skin was pulled back and held with clamps and the flesh had been expertly carved to expose the man's spine and some of his ribcage. Charley deposited the towels and departed to the balcony for some air.

"Close that door," the Chief surgeon commanded.

"Beth, is everything goin' all right over thar?" Charley said with teary eyes, trying not to heave dinner over the railing.

"Everything is all right now," Beth soothed. Closing the door and standing a moment with the stricken friend.

"I ain't never seen anything like that, but butchered chickens and hogs . . . but that . . . that's my friend!" Charley said with a tear.

"Stay calm. You can't do any one any good by getting over excited. Dr. Scherer is a great doctor, and my brother is a very good surgeon," Beth comforted.

"I got to lay down," Charley said breathing deeply.

"I'll let you know when they are done," Beth added, walking Charley to his bed.

"Is every thing going all right?" Beth asked her father and brother.

"Yes, we got the bullets out, I believe we are almost finished here," Martin answered. "Beth, you and father should go on home and try and rest, I can finish up," the young surgeon advised.

Martin took up the balance of the night sleeping off and on, in the chair in the sitting room and monitoring his patient, until at last the dawn broke and shed its splendor onto the balcony.

The dawn's light caused Charley to stir from sleep; he rose to see his friends both resting comfortably. Charley threw on his coat and trotted down stairs to the tavern once again, after first stopping at the most remarkable indoor outhouse, called a water closet. He proceeded to the dining room and conferred with a waiter of the establishment and ordered two steak and egg breakfasts with juice and coffee. He ordered them to take to the room.

"Take? You mean want them sent to your room? Room service?" the waiter asked.

"You mean I coulda ordered food and had it delivered?" Charley questioned the young man.

"Yes of course, sir! We have service to all the rooms," he responded.

"Damn . . . I wish I'd known that last night. It would'a saved a heap of leg work!" Charley sighed. "Geez . . . This is really full service here! Yes, please, send that order to room 6. I must say that you have mighty fine rolls in this establishment," Charley added in a friendly way giving the man a dime for a tip.

"Thank you very kindly, sir, I will have your breakfast there for you quick as a wink," the waiter smiled and set off with renewed enthusiasm.

Charley trudged back up the stairs, confident that breakfast would be arriving soon. He cleared the table in the sitting room for dining. Noticing the pot full of bloody towels next to Will's bed, he placed them near the door in hopes of having them laundered. Charley tiptoed about the room, trying in vain not to wake either patient or doctor. At last, the knock came at the door that meant breakfast. Charley ushered in the young man in charge of the delivery and asked him to be quiet. After he placed the food on the table, Charley then gave him a small coin and bid him please return for the dishes in an hour and see to the laundry, which was rather startling, given all the blood. However, a reevaluation of the coin gave the boy new courage. The voices and the aroma of food roused the tired doctor.

"I ordered breakfast, Doc. I had it delivered, I'm sure you must be hungry," Charley said.

"It smells very good, thank you," Martin replied.

"What about Will? Should I order something for him?" Charley asked his friend.

"He won't want much to eat today, but he must be made to eat later. Eggs are good for a start, liver, any rich meats that you can get him to eat is good. He will need to lay still for a few weeks, a month before he does any traveling. The first two weeks are critical to his healing. I want him to stay here, where I can keep an eye on him. It's very important!" Doc warned. I don't want him to get sick."

"Whatever you say, Doc!" Charley said enjoying the food.

CHAPTER 50

The next few days became a routine, with Doc checking in on his patient once a day. Charley read the newspapers for things of interest to see in New York City.

"Well, I'll be damned! Little Lotta Crabtree is playing in the theater here this Saturday, with two performances on Sunday. Imagine that, little Lotta!" Charley said with pride. 'La Petite Fadette' is the name of the show," Charley added. "Starring Lotta Crabtree as Fanchon.

"You should go Charley," Will advised. "Then tell me all about it."

"I'd like to, but I feel bad that you're not up to goin' yet. Of course if I go, I could tell you all about it, that's better than nothin'. I wonder if'n the Doc would like to go?" he pondered. "Shit! I ain't got a thing to wear!" Parkhurst pointed out. "Geezz, she's got to be about sixteen or seventeen by now. I remember when she was just a little squirt dancing on an anvil!" Charley reminisced.

"Well, you gonna just sit there or are you gonna go out and get yourself a ticket?" Will chided. "Pick me up a couple of good cigars while you're out too," he added.

"Right then, I'll be back in about an hour." Parkie beamed. Charley was so caught up in the idea he even stopped off at a tailor and purchased a new shirt, tie, and vest for the occasion. When he got back to the hotel, he sent his traveling suit to the laundry for a good pressing.

"Hand me that bed pan, Charley," Will called out.

"Good, it's about time you had to go, you been as tight as a stopped up bottle of wine. Them greens musta helped," Charley rambled, as looked over his purchases.

"Just hand me the pan," Will scolded.

"Here, I'm gonna try on my new duds," Charley said, handing over the hospital issued bedpan. He retired to his corner of the room and stripped down to his long johns, making sure to face away from Will until the vest was on. "You want me to get some coffee? I could do with some, might loosen you up . . . There, what do you think of that?" Charley said adjusting his new tie.

"Very nice. I like the fabric in that vest. Shirt needs a press though. Yes, I would like some coffee, thank you," Will said, trying not to waste any breath, his ribs hurt.

"You want your laudanum, before I order coffee?" Charley asked.

"Whatever possessed you to become my nurse maid, Charley?" Will asked, as he set the pan with the token deposit on the floor. "This is so degrading," he sighed.

"Well, that's what friends are for William," Charley answered, taking the pan to the water closet.

Will wanted deeply to confess that he knew Charley's true gender, yet the thought of disrupting the dynamic of their friendship seemed unfathomable. Especially since he was now totally dependent on her for his well being. He couldn't even take a shit right now without her help. He felt her love and figured that was enough.

"I just love this indoor plumbing thing!" Charley remarked, as he reentered the room. "S'pose only a friend would walk a turd down the hall for ya!" Charley laughed, as he returned with the laudanum and a spoon. "Wait I'm still laughing, I'll spill it."

"Just hand it over, I can do it!" Will grumbled.

"Good to have you back amongst the living, my friend." Charley laughed, handing over the bottle. "Damn, it stank too!"

"Cheers!" Will saluted, as he drank from the bottle. "Not only that but you dawned your finest attire for the task!" Will laughed, as the burning liquid melted down his throat. Charley took the bottle from the man and shoved the cork back in the neck.

"Doc will be along soon, I'm gonna order some coffee and supper sent up, anything special you want?" Charley asked when he quit laughing.

"No, I don't expect I'll want anything 'til much later. I'm just gonna sleep now," he said drifting off. Charley took care to put the laudanum safely out of Will's reach; he was becoming very dependent on it. Charley grabbed his coat and walked down to the tavern below for a well-earned drink and a chance to see what looked good on the menu. He was excited about the tickets in his new vest and set them on the bar to look at them. Two tickets next to the orchestra; Parkhurst was very excited about seeing his little fairy dancer; troding the boards once again. Charley intended to invite Doc to see the show with him, partly in gratitude and partly because he found him to be such good company. He planned to ask him when he came to check on Will and wanted things to be just right for some reason. Parkhurst supposed that she had a small infatuation going for the doctor, but if he was too busy to go, she would understand that too. Charley looked around the room until he spotted a familiar waiter and ushered him over with a smile and a wave.

"I want some supper sent to my room in about half an hours time. Send up some coffee with cream and sugar. Also some of that smoked salmon with some rye bread. Bring up some cheeses and some butter. That ought to hold me for a while. I want enough fish for three. Here's for your trouble," Charley said tossing the boy a silver nickel. "Put the supper on my room account, number 6."

"Yes, sir, I'll take good care. You want three cups for the coffee?" The young man asked.

"Very good, yes, three cups." He smiled.

"I like your vest." The young man smiled back. "Very sharp." He winked.

Charley was not quite sure what the wink was about but was flattered just the same. He then bought three cigars from the bartender and made his way back to number 6. Will was snoring away, so Charley took out a deck of cards and amused himself shuffling and laying out hands for the fun of it. He kept an ear cocked for the rattling of trays or

Doc's arrival. The young waiter soon arrived and laid the plates out on the table and instructed his host to feel free to call for anything else at all, then quietly left.

"Will, are you hungry?" Charley called out.

"No, I'm sleeping," he replied.

"Well, I'm just gonna have a taste of this fish then I'll wait for the Doc," he said pulling off a piece of fish and a slice of fresh bread. Charley finished looking at the paper as the doctor knocked respectfully on the door. "Come in, it's open," he responded.

"Hey, new vest? Very nice," Doc said, politely. "How is Will this evening?" he added.

"He's had his laudanum and is resting quietly. Can't get him to eat much of anything, Are you hungry?" Charley replied.

"Hmmn, I can't say I'm suprised. Yes, I could eat something. Looks like you got some nice lox there," Doc remarked.

"He did have a turd this afternoon if that's important?" Charley injected. Looking at the food he then turned red with embarrassment.

"That's good . . . I'll just change his dressing," Doc replied.

"Well hello, Doc." Will whispered. "How am I doin'?"

"That's what I was going to ask you," Doc said, cutting the stained bandages with his sharp scissors. "This is healing up very well." He smiled. Charley was standing by with clean bandages that had been freshly cut and rolled.

"Say, Doc, I got tickets to a show in town, next Saturday, that's featuring a friend of mine. Would you like to see it? She's a great little performer, named Lotta Crabtree, maybe you heard of her. Anyway, I got an extra ticket if you'd like to go?" Charley said, turning red again.

"I would, I just need to check my schedule first. I'll give you an answer tomorrow if that's all right?" he politely replied.

"That's all right with me, Doc," Charley said, cutting off slices of smoked salmon and laying them on top of slices of bread.

"You got to eat some of this Will, it's delicious," Doc said, fixing up a plate for the patient. "The hospital food has got nothing on this fare!"

"It is good!" Charley said, fixing up a second helping.

Will sat up and gave it his best effort.

"I'm thinkin' while I'm this far East, I might drive to Providence and visit my old stomping grounds and look in on Ol' Ebenezer Balch," Charley pondered while he ate.

"That's a good idea, you should," Will added. "I could hire a nurse to look after me while you're visitin'." He was eating more than Charley had expected.

"You could take a train," Doc offered.

"Train might be easier," Charley said. "Maybe we could work out some arrangements. You know, it seems strange to be on my own time, instead of somebody else's schedule. Somehow I'm not looking forward to traveling alone."

"Ha, you'll get used to it," Will said, settling back for a snooze.

"We can set up a nurse to look in on Will here, and I'll have my supper delivered up here when I make my rounds. Go ahead and go," Martin said, sopping up the last of his dinner with a piece of bread. "Much better up here, than in any restaurant," the doctor said, looking out the balcony windows, at the traffic in front of the hospital across the street. He sighed. "Well, boys, I've got to get back to work. Will you're doing just fine, we'll have you up and around in no time."

"Thanks, Doc. I'll be looking for you tomorrow then. Don't forget about Saturday at eight, Lotta Crabtree." Charley smiled.

"Oh yes, I'll be sure to check. See you soon," Doc said putting on his hat and gloves.

That Saturday the doctor did indeed find time to attend the theater with his friend; however the overworked doctor slept through most of the show. Charley, who was enchanted with the show, nudged him awake when he snored too loud.

Little Lotta had blossomed into a beautiful rose, she filled the stage with charm and grace and humor; Charley couldn't take his eyes off of her. He would have liked to try going backstage, but did not wish to deprive Doc of any more of his much-needed sleep, so the pair went straight home.

Charley sat up telling Will the entire evening's entertainment, until Byrnes was snoring away as Doc had been.

A week later, Charley had butterflies in his stomach, as he bid farewell to his recuperating friend, for a trip back to Providence Rhode Island.

"Take it easy on them nurses now. I'll see you in a week or so. Take care," Parkhurst said, shaking Byrnes hand.

"I'll hold down the fort. Have a nice trip," Will replied.

Charley walked out of the hotel with a bag and hailed a cab to the railway station.

Upon arrival to his old haunts, Charley was suprised to find that it had changed very little. He began to get nostalgic, as familiar streets came into view, he missed Felix. At last, before him was the What Cheer public house. The teamster had to conceal a tear welling up in his remaining eye. It was strange to be home after so long, about ten years. It felt like a dream, somehow. Charley walked up the familiar steps to the tavern, every thing looked just like he remembered it. He opened the old door to a flood of memories of James Birch, Felix, and Eb. It even smelled the same! Charley was not the same though. He felt it, as he entered the room; it was as if he no longer belonged there, like a ghost from long ago. He walked with anonymity to the bar. Charley scanned the room for a familiar face, but there was none; only the pictures on the walls were the same. A young bartender stepped up to the new patron and asked him for his order.

"I'd like a flip," the teamster ordered; after which the bartender rolled his eyes at the old-fashioned concoction. "Can you tell me where Ebenezer Balch is?"

"Oh, you mean the old man? He's probably upstairs in bed," the bartender replied. "This is gonna take awhile. I haven't got a hot poker."

"Oh, just make it a beer then."

"You a friend of old Eb?" the relieved barkeep said, setting down a draft.

"Yes, a good friend of him and his wife, Mary. My name is Charley Parkhurst."

"Mary was in the kitchen a few minutes ago, I'll go get her."

Charley felt like a stranger in his own home as he sucked down the beer. Soon, a fat old lady, seemingly tough and frail at the same time, came bustling in from the kitchen, with tears of joy and laughter on her face. Charley rushed to greet his second mother; tears of happiness streamed down his leathery face, as he hugged Mary.

"It's sure good to see you again!" he sighed.

"Oh, I'm so happy to see you, my boy!" she cried. "Let's go up and wake Eb!" She smiled, as she ran her hand over Charley's face, caressing the eye patch tenderly.

"Yes, let's."

"You can have the room next to ours, your old room. I got it ready the instant I heard you were coming," the old woman wheezed, as they climbed the stairway.

Eb had become frail and was in ill health, but the family had amassed enough money to keep them in the style with which they had become accustomed. He stayed in his bed upstairs most of the time.

"Eb, wake up, Charley's here!" the old woman said, lighting the candelabra next to the bed.

"What? Who's he?" the man said, looking at the stranger in his room.

"It's Charley, Pa!" she said loudly to the old man.

"Yes, it's cold in here. Who is he?" Eb said, shaking off the sleep.

"It's me, Eb. Charley Parkhurst," the stranger said, leaning in close to the bed.

The old man reached for the spectacles on the top of his head and adjusted them in front of his eyes, then had a close look at the man with the eye patch.

"Is that you, Charley? Mary, Charley's here!" Eb proclaimed.

"Yes, Eb, it's Charley. He's come home!" Mary smiled, grabbing hold of Charley's strong arm.

The three visited until Eb became tired. Charley settled in and tried to sleep; he felt pangs of guilt for the time he would once again say good-bye, for he knew that it would be for the last time. It made the time spent there bittersweet, and it went by so quickly.

"You look like you're fairing well," Charley said to Will, when he returned to New York.

"I feel pretty good, I have to admit." Byrnes smiled at his friend and shook his hand. "How was your visit?" he asked.

"It was fine," Charley said, with a quiet refection. "How soon did Doc say you could travel?" he said, changing the subject.

"He says I should be able to travel in about a week, maybe," Byrnes related. "Wants me to start walking a little each day."

"Have you been for a walk today?" Charley inquired.

"Sure, I made it to the Crapper all by myself this morning," Will said boastfully.

"Well, I'm surely glad of that." Charley laughed. "Oh, look I picked us up some traveling equipment for the train ride home. First, a copper pot, with a lid, for collecting up our dinner at the stops. Then, I got some decent cutlery and pewter plates, napkins too, see? I got a good deal on some tins of smoked oysters and sardines," he said putting down some boxes and setting the new treasures out on the table. "They all fit nicely in the pot see?" he added.

"Very nice, and very convenient as well, I might add," Will said, as he examined the booty. "Say I think it's time for another stroll down the hall. You want to go downstairs and have a drink?" Will asked. "It'll be part of my exercise if nothing else."

"I even bought some twelve-year-old Scotch whiskey. How much laudanum have you taken?" Charley inquired.

"Not very much, about a teaspoon two hours ago," Will lied.

"I guess it would be all right if we go down stairs for a bit, but you better stick to beer," He cautioned like a mother hen.

"Yes, mother," Will answered, as he examined the bottle.

"We're savin' that for the drive home. God only knows what kinda whiskey we'll have to put up with back out there," Charley said retrieving the Scotch.

"Yeah, I'm gonna go sit on the Crapper," Will announced rising slowly from his chair. "Hand me that cane," Will asked. Charley quickly obliged.

"You need any help?"

"Sure! You just gonna stand there?" Will asked. Charley snapped into action, taking Will's arm and helping him to the water closet. As Will occupied the commode, Charley reflected on the frailty of his friend and the responsibility of transporting him home.

"Mother of Mercy, you surely do not want to go in there!" Will cautioned, when he emerged from the closet. "Let's go get us a beer."

A week later, the pair was back on the train, bound for St. Joe. Charley had wired Holladay that they were heading back and there was a coach lined up there, ready for the teamster to drive back to Carson City, Nevada, complete with mail and passengers.

A dismal tide of humanity was flooding in from the raging war in the South, but the plains were like another country far removed. Thundershowers danced merrily across the rugged landscape as the driver, and his chargers rolled on, making their way back to the land of milk and honey. Charley looked forward to being paid off and then on to greener pastures of the California coast. He would be leaving Will with his family at Carson City.

As the coach approached the Sierras, Will telegraphed a message to Marion, to let her know when they would arrive. She met the travelers in Carson City with the family buggy and their daughter Nellie. It was a glorious reunion. Charley was moved to tears and had to leave the scene. He loaded Will's bags onto their buggy and swore at himself for being such a sentimental old fool. Just then the afternoon coach pulled up to the Express office.

"Well, if that ain't Charley Parkhurst as I live and breath!" Hank Monk called out. "Whoa, now," he purred to his team.

"Hank if you ain't a sight for a sore eye. You done for the day?" Charley grinned.

"Tomorrow is Sunday, I am in Carson, yes, I am definitely done. My brake'n leg is in need of some lubrication, as am I," Hank thought out very carefully. "Parkie, won't you join me. I believe you just entertained quite a long journey yourself if I'm not mistaken," he added.

"Amen to that!" Charley smiled, as they entered Ormsby's tavern.

"I was not aware that you were a religious man," Hank chided.

"Well, the older I get, the more thankful I am that I am still relatively all in one piece," Charley reflected.

"I guess you seen a lot of them men who was fighting in the war," Hank reflected, as he seated himself at the bar.

"Hundreds of men with limbs missing and such . . . Such a shame," Charley sighed.

"How is Byrnes?" Hank inquired.

"See for yourself. He's doing well. We had a doctor aboard the coach that took an interest in him. He'd never seen a man that had been shot so many different times. Even did the surgery, when we got to New York. The doctor we drove all the way to New York for had rode off to Atlanta because of the war. Byrnes seems to be healing up well enough though. He survived the trip and that was half the battle," Charley reflected as he hailed the bartender.

"Hey, Charley, nice to see you! What will it be?" the big man asked, shaking hands with the driver.

"Just a beer and your dinner, a steak with some spuds," Charley ordered.

"You having your usual?" the bartender asked Monk.

"You bet," he replied.

After receiving their beer, the two descended on the domestic scene at the tavern table, featuring Will and his reunited family.

"Nice to see you again, Hank," Will said politely.

"You look real good," Hank said, with real amazement.

"Thank you. This is my wife Marion and my daughter, Nellie," Will added.

"Pleasure to meet you, ladies," Hank said, tipping his hat,

"I'll be traveling home with Marion, so I guess this is the end of the line my friend," Will said sentimentally.

"I can take him the rest of the way," Marion said with a grateful smile to the driver. "Thank you for everything you have done for Will, Charley," she said bursting into tears. "Of course, you're welcome to stay with us anytime."

"I'm sure you'll make it home safe." Charley smiled.

"Too bad they don't have one of those Crappers out here," Will mused, to the wonder of those present who did not know what the heck he was talking about. He stood and made his way to the crude outhouse in the back lot.

"You must be very careful about how much laudanum he takes. He needs to take less and less, not more and more. It's dangerous in high quantity, and he cannot be trusted to administer it himself. For God's sake do not let him drink strong spirits with it, might kill him!" Charley instructed Marion when Will left to relieve himself.

"Thank you for all you have done. He would have died without your help," Marion said squeezing Charley's hand.

"Are you making love to my wife?" Will teased upon his return.

"No, I am discussing your medications with your nurse," Charley said kissing the small woman on the hand.

"I'll see you around, my friend," Will said, as they left the establishment.

"Your dinner's ready, Parkie," Hank said, setting his hand on his friend's arm.

"Fine," Charley said turning back to the tavern, leaving his friend to his family and his home. "You seen Thompson around?" Charley asked, setting down to dinner.

"Yep, he's around. Probably at his ranch, he's busy digging up taters. I reckon you're eating some of his spuds now," Hank said, trying to lighten the conversation.

"Maybe I'll look him up on my way back to California," Charley said shoveling his face full of potatoes.

"You gonna buy that big ranch, like you always spoke of?" Hank said, buttering his biscuit.

"I think I'll head back to the coast and look around. I just don't know what I'll do yet, I still enjoy driving. I've had it with the plains though and I'm tired of the snow and hard driving at night, with one eye. The coast seems right for me somehow," Charley reflected as he looked over the menu for a suitable dessert. "Maybe I'll go back to San Francisco."

"Well, I like the lake. It's a nice drive for me; most anything else seems too tame and boring now. Tahoe is such a feast for the eyes, I never tire of the view," Hank related.

"I'm glad for you, my friend," Charley said lighting a cigar. "I suppose I am ready for a quieter lifestyle," he said tossing the match into the spittoon. "Maybe I'll head out to Placerville on your coach Monday," he said, puffing on the stogie. "Be nice to ride along and just look at the scenery for once," he sighed. "Oh, here I brought back some of them sardines you like," Parkie said, digging in his great coat, then handing over a few tins.

"Why, that's right kind of you, Parkie." Hank smiled, as he took the present. "Yep, these are the good ones! I think I'll have these later. Thank you," he said as he examined them, then stuck them in his pockets. "You want to take a ride to Virginia City tommorra? We can stop off at Gold Hill and look in after Will?" Hank reasoned.

"Yes, that sounds real good. What is this 'Mazeppa'?" Charley asked noting the waybill tucked in Hank's pocket.

"Oh this, I met this gal Idah Menken in Placerville, you never saw such a creature. That's her there," he said, examining the picture of the actress, wearing barely any clothing, laying across a rearing wild stallion's back.

"There's a gal I'd like to meet," Charley said, getting a closer look.

"I seen the horse too, he's a beauty. Anyhow, she's performing tomorrow in Virginia City." He smiled longingly at the waybill.

The next day was a cheerful one, starting early for the ride to the raucous boomtown. The two rode higher and higher on the desert road, stopping at a steep rock pass called the Devil's Gate, to pay a toll. At Gold Hill, they looked in on the Byrnes family and were invited to lunch, before they headed out to Virginia City. The stamp mills stomped a rhythmic, bone pounding, percussion, that you could feel in your chest, as you drew near the mining town. It was so full of rough men that it was an unusual day that someone was not shot or stabbed to death.

It had been a few years since Charley had first been there and was impressed by its rapid growth. Everyone was abuzz about the "Mazeppa," and there was a long line around the new Pipers Opera House for tickets.

"You stand in line Charley, and I'll look and see if'n I can't scare up some tickets some other way," Hank instructed.

"You mean like a card game?" Charley said glaring with his one eye.

"Well no, I hadn't thought of that, but that is a good idear," Hank mulled. "Here is my money for a ticket. I'll be back soon, if I can't get any," Hank promised.

"All right, but bring me back something to drink, it's gonna be hot out here," Charley whined. Believing his partner would head to a tavern and drink beer, while he steadfastly waits in line. Parkie was suprised to see Hank returning soon, with a large grin on his face.

"Let's go, I got them," he said patting his breast pocket. "You can buy me a beer. Oh, and I'll have my money back as well."

Parkie laughed at his resourceful partner, as they clunked down the boardwalk, past the men in line.

"Where did you get the tickets?" Charley inquired.

"Oh, let's just say I called in an old debt and leave it go at that," Hank said with a sly grin.

The evening's entertainment was quite remarkable. Idah Menken held the men spellbound with her performance. The last scene brought down the house. Beautiful Idah appeared on stage clothed in a flesh-colored garment that made her look quite nude, draped only with a small toga. A spirited stallion was led prancing onto the stage and the young actress was miraculously tied onto his back. The set was specially constructed, with a conveyer belt flooring, enabling the horse to run in place, as the floor moved beneath him. It made tremendous noise as the horse pounded on the wood contraption, and it drew thunderous applause from the excited miners. The woman bravely held her composure as the effect reached its climax. At the curtain call, Adah Menken was showered with flowers, a rare commodity in Virginia City and coins of every denomination.

Hank insisted they wait backstage, to call on the lovely one herself, and Charley agreed to go. Many men had the same idea; among them were Dan DeQuille and Samuel Clemens.

"Hey, fellas, it's been a long time!" Hank boomed out.

"Well, if it ain't Hank Monk and Charley Parkhurst as I live and breath!" Dan DeQuille called out.

"Dan, Sam, good to see you again," Charley said shaking the men's hands. "Ol' Hank here says he knows Idah Menken, ain't that right?" Parkie boasted.

"Well, I've met her before. Thought I'd just say hello." Hank blushed. "You writin' a column about the show, Dan?" Hank said changing the subject.

"Yes, I am. Thought I might get a few words from Miss Menken herself," DeQuille responded.

"How do we know the lady will be coming out this door?" Clemens remarked.

"Maybe two of us should stand at the front door," Charley added.

"No, I'm pretty sure she will use this one," Dan said with confidence.

Minutes later, the door opened, and a large man exited the building, followed by a small man in a fine evening suit and a silk top hat pulled down over his face. As he passed Hank, he stopped and then smiled a beautiful grin and winked.

"Hank, you made it," the petite man cooed.

Monk beamed at the disguised woman, as they shook hands. Charley then recognized the young woman and played along, pretending not to notice.

"I told you I wouldn't miss it!" he said, strolling down the boardwalk with the actress. The three other fellows strolled along behind.

"We were just heading out to get us a beer. Would you like to join us?" Hank said with as much charm as the old Jehu could muster.

"Well, I was hoping to go somewhere private," Adah said, worried that she would be discovered and mobbed by her fans.

"We can have a drink over at the newspaper office, the Enterprise," DeQuille offered from behind Monk.

"Oh, these are my friends, Charley, Dan, and Sam. This is, well, I think you know who this is," Hank said, looking around the street suspiciously. "Yeah, let's go in there!" Hank said, spotting the familiar sign for the budding newspaper. "Charley you got any of those sardines on you?"

"I got crackers too!" he offered.

"Splendid! Perhaps we can even play some cards," Adah exclaimed. It brought a frown to her large protector. "You may go back to the hotel, I'm in safe hands now," she confronted him.

DeQuille was so excited, he had trouble getting the key in the door. When he did, he held it open and welcomed the small party inside.

The woman was mesmerizing. Even though she was wearing a man's suit, she was an incredible dark-haired beauty. Charley was completely amused. Dan DeQuille livened up the party by dragging out his stash of aged rye. Monk in turn broke out some tins of sardines and set the crackers in a plate that DeQuille had found.

Clemens produced a shot glass he had pilfered from the Bucket of Blood, earlier in the evening. He wiped it out with his clean handkerchief and offered it to the lady. Soon odd glasses were collected for all and a toast to the "Mazeppa" and Adah Menken were made.

Hank and Charley were quiet most of the ride back to Carson City. Charley amused himself thinking about the lovely entertainer, dressed in the man's suit. Hank thought about her without it.

CHAPTER 51

Fall 1863

Charley rode back to Placerville with Hank the next morning. The scenery quenched Charley's thirsty eye; he was happy to be back in the wooded mountains of California. Even the miners' careless disregard for timber did not destroy the beauty of the foothills. Many of the hoards had moved on to other diggings, so Placerville, while still an important city in the West, was almost peaceful now, it was in danger of becoming civilized. Charley decided to play it by ear and stay in town for a few days, maybe rest up a bit before moving on to the coast. It was fun visiting with Hank; Charley was hoping to run into Thompson too.

Meanwhile, he sat on the porch of the local hotel and watched the horses and wagons roll by, as he scratched a wooden match on the wall and lit his cigar. San Francisco seemed the place to go to from here, he mused, blowing a smoke ring and scratching his vest, which was heavily lined with gold.

"Hey, Charley, I think I seen Snowshoe a goin' into the dry goods emporium," Hank said pointing down the street with his thumb, as he came out onto the porch.

"Oh really?" Charley smiled. "Well maybe I'll go on over and see if they got some socks over there. I'm plum out. Maybe I'll say hello to Thompson while I'm at it," Charley rambled. "You comin'?"

"Sure, I could use some new socks too," Hank agreed, looking down at his dusty boots.

The two sauntered down the planked sidewalk, until they got to the dry goods emporium and went in. A small bell above the door heralded their arrival.

"I'll be right with you fellers, feel free to look about the wares," the jovial proprietor sang out.

Thompson was busy at the rear service entrance, stacking up sacks of potatoes; he had just sold the proprietor.

"Looks like you had a good year with yor tatters," Hank said watching the man working hard.

"Ya, I guess I have. Hey, Hank! Charley!" the strapping Norwegian man laughed, standing to greet his friends. He shook hands like a great bear might. "It's zo good to zee you and both at once, dis calls for a beer!" Thompson sang out.

"It's good to see you too!" Charley laughed.

"Say, we're heading over to the hotel for dinner, why don't you join us?" Hank offered.

"Why sure," Thompson agreed.

"Good, we'll see you over there, then." Hank smiled. "You gonna pick out some socks, Charley?" Hank asked.

"Why yes. I had planned on it, thanks. See you when you get done with business there, John." Charley smiled.

"Yes, I'll be dere soon." Thompson grinned at his old friends, turning then to retrieve another sack of potatoes from the wagon bed.

"It's good to see that he hasn't changed," Charley said, setting down three pairs of socks on the counter.

"No, I'd say he looks just fine," Hank said smiling down at the pair of socks he had picked out. They were a fancy checkered pair, made of fine wool.

Upon arrival back at the hotel, Charley retreated to his room and stowed the socks in his shirt bag then proceeded back to the tavern, to await his old friend's arrival. Charley found Monk sitting at a table attempting to remove his boot.

"Give me a hand now, Parkie, if you will?" Hank said struggling with the offending footwear. Charley grabbed the heel and pulled the boot off with the help of Hank's foot on his posterior. Charley turned with a frown.

"Thank you kindly," Hank said peeling off a most offensive piece of woven footwear, which had been worn beneath his boots for an ungodly amount of time. Hank tossed the worn sock into the spittoon, where it festered with its mate, until customers could take the smell no longer and complained to the bartender to please bury the dead.

Hank proudly adorned his feet with the new and improved checkered socks, and Charley handed the Jehu his boots. Just as he slipped the left boot on, a great outdoorsman entered the tavern.

"So tell me, vhat is happening out dere, my friends. It is surely something to zee you both together again dis way," the Norseman smiled at his two comrades. Hank was still fumbling with his right boot.

"We just left your friend, Captain Byrnes, to recuperate with his family. Charley could tell you all about that. Then we went and saw a show called 'Mazeppa'! You never seen nothin like it before! There have a look at that," Hank said pulling out his waybill and smiling in reflection.

"It smells like a skunk valked through here," Thompson remarked sniffing over at the spittoon.

"Are you still carrying the mail in the dead of winter?" Charley asked the big man.

"Well, ya, no von else can or vill do it, it zeems." Thompson smiled shyly.

"Is the government giving you a paycheck for your services, John?" Hank nosed in.

"Vell, not exactly. I get zome money from people dat vill pay me for my zervices, but it's hard to collect. I even carried zome of the Territorial Enterprise printing press over da Sierras, but dat vas by private contract, and I got da money up front," The man boasted with a smile.

"Tell you one thing, John, you still grow the best spuds this side of heaven, and you do a damn fine job raising beef cattle as well, I'm here to tell you!" Hank said salivating as a plate of food was set on the bar, in front of another hungry customer. "I'll have whatever that was, bartender," Hank ordered. The server then turned to Charley and John, who both replied in unison, "Yes, I'll have the same."

"Thanks, Hank. Do you plan to stay in California, Charley?" Thompson asked.

"I think so," Charley conceded. "I've missed these wooded hills," Charley confessed. "I've surely had my fill of the plains."

"Did you zee a lot of buffalo and Indians?" John asked innocently.

"Yep, I saw a lot of both, and they can have the plains. It's theirs anyhow . . . . I surely won't miss those damned tornadoes!" Charley sighed, "they can have those too!"

"Vat about da war?" Thompson reflected.

"Well, it's a shameful thing to be sure. I seen a lot of the men returning home with legs missing and arms gone, butchered up something terrible, for to live out the rest of their lives in a pitiful existence," Charley said looking at his glass. "It's a damned shame!"

Thompson pictured Sisson and his amputated feet and shuttered at the thought.

"Well, I sure as hell ain't gonna get mixed up in all a that, I'm staying right where I'm at, I like driving my route," Hank said punctuating it with a well-aimed shot at the spittoon; it made a nice ring.

CHAPTER 52

February 1864

William Byrnes recovered from his surgery beautifully, with the loving care of his personal nurse and wife, Marion, and his sweet daughter, Nellie. He was even able to hold down a job at one of mines near Gold Hill, leaving the law and the pursuit of Indians to someone else. Marion was doing well as a baker and seamstress; she had become quite resourceful while Will had gone to New York for his operation, needing to keep busy to prevent worry and make extra money. Little Nellie had become a good helper.

Will on the other hand was really not suited to the domestic life; he had been on his own and roaming around most of his life, sitting still was strange. He lost money playing cards and was soon longing for the adventures he had always pursued.

That spring, William Byrnes fell in with a couple of prospectors, named Mathews and Crow, that had heard of rich diggings in the new Aurora gold mines, down South a ways. He kissed his girls farewell and set out in search of untold riches.

The men first tried their hand in the new settlement of Aurora, but by summer had crossed the border into California, to the Deep Spring Valley, near the Owens River. It was a high desert valley that was being used to raise cattle. The settlements were mostly set next to the river, where the runoff of the Sierras, bounded down in various creeks. To the south of their mine, in the distance, was the snowcapped, mighty Mount Whitney, which rose to over fourteen thousand feet. The three men found a promising piece of land, about ten miles from the nearest town. They named their mine the Cinderella after a story William had read to his daughter, Nellie, from an old book. He wanted to name it Nellie, but since they all had kids; they picked a name that was neutral, so to speak. The Cinderella was a good mine and was beginning to pay off. The three had worked hard all summer and had managed to dig down about seventy feet; it was what the prospectors called a "coyote hole." A simple shaft set straight down into the ground from which veins of gold were followed.

The men took turns digging in the shaft and working the windlass, which they used to transport buckets of dirt to the surface to be panned. The windlass was the only means of getting in and out of the shaft.

Al Crow had just returned to the mine that evening, with the partners water wagon and a load of provisions. He was a big Irishman, who had engineered the cabin and the windlass. The oldest partner, Mathews, was a pretty fair cook. He had come to

California, a young man in 1831, supporting himself as a trapper and prospecting in the mountains ever since. He was ever so happy to see Crow with the needed supplies.

Byrnes was certainly the armed support that the trio needed, in case of claim jumpers and native uprising, but he was happy to do his part of the hard labor. It felt good to be able to do any work, after the trauma his body had endured. At least he was not making his living at the end of a gun, and for that Marion was happy, though she desperately missed him. Each month when he went home for a visit, he brought his share of the toils back to deposit in the bank in Carson City. It was beginning to add up to a nice figure.

The threesome took advantage of the dry weather, while it lasted and worked all the next day. It was quite warm for November, though deep in the shaft it was always cool. The weather was beginning to take a nasty turn however; dark clouds were beginning to pile up.

It was Byrnes turn to go down the dark shaft next, as he and Crow hauled Mathews out into the sunlight.

"I'm gonna go get dinner started, soon as we lower Will," Mathews said, as he squinted into the bright light. "I left the water bag down there. It's still plenty full," he said, handing over the tin oil lamp to the next in line.

Byrnes stepped onto the bucket, securely holding on to the attached rope as the two partners slowly lowered him down into the deep, dark hole. Once down there, Crow would crank up the dirt whenever Byrnes rang the bell, rigged up at the top of the windlass. The dirt was then panned out with a rocking sluice box, using water from the water-wagon.

Crow was singing to himself, as he ran his hands through the wet gravel, picking out stones here and there and rejecting common ground. He did not notice the two Paiutes watching him from the hillside near the shaft.

Mathews was also in his own little world, as he molded dough into biscuits. Byrnes of course was down deep in the earth, with only the damp darkness and the friendly flicker of his oil lamp to keep him company. He was inspired by the gold colors he was seeing.

Mathews was inspired by the beauty of his biscuits, as he took them from the fire. He was so impressed with himself; he did not hear the wiry native, climbing on the roof of the cabin. He did eventually notice a Paiute woman near the door. She was looking around to see if the man at the windlass had seen her, and tried to keep from his view by crouching behind some supplies. The woman called softly at the door, as Mathews came to see what she wanted. Motioning for food, she looked destitute in her ragged cloths and missing teeth. Mathews stepped outside to get a better look at the woman, when the Indian, who was crouching on the roof, fired his rifle at the miners head. The bullet pierced his scull at the temple and proceeded out though the man's lower jaw near the front of his face. The native then turned his attentions to the now-alerted Crow and without hesitation, shot him dead as well, piercing him through the chest. The Paiute jumped from the roof and gave the woman orders to search the house, as he proceeded with caution to the mineshaft. The woman stepped over Mathew's still body, past an expanding puddle of blood and began collecting goods.

The Paiute kicked Crow in the face, to make sure he was dead, then took the white man's pistol and tucked it in his belt, as he listened down the hole.

"Crow? Are you all right?" Byrnes called, without thinking.

The murderer peered into the abyss and could vaguely make out a flicker of light down there. He looked over at Crows dead body, taking whatever possessions he could find off it, then thought it wise to dispose of it in the large hole, thoughtfully provided. He rolled Crow to the mouth of the shaft, then down it bounced, snapping and breaking on its way to the bottom.

Byrnes, who had blown out his light, was listening with great alarm, until the untimely visit from Crow startled him into a yell. The body smashed hideously against him, causing horror and panic to well up inside. It did not go unnoticed. The native laughed and fired Crow's pistol at Byrnes, striking him once in each arm. He then pulled the rope and bucket out of the shaft and cut it off the windlass, setting it with the other things the woman was collecting. He spotted a wheelbarrow full of rocks and emptied it down the shaft, laughing as he did. The deep abyss greatly amused him and he tossed big boulders down at the suffering man, trapped below.

Byrnes was terrified and huddled close to a new lead in the shaft, forced to use Crows dead body as a shield, along with his shovel. It sickened him when he heard the bones of his dead partner cracking from the boulders that bounced off the crude walls, sending more and more debris upon him.

The trapped and wounded man pulled his shirt over his face, trying to breathe slowly so as not to cough; the dust was terrible, he was being buried alive. Will could faintly hear some voices talking from above, when the debris finally stopped falling. The man was ordering someone to do something. He distinctly heard the Paiute word for horses and horses stamping and pawing in excitement before they rode off.

Byrnes lay still, assessing his damages. He was seriously hurt, nothing seemed broken, but both arms were torn up pretty badly, and he had a bullet lodged in one shoulder. After hearing nothing for quite some time, Will pulled himself out of the rocks and into the open black grave. As the dust settled, he pawed around the shaft in the darkness and dislodged some rocks that had settled above him, causing more rocks to rain down in the pit. A fist-sized rock hit him on the head and Will fell. He did not know how much time had passed, when he finally woke up to a pitch-black nightmare.

He once again realized the horror of his situation, as he lay in the dusty darkness. He felt his bloody wounds and tried not to panic. The pain was searing, and he had lost a lot of blood; he was covered in a sticky, gory mess. Attempting to climb out might be fatal.

Byrnes had to search for his missing oil lamp. In broad daylight, the light from the opening shed almost no light down this deep shaft. He was forced to search the rubble on his knees but had to stop and tie his shirt around his arms to keep from bleeding to death. It was easy to get disoriented in the blackness. Will struck a match to assess his surroundings. He must be frugal with them as he would have no way of knowing how long he would be down there.

Crow's smashed-up face was enough to make the seasoned warrior vomit.

It was better in the blackness, he thought as he sat back down in despair. He presumed that Mathews was dead, and the thought of Crow's mashed-up presence wasn't a bit comforting. He had to take care of his dead partner, at least get him stored away and covered up. The sight was as gruesome as Tres Dedos' severed head. The past came flashing back in his mind's eye so clearly, the sensory deprivation of the blackness exciting his imagination, to a dreamlike state. He lit another match and searched desperately for the lamp; then he remembered his vest pocket.

Byrnes pulled out Marion's letter, which he had just received and had only read twice, twisting it tightly into a wick, then lit it with the match. He continued his frantic hunt, pulling Crow to the side of the shaft and searching around his body, before burning his fingers. Finally success, he grabbed the desired object and lit the lamp with the remaining embers of the letter. Byrnes swirled the lamp to find out how much oil was left. It was about half full.

"Thank you for writin' me a letter, my beloved," Will said aloud. Remorseful that he could no longer read it.

"I can't win," Byrnes spoke to himself while dressing his wounds. "Seventy feet down a hole, and I still get shot."

After stowing away Crow and recovering the precious water bag, Will sat back down on the rocky ground and mulled over his situation, tending to his still bleeding wounds. He then took out a cigar from his vest pocket and lit it from the lamp. He extinguished the light to save the precious oil. This was going to be a long night, he figured; his stomach was starting to protest as well.

Byrnes tried not to think about the opiate cravings that were beginning to set in, for he was hopelessly addicted and was beginning to sweat and shake. He was only about seventy feet too far away. He closed his eyes and tried not to panic, desperately trying to remember the contents of the burned up letter.

Mathews lay at the entrance of the cabin, in the dirt; he twitched in pain as his last memory flashed though his brain. He could feel the earth with his hands, soft like lumpy flour. It seemed impossible. Was he dead? Surreal thoughts flitted through his pain, racked head. Everything was sticky as he raised his hand to his face. "I'm a dead man!" Mathews screamed in his mind. He slowly tried to get to his feet, the loss of blood making him dizzy. Pure adrenaline from the thought of death kept him moving. He could only see out of one eye, but it was enough to tell him he was alone. There was no sign of Crow, not even a body to be seen. Mathews looked to the cabin for whisky, but the place had been cleaned out. The horses were gone, as were all the guns and ammo. The man sat down in agony, as helpless as a newborn babe. He would not even be safe from the wolves or bears now, that is, if he didn't bleed to death first. He must not pass out, he realized.

Mathews only chance of survival now was to stay awake and get help. If he could just get help. The man wrapped his head up in some cloth left in the cabin and set out to see if anyone was alive in the mine. He looked at the windlass, naked of rope and heaved another bitterly painful sigh. He peered down into the blackness and saw no signs of life. He tried to call out, but could not produce any voice; the blood and pain of his broken jaw prevented any more attempts. He would be on his own. If the Indians came back, he was a dead man for sure. Mathews would have to walk to town, or die.

For a time, as Mathews sat by the entrance to the mine, resting, he felt that maybe it would be more pleasant to die right there, instead of enduring all the pain and suffering, just to die in some ditch on the way to town. After all, his partners were already dead there; it was good enough for them! The miner debated himself; then a small voice inside his head told him it was time to go and the man got up, with all his strength and walked away. He would head for the river. He could get a drink of water. He longed for just one long drink of cold water; the Paiutes had drained the waterwagon.

Placing one foot in front of the other, Mathews made his way; maybe some prospector or cowboy would come along and help him, he prayed. Yet, he saw none. For two days he walked through the rugged mountains, but his search for water was in vain. He was disoriented and a feeling of utter loss was creeping in. Still, the man pushed on, using every last reserve of his mountain man strength to carry on. At last, he spotted the Owens River; he paused to thank God as he crawled down to the water. When he was on his belly at the river's edge, he splashed the cold water on the angry flesh that was once his face. He set his mouth in the river, but tasted only blood. His throat was clotted up so terribly that the water could not go farther than his mouth. The cold water touching his face caused waves of new pain to assault his brain. Mathews climbed to his feet and tried to remain alert. He endeavored to ford the river, in hopes of finding some help on the other side. The icy water was bracing enough, but when he was up to his waist, the current and the slippery footing swept the weakened man into the cold current.

"I have come all this way to drown myself! Shooting wasn't enough?" the man scolded himself, in the recesses of his brain, as he was swept along in the rushing water. When he came up for air, he began coughing; it was uncontrollable and felt like he was being shot in the head again repeatedly. He choked on the mass of clotted blood that was loosening up in his throat. He regained his footing and barfed up a very bloody clot that had been preventing his drinking. The man plunged back into the water and let it flow around his pitifully damaged face, spitting out several teeth. The icy cold water could at last flow down his throat and lessened some of the pain, as he drifted across the river. When he reached the other side, Mathews crawled up on the riverbank in misery and exhaustion, oblivious to his surroundings. A shadow spread upon him, but he was too feeble to even look up, to see if was a savior or death, until he heard a young man's voice from above.

"Don't worry I'll get you some help."

Mathews rolled over, onto his back, to see the voice coming from a young man on a horse, who was determined to deliver him from the clutches of death.

"Don't try to talk. I'll take you to our ranch. It's not far, can you get up on my horse?"

Mathews nodded, with a horrifically gruesome smile, his face redesigned by the bullet's path.

"I think it's better if you ride behind me, that ways we can go faster. We'll get you up on that stump there and then I'll just pull you aboard," the young man said, helping the wounded man to his feet.

Will lay in his tomb for days, his light nearly exhausted. He had resigned himself to a slow and miserable death. His water was very low, when it ran out, he would die of thirst, if the cold didn't kill him first or he didn't bleed to death. Shaking uncontrollably from the cold, shock of blood loss and from his body's addiction to opiates, Will tried to keep his mind filled with thoughts of Marion and his little Nellie. Tres Dedos' ugly misshapen face, along with poor unfortunate Crow, with his bashed in scull, kept mocking him in his waking sleep, sending him into fits of insanity.

Time had lost all meaning. How much longer until he would cross to the other side and face the great mystery of the shrouded beyond. He had survived worse than this; he tried to reassure himself.

"I'm afraid I'm gonna need your clothes, Al," Byrnes called out in a delirium. "You don't mind do you?" he said, crawling over to where Crow's body was. Will had placed rocks over him so as not to have to look at him. The lone survivor was freezing to death and had come to retrieve any source of warmth he could. It had been raining and the shaft was very inhospitable. It was a grisly task and the starving man even entertained notions of having Crow for dinner. He resisted because of the hallucinations that Al was still alive.

"I have some tobacco in my vest pocket, help yourself," the mangled corpse offered.

"Thanks, Al. You're all right in my book, always said that. Oh, look you've got matches and everything." Byrnes smiled a strange smile.

He respectfully recovered his partner with stones, then set about trying to collect rainwater, using the shovel and water bag, as the light began to flicker dimly. Will gave up and extinguished the lamp, then curled into a pocket in the wall and tried to rest, or perhaps die.

Byrnes was in a deep sleep for days it seemed, painfully stranded in a hallucinatory nightmare. His dreams were fitful and vivid, the battles he fought, mixed with his little daughter's smiling face. At last, the dream turned less violent and horrible, as his wife and child continued to beckon him home. All the while a recurring song kept playing in his head.

"What is that song?" he kept shouting in his dream, or was he really shouting? He just didn't know. "What is it?" That song, over and over the same notes played, getting closer and closer, almost on the tip of his tongue. Was he finally passing out of this earthly existence? The gates of hell were creaking open to receive another resident? No. This song was so familiar, so happy. It was beautiful, a beautiful song! It was the windlass squeaking and the bell ringing! Byrnes was not sure if he could trust his senses, as men's voices once again played in his ears, friendly voices! He opened his mouth to call to them, but no sound would come out. It was a beautiful sight, light was approaching. At last they had come for him. In his delirium, he knew not who they were, but he was sure happy to hear them. It was like an angel descending, to deliver him from darkness. At this point, the devil himself would have been a relief, to the monotonous agony of a slow death in the blackness.

The man that came down was shocked to see Byrnes was alive and called up the shaft. He tied the rope around Byrnes waist and secured him to the makeshift rescue lift, so he wouldn't fall off, then yanked on the rope and up they went. The sun blinded him, as the windlass delivered Will to the surface. The men around him were astounded that anyone could have survived such an ordeal, for five days! Byrnes wore the grin of a deliriously happy man, as he was loaded onto the back of a wagon; the rescue party returned him to the ranch. The bounce of the wagon reassured Will that he was indeed still in this world; he knew he would survive to see his wife and daughter now.

His partner Mathews made a recovery, but was greatly affected for the rest of his life, in the long run, so was William Wallace Byrnes.

CHAPTER 53

1864, San Francisco

Charley Parkhurst had gotten a job on a familiar route, on the coast of California, driving the Wells Fargo stagecoach. He was getting close to San Francisco for the night and was tired and hungry. It had been a long day, starting in the small town of San Jose, but it was good to be in civilized country. The horses were working hard, but they knew they were getting close to home too; the driver could feel them wanting to pick up speed, as they got closer to chow time. Soon Charley would be sauntering into a tavern, for a bit of refreshment and relaxation in the finest city in the West.

It was summer, which meant that it was still light in the evening. As the coach reached the top of the grade and could look down on the growing city by the bay, the driver pulled up the team briefly to catch a good glimpse of the unusually fogless vista. As they paused a moment, so the horses could catch their breath, Charley witnessed the most earth-shattering explosion! The horses all jumped and danced in unison. From afar Parkhurst saw a gigantic cloud of debris heaved into the heavens. Even from a mile away, he estimated that the explosion took place close to the mail depot. In fact, it almost looked to be "snowing" mail. Charley steadied the team, then consulted with his shotgun partner, as they watched debris raining down from the sky.

After a minute, Charley called the horses into action and galloped in, to learn the fate of their destination. People were swarming all over—screaming, shouting, and crying. What the driver saw stunned and shocked everyone around. People were shouting that the Parrott building had blown up! Charley guided his road weary partners in locomotion through the mayhem, to the depot office. People were running in different directions; some were putting out fires. As the coach pulled up to its final destination, Parkhurst could see that the back of the building was now missing! In its place was a crater and a ghoulish assortment of mail, rubble, and body parts! As the passengers climbed out of the coach and saw the effects of the explosion, most had to stop and vomit at the carnage. Even Charley had to hold back the dry heaves, as he saw part of a human face hanging off a light pole! The whole back end of the building, which Mr. Parrott had so painstakingly shipped all the way from China, had been blown away! It was solid granite and could withstand fire, but this was something new!

Parrott had envisioned a grand building that would withstand anything that could occur, be it a fire or earthquake, so he sent his architect to China to have the granite cut to his specifications. The blocks were then shipped to San Francisco, along with the Chinese laborers to assemble it. However, trouble began right from the start of construction, as the laborers became anxious and disturbed from the onset.

"Bad Feng Shui!" the oldest laborer spoke to the foreman during the construction.

"That's the only thing he keeps sayin', but the China men just won't work. Bad Fung Sway!" the foreman explained to Parrott.

"Well, offer them more tea and rice. All the markers on the blocks are in Chinese, so we have to have the Chinese workers build it," Parrott said with exasperation.

Finally a bargain was struck and the elaborate building was beautifully crafted. It was splendid, with its elegant archways and polished marble columns.

Parrott was startled from his recollection, as a letter floated from the heavens and hit him in the nose. He grabbed the paper and stuffed it in his pocket as two Chinese men stopped to marvel at the gaping hole.

"I say him, bad Feng Shui!" the elder Chinese man said to the younger, as the two continued about their business. Charley spotted Parrott walking back and forth up and down the walk, scratching his head and mumbling into his hat. Papers and mail of all sorts were still floating down from the heavens like giant snowflakes and occasionally he would snap up a document or letter.

As soon as the horses were seen to, Charley looked for the expressman to find out what happened. He found him in the nearest tavern, which was about as full as it could be, with people who all had the same ghastly look on their faces, as if the Devil himself had come up from Hell and had given them all a preview.

It seemed that some miners had ordered some new fangled explosives, called "Nitro something or other" to help extract their precious gold. The poor mail handler, having no knowledge of the instability of the liquid, leaking inside the wooden box, took it upon himself to try and open the package to remedy the leak. Needless to say, a hammer and chisel were not the right tools for the job! The first blow with the hammer was the last they ever saw of the poor unfortunate postal worker and everyone else in the room at the time. Later they found the man's hand in the street, identified by a ring he always wore. Unfortunately, the line for receiving mail ran past the back of the building and anyone caught there, was blown up as well. Lots of folks didn't get their mail that day.

Folks were in shock over that for days. As hungry as Charley was that evening, he fairly drank his supper, couldn't even look at a steak for days afterward! It seemed that there had been a few other mysterious explosions in the news that he could recall. He thought he had remembered a familiar name, Nobel, a scientist of some kind, had shipped some products from his laboratory in Sweden.

Charley Parkhurst took it as a sign to look for a more peaceful part of the country. He soon after ventured farther South and found a beautiful route to drive in the mountains of Santa Cruz.

CHAPTER 54

Santa Cruz Mountains, April 1865

Charley woke one morning, at first not knowing quite where he was, and then a reassuring wet nose nuzzled the weathered driver's face as he smiled.

"Morning, Buster," Parkhurst said to a young spotted pup. "Come on, let's git some breakfast."

The coachman now lived by himself in a cabin, near the small town of Santa Cruz. Charley could walk to the stagecoach depot from home.

Parkhurst had saved up for a retirement, but just couldn't bring himself to quit driving; it was all he had ever known. It felt strange to set the brakes and stay in one spot for long.

"You comin', Buster?" Charley called to the pup as he headed to work. The little dog sat in the middle of the cabin near the stove, then whimpered, and lay down. "All right, suit yerself. I'll have the Miller boy take you for a romp after school." The little dog whimpered again, then yipped, as Parkhurst shut the dog in the cabin.

Frank Woodward, the expressman, was already in the depot when Charley arrived.

"Where's Buster?" Woody asked.

"Oh, he decided to stay home. Maybe its gonna rain, he don't like the rain. Some dogs got a six sense about storms and such," Charley explained. "Would you tell the Miller boy when he comes by to look in on Buster?" Charley asked the clerk.

"Sure, if he don't come by, I'll feed him myself, on my way home," the young mail clerk smiled.

"We 'bout ready to go?" Parkhurst asked his driving companion.

"I reckon," Woody said looking at his watch.

It was a good day to drive, Charley thought to himself. The Coast Line stage route was a simple one for the seasoned driver. After braving the Devil's Dip and Peavine Ridge, this was just a jaunt over the hills.

The fog was thick and bracing this morning, in the little coastal town; it felt good on Parkhurst's leathery face. Charley pulled the worn felt hat down on his gray frosted hair and adjusted his leather eye patch with his gloved hand. The horses were in eager anticipation of their oncoming run in the mountains, the damp weather made them frisky. The route started low in the fog, then climbed up along the crest of the ridge, higher and higher, until they would finally burst through into the glorious sunshine above the clouds. When they reached a clearing on the knoll, the company could see the pillowy fog below them covering the foothills, spreading out like a soft, puffy blanket to the vast horizon. On days with no fog, the Pacific Ocean lay stretched out in its place.

Occasionally, the coach would dip back down into the fog, as the road twisted through the mountains and gullies, where the dense redwood trees turned the fog into fat raindrops. The route had plenty of places an inexperienced driver could get into trouble; it had some tight turns that caused the driver to lose sight of the lead team, as they maneuvered around the side of a steep mountain. Charley always held his breath and chewed hard on his tobacco, until they got through those rough spots. He put in a fresh plug of tobacco in preparation for the first hairpin turn.

It was not at all uncommon for passengers inside the coach to become sick to their stomachs at this portion of the ride. The next turn was another switchback that turned again around the face of the mountain, then got very steep, as you made your assent from the gulch. There were tall trees growing all over the steep rocky terrain and one could even look at the tops of trees, rooted far below.

The six coach horses stretched out thirty feet from the driver's box and would soon start disappearing around the last treacherous turn. Just before they approached the hazard, Charley noticed nervous behavior from the leaders, and prayed it wasn't a bear.

"Come on, girls, one more turn, it's all right," Charley called out to the horses. They responded in kind and threw themselves into the turn. As they did, the coach felt the violent repercussions of the front team sliding to an immediate halt. Outside of Charley's view, around the corner, was a herd of pigs being shepherded down the road by a resident of the area, named Mountain Charley.

The lead horses, encountering such a horrible smelling sight, stopped cold and then began backing up on the narrow road, causing a hideous chain reaction. The middle pair, or swing team of horses, had no recourse but to begin backing up as well, which caused a great stress on the pole between the wheel horses nearest the coach. The coach was beginning to jackknife and the rear wheels were starting over the edge of the road, which had been cut into the side of a mountain. Beyond the road was a steep, rugged, drop off. The road was so twisted, that the driver had no way to back the vehicle out of danger, with the horses in a blind panic. Charley reeled in the leather lines and tried in vain to straighten out this mess.

"Get out! Get off! Someone grab the lead horses! The coach is going to go over the cliff!" Charley yelled to his passengers, fearing the worst. He cracked his whip and swore at the horses, but it was happening too fast! It was his worst nightmare coming true! The swing team was retreating much too close to the edge of the road. It was forcing the wheelers to turn or break the pole, which was now creaking with distress. The pole, which was connected to the front axle, was turned at a very sharp angle to the front of the vehicle, causing the body of the carriage to rise up, pushing the coach over the edge of the precipice. Charley stood with all his weight on the brake bar, swearing at his horses, trying to hold things together, until they could be straighten out, but it was to no avail. The back wheels dropped off the road and began to slide down the mountain, thus making the brake useless and freeing the horses to bolt backward.

"Oh God! We're going over!" Charley cried out, not willing to let loose the lines to his beauties. When the horses flew back and the front wheels went over the edge, the weight of the coach dragged the horses over the side with it!

The coach, top heavy with baggage, rolled over onto its side, as it slid down the steep mountain. Charley was ejected from his seat but was still holding tightly to the leather lines and a fist full of the rear wheel horse's tail.

He could hear the shrieks of terror from passengers still inside, as the coach slid on its side. Those who had not gotten out in time, including two women, were tossed about like rag dolls as the horror of their situation dawned. The left window's scenery had suddenly come too close for comfort. Charley refused to let go of the frightened horse's lines; he tried to steer any horses that had found their feet into some shrubs to slow the pull of the sliding coach. Several of the six horses had fallen and were dragged about by their partners. Fallen horses miraculously found their footing, as the upset coach soon slowed. The panicking horses tried to run, dragging Charley and the coach along, bouncing his body against sharp rocks, until they came to a thick patch of chaparral and could go no farther.

The men on the ground began charging down the mountain to see what was left of the wreckage. They found Charley, lines still in hand, laboring hard to breathe.

"Leave me be and check on the passengers and horses," Charley said, just barely able to whisper.

"Looks like you busted some ribs, Charley, you just lie still and breathe real slow," Frank Woodward said, as the coachman blacked out. Charley woke briefly, as the men loaded his broken body onto a makeshift stretcher. They rested him on the road in the shade, with the two ladies, who had ridden down the cliff inside the coach. The men then assessed the situation and managed to use the horses to drag the coach back onto the road. The horses that were scraped up were attended to, while the men foraged around for wood to use as a lever to right the coach to its wheels.

Charley dragged himself to his feet and ambled over to inspect the horses. Holding his sides, he began to untangle harness and examine injured animals.

"We'll drive a spike hitch to the next station," Charley gasped to the express guard. "It's mostly downhill after the crest, some'll have to walk to the top of the grade. We'll tie these three horses to the back of the coach. They're banged up pretty good," Charley said, reeling in the afternoon sun. He hit the ground, as the words left his mouth.

"Good God, why did you let this man wander about?" growled Mountain Charley. "Can't you see his ribs is broken?" The hulking man bent tenderly over the driver and wiped the blood from his mouth. He grabbed his water pouch and gave the driver a small drink. Charley coughed up more blood as he labored for breath. The mountain man carried the valiant driver back to the shade and instructed the women not to let him up. "Now don't worry, we'll take care of things from here," the big man comforted the driver.

Charley was vaguely aware of being placed inside the coach, then only woke again as they neared the station. He was given a shot of whiskey to dull the pain, from a man riding beside him, then lapsed in and out of consciousness from there.

It was queer to be riding on the inside of the vehicle. Who was driving? Parkhurst wondered. He could barely breathe. It felt like a hot poker in his chest, each time he coughed it burned more, until he passed out. Parkhurst spotted Mountain Charley sitting in the driver's box, as the men carried his broken body from the coach.

Charley felt the familiar taste of laudanum, as she opened her eye and looked up at the doctor who was cutting open her shirt for examination. Parkhurst was just in time to see the suprised look on his face, when he saw his patient's breasts. It struck Charley as hilarious, compared to the rest of the day. It made her cough, instead of laugh. It brought a look of concern back to the astonished doctor's face.

"Be as still as you can. I know its hard not to cough, but at least two of your ribs are broken. I will have to put you out to set them," the doctor said, trying not to appear shocked. "My nurse will assist me."

Charley hadn't noticed the woman, as she stood on her blind side. The nurse too was stupefied to find a well-developed woman on the bed.

"Please don't tell anyone I'm a woman," Charley whispered to the doctor, grabbing him about the wrist, as the light in her eye dimmed to black.

When she woke, she found herself tightly bandaged, with her arm in a sling. She was in the doctor's room with only a cloth gown, a sheet and a blanket covering her. But she felt clean and somehow safe. A young woman sat sewing on something in the corner of the room. As Charley stirred, she looked up.

"Would you like some water?" she softly asked, appearing like an angel, as she stood and walked to the bedside.

"Yes," Charley croaked out.

She placed her hand on Charley's forehead, then turned to a pitcher and poured some water for her patient. The cool water felt soothing as it went down her throat.

"I'll get the doctor now," the nurse said, setting the glass back on the table.

The doctor smiled at Charley, as he entered the room. He rested his hand on her forehead as the nurse had done.

"How do you feel?" he asked, expecting the obvious.

"Better than when I came in here," Charley managed in a whisper. The doctor smiled in return.

"You had three broken ribs and received several stitches in the head. You nearly punctured a lung. I shall have to watch you carefully for sighs of internal bleeding. I don't want you to move for at least another day. You will stay here. The stage company has been notified and will pay for your injuries, I have seen to that," the doctor said thoughtfully.

"How long have I been out?" Charley asked.

"Oh about six hours, I suppose," he answered. "Are you hungry?"

"Yes, very," Charley groaned pathetically.

"Good!" he laughed. "We'll get you some soup. Oh and though I might not approve of your lifestyle, my sacred oath as a doctor will protect your secret."

"Thank God!" Charley smiled.

A day later, Charley was home again at his little cabin, resting in his own bed.

"Hey, Charley, you up?" a friendly young man said, looking in the rustic house. "Have you seen the papers yet? President Lincoln has been shot and killed!" Frank Woodward said, as he sauntered into Charley's room. "I don't suppose you've seen the paper. Here. How you feeling, Charley?" Frank rambled on. He and Charley had met on the Coast Line and had become good friends. Woody was very enthralled with Parkhurst's vast experience on the open road.

"Oh, Woody, I just been laying around in here, I'm pretty beat up. My ribs got stove in some. What's this you said about the President?" Charley said, rousing from his sleep, and looking at the news.

"No kidding! The president has been assassinated! They say it was John Wilks Booth, Edwin Booth's own brother," Woody said with great excitement. He handed the paper over to the wounded driver.

"Damn! That's just awful!" Charley said, with amazement.

"It says here about your accident . . . Here," Woody pointed to a few lines on the second page.

Charley gave out a heavy sigh, as he reflected back to his own tragedy, realizing the seriousness of the situation. He would not be able to drive again for a long while, if at all.

"You know Charley, that kind of accident could have happened to any driver. You saved the horses, and the passengers. You were the only one seriously hurt, because you steered the horses to safety. You'll be up and around in no time, you'll see," Woody consoled. "I brung you some pie from Mrs. Harmon. I'll set it over here, on the table."

"Thanks, Woody." Charley smiled.

"You want me to make you some coffee?" Frank offered.

"Sure," Charley said, trying to sit up. "Help yourself. You know where I keep it, don't you?" Charley groaned. "Doctor will be along soon, he'll want some. Good God, I feel so weak," he said, lying back down on the bed. "Thanks for the paper," he called out to Woody.

"Mrs. Strosser cooked you up some o' her baked beans. Come on little Buster, you want some baked beans?" Woody said, directing his attention to Charley's little dog who was scurrying about underfoot.

"Don't give him too many beans. Makes him fart bad," Charley warned.

"Come on, Buster, you can have some beans!" the young man said, spilling beans into a small dish.

"He's a little dog, now don't give him too much!" Charley scolded. "People always a feedin' that dog. It's a wonder his belly don't drag on the ground!" Parkhurst mumbled to himself. "Good thing you stayed home the other day," he reflected.

"Charley you look like you need a shave, you want me to give you a shave?" Frank said.

Charley laughed hysterically inside, outwardly he merely coughed with a smile.

"Yeah, sure, I guess I could do with one, why not, you ain't got the shakes now do ya?" Charley said still coughing

"Heck no!" Woody laughed.

"I been thinking for a time about running a station," Charley said, as Woody lathered his friend's face.

"You could run a fine station, Charley," Woody concurred.

"I got some money set aside. I was thinking of maybe buying a ranch, raising some horses and cattle. Or maybe open a station," Charley mused aloud.

"That sounds real good. You still need time to rest though, you're ribs and all," the man replied, scraping the straight razor across the old driver's chin. "Now you just be quiet now," he warned, taking another swipe and wiping the lather on a towel. "You could run the best tavern. My cousin is a good cook, she's a widow, just loves to cook!" Woody rattled on. "Bakes the best pies! I'll have her bake you one!"

"Might be rather amusing at that!" Charley smiled.

"No! Don't smile, just keep your lip still," Woody continued.

The next few weeks found Charley riding into Santa Cruz, to discuss with people that knew, about the possibilities of ranches for sale and locations for stage operations. On one occasion, he happened to run into his old friend James Hume who was now working for Wells and Fargo, full time.

"Real nice to see you again Sheriff! Charley said.

"Hey Parkie!" Hume said, looking at the teamster. "I read about your accident."

"How did you know it was me? The news only mentioned the briefest facts." Charley smiled.

"Wells Fargo is very thorough, I saw in the report . . . that it was you driving."

"Well . . . what do you know!" Charley marveled. "It's a shame about the president!" he added.

"Yes! Can I buy you a drink to better times?" James asked, pouring himself a drink, and then another.

"You bet!" Charley replied, as they drank a shot together. "I'm thinking about opening my own station," he added. "I was out at the Seven Mile House outside of Watsonville on the old Santa Cruz road, the man that runs it is figuring on sellin' out."

"We'll drink to that too!" James said, pouring another shot. "To Charley's station!" he cheered.

Charley sniffed around and soon found a new home. He thought the name Seven-Mile House a bit to impersonal, so he rechristened it Sandy Station, due to its close proximity to the beach, and set up shop. The name proved especially appropriate as the sand got into practically everything.

The station was a string incorporated in the Coast Line Stage Company. It was a swing station and provided a noon time meal, which got rave reviews amongst the frequent travelers, except for the sand of course. Charley kept a low profile and depended on people to run the kitchen and bar. Frank Woodward came on to help run things with the horses and they had a few other stable hands, but Charley still longed for the open road. The station was close to the ocean and he took frequent rides on the surf, it reminded him of the old days with Mozo.

Charley often reflected back on the first adventures in this new country and how much it has changed. He remembered his first sighting of a wild herd of horses, running free in the foothills. The stallion standing guard over his harem. Young colts running friskily by their mother's sides, tails flagging straight up to the heavens. The stallion tossing his head and pawing the ground as the coach came nearer, then challenging the oncoming herd of captive horses with an explosive leap and driving his mares away from danger in the twinkling of an eye.

CHAPTER 55

Carson City, May 1866

John Thompson entered Ormsby's Tavern after unloading his produce. He scanned the room for any familiar faces and found Hank Monk, sitting in his favorite spot, near the large potbelly stove.

"Hank, I've got good news! I'm getting married!" the Norseman announced to the world.

"I thought you said you had good news," the droll teamster remarked.

"It's vonderful news, I'm zo happy, I never been dis happy before," John said, glowing with the glory of his new love.

"That's just fine, Snowshoe! Have a drink on the house!" Big John, the bartender said, pouring a beer for the mailman.

"Tank you."

"So how did you meet the soon-to-be Mrs. Snowshoe?" Monk inquired.

"I met her on da mountain zide. I vas teaching zome of da young boys to ski, and she came out to vatch. Her name is Agnes Singleton, she is from England."

"You just swept her off her feet?" Hank inquired.

"Vell not really, I hired her and her mother to be my housekeepers, at my ranch. Ve vill be married at her brother's ranch in Sheridan, next Sunday."

"That's good thinking, John, at least you got to test out her cooking and cleaning skills first. Sounds like you got the two fer one package too," Monk chucked to himself, as he raised his glass. "A toast to Snowshoe Thompson, who's gettin married! May God have mercy on the man!"

The wedding was a lovely one, simple but friendly. Folks came from all over, bringing food and gifts for their beloved hero's nuptials. Anyone who could play an instrument brought theirs and folks sang and danced the day and night away, many leaving the party after breakfast the next morning. People around there enjoyed a good wedding.

At last, Agnes and John Thompson left the celebration, climbing in his wagon that had been decorated and filled with gifts. He put the leather lines in one strong hand and put an arm tenderly around Agnes's waist and clucked to his horses as he kicked off the break, eager to be alone with his bride, at his new home in the Hope Valley, he named the Diamond Ranch.

Anne, Agnes's mother, would be staying with her son Sam for a month or two, until the newlyweds got settled and an extra room added to the Thompson house.

Nine months later on February 11, 1867, little Arthur Thompson was born.

"Hank! I'm zo happy! I'm a father, I have a son!"

"Well, that is good news! What did you name the little nipper?" Monk inquired.

"Agnes vanted to name him Arthur, dat's my middle name," John said beaming with pride.

"Hey, Lenny, set everyone up and we'll have a drink to Snowshoe's new son, Arthur," Monk said, setting a few coins on the well-worn bar. "Top the whiskey off with some of that hunert proof peppermint schnapps you got there, we'll call that a Snowshoe! There now, three cheers for Snowshoe Thompson!" Monk said looking at the potent shot. The bar shouted their cheers and tossed down their liquor.

"Boy, howdy that's pretty good stuff!" Monk said enjoying his concoction.

"Zet 'em up again, Lenny, you can't ski on von snowshoe!" Thompson said setting down a few more coins to treat his friends. The men gave Thompson three more cheers, as the busy bartender poured out shots to the men at the bar, who were holding out their thirsty glasses.

CHAPTER 56

Santa Cruz, California, 1868

"My father taught me that it was every man's duty as an American to vote!" Woody preached.

"I'm an orphan." Charley smiled sarcastically. "Who are you going to vote for?"

"Well, I'll tell you, I'm leanin' toward Grant. He's definitely a strong leader," Woody commenced.

"I don't know, I hear he's kinda a hard drinker." Charley grinned.

"What? What about all his experience in the war and the like."

"Well sure, that does make a man add up of course. I tell you I'll have to give this some thought. When is votin' day?" Charley asked.

"Tomorra'," Woody sighed.

The next day, Charley and Woody stepped up to the town hall, to cast their vote along with the rest of the men folk. The women stood around outside in a group, waiting for their husbands to do their duty, as Charley walked past them, he smiled. Maybe someday they would all have the right to vote.

The line of men wound around the inside of the meeting hall. It was very solemn and orderly. Many official men were busy manning the wheels of democracy. An elderly gentleman was sitting at a desk with a ledger, taking down the name of each voter, who then stepped to another officer, who handed over a ballot, then off to the voting booth and the ballot box. As the line of voters progressed, the two friends could hear the elderly recorder clearly asking each man:

"Plainly state your last, first, and middle name. Age? Country of nativity? Occupation? Local residence?"

"What's he mean by middle name? You have a middle name?" Charley whispered to Woody.

"Sure everyone's gotta middle name. Mine's Albert. Frank Albert Woodward. Don't you have a middle name?"

"Well, Hank always called me Parkie," Charley reasoned.

"That's a nick name, ain't you got a Christian name?" Woody inquired.

"That's the only other name I got," Charley whispered anxiously, as the two grew nearer to the recorder. Maybe you ought to go a head of me?" he said, getting nervous about no middle name.

"Oh, for crying out loud, go on," Woody said shoving the teamster ahead.

"Plainly state your last, first and middle name," the elderly man said, looking over the tops of his frail glasses, pen at the ready.

"Cha . . . Um . . . aaa . . . Parkhurst, Charley, Parkie, sir."

"Parkhurst, Charley, Darky," the recorder mumbled, as he scribbled on the ledger.

"No, that's Parkie." Charley pointed out.

"Age?" the man relented.

"Fifty-five. I . . . um . . . I think you got my middle name wrong."

The recorder was not about to mess up his nice scroll for such a small error.

"Yes, well . . . Country of nativity?" he continued.

"New Hampshire," Charley grumbled.

"Occupation?"

"Uh . . . Farmer?"

"Local residence?"

"Soqual."

"Sign here." The recorder handed over the pen. "Over there, please. Next!" he hollered. Charley turned and was handed a ballot and a pencil, then entered the booth.

"Damnation, I can't believe he got my name wrong!" Charley said lighting up a cigar outside the election center.

"Your nickname! Darky! Ha ha! That's hilarious," Woody said doubling over. "Darky!"

"Keep it up, and you'll get a punch in the snout!"

"Oh, I'm sorry. But it was funny! I won't tell anyone, if you don't want," Woody said seeing Charley's feelings were hurt. "Say, who did you vote for?"

"I ain't a tellin! So there!" Charley said, smiling.

"Come on, I'll tell you who I voted for?"

"I don't want to know!" Charley teased, as they headed back to the buckboard.

"Please? I'll tell folks what your middle name is?"

"Grant."

"Ha! Me too! He'll be a grand president, I just know he's gonna win!" Woody rambled on.

CHAPTER 57

1869 Sandy Station

"Don't tell me you're tending bar tonight, Charley?" Dave, a dairyman from a near by ranch teased, as Parkhurst walked behind the bar.

"Well . . . What's wrong with that, I sat at enough bar stools! Besides, Jesus' wife is having a baby, their first. What can I do? The man's a nervous wreck. So you guys are stuck with me." Charley smiled.

It was queer to be on the other side of the oak planks, for a change. It reminded Charley of Ebenezer Balch. Sandy Station was Parkhurst's best imitation of the What Cheer, but somehow Charley's heart just wasn't in it. Since the coach accident, it was too painful to drive, so he was compelled to run a station. He lived over the tavern there and saw to the livestock and provisions and hired a bartender and a cook. It was a reasonable business, but it had become a full time job, much harder than driving the coach, he found out. As a coachman, you had the road and the horses to worry about, once in a while the odd hold up, but that was it. It was much different running a stage stop. However, the local people enjoyed the food and drank there, as well as the travelers and as a business; it made money.

"So, Charley, can you shake up drinks like Jesus?" Dave asked.

"Sure, I can make what ever you want, as long as it's a shot or a beer! Oh, I got wine and cider too," he added proudly.

"Say bartender, we'll have two beers here," a thirsty-looking patron called out. He seemed to have a coarse roughness about him that Charley didn't like. Parkhurst was not used to being talked down to, as a bartender sometimes was.

"All right, gentleman, two beers coming up." He smiled, holding back his contempt. Charley knew that the local men were all fond of Charley and would always be there to back him up, never the less, he always kept a loaded shotgun under the bar counter and a loaded Derringer in a specially tailored pocket, for emergencies. Thankfully, he had never needed to use it. Charley's weathered face and eye patch, along with his proud stature and confidence, commanded most men's respect, even those who didn't know him in his lofty driving days.

The coach would be arriving any time now, Charley surmised, as he gazed upon his faithful pocket watch. His friend Woody was in charge of the horses. It would not be a fast change as it was a lunch stop.

Cathy the cook and her daughter, Pearl, buzzed around the tavern, setting up the buffet table. The patrons would pay fifteen cents and receive a plate to take to the buffet, then retire to the rustic dinner tables to eat, before they were whisked away again. The station tavern always had stew and bread with gravy and fresh game from the area, duck or goose, fish, and clams; today they were treated to Cathys' special dumpling soup. The Monterey coast was a culinary cornucopia; the buffet also had fresh local cheeses and fruit.

When the stage arrived, the passengers poured into the station dining room and bar. Finally a young man entered lastly. Charley's eye poured over the coachman, as he entered the tavern. He was regal in his sand blown great coat and hat, as he stood in front of the fireplace and warmed himself, taking his time to the buffet table, letting the hungry passengers go before him. He seemed most noble. Charley remembered his driving career sentimentally for a moment.

"Full load, it looks like," Cathy said, as she put out extra plates.

The hungry horde soon departed, as quickly as they had arrived, leaving the station a mess with dirty dishes.

Charley then noticed a disheveled man who had entered the establishment, as the coach riders departed. He had stepped up to warm himself at the fire in the stone hearth, as the fog had hung thickly all morning. Charley was carrying a load of dishes to the kitchen.

"Hey, barkeep!" the short man called.

"Oh, hello, I'll be right with you," the bartender greeted the potential customer. "Pearl help your mother with these dishes," he said, handing the plates to the girl and heading back to the bar.

"Now then, what can I get you?" Charley said, with as much charm as he could muster. Given the eye patch it was a little scary.

"Can I get something to eat, and some coffee?" the man asked, looking at the picked over buffet table.

"Sure! We can get you fed. I'll get Cathy to fetch you a plate, then you can help yourself to what's left over there." Charley smiled, then fled back to the kitchen.

"I need to get a clean plate for a customer," Charley pleaded.

"Here I'll get you one. Keep stirring this pan," Cathy said, handing the proprietor a large wooden spoon and going over to the sink.

"What are you cooking, Charley?" Woody asked, as he came into the kitchen, with his two stable mates.

"Hell, I don't know," Charley said, concentrating on the pan, "but if I burn this, Cathy is gonna skin me alive and I might miss out on some wonderful dessert. So leave me to my stirrin'."

"You ain't burning that are you?" Cathy said, as she returned from the bar.

"No, looks good what is it?" Charley asked, licking a finger full.

"It's a glaze for my cake. See?" she said, pointing to the cooling masterpiece on the windowsill.

"Oh well I certainly hope I didn't spoil it," Charley said, with high expectations.

"I hope not too," Woody spoke from the back of the kitchen.

"Well I got a job to perform, Don't you fellers have some horses to look after or something?" Charley said, as he returned to the bar.

"No, we're done for a while. We come to watch you be bartender." Woody smiled. "Come on, Charley, I'll shake dice with you for a round of beers."

"Not right now fellows, you shake among yourselves, I'll join you later," Charley said, getting out the dice cups, then back to business. "Sir, can I get anything else for you?" he asked the bearded man at the end of the bar, who was now eating.

"Say this looks like a horsy type of a place. Do you know anything about horses or could you direct me to someone who knows about horses?" Dick Fellows asked the bartender, as he looked at the pictures of racehorses and stagecoaches that were framed and hanging on the walls of the tavern.

"Well, I might know a thing or two. What is it you want to know. Maybe I can help you?" Charley responded, his interest peaked.

"I got a problem with my horse." Fellows laughed nervously.

"My names Charley Parkhurst, you can call me Parkie. I've been a coach driver for over thirty years. I guess I know a thing or two about horses," he said with pride.

"Dick Fellows, pleased to meet you."

"What kinda trouble you having with your horse?" Charley asked.

"Well, he's predisposed to jumping up and down at the worst possible times, going down hills and such," Fellows said, rubbing a tender spot on his head. "He's also pretty good for running off at untold opportunities as well."

"Hmm . . . Is he outside, maybe I can have a look at him?" Charley said, scratching his head.

"Be my guest, he's out on the rail. He's the mustard-colored nag with the gray mop," the short, bearded man said, savoring his leftovers.

"Out on the rail, well, I'll have a look then," Charley said, taking out a thin cigar and lighting a match. "Woody keep an eye on things, I'm goin to step outside for a minute." Charley walked along the porch until he stood in front of a seedy looking mustang. The horse snorted his disapproval. He was a mean little son of a bitch, probably kick you or bite you if given any chance, Charley thought to himself, as he stepped down the stairs to the front of the hitch rail and looked over the small horse. He was lean and mean, and he looked hungry. As Parkie felt sympathy for the animal and let his guard down, the miserable beast bit him on the arm.

"Damn! You little cussword, I was going to get you some supper and see how you treat me?" Charley growled, rubbing the arm, which was developing a great welt. "You're probably some offspring of Clemens long-lost nag!" he pondered, as he examined the animals' bridle, to find no chinstrap on the bit. "No wonder you run off and carry on. You just open your mouth and do what you please. Well, maybe I shouldn't give this guy the upper hand, but if I don't, he might just shoot you in the head someday, and then where would you be? Vulture food, that's where. You don't want that, do you?" Charley said, scratching the nag behind the ears.

"Well, I think I see what your trouble is with the horse. You've got no curb chain on your bit," Charley said with obvious expertise, as he settled back behind the bar once again.

"I've got no what?" Fellows said blankly.

"No curb chain on your bit," Charley said, as if everyone should clearly under stand this. Woody was nodding with approval. At that time the cheese man Robert had arrived with his deliveries.

"Robert, you always have a curb chain on your bits, don't you?" Woody asked the man, as he stepped into the room.

"Why of course, I always drive with a curb chain on my bits, doesn't everyone?" he asked in return, setting the box on the bar. "Charley, don't tell me that you're bartending tonight?" Robert asked incredulously.

"Yep, Jesus' wife is having her baby." Charley nodded, putting clean glasses on the back bar. "What'll it be Robert?"

"Hey, whatever is your specialty, I feel like living dangerously tonight," Robert said shaking hands with his friend.

"Well, how about a beer?"

"So, Charley . . ." Dick Fellows motioned for the bartender to come close. "What the hell is a bit and curb chain?" the Easterner whispered.

Charley stared at the man for a moment in disbelief, then answered, "Oh, I'm sorry, I'll show you if you'd like."

"Yeah, but not in front of all these folks," he whispered in confidence.

"Oh sure." Charley smiled with a wink. He left the bar for a moment then returned to the disheveled man caring a curb chain. "I'll adjust it for you for no extra charge. It will be just two bits for the chain," he added.

"If you think it will do any good, it's worth it," Fellows said in complete ignorance.

"Oh it will be a big help, believe me," Parkhurst said heading toward the tie rail outside. "When he starts carrying on just pull the reins up . . . These," he said, running his hands down the leather trying to avoid being bitten again. "Look this is the bit, and these are the reins, and this is the curb chain. It goes on here," Parkie said pointing to the top hole on the metal mouthpiece the nag was grinding on in boredom and hunger.

"I thought this was the bridle," Fellows tried to bluff.

"The whole thing is the bridle. The chain is attached with these leather straps. Like so." He buckled the short chain around the horses' chin, to the top holes in the metal mouthpiece. "By the looks of him, I highly recommend that you feed him, and you can do that here as well. Tell you what, you buy another beer and I'll throw in that nags' dinner for free," the tenderhearted teamster added.

"You got a deal!" Fellows said, knowing he would imbibe more than one before he left tonight; he had many bruises to relieve, before he would dare climb on that bone-jarring mode of locomotion.

"Alejando, take that horse to the livery and feed him bueno," the superintendent ordered. "And watch out, he bites, probably kicks too," Charley called out. Fellows nodded. "Yes, he definitely kicks too."

Alejando waved as he grabbed the nag by the reins and led him off.

Charley sighed; it was going to be a long night. There would be two more coaches coming through tonight, a dinner stop and a late swing through, a fast change. After that he could close the station and sleep. Until then Parkhurst would have to be pleasant and make nice behind the bar.

Charley began to seriously consider retiring to a ranch, to raise cattle or horses and not have to deal with the public any longer. That thought gave him new strength. Charley sauntered back behind the oak bar and settled into a discussion with Robert.

"You want a fresh beer?" Charley asked.

"No, I got to be on my way. I got two more stops today," he said finishing his glass.

"Robert, do you know of any ranches in the area coming up for sale?" Parkhurst said quietly,

"You fixin' on buying a ranch, Charley?" Robert responded.

"Yeah, I reckon I am," Charley replied calmly, as if receiving a revelation.

"I know of one, I can ask around if you like. It's in the Pajjaro Valley. Nice piece of land, I'm told. Lot's of big trees," Robert offered.

"If you could look into that for me, I be greatly indebted," Charley replied.

"No trouble at all." Robert smiled.

That night, Parkhurst dwelt on the idea of a simple cattle ranch, with no bartending required.

Robert did help Charley find the ranch that he wanted. In fact, it was not far from where his horse Mozo was buried. It gave Charley a sense of peace to be close to something he had loved so dearly. Parkhurst sold Sandy Station and set about fixing up a log cabin and acquiring cattle. This was a much more liberated lifestyle; no clock to watch or timetable to meet, or customers to please, just the land, the livestock, and the dry goods bills.

Charley and Frank Woodward became expert lumberjacks and purchased and trained good logging horses. The property boasted groves of enormous redwood trees. Parkhurst's skill snaking logs out of the forests with his beautiful new gray Percherons was soon well known. The horses were voice trained and had a great working attitude, not to mention their brute size and strength. Charley made sure they were always well fed and in top condition.

The only problem was the grizzly bears that would frequent the ranch. They were especially dangerous when the cows were calving in the spring. The bears were quite hard on the newly born calves; there was no fence that Charley could device that could stop a grizzly bear. Keeping them up was a full time job in itself. Woody was a partner in the ranch, and the two were good friends, but Parkhurst was feeling his vital energies slowing down and growing weaker, then there was the persistent cough that plagued him.

"Man, I am dog tired," Charley said, as they rode the great draft horses back to the barn, from the logging site.

"I'm right there with you partner," Woody said, from the back of the other great horse. After we put these fellows to bed, what say we go to town and get a good dinner? We deserve it!" Woody said with pride.

"I don't know if I have enough strength for even that. I think I'll just scramble a few eggs and some bacon and go to bed," Charley said, with tired eyes. "Wake me when we get to the barn," he said turning around on the back of the giant logging horse, until he sat facing the tail. He stretched out onto the horses' wide rump and made himself quite comfortable, shutting his eyes. The beautiful horse knew the way home and so did Woody, so the aging teamster napped, as the light-footed conveyance rocked him to sleep.

The next morning, Charley read the news of his friend John Rollin Ridges' death, at the age of forty. It further depressed the teamster.

"I can't believe that John is . . . passed on!" Charley said looking at the paper. "Damn, he had so much to say and to offer people. He was so young. I didn't believe that everything the man wrote was right; he believed in the right to have slaves. I certainly can't agree with that . . . But he was my friend," Charley said quietly. "A good friend. Geez I wonder how Will is doing? I ain't heard from him for a long spell," Charley said, quite unaware he was carrying on a conversation with himself. "Say, it might not be a bad idear to check in on my old patient. Maybe I ought to write him a letter see how he's holding up," Charley said aloud to himself. "Sherry I'd like to settle up here," he called to the waitress at the counter.

"Are you sure you wouldn't like some pie, Charley?" Sherry said with a smile and a wink.

"No, I'm afraid my sweet tooth is kind of painin' me. I'll have to forgo the pie tonight," Charley said, in an off-handed manner, rubbing his jaw. "Thank you very kindly anyway, just the bill if you don't mind," Charley said, wincing from the aching mouth. When he arrived home he took a swallow of laudanum and retired. He had bizarre dreams of John and Will and Joaquin.

The next day, Charley's mouth still hurt, but he had no plans for the day, as it was Sunday, and he seldom went to church. Charley found it simpler to remain a recluse on the ranch with Woody. Occasionally having dinner in town with him or Otto. Otto was a businessman in town and had become a good friend too. He even offered to sponsor Charley into the fellowship of the Odd Fellows. Charley found that completely hilarious. She contemplated that there was never an odder fellow than herself and accepted his invitation. After all, Charley had been a member in good standing with the E Clampus Vitus clan or "The Clampers" as they were sometime referred to. They were a fraternal brotherhood started by a Hell-raiser named Sam Hartley in 1857, in Sierra City.

The Clampers were a good hearted fraternity that made widows and orphans their charitable benefactors, while playing practical jokes on any unwary stranger or passer by. Traveling salesmen could not sell their wares in many frontier towns, unless they became initiated into the fraternity. The initiation itself was a most humiliating experience. Charley's own initiation was mild, as James Birch, himself a high-standing member, presided over the event and had the final say on all of the pranks pulled on the new initiates that night.

The Odd Fellows were quite mild compared to the Clampers.

CHAPTER 58

Placerville, winter 1870

As the gold towns of California emptied out to the newly expanding gold fields in Nevada, Placerville continued to flourished as a stop on the cross country route. But still, the winter snows kept the mail at a standstill across the mighty Sierras, until John "Snowshoe" Thompson picked up the mail sack and carried it on his back, over the untamable mountain peaks to Carson City, Nevada.

Thompson stamped the snow from his boots, in front of the Express office. He had his twenty-five pound skis in one hand and rested them against the front of the building before he entered.

"Is the mail ready to go?"

"Thompson, you're right on time. Hey how did that race go, you was in?" the mail clerk chimed.

"Terrible, I didn't win," Thompson said, smarting.

"What? I don't believe you, now don't you kid me," the clerk laughed.

"It's true," Thompson said, trying to end the conversation.

"Oh gosh, wait till Hank hears. He had twenty dollars on you," the man tittered.

"Is da mail ready? I just vant to go." John glared at the puny man.

"Yes I said it was." The man pointed to the bundle. The office door then swung open unceremoniously, and in came James Hume and the Wells Fargo Expressman.

"Hey, Thompson! I thought I spotted your planks out front. Going out?" Hume said, slapping John on the back.

"Yeah, I'm just leaving," he said, lifting the mail sack to his back.

"Well then, good luck to you. Hey, how did you do in the race?" Hume inquired.

"I didn't win," Thompson said, solemnly.

"What? I don't believe it! You're pulling my leg, how could anyone beat you?" James Hume said laughing.

"Dey put zomething on deir skis to make dem zlide faster. I don't know. Da man dat beat me vas from da old country, Germany I tink. He vas very fast," Thompson said humbly.

"Well, I just don't believe it." Hume shook his head. "Oh hell, Hank will be in a minute, no doubt."

"Hey, Thompson! I thought I saw your snowshoes out front! How much money did you win at the race?" Hank cheered, shaking the snow off his hat, creating a puddle on the wood floor.

"I didn't vin," Thompson grumbled with a sigh.

"You didn't win?" Hank laughed heartily. "What do you mean you didn't win? You're pulling my leg!" Hank laughed sizing up the miserable mail carrier. "Shit, you mean to tell me that you really didn't win?"

"Dat's vat I zaid," Thompson said, again trying to put on his mail sack. "I've got to go," he said turning to leave. As he jerked the door open, Edgar appeared in its opening.

"Hey thanks, John. It's really cold out. Oh, how was the race?" Edgar rambled.

"Vhy does everyone keep asking me dat!" Thompson hollered, grabbing his planks and marching off into the night. "How vas da race, how vas da race. I'll vin da next time, just you vait and zee. I'll put vax on my skis dat's vat I'll do!" Thompson said to himself, as he kicked his boots into the ski bindings, then went off into the snowy landscape, faithfully carrying the mail across the Sierras in the dead of winter.

CHAPTER 59

Stockton, California 1870

Charley had come to Stockton to pick up some supplies for the ranch. While waiting for the goods to be loaded, he thought he spied a familiar face walking into a nearby tavern.

"Jim, I want to go say hello to a friend I'll just be a few minutes," Charley said to the hardware man, before walking away. He stepped into the dimly lit tavern and squinted his eye to adjust to the darkness. Then smiled from ear to ear as he spied the quarry. A tired-looking man was looking wistfully into his glass of whisky and appeared to be deep in thought.

"Will? William Byrnes?" Charley said, smiling. The man shifted his gaze angrily toward the inquiry, slamming the glass down against the table.

"Yes? What do you want?" Byrnes said with no recognition of his old friend and more than a little hostility.

"I just wanted to say hello," Charley said, the lack of recognition was extremely painful, he hardly knew what to say, as his throat seemed to tighten.

"Well, you said it, now move along," Will said coldly, reaching for his gun.

"Sorry, Will. It was nice to see you, I reckon," Charley said making a hasty exit. "Damned if that wasn't the strangest thing," Charley said, scratching his head and walking back to the wagon. "Ready to go yet?" Parkhurst asked quietly, feelings hurt.

"Did you see your friend?" Jim asked.

"Yeah," Charley said quietly. He didn't know what to think, as he climbed into the driver's seat. "How could he not know me?" He kept asking himself. Charley kissed at the horses, and they were off. As the wagon reached the corner of the street, Charley spotted William Byrnes stepping aboard his horse.

"Hey, Charley!" he waved at his old friend and rode off in the opposite direction.

"Will?" Charley said with a smile, as they turned the corner. "Well, I'll be damned. If that wasn't odd," Charley mumbled, wanting to turn back and chat with his friend, but he was gone.

Charley could not help thinking about Will nearly the entire trip back. How deep in a fog was he? He would find some reason to return to Stockton.

CHAPTER 60

Reno, Nevada, January 1872

John Thompson picked the harshest time of year to make this pilgrimage to the nation's capital, possibly to make a point, by simply not being around to deliver the snowed in mails from Placerville. He had made his mind up about going; he was at the train station in Reno, a small knapsack with some clean clothes strapped to his back.

Snowshoe Thompson climbed onto the puffing iron horse, knocking the snow off his boots with each step. He paused on the step for a moment, to adjust the parcel of biscuits in his shirt that Agnes gave him, when they said fair well in Carson City. He noticed the iceman shoving great blocks into compartments underneath the nether reaches of the dining car. The porter at the top of the stairs took his bag and followed him inside the train. Thompson stood out from the rest of the passengers with his great physical size and bearskin coat. The porter tapped the huge man and asked to see his ticket so he could stow his luggage. Snowshoe meekly turned and fished through his pockets with an embarrassed blush creeping up his cheeks. At last he procured the missing paper and thrust it with enthusiasm at the porter, causing him to cower. The porter soon regained his composure and guided Thompson to his seat on the train, then placed Thompson's bag in a rack, above the seat and hustled off to help others settle in for the long ride across the country. The stagecoaches had been replaced by the steam engine at last.

The outdoorsman was duly impressed with the fine craftsmanship of the new train car. The seats were richly upholstered with burgundy colored damask and the curtains were of deep red velvet, with gold-colored trim. The woodwork of the car was quite fancy with rich mahogany, inlaid with lighter woods depicting, flowers and ferns. Above the windows, the walls were also mahogany and had woodland paintings set into the panels and trimmed with lavish moldings. The luggage racks above the seats were highly polished brass and were on hinges, to be folded up when not in use. The center roof rose up into a high arch, above that, was thin rectangular etched glass windows. The ceiling was also impressively built of fine wood, then lit with suspended brass oil lamps. Snowshoe felt it was the fanciest place he'd been to in a long time and felt somehow inappropriately attired, as he sat on the fine fabric of the new train, in his well-worn fur coat.

Thompson felt around in his coat and retrieved a hard biscuit that Agnes had baked and began to gnaw on it. His mind wandered about what he would say before the politicians in Washington. He had never felt very comfortable talking in front of a crowd, but had made up his mind to go get what was rightfully his. His friends had signed a petition and the list of signatures was impressive. It was a resolution that asked the U.S. Congress to pay Thompson $6,000 dollars for his past services. Up until this day, all he had ever been paid for his years of mail carrying had been $80.22 from Chorrpenning, who then lost the mail contract and ceased to pay Thompson. Yet the mail was still in need of delivery, so Snowshoe continued to carry it across the Sierras in the dead of winter. Thompson got the mail through the snowed in mountains for over fifteen years, when no other man could and had earned compensation, yet had never received it. The document was signed by the Governor of Nevada, and the Nevada Senator, William Stewart, with over a thousand other signatures.

John's eyes roved up and down the aisle, taking in all the different people, stowing luggage and, making themselves comfortable in their seats. Other cars contained sleeping berths; then there was the dining car. Thompson had his bench seat to himself for the time being, but soon a man came trundling down the aisle, looking for a place to light, as the train lurched from the station.

"May I?" the odd little man asked, as he swayed in the aisle.

"Surely," the big man replied, sliding over to the window. "I never rode on a train, have you?" Thompson added, looking out the window.

"Oh my, lots of times. I'm from the East. I travel around all the time," the man responded. "My name is Rufus Turner."

"John Thompson, my friends call me Snowshoe," he said, holding out his bear paw.

"Oh my, I have heard of you! The man that carries the mail! Yes, siree, it's a pleasure," Rufus said, pumping the big hand up and down.

"Tank you, I'm sure," Thompson said humbly. "Vould you like a biscuit, my vife made dem," he said, fishing around in his coat.

"Your wife made them, well. Don't mind it I do," Rufus said, examining the baked goods. The biscuit was hard as a rock. That made them good for traveling purposes, but not necessarily good for eating. Rufus tried to eat the snack, but soon decided politely to save it for later.

"I'll just keep it here for now and enjoy it later."

"Let me know if you vant anymore. I got a whole bag of dem. Agnes always vorries dat I get hungry. My vife is so sweet," Snowshoe said, gnawing on his lover's gift.

Turner had two large cases that he was trying to fit at his feet. Thompson rose and heaved the cases up on the brass rack. He towered over Rufus Turner who was a short man, rather on the fat side and appeared to be about forty. He may have been younger but was fairly bald, and it made it hard to speculate, Thompson thought.

"It smells like it vill snow," John said, sniffing the windowsills. "I bet it snows by night fall," he said confidently.

"Say, that can't be good. This train can't roll if it snows, can't it?" Rufus asked nervously.

"I don't know anyting about trains Rufus," Thompson said, looking out the window.

"I came in through the dining car. I think I'll head back over there and see what they have," Rufus said changing the subject.

"All right Rufus, I'll zee you later," Thompson said, stretching his legs and closing his eyes. He had tried to save some money by purchasing a general ticket without a sleeping berth. Trying to conserve his resources, he had no idea how long he would have to stay in Washington and that meant paying for hotel rooms. These train seats were deluxe accommodations compared to some of the places that he had camped in blizzard conditions.

John sat trying to get some rest, but his long legs were becoming rather cramped. A child in the seat behind him was crying and getting ready to pitch a fit, so the lanky man got up and decided to explore the dining car too.

It was a strange new feeling walking along the moving train, as it jiggled along, swaying lightly to and fro. It was like being drunk, almost, he thought, as he passed through the doorway and stood out on the vestibule, drinking in the fresh crisp air flying around him. It was definitely going to snow. He paused for awhile before going into the pie car, a friendly nickname for the diner. He was in awe of mankind's inventive and gung ho spirit that was bringing this country's shores together. The Iron Horse, the herald of the new age, may someday even carry the mail in his place, across the mighty Sierra.

As he opened the car door, a great rush of smells flashed into his face. The room was full of people in all stages of dining, from looking for the waiter to order, to men smoking cigars and drinking brandy with full stomachs. The man stood at the doorway looking down the aisle at the booths, lining the pie car, trying to find a place to sit. He spotted Rufus on the other end of the car; busy dunking a biscuit in a cup of something that looked like coffee.

"Rufus!" Thompson called out. To his chagrin, most everyone in the car stopped what they were doing and looked around at the outdoorsman, who was turning red. "Hi ya there, Rufus," He waved.

"Thompson! Come on down." Turner laughed, as everyone went back to business. "Sit here. Your wife's biscuit was just delicious. Have you ever dipped them in a cup of coffee?" he asked seriously.

"Yes, I confess I like dem dat vay myself," John confided.

"May I buy you a cup of coffee, my friend," Turner said, eyeing the last piece of biscuit left in his hand. Then gobbling it up with a smile.

"Sure Rufus, dat zounds fine." Thompson smiled broadly at his new friend.

Rufus quickly leapt up and whirled around and headed to a small counter and purchased a steaming mug for his biscuit toting friend and a small pitcher of cream and went back to his seat.

"I have some dairy cows at home, a small herd. I raise beef stock too," Thompson said proudly, as he poured the cream into the cup. "Oh here," he said, reaching into his stash and pulling out a fist full of biscuits. "Tanks for da coffee." The two had a regular tea party, except of course for the coffee.

"You know, it is starting to snow," Thompson said casually, looking at the fine silverware on the table.

"Is it?" Rufus said with concern.

"Yes, I tink dat it vill get very bad. I can smell da strong veather coming," Thompson said grimly.

"Well, that is news, strong weather, indeed," Turner said, not knowing what else to say. "Look you can order a whole dinner right off this menu, anything you could think of," he added, trying to change the subject. "Oh, here comes the waiter now," he said with glee.

"Are you ready to order, gentlemen?" a man in an apron asked. He had a small board with some paper fastened on and a small pencil in his hand.

"Vhat is da special here?" Thompson asked.

"Oh, we have some very lovely quail," the waiter replied, smiling smugly.

"No, I don't like quvail, too much shot and too many bones. Vat else do you have?" Snowshoe asked.

"I'll just let you look at the menu, a bit longer. I'll be back around in a few minutes," the waiter replied, rolling his eyes.

"That would be just fine," Turner injected. "They have a buffalo steak here and antelope cutlets as well."

"Vat are you going to get, Rufus?" Snowshoe asked, looking at the fancy menu.

"Oh, I think I'll have the antelope," Tuner said, with a smile at his new friend. "They have turtle soup and crab bisque. Broiled teal with olives," Rufus rambled on. Generally he didn't have many friends.

"I'm pretty hungry, I tink I'll get da buffalo," Thompson said with resolve. At that time, the harried man in the apron darted by, briskly delivering hot food to hungry customers. "Sir!" was all Thompson was able to manage, before the man was gone to the back of the car, making his deliveries and juggling empty plates.

"I'll catch him next time." Snowshoe smiled to his friend.

"He'll stop back Snowshoe, don't worry," Turner soothed.

The man did appear shortly after, with armloads of dirty plates and fist fulls of empty wineglasses. It was a remarkable balancing act that was only designed to be carried a short distance.

"I'm ready to order," Thompson said stopping the waiter.

"I'll be right with you!" the waiter said, smiling an agonizing smile, as he kept on to the tiny kitchen. Before he could reach the kitchen, which was really a large triangular closet, the train hit some bad track and the flooring bucked like a newborn colt. It was enough to upset the waiter, who went crashing to the ground.

"Damnation!" the waiter said, hitting the floor. Thompson was soon on his feet to rescue the waiter.

"Are you all right?" Thompson said, helping the man to his feet.

"Yes, yes I'll be fine," the waiter cried, brushing the food and broken glass from his cloths. "Thank you so much. Miguel! Come and clean this mess up!" the waiter screamed.

"Yes, sir," cried, the dishwasher.

"Get me a clean apron," the waiter said with exasperation.

"Here!" Miguel handed over the clean apron, having been involved in previous bouts of bad track before. The waiter retreated to the bowels of the pie car to compose himself, then made a fresh appearance.

"Yes, sir, you seemed quite eager to order?" the waiter said with confidence.

"Well, could you just tell me about the special again?" Rufus said rather timidly.

"Vait, come closer," Snowshoe beckoned. "You've got zometing dere in your hair," he said, reaching into the man's greasy hair. "Dere, dat's better."

"Oh, thank you ever so much!" the waiter said with chagrin. "Yes, well, the special. Yes, yes, oh I know this! Just be assured of that!" the waiter said getting himself into a lather. "Tonight's special is two roast quail, with potatoes and gravy and fresh string beans," he said with dignity.

"I don't like quvail," Snowshoe said butting in.

"What about the antelope?" Rufus asked.

"It' comes with potatoes," the waiter said relaxing

"Vat about da buffalo? Thompson asked.

"Well, it has one bone but I can guarantee no shot!" the waiter said, winning over a friend.

"Vell, in dat case, I will have the buffalo and da potatoes. Do dey keep da skins on?" Thompson asked.

"What do you mean do dey keep the skins on? There's no buffalo hide, if that's what you mean," the waiter said haggardly.

"No, da potatoes, do dey keep da skins on?" Thompson asked.

"Do they keep the skins on? Let's see . . . the skins . . . ugh," he said as if he was searching for the meanings of the words. "Do you want skins on?" the man said defensively.

"Ya, I vant da skins, with a plate of butter with some bread," Thompson ordered.

"And you, sir?" the waiter asked, turning to Rufus.

"I'll have the antelope dinner, thank you," Rufus added, as the waiter scribbled something on the paper and whisked off. "And some more coffee," he hollered down the aisle.

"Vere are you headed, Rufus?" Snowshoe asked bluntly.

"I'm headed to New York on business," Rufus said finishing the last piece of biscuit. "I just love these, I would love to get the recipe for them."

"My vife just mixes tings from her memory, I tink." Snowshoe was puzzled.

"Tell me, John, why are you on a train headed East, I thought you delivered mail in the winter?" Rufus asked inquisitively.

"I am gong to Vashington to present a petition to receive money I am owed for carrying da mail," Thompson said in one breath. Rufus stifled a laugh, and almost choked to death on a piece of biscuit. Thompson immediately swatted Rufus on the back, causing him to cough loudly.

"Are you all right, Rufus?"

"Can I see the petition?" Turner asked after he composed himself. "If you don't mind?"

"Please, I'll show you, it's here," Thompson said reaching inside his vest for an envelope.

"I'll have your dinner for you in just a moment," the harried waiter said, setting two bowls of soup on their small table, then trying to dash off.

"I didn't order any soup," Thompson said, holding the man fast by the arm.

"Oh, it's included in the dinner," the waiter said, trying to gain relief from the viselike grip, as well as balance the other cups and plates on his tray. It was an amazing feat of juggling as the train jostled through more bad track. The waiter disappeared back to the kitchen to retrieve more food.

"You see? This is a first class establishment. Turtle soup," Rufus said slurping up a spoonful.

"Are you sure?" Thompson said tasting the broth.

"It says turtle soup on the menu see?" Rufus said passing over the thin book.

The aisle down the center of the car had become slippery due to previous upsets; Thompson spotted the sliding waiter, navigating down the aisle with two plates. He leapt up to save his dinner when the train hit some bad track, catching both plates in midair, as the poor waiter landed flat on his back.

"Are you all right?" Snowshoe asked, setting the plates on the table and helping the man up.

"Yes, yes, I think so!" he said dusting himself off. "Good catch!" he smiled and darted off.

"Here, I tink dis 'uns yorn, Rufus," Thompson said, pleased with himself. The other residence of the pie car responded with good-natured applause.

Thompson slept soundly when he returned to his seat on the next car. The rocking motion of the train and his dinner soon had him snoring away.

The next morning, the windows were covered with snow and the train was moving along very slowly. They were pulling into Salt Lake City and would pick up another engine to help pull through the relentless snow. When the train stopped, Thompson was eager to get off and watch them adding the engine. He found it quite impressive. They took on fuel and water and a few more people, then were off again, sluggishly chugging through the winter storm. The second engine helped, but at the next station it was agreed to add yet another. The three engines labored along as the weather got worse.

Turner fidgeted and felt fairly pessimistic, as Thompson was prone to stepping out on the vestibule, then returning with dour weather reports. So far he had always been irritatingly correct.

On the third morning, Snowshoe woke to a still locomotive. People on board were beginning to wake. They began to softly worry to each other. Thompson stood up and shook off his sleep. He tightened up his coat and wrapped his blanket over his head and shoulders and went outside. The blast of freezing air was waiting for him when he cracked opened the frozen door. The sleepy passengers wailed in discomfort, as the snow blew in when the door came open. Thompson kicked the snow out as he left, then slammed the door closed and trudged to the front of the train. Men were arguing and shoveling. Thompson scratched his head at the sheer impossibility of the situation. The drift ahead of the train was at least twenty feet, and there was more snow on the way. He listened to the men argue about the best way to deal with the snow, then turned and trudged back to his car, disgusted with technology.

"It doesn't look real good, Rufus. I'm going to get zome breakfast, you vant to come?" Thompson said solemnly upon his return.

"Yeah. Wait up, I'm coming," Rufus said wanting a full description of the drama.

"Better put your coat on, it's freezing out," Thompson warned. Other passengers taking heed and covering up for the cold blast that was about to rip inside, when the door opened yet again. Thompson waited and the two blasted across the vestibule together. The pie car was practically deserted except for two of the conductors, who were at wits end and tossing a coin for the privilege of informing the passengers that they were stranded for an unknown period of time.

Turner and Thompson sat close to the kitchen at the small counter. They spotted the waiter asleep in a booth.

"The thing is, see, that I really have to get to New York. I'll be in serious trouble if I don't get there by next week," Rufus whined.

"I don't vant to be stuck here either," Thompson protested. The two conductors, settling their wager, looked over and smiled apologetically. The waiter was soon roused by the sound of a potential customer.

"Oh, it's you! Good morning, I'll be right with you," he said with a practiced tone, rolling up onto his feet and running his fingers through his greasy hair, then disappearing to the bowels of the car. He returned in an instant with a clean apron and his order board.

"You both want coffee with cream?" he asked.

"Yes, I vould like to have five eggs scrambled and five pieces of bacon, zome bread, and two potatoes if you got dem," Thompson added.

"Yes, and you?" He indicated to Rufus.

"I'll have two eggs scrambled and a piece of ham. That's all," Rufus ordered.

"I'll have that for you right away!" the waiter, who was doubling for a cook at this time, said flying into action. He was greatly unimpeded by the now still train.

"I don't tink dis train vill be moving for qvite a long time," Thompson said, with all seriousness.

"Damn!" Turner burst out, turning a bit red in the face.

"I tink I could valk to da next station before dis train arrives dere," Snowshoe boasted.

"You're not really thinking of going out there and walking?" Rufus joked.

"I might give it some tought," Snowshoe mused. "It's pretty flat. I make it up over mountains no man dares to climb in da snow. Dis cannot be so hard," John was beginning to seriously consider.

"But it must be below freezing outside!" Rufus said, backing down.

"It might get even colder if da vind starts up," Thompson said solemnly.

"You're really thinking about going aren't you?" Rufus said incredulously.

"I don't know yet," Snowshoe said looking out the window at the white scenery.

"I left the skins on the potatoes," the waiter said triumphantly returning.

"Tank you, dat looks good," Thompson praised.

"Eat hearty, I just got word we may be here for a while, we may have to start rationing food," the waiter said, spilling a big headline.

"You men there, the Engineer is organizing a crew of volunteers to clear snow from the tracks. You should check in when you're done eating," the porter announced. "Say I could use a cup of coffee. Waiter!" the porter called.

"I'll be right with you!" the waiter called back.

"Maybe I'll varm up by moving zome snow, den head out. I vould rather valk to Vashington dan to shovel my vay," Snowshoe said between mouthfuls. Rufus laughed, and shook his head in disbelief.

The men at the front of the train were feebly trying to make a dent in the enormous snowdrift, but the snow was coming down almost as fast as they could remove it.

"This is ridicules!" Rufus said in a whine. "We'll never dig through this. We'll have to wait for the spring thaw to come, till we can get out of here!"

"You may be right Rufus, I tink I'm varmed up enough. Are you going to come wid me?" Snowshoe asked directly.

"I don't know if I can make it Thompson," Rufus said with some fear in his voice.

"Zuit yourself, Rufus, I'm going to get my stuff and go," Thompson said walking back to the car.

"Hey, where are you goin'?" the Engineer shouted.

"He says he can out walk your iron horse here. He's going to walk to Washington and beat this here train!" Rufus called back to the Conductor, as he laughed. "And I'm going with him!" Rufus blurted out before he could stop himself. He ran after Thompson like an excited dog.

"Put on all of da clothes you can. Ve need two extra blankets and zome bacon and a few tings. Den ve go. Right Rufus?" Thompson coached.

"You sure you know what you're doing, John?" Turner said hopefully.

"I've never gotten lost yet. I'm sure I can get us trough. I'll not stay here and shovel; I am at home out in da snow. It's not too late to change your mind, you don't have to come vith me. But once ve start, I'll not turn back," Snowshoe cautioned.

"I believe you, Thompson. I'm ready," Rufus said lightly.

"I don't advise you to carry those," Thompson said, pointing to Turners two bags.

"I have to bring them. They are the reason I have to go to New York, to deliver them. If I leave them, I may as well stay here too! See?" Rufus explained. "Don't worry I can carry them myself," he added.

Thompson looked skeptical. "Let's go." The two entered the pie car for the last time. "Remember to take your plate and cup when we leave."

"What about the silver wear?" Rufus smiled.

"I don't tink ve need da silver wear," Thompson reasoned, trying to be fair.

"I'm going to take mine anyway. What else do we need?" Turner asked.

"Lots of Lucifers, lots of cloth napkins, newspaper, candles. Den of course some food. Have dey begun rationing out da food sir?" Thompson called out to the waiter, almost causing a panic amongst the other guests.

"What? What? Don't be stupid, everything is all right. Just relax!" the waiter soothed the ladies in attendance.

"Rufus and I are going to strike out on foot, instead of trying to shovel out, I vant to get zome food for da trip," Thompson explained.

"You mean you are going to walk out into that? You got to be out of your head, you'll freeze to death!" the waiter carried on, pointing out the window.

"It vould be crazy for you to go, but not for me, I'm going," Thompson replied.

"Well, order what ever you want, I can't believe you'd go out in that," the waiter marveled.

"This is the great Snowshoe Thompson, the mailman of the great Sierras!" Rufus said proudly. The two ordered the prescribed bringings and swiped the Lucifer's matches off the table, along with the small wooden holder, that contained a small flint striker. Thompson divided the newspaper into two, then folded it over his plate and stuffed it in his shirt, and motioned Rufus to do the same. There were snickers from the other patrons, as the two prepared to leave. Rufus handed the waiter a gold coin and shook his hand, as the man delivered to them a bundle, wrapped in cloth napkins.

"I threw in some boiled eggs. Take care!" the waiter gushed. Examining the coin and dropping it into his vest pocket.

"Are they really going to walk?" a passenger asked, as the door closed behind them.

"That's what they said, can you believe it? That was Snowshoe Thompson!" the waiter said wistfully.

Thompson strode out into his element, with Rufus ambling along behind, a bag in each hand, trying in vain to walk in the footprints of the great athlete. For one thing, the strides didn't match. Thompson was over six feet tall. Rufus was four foot eleven. It took a while, but Thompson soon noticed and took smaller strides. He felt liberated by the lack of seventy-pound mail sack, carrying only his small bag of cloths and the food, it was relatively flat terrain. The freezing temperature had caused the snow to crust over so the two didn't sink much. Thompson's intimate knowledge of snow travel allowed him to choose the best way through the frozen landscape.

As footfall followed footfall, the two marched onward. Snowshoe noticed the struggle Rufus was having with his load and fitted his two bags with a napkin tied around the handles, so that they could be carried across his shoulders like saddlebags. Turner's hands had gotten dangerously cold transporting his precious bags. Snowshoe wore his finely knitted wool mittens. He pulled out a spare pair and placed them over Turner's raw hands. He then slung the man's bags over his own broad shoulders, and they began the journey anew. It somehow felt natural to carry the baggage anyway, he remarked to himself, looking back at a still struggling Rufus.

They would make camp before sunset, until then they, trudged on. At last, they came to an enormous drift and Thompson stopped. He took the newspaper from his shirt and retrieved his plate then put the paper back. He used the plate as a shoveling tool and begun to tunnel into the snow. Rufus fumbled for his plate to help his scoutmaster. Soon the two were sitting in a fairly comfortable den, liquefying snow in their cups over a candle. The pair slept quietly in their make shift igloo, after dining on food from the train. The extreme weather making their deliciousness tenfold.

Thompson woke several hours later and began preparing for the journey ahead. He was now responsible for his friend's life and the mistake he may have made in allowing him to come along. Turner's shoes were not the best suited for this environment, and he feared that frostbite might set in. John set about trying to augment his traveling ability by waxing his boots and putting wool insulation in the feet and ankles. He used pieces from his spare underwear, which was thick wool and tightly shrunk up, until it was like thick felt. When Rufus woke, the two feasted on hot biscuit mush and bacon.

"I see you kept your spoon." Rufus laughed.

"I fixed up your boots, try dem on Rufus. Thompson said handing them over.

"Wow! These look great!" Rufus said, with a smile that wavered when he rubbed his feet. Thank you for carrying my bags, John," Rufus said apologetically. "I have to get that stuff through. I'd gladly pay you."

"Ve'll get trough, don't vorry Rufus, just try on your shoes, ve may need to make zome adjustments," Thompson said humbly.

They finally collected themselves and used their plates to tunnel back out to the snowy landscape. It was ever so bleak to Rufus, but Snowshoe got his bearings and started out. Rufus sensing the desperation of the situation, clung close behind the outdoorsman and followed in his large boot prints, not bothering to look ahead at the stark white vastness that lay ahead. Rufus was amazed that he was actually getting rather warm, with the physical exertion.

"How far do you think we've come?" Rufus asked when they took a break.

"I tink about ten miles dis morning," Thompson said quietly.

"How far till the next station, I wonder," Rufus said not really expecting the answer.

"Maybe tventy more." Thompson blurted out.

"Oh God, please have mercy!" Rufus sighed. "Well we won't get there standing around I'm getting cold," he added.

"Dat's da spirit, Rufus!" Thompson said, patting his pal on the back. "Let's go. Here's a biscuit to chew on." Snowshoe fished out a snack.

"Thanks, John!" The man snapped up the biscuit like a mongrel dog, and stepped in line.

The two kept a steady pace, as the snow seemed to ease up a bit. They walked along the path of the tracks, losing sight of them in large drifts. By looking out to the horizon, one could see the path they took above the Platte River that lay in the canyon below. The landscape took on its pristine grandeur, the snow erasing man's telltale handiwork with winter whites. Thompson watched snowshoe hares and white fox running around the frosty trees, near the river, as he kept ever onward.

He spotted a good looking place to camp for the night and after setting up, proceeded down to the river to get some wood for a fire. Thompson was worried about Rufus's feet; they were getting bad. When he returned, Rufus was trying in vain to remove his boots.

"Let me get a fire going, den I'll help you," Thompson said, snapping a branch into pieces, it was freeze dried and would burn well. The camp butted up to a ledge and was protected from wind by another ledge about twenty feet away. The hillside had been blasted through to make way for the railway bed. It was quite doubtful that a train would be along any time soon.

Rufus had been quite brave in his travels; he had gone well beyond the usual threshold of pain for a soft desk jockey. He went from ice stabbing pain in his feet, to not being able to feel his feet at all.

Thompson peeled the frozen socks from the swollen feet, setting them near the fire to dry.

"Let me know when your feet starts to ache again," Thompson said wrapping Rufus in a blanket, then setting cups of snow next to the raging fire to thaw. "You must keep drinking water, Rufus. Here have an egg, and a potato. I tink ve can get to da next station tomorrow. Don't be scared, ve'll make it. Have zome bacon," Snowshoe encouraged. "I vish I had my skis," he said wistfully.

He got more wood for the fire, then Thompson applied wax to the boots, from the last remaining candle, and wiped them down with the greasy napkin that held the bacon.

The next morning, they headed out at the crack of dawn. Thompson became frustrated at how slow Rufus was. He turned and beckoned Rufus to climb on his back, the shivering Rufus did not have to be asked twice. Thompson carried him piggyback down the rail bed, as the snow started to come down faster and faster. The two suitcases still dangled across the trudging man's shoulders as he slowly carried his load through the snow. Nevertheless, it was still faster than having to wait for Rufus. He would make Laramie station before nightfall.

The weather in Laramie, Wyoming was no better than any of the frozen pioneer towns in the West. The snowdrifts piled up, bringing everything and everyone to a standstill. The train station was full of people going nowhere. It was a tremendous snowstorm that gripped the plains and just wouldn't let up.

A Conductor, who had been scheduled to conduct, stood out on the weather blown depot deck, looking out at the frozen landscape with his Engineer. The two shared a pint of brandy, as neither would be going anywhere, anytime soon.

"Damnation! We're gonna be stuck here for at least a week, if'n we're lucky!" the Conductor said, spitting in disgust. "What in the name of mercy is that! Is that a bear?" the man said, spotting the white apparition lumbering down the tracks, toward the station. "Get me my rifle! I think it's a bear!"

"I thought bears sleep all winter?" the Engineer said, taking a pull of the bottle.

"Well, what fool would be out walking . . . out there?" the Conductor said, taking back the pint.

"I suppose it could be a bear at that! It looks like a great, snow covered, bear, walking on his hind legs . . . and he's got luggage! Good God Almighty!" the Engineer gasped as Thompson got closer.

"Where in the hell did you come from? Come, help him to the station," the Engineer said, as Thompson, at the utmost edge of exhaustion, stumbled and fell before the two astonished men.

"Holy Mother of God! He's got another guy on his back, under the blanket!" the Engineer hollered, as Rufus groaned and rolled off Thompson's back.

"We made it, we made it! I'm so glad we made it. Thank you, Thompson, you didn't leave me," Rufus said, kissing Snowshoe on the face. "You've saved me!" Rufus tried to stand but couldn't. His feet were frostbitten. Men from the station carried them inside. Thompson was treated to a hero's finest dinner and a good night's rest.

The general population, who were all bored beyond measure, were excited about the strange, heroic new guests of the station. One man was a journalist and began taking notes, as information about the snow covered strangers emerged. Thompson set about making sure his boots were dried out and waxed thickly. He replenished his food supply; sadly he was out of biscuits. He had given the last one as a present to his friend, who was resting comfortably under a doctor's care.

"So you're going back out there?" Rufus asked.

"Yes, it vill be much easier now dat I don't have to carry you, Rufus," Thompson said with a wink.

"You sure you don't want to take my bags?"

"I'm sure." Thompson smiled.

"Well, Snowshoe Thompson, thank you and good luck in Washington. Send a telegram back to this station when you get to Cheyenne, so we'll know you made it," Turner said shaking his friends hand and getting a bit misty eyed.

"Don't vorry, Rufus I'll make it all right," Thompson said standing. "I vill send a telegram. If da vire is still up. Good-bye Rufus."

"Good bye, John. Thanks again." Rufus smiled at his friend.

John adjusted the pack on his back and walked out. Stranded passengers watched in awe as he departed from the station.

Rufus watched out the window, as his friend disappeared into the swirling white landscape.

"Well, if'n I didn't see it with my own eyes, I woun'ta believed that a man would leave some perfectly good shelter, to go a walking around in that there blizzard," the Engineer remarked to the Conductor, as the outdoorsman strode off into the blinding snow.

Thompson was well rested and soon hit a comfortable stride with his greatly lightened load. The exercise kept him warm, even though the weather was well below zero. He was like some sort of a polar bear, impervious to the weather, relishing the white solitude that the rest of mankind had vigorously shunned. In a few days, he had reached the station in Cheyenne, some fifty-six miles and was none the worse for wear. Some trains were just able to move about again, and Snowshoe was able to take the next train toward Washington, but not without notice. News of his great trek had reached the media, and Thompson's name was a sensation. "The Mail Man from California that beat the Iron Horse."

But even the newspaper, it seemed, could not help him with his request for the money he believed owed to him. His heroic efforts had little effect on Congress. They constantly put him off and delayed his stay in Washington much longer than he had expected. He was forced to take up residence in a hotel, and it was becoming expensive.

At last, it was determined that John Arthur "Snowshoe" Thompson had never had a legal contract with the United States Mail Service and was not legally entitled to be paid. And so the trip had been for naught, and the man, after risking his life and hard-earned money, went home no better for his efforts, with a feeling of disgust. He continued to carry the mail when it was needed however, and his legacy of downhill and cross-country skiing is still with us in the Sierras.

CHAPTER 61

1872

Hank pulled his coach into Placerville; the street was a quagmire of mud and snow. After tying off the lines, he nimbly climbed down the vehicle and stood perched on the muddy, steel tire of the yellow wooden wheel, then leapt to the plank sidewalk to avoid the slush.

"Evening, Hank," Sheriff Hume said, as they entered the Express office. "You made good time."

"Yep, but I don't know about tommorra, big storm up there. Hey, Edgar," Hank said signing a ledger after first shaking his hat off, much to Edgar's chagrin. The clerk took out a handkerchief and mopped up the water that soiled his desk.

"Must you shake your hat off over here?"

"Oh, sorry."

"Say you read that new book *Roughing It* by Mark Twain yet?" Edgar snickered. "It's real funny!"

"No, I ain't. But someone told me I was mentioned in it."

"That's what I hear, I haven't read it yet," Edgar snickered, pulling on his gray oily mustache.

"Hmm." Monk shrugged, as he turned to seek out his well-earned leg oil. "See you later Edgar. Evening Sheriff," he said scuffling out the office.

"I'll see you later, Hank. Edgar, here are the new ordinances for you to put up."

"Hey, Sherriff, I lied, I did read all of *Roughing It.* you want to borrow it? It has one hell of a chapter on Hank, even calls him a liar and such, he's gonna get such a goin' over!" Edgar confided.

"You bet I'll borrow it, take good care of it too."

"I sure wish I could see Hank's face when he reads it!" Edgar clucked.

"I'll bet you five-to-one some man jacks got a copy of the book right now, awaiting to hear how he takes it," the lawman deduced. "If you close up quickly you might still catch the show! I better go on down to Jake's to keep order," he said, beating a hasty retreat and not wanting to miss any of the fun.

"Hey there, Hank!" Jake the bartender said greeting the driver and pouring a beer into a mug as the teamster drew up to the bar. "Hey I got a copy of that book, *Roughing It*, you're in chapter ten. Look." With that said, the chubby barkeep handed over a brand new book and flipped it open to the corresponding page. "Hey, Hank, would you sign the page there?" he said handing the driver a freshly dipped pen.

378

"Well, let me read it first before I get ink smudged everywhere. Get me a shot of rye too," Monk said holding court, as the bar began to fill up. The Jehu downed his first shot, then fixed his concentration on the pages, chuckling and smiling.

"He keeps saying the same Horace Greeley story over again!" Monk protested, but kept reading, and kept chuckling. When he concluded his reading, he said in a most wistful tone, "I didn't know they's a writing a song fer me?"

"I didn't either. Are you done? Here, sign it all right?" Jake said putting the pen in his hand.

"Hey what's this fine print at the edge of the page there?" he said as he scribbled his name at the top of the page. "What the hell? What does he mean never occurred! He doesn't know what the hell he's talking about! What does the thirteen chapter of Daniel say? Aha? What the hell is that? Any of you heathen know?" Hank said polishing off his beer as he looked around the room for an explanation.

"Why, I'm sure that there is no chapter thirteen in Daniel," a quiet man in the back of the bar spoke. The bar broke up with laughter.

"I don't know!" the bartender said in sympathy with the driver. "I heard Snowshoe Thompson say that Mark Twain is really Sam Clemens, that used to work at the Territorial Enterprise, said Dan DeQuille told him."

"Sam Clemens? I knew a Sam Clemens in Virginia City, got threw out of his boarding house for hanging his landlady's cat out of a window," Hank reminisced. "You know that's the first I ever heard of a song, though. I like that idear."

"I'll ask around." Jake seemed quite relieved that the teamster was not in a mood to pitch a fit. Instead the man had resigned himself to a life of fame and notoriety. Many asked for his signature and many more would buy the famous driver a drink.

CHAPTER 62

Stockton 1873

In the summer of '73, Charley Parkhurst and his partner, Woody, took a herd of young cattle to the auction in Stockton, where an acquaintance remarked that William Byrnes had been locked up in the city's new booby hatch.

"What?" Charley's face went white for a moment.

"I heard his wife had him committed to the insane asylum," the man chuckled.

Charley was filled with mixed emotions deep inside. He so wanted to see him, yet was afraid of what he might find or another cold reception. The thought that he was in an institution for the insane; it got under his skin. Parkhurst made up his mind to go and say good-bye.

The teamster noticed the size of the institution as he approached. The grounds were large and surrounded by a great tall fence, made of brick and stout timbers, solid to keep prying eyes out, and crazy people in. The buildings inside reminded you of a castle, with steepled corners and pointed spires that stabbed at the sky. The middle building had a steep cupola on the roof, which looked like it might contain bells. The whole place looked more like a great church than an asylum. Charley rode his horse to the front gate and explained to the guard that he would like to visit a patient. The guard instructed him to tie the horse at the post, inside the ground reserved for visitors and go on in.

It was an odd feeling walking into a locked facility. It was a little hard to tell sometimes just who were the staff and who were the inmates. Many of the people out in the gardens working, were less severely afflicted residents. The gardens were quite lovely and immaculately tended. The establishment seemed bright and cheerful.

As he entered the main building, Charley encountered a nurse and asked about Mr. Byrnes. She pointed to an elderly gentleman behind a counter.

"I'm looking for William Wallace Byrnes, sir," Charley inquired.

"Byrnes, I see. Well, let's just see what room. Yes, I see, that would be number 72. Now you just follow that hallway to the end, see, then you turn left. Keep a going down that hall till you come to a door-72. That ought to do it." The gentleman looked directly into Charley's eye, as if waiting for any questions.

"Yes, I guess that will do it, down the hall, then to the left," Charley repeated.

"If I'm not mistaken, 72 is on the right side," he called, looking after Charley, as he made his way. Parkhurst walked by an open room with old ladies busy rocking and knitting, he tried to look relaxed, though it was strange at times. He met an orderly at the crossroads of the hall. She was collecting linens from the rooms. Charley tipped his hat and turned down the next hall. He could feel his heart pounding in his throat and for a split second thought about turning around and leaving. He found himself knocking on the door instead. The response at first was only some coughing.

"Crow?"

"Will, it's me, Charley Parkhurst. May I come in?"

"Come!" A familiar but somehow distant voice called out from within the darkened room. "Why, Parkie, my dear friend, please come in. Why what a suprise!" Will said slowly. He had been sleeping in his rocking chair, in the corner of the small room. There was one small oil lamp on the table.

"Please pardon the dim lighting. Bright lights bring on fierce head aches," Will explained. Charley could see the traces of a bullet wound to the head, as his eye adjusted to the dim light.

"Its good to see you Will, I've missed you." Charley prattled on, not wanting to seem shocked at his appearance. "How is Marion?"

"She's fine . . . She put me in this place," he added with some measure of indignity.

"Seems like a nice place to retire, you have the run of this place, I imagine," Charley smiled hopefully.

"Well, I am partial to a smoke on the verandah in the evenings. What time is it?" Will asked.

"It's 3:30," Charley said, consulting his watch. "I brought a few cigars. Would you like to give me a tour of your verandah?"

"Just give me a hand getting out of this infernal rocking contraption and I'll get my coat," Byrnes groaned like an old man as he got up. He was only forty-seven. Charley grabbed his frail hand and helped him up. The two walked slowly from the room to the porch.

"God, last time I seen you was Gold Hill. You was headed west, after our big ride, I think," Will recounted. "Gone to buy the ranch of your dreams, I believe."

"Yes, I think you're right. It has been a long time," Charley added, as he bit the end off his cigar and lit it.

"Became a prospector after I seen you last. The Cinderella Mine! Had some trouble with some Injuns though. Sneak attack. Shot one partner in the head, then got t'other in the chest and killed him and tossed him down the shaft on top of me, while I was working away, down about seventy feet. The bastard's got a few shots in on me, then tried to bury me alive. By some miracle, my first partner who had been shot in the head, came to, after the red bastards left. He managed to walk to safety. After they patched him together, they came and got me out, after five days."

"Geez, Will, how many times have you cheated death? You must hold some kind of a record."

"I believe I have thirty-two gunshot wounds, I know I have at least three arrow wounds. It would seem that the Almighty simply has no use for me, and the Devil likewise, I reckon," he said, as a matter of fact. "That is my new lover," he said, pointing to the nurse Charley had passed in the hallway. William's eyes were twinkling.

"She's a nice little filly," Charley smiled back. The two had made themselves at home on a couple of chairs on the porch.

"I saw Joaquin the other day. He sure looks good." Charley's face grew serious as Byrnes continued. "I rode on out to Post Office Rock. I was ever so suprised to see him," Will said looking dreamily into his smoke.

"Really, that's just fine, If you see him again, please send my regards. I didn't think he was still ali . . . around," Charley tried to reason.

"But I saw him only the other day," Will insisted.

"He didn't have Tres Dedos with him, did he?" Charley tried to kid.

"Why, Charley, you know I killed that vermin with my own hands just for you. Then I cut off his head. That man will never walk the earth again and you know it." Will was almost offended.

"I was just havin' a little fun, Will." Charley laughed nervously. "Have you heard from any one else?" Charley tried to change the subject.

"Have you heard about Harry Love? He was killed in a shoot out with his wife's boyfriend or some such nonsense," Will related.

"No, I haven't," Charley said, as he took a flask of brandy from his breast pocket and passed it to his friend after checking for prying eyes.

"Oh, he married a big Ol' gal named Mary, who swelled up to about three hundred pounds after the wedding. But she had a lot of money and property because she was a widow, and Harry wanted to get his hands on it. That old thing was tough as an Ol' red rooster though, and Harry had to hide out at his sawmill to get away from her bitching and nagging. Well, she goes and gets so big around the girth that she hires a man just to help her get around. She called him her valet. She complained that Harry was never around to help her get in and out of carriages and to shop, so she hired this man named Iverson, whom Harry hated and called Fred. Harry had decided to try and appease his big, fat wife with a new house, one as big and fat as her, and was in the process of havin it built in Santa Clara, but he wasn't havin' any luck getting rid of the fat wife's man. Well, Harry gets a belly full of this Fred character and gets a snort full and decided to run him off," Will said, slowly puffing on his cigar.

"Don't tell me they had a duel?" Charley asks.

"Well, not exactly, when Harry came home, his wife and her man, Fred, were out, so he gets his shotgun and a revolver and waits in ambush down by the gate."

"That's not very sporting," Charley remarked.

"No, not really. Well, the way I heard it was the stepdaughter, Clementhia, came home first and found Harry drunk at the gate. She drove her pony cart up to the house and watched out the second-story window; for signs of her mother's arrival. When she sees the carriage coming, she ran down to it, past Harry, who was probably really drunk by now, and tries to warn them of the ambush. Pretty soon Mary spots Harry in the bushes by the gate, with his shotgun drawn, and she starts screaming. So

Fred jumps out of the carriage and pulls a gun on Harry, who fires one barrel and just grazes Fred, who shoots Harry in the arm, breaking it. The two carry on this way, as they shot their way to the house and ran out of ammunition. Harry was too drunk to hit Fred, and he was bleeding like a stuck pig. The two slugged it out, until the wife ordered the workman to break it up and get a doctor. Fred had come out all right and Mary told him to hightail it out."

"My word!"

"Yep, it was pretty bad for old Harry! When the doctors got there, they told him that his arm would have to come off. But the captain wasn't havin' any of that, even though he was bleeding to death. Pretty soon there was two more doctors there, and they said the same thing, the arm had to come off, only these doctors brought some chloroform. Ol' Harry he starts screaming and hollering at them, as they tried to put the mask on him and knock him out, but he wasn't going down without a fight!" Will reflected.

"I can just imagine, what a sight!" Charley sighed.

"Harry must have thought that Tres Dedos had returned from the grave for his head, the way he fought those doctors. He came to as they were removing his arm, and he started screaming incoherently about the tins of whiskey. But I guess the old warrior had lost a lot of blood during all this time, as they were put'n in the last stitches, with his dying breath, he pleaded to the men, 'Please don't let them put my head in a jar!'"

The two men shared a drop to their old comrade. "So ends the great and powerful Harry Love . . . Yep."

"And you, Charley, what have you been doing these days, my friend? Still driving stage?" Will asked.

"No, I don't hold a route any longer. I had a bad wreck a few years back, it stove in my side," Charley said rubbing his hand over his ribs. "It was a bad one, I reckon. After I got back on my feet, I bought a station and ran a stage stop for a while. But I reckon I wasn't cut out for that kinda work. So now I got myself a small ranch, and I cut a few trees and I raised some horses and cattle. Nothing much, just enough to make ends meet. I'm afraid my driving days are behind me now." Charley took a deep drag off his cigar. It was followed by about three minutes of coughing. "Shit, I can't even smoke anymore."

"You don't sound very well, Charley. Tell me about the crash. Wasn't the doctor shocked to find you were a woman?"

Charley sat for a moment with her mouth open, then resumed coughing. When she stopped, she stood looking out onto the lush green lawn. Finally, she turned to her longtime friend.

"You knew, and you never said anything?" Charley said, with disbelief in her face. "When . . . did you know . . . I mean how long have you known?" Charley said quietly.

"Well, after I killed Tres Dedos and then got myself shot up. You visited me in the hospital. The fat nurse made a rather great faux pax. Marion apologized for her and asked that I forget about it. Yet you see, I have not." Will smiled.

"You old son of a bitch!" Charley said still incredulous.

"Did you ever git married?" Will laughed.

"No, all the men I ever loved either died or are locked up in a loony bin," Charley said still smarting, as she glared at her friend.

"It ain't too late still, I got a room," Will said smiling. Charley turned and looked out across the lawn and gardens again. Breathing hard and stifling another bout of coughing. She had loved him for so long. Here they were, a shadow of their former selves. Charley heard a voice from deep within that cried out. "Yes, go, you want him so much, do it." Charley turned back to Will; she studied his scarred face, careful to wear her own best poker face.

"I don't want to cut in on your girlfriend's action," Charley said sarcastically.

"I'm sure she won't mind," Will said dreamily.

Charley smiled and laughed to herself. "God, Will, I've loved you for so long," she said quietly.

"I know. In my way, I've loved you too," he responded.

"Why didn't you ever tell me you knew?" Charley asked; Byrnes' face seemed somehow to be clouding over.

"Tell you that I knew what?" Will said with a puzzled look. "That I seen Joaquin?"

Charley stared into the confused man's face and realized that his mind was becoming shattered.

"Yes," Charley said hesitating.

"I seen him just the other day at Post Office Rock," Will repeated. The other conversation had been dashed from his broken memory. Charley just smiled and humored him. The subject of Charley's gender never came back up, as if it had never occurred. As the sun got low upon the horizon, the nurse interrupted the visit and informed them it was time for Will's dinner. Charley embraced her friend as they stood and said their final good-byes. She had a very hard time fighting back her tears, for she knew that she would probably never see him again.

"You take it easy on those nurses now, you hear," Charley said in parting.

"Remember me," Will said, turning to leave. It drove a nail through her heart.

Charley slowly walked back down the hallway. Her eye was blurry with moisture. She felt as if a great pain was welling up in her throat, if she coughed, it might come crashing out. She passed the man at the desk and tried bravely to smile at him. The best she could do was to wipe away the tears streaming down her face. It was hard to see, as she turned from him toward the grand doorway, and nearly stumbled down the stairs. She stopped to look back at the institution, not knowing what to do or say and feeling so utterly helpless to do anything. All their adventures together had come to an end forever. It seemed unbearable, as she slowly walked out the main gate never to return. She felt as if she had a gapping wound in her chest, as she rode back to the mountains in Santa Cruz.

CHAPTER 63

1875

James Hume lit his pipe, as he stood on the depot deck, watching the train from San Francisco glide to a halt. He had come up in the world from his dog licensing days in Placerville; his skills as a Deputy Sheriff had landed him a job protecting Wells Fargos' gold. It was arriving at Caliente, $240,000 to be exact, to be taken to the bank in Los Angeles by stagecoach. He and three other men would see to its safety.

"Say, isn't that little guy on the corner in the fancy dud's, the Bible thumper you used to joke about. You know, the con at San Quentin, who was always brown nosing and making like the good little man that had the raw deal, Perkins?" James Hume quizzed his guard.

"I don't know, I suppose it could be." Both lawmen studied the bearded fellow as he looked over the train schedules and hid his face, by taking off his fancy silk top hat. The Bible thumper looked like a misplaced easterner. "I don't think that we have much to fear from him, even if it is," replied Chief of Stockton Police, Jerome Meyers. "I remember the case well, we all had a good laugh over it! Perkins held up the Coast Line stage, outside of Santa Barbara. He was ridin'a green-broke colt and was having a hell of a time keeping it steady. The driver said it was dancing a fandango in front of the coach. He threw down the box and then cracked his whip, as he drove his team home, said we'd probably find the robber trampled to death from his own horse. Well, the posse found Ol' Dick in just about the same spot that he held up the stage, still aboard his colt, but swearing like a jay bird, and trying to choke the life out of the fool nag!"

Hume watched as the dandy turned and climbed on a scruffy looking horse, then trotted off.

As it turned out, they had little to fear from the diminutive con man, who was now traveling under the name Dick Fellows. Dick had made plans to rob the treasure that the men were securing on board the coach, but due to Fellows' poor choice at the Caliente livery stable, the robbery did not take place. Instead, the headstrong horse had left the robber unconscious, about a mile outside of town.

"Goddamn it! Where's that flea-bitten nag gone with my new shotgun! Goddamn him!"

Dick Fellows stumbled out of the brush and dusted himself off and ambled back into town, swearing and keeping an eye peeled for his shotgun. He spotted the regrettable mode of locomotion back at the rental barn and had words with the proprietor, who knew nothing of a shotgun.

"You sure you didn't find it?" Fellows said, his hand reaching in his brocade vest and his fingers resting on the fifty-caliber Derringer in the breast pocket.

"No, mister, honest, go look at the leather ties, they're ripped from the saddle, go and look," the shifty-eyed man pleaded. Fellows turned and looked the saddle over, as the clever stable proprietor covered the concealed shotgun with a saddle blanket. He would replace the beast. The best that the stable had, at no extra charge. "This is a quiet animal," he told Fellows.

"I'll have this horse back later today," Fellows lied. "I've already lost the best part of the day, as it is!" he grumbled, stepping out to mount the new horse. He dusted his dirty, silk top hat and straightened his brocade vest, before climbing onto the saddle. The new mount seemed mild mannered. Dick had missed the big payload, but felt confident he could at least get some pay off, so he tried for the next best thing, he intended to rob the next available stage.

The stage robber chose his ambush location carefully and after securing his kinder, gentler mount to a tree, had plenty of time to spend reflecting on his earlier attempted robbery, as the sunset lit the foothills in vivid pinks and purples. The stage was not due for some time yet.

It seemed to him that he recognized the man in charge of the earlier coach as Sheriff James Hume, whom he had seen often, while Fellows had been incarcerated at San Quentin, a year ago. Dick had been very resourceful in prison. He had effected a new religious outlook and even coordinated Bible studies for the inmates. He had been so convincing that he received a full pardon from the governor, after only serving half of his eight-year sentence for armed robbery, with intent to commit murder.

At last, in the darkness, Fellows could hear the jingling traces of the coach approaching, and he sprung into action, jumping to the center of the road, his small Derringer in hand, at the ready. He missed his shotgun dearly at this moment and was nearly run down by the lead team, as the stagecoach rocked to a halt. Fellows played the part of a stranded traveler, as he made his way over to the driver, then pointed the small, fifty-caliber pistol at the reinsman's head and demanded that he "throw down the box!"

Driver Dugan later reported the diminutive bandit whistled "The Arkansas Traveler" during the entire robbery.

At last Fellows had secured some treasure, or at least, he had gotten the box. Opening it would be another story, for Dick had neglected to bring any tools, with which to open it. He had thought of shooting off the lock, but the percussion cap had fallen off the gun, and he could not find it in the dark. After searching the darkness for a large rock with which to smash the box and finding nothing suitable, Fellows decided to leave the area on horseback with hopes of opening it elsewhere. A posse would be coming soon.

The mild-mannered horse now became a wild-eyed mustang, at the prospect of carrying such a menacing looking box; he soon had the upper hand with the unfortunate Fellows and was galloping off into the black night, without Dick Fellows or the nasty box. Dick knew that a posse would be upon him before long, so he shouldered his prize and began trudging down the dark road.

Unfortunately, Fellows had chosen a path that intersected with the workings of the Southern Pacific Railroad and in the blackness of night, had failed to see the eighteen-foot hole in front of him. After much moaning and swearing, at his newly broken foot and ankle, caused when the box landed on his left leg, Fellows discovered himself in a newly constructed railroad tunnel. He dragged his broken body and his treasure along, until he came across a Chinese work camp. With a great degree of stealth and agonizing pain, he appropriated some tools, then splinted his broken leg, using the handle of a shovel and a hoe.

When Fellows finally opened the box, he was pleased to find that it contained $1,800. He then fashioned himself a pair of willow crutches. Fellows then hobbled his way along, until the morning work crews arrived, when he hid in thickets. When he reached the Fountain Ranch, he hid in some bushes for the cover of darkness.

As night descended on the ranch, Fellows crept from his hiding place to the barn, where he found a friendly workhorse tethered in his stall, lazily munching on his dinner. Fellows took the bridle off the hook on the post and placed it on the horse with a minimum of effort. Then after locating a mounting block in the form of an old saw horse, Fellows climbed on board the horse and was gone. The next morning, young Tommy Fountain discovered the horse missing and put his amateur sleuthing to the test. It was not hard to track the missing animal, for it was wearing one mule shoe, which Tommy's father had put on the horse as a temporary measure, until a proper one could be procured. While on the trail of the missing animal, he came upon a posse, headed by County Deputy Edward Mahurin and explained his plight. It was not long before the missing animal with the crippled rider was spotted and Fellows was arrested.

While incarcerated in the Bakersfield jail, James Hume was summoned to collect the stolen Wells Fargo money; he found it lacking five hundred dollars. Fellows insisted he had hidden none of it and had told the detective to inquire to Mahurin for the rest. Dick claimed that the deputy had cleaned him out of all his cash even that not belonging to Wells Fargo. James sized up the robber, assessing that he had nothing to gain by withholding the bank's money and looked into the matter further. He then approached the deputy, who blustered around like a hen, then spouted off about going back and searching the grounds for money that may have been lost at the time of the arrest. Upon his return, Deputy Mahurin had miraculously found another three hundred dollars, stupidly thinking that it would appease the suspicious detective, it did not. James Hume soon had the deputy dismissed from his position.

Dick had his broken leg attended to, then was sentenced to eight years at San Quentin. The thought of going back, inspired Fellows to look for a means of escape. The Bakersfield jail was not the fortress that San Quentin was, so it would be now or never. Fortunately for Dick, the floor of his cell was dirt, so he took his crutch and began to dig his way out.

The next morning, when the guard brought the convict his breakfast, he was amazed to find the cell empty, with an oversized gopher hole in the corner.

Wells Fargo posted a five-hundred-dollar reward for Dick Perkins, alias Dick Fellows, that after noon.

Dick made his way to the Kern River, outside of town and managed to hide himself there for two days, while trying to formulate a plan of escape. He would need another horse. There were many Chinese living out on the slough, but not a lot of horses, at least ones Dick could get his hands on.

After unfortunately rebreaking his leg, Fellows managed to steal a nag and was on his way moaning and groaning along. Until he was stopped and questioned by a group of shepherds. It was no use; Dick was outnumbered and in great pain. His capture was practically a relief. Fellows lay in the grass looking up at the shepherds who were busy deciding who would get what percent of the reward, as the lights mercifully went out.

Fellows was sent to San Quentin prison to recuperate. He would further his education working in the prison library, as he was to reside there for eight long years.

CHAPTER 64

Hope Valley, Spring 1876

"Agnes, Arthur, come and look at dis piece of quartz I found," Thompson called to his family, as he set the rock on the table and began stripping off his coat. "It's varm in here."

"Daddy's home! Mamma, Grandma!" The boy, now nine, wrestled with his proud papa as the mountain man picked up his son.

"You're growing zo big I can hardly lift you Arthur," John said hugging his son. His side ached. "Look I picked dis up as I vas riding trough da canyon, on da vay home. It shows real nice color. See dere," he said showing his wife and son the gold veins running through the white rock. "Agnes, zomething smells very good. I'm zo tired, I tink I'll go to bed right after dinner. I got a pain in my zide."

"I'll get your supper right away," Agnes said, kissing her husband on the cheek. "You are very warm, John," she said, setting his dinner on the table.

The next day, John rose early and set about plowing the last piece of ground before planting. He felt sick to his stomach, as he sat on his new riding plow behind his mules. The air was crisp and he could see his breath, he was sweating profusely. At the end of the day, when John came in for dinner, he was near exhaustion.

"I want you to stay in bed tomorrow. The planting can wait, I don't want you catching your death with the fever," Agnes scolded.

"I'll have Arthur and Bobby from across da road help me, and I'll ride Ol' Sally, but I must get da barley planted. If I plant now I can get in a zecond crop dis zummer," Snowshoe reasoned with his wife. The sweat was beading up on his face and he was starting to shiver.

"John the crops can wait till your feeling better!" she scolded her husband, then kissed him tenderly on the forehead. She draped a quilt around his broad shoulders, then set his dinner in front of him.

The next morning, John rose slowly before dawn and crept from his bedroom, leaving his wife to sleep. He put on his clothes in the front room and then went out to the barn.

The sky was deep blue, except on the horizon in the east, where a swath of red sky changed subtly, as the sun rose slowly, just beyond the horizon. With great effort, John saddled his white mule Sally and slung the grain sacks across the saddlehorn. The pain in his side ripped though his body, as he tried to climb aboard. He rode out to his newly plowed field and began to throw the barley seed, as the sun climbed over the mountain peaks.

"Pa, Mama wants you to come in and have breakfast, she's going to fetch the doctor," Arthur said, while trotting alongside the mule.

"Go back to the barn and feed the chickens Arthur," Thompson said curtly, though the searing pain. "I'll come in soon."

"All right, Pa," the boy said obediently and galloped away on an imaginary horse, back to the barn.

Agnes put on her coat and met the boy, as he was pouring grain in the chicken feeders.

"Ma, is Pa sick?" Arthur asked, as she saddled her horse.

"Yes, son, he is, and I'm going to fetch Doc Benton. You look after him, with Grandma, while I'm gone. Get Bobby to finish the seeding, so your Pa won't fret. I'll be back this afternoon. Be a good boy and mind your Grandma," she said, hugging her young son.

Agnes climbed on the horse and rode out of the barn. She galloped over to her husband, who was slumped over in the saddle throwing grain.

"I'm getting you to bed husband! Then I'm going for the doctor," she said with her sharpest voice.

"All right, Agnes, you're right as always," John softened. He was no match for the feisty English woman. She grabbed the lead rope, which was wrapped around the saddle horn and lead the mule to the house, then helped her husband down and up the steps to the house.

"Mother, please get John to bed, I'm going, I'll be back with the doctor as soon as I can." She kissed her husband on the cheek. "Good Lord, you're burning up."

With her mother carefully looking after her sick man, Agnes remounted her horse and sped off.

When she returned later with the doctor, she found him no better. The doctor examined John and could only give him some pain relief for now.

"I gave him something that will help him rest. Was he able to eat at all today?" Doc Benton inquired.

"Just a few spoonfuls of eggs and some soup." Agnes's mother, Anne, replied.

"Try and keep him quiet and don't let him get out of bed, till I'm sure what we're dealing with. It might be some sort of fever and contagious. I need to see how he does tomorrow morning," Doc Benton advised. "Try and get some more soup down him if you can."

The next morning, John was even worse. He was sweating profusely and weak as a newborn. Agnes stayed by his side the entire day.

"My colleague and I agree that it is probably his appendix. The sever pain in his lower abdomen is suggesting that it is. If that is the case there is little I can do," Doc Benton confided to Anne.

After a few agonizing days, John "Snowshoe" Thompson was dead.

"Where you been, Doc?" Monk asked as he climbed from his perch.

"Oh, hello, Hank. I been out to the Diamond Ranch." The doctor was choked up tight.

"Ain't that Snowshoe's Ranch? How is that old grizzly bear?" Monk said in a friendly way.

"He's dead, Hank," the doctor said, with tears rolling down his face.

"What? Snowshoe Thompson? Dead? Lord, have mercy! I can't believe it!" the stunned man said, as the doctor walked away, towards his office. "He was younger than me!" Monk stood on the plank and stared in disbelief, then stumbled after the bearer of the horrible news. Monk followed him into the office, as the doctor opened a drawer and pulled out a bottle of brandy and a couple of glasses.

"Geez, Doc, what happened?" Monk said quietly, as the doctor poured out two shots.

"I think his appendix burst."

"God, that's awful! What's an appendix?"

"It's a small bit of your guts. It leaks into your body cavity and makes you sick. In layman's terms," the Doc said patiently.

"To our friend Snowshoe," Hank said, lifting his glass to heaven. "I bet he's testing out the heavenly slopes as we speak," Monk said, wiping away a tear.

CHAPTER 65

Pajjaro Valley 1878

"I got it for you, Charley. 'The Hank Monk Schottische' by J. P. Meder, Carson City Nevada." Woody said with a grin.

"Well now, that's right thoughtful of you, but do you know any one that can play it?" Charley asked, as he spit into the spittoon. "Looks complicated!"

"I'll find someone to play it, don't you worry," Woody reassured.

Charley smiled at Woody's enthusiasm. For years Woody had heard of the outlandishness of the irrepressible Hank Monk. Charley had glorified him into a downright legend.

"Mark Twain helped build the Jehu into the fabric of gold and silver rushing into history," Charley reflected.

The sales of Twain's book *Roughing It* had spurred Hank's notoriety into the sky. Everyone wanted to ride with the famous driver. He did very well with his popularity. Even the local composer did well, by cashing in on the newfound interest in the coachman. "The Hank Monk Schottische" was quite an elegant tribute to a very ribald and earthy sort of a man.

It took Charley a year before he could find someone to play it. When he heard it for the first time, it brought a tear to his eye. It was so beautiful, and oh so Hank Monk.

CHAPTER 66

Deadwood, North Dakota, February 10, 1878

The stagecoach rocked along in the icy rain on the muddy road; it was early evening. The coach was slowing down, as the women snuggled close together under a robe.

"We are slowing down, it's too soon for a relay stop," Lurleen said whispering to the older woman.

"I'll look." Eleanora wrapped her cape up close around her neck and peered behind the leather curtain and out the coach window. All she could see was the snowy drifts next to the road, as she called up to the shotgun rider.

"Why do we slow?"

"Wagon train a head of us," the man called back.

"It is a wagon train. That is always a good sign, especially if they are headed in our direction," Eleanora explained to the vivacious young prostitute.

"I don't see why we couldn't stay in Bismarck," Lurleen complained.

"Because there is more loose money and less competition in Deadwood, that's why," the experienced woman advised her young working girls. "I think maybe this is Charley Utters' train. If it's going to Deadwood, it's a good sign indeed," the Madame explained.

The coach began picking up speed as the road widened enough to pass. The wagon train was huge, fifty-two wagons in all. "They were big and full, pulled by large draft mules. Each wagon had at least two men," Eleanora thought out loud.

"That you, Charley Utter?" Mme. Dumont called out from the window.

"That you, Eleanora?" the snow-covered teamster called back.

"The one and only. Where are you going?"

"Deadwood."

"See you soon!" she called, closing the curtain as the stagecoach pulled away.

"Now I know we will make money, girls," Eleanora said taking out her silver flask and a thin cigar. The girls roused from their wraps and the passengers aboard had a brisk cocktail hour.

Fate has a way of dealing the most unexpected hands, and it so happened that the coach to Deadwood was delayed just long enough to arrive just ahead of Utters' wagon train. Thus the town folks were turned out royally to witness the new bounty. The girls aboard the coach rode upon the roof of the vehicle, with petticoats waving in the stiff breeze, to the enchantment of the crowd.

"Now this is a warm reception," Madame Dumont called to her girls. "Don't forget to speak to the newspaper man, Lurleen, you know what to do," Eleanora whispered to the lovely blonde, as the coach pulled up to the express office. "Look there's one, he has a pencil behind his ear and a notepad."

The young man was waiting to take notes on the newly arriving to this budding boomtown. He was taking great interest in the lovely cargo aboard the Concord coach.

"Oh, Lurleen," Eleanora called.

"Yes?" the blonde replied, as she began to climb from the roof.

"Don't forget to get his wallet."

The newspaperman was dazzled and fleeced, without the slightest bit of pain. He managed to write down Lurleen Montever and Eleanora Dumont, before he lapsed into ecstasy and the flurry of lovely creatures evaporated into the town, and Charley Utter occupied his newspaper duties. It was hours later that he discovered his money was missing.

The women settled in to a house on Tough Nut Street, and the next few days they were busy beyond belief.

The local women and their pimps did not take too kindly to this invasion. Deadwood was a coarse town and one lived there by using harsh survival skills. Eleanora had learned years ago as her beauty faded that to survive, she must offer more than a card game. She herself would work on her back if she had to and often did. Her thin but distinctive black mustache, adding an element of freakishness to her once-lovely features.

"Lurleen?" Eleanora called through the door.

"Yes?" the girl replied in a dreamlike voice. She lay on her bed in nothing but a robe, smoking an opium pipe and was just about to drift off. Eleanora opened the door and found the whore with the pipe dangling carelessly from her fingers, on the fabric of her robe. In another moment she would light herself on fire.

"Lurleen, what is that shit? You know I don't allow that. Don't you know it will poison your mind? You will end up in the gutter!" Eleanor said, taking the pipe and emptying it on the floor, then grinding the pellet into the wood with her boot.

"I can't take it anymore, Ella," Lurleen said, with tears rolling down her face.

"I know," the Madame said, putting her arms around the frightened woman.

"Why are you still out here? Why don't you have a home somewhere? I can't end up like you!" Lurleen sobbed.

Eleanor was stunned by what she heard and slowly released the woman from her grasp and set her limp body on the bed. Lurleen curled up in a fetal position and cried.

"I wanted to have a home once . . . and I had one too. I was once fabulously wealthy, I drank champagne every night," the Madame said, turning away from the girl. "I had acquired a fortune in the mountains of California and then the Comstock lode. I was going to retire in style. I bought a ranch near Carson City. It wasn't long after that, I met a very charming and handsome man, who said he was a cattle buyer and was eager to get my business . . . if you know what I mean," she said, lighting her thin black cigar. "Jack McKnight . . . He was sure something. Smooth talking, like the serpent in the

Garden of Eden. We soon married. I loved him so very much and trusted him with every dollar I ever earned . . . like a fool . . . And then he changed. There was an evil man hiding behind a sweet veneer, just waiting to appear when the papers were all signed. A month later, without my knowledge, Jack sold the ranch and left me, taking all of my money, every cent, leaving me only the bills," Eleanora sighed, taking a long draw off of her cheroot. "I had nothing . . . and no sign of Jack. I had to go back to work, I had to call in a few favors, I scraped along, but I . . ."

"I'm so sorry, Ella!" Lurleen said turning to the stoic Madame who was now crying.

"I learned only to trust in myself and I get along," she said, looking at the pipe. "You smoke that, and you won't even be able to trust yourself, believe me," she said turning to leave.

"I'll be down in a few minutes, Ella," Lurleen called to her employer.

"You go take a bath and get yourself some sleep. I'll tell the boys your feeling indisposed tonight," Eleanora comforted the girl.

"How many fellas down there?"

"About four, got money too." Eleanora smiled. "And they have teeth."

"I'll be down soon," Lurleen sighed.

CHAPTER 67

Lake Tahoe, March 1879

It was just after four in the afternoon when Hank Monk arrived at Cobb's Hotel in Glenbrook, driving Doc Benton's stagecoach. It was very picturesque this time of year, as the hotel looked out over the beautiful blue water of Lake Tahoe; the mountains surrounding the blue body were still frosted with snow.

The hotel had an ice-skating rink landscaped into the lovely grounds, which was a popular attraction and was currently in use by two very lovely young creatures, their full skirts catching the breeze as they glided around.

Hank slowed the coach for a moment to appreciate the young women practicing their turns on the ice. He noticed an old geezer, who was grinning the grin of a lustful old sot, approaching the two girls. Monk sneered at the old coot, who was distracting the girls, sized him up, and then knew just what to do.

After parking the coach, Hank stomped the dirt off his boots and entered the hotel.

Monk spotted an old woman sitting alone in the front room, looking small and frail, as she sat saying nothing. The teamster walked up to her and began, "Madam, your husband went out to see the lake, didn't he?"

"Yes, why?" she asked, turning pale.

"He was a tall man, wasn't he?" Monk said fumbling with the brim of his hat.

"He was?" she replied standing up and beginning to panic.

"He had red hair?" Hank said running his fingers through his hair.

"He had? Oh, what has happened?"

"Weighted about one hundred and eighty pounds?"

"Yes, yes, where is he? Where's my husband?"

"Couldn't swim could he?" Monk relented.

"He's drown! He's drown? My husband is drowned?" the old woman wailed.

"He had on a silver chain?" continued Hank, looking down at his own watch.

"Where is my husband? Where is his body?" the woman said, almost in a swoon.

"Do not get excited, Madam. Did your husband have on a gray suit?

"Yes! Oh my poor Thomas, my Thomas!"

"And boots?"

"Let me see him! Let me see him!" she cried.

"Come this way, Madam, but do not get excited. There, is that your husband across the street at the skating rink?" Hank said pointing through the window.

"Yes, yes, that's him, that's my husband!" she sighed joyfully. "I thought you said he was drowned," the old woman said, raising an eyebrow.

"No, Madam, I kinda thought that for so old and dilapidated a cuss as him, to go after those young gals and leave a nice old lady, such as yourself, all alone, was just a little too rough!" the coachman smiled, as the old gal set off in search of her straying husband.

"Oh, Thomas! Hank, you old rascal," the hotel clerk said, laughing at the prankster. He again tried to mimic the old woman.

"Evening, Chester," Monk said fitting his hat back on his head.

"Oh, Thomas, he's drown! Did he have a silver chain?" the young man laughed again out loud.

Hank winked and walked through to the hotel bar and ordered up.

"Coach leaving for Carson City in ten minutes. Get me a beer there, John, I'm parched as a prairie fire," Hank called out.

"I see DeQuille put another one of your whizzbangers in the Enterprise," the bartender said, setting down the beer. Monk drank the cold libation down.

"Yep, he always hovers around Ormbys when he needs some filler. I might just have another humdinger for him. See ya later, John," Monk said, setting a coin down on the bar and turning to leave.

"But what is it, Hank?" John called out.

"Ask Chester the desk clerk, He'll tell ya," Monk said, as he looked at his watch and left. He passed the young clerk who was chuckling to himself and grinned even larger as the teamster walked by.

"Oh, Thomas!" the young man mimicked.

"See ya tomorrow, Chester."

"Bye, Hank!"

"Hey, Chester! Get in here!" Big John, the bartender, called out from the tavern.

CHAPTER 68

September 1879

Eleanora worked her way back to California, by way of Tombstone, while big talk was made about the mines in Bodie, California. The high desert town swelled to more than twelve thousand people that year. Madame Dumont was eager to get back to a more civilized city. While Bodie was crowded with miners, it was far from civilized; Eleanora Dumont took her place in the red light section of town, on Maiden Lane, playing cards and whoring.

The parlor of her saloon was thick with cigar smoke, as the dawn's light played through the window, illuminating the smoke clouds swirling overhead. Eleanora was exhausted. The night had seen her ruin, and she was about to lose everything in this card game. Two men had come to town several days earlier and had cleaned out several small card parlors already. They had set their sights on Madame Mustache, the name miners callously used, who had not aged well and now sported very prominent dark hair above her top lip. She had grown hard and tough, gone were the sumptuous curves; they were replaced by sagging flesh, held up with tight corsets. She had become a horrid caricature of the lovely woman she once was. Her mesmerizing eyes had grown murky and red, from years of alcohol, with deep circles beneath them, accentuated by misplaced mascara. Her eyes wandered back to the cards in her hand; she held a Jack and a three. The card face up on the table was a Queen.

"Well? You just gonna sit there all morning, or you gonna do something?" the card shark said impatiently. It snapped her back to reality.

"I'm afraid I'm finished, gentlemen. Just let me go upstairs and get my things, and the place is yours," Eleanora said, with a far away voice, as she set down her cards. She had been losing steadily all night and had lastly put up the deed to her parlor. Rising with her last remaining dignity, she walked slowly up the steep stairs to her room, oblivious to the laughter of the callous gamblers.

Sitting on her bed for a moment, with her face in her hands, she cried. With nothing left, no home, no money, no man, no friends, this was it—the end of the line. Not even the loser's glass of milk was offered. Thoughts of suicide swirled about in her foggy mind.

Feeling her leg garter, she realized that she had even lost her derringer in the game. Eleanora rose and walked to a small table by a window and poured the last shot from the bottle of brandy there, swallowing it in one gulp. She looked down at a small wooden box, under the table, something she had forgotten about, but had saved such a long time, dragging it from boomtown to boomtown, for a special occasion, from the old days. Opening it she took out a bottle of French champagne, the last link to her successful past. She found her carpetbag and put in the bottle of sparkling wine, along with a glass. Eleanora took one last look around the room and walked back down the stairs. She left without saying a word.

The morning sun was painfully shining; it would be another hot day in Bodie. She stood for a moment and looked down the sleepy street. A merchant was just unlocking his door for the day. The beaten woman slowly walked in his direction. Entering the dry goods store, Eleanora glanced around, spotted what she wanted, then walked to the counter.

"Got rats at your place?" the merchant sneered, looking down at the small bottle the woman had placed on the counter.

"Yes, rats . . . Put that on my account," she sneered back.

"Your account is due tomorra!" the merchant said, blowing smoke at the old Madame.

"Don't worry, you'll get what's comin' to you," Eleanora replied, as she left the store. "Ugly son of a bitch!" she grumbled, as she walked slowly out of town. She reflected back on her life, the places she'd seen and the people she had beaten at the poker table. Her life had been adventurous, though it wasn't always easy; she had lived it on her own terms.

About a mile outside of town, she spotted the only remaining tree and sat in the morning shade. She pulled the glass and the champagne bottle from the bag. Eleanora was still clutching the small bottle she had gotten from the store and set that next to the tree. Slowly she proceeded to open the champagne, for it was warm and would come rushing out, if she was not careful. She poured herself a glass and drank a toast to her life, tears rolling down her creased face. Then Eleanora opened the small bottle and poured a shot of strychnine in her glass, topping it off with the sparkling wine. She toasted to a better future, then drank the cocktail.

Miners found her lifeless body about an hour later.

CHAPTER 69

Watsonville, October 1879

Charley had settled into a simple lifestyle; he had sold his ranch and rented a small cabin on the same property that he had cultivated. The young folks who bought the place, the Harmons, fell in love with the land and all the apple trees that Charley had planted, but were now too much work for him.

The couple had a six-year-old boy with a face full of freckles, named George, who took an instant shine to Parkhurst.

Charley lay in his bed, in the small cabin to the rear of the main ranch. It was ten in the morning. He felt guilty for not getting up, but he had no real reason he could think of, not to remain in bed. The fall weather was bringing on stiffness and pain in all his joints; the thick, wool flannel, long johns helped only a little. Charley's throat was still sore and his tongue was aching, as tears streamed down old, leathery cheeks. He simply couldn't get warm enough and rolled over and grabbed the bottle of laudanum and took a swallow. Setting the bottle back on the table, he rolled back and gave up for the time being.

"Charley?" a young boy called into the small cabin, some time later. "You sleepin', Charley? My Mama sent me to see if'n you want some lunch?"

"Oh, come in you rascal!" Charley croaked out.

"How are you feelin', Charley?" the little boy said, sitting on the bed next to his best friend.

"I'm just a might tuckered out today, youngster. How are you?"

"Fine, you gonna have lunch with me today?"

"Why sure, hand me my blue shirt there, George," Charley said, sitting up slowly.

"Oh boy, you'll like it too, Ma made pie," the small boy said, grabbing the eye patch off the bed table and placing it on the old man's face, as he was buttoning his shirt.

"Your Mama is a right good cook. Hand me over them coveralls." Charley's head spun for a moment, as he still felt the effects of the drugs. The pain was quiet a bit relieved though.

"Here's your boots and socks."

"Not those socks, get me a clean pair from the drawer."

"You sure got a parcel of socks in here, Charley."

"Yep, I guess I have."

"You got a baby dress in here too. How come?" George asked innocently, looking at the faded, red, silk baby gown and petting it gently as if it were alive.

"Just toss me the socks mister nosy blivins," Charley croaked affectionately. The boy turned and laughed and ran to his friend with the garments requested. Charley laughed too, it brought about a coughing fit. He spit up a wad of flem mixed with blood and spit it into the spittoon next to the bed, sensing the seriousness of the situation. "Let's get our lunch shall we?" he said to his young companion. "What else besides pie?"

"Come on, Charley, you'll see!" the boy said, pulling on the old man's hand.

"There you fellows are!" Mrs. Harmon smiled as the hungry pair entered the house. "I hope you're not feeling too poorly today, Charley."

"I'm afraid I just can't get any wind in my sails, my throat is still sore. I might go to town and get me some throat oil."

"You should go in and see Dr. Plumm. He's a throat specialist."

"Something surely smells good, Ma'am," Charley said, changing the subject.

"It's vegetable soup with ham. I made biscuits too, sit down," Mrs. Harmon clucked. "George, did you wash your hands?"

"Yes, Mama."

"Well, go wash them again, young man. You didn't get a bit of dirt off'a them the first time! Now scoot," the young mother scolded, as she ladled Charley a big bowl of soup.

"Thank you kindly, it smells divine, your pie smells heavenly too," Charley praised.

"When is Daddy coming home?" little George said, plopping himself down triumphantly next to his pal."

"Your father will be home this evening some time, you may stay up until he comes home," she reassured.

"Oh boy!" he said, digging into his soup.

"I was hoping to talk to Mr. Harmon when he gets back, it's nothing important. Just something I wanted to discuss," the retired coachman mused. Charley dunked his biscuit in the broth and let it dissolve in his mouth. It was difficult to chew anything.

"Oh, Frank Woodward was by this morning. He said he'd stop by later to see you," Mrs. Harmon related.

"Thanks," Charley said finishing the soup. "Your little George has been a great help to me in these past weeks, I want you to know."

"Well, I'm glad to hear that he hasn't been making a pest of himself," Mrs. Harmon sighed.

"No." Charley smiled. George adjusted his friends eye patch, as his mother cut them all a slice of pie.

"Would you like some more coffee?"

"Yes, please. I think I'll ask Woody to take me to town, do you need anything? Perhaps you'd like to go with us?"

"No, I had better stay here in case Charles gets home early, but I would like to get a few yards of fabric. Maybe you'd pick that up for me?" Christine asked.

"Surely, what color?"

"Can I come?" George called out. "Pleeeeaase?"

Charley nodded at Christine from behind the boy. She smiled and agreed.

"But you better hurry after you eat your pie and finish your chores, before Woody comes by."

"Oh boy!"

After the boy had vanished to his work in the yard, Christine sat next to the quiet old man. She familiarly felt his forehead for signs of a fever. "You really should go and see a doctor, Charley. I'm worried."

"I suppose," he sighed. "What's his name?"

"Dr. Plumm. He's in Soqual. I'll go with you if you'd like?" she added, tenderly holding his hand.

"Thanks," Charley said, bringing the soft hand to his mouth and kissing it. "What color?"

"What?" Christine was puzzled. Charley tapped on the table.

"Oh! I saw some light blue at Lyman's Dry Goods. It has little white flowers, I need two yards," she said kissing the top of his head, as she stood.

The following week Christine was walking Charley up the ornate stairs of Dr. Plumm.

"His house is certainly a plum!" Christine smiled at her pun.

"He must be very expensive if he can afford such a place," Charley groaned.

"Well, I'm sure he can do something for you." Christine frowned at the balky patient. "Come on."

The woman that answered the door wore a very plain starched white dress with a soft gray tie, her features were quite severe, and she smiled not a bit. She ushered them to a small waiting parlor, until the doctor could see them. It was a pleasant room with a window and some paintings of sunny landscapes on the walls. The severe woman returned with a teapot and reported that the doctor would be a bit longer and recommended a cup of mint tea while they wait. It smelled good and no doubt was more for the benefit of the doctor as well.

"Ah, Mr. Parkhurst, I am Dr Plumm. I'm sorry to have kept you waiting. If you would be so kind as to step into my examining room, we can have a little talk, then have a look at you," the doctor said, shaking Charley's hand.

"Sure, Doc," Charley said, turning to his lady friend and nodding. The two disappeared into the next room leaving Christine to contemplate the landscapes.

"I'm on my last legs, I know. I'm just here to please her." Charley motioned to the door with his hat.

"Well, let's leave the diagnosis to me, shall we? You have a sore throat that persists?"

Charley nodded.

"Here have a seat." The doctor motioned to a very comfortable and by the looks of it a very expensive chair. Charley shuddered at the cost of sitting in this plush seat. "That's right. I'm just going to have a look in your mouth," he comforted.

Charley noticed that the severe woman had reappeared, this time equipped with a pencil and paper. She set it on the table next to the chair and adjusted the light for the doctor.

"Get me the oil of cloves . . . . I'm just going to give you some syrup I want you to swish it in your mouth and throat, then you'll be more comfortable," he said, handing Charley a shot glass of dark thick liquid.

"That's good." Charley smiled, settling back in the chair and opening his mouth.

"It should help the throat pain some. Yes, I can see you've got quite a problem there, I'm afraid this does not look good," he continued to stare into the mouth, taking note of each malformation and reporting it to the nurse who wrote it down. The doctors' scientific jargon was enough to convince the patient that hope was lost. At last the examination was finished and the Dr. Plumm had the grim task of summing up situation.

"Mr. Parkhurst, I'm sorry, but I'm afraid that you have what is called a cancer. It has grown into a tumor on your tongue and goes down your throat. I cannot tell how far it goes with this examination. The best I can offer is surgery to remove the cancer, but there is no certainty that it will not reappear. I'm afraid I will not sugar coat it for you. The surgery involves the removal of your tongue and voice box. I would have to insert a silver tube to assist in your breathing."

Charley sat in stony silence. He slowly rose from the chair and stood facing the doctor.

"Thanks for lookin," he said, as he shook the man's hand, then walked toward the door, slowly placing his hat back on his gray head.

"The surgery will buy you more time," the doctor offered.

"Can I get some of that clove syrup?"

"Of course, I'll have my nurse get it for you. Think about it," Dr. Plumm said, resting his hand on the doomed man's shoulder. "You can not afford to wait, I'm afraid."

"How much longer do I have without the operation?"

"I can't say for certain maybe a month or possibly two. I just don't know how fast it is spreading," the doctor sighed.

"Thank you for being straight with me, Doc," Charley said, opening the door.

"Nurse, get Mr. Parkhurst a bottle of that clove syrup," he said, as they returned to Mrs. Harmon, who was searching Charley's face for some glimmer of hope, yet found none. The nurse set the bottle on the desk and wrote up a receipt for the patient who glumly settled up. As the two left the office, Christine could hardly bear it.

"What did he say?"

"'Bout what I thought. It's queer though when a stranger says it," Charley pondered.

"Can't he do anything?" she pried.

"Yes, he wanted to operate, but I said no."

"Why? He might save your life."

"We all got to go some time, Christine. I want to be able to taste your pie till the day I die."

"You mean?"

"My tongue, voice box, throat . . . was gonna give me a silver tube to breath through," Charley said, as a trickle of saltwater ran down the rugged face. Charley's talking set him to coughing.

"Oh, Charley . . . I'm so sorry," Christine cried, hugging her friend.

"Now don't you cry, Christine. I had a good life and I'm getting mighty tired," Charley said softly. "It ain't gonna be so easy for little George though. Damn! Let's go."

"Did he say how long?"

"Couldn't be sure, maybe only a month."

"Shit!" Christine forgot herself. "I'll make you some pie when we get home. Thank you for planting that apple orchard."

"Cider's good this year. I reckon I could use a belt when we get back."

"Me too."

"I want to see Otto Strosser. I need to make up my will."

"We can stop at his house on the way home, if you like. He might be there today."

"That would be fine."

"Why don' you let me drive, Charley," she offered.

"If you please," Charley said handing over the lines.

Otto and his wife were sitting on the porch, when they pulled up. They were delighted to see the teamster, for he had been staying close to home for quite a while.

Otto insisted they have tea, and Charley revealed the nature of his visit.

"Of course I can help you make out a will. I hope you're all right, Charley."

"Doctor tells me I'm not long for this world, Otto."

"I'm so very sorry to hear that. Can I get you a real drink, I know I'd like one," he said with great sorrow.

"Why yes, I really would. I know Christine here needs a snort too," Charley sighed. "Sorry to put a damper on your afternoon Otto," Charley said, setting a tired hand on his friends shoulder.

"To you, Charley," Otto said when he had glasses filled with brandy. "Would you care to stay for dinner?"

"No, we gotta get back, Christine's fellas'll be lookin for their supper," Charley said relishing the drink.

"I can stop by anytime and take care of your will. How about Monday evening?" Otto offered.

"That would be fine, you can sample some of the cider Woody and I set up."

"I've heard that it's good!"

"Well, thanks, Otto, for the drink and for everything. We better be heading out, we'll be looking for you Monday then," Charley said setting down the fine vessel.

"Yes, take care." Otto smiled bravely. He escorted the pair to the porch and watched as the two drove away.

"There is plenty of room for him in the Odd Fellows Cemetery, he's a member in good standing. I will bring it up at the next meeting. I doubt he will attend many more meetings himself. He really looked very poor," Otto confessed to his wife as he sat on his rocker and lit his pipe.

The little surrey kicked up a cloud of dust as the pair turned off the main road to the ranch.

"Do you want me to tell George?" Christine asked, as they turned into the driveway.

"Yes, I'm afraid I haven't the heart. Would you mind telling Frank Woodward too."

"Oh God, I don't know, he's a bigger baby than George."

"Maybe tell them both at the same time, kill two birds at once," Charley kidded. "I'll unhitch Ol' Sarah here and then I'm gonna call it a day, sweetness. Thank you for comin' with me," the teamster said softly, as they drove up to the familiar barn. They parked under the barn roof, which extended out from the structure. Little George ran out to greet them, helping Charley unharness the horse and feed her. It felt good to do this simple job, even as the exhaustion set in.

"Ain't you comin in fer supper, Charley?" the youngster said, tugging at the old man's hand.

"No, I think I'll just go lay down a spell," the tired teamster sighed.

"But you gotta eat," George nagged.

"Maybe later," Charley said walking slowly to the small cabin. "Be a good boy now and run to your Mama."

The next evening, the boy knocked on the door.

"Charley, I brought you some soup, are you sick?" George asked opening the door.

"Yeah, I'm afraid so, little man," Charley whispered. "I'm gonna be going away."

"I don't want you to go," George sobbed as he lifted the worn hand to his soft young face.

"I know you don't," Charley said, putting his arms around the young life.

"I love you, Charley!"

"Love you too, George," he softly spoke, tears coursing down his wrinkled and scarred face.

"Oh yeah, Mama said to tell you Otto was coming down the road," the little boy said, looking though teary eyes at his friend.

"Well, get my eye patch then!" Charley said releasing his grip on the boy, who then sprung into action, lighting the lamps in the cabin to look around. "Get my neckerchief too." The boy then combed the gentleman's hair in preparation for his guests. After putting the boots on his elderly friend, he helped him walk down the path to the main house. Christine was busy setting out coffee cups and plates of pie to the delight of the rotund Otto and his plump wife. Charley was greeted at the door and given a comfortable chair. The young mother draped a blanket over the ailing man's lap then set down a mug and a piece of pie on the oak table next to the chair.

"Thank you, Christine. Where's Mr. Harmon?" Otto inquired.

"He had to go to Stockton to sell some cattle," she politely responded. "George after you finish your pie, you say good night and go to bed."

"Yes, Mama," George complained.

The ladies departed shortly after the boy and left the men to talk.

"We have a burial sight in the Odd Fellows cemetery. That is unless you had other ideas," Otto offered. "You've always been a member in good standing."

"Why, yes, I think that is a fine idea. I'd like that," Charley said, the smile on his face beamed at her inside joke. "Here is my bank account. I own no real property. This is my bankin' book. I'd like to take out the money for the casket and maybe some flowers. What's left over should be about four thousand dollars. I want all of that to go to George Harmon. Entrusted to his mother until he is eighteen," Charley said laboring over the words. "I wrote it all down."

"That's just fine then," Otto said, smiling at his friend. He picked up the paper and looked it over.

"You can just sign it at the bottom, and we'll have Christine and myself witness it, and it will be taken care of." He set the paper down and stood up, pouring Charley another glass of his special peppermint schnapps. It felt cooling as it flowed over the afflicted throat. "I'll get Christine," Otto said replacing the bottle on the table.

The will was signed, when a small voice from the hall stairs spoke out, "Woody's coming down the road."

"Back to bed, Georgie," Christine called out.

"Thank you, Otto," Charley said holding out his hand to the plump lawyer.

"We really should be running along home. That pie was divine, Christine," Otto said turning to his hostess.

"Hey there, Otto, Mrs. Stosser, Christine," Woody greeted, as little George opened the front door. "Hey, Georgie, your Ma is gonna tan your hide if you don't get back to bed," he laughed, shaking the executors hand. "Good to see you, Otto. Tried any of this years batch?" Woody offered.

"Maybe some other time, Woody, we got to get home. Mama's getting tired," Otto said turning to his plump wife.

"Come on in, Woody, I saved you a piece of pie," Christine said, hanging the hat on the hat rack.

"Hey, Charley, you look all dressed up for town. You want to take a ride in?" Woody asked his friend.

"No, I'm kinda tired right now. Have a drink. Otto left his Schnapps for us." Charley motioned to the table.

"Smells like mint!" Woody said, smelling the bottle, his mouth full of pie.

Charley looked imploringly at Christine, unable to tell his friend the grave news. He pulled himself out of the chair and headed for the door.

"I'm gonna call it a day."

"I'll see you tommorra then, Charley. I'm sorry you're feeling poorly again. You want me to help you to your cabin?"

"No, I'll be fine, night, Christine, thank you, sweety," Charley said, as the young woman kissed the old man on the cheek.

"Good night, Charley," a small voice from the stairs whispered.

"Get to bed, George," Christine called almost in tears.

As Charley ambled toward the familiar cabin, he heard the familiar rustle of a small boy's gallop coming from behind.

"I climbed out the window, I'll help you with your boots." George panted as he caught up to the tired man.

"I'll let you. Get the door," Charley sighed.

As little George finished tucking in his friend, the way his mother always did to him, the two heard Woody swearing an oath and cursing aloud from the Harmon porch. Charley swallowed hard and awaited the distress of his friend and partner, as the boy kissed the forehead of the old man and neatly hung the eye patch on the bedpost.

"Good night Charley," the boy said, blowing out the light and tiptoeing from the bed.

"Good night, little man," Charley said closing his eyes.

The boy tiptoed to the door, opened it, then shut it without leaving, creeping silently back to the bed and curled up on the rug next to it, like a faithful dog.

Moments later, Charley lay very still and heard another set of footfalls coming to his porch, followed by a gentle wrapping on his door.

"Charley, it's Woody. Can I come in?"

"Yeah, come in," he croaked, as little George rolled beneath the bed.

"I . . . I just wanted to say . . . I'm sorry," Woody said fighting back tears in the dark, as he approached the bed.

"Don't be sorry, I've had a good life, I'm just worn out," Parkhurst said, trying to sit up.

"Don't get up," Woody said, putting his hand on his shoulder.

"You're a good friend, Woody," Charley whispered. He could feel the man's shoulders shake in the dark, as he cried. Woody was embarrassed and hung his head, as he sat on the edge of the bed. As his eyes adjusted to the dark room, he spotted a small foot sticking out between his own boots.

"Is that you under the bed there, George?" Woody said lifting up the bed spread.

"Hey, Woody," the boy sheepishly replied.

"Get under the covers here before you catch a chill," Charley croaked, pulling his blankets up and patting his bed.

"Better get the dust bunnies off him first," Woody said, lighting a candle.

The next day, Woody and George rigged a bell in George's room, with a long thin rope, strung through the apple trees with pulleys, all the way to Charley's cabin and to his bed, threading the rope through a small hole in the wall. Christine figured it might keep the boy in his bed at night, waiting for the bell to ring for service, thus giving Charley some peaceful time to himself.

CHAPTER 70

Ormsby's Tavern, Carson City, Nevada, January 4, 1880

"Here he comes," Dan DeQuille said, getting his note pad and pencil out. "Do you think he knows yet?" he asked the bartender.

"I hate like hell to have to tell him, no tellin how he'll take it. When Snowshoe Thompson died he was melancholy for weeks, just moped around," Jake, the bartender, sighed.

Hank Monk stood in the doorway, dusting the snow off his hat and coat, then trudged toward the bar.

"Set me up, Jake!" Hank said, flipping a coin on the bar. The barman set into action, setting a glass, a bottle of whiskey and a cup of coffee in front of the coachman. "I'll shake you for a cigar, Danny?" Hank said turning to the talkative newsman, who now sat silent. All eyes were on the coachman.

"Sure, Hank, what's new?" DeQuille asked, reaching for the dice boxes, studying the challenger's face for signs of sadness, as was the bartender.

"Not a damn thing, 'cept that its cold'n a witches tit outside. You can quote me if you like," Hank said, inspecting the cigar selection. He pulled out a fine specimen and cut the tip off with a lewd cigar cutter. She was a bronze nymph, naked except for a belt and lay stretched out on her side, on a small slab of marble, anchored firmly to the bar. One hand was shyly concealing her eyes while one leg hung in the air, awaiting the next patron. The cigar was inserted between the woman's legs and the limb pushed down upon, cutting the tip off, neat and clean.

DeQuille watched Hank playing with the cutter, oblivious to the attentions on him.

"I don't reckon he's heard, Jake," Dan said, shaking the dice nervously.

"You don't reckon I heard what?" Hank asked, slamming his dice box on the bar, then peeking beneath to see what he had rolled. "Two fours."

"Here, better have a drink first, have one on me," Jake said, pouring a shot.

"Yeah, I think we all better have one," Dan added, lighting Hank's cigar.

"Yeah, all right," Jake said getting himself a glass.

"What is this? What haven't I heard?" Hank asked, looking around the room, which had become very quiet.

"You gonna tell him, Jake?" another man at the bar asked.

"Yep, I reckon I got to," Jake said sighing.

"Well, I hope somebody gets around to tellin me?" Hank said, slugging down his shot in one motion. "Yer give'n me the creeps."

"It says in the newspaper that your friend Charley Parkhurst died a few days ago," Jake began. He paused to see his face go completely white and tried to find the courage to tell the rest. "The newspaper goes on to say that . . . Ugh . . . Charley was not a man, but a woman, they made no mistake about it . . . . Here is the paper. You can read it for yourself if you don't believe me," Jake said. He then picked up his glass and threw back his reward for stunning his friend so completely.

Hank just sat there with his jaw hanging down for what seemed like several minutes, to those waiting with baited breath for his reaction, as he read the *San Francisco Call*:

DEATH OF A WOMAN WHO FOR TWENTY-FIVE YEARS PASSED AS A MAN

The following remarkable story is creating considerable stir in the newspaper line. If true, the subject was indeed an extraordinary character: On Sunday last, in a little cabin situated on Moss Ranch, six or seven miles from Watsonville, died a person sixty-seven years of age, and well-known to old-timers here and stage drivers and stage men generally as Charles Parkhurst. He was one of the best drivers in the early days in various parts of the state from Stockton to Mariposa, from Oakland to San Jose, and from San Juan to Santa Cruz when San Francisco was reached via San Juan. For fifteen or twenty years, he had been engaged in farming, working in the woods, etc., and it is said that he accumulated several thousand dollars. For several years past, he has not done much, being greatly troubled with rheumatism, which caused great suffering as well as considerable deformity. The immediate cause of his death was a cancer of the tongue. It was found when friendly hands were preparing him for his final rest that Charley Parkhurst was unmistakably a well-developed woman. It could scarcely be believed by persons who had known Charley Parkhurst for a quarter of a century. It is one of the most wonderful of the few such cases on record. That this woman living among men for thirty years or more, going through all the dangers and vicissitudes of California life, should conceal her sex could hardly be believed, but this is a fact. On the greater register of Santa Cruz county of the year 1867 appears this entry: "Parkhurst Charles Durkee, 55; New Hampshire; Farmer; Soquol." Where he then lived, it is said by several who knew her intimately that she came from Providence, R. I. Of course, great curiosity is excited as the cause that led this woman to exist so many years in such strange guise. There may be a strange history that to the novelist would be a source of inspiration, and again, she may have been disgusted with the trammels surrounding her sex and concluded to work out her fortune in her own way. More light may be thrown on this wonderful case. The female stage driver, Charley Parkhurst, left $4,000 to a little boy who had been kind to her.

"Goddamn it, goddamn it, Parkie! I can't believe it—Jehosiphat! I camped out with Parkie once, for over a week, and we slept on the same buffalo robe right along!" Hank finally blurted out. "Now I'm startin' to wonder about Curly Dan!" It broke up the silence and they all had a drink to the amazing one-eyed woman. Hank sat in stunned silence most of the night and was visibly affected by her death.

The old-timers that knew Charley swapped stories of her illustrious driving career throughout the night. Even Curly Dan revised his classic coaching song "Comin' Round the Mountain" to pay tribute to his friend.

"She'll be driving six white horses when she comes!"

CHAPTER 71

Tahoe, August 11, 1881

The summer air was sweetly scented by the pine needles, baking in the hot August sun. The Glenbrook garden was beautiful and bright this afternoon and the hotel was full of guests and gaiety. Hank was resting with a lemonade in the shade of a whispering pine, his clothes soiled from the dust of his morning drive to the Lake Tahoe resort from Carson City. He had finished his lunch and was awaiting the afternoons jaunt back down the mountains. His exploits and anecdotes, published in the Territorial Enterprise, were turning him into a sought out celebrity with the travelers; it was a bit tiresome at times. Hank had recently tried to cut back on his alcohol, his boss Doc Benton's orders. For an old-timer set in his ways, it wasn't easy. If he went into a bar, invariably some tourist wanted to buy him a drink and it was too tempting.

At last the old teamster rose from the swing and ambled back to the hotel, to return his empty glass and announce the impending departure of the afternoon stage. Pulling his gold watch from his vest pocket, he spotted the tremble in his hand, as it held the timepiece.

"Bentons stage for Carson City leaves in fifteen minutes," Hank announced loudly in a well-practiced call. He then turned and sauntered out to the bright sun, lighting his cigar, on the way to the livery. He could see the tourists looking at him and talking, so he smiled to them, as he went about his business. When he pulled up to the hotel on the fine concord coach and six, he was hailed by a large group of travelers on holiday, in various stages of inebriation.

"You got yourself a full load this trip, Hank," Curly Dan remarked, as he loaded the extra trunks on the roof of the coach. "Geez what does he have in this one, rocks?"

The passengers began the clumsy climb, up to the roof seats of the rocking conveyance. Several of the passengers were ladies, who longed for the thrill of riding on the top. The men helped the women navigate up the cleverly arranged steps that lead to the hurricane deck. The final tally of passengers was twelve.

"Oh, driver, I say, it's such splendid weather, we would like to ride topside, as well." A fat British man, who had obviously had too much to drink, slobbered.

"Well, I don't know where you're gonna sit!" Hank said looking at the load.

"Oh splendid!" The British chap smiled incoherently, as he eagerly scaled the vehicle in search of a perch.

The teamster sat impatiently, as the man jostled for a place.

"Hey, Curly, fatso, get a seat yit?" Hank asked. The woman seated behind Monk tittered at the driver's language.

"I dunno, hey Fatso, you got a seat back there?" Curly called out, to the laughter of the happy travelers.

"I say!" the man objected.

"Well, hang on to it then! Git up there, boys. Let's go!" Hank whistled a familiar tune to the horses, which were waiting in eager anticipation of their master's command to move out. He let the leather lines slide through his fingers, as the horses stretched their necks into the collars and took off, causing the coach to rock back with a great sweep. The fat tourist realized that he may have chosen poorly, as he gripped the top rail of the luggage rack with all his might, sobering up in the process. The passengers were exhilarated as the vehicle sped off down the twisting road, out into the wilderness.

Hank was now in his glory and could think of no better place to be, nor could he ever imagine one, he felt. The horses were the finest around and the coach kept in perfect order. Monk loved to tell his tall tales to strangers who believed every word, stories of fierce bear attacks or lions or perhaps bewilder them with the tale of his friend, Charley Parkhurst.

The coach passed drifts of snow piled in the shady areas and rocks that had tumbled down the mountains with the melting slush. The coached churned on through the muddy roadbed, rocking and swaying with the rhythm of the road.

"You must have met just about every important person who has come through here," a young woman asked Monk, leaning forward so she could hear his reply.

"Why yes, Ma'am, I suppose I met em all!" he boasted. "President Grant and the rest, even met the Emperor Norton!" Hank said, leaning forward to grab for more leather, as the horses rounded a corner and descended on the rocky road. As the top-heavy vehicle swayed into a curving stretch, the passengers leaned away from the steep bank on the left side of the coach. The vehicle swept around in a right hand turn, causing them to look down into a steep wash on the right side of the coach, before they would climb up to the crest of the mountain. This gully was prone to falling rocks and flash floods, the road having been cut out of the mountain. The spring run off meant steady work for road crews; rockslides were a common occurrence.

"Get over there, Conklin!" Monk hollered to his swerving lead horse. The swing horse followed Conklin, as did the wheeler, just as the weathered teamster cracked his whip. A large rock in the road that the horses were avoiding caused the front coach wheel, beneath the driver, to bounce up with a crash, followed closely by the rear, causing the coach to buck on one side. The force of the large rock against the right wheels caused the driver to be flung from his seat, as the vehicle tipped over onto two wheels against the side of the mountain. Monk landed on the break lever and narrowly escaped being dragged. He pulled hard on the lines, still tight in his grip and called the horses to whoa, which they did. It all happened so fast. The horses stood obediently, as Monk climbed to the roof, which was leaning on the side of the mountain face, like a drunken sailor. Several of the passengers had been thrown from the coach roof, but miraculously no bones were broken. The women were all crying from the shock.

"I don't know how it happened!" Hank kept saying over and over to himself.

"We should be able to pull her back over without any trouble," Curly said trying to comfort the driver, who was examining the mangled luggage rack, then the wheels.

"Help me unhitch these horses first," Monk reasoned. "Was there anyone seriously hurt?" The man asked the passengers, now all standing around.

"Only cuts and bruises," a young woman said, as she dabbed at the fat man's elbow with his handkerchief.

"My dear, I never meant to harm a hair on your lovely head, my sincerest apologies for this inconvenience," Hank said to his passengers. "Let's get this coach back on the road!"

The men set into action and in little time they were back on four wheels and trotting along; only one side of the roof was damaged. Hank's pride was another story. He dreaded the newspapers, for he knew they could not pass this up.

"I've never had a single wreck in all the years I been driving! I just don't know how it happened!"

"The wheels hit a rock. I'm sure that's it," Curly tried to explain. Hank would not be satisfied. He hated the thought of everyone questioning him about it at Ormsby's.

"See what happens! I quit oilin' my brakin' leg, and it lands me off my seat and onto the brakes! Might even put an end to my career. Nobody will want to ride with me," Hank said sullenly.

"I'll still ride with ya, Hank."

"Thanks, Curly."

When they arrived in Carson City, the late coach was a beehive of interest. Hank wanted to stay clear of the press, so he hid out in the livery. Curly braved the inquisition and stuck up for his unusually shy partner, reminding them of his perfect record and stating for the record, that Hank had taken the pledge and had been completely sober. Another passenger spoke up and insisted a large rock had been the culprit.

Sure enough, the next day it was in the papers.

"Well, here it is, the *Carson Morning Appeal,* you're sure in here, you want me to read it to ya?" Curly grinned.

"No, I'll read it myself:"

"A dispatch from Virginia City says that Hank Monk had his first upset last Monday. In driving down from Lake Tahoe, his coach containing twelve passengers was overturned. It has been rumored lately that Monk had joined the Good Tempars. If this is true he may have been sober, and the accident is thus easily accounted for. One of the strangest things in the world is the immunity that Hank Monk has enjoyed from accidents in his driving. In the days of the Pioneer Stage Line, he was often so drunk that he had to be lifted up to the box and the lines places in his hands, but once his fingers clutched the reins he had perfect command of his six horse team, and sent the horses spinning down the steep grades and in and out of among the huge prairie schooners and wagons of every description with which the roads were lined. His driving appeared reckless, but was really scientific, and no matter how drunk he was he always got to the end of the route in safety, and during all his career his driving has never resulted in so much as a bruise to but one passenger. This one was Horace Greeley on his famous ride from Carson to Placerville, which caused Mr. Greeley to remark to the chairman of the meeting that he addressed at Placerville that he much preferred a standing position during the exercises. The story of Mr. Greeley's ride was once printed in a Nevada paper, but as it is not familiar to latecomers to this coast, the *Daily Report* will republish it at an early day. We shall print an extra edition. Send in orders early for copies."

"Well of all the nerve! First they call me a drunk then they try and make money off of it!" Hank fumed as he threw the paper on the bar.

"You gonna give them what for, Hank?" Curly said, snatching up the paper and looking it over for himself.

"I reckon I ought to give them pencil slingers a piece of my mind. Why the other night I had a horrible dream about Greeley's ghost, he was laughing at me and askin' "What do you think of yourself now?" Monk said, finishing off a beer. A few of the fellows around laughed. "They keep following me around asking me what happened, they're tryin' to ruin my reputation!" Monk said, scanning the room for the offensive pencil pushers. "Why I bet money that those two over there are reporters, look at 'em getting out their scratching paper," Hank said, sauntering over to the men. "You want to know what happened to upset my coach?" Hank said, looking at them with mock menace.

"We sure do, Hank," the men said in unison.

"Well it was a this away, we was makin our way though a hair pin turn see, and my lead horse Ol' Conklin gets an eyeful of this seedy lookin' character a sittin on the roof up ere, and he decides naturally, that he was a pencil slinger, such as yourselfs, and lunges out to attack him, see? Well that there aggression was what done spilled over the coach. No matter how he dresses up, or tries to disguise himself, an animal can always detect the smell of a pencil pusher . . . . Now I dare you to print that! Ha!" Hank said, slurping down his shot, as he walked proudly back to his barstool.

The next day the *Nevada Tribune* did print it, nearly word for word.

"I see ya got a good one in." Doc Benton smiled at the old teamster.

"Do you think I ought to retire, Doc?" Hank asked morosely.

"I think you ought to do what makes you happy, till you can't do it anymore. Can you still drive and do you want to?" Doc said reasoning with the depressed man.

"You know I was having the best drive, up until that accident. I was really enjoying myself," Hank thought out loud.

"You have your answer then, unless of course, you're not fit," the doctor said, eyeing the shot in front of Monk.

"Oh here, I bought you a drink," Monk said passing the glass to the man.

"Good, let me buy you a beer. And say, you ought to buy them two reporters a beer if you see them," Doc said sipping the brandy.

"Already done that," Monk said tipping his hat to the scruffy young men.

Hank drank more and more and drove less and less. His health was deteriorating. He was most often found at Ormsby's Tavern, retelling stories from his colorful life.

"Say, Hank, you shore do read good. Did you get much schoolin'?" the young bartender quizzed the old man.

"I was eddicatted on the compulsory plan. My layout for grammar and 'rithmetic was cussed slim. One day I was ketched throwin' spitballs at the girls and the teacher shut me up in the fireplace and closed me in with the fire screen, along with two other fellers who wouldn't study. Well, we thought it would be a danged good joke to climb up out of the chimney onto the roof and run off. We stuck our bare toes in the cracks of the chimney and climbed up. Pretty soon the top feller he sung out 'Boys, I've Stuck Daylight' and gave a whoop. Then he slipped somehow, and the two fellers come down on the top 'er me. They must'er weighed two or three tons and we fell sixteen feet and rolled plum though the fire screen, tumbled into the geography class where a boy was just boundin' Maine. It broke up the whole class and damn near broke up me. My collarbone was smashed, and the other fellers had their ribs stove in. Next day one of them died, and he was the most promisin' boy in the school. He could do fractions rite in his head just as easy as anything, and maul the daylights out of any multiplication table you ever saw. We all attended the funeral, and I was pallbearer with my new blue britches on. He was an awful good boy and got shut up in the chimney because I pretended he was throwing spitballs too. He was too good for this world anyhow and blamed if I wasn't glad to see him taken to a better land before he got time to git wicked."

CHAPTER 72

May 1881

Dick Fellows stepped from the brick fortress at San Quentin, to freedom at last. His thick brown bushy beard was now trimmed short and was frosted with white; it was topped with a thick sweeping mustache, also frosted. If not for the clothing, which was clean and pressed, but well worn; he looked like a businessman or lawyer, as he walked along to the docks. He was looking to get a ride back to San Francisco to find employment as a teacher. Fellows had kept busy while he was incarcerated, reading law books and teaching the illiterate to read. He soon went south to Santa Cruz and got work at the local paper, the *Echo*.

"Hey there, Dick, fancy running into you. I heard you were out. How are you doing?" Detective Hume remarked.

"Fine, I'm working on the paper and I have some pupils I'm teaching to read. I heard that you have a tough case in that Black Bart fellow, is it Detective Hume?" Fellows smiled.

"Yes right up your alley, in a way, he calls himself a po-eight." Hume smiled.

Dick Fellows recited the following:

> Here I lay me down to sleep
> To wait the coming morrow
> Perhaps success, perhaps defeat
> And ever lasting sorrow.
>
> I've labored long and hard for bread
> For honor and for riches
> But on my corns to long you've trod
> You fine-haired sons of bitches.
>
> Let come what will, I'll try it on
> My condition can't be worse
> And if there's money in that box
> Tis money for my purse

"I taught the inmates to spell with that poem, it was very popular," the man smirked.

"Well at least you're staying free of trouble. Take care, Dick."

"See you in the newspapers, Detective." The seasoned convict saluted.

The paper did not pay well, however and teaching proved more frustrating than profitable, soon Fellows was considering his previous occupation. He made his way to San Luis-Obisbo and on July 19, set his sights on the Coast Line Stage.

Picking out a good location, he set his hat and coat up as a decoy and set out sticks to look like gun barrels amongst the rocks, then hid in some brush and rocks beside the road, hiding his horse out of sight.

"Hold up there, driver," Dick called out with authority.

"All right," the coachman said, calmly halting the vehicle in a cloud of dust.

"Steady, boys!" Fellows called to makeshift gang. "Throw down the box!" the bandit demanded.

The coachman indifferently tossed down the strong box and was ushered away by his assailant.

Fellows was extremely pleased with his accomplishment and shot the lock off with his derringer.

"Shit!" Fellows said, stomping around. "Ten dollars! Goddamn it! All that trouble for ten dollars." He shoved the money in his pocket and kicked the strong box into a bush. "Damn!"

It was then the robber decided to look for greener pastures, perhaps using some of his hero Black Bart's strategy, Dick roamed north to Duncan's Mills on the Russian river, to try again.

Again Fellows successfully relieved the coach of its strong box without trouble.

"I don't believe this! There is suppose to be money in here! What is this?" Dick examined the box, shaking his head and pulling out a piece of paper with some scribbling on it. "What is this shit? One lousy letter? It looks like Chinese, for God's sake!" Fellows fumed. It never occurred to him to high tail it out of there. He found a likely looking hideout near by and waited for the next coach to rob, determined to leave the area with some money. What he did not know was his detective nemesis had already been summoned to find him.

Hume sent a telegraph instructing that a man wait at the scene of the most recent robbery, until he could arrive on the stage. A young man walked out to the sight, about two miles from the station and waited, much to the frustration of Fellows who was waiting in the rocks and brush near by.

"What is that jerk doing, he's just sitting there, why doesn't he leave?" Fellows whispered to his horse. "Let's go find out," he said, unable to stand it any longer. He climbed aboard and casually rode along, pretending to be a traveler.

"Say, what are you doing sitting way out here?" Fellows said pleasantly.

"Oh, I'm a waiting for Detective James Hume to come on the stage. This was the sight of a holdup," the young man boasted.

"Oh, well you keep up the good work," Fellows said, cantering out of sight. "Shit, Detective Hume, now what am I gonna do? I gotta buy some time. I'll tell ya what I'm gonna do, I'm gonna get rid of that kid, before Hume gets here, that's what! Come on!" Dick said, still talking to his horse.

Fellows rode the horse back to his hiding place and covered his face with his bandana, then snuck around the rock so he could spring on the waiting stool pigeon.

Fellows jumped out from the rocks with his gun pulled, it was a small derringer, but it was fifty caliber and demanded respect.

"What in the hell are you interfering in my business for?" Fellows bellowed at the youth, scarring him half to death.

"Please don't kill me!" he pleaded.

"I ought to kill you! You got any money?"

"No."

"Well, you better start running then, before I blow a big hole in your soft head!" Dick Fellows growled, as he ran the kid off, pointing the unloaded gun. He watched him take off into the woods, then walked back to his hidden horse. Climbing aboard, he galloped off into the surrounding forest.

"That boy will be running for miles, pissin' his pants, while Hume's coach just keeps on riding along," he laughed.

As it turns out, the young man did run, for about two miles, back to the station. He then informed all present, including the newly arrived detective, about the bandit. They set out in hot pursuit.

The fog was billowing into the hillsides from the ocean and condensing in the towering trees that had not yet met the sawmills. It began to rain in thick fat drops. Soon it would be impossible to follow a trail, Fellows had been very lucky indeed. He wandered back to San Luis Obisbo.

A soaking wet detective arrived at the tiny town of Sebastopol and checked his posse into a drink and supper in a tavern and gave up the search for the night.

"Tell me again what happened at this scene of the stage holdup. The man that had the gun, was it a derringer?"

The young man was drinking a tin mug of beer and warming his butt by the large fire.

"I do reckon that it was, small gun, short thick barrel, forty-five maybe fifty caliber."

"How tall was he?"

"Oh, he wasn't tall at all, kinda short, but he was real feisty," the young man said, relishing his beer.

"What about the first man? The one that asked you what you were doing there?" Hume asked

"Well, I couldn't tell how tall he was, he's ridin' a horse. Perty horse too."

"What color?" Hume said taking notes.

"Red with three white socks and one white leg with a nice star on his forehead. Oh, and the two fellers had on the same kinda hat. Come to think of it their shirts was the same color too."

"Did the first fellow have a beard?

"Yep, and a big gray mustache."

"I am going to have you look at some pictures, maybe you could recognize his face?" the detective asked.

"Golly, sure, I'd be happy to," the young man said with pride.

"If I can get a positive identification, Wells Fargo will put up a wanted poster, and it will be easier to catch him. Tell me again, everything you can about both men. Waiter can I get a few more beers over here."

After the trail dried up on the Duncan Mills robbery, Hume followed up by showing the witness a series of prison mug shots. Dick Fellows seemed the likely culprit. The ex-convict was keeping his hand in close to his old stopping grounds by robbing three stages in San Luis Obisbo. The detective ordered wanted posters with Dick's likeness plastered all over the countryside, in hopes that someone would see him.

Dick had been hiding out in the woods and wherever he could find shelter. His horse was in need of a shoe, and he was forced to seek a replacement. He found a ranch with a corral full of horses and waited for the cover of night to make the switch. The owner of the ranch was in his home, avidly reading the paper after his hard day's labor. He heard his horses making a bit of a fuss but was only distracted momentarily, for his supper was on the table. While he dined, he noticed the animals in the corral were becoming quite agitated and stopped mid chew to listen closer. He got up and walked to the window and noticed an odd man getting pretty well trampled in the corral. The rancher grabbed his Henry rifle and ran through the doorway.

"Don't move!" the rancher said in a loud, authoritative voice, as he leveled the rifle at the grubby man.

"You got me fair enough, don't shoot me please."

"Come out of there. Slowly," the man with the rifle ordered.

"My horse accidentally got loose with your horses."

"We'll see about that later. What's your name?"

"Richard Lyttle."

"You look like Dick Fellows to me. Come on, let's get you to the barn, you can wait in one of the stalls, till the constable comes. Then we'll sort this out," the rancher said motioning to the barn with the Henry.

The ranch hands roused from their meal and all heavily armed, watched the man in the stall as if he was a form of amusement, while waiting for Constable Burke. When the Constable arrived, the prisoner was handcuffed in the front and set upon his horse, which had been newly shod, and the two set off for San Jose. Burke was a likable fellow Dick thought and maybe even a little gullible, he hoped.

As they approached town, Fellows used all of his charm to persuade the young lawman to allow him one last drink, before he would most assuredly be sent to prison, for life. Much to his suprise it worked and young Burke offered to buy him a drink.

They stopped off at a seedy little bar, just inside town and had a beer. On the way out, Fellows quickly turned and smashed the Constable over the head with his handcuffs, dropping him to the ground. Dick ran as fast as his short chubby legs could carry him, down a back alley and gone. He ran, then hid, and tried to avoid being seen, taking refuge in haystacks and buildings shut down for the night. He stole some tools and managed to relieve himself of the cuffs, but he did not sleep easy. The episode made the evening paper, and Dick Fellows was again big news. Everyone in the countryside was on the look out for him, and it was not long before he was in custody again, this time in the San Jose Jail.

On February 5, five hundred gawkers filed by his prison cell window, just to get a glimpse of the slippery outlaw. The *San Jose Mercury* sent a reporter to the jail, to get Fellows first hand accountings. Fellows created an even bigger stir when he signed on as his own lawyer. He was found guilty in the Santa Barbara Courts and sentenced to life, at the new state prison at Folsom. He would be transported from the Santa Barbara jail to Folsom Prison, on April 1. From there, he knew there would be no escape.

The morning of his transfer, Dick waited nervously in his cell awaiting his breakfast. He had not sleep well the night before. The armed guard finally arrived with the morning meal, and Fellows acting very sleepy at first, quickly pounced on the unprepared guard and grabbed his gun.

"I'm a desperate man, don't try anything you'll be sorry for!" Dick growled as he knocked out the guard and fled though the jail, waving the peacemaker at anyone about to interfere. He made it out of the jail and ran for dear life. He spotted a horse tethered to a tree, at the end of the street, quietly munching on some grass. Dick shoved the pistol inside his shirt and untethered the animal, which wore only a halter. The horse did not object as Fellows swung aboard, but seemed very confused at Dick's thrashing about, once aboard. He trotted around in a circle, unable to understand the urgency of the situation, until at last he had endured enough of Dick Fellows. The horse pulled his nose to the ground and commenced to buck and pitch a fit, sending Fellows from side to side, until at last, he lay on his back in the dirt, near the steps of the jail, where he was once again apprehended. This time there was no escape.

CHAPTER 73

Carson City, February 1882

Hank Monk trudged along the Carson City boardwalk; his worn-out old bearskin coat wrapped tightly around him as he pushed open the Post Office door and walked inside.

"Hank you got a package here," the clerk said, as the familiar figure entered the office.

"Yep, I got word. Does it have postage due?"

"No."

"Good. Let's see it."

"It's from a lady." The clerk smiled.

"Sallie Morgan from Illinois. Must be one of my many admirers," Monk boasted. "Looks like a book of some sort."

"You dropped the letter there," the man behind the cubby hole said, pointing to the floor, eager to learn new gossip."

"Thanks, Edgar. Think I'll read this over a beer," Monk said, smiling at the disappointed man.

Hank plodded along, until he came to Ormsby's Tavern. He set his hat and old worn out bear coat on the familiar rack and settled into his favorite chair, leaning it back against the wall and warming his feet on the potbelly stove in front of him. A familiar face set a glass of beer on the table next to him and smiled at the teamster's mail.

"Got a package from one of your sweeties?" she cooed.

"Yep, Sallie." The old man grinned lustfully at the young waitress.

The barmaid laughed. "Well aren't you gonna open it?"

"You jealous, sugar?"

"Of course!" she laughed, flouncing away.

The man took his time opening the letter and the package. It was a book, a novel entitled *Tahoe or Life in California* by Sallie Morgan."

"So what does your sweetie have to say?" the waitress asked, as she set down another beer.

"She has asked me to be her literary agent on the West Coast," Monk said, with a solemn look across his face.

The bartender who was listening intently, along with the waitress was stunned.

"Well, I wasn't expecting that!" she said, turning to the bartender.

"What's a literary agent do, Hank?" he asked.

"Damned if I know, I'll have to ask DeQuille," Monk said with resolve, as he thumbed through the book.

Later on, Hank wandered over to the restaurant and left word that he was looking for Dan DeQuille, who was always eager to hear some new anecdote and would soon look him up for questioning.

That evening Dan found Monk in his usual spot by the stove, dozing in his chair.

"I heard you wanted to talk to me?" DeQuille said warming his hands.

"Oh sure, here, pull up a seat. I wanted you to have a look at this and tell me what you think," Monk said pulling the letter and book from his grubby vest.

"Hmm. How interesting!" he said at last, reading quickly and looking at the literature.

"But what does it mean? Literary agent?" Hank asked with embarrassment.

"Oh, well, I think that she wants you to take her book to towns and sell them to the stores for her. For a percentage usually," DeQuille replied.

"I see, I thought maybe she wanted me to make corrections." Monk smiled. "Do you know anything about bein' a book agent?"

"A little, I can introduce you to someone who knows a bit more if you like."

"That would be fine, Dan, have a drink on me!" Monk cheered.

That summer a deal was struck, and Hank Monk started on his new career as a literary agent.

Doc Benton dropped him off at the Carson City train depot. After they said their good-byes Hank rested on one of the benches, until he spotted a familiar face.

"Hey, dog catcher, I heard you caught yourself a bad dog!" a neatly dressed and carefully groomed Hank Monk called out, on the crowded railway platform. The detective turned, recognizing the voice, but not able to believe the source.

"Well, look at you, what happened. Did you get married?" Hume laughed.

"Hell no! Good to see you, Jim!" Monk smiled, as the two shook hands.

"You sure clean up good, Hank!" The detective smiled back.

"These are my literary agent duds, I started a new career, even at this advanced age." Monk grinned. "Where are you off to?"

"I'm headed to Sacramento."

"I'm headed that way myself. Say, I heard that Dick Fellows got the upper hand of you folks two or three times, but I guess he's locked up fer good now."

"Yes, I saw to it personally."

"Well, you're tenacious and persistent, that's fer sure," Monk said, slapping his old friend on the back. "I think that's our train." Monk smiled, as the conveyance steamed into the station. "This is my first train ride, it should be enjoyable," Hank chuckled. "I see you're not having any luck at all with that other road agent, Black Bart the po-eight," Monk cackled, as they boarded the locomotive.

James Humes sighed, it was going to be a long ride, and Monk hadn't changed a bit.

"Look, here is the book I'm peddling, *Tahoe or Life in California.*"

"Do you have a peddlers license?" Hume smiled.

"I got a dog license."

"I'm just kidding, I'm working for Wells Fargo now." The detective smiled.

"Here you can have this book as a present, for old times sake. I got a whole case of em." Monk grinned. "Tell your friends about em too," he said, practicing his sales pitch.

"Why thank you Monk that's real nice, here have a cigar," Hume said, fishing in his pocket.

The two passed the ride talking about old times and past friendships, until they at last went their separate ways. Monk had gotten fairly drunk that afternoon.

"Take care, dog catcher, that one of them dirty dogs don't getch you," Monk slurred as he teetered off.

"You take care, Hank Monk, and watch those steps," Hume called, as he watched the teamster tottering off.

Unchaperoned by Doc Benton's watchful eye, Monk returned to his bottle unabashed. He kept his flask ever ready and stayed well oiled most of the time.

He rode the stagecoaches to the major cites, hoping to be rid of a job he had grown bored with at the first stop. Though he had always had an easy time talking to people, he had never been a salesman before. His rough veneer did not mix well with polite business atmosphere.

"So this gal sends me this letter and here I am!" Monk pronounced proudly.

The young salesman, who was trying his best to remove Monk's friendly arm, which was resting around his neck, was recoiling in horror over Hank's breath.

"Well, that is quite a story I'm sure. But I am not authorized to purchase any books. You have to come back next week to talk to the owner," the ruffled clerk pleaded.

"Well that surely is a shame. What about you? You ought to buy one of these books yourself. Why there's some real knee slappers in there, like the part where the Chinaman lights a fire popper under a Negro lady's chair," Monk said, sidling in close again.

"I don't have any money on me," the clerk said, holding Monk at arm's length. "I haven't been paid this week."

"Well, I will be sure to come back," Monk said slapping the man on the shoulder.

"Wonderful," the man sighed.

Hank went from town to town, but did not find this line of work to be very fulfilling. He hated riding on the coach as a mere passenger and found his brake leg pushing down as if automatically on the job. Riding inside was worse, for he found it made him sick in spirit and in body. Traveling this way was eating away at his health.

By the time he got to Bodie, he was weary and ready to retire; yet he still had half a suitcase full of books. When he realized that many of the men there could not even read, he formulated a plan to rid himself of the goods. By informing an illiterate that they were full of lewd and exciting tales, a buyer could make a tidy profit selling them himself. Hank pointed out pages and recited passages from his own imagination, to flesh out the mediocre ladies' novel. The ruse worked and Monk was finally free of his obligations. He fled town quickly, drinking an oath never to delve into book sales again.

As the train slowly chugged into Carson City, Hank Monk was very happy to be returning home. He realized it probably hadn't been a good idea to undertake such a new career. Worn and thin, Hank had a very nasty cough setting in. As the train settled in at the station, he grabbed his suitcase, which seemed to weigh a ton, even though nearly empty and dragged himself out of his seat and off the train. Doc Benton was standing on the platform, anxiously looking for his friend, his face fell as he took in the pitiful sight, laboring to get down the stairs, dragging the case behind him. A young porter seeing the frail man's plight, grabbed him before he fell flat on his face.

"Easy does it, sir," the porter said politely, as he settled the man on the platform. He picked up the suitcase and dusted Monk off.

"Do you have a carriage waiting? I'll carry your bag for you."

"Oh, I do appreciate that, I nearly landed on my face," Monk said, as Doc Benton made his way to the sick man.

"Here's two bits," Monk said fishing in his vest. "Oh, Doc. Are you a sight for sore eyes!" he said coughing.

"Hank Monk, you look afright! You're burning up!" Doc scolded, putting his hand on Hank's forehead. "Help me get this man to my carriage," he said, turning to the porter.

"Is this 'the' Hank Monk?" the strapping young black man asked.

"I am the one and only!" Monk smiled in a fevered delirium.

"Hell, I'm gonna carry him!" the porter said, scooping up the frail teamster. He followed the doctor to his vehicle. The porter gently set the man in the seat, as the doctor got out blankets from the rear of the vehicle and covered him up snugly.

The porter set the bag in the back and then returned to the famous coach driver.

"I hope you get well soon, Mr. Monk. It sure was nice to meet you."

"Thanks for the ride, young man, here's a dollar," Monk said smiling at the dark young face.

"Thank you, sir, thank you!" the man said, turning around and smiling at the money. "Wait tell I tell Wanda Jean!"

"I hate to ask, but how was the trip?" Doc Benton asked after he got under way. Monk was dozing off, snug beneath the blankets.

"Oh, it was fair, as trips go," he said, after a coughing fit.

"You sound terrible," Doc said slowing the vehicle. He reached under his seat and pulled out his doctor's bag and set it on his lap, then lit a small lamp suspended from the center of the buggy top. He pulled out a bottle of medicine and poured the man a measure. "Here drink this."

"That tastes bad," Monk protested.

"Wash it down with this."

"Is it brandy?"

"No, water."

"Figures!"

"My wife got your room ready for you, are you hungry?"

"Yep," Monk said, as he drifted off. When he woke, he was at Doc Benton's home, his wife was waiting at the gate.

"Help me get him in the house, he's very sick."

Doc Benton had an extra room in his house that he let Hank call home; they were after all these years, like family. They helped the man to bed, where he was soon fast asleep.

"My God, it's good to be back." Hank smiled, as he open his eyes to the familiar setting. He could smell Coras' cooking, as it wafted in from the kitchen downstairs. It beckoned him, so he swung his legs down to the floor and sat up. His head was swimming and he felt nauseous, it did not mix well with the hunger pains, and it made him feel weak and light headed. Just then a knock came on his door.

"Hank, are you up?" Cora called from the hallway.

"Come in," Monk coughed.

Cora opened the door, then turned and picked up a tray that she had set on the hall table.

"You just get back in bed this instant. Doc ain't given you the all right yit!"

"Oh, that smells heavenly, what is it?" Monk said lying back in his bed. Cora had set down the tray on a table and then helped Monk arrange his pillows.

"It's all your favorites, hot cakes and sausage and eggs and some coffee." She smiled.

"Aww Cora!" Hank cooed, as she set the bed tray on the bed and uncovered the breakfast. "You're an angel of mercy!"

Doc Benton stopped in, as Cora returned for the coachman's dishes.

"Oh, I almost forgot, you got a telegram from Buffalo Bill, here," Doc remarked as he felt Hank's forehead. He fished out a folded paper from his inside pocket and set in on Monk's bed.

"Billy Cody! What the hell does he want!" Monk belched. "God I been dreamin' about Cora's flapjacks, but I'm as stuffed as a Christmas goose!" he complained, as he unfolded the paper.

"You look better than when we dragged you in here. You have a fever; you have to stay in bed . . . What does Buffalo Bill have to say?" Doc inquired.

"Ha! Says he has a big starring role for me in his new Wild West show. Ain't that a hoot?" Monk laughed, causing him to cough painfully.

"Well, think of what being a literary agent got you. A Wild West show should finish you off!" the doctor sighed. "Here take some of this and go back to sleep," he said, pouring a shot of medicine in a glass for his patient.

"You're probably right, I would have to rest up. You gonna give me a whiskey chaser for that shit?"

"No, just water. I'm going to the office, behave yourself," the doctor admonished.

"Yes, sir boss!" Hank said downing the noxious liquid with disgust. "Don't you have any branch water?"

"Go to sleep, Hank." Doc Benton smiled, as he set a tumbler of water on the nightstand.

After a few weeks of rest and good care, Hank was again at his familiar seat at Ormsby's Tavern with his chair cocked back against the wall, warming his feet on the stove, drinking his own brand of medicine.

Doc Benton would look in on him and take him home on many occasions.

"Hey, Hank, tell my cousin Lou about Mrs. Rollin Daggetts' Saratoga trunk," the bartender asked, setting down a shot of rye in front of the teamster.

"You know what a 'Saratoga bandbox' is?" Monk said turning to Lou.

"No," the cousin remarked expectantly.

"It's a trunk so big, you could fit a band and all the instruments including a piano inside."

"Gee whiz!"

"Well sir, Mrs. Daggett had one of these monstrosities and she desired to have it brought up to Glenbrook for the summer. It was about eight feet tall and five feet deep. It had to weigh a ton. Every morning she begged me, 'When will my trunk be delivered?'" Monk sang in his best imitation of Mrs. Daggett. "'Oh should be up next trip for sure,' I stalled. Truth was, we couldn't fit it on the coach, it was too big. Curly was arranging a freight wagon to bring it up next day. I arrived again at the Glenbrook, and there again was Mrs. Daggett waitin' on the verandah, givin' Rollin a bad time over one thing or another, when she notices I ain't got her trunk once again. She marches off the verandah and gets ready to pitch a fit with me," Hank said sipping his shot and reflecting back. "Rollin, didn't know of the new arrangements and watched his wife from the verandah."

"Where is my trunk? You promised it would be here!" she laid in.

"Well, Marm, I haven't brought it, but I think some of it will be up with the next stage." Monk began.

"Some of it?" She screamed.

"Yes; maybe half of it or some such a matter." Monk smiled at Rollin Daggett on the porch.

"Half of it?" She shrieked at the top of her lungs.

"Yes Marm; half tomorrow and the rest of it the next day or the day after." Monk persevered.

"Why, how in the name of common sense can they bring half of it?" she said, nearly fainting.

"Well, when I left they were sawing it in two, and."

"Sawing it in two! Sawing My trunk in two?" She was stunned, Rollin was trying his damnedest not to laugh out loud.

"That's what I said. Two men had a big crosscut saw and were working down through it—had got down about to the middle I think." Monk reflected.

"Sawing my trunk in two in the middle!" she shrieked in a panic. "Sawing it in two with all my best clothes inside! God help the man that saws my trunk, I say!" she said, screaming with hostility and running inside.

"She never did see one bit of fun in that prank!" Monk said, finishing his shot. "Rollin thought it was hilarious! Bought me several drinks that night, much to the disgust of the missus."

As springtime was renewing the Nevada desert, Hank Monk began to slide downhill at a faster pace. His cough was now very bad; Doc Benton feared it was pneumonia. Hank was completely bed ridden and his condition was grave. Finally, on February 28, 1883, Hank Monk breathed no more. The Bentons were grief stricken, as was the rest of Carson City, as the news spread. They had lost a most colorful piece of their history and identity with him, from the spirited old days in the Wild West, before the railroads tamed the frontier.

People came forward to help prepare to send off their friend in grand style. Flowers came in from all over the countryside. Hank was dressed in a new suit and manicured to his handsomest. He was then placed in a fine coffin and transported to the Episcopal Church in a hearse pulled by black horses. At one o'clock he was laid out for all to view, his coffin was barely visible with all the flowers placed over it. The choir, who were helped by the hundreds of people coming to pay their last respects, sang a heavenly rendition of "The Sweet Bye and Bye." The church was filled to overflowing, as the Reverend Davis took the podium.

"During many years of my ministry in this city few sadder tasks have been allotted me than the one placed in my hands today. Death brings to our minds many truths not realized before. How often do we lay away the body of someone highly honored in his lifetime. We perform the last rites with due pomp and circumstance of detail, yet before we reach our homes we become aware of the fact that after all the man really deserved but little of the world, and despite his high station, he was easily spared and but little missed. Men cringed and fawned before him, and he is gone. Some simple minded man, furnished with but little of the world's goods and hardly any of the blessing of life, disappears from our daily walks, and we are startled at realizing how much we feel his absence and how much we lacked in a true appreciation of his merits while he lived.

The man who knows his own natural capacities and strives to occupy the position in life best suited to his gifts, however humble, which will result in the fullest measure of usefulness to his fellow men, is a man of brains and honest purpose. A man who strives to fill positions beyond his powers is either a knave or a fool. How few of us have the good sense or modesty to know our place in life.

It is often through senseless ambition that ships are wrecked, that strong organizations are wiped out. I hold that our friend lying before us filled his mission well. While with sure eye and steady hand, he guided his human charges over the dangerous grades of the mountains; he was more deserving of his fellow than some vain prince overrating his capacities and leading an army into the jaws of needless destruction. Too much credit cannot be given a man who follows a humble calling and takes an honest pride in doing his work well. I had the pleasure of an acquaintance with the deceased, and now as we lay him away in Mother Earth my mind recalls the pleasant journeys I had with him though the canyons and the solemn old pine forests of the Sierra. Beneath his rough exterior I found a sage and philosopher. He was a man of simple tastes and gentle heart, and many of the throng who gather here today to pay the last tribute of respect and friendship will pass from this sacred house, realizing perhaps for the first time how much Hank Monk can be missed. His long exposures in the service of the public brought on bodily infirmities during the past few months of his life, which perhaps made death not unwelcome, and which calls to mind the word of the poet Omar:

> What if the soul can fling the dust aside
> And naked on the air of heaven ride,
> Wer't not a shame—wer't not a shame for him,
> In this clay carcass so crippled to abide?
> And fear not least existence closing your account and mine,
> Should know the like no more,
> The Eternal Saki from the bowl has poured,
> Millions of bubbles like us, and will pour.

Amen.

"Please all sing "The Peace That Flows Like a River."

The whole town and then some, filed by to say good-bye to their friend. The local musicians rallied together and played a magnificent rendition of "The Hank Monk Schottische." There wasn't a dry eye in the house.

Hank was then taken with great solemnly to his final resting-place, as a long line of carriages followed, to the Carson City cemetery.

Afterward, local people couldn't believe he was really gone. In fact, some people believed that his spirit had never really left. Henry Sharp, who operated Ormsby's, swore that every night when he closed up, he hung all the chairs on the walls to sweep and every morning, he found one chair, leaning back against the wall, next to the stove, in Hank Monk's favorite spot.

The end